E Q U A L S

"I love you," was all he said before he kissed Clare deeply and nuzzled her neck. "I don't care about your memories, I don't care about anything but making sure I don't lose you."

She wrapped her arms around him, the feel of his lips lingering on her neck. Mark was different from any man she'd ever known. He was honest and open, and he treated her as an equal, in business as well as here in her bedroom.

"There's only one rule for success," he whispered conspiratorially, "and it's the same for men and women . . . Know what you want and go after it . . ."

Clare wanted Mark Lyons with all her heart and quickened senses . . . but a chill went through her as she remembered, first, how much she would have to give up for this love . . . and then, how much she stood to lose without it . . .

SUCCESSION

Romantic Reading from SIGNET

Succession

Joyce Carlow

A SIGNET BOOK

NEW AMERICAN LIBRARY

NAL BOOKS ARE AVAILABLE AT QUANTITY DISCOUNTS WHEN USED
TO PROMOTE PRODUCTS OR SERVICES. FOR INFORMATION PLEASE
WRITE TO PREMIUM MARKETING DIVISION, NEW AMERICAN LIBRARY,
1633 BROADWAY, NEW YORK, NEW YORK 10019.

This book was created and produced by Larry and Helene Hoffman,
Authors' Marketing Services Ltd.

SIGNET TRADEMARK REG. U.S. PAT. OFF. AND FOREIGN COUNTRIES
REGISTERED TRADEMARK—MARCA REGISTRADA
HECHO EN CHICAGO, U.S.A.

SIGNET, SIGNET CLASSIC, MENTOR, PLUME, MERIDIAN AND NAL BOOKS
are published by
New American Library,
1633 Broadway,
New York, New York 10019

First Printing, September, 1984

1   2   3   4   5   6   7   8   9

PRINTED IN THE UNITED STATES OF AMERICA

For

Tom Canagiano

I

1898–1904

1

Friday, July 1, 1898

BROOKLYN

The hot summer sun beat down on Bedford Avenue and in spite of the multicolored awning that extended out over the curb, the heat was oppressive.

"The lettuce will wilt," Domenico Tonelli complained as he wiped his brow with the corner of his green apron. At sixty-two, Domenico was short, bald, and round. His bushy eyebrows glistened with perspiration and he waved his arm, dousing the lettuce with cool water from the sprinkle can.

Donato Ferrante, the husband of Domenico's only daughter, Maria, stood nearby. He shook his head dejectedly as he took refuge beneath the awning. Inside the grocery, Paolo, Domenico's son, worked in the back room uncrating cabbage, while Gina Tonelli, Domenico's diminutive wife, sat perched on a high stool behind the counter, her long skirt falling about her so that she looked like a doll on display.

The Tonelli house, a large two-story clapboard dwelling with a small front porch and a back-porch room which had been added on after Donato and Maria were married, rose two stories behind the store. The trim on the house was bright green and Gina Tonelli was cheered by it, since Agosto, her eldest son, had painted it just before going to Cuba to fight for the United States and help liberate the Cuban people from Spanish domination. "Whenever I look at the shutters, I think of Agosto," she frequently sighed.

"It's too hot for you here, Mama." Domenico came into the store, arms flying and eyebrows raised. "Go back to the house, send Maria down."

Gina smiled faintly. "It's all right as long as I'm sitting down."

Domenico unconsciously glanced at her skirts. Beneath them

he knew her legs were swollen and puffy from the heat, and her feet were packed into her high-topped black laced shoes. "You should be lying down," Domenico added. "Not just sitting, lying."

"If I lie down, I think," Gina confessed. Her face was round and soft, her black eyes serious and contemplative.

"Why don't you want to think?" Domenico questioned.

Gina shrugged. "There was no letter from Agosto this morning. I'm worried."

"You've been worried since the day he left."

"This is special worry," Gina replied. She was looking at her small hands and twisting her wedding ring around in circles.

"There's nothing to worry about! Agosto will show those guys! We've got the best army in the world!"

Gina smiled. If Domenico had been talking to Salvatore, his language would have been spicier, but he was careful when he spoke to her, careful always to be a gentleman. But the smile faded from her face and she shook her head. "Domenico, Agosto is my son. I have a feeling today . . . a feeling only a mother knows."

Domenico frowned. He remembered when Agosto was a child and had been lost. A curious little boy, he had crawled into a large drain pipe and became stuck. Gina had found him straightaway, knowing just where to look. She had a certain psychic power where her children were concerned. But he had no intention of letting Gina know her worry troubled him. "Agosto will be safe," Domenico muttered. "The Virgin will protect him, Gina. Remember, you had the medal blessed yourself by the priest."

Gina did not answer, but she still twisted her wedding ring.

"It's only the heat," Domenico told her. "You need to rest. Gina, go lie down."

Gina slipped down from the stool. "A mother knows," she said to her husband. "You laugh at me, but I know."

Instinctively Domenico hugged her tightly and kissed her cheek, rubbing his unshaven face against her soft skin. "I don't laugh at you, Gina. I never laugh at you."

"I'll go pray for Agosto," she answered solemnly. "And, Domenico, I'll pray that you can laugh at me."

Domenico's weathered face reddened and he nodded sheepishly. "Send Maria to tend the counter," he told her. "And say a prayer for me too."

One day Agosto Tonelli had been on the sidewalk in front of his father's store in Brooklyn, and the next he found himself in a mobilization camp in Tampa, Florida, one of a hundred and twenty-five thousand volunteers who had responded to Assistent Secretary of the Navy Teddy Roosevelt's call to arms.

Agosto admitted to himself that he had been filled with patriotic fervor; he believed in America and in freedom; he believed in the Cuban cause. He had just read *The Gadfly*, a powerful and adventure-packed novel about Italian unification, and inspired by the heroic tales of the Italian warrior, he enlisted. Garibaldi had united Italy, been welcomed to New York with a tumultuous parade; he had gone to Uruguay to help that tiny country achieve its independence. Garibaldi was a freedom fighter, and on the day Agosto joined the army, and indeed during his first year in Cuba, Agosto was a freedom fighter too. He had not lost his belief in freedom, or in America, but he now recognized that freedom was an ideal and war a bloody reality.

He marched up the narrow jungle road they were taking this morning, to the San Juan hills. *Hills,* he repeated to himself. The press called it San Juan Hill, but of course it wasn't a single hill, it was a ridge of hills—the highground over Santiago de Cuba.

The heat was torrid and even if he had been lying stark still as Major General Shafter was doubtless doing, he would still be roasting and soaked with salty sweat. Confusion became the order of the day and the word that Agosto would forever associate with war.

"It's your damn fault, you stupid dago!"

Agosto turned to his fellow soldier and grinned. "I'm just as hot as you are!"

"You're quartermaster, you bastard! Why the hell are we marching through this goddamned jungle in winter uniforms?"

"Because this army is run by a bunch of bluenose idiots like you! They don't have any other uniforms!"

"Then they should have bloody well let us go naked!"

Uniforms, Agosto thought. Hell, not only did they not have summer uniforms, but they also had ancient Springfield rifles, and some of the men didn't have guns at all. Worse yet, most men, including himself, had no battle training.

And they had no commanding officer, either. Major General Shafter, their name-only commander, was old and afflicted with gout. He was so damned fat he had to be helped on and off his horse, when on rare occasion he attempted mounting. He spent most of his time sleeping in his hammock complaining of heat prostration.

Agosto wondered if Garibaldi's troops had been so varied, so ill-trained, and so miserably equipped when they attacked Sicily to defeat the Bourbon royal family and unite Italy. No, Garibaldi was a real general. He fought with his men, didn't have gout, and he wasn't fat and soft. Moreover, Garibaldi's men were homogeneous: all good peasants, with a single aim. That was a comment that definitely couldn't be made about either Shafter's V Corps, the First volunteer cavalry, who were called the Rough Riders, or the New York Seventy-first. This army came from all parts of the United States and every possible walk of life. There were cowboys, hunters, Civl War veterans from both sides, and drunkards from everywhere. There was a contingent of bankers and stockbrokers from Wall Street and farmboys from the Midwest and the South. If the ragtag army shared anything on arrival, it was overconfidence and enthusiasm. Now they shared homesickness, rotten food, and fever.

"Up and at 'em!" a bearded, puffing, sweating man screamed. He was one of the Rough Riders who was not riding, but who was on foot, having been forced to dismount because his horse could not negotiate the narrow winding jungle path that led to the San Juan hills. They'd been ordered onto this road at four P.M. Twenty thousand men, brass bands, artist Frederic Remington to record the battle, a press corps that was two hundred men strong and armed, and a man called J. Stuart Blackton with his sixty-pound Vitograph camera and tripod. "This will be the first war of a new united nation! And every bit of it will be recorded in real-life motion pictures!" Blackton proclaimed loudly and often. Teddy Roosevelt had posed for Blackton, and then, remembering the pictures would move, he waved and mounted his horse.

"Get them damn Yankee boys!" Fighting Joe Wheeler shouted as he ran up and down in front of the bedraggled column shrieking his lungs out.

Yankees? Agosto thought. The stupid son of a bitch didn't even know what war he was in. He was an ex-Confederate and still full of it.

The path narrowed and it seemed the jungle was closing in on them. The shallow roots of trees transected the path as if the earth were vomiting them up, and prickly branches from low brush tore at them as if made angry by the intrusion and noise.

"Open up!" The cry from the unidentifiable voice preceded the first shot from hostile rifle fire by only seconds. Agosto hit the ground and grasped his ungainly Springfield. Men crawled toward the jungle and Agosto did so too, aware that the smoke from the miserable rifles would clearly give away their position, and whatever else might be said of the Spanish, their sharpshooters were good.

Agosto, like a few others, took a still narrower path that led off into the bush. "Try that direction!" he was told.

Men fired aimlessly and hacked at the thick brush with machetes. Darkness and shadows—but no relief from the heat. The jungle was lush, and since the day they arrived in Cuba it had been their nemesis. There were no poisonous snakes, as many had feared, but there were land crabs: huge ugly crustaceans that lumbered around in the dark, rustling the leaves on the forest floor and sounding like an enemy intruder to the sentries who nervously stood guard duty at night. Agosto's only thought on the crabs was how disappointed his mother would have been that so large a crab was not edible. "God's waste!" she would have proclaimed. In fact, on those long hot days encamped on the beach with the jungle in front of them, they had discovered there wasn't much that was edible and desirable, though there were fruits and plantain. The latter was rejected by most, but Agosto's southern Italian palate welcomed the plantain gladly as a salvation from the putrid tinned meat—left over from the Sino-Japanese War of 1894—and the dry, tasteless hardtack. Unhappily, the jungle had no game, and it was fresh meat the men desired most. Some told of seeing a few timid deer that wild dogs stalked through the dense underbrush, but no deer were caught. The animal most evident was the huge winged buzzard that fed on the land crabs killed by nervous sentries. Learning that the Americans would kill their prey for them, the great birds followed the army, hovering above them or gliding through the air above the tall trees with watchful beady eyes on the strangers below. Dead crabs or fallen men—they were the same to the circling flesh eaters.

"Shit!"

Agosto turned to the sound of the curse and heard a bullet whiz past his ear. The man in front of him screamed and he saw the blood gushing from a chest wound. The wounded man was a six-foot-two Texan. Instinctively Agosto touched his medal of the Blessed Virgin and crossed himself.

"Shit! Get me out of here!"

Agosto turned back to the voice in the thicket. It was Ainsley. He was caught in barbed wire and his pale face was scratched and bleeding. The goddamned Spanish had strung barbed wire along the jungle trail, fastening it to trees and covering it with brush. Ainsley was struggling with his gun even though he was partially blinded by the blood running from his forehead down into his eyes.

"Don't fire!" Agosto hissed. "The smoke makes a perfect target!"

"I'm already a perfect target. Get me out of here!"

"Trussed up like a pig." Agosto grinned. It was a rather pleasant sight. Philip Ainsley, son of one of America's wealthiest families, caught in barbed wire, scratched up, mussed up, and terrified. "You look like a grubby immigrant that just got off the boat!"

"Shut up, you dumb dago, and get me out of this mess!"

"Hold still." Agosto fumbled with Ainsley's wire-entangled clothing. "Damn! Will you hold still!"

"We're going to be killed!"

"There." Agosto pulled the last bit of clothing free.

Ainsley nodded. It was his way of saying thanks.

Agosto searched the trees, his eyes adjusting to the shadows. The light filtered through the leaves of the mahogany forest and fell on the ground in dim lacy patterns. Agosto motioned Ainsley to follow him. Silently they crawled back toward the main trail, passing three dead men and four wounded. Agosto promised to send stretcher-bearers.

"The cavalry's dismounted and the Rough Riders are headed up the heights. Come on!" The voice came from one of the volunteers who had been in the rear.

"I'm going back for medical attention," Ainsley announced.

"For a few little scratches?" Agosto shook his head. Garibaldi fought for an hour after he had been shot.

"I'm going with Wheeler!"

"Good combination, a stupid dago and an old Confederate bastard!" Ainsley shouted.

"The Cubans deserve their freedom and we're going to help them get it. The way we got ours in 1776! The way Garibaldi got it for Italy in 1860!" Agosto pulled himself up to his full five feet, eleven inches. He felt the way he had the day he enlisted, full of patriotic fury. And it was all doubly satisfying. First he was fighting for the United States of America, and second against a Spanish Bourbon king—the same Bourbons his hero Garibaldi had fought against to free Italy.

"Dumb dago!" Ainsley mumbled even as he waved his hand and started off toward the rear.

Agosto turned toward the fighting and started running. "Vittoria!" he shouted. It seemed as appropriate as "Get those damned Yankees!"

Saturday, March 3, 1900

BROOKLYN

Gina Tonelli walked around the living room and paused for a moment in front of the mantel. She picked up Agosto's picture and studied it. He looked so handsome in his uniform. He was tall, five-foot-eleven, and well-built. His hair was thick, dark, and straight, his eyes deep brown and expressive, and his face was square with a nice cleft chin. Gina kissed the photograph tenderly and put it back on the mantel. She walked across the room to the front window. The Tonelli house on Bedford Avenue looked out on the deserted street. It was six A.M., and the first gray light had only just begun to break in the eastern sky, revealing heavy dark clouds overhead, and threatening rain. But even if it did rain, the street below would be bustling with shoppers by ten o'clock. Saturday was a big market day, but for Gina this Saturday was important for other reasons. Agosto was coming home.

She clutched the curtain and thought that Domenico was wrong not to take her seriously. On the very day she had experienced her "feeling," Agosto was wounded. His letter said it was not a bad wound, but she longed to see him and confirm his denials that there was anything wrong. She sighed deeply. After Agosto was wounded, he contracted the fever and was sick for weeks. She had "felt" that too, and she worried without ceasing till she had a letter in his own hand, telling her he was well. "He's probably too thin now. And maybe he limps," she said aloud.

"Mama, what are you doing up so early?" Maria's voice cut through the silence of the deserted living room.

"I can't sleep," Gina said, turning to face her married daughter. "I was just lying in bed tossing and staring at the ceiling. I didn't want to wake your papa, so I got up."

"It's cold in here," Maria replied, pulling her robe around her. "Mama, you need your rest, and it's too cold to be up."

Gina smiled. "I'm too excited to sleep. All I can think of is that tonight Agosto will be home. Home, Maria. Home safe."

"We're all excited," Maria responded. She was busy in the kitchen lighting the lamp and turning on the gas stove. "Come in the kitchen, Mama. It's warmer by the cooker."

Reluctantly Gina followed. It was peaceful-looking out the

15

window on the deserted street. In her mind she conjured up images of her neighbors as they would look when they came to the store midmorning: young women in long colorful skirts with scarves covering their heads, old women in black who would squeeze the melons and examine the cabbage, small children who were sent to pick up vegetables for their mamas and those who would try to steal an apple when Domenico wasn't looking. She could envisage the rows of baskets in front of the store filled with fresh eggplant and tomatoes. In her mind she could picture Agosto working in the store, even though he'd been gone two years.

"I wonder where he is now?" Gina mused.

Maria frowned. "You know where he is, Mama. He's on a ship on his way home, and probably asleep. They said the ship would dock at three o'clock."

Gina felt impatient. Nine hours! And then the trip home from the Brooklyn Navy Yard. It would be ten hours before Agosto would hold her and kiss her, ten hours before she would have her son again. "I wish I could go to the docks," Gina said wistfully. "I'd like to be there, I'd like to see him before anyone else!"

"The ship will probably be delayed, Mama. You know it's not good for you to stand for so long. It's better that you stay home."

Gina glanced at her swollen legs. Without her black stockings you could clearly see the veins and the puffy redness. Sadly, Maria was right. The trip on the streetcar to the Brooklyn Navy Yard would have been difficult. She'd have shooting pains all through her legs, and by the time Agosto came, she would be in such pain that she could hardly stand. "Will you kiss him for me, Maria? Will you kiss him and tell him the first kiss is from me?"

Maria nodded impassively as she watched the coffeepot on the stove; dark black Italian coffee with its distinct aroma. Its odor filled the room.

Maria's hair was loose now, but when she dressed she would pull it back tight and pin it up. Then she would carefully cover it with a scarf. With her hair loose she looked her age of twenty-two, but when it was tied back, she looked older and more severe. But it was more than imposed severity, Gina reflected. Maria wasn't happy; seldom did her face break into a smile, and she almost never laughed.

"Aren't you excited that Agosto is coming home?" Gina prodded.

"I'm afraid," Maria replied without turning.

"Afraid? Afraid of what?" Gina pressed. She felt terribly

distanced from her daughter, even though Maria and her husband, Donato, lived with her and Domenico.

"He'll be changed," Maria said flatly. "Nothing will be the same."

"Agosto will be the same," Gina said confidently. "I know my son, he'll be the same. Of course, he'll have to be fattened up and he'll have to have a good rest, but he'll be working in the store with your papa, Paolo, and Donato. It'll all be the same, everything will be the same."

They called it "a splendid little war," though Agosto hadn't thought it so splendid. He was willing to admit there were splendid moments: the Spanish surrender was splendid, the treaty that brought peace was splendid, and the magnificence of Havana was splendid. The heat, the insects, malaria, yellow fever, putrid food, infections, the slow death of the mortally wounded under the tropic sun—these were not splendid. They were, in fact, a horrific memory that had changed forever Agosto's romantic visions of battle.

He could see the skyline of New York on the distant horizon and from his vantage point on the deck of the rusty old transport vessel, the city appeared in miniature, as if it could be held in the palm of his hand; it was a huddle of toy buildings looming out of the gray water and blanketed in fog and smoke.

Agosto smiled to himself. He had sometimes visited Manhattan, journeying across the Brooklyn Bridge and heading up to Mulberry Street, an area inhabited largely by recently arrived Italian immigrants, just as adjoining areas were inhabited by Germans, Jews, and assorted people from the Balkans. It was a fragmented city, and not until this moment had he thought of it in its entirety; rather he remembered paper-strewn streets, old women dressed in black from head to foot, and the demarcation lines— invisible lines that separated the Italians from the Jews, the Germans from the Greeks, and most striking, the rich from the poor. And pickles. Agosto remembered pickles, even though pickles weren't Italian food. But nonetheless the smell of pickles floated across the demarcation line, just as the old women dressed in black often walked across it, invading the territory of elderly Jewish women whose wigged heads wobbled on their shoulders and whose eyes were firmly fastened on the ground as they made their way from one shop to another, haggling with the street vendors and filling their tiny wicker baskets with bagels and great long loaves of twisted bread.

"Homecoming," Agosto mumbled under his breath. He inhaled the smells of the city as its odors wafted across the choppy waters. New York seemed different, but in his heart Agosto Tonelli knew that New York was unchanged. It was he who had experienced a metamorphosis. He knew as he looked at New York that he didn't have to remain in Brooklyn. The city was whole, it was exciting, and it offered rare opportunities to those willing to take a chance and seize them. No, the streets were not paved with gold, as so many new immigrants thought, but there was wealth, and gaining that wealth depended on a man's imagination, on his willingness to take a risk.

Agosto glanced toward the vessel's bow and his eyes fastened on Philip Ainsley, who leaned over the rail just as he did. He stared at Ainsley's patrician profile, and as if feeling eyes on him, Ainsley turned and walked down the deck to join him.

"You surprised me, Tonelli!"

Agosto thought Ainsley was close to his own age—maybe a few years younger, maybe twenty-one or twenty-two. Ainsley had dark straight hair that didn't blow in the brisk breeze because it was slick with Vaseline or some other kind of grease. Who could know what bluenoses put on their hair? And Ainsley *was* a bluenose, a true snob. But Agosto could pay Ainsley one compliment. He was always neat. In Cuba he had hired a houseboy to wash and iron his uniforms and shine his boots. Agosto could have afforded that on his officer's pay too, but unlike Ainsley, Agosto sent all his pay home to his father. Ainsley didn't. But then, Agosto reasoned, what would Philip Ainsley's father want with a few miserable dollars a week? The Ainsleys lived on Park Avenue, had a home in Westchester, and summered in Newport. They owned a bank and Agosto wasn't sure what else, but he was certain that Philip Ainsley's future was assured, even though he wondered why Philip Ainsley had volunteered to fight in Cuba in the first place.

"How did I surprise you?" Agosto finally replied.

Ainsley shrugged, but it wasn't a good Italian shrug. It was a half-interested bluenose shrug, and it was augmented by one arched eyebrow.

"Never thought of dagos as fighters. Frankly, I suppose it surprises me that a dago would join the military to fight the Spanish. They're all the same in my mind."

Agosto smiled. Ainsley had gone to a fancy prep school and attended Harvard. But Harvard or no, he was an ignorant son of a bitch. What Ainsley knew about American history was little enough; what he knew about Europe was nonexistent. If I say I fought the Spanish because Alfonso, King of Spain, is from the House of Bourbon, the stupid bastard will probably think I mean Alfonso's family drinks a lot, because he sure as shit doesn't know the difference between a Spanish Bourbon king and Kentucky bourbon on the rocks.

"I'm just patriotic," Agosto answered, deciding not to explain Garibaldi, the Bourbons, or the unification of Italy. "I was born on the fourth of July in 1876, the hundredth anniversary of the American Revolution."

Ainsley smiled sardonically and his eyebrow went up again. "The Centennial," he half-corrected in his clipped, somewhat annoying Massachusetts accent. "Well, I suppose your gratitude toward America is understandable. No matter how you live here, it has to be better than Italy."

Agosto didn't answer, nor was he annoyed. Actually, Ainsley had the opposite effect on him. Ainsley made him feel strangely superior. He vaguely thought that Ainsley's family probably had box seats at the Metropolitan Opera; it was one of the places to be seen. Doubtless Ainsley didn't think of Verdi or Puccini as being Italian. And Ainsley's family probably paid a fortune for Italian paintings. Agosto, still smiling, took a step toward Ainsley and watched as Ainsley took a step away from him. Bluenoses always did that; they always moved away as if they had to be surrounded by empty space.

"You're slick." Agosto said good-naturedly.

"I pride myself on being a bastard," Ainsley answered.

"Going back to Harvard?"

"Probably."

"You're how old?"

"Twenty-three." Ainsley symbolically ran his hand across the top of his slick hair.

"So you volunteered to fight the Spanish in Cuba when you were twenty-one."

Ainsley nodded. "I have two years more before I graduate. I expect I'll go into the family business."

"You could have stayed and just finished. What made you join the military?" It was a personal question and Agosto felt a wave of pleasure. Men like Ainsley hated personal questions.

Ainsley looked uncomfortable. "My father thought it would be good for me."

Agosto shrugged. A good Italian shrug from the waist up. Ainsley's answer satisfied him. Ainsley was no mystery at all: he was a rich little spoiled bluenose and his father had made him join the army so that he could be disciplined. That was typical. Bluenoses let their children run wild and spoiled them rotten, then sent them off to a military academy or to the army to learn respect. But Italian kids always had respect; they didn't need to be disciplined.

Agosto smiled to himself because the thought conjured up the image of his own father, Domenico. "You have respect," he could hear his father saying. "You're a good boy, you have respect. And you remember, you remember always, everybody else will let you down, but the family is everything. You can count on family. And you remember: *Senti tutti i consigli, ma il tuo non lo lasciare*. It's an old proverb. It means, 'Listen to all counsel, but keep your own.' We learned the wisdom of that proverb. Puglia, where your mama and I come from, is a poor province. It sits right on the heel of the Italian boot. Right out there in the sea. And everybody for centuries invaded us and we were dominated by foreigners, so we learned—we learned to keep our business in the family and we learned to keep the proverb."

"And what are you going back to?" Ainsley asked pointedly.

The question interrupted Agosto's thoughts of Domenico. It was a more important question than Ainsley realized; it was a question Agosto had been thinking about for the past year. He had met and talked to people from another world; he had a commission, a medal for bravery, and he felt he had learned a lot, especially about the world of money and finance. It intrigued him, there was no denying that. His father, his mother, his brother, all the Tonellis worked with their hands and backs, but Agosto now knew a man could earn money in other ways. It was a valuable lesson.

"My father owns a store," Agosto replied.

Ainsley didn't ask what kind of store. He probably didn't have to ask. All the greengrocery stores in New York were owned by Italians. "The bluenoses have the money," his father would say, "but we got the lettuce."

"There are other kinds of businesses," Ainsley suggested, almost echoing Agosto's own thoughts.

"I'm giving them some thought."

"Frankly, Tonelli, I suspect you're smarter than you should be. And I'll do you a favor, I'll tell you honestly that there's no money in fruits and vegetables. If you want money, you have to go to the source. Banking, investments, that sort of thing. You've made some connections in the past two years, connections that could do you some good."

"Maybe."

"Mind you, you ought to change your name. How about 'Augustine Turner'? That sounds right. God knows, with the right tailor, a haircut, and a name change, you could make it."

Agosto shook his head. "You don't get respect by changing your name, you have to bring respect to your name."

Philip looked at Agosto with his watery blue eyes, eyes which seemed to look past you. "Have it your own way. I was only trying to be helpful."

"An unusual act for you."

"Damn right. I'm not as terribly keen on the poor and tempest-tossed' as she is." Ainsley pointed off toward the Statue of Liberty, which loomed in the distance, and surprisingly, he quoted from the poem on its base.

"But you lift the lamp beside the golden door," Agosto proposed, as he also quoted from the poem.

"You were quartermaster, and a lieutenant. You're good with figures. You could start as a teller in a bank, and who knows, maybe after ten or fifteen years you could become a manager."

Agosto smiled and turned to lean on the railing. The blue-gray water of New York City's harbor lapped against the side of the transport, and the escort tug on the starboard side gushed out puffs of sooty dark smoke in welcome.

"Are you offering to write me a reference?"

Ainsley nodded. "I imagine my father would hire you."

"I'll give it some thought." A recommendation, Agosto mused. It was the very least he might expect from Ainsley. But there was someone else who might write him a recommendation, and that someone was Teddy Roosevelt himself. After all, he was now the Governor of New York. And why go to work for the Ainsley National Bank? There were other banks.

"Is your family meeting you?" Ainsley asked.

"Some of them," Agosto replied. "Someone has to stay at the store. It's Saturday, a big day."

"I wouldn't know," Ainsley answered.

Agosto nodded and shouldered his heavy pack. It was full of small presents. An Italian boy didn't come home without gifts; not even from a war.

Agosto's eyes searched the crowd until they found his father, brother, and sister. His mother wasn't there, and his heart sank. She wasn't well, only her health would have kept her from this reunion.

"Where is Mama? And Donato?" Agosto asked as soon as he reached them.

"Mama's feet are swollen, so she is waiting for you at home. Donato had to stay with the store," Paolo replied.

Agosto pressed his lips together. It was his mother he had wanted to see most of all.

"Is it so bad?" he asked.

"She has pain standing," Domenico replied. "But seeing you

will change her. Having you home will make her smile again. And you won a medal! She's proud, Agosto. You are her medicine! Better than all the doctors.''

Agosto nodded and studied his father just before embracing him. It was Domenico's face that was most changed. In the time he had been gone, his father had visibly aged, and his face bore a network of deep lines. But Domenico's eyes were still soft brown, and just as he had when Agosto left, he wept openly, allowing his large tears to run down his face.

Domenico hugged his son and held him close. He kissed his cheeks and hugged him again. ''Proud,'' he whispered. Then he repeated the word in a roar. ''Proud! We're proud! You make your mama and me proud! You do honor to your dead brother, Ulysses S. Tonelli! You do honor to the whole family!''

Agosto felt the tears in his own eyes, and he kissed his father and returned the bear hugs.

''Good thing you come home now,'' Agosto's brother Paolo put in. He was dressed in his Sunday suit and he shifted his weight from one foot to another. He waited till Domenico hugged Agosto one more time, then stepped forward and hugged his brother. ''We're going to build an addition on the store! There's plenty of work! And I joined the Columbus Society. I get to know people, and then they shop at our store!''

Maria stepped closer to her brother. She crossed herself reverently. ''We thank God for your safe return,'' she said in a low voice; then, like her father and brother, she hugged Agosto and kissed him, whispering, ''That kiss is from Mama. You don't limp?'' she asked, stepping back to look at him. ''Mama was afraid you'd limp.''

''Just a little if the weather is damp.'' Agosto allowed. ''It's really a small wound, nothing to worry about.''

''But you got a medal!'' Domenico boomed. ''And the letter said you saved two lives!''

Agosto blushed. One of them had been Philip Ainsley, the other Teddy Roosevelt's first lieutenant. ''An accident of war,'' Agosto replied modestly.

''Politics!'' Maria muttered. ''Men get killed because politics causes wars and killing. It's no good!''

Maria's long black hair was covered with a green scarf that had large red roses on it. She wore a loose-fitting long dull dress and her eyes were downcast. Maria seemed tight and tense; she didn't look youthful and vibrant as she should. Momentarily Agosto's mind strayed to the women he had known in Havana— wild, happy women who sang and danced; women who even drank and who seemed to live each moment as if it were their last. He had enjoyed the favors of some of those women, though he disapproved of them. He often thought that they should be like Maria—moral and staid. But now as he looked at Maria he wondered if there were a middle ground, women who enjoyed life and love and who were still moral. He had always felt his mother to be such a woman, but he could not see it in his sister. Maria didn't seem to have any joy in life, and little curiosity about what lay beyond her own small restricted world.

"Wait until you hear the plans for the addition! It's big, Agosto! We're going to be the biggest store on the street!" Paolo put in.

"It's an honored name—Tonelli is an honored name!" Domenico said again.

They were all talking at once. They always talked at once. Agosto forced a smile. "Don't cry, Papa," he said softly, putting his arm around his father's shoulders.

"Don't cry! I always cry when I'm happy!" Domenico grinned and Agosto nodded. "Let's go home, Papa. Let's all go home."

Agosto sat on the bed in his mother's room. It was their first moment alone since his arrival, and he savored it as he watched her try on his gift.

"It looks stunning on you," Agosto said, admiring the delicate Spanish black lace veil. He had brought his father real Havana cigars, his sister handmade silk flowers, his brother a bright shirt, and Donato a painted statue of the Virgin.

"Are you sure you feel up to Mass on Sunday?" Agosto studied his mother, who in turn studied her image in the old gilt-edged mirror that hung over the dressing table Domenico had made. Her image was drawn and the tight lines around the mouth indicated her pain.

"I've missed too many Masses. I missed meeting you at the docks. No, I won't miss Mass this Sunday. I want to see my Agosto in church sitting between his father and mother. I want to show how proud I am. I want to see Mrs. Torroni. She'll be so jealous that her son is not as brave as my son!" Gina smiled and adjusted the black lace. "It's beautiful!" she said, running her hand across it. "It's the most beautiful thing I ever owned."

Agosto basked in her pleasure.

"No, I wouldn't miss the look on Mrs. Torroni's face when she sees this lace!" His mother giggled like a young girl and turned away from the mirror. "Did you really meet the Governor? Do you really know him? He's such a brave man! Is he really like Garibaldi?" Her black shoe-button eyes shone. Like a treasure, she had hidden her hoard of questions for the moment when they were alone. She was from the old country, and in Domenico's presence she kept her silence, leaving the conversation to the men. But for this brief moment she found her tongue and her questions.

Agosto walked to her side and patted her shoulder tenderly. "If anyone is like Garibaldi, it is Teddy Roosevelt." Agosto, in his own mind, didn't really believe anyone in Cuba measured up to his hero, but he conceded that Teddy Roosevelt came the closest.

"I want you to take some time alone with me and tell me everything," his mother declared. In spite of her pain, her eyes danced. She was always inquisitive; it was a part of her. She was deeply religious, bound to the old ways, but somewhere within her was a spark, a desire to know about the world beyond Sheepshead Bay. It was, he surmised, that spark that had led her to answer the letters written by Domenico, to come to America alone, and to marry a man she knew only through friends. She was, he suspected, not to be influenced by the outside world, but she longed to know about it.

"You can have all the time I have," Agosto promised.

"You're a good boy. I missed you."

"You had Maria, Paolo, and Papa."

Gina pressed her lips together. "Your papa, yes. Your papa is a fine man, a good husband." She frowned, then whispered, "But Maria is a young stick-in-the-mud!"

Agosto roared. "Mama! Where did you hear that expression?"

Gina smiled conspiratorially. "I may be half-crippled, but I hear good. And I know what it means. Maria is too young to be old! I failed her, Papa failed her, and Donato failed her. He's so somber. He only thinks of business, and he thinks so much he gets nowhere. As for Paolo . . . well, he is involved with his clubs and his meetings. He wants to be a neighborhood leader, so his father will put him in charge. But I know he doesn't care that much. He should have been an actor."

"Mama!"

"A good mother knows her children. I love you all, but I know your faults." She shook her finger at him mockingly. "You got things on your mind you can't tell me."

Agosto blushed, thinking of the women of Havana and his lost virginity.

"Never mind, you'll tell me everything else." She smiled knowingly.

"I'll talk to you all you want, Mama."

"I want to know what Havana is like, Agosto. I want to know

what the fighting was like. I want to know everything. You tell me about Cuba, because I can't go there."

Agosto touched his mother's fine hair. "Papa should take you on a trip back to Italy."

"Oh, we'll go," Gina answered. "In time, when your papa retires. Then we'll go to Puglia and visit all the family in Lecce."

"You want to travel, don't you, Mama?"

She smiled and nodded, then whispered, "You can help me travel to Cuba in my mind, Agosto. You tell me stories and I'll imagine what it's like. You know that imagining is sometimes better. I used to imagine about Manhattan, but when I went there with your father to visit the Draganis—you remember, they moved to Manhattan—I was disappointed." She paused. "It was much nicer in my mind than in reality."

"Supper!" Maria's voice rang through the house.

Agosto took his mother's arm and kissed her on the cheek. "We'll have lots of time to talk," he promised.

Sunday, March 4, 1900

SHEEPSHEAD BAY

"Let's hurry," Agosto suggested. "So Mrs. Torroni can see you coming into church."

He took his mother's arm and helped her toward the front door. The others were gathered on the sidewalk. Domenico had lit a Cuban cigar and proudly puffed smoke into the morning air.

Agosto forced a smile. It wasn't as it should be, he thought. In the last twenty-four hours, nothing was as it should have been. For two years in Cuba he'd longed to come home; longed to be with those who understood him, those whom he understood. He'd been with a hodgepodge of men: men with soft Southern accents; men with Western drawls who talked about cows and sheep; men who were in a hundred different businesses. And there were those he found most interesting, the men who discussed stocks and bonds, banking and finance. They spoke a flawless English like Philip Ainsley. They read books and newspapers; some even read novels.

In the beginning he felt like a misfit, with nothing to talk about, so he listened and learned. But all the time, he had yearned to come home, to talk to people like himself. Now he was home, and apart from his parents, everyone seemed a stranger. No, his mother was special. She knew who and what she was, knew well enough to risk hearing about all other experiences and kinds of people. A sadness swept over him and he realized he envied her because at this moment he wasn't at all sure who or what he was. All he knew for certain was that Paolo, Donato, and Maria bored him, that the evening before, they had cut off his stories and returned to the familiar as if they couldn't stand to be reminded of life beyond the street on which they lived.

"Good cigar!" Domenico puffed away as they all walked off toward the church. He nodded proudly at the neighbors and

26

waved his cigar conspicuously "It's a real Havana cigar!" he told Roberto Marcucci, whom they met at the corner. "And look at Agosto in his uniform! See his medal!" Domenico flicked the medal with his finger.

Agosto felt himself flush with embarrassment, but he made no comment.

"Welcome home, Agosto!" Roberto embraced him. "You come over later, the wine is ready!"

Ainsley would have called it "dago red," Agosto thought.

"I'll come."

"You had better!" Roberto roared, slapping Agosto on the back.

On the steps of the church, they encountered old Salvatore Giuliano, who embraced Domenico and then Agosto. "It's good to have you home," old Salvatore said warmly. "Your papa needs you."

Agosto embraced Salvatore in return. The Giulianos were old friends. When Domenico first came to America, Salvatore gave him a job. The two of them invested in a fishing vessel and together profited. Then Domenico sold his half of the business to Salvatore and bought the greengrocery. Agosto remembered asking his father why he had given up the vessel when he loved the sea so much. "It's no life for a married man," Domenico answered simply.

"Where is Sal?" Agosto asked. Sal was Salvatore's son. He, like Roberto Marcucci, was Agosto's age; the three of them had grown up together.

"He's away just now. Back next week."

Agosto nodded. He caught the expression on Maria's face. Her small white hands gripped her purse, and her dark eyes studied the stone steps. Pressed lips betrayed her thoughts; there was clearly something on her mind. The others began moving into the church, and Agosto lingered with Maria.

"What's the matter?" he asked bluntly.

"Stay away from Sal," Maria urged. "His soul is black, like the night."

Agosto laughed. "You always liked him."

Maria didn't elaborate, she only shook her head darkly. She forged on ahead to catch up to Donato, leaving Agosto to bring up the rear.

The little church was unchanged, Agosto thought as he took his seat between his parents. It was a typical fisherman's chapel, brightly painted and filled with ornate statues. Philip Ainsley would have called it gaudy.

When Philip Ainsley thought of Italians, he thought of Little

Italy, where the newly arrived immigrants flooded, living on top of each other, struggling for a better life. Domenico was different. He had come to the United States much earlier, in 1853, when he was only seventeen years old. He settled in Sheepshead Bay with its little detached houses, each with its own plot of land so that a family could grow vegetables in the summer. And if anything symbolized the difference between families like the Tonellis and the newly arrived immigrants, it was this little church where the fishing fleets were blessed before heading out to sea. Most new Italian immigrants had grown away from the church, though they retained their religion. The newly arrived immigrants, were largely from the regions of Abruzzi, Calabria, and Sicily, as well as from the city of Naples. In those areas the church was one of the biggest landlords, controlling vast estates on which the *contadini* labored. The church dispensed no charity, but it expected donations, and because of the poverty, there was hostility toward organized religion. Moreover, in America the new Italian immigrants encountered a clergy that was largely Irish, who tended to ignore those special Italian feast days and festivals that were the major expression of the people's faith.

Agosto smiled as the priest began to chant the Mass. He was an Italian priest, the only one in Brooklyn, and he had been brought to America by the Italian fishermen of the area, who had raised money to ensure that their religious needs would be looked after. Agosto, who had been baptized and confirmed by him, always remembered his parents' pride. ''You're especially blessed because Salvatore and I raised the money to bring Father Carolo to this very church!''

Yes, Agosto thought. The Italians of Sheepshead Bay were different from the Italians of Little Italy—but they were all dagos to a Philip Ainsley.

The Sunday dinner table looked as Agosto always remembered it. I daydreamed about this, he thought. In Cuba each man was responsible for his own cooking. The rations were passed out, and consisted mostly of hardtack and tins of gristly meat. Mealtime was a time of grumbling and of complaints. He sometimes fed himself solely on the memories of Sunday dinner, for Sunday was a day of nonstop eating and drinking, a day when the long Tonelli table all but groaned under the weight of various pastas, of salad, cheese, olives, and of bottles of homemade red wine. And loaves of bread! Loaves that were nearly three feet long; hard on the outside and soft on the inside, they melted in his mouth and were used to sop up the rich sauces that spilled over the pastas.

"You eat," his mother instructed. "You lost a lot of weight! You don't even look like an Italian anymore! You look like one of those men from Manhattan, all skinny and pale."

"I feel fine."

"I'm telling you how you look." She smiled.

The table was covered with a long red-and-white tablecloth. It wasn't the Tonellis' best tablecloth, it was their only tablecloth. There were two large bottles of red wine, two giant loaves of bread, and three kinds of pasta, one with a sauce as red as the red squares on the tablecloth.

Domenico poured the wine. "A toast to my son! A toast to Agosto, who honors us with his Silver Star!"

The glasses were lifted and clicked together, and there was kissing and more hugging.

"To Agosto's homecoming! May he never leave again!"

As cheerful as Domenico's words were, and as well-intentioned as Agosto knew them to be, they sounded like a death sentence. Never to leave, never to be a part of the world beyond this neighborhood. Even Garibaldi traveled! He had gone to fight in Uruguay. He had been feted in New York, Paris, and London. A vague feeling of rebellion seized Agosto.

"And to the new addition on the store!" Donato added. It was dropped into the toast as a reminder. Donato's tone was good-natured, but it had a pleading quality, Agosto thought. Poor Donato, he'd never left, so his homecoming couldn't be feted.

"I'm looking forward to more time off." Domenico laughed. "Now that you're home to run things."

Agosto stared at his glass of wine. He felt uncomfortable. For two years Paolo and Donato had been running the store. Now they were cheerfully being told that they would no longer have that responsibility. Agosto waited for one of them to say something.

"Now you don't have to work so hard, Paolo." Maria's sharp voice filled the unusual silence. "Now you can find a wife and get married." Her tone seemed less than friendly. But she was smiling with her narrow lips. And her dark eyes flashed and fastened on her brother as if he were an insect she wanted to swat down, even though one wing was clearly broken.

"Maybe Agosto doesn't want to be in charge of the store," Gina suggested.

"What do you mean?" Maria snapped before anyone else could speak.

"She means I might want to go into some other business."

"What other business, for God's sake? This is our family business we're talking about here!" Paolo shouted. "It's the business our own father started!" Paolo's voice was suddenly defensive and a little higher-pitched than usual. Agosto frowned. Of course he'd sound defensive. First Domenico passed him over; now the chosen was rejecting what Paolo desired most.

"I know. I know what the business means to all of you. But I want to look into something else."

"In competition! Hey, Agosto, there're already too many stores in this area!" Paolo scowled.

"Not a store," Agosto said firmly.

"What, then?" Domenico spoke for the first time. His heavy eyebrows were lifted and he looked almost bemused. His eyes bore the same light of curiosity Gina often exhibited. Perhaps this conversation didn't come as a surprise to his father. Perhaps when his father had told his parents he was leaving Puglia and coming to America, there had been a similar conversation.

"I think I want to look into banking," Agosto replied.

"Banking! You are suddenly crazy, like young Salvatore! The only 'banking' for an Italian is with the . . . the Black Hand. You'll end up like young Salvatore! Godless!" Maria shrilled.

"Don't talk that way about Salvatore Giuliano's son! He is our friend! And what do you know of these things anyway? You're only a woman!" Donenico's eyes had gone suddenly hard.

Maria's silence was instant. Her eyes fastened on the tablecloth, her lips pressed closed.

"They keep it to themselves," Paolo said solemnly. "There's no room for Italians in that business. No one will let you do this."

"And the store! How can we build the addition? Come on, Agosto, you know you can't be a banker! People will laugh at you. You'll go in the front door and be thrown out the back! That's shame! They'll shame you!" Donato predicted.

"A man can only shame himself," Agosto replied.

Domenico leaned forward and banged his knife on the table. "How you going to do this?" he asked.

"I met some people in the army. First I want to try working in a bank for a while—to see if I like it. Then . . . well, I'm not sure yet."

Domenico nodded thoughtfully. "And will you get paid for this work?"

Agosto suppressed a smile. His father couldn't imagine a man getting paid for anything save manual labor. The work done by those in Manhattan offices was a mystery, and doubtless a mystery with ill feeling attached to it. Those who had money and no calluses on the hands were not trusted by a man like Domenico.

"I'll get paid for it," Agosto confirmed.

"Is it honest?"

Agosto nodded. He hoped his father would not ask for an explanation of the actual work.

"And can you one day open your own bank?"

Agosto smiled. "I suppose it's possible."

"Good," Domenico agreed. "It's not good for Tonellis to work for other people. We like to work for ourselves, for family."

"And how will we pay for the addition to the store? How can we manage?" Paolo sounded defeated.

"I'll give some of my salary—I don't need much to live on."

"At home you don't need anything," his mother said.

Agosto shook his head. "I'll have to live in Manhattan, near where I work."

"Not here?" Maria questioned, raising her eyebrows.

"Oh, Agosto . . . I just got you back," his mother said sadly.

Donato shook his head. "You're going to become like a stranger. You're going to move to New York and wear one of those hats and a big overcoat. You're going to talk funny."

"I know where I belong," Agosto answered. Even though it was a lie. He wasn't certain where he belonged.

Domenico banged his knife again. "It's good!" he bellowed. "I've decided it's good! Agosto must spread his wings. I trust Agosto to bring honor. Agosto has respect, he's always had respect! I give you my blessing. You become a banker. You become the best damn banker in New York City!"

When Domenico swore, Gina crossed herself. But she smiled. She handed Agosto the wine bottle. "Your glass is empty," she said softly. Then added, "I think banks are a good idea. They keep money safe, like the church keeps souls safe."

"We don't have any money in a bank," Paolo said in mild disgust.

"It's not right for you to do this," Maria warned. "You'll meet evil people. You'll forget our ways, you'll become a stranger."

"I've given my blessing," Domenico said with a warning glance toward his daughter. "Pass the pasta!"

Monday, April 30, 1900

MANHATTAN

Agosto paused to look into the deep pit, which was surrounded by a makeshift fence. He was not alone. The fence was lined with the denizens of Manhattan's offices. Dressed in their conservative suits, their hair held firmly down by their felt hats, their spring coats flapping in the breeze, they leaned over the fence and peered into the hole silently with expressions of near-reverence. The sight was obviously gripping, though Agosto himself was not at all sure why. The pit was filled with Irish construction workers; at least he assumed they were Irish. The laborers were stripped to the waist and their curses drifted upward, muted by the street traffic and the distance. They climbed over girders and worked diligently on the masonry. But it was not the construction that intrigued Agosto; it was the impeccably dressed, manicured, and somber observers. They were rapt in fascination as only those who had never bent their backs could be. They were as intrigued as he imagined the pharaohs must have been watching a hundred thousand slaves erect the pyramids. No, Agosto thought, a man who had carried bricks could never be mesmerized by construction.

"Another tall building," the man standing next to Agosto commented authoritatively.

"A wonder," Agosto replied blandly. Personally, he venerated God, not buildings, but he was interested in this phenomenon. He had been working in Manhattan for three weeks, and each and every noon hour he noted that the fence around the building site was crowded with silent worshipers who gave up free time to stare into the construction pit and comment in low tones on the progress of the work.

"Wonderful." the man next to him enthused. "Bloody wonderful!"

Agosto almost laughed. The first tall building had been finished in 1889—a tower at 50 Broadway. It was thirteen stories high—an unlucky number in any case—and had been built by John Stearns, the silk merchant. Just as the building—which no one believed would stand—was nearly completed, a hurricane hit the city. People stood on Broadway, Agosto had been told, in the high winds and drenching rain, just to see if it would topple over. But John Stearns himself climbed the ladders to the tenth floor to show his faith, and Bradford Gilbert, the architect, went all the way to the top. It didn't topple over, and now everywhere you went, tall buildings were being constructed.

Agosto turned and began walking. He too had forgone lunch, but not so he could stare into the pit. He had gone without it to save money. I'm turning into a regular miser, he conceded. But under the circumstances there was no alternative. He had his own rent to pay, and he took money home. Moreover, in the past several weeks he had spent a good deal on clothing, but the expense was easily enough rationalized; it was necessary for him to "look right."

On the matter of taking money home, Agosto felt some guilt. He didn't tell his father or any member of his family how much he earned. He took home little more than he had sent while he was in the army, though he made considerably more. But he was not being wasteful. He hoarded every cent and kept careful accounts, he ate only one meal a day and put every spare cent into stocks. But Domenico didn't know about the investments. Perhaps he would approve, as he unexpectedly approved of Agosto taking the job in the bank, but more likely he would have considered it a form of gambling. Certainly Maria would disapprove, even though her disapproval would be couched in words of concern. He imagined her saying, "Agosto, this is bad. You will lose everything."

Agosto headed back toward the Morgan Bank on the corner of Wall and Broad streets. In the short time he had been home, his life had taken unexpected turns.

Two days after he expressed his intentions at the dinner table, he had written to Vice-President Roosevelt. He only half-expected an answer, and when a warm friendly letter arrived a mere two weeks later, Agosto was taken aback. It contained a carbon copy of a letter written to the Morgan Bank, a carbon copy Agosto had read again and again.

He had the letter memorized. Even the carbon copy was on official White House stationery headed "From the Office of the Vice-President of the United States." It read:

Mr. Jonathan Wentworth
Personnel Manager
Morgan Bank
Wall and Broad Streets
New York City, New York

Dear Wentworth:
 Let this letter serve as the highest recommendation

of the bearer, Mr. Agosto Tonelli, an outstanding officer (field commission by yours truly) in the New York
Seventy-first and honorary "Rough Rider" (also a field
change of status by yours truly).

Mr. Tonelli is a bullie young man in all respects! He
distinguished himself in the campaign, won the Silver
Star for outstanding bravery, and showed not only
battle know-how, but did a splendid job as quartermaster of his corps. Not an easy job, I can assure you. He
kept good accounts, is scrupulously honest, and put
up with a good many complaints. I know you will hire
Tonelli. He's a good man.

My regards to J.P. (Tell him I'll be meeting with him
soon!)

Yours sincerely, Theodore Roosevelt
Governor

Agosto had handed Wentworth the letter and watched his
facial expression as he read it. Wentworth's steel-blue eyes
scanned the page quickly, then returned to the top and began
reading more slowly, as if the first time it had all been
incomprehensible. During the second reading he ran his finger
around his high white collar and shifted in his chair uneasily.

"It certainly is a good recommendation," Wentworth finally
managed.

Agosto nodded appreciatively. It wasn't exactly what he would
have called a recommendation. It was more akin to an order to hire
him.

"Tonelli." Wentworth rolled the name on his tongue as if it
were an extra long piece of pasta. "Is that Italian?"

"It's American," Agosto answered. "I was born here, in
Brooklyn."

"Naturally," Wentworth replied. "Your English is obviously
too good for you to be an immigrant."

Agosto didn't answer.

"Tell me about your education, Tonelli."

"I graduated from Brenden's High School. I was trained as a
quartermaster in the army."

"And between your graduation and the army?"

"I worked in my father's store in Brooklyn."

"And why do you want to work in a bank and learn banking?"

Agosto grinned. "I like money."

"Not everyone who works in a bank gets rich, although
certain opportunities for good investments present themselves if
you work in the right department."

"I want to learn everything about banking."

"How ambitious of you." Wentworth sounded sarcastic.

"I *am* ambitious," Agosto allowed. In point of fact, he saw no need to hide it.

"There aren't any Italian bankers in America," Wentworth said flatly. "Personally, I have nothing against immigrants, but I suppose it's a matter of public trust. People trust those who already have money. They trust good stable firms, firms with a reputation. After all, they put their money in banks as a safeguard, they lend it to us so we can invest it. I don't know if the average American would trust an . . ."

"Italian," Agosto finished.

Wentworth nodded. "Mind you, this has nothing to do with your working here. It's just a caution to your confessed ambition. I don't know if you could fulfill your ambitions in this field. I mean, generally your people have been small businessmen."

Agosto smiled. "Italy has more than small businessmen. The Bank of Milan is run by Italians. Indeed, Mr. Wentworth, it was Italians who invented banking."

Wentworth cleared his throat. "But they stayed in Italy," he blundered.

Agosto ignored him. "If you give me a position, I'll worry about my own ambitions."

"I only wanted to be honest with you."

"I appreciate your honesty."

Wentworth smiled weakly and stood up. He walked around his large desk and slapped Agosto on the back gingerly, as if afraid Agosto might touch him in return.

"Well, see here. I can't turn down the Governor. J.P. would never forgive me. So, I'll tell you what. I'll start you off in margins. If you survive there, I'll move you around to different departments till you've got the whole thing under your belt. How's that?"

"Sounds good."

"All right. You be here tomorrow at eight sharp. Sharp, Tonelli—I know about Italians and time."

Agosto grinned. Wentworth was not entirely without humor.

"And, Tonelli, go and get yourself a suit. It doesn't have to be as expensive as this one"—he fingered the cloth of his own apparel—"but try to get something that looks like this." He glanced down at Agosto's shoes. "And not so much shine. People don't trust men with shiny shoes; it identifies you as a flashy Italian. Dull finish, Tonelli. I want everything about you to look staid, stable, and dull. And no more garlic. You can't lean across a table and gve someone investment advice smelling of garlic!''

Agosto frowned.

"I mean it," Wentworth said seriously as he picked up a sheaf of folders. "Here, take these with you and study them tonight. I want you to pick out ten stocks and tell me why you think they're good investments. No, let me rephrase that. Tell me why you *know* they're good investments. Bankers don't think, Tonelli. That's your first lesson. Bankers don't think, they know. And one more thing, Tonelli.''

Agosto turned back to face Wentworth.

"A letter from Teddy Roosevelt can give you a chance, but if you can't make it, we'll dump you. The House of Morgan can't afford incompetents, and frankly, with your name a lot of people in this organization will be gunning for you.''

"Does that include you?''

Wentworth didn't smile. "It includes me,'' he answered.

Agosto remembered that night with considerable pain. He had drunk more cappuccino than his stomach could handle. He hadn't had diarrhea in Cuba, but he had it on Tuesday morning. He was also overtired from reading so many reports and from studying the newspapers and stacks of back issues of *The Wall Street Journal*. He had selected ten stocks and managed to justify them as "comers.'' But one, the last, was a flier. He suggested the bank make a large investment in George Eastman's company, Kodak. The little camera was already a success, but that was not why Agosto recommended it. First, he maintained, Kodak was a well-run company because Eastman had himself been a banker; second, although the various motion-picture firms, Vitograph, Biograph, and the others, were suing each other, he felt that when they got together they would have a monopoly on the production of films, and in turn, Kodak had a monopoly to supply the film. So enthusiastic was Agosto that he had decided to invest a hundred dollars of his own in Kodak. The decision gave him a kind of apostolic power of persuasian when he sat down with Wentworth to recommend his choices.

It was a grueling morning of discussion, but Wentworth finally conceded that the recommended stocks were wise selections.

"That's your first hurdle,'' Wentworth told him begrudgingly. "But only the first. Every day will be a test for you, Tonelli.''

And it has been, Agosto thought as he climbed the steps and entered the Morgan Bank, taking in its spacious elegance. The many-tiered crystal chandelier cast a muted light on the huge room, and Agosto's shoes clicked as he walked across the inlaid marble floor. This gray stone building looked unimposing from the outside, but inside, its art treasures hinted at its true worth. This, Agosto thought, is the center of America's financial power.

Friday, May 11, 1900

MANHATTAN

Agosto sat on the edge of his narrow bed and surveyed his room. It had all the grandeur of a clothes closet, but he knew he was fortunate to have found it. It was on Prince Street, near the corner of Sullivan, in the heart of Little Italy, three floors up a rotting flight of stairs. Its only favorable attractions were a tiny window and a somewhat yellowed sink. The bathroom, down the hall, was shared with twenty other tenants; thus he was often obligated to use the chamber pot under the bed. The furniture was as nondescript as the room. The only furnishings were a bed, a table, and one straight-backed chair. On the cracked wall, Agosto had hung the picture of the Virgin that Maria had insisted he take, and in the corner was a tintype in a cardboard frame. It was a family portrait taken some five years earlier.

Agosto wiped his brow and took a spoonful of the white powder prescribed by his doctor, washing it down with a glass of water. There was no question about it: he had a high fever and he was already beginning to get chills, a sure sign he was going to have a slight malaria attack. They had warned him about it when he left the army. Agosto sank back onto the bed and extinguished the lamp. He huddled under the heavy woolen blanket and thought about the time he and Philip Ainsley had been stricken.

"You must be immune," Ainsley had muttered. "The Cubans are carriers, and so are the Spanish! Are you a carrier too?"

Agosto shook his head. "You're delirious."

Ainsley's watery blue eyes were bloodshot, and beads of perspiration lined his brow. He shivered uncontrollably. "My head is killing me. Do something."

Do something? What could possibly be done? Three thousand, seven hundred and seventy men were down: Nearly three thousand had the dreaded malaria. The rest either had stomach ailments or yellow fever, and new cases were reported at the rate of some six hundred a day. At first the army responded by sending two regiments of black soldiers. "Blacks are immune to yellow fever and malaria,'' General Shafter proclaimed. But they were not immune.

Agosto doubted anyone was immune, although the men teased him. "Southern Italian blood!" they shouted. "You won't get the fever.''

"It's the unsanitary conditions,'' Shafter proclaimed next. He insisted on daily inspections until there weren't enough men well enough to stand. Everything possible was done to keep things clean, but nothing worked. The fever rampaged through the camp, striking officers and enlisted men alike; it struck regardless of cleanliness or background, in spite of diet and the amount of rest received, and to make matters worse, supplies of quinine were insufficient—and the use of quinine didn't affect yellow fever in any case. It seemed to work only for malaria, even though the cause of malaria was unknown.

"You'll die if you lie down,'' Agosto advised Ainsley. "Keep going, even if you have to crawl around.''

Ainsley crawled, Ainsley vomited, Ainsley shook, and Ainsley suffered high fever for over a weak. Then he seemed to recover.

"Your turn,'' Ainsley told Agosto when he was finally stricken. "Keep going, or you're going to die.''

Agosto kept going. Since Ainsley had kept going and recovered, Agosto could do no less. It became a matter of honor. As sick as Agosto was, he wasn't going to let Philip Ainsley prove himself stronger or more courageous. Their competition with each other served to keep them both alive.

"Snakes as long as Halstead Street,'' the bitter soldiers sang around the campfire, "Flies and skeeters that can't be beat! Oh, how we want to leave Cuba, Lord, How we want to go home!''

Agosto's eyes snapped open and he wiped his brow. "Damn,'' he grumbled. There was no question about it. He was having an attack, doubtless the result of the spring cold he had been developing. "A souvenir of Cuba,'' he muttered.

He struggled with the lamp on the table beside his bed. His shaking fingers finally managed to light it. The room came into focus in the dim light, and Agosto fumbled about, looking for more quinine powder. A second dose would send the chills away. He swallowed the powder with the remaining water in the glass. He glanced uneasily at the clock; it was almost midnight, and he wondered how he would get up in the morning to go to work. Fortunately, Saturday was only a half-day. On weekdays the stock market and banks were open till four; on Saturdays they were open till two. "I'll have to rest all weekend,'' Agosto said aloud.

He snuggled down under the blanket again and extinguished the lamp. He smiled to himself in spite of the chills. How stupid they had been to think that there were "immunes"; no one was immune. In a sense, he felt he had the last laugh. Malaria, it had now been proven, was carried by the mosquito, and that medical fact had been discovered and confirmed by Amico Bignami, Giovanni Battista Grassi, and Giuseppe Bastianelli—three Italian scientists in whom Agosto felt a certain pride. Probably yellow fever was caused by mosquitoes too, and if not mosquitoes, some other sucking parasite. It was all those insects, those damn biting, buzzing pests that were so impossible to escape. He thought of his half-dream and of his competition with Philip Ainsley to stay alive. He wondered if Ainsley knew of the Italian medical discovery; he wondered what Ainsley would say if he found out how advanced Italian medicine was compared to medicine in America. "Probably wouldn't admit it," he mumbled, suppressing another wave of violent chills.

Ainsley could be back at Harvard now, or he might be in Westchester or Newport. Maybe I should call him, Agosto mused. "I could ask him if he still has chills," Agosto said aloud. Vaguely Agosto acknowledged the fact that he rather missed Ainsley. After all was said and done, they had made a good team in Cuba, keeping each other going with insults.

Morning came too early, but Agosto forced himself to get up. His head still ached and his eyes felt as if they were full of sand. He wanted nothing more than to remain in bed, perhaps for the whole weekend. But that was impossible. First he had to work till two, then he had to go home to Brooklyn, and like it or not, he couldn't let on he was sick. His mother would surely deliver a lecture on his living habits; his sister Maria would seize on the opportunity to discuss the inherent evil of living away from home among strangers.

He dressed and abstractedly pulled the odd collection of covers up over the bed in a halfhearted attempt to make it. The early-morning light was pouring through the window, and the best Agosto could say was that it looked like a nice spring day, a warm spring day. He longed for warmth, more so after his chills and fever of the night before.

Yes, Agosto thought, looking out the window. It was warm, the kind of day that would make his father happy. Whenever Agosto or any other member of the family complained about the cold, Domenico said, "Sometimes I wonder why I ever came here? In Puglia the sky is always blue, the sun always warm. And the sea—the sea is like blue-green glass—*clare marina,*

brilliant.'' Domenico used the Latin phrase. ''But the sea can
also be unpredictable; moody like a woman, and fickle.''

''Are you really sorry you left?'' the young Agosto always
prodded.

''No, not sorry. I just wonder, that's all. Just like I wonder
sometimes why I gave up the ship with Salvatore. I like the sea,
I always dream of the *clare marina*, of the cool ocean breeze, of
the waves dashing on the rocks of a distant shore. Here, take this
conch.'' His father would hand him the beautiful spiral shell. On
its front a Roman chariot scene was hand-carved by a craftsman,
and the shell itself was embedded on an ebony stand so it could
be displayed. Agosto, following his father's instructions, would
hold the conch to his ear and listen.

''Listen . . . listen! It's been out of the sea for many years;
it's been made into a work of art! But listen, you can still hear
the roar of the sea, the waves as they come ashore in our
homeland.''

Agosto smiled at the memory, and in his mind he could see
the conch. It was sitting on the mantel in the parlor of his
parents' house. It was on the far left, near the painted satin
pillow Roberto had brought Gina from Philadelphia. The mantel
was a museum of treasures dominated by the graceful Virgin in
her light blue flowing gown, her heart bloodred, her face knit in
delicate pain. His mother had brought the statue from Puglia
wrapped in her wedding dress. She touched it now and again,
and when she was troubled, she stood in front of the statue
and prayed silently. Agosto shook his head as he glanced at the
clock. It was time to leave. Past time. He would have to hurry.

He put on his jacket. It itched, but it hung well on his body
and it gave him an air of confidence, a feeling that he was
somehow indistinguishable from the others, that he belonged
now to that fraternity of men who ran the nation's business.

He closed the door behind him. Tonight I have to go home, he
thought, but the thought was not as pleasing as it should have
been.

3

Saturday, May 19, 1900

Agosto worked in a tiny cubicle in the margin department, a windowless office furnished only with a massive oak desk, two chairs, and a telephone. Beyond the open door, the continual sound of the ticker machines clicked out the latest quotations in an endless monotonous rhythm, punctuated only by occasional lulls. Each transaction on the market was reported as the tickers printed out the stock symbol, the number of shares bought or sold, and the price. Every few minutes, a messenger was sent to Agosto's office, bearing the tapes for his perusal.

He put down the last batch of tapes and scribbled a note to himself on a large yellow pad. Sometimes he wondered what communications must have been like before the ticker machine was introduced in 1867. Visions of slow mail and running messengers ran through his mind, together with thoughts of the chaos slow communications could create. Of course, he contemplated, that could happen now. On a busy trading day the tickers often ran behind, leaving a vital information gap.

"Agosto Tonelli?"

Agosto looked up. The man who stood in the doorway of his office was expensively clad in a dark gray suit. He wore a fashionable felt hat and carried a lightweight coat over his arm. Definitely a banker; his skin had the pale hue that marked those who spent their days away from the sun. His hair, what could be seen beneath his hat, was thick and brown, with just a touch of gray near his sideburns. His eyes were blue and framed with gold wire glasses.

"I'm Agosto Tonelli." It was rare that he had a visitor, unless it was one of the senior supervisors coming to bring him extra work. More often than not, that was how the prejudice toward

him was manifested—extra work just before closing, usually
something that kept him at his desk for an additional hour.

The well-dressed gentleman extended his hand across the desk.
"Barton Pierce Ainsley," he announced, smiling. "I believe
you served with my son in Cuba."

Agosto smiled back. It was his best conservative banker's
smile. "Yes, sir. We served together."

I was only thinking of Ainsley last week, he remembered.
Somehow his brief attack of chills and his dream of Philip
Ainsley now seemed prophetic.

"How is Philip?"

"He's planning to go back to Harvard in the fall. At this
moment he's enjoying the social life of Westchester."

Barton Ainsley's expression was both friendly and questioning.
He seemed to be studying Agosto with his watery blue eyes; they
were eyes like Philip's, and Agosto could clearly see the similari-
ties between father and son.

"Philip told me a great deal about you," Barton Ainsley
continued. "And since my office is only down the street and I
was in town this morning, I thought I'd drop in and invite you
out to Westchester for the weekend. Philip would like to see
you."

Agosto raised an eyebrow. Barton Ainsley seemed genuine,
and his invitation and manner took Agosto completely by surprise.
But he forced himself not to act surprised.

"That's very kind of you," Agosto managed.

Barton Ainsley smiled again. "I wanted to meet the man who
saved my son's life. Frankly, Philip's sister would like to meet
you too. Philip's full of stories. You're rather famous in our
household, Tonelli."

"I didn't really save his life," Agosto protested. He felt
puzzled by Barton Ainsley. Philip spoke glowingly of him? He
and Ainsley had rarely had anything more than a barbed conversation laden with a kind of friendly contempt they felt for each
other.

"Don't be so modest! I've heard the story at least fifty times!
He was caught in the wire, you got him out in spite of enemy
fire. In any case, I'm told you received a Silver Star for saving
Philip and another chap later in the day—on the charge up San
Juan Hill, was it?

Agosto nodded and was certain his face revealed nothing short
of total disbelief. Ainsley hadn't even said so much as thank you
at the time.

"And I know you nursed him back to health when he had
malaria."

Agosto's mouth opened slightly. "I think Philip must exaggerate."

Barton Ainsley grinned. "More likely he understates. Will you come? It's nothing special, just a quiet weekend. Dinner, perhaps a little tennis, and some good conversation."

Agosto cónjured up an imaginary vision of the Ainsley mansion in Westchester. It would be a rambling, elegant mansion and he'd be totally out of place. As for tennis, he hadn't the dimmest idea of how it was played. Street soccer was the only game he knew, and since the teams were usually made up of immigrants from various Italian provinces, between whom there was often animosity, it was a rough game.

Barton Ainsley pressed his lips together. "I'm told you're doing very well here. I'm sure no one will ever tell you, but word has it you're a 'natural.' Wentworth says you're psychic." Ainsley laughed. "He can't admit to himself that you're capable of making the right decisions."

"You're right, he wouldn't tell me," Agosto said pointedly.

"He doesn't like foreigners, prefers to think the purebred have cornered the market in brains."

"I'd have thought your son felt the same way."

"Philip was born with a silver spoon in his mouth, and frankly, he soon learned to replace it with his foot. He's spoiled, immature, and reasonably uneducated. He has a lot to learn, a hell of a lot. But he's honest. He gave you the credit I expect was due. Just because he didn't give you credit to your face doesn't mean a thing. He's quite fond of you."

Agosto grinned. "I rather like him too."

"I suspect you'll go far in this business. I know you could benefit from the kind of men you'll meet this weekend. Will you come?"

"How will they feel about a foreigner—as you put it?"

Ainsley grinned and shifted his weight from one foot to the other. "My dear Tonelli, the Baron Rothschild is a foreigner."

"Not from Brooklyn."

"A little spit, polish, and guidance and you won't be from Brooklyn either. If you're the man Philip says you are, you won't turn down opportunity."

"I'm not a social climber."

"I wouldn't invite you if you were."

"And I don't consider myself a foreigner. I was born here."

"Oh, I know. On the fourth of July. Don't be defensive. Listen to the advice successful men can give you. Make the most of it and then follow your own instincts."

Senti tutti i consigli, ma il tuo non lo lasciare. Barton Ainsley's words were nearly identical to Domenico's proverb: "Listen to all counsel, but keep your own."

"I'll be glad to come," Agosto agreed.

"Good," Barton Ainsley said, pressing his lips together. "I'll pick you up at two-thirty in front of the bank."

Agosto reached across his desk and shook Ainsley's hand. "I'll be there." He glanced at the clock on the wall; it was a giant clock for such a small office and it was framed in oak, the same kind of oak his desk was made of—light wood with dark grainy lines. It was nearly noon.

Agosto eyed the black telephone on the corner of his desk. Its gaping mouthpiece seemed to be looking at him accusingly. "Damn," he cursed. He couldn't call his mother because there was no phone in the house, and although the Giulianos, who lived down the street, had a phone, there was little likelihood of anyone being home. He'd have to call the store, and in all probability he'd get either Paolo or Maria.

For a brief moment he considered telling them he was sick. But that wouldn't do. A hint of illness would bring his sister immediately, and no amount of reassurance would prevent her from insisting it was her duty to nurse him back to full health. Besides, even if he succeeded in dissuading Maria, his mother would worry needlessly.

"The truth," he said aloud. "And there's no use putting it off."

Agosto reached for the receiver and lifted it off its hook. He pulled the phone closer so he could better speak into it. The store would be noisy; it was always noisy.

Agosto got the number and listened to the ring of the party line the store shared with the butcher down the street. Miraculously, Antonio the butcher didn't answer the phone as he usually did. Both Antonio and Domenico had just gotten phones, but neither had mastered the long and short rings that distinguished one number from another on the three-party line. The third party who shared the phone was old Mrs. Solari, who was deaf and never answered even her own ring. Mrs. Solari's phone was a Christmas gift from her son, and for her the phone was an object of worship rather than an instrument with a utilitarian purpose. It stood on her mantel next to her plaster-of-paris statue of Christ, and sometimes she'd lift its receiver and pray aloud into it, interrupting whatever conversation might be in progress.

"Yes," Maria's high voice answered.

"It's Agosto."

"Who? Speak louder!"

"Agosto!" Somehow he felt angry. In the background he could here someone haggling with Paolo over the price of onions.

"Agosto? What's the matter? Why aren't you on the way home? Mama's expecting you for dinner."

"I'm not coming home. That's why I'm calling."

"What do you mean? I told you, Mama's expecting you! And all week Papa's been saying, "Wait till Saturday when Agosto comes.' "

Agosto closed his eyes and tapped his fingers on the desk. The phone was a damnable object. One couldn't see people's faces or gestures. Shouting meant nothing—you had to shout anyway.

"I can't come home! It's business. Important business. I have to go to Westchester!"

"Where?"

"Westchester."

"Why?"

"I told you, business!"

"I knew this would happen. I knew it. Mama will be so disappointed, and so will Papa. And now I'll have to wait another week!"

"For what?"

"To tell my news! Papa said I should wait till you came home on Saturday!"

"Well, you can tell me now."

"No! It's family news!"

Agosto let out his breath. "I'm sorry, but I can't come home this weekend."

"Are you going out with one of those women?"

"Those women," as his sister called them, were defined as any women whose hair was uncovered and who weren't Italian. "No, I told you, it's business."

"Mama will be disappointed."

"Tell her I'm sorry. Tell Papa too. Tell them I'll be home next weekend for certain."

"Holy Mary, Mother of God . . ." old Mrs. Solari's cracked voice interrupted.

"What?" Maria said.

"Tell them I'm sorry!" Agosto hung up just as Mrs. Solari began her rosary anew. *"Cristo,"* he muttered. It would have been better if Paolo had answered. In fact, he reflected, it would have been better if Antonio the butcher had answered.

Agosto felt a little apprehensive as he waited in front of the Morgan Bank. He had hurried around and bought a few necessities, and these he packed into a newly purchased satchel.

In the back of his mind he harbored the fear that he might require some formal attire. God knew what a "quiet" weekend in Westchester meant to Barton Ainsley. He reviewed the various excuses he could use to explain his lack of clothing. "Didn't have time to pack," he could say, or he could claim his suitcase had been lost or stolen. Somehow admitting that he owned only one suit and a hundred dollars' worth of shares in Kodak seemed out of the question.

And what could he discuss with Barton Ainsley and his friends? Garibaldi's conquest of Sicily? The price of onions? His own day-to-day work in the margins department? No, he decided. There was little he could discuss, but there was much he could listen to, or at least he hoped there would be much to listen to. In any case, Philip would be there, and if nothing else, they could trade insults. There was no need to fear discussions with Philip Ainsley, because with Philip he could hold his own.

"Ah, there you are." Barton Ainsley waved casually. "It's a nice day, let's walk down to the foot of Wall Street."

The foot of Wall Street? Why were they going down to the foot of Wall Street? Weren't they going to take the streetcar or the train?

"My yacht's anchored there," Barton Ainsley said matter-of-factly. "It's the perfect day. We'll just hop aboard at the dock, go around the Battery and then on up the Hudson to Westchester."

Agosto nodded. The only ships he'd ever been on were the transports that had taken him to Cuba and back. The only small boat he'd ever been on was Salvatore's fishing vessel, which smelled perpetually of mackerel and which was in no way a pleasure craft.

"My father has a friend with a boat," Agosto ventured.

"What kind?" Barton Ainsley asked.

"A fishing boat," Agosto answered, smiling. "Strictly practical. A lot of the Italian families that live in Sheepshead Bay are fishermen."

"It's an honorable occupation. Fishing and furs made the economy of this country. John Jacob Astor was, after all, a glorified trapper."

"He owned a trading company."

"People who make money, real money, have usually worked in their business. They know their investment from the ground up. It's quite true that I inherited money, but I started out as a teller. You can't run a business without knowing what's involved, without knowing the day-to-day problems and workings. Investments aren't abstract either—it's vision. You have to have the vision to know when a company has potential and when a product is going to sell. There's a lot of knowledge involved and, I willingly admit, a certain amount of luck.''

"It helps to know what's going on in Europe too," Agosto added. "We're not so independent as we think.''

"Damn right! This country needs trade. International free trade and commerce. We're an industrial giant and we're going to need expanding markets.''

They reached the docks. Agosto looked around in awe. He often walked down to the docks on his lunch hour, but he had never dreamed he would have the opportunity to sail on one of the vessels.

"Ahoy!" Barton Ainsley called out with joviality. He stopped in front of a blinding white seventy-foot yacht. She was trimmed in red and flew an American flag together with another insignia.

"This is it, the *Boyington*, named after my maternal grandfather, Clifford Philip Boyington.''

"She's beautiful.''

"Welcome aboard, Mr. Ainsley!" A young black steward appeared from below deck. His uniform was decorated with bright gold buttons and was as spotless white as the vessel.

"Thank you, Charles.'' Ainsley smiled. "This is my guest, Mr. Tonelli. He'll be joining me in the stateroom.''

"Yes, sir!''

"What do you drink, Tonelli? Scotch, bourbon?''

"Scotch and soda," Agosto returned. Actually, he hated Scotch and soda, but he was aware that men like Ainsley usually only drank wine with meals, and Scotch and soda was what Philip had drunk in Cuba—when it had been available.

"A Scotch and soda for Mr. Tonelli too, Charles.''

"Yes, sir!''

"This way, Tonelli. I think you'll enjoy the view from inside. The breeze on deck is a bit much, and it'll pick up when we're under way.''

Agosto followed Barton Ainsley into the stateroom. It had windows on all sides, offering a panoramic view. Below the windows were low-slung blue-and-red plush velvet sofas. And there were several small tables scattered about, though they were fastened to the floor.

"Make yourself at home, Tonelli. It's not as luxurious as old Cornelius Vanderbilt's yacht the *North Star* or Morgan's *Corsair*, of course. but I like to think of it as homier. See that monster over there—third one down—that's Cornelius' yacht.''

Agosto followed Barton Ainsley's pointing finger. The Vanderbilt yacht was a monster indeed; it was at least a hundred and fifty feet. "Impressive," Agosto said honestly. There just wasn't another adjective that would do.

"Money doesn't buy happiness, but it makes misery bearable," Barton Ainsley joked.

"That's a time-worn saying," Agosto replied cheerfully, "but are you and Cornelius Vanderbilt miserable?"

Ainsley looked surprisingly thoughtful, "No," he finally answered, "but sometimes it seems that personal tragedies stalk the rich, as if some higher power wants them to remember they're human."

Agosto gave Ainsley's answer some thought, then asked, "What would you do without money?"

"Probably what your father does, or something like that. I certainly wouldn't like to work for other people."

It was the second time that day that Barton Pierce Ainsley had sounded like Domenico speaking in another language.

"You have a partner, don't you?" Agosto asked.

"William Bentley Stearns. But he's my brother-in-law. We tend to keep things in the family."

Agosto smiled. "That gives us one thing in common."

"More to the point, Tonelli, what would you do *with* money?"

"I think I'd start my own bank. But I have to learn a lot more first."

Barton Ainsley nodded. "You'd have it rough, banking is an establishment enterprise, and what's more, bankers have an almost universal profile in America."

"Staid, stable, dull, and Episcopalian," Agosto returned. "My father says that overcoming obstacles gives a man greater satisfaction."

"I agree. And I must say in a way I envy you. When you're born with money it's different, of course. You don't have that need to conquer, you only have a need to hold on to it. I have a theory that innovation dies in the third generation unless there's an infusion of new blood."

"Is Philip the third generation?" Agosto queried.

Barton Ainsley nodded, and at the same time his face clouded slightly. "If Philip is to survive, I'll have to make it difficult for him. He's soft, too soft."

My father feels that way about my brother, Agosto reflected. But he kept the thought to himself.

Charles knocked on the door and brought in the drinks. Ainsley motioned him to put them down on one of the tables.

Barton Ainsley lifted his glass. "Here's to a pleasant weekend," he toasted.

In the distance Agosto could see the Ellis Island ferries. Laden with new immigrants, he thought. More Italians, Irish, Hebrews, Greeks—masses of people to toil in the growing industries.

Then the rising palisades came into view, the lush greenery that lined the shore. The yacht sailed on up the Hudson and they passed huge barges loaded with rail cars which carried food into the city, food to feed the millions of workers.

Agosto was overcome with the same feeling he had experienced on his return from Cuba. New York City seemed like a toy city fueled by people who appeared to be constantly building and building. He smiled to himself. Those people didn't earn the huge salaries of Barton Ainsley, nor did they individually possess the resources to become their own financial masters. The existing banks ignored them and catered to the wealthy. But collectively, Agosto thought, they have millions. He thought of the old women he knew who, like his own mother, constantly saved pennies and nickels, hiding and hoarding them, "a little something put aside, just in case." Why couldn't such people earn interest on their pennies just as Barton Ainsley earned interest on his millions? Why shouldn't such people be able to get loans? Surely a man willing to work twelve hours a day wasn't a risk.

"You seem pensive," Barton Ainsley commented.

"Just enjoying the scenery," Agosto replied. "The view from this vantage point is different."

"Distance clarifies things," Ainsley answered, as if he could read Agosto's mind.

They descended the gangplank onto the private dock and were met by an elegant surrey drawn by two shiny-coated chestnut-brown stallions. The surrey was trimmed in gilt and its seat, like the sofas on the yacht, was red plush velvet. An elderly black drove. He was dressed in white breeches, a red coat, and a top hat. He might well have been a slave on one of the great Southern plantations of fifty years ago, but then, the rolling manicured lawns of the Ainsley estate on the east bank of the Hudson might well have belonged to a plantation mansion.

"Hop in," Barton Ainsley invited.

"Is the house that far?"

Ainsley grinned. "We could walk, but to keep up appearances, we'll ride."

Agosto climbed into the seat beside Ainsley, and the driver set the horses in motion. The surrey ambled slowly up the long winding drive, and beyond a barrier of stately weeping willows, the portico of the large white house emerged on the crest of the hill.

"It looks rather like the White House," Agosto commented.

"I tried politics when I was younger," Ainsley confessed. "Having failed to become President, I decided to build my own White House."

The surrey came to a halt in front of the wide white portico and the driver, carrying Agosto's satchel and Barton Ainsley's briefcase, fell in behind Agosto and Ainsley as they strolled toward the front door.

"Where's Philip?" Agosto queried. What had he expected, that Philip Ainsley would fling open the door and come running down the steps to embrace him?

"I hope he's resting," Barton Ainsley replied with a slight frown. "I didn't mention it before, but he's not been too well."

"Malaria chills?"

Barton Ainsley nodded. "Yes. I have him seeing a specialist, of course."

"I have them too," Agosto confided, hoping that his revelation would assuage Barton Ainsley's obvious concern.

"Yes, but you look healthier. Philip looks . . . well, peaked."

A black maid opened the door and smiled broadly. Her hair was hidden beneath a white dust cap and she wore a long gray-and-white-striped dress with a lacy apron over it. Her dress, Agosto could not help thinking, was of a better quality than any owned by his mother or his sister.

Agosto took in the mammoth entryway in one sweeping glance. It had a highly polished inlaid tile floor, an ornate hanging crystal chandelier, a winding white staircase that led to the second floor.

"Let's go in here," Ainsley suggested, leading Agosto through heavy double doors.

The room behind the doors was large, larger than the Tonellis' house, but its furnishings gave it a warm feeling in spite of its size. The rich oak floor at the far end of the room was partially covered by a deep pile carpet which was a subtle combination of deep greens and golds. Graceful ornate mahogany tables with gold accessories held golden Tiffany-shaded lamps. The chairs and the love seats were covered with green or gold satin, and paintings by Cézanne and other French moderns were on nearly every wall. Agosto looked to the far end of the room. There the floor was bare and the walls were lined with ferns in giant red-and-white pots. It was a moment before Agosto saw that the room could be divided by a great folding door. In all, it reminded Agosto of a display in a Lord & Taylor window; he half-expected posed mannequins to be lounging on the settees.

Ainsley walked directly to a small lacquered tray on which a silver decanter and small silver brandy snifters sat. "I'll pour you some brandy."

"This is a huge room," Agosto observed.

"Why don't you pull the doors closed. It tends to make it a little cozier, not that anything in this house is actually cozy."

Agosto walked to the folding doors. He felt that he was alone in a museum, an interloper after the public had been turned out for the night.

The doors slid easily and silently on ball bearings and the giant room was instantly cut in half, though the remaining half was still a formidable size.

Ainsley handed Agosto the brandy snifter. "Art Nouveau," he commented dryly, "My wife, Aggie, decorated it before she died three years ago."

"I'm sorry. I didn't know. Philip never said anything . . ." Agosto felt awkward.

Ainsley pressed his lips together and smiled tightly. "It's all right, it's been some time now."

"I like the use of color," Agosto said. They were the colors of fall, his favorite season. "Do you, Philip, and your daughter live alone here?" he ventured.

"My daughter, Sarah. I suppose Philip never mentioned her either."

"I'm afraid you're right. The first I heard of her was when you mentioned her."

"I expect she'll join us momentarily. She must have seen us drive up. But Sarah likes to make an entrance. She's a trifle dramatic."

Agosto smiled and swirled the amber liquid in the silver snifter. He felt as if this experience was happening to someone else, was a fiction woven from a daydream. The yacht, the house, even this room, was so far from his experience that he couldn't put it all into context. It was as if he had stumbled onto the set of an opera and quite accidentally become one of the singers. Yes, that was it. He felt as if he had moved from standing in the back of the Metropolitan to a position on center stage.

"Ah, Father!"

The double doors opened and Sarah Ainsley swept into the Art Nouveau room like a prima donna. Her long golden hair was pinned up and framed her face; her blue eyes studied him quizzically. She wore a long mauve taffeta dress with a tiny pinched waist, and mauve ribbons fell from her hair. Philip's sister was a very attractive young woman, Agosto noted.

"Sarah, this is Philip's friend Agosto Tonelli."

She smiled a brilliant smile and fluttered her eyelashes. "Philip didn't tell me you were so handsome," Sarah Ainsley said flirtatiously. "You have a cleft chin, very handsome."

Agosto flushed. Her comment was rather bold. The women in Havana had been bold too, but they were professionals of sorts. This was a well-bred, obviously educated, wealthy young woman. Yet she had the coquettish manner of a harlot. Agosto didn't quite know how to respond. "Philip didn't tell me he had a sister," he finally said.

"He's such a silly, and that's so like him." Sarah produced a gaily painted Japanese fan and spread it out with a flip of her wrist. She smiled at him from behind it; her eyes twinkled as if she enjoyed his obvious discomfort.

"Is Philip up?" Barton Ainsley asked.

"He's dressing," Sarah said, gliding toward the brandy tray. Agosto watched her as she poured herself a drink. He had never seen a woman drink brandy before. His mother and sister drank a little wine with meals, of course, but never anything else, and never would they help themselves. He could not have been more surprised if Sarah Ainsley had pulled out a cigar.

"Agosto!" Philip came through the doors and Agosto looked at him in surprise. In only two months he seemed to have withered. His young face was sickly white and drawn; he had dark circles under his pale blue eyes, and he looked to have lost fifteen or twenty pounds.

Instinctively Agosto stepped forward and embraced Philip. It was a bear hug of an embrace, but in a sense it was protective too. Agosto struggled with his shock at Philip's appearance. What could he say? More important, was there anything he could do?

When he withdrew from the embrace he looked at Philip Ainsley carefully. He masked his real concern, but commented, "You've lost weight."

"A touch of the malaria," Philip said offhandedly. "I suppose I should reprimand you for that clearly dago greeting. You're supposed to shake hands, you know."

Agosto extended his hand with a wide grin. In spite of his ailment, whatever it was, Philip was still Philip. "How do you do, you bluenose bastard."

Philip Ainsley laughed. "That's better!"

Saturday, May 26, 1900

B R O O K L Y N

Agosto reflected on the weekend at the Ainsleys' and decided it was both stimulating and perplexing. On Saturday night Barton Ainsley hosted what he called a "small dinner." Among the guests were William Bentley Stearns, Ainsley's partner in The Ainsley National Bank, his wife, Martha Pierpont Stearns, and a cousin, Creighton Stearns, who was in his early twenties, and obviously a young man smitten with Sarah Ainsley. In addition to the members of the Stearns dynasty, there were other well-known names, the Whitneys, the Lamonts, and J. P. Morgan Jr.

"No man owns a fortune," Morgan intoned. "It owns him, dictates his hours, his tastes, rules him completely!"

Early in the evening Agosto tried to remain in the background. What was he to say to these men? But later, as the conversation became more casual, he began to participate, choosing his words carefully. He did, in a sense, work for J. P. Morgan Jr. And, he contemplated, if he was prejudiced, it was well hidden and not at all like the bigotry he encountered daily at the bank. In the hall beyond his cubicle, he often heard Fredericks, the supervisor in the margins department, say, "Ask the dago what he thinks." Or, "Have the dago do it, he's got plenty of time." No, nothing so overt from Barton Ainsley's guests. They seemed to regard him as a mere oddity, a person so foreign from their way of life that he was, as Mrs. Whitney kept saying, "interesting." Indeed, by the end of the evening the conversation had come close to a "tell-us-what-the-common-man-thinks" invitation to express his opinions.

On the positive side, Agosto could honestly admit that he picked up some vital stock information, and in addition learned more about each man's holdings and outlook. What perplexed him was the isolation in which these men who ruled finance lived. Every single day they made decisions that affected millions of people, yet they seemed to know nothing about those people and, he guessed, cared little either.

On the negative side, the weekend had caused him still further difficulties at work. J. P. Morgan Jr. kept speaking to him, and so did Whitney when he was in the bank on Tuesday. That brought on a round of comments from the other staff—whispers that were uttered just within earshot: "The dago is a real climber," or "I suppose he thinks he'll be running the bank soon."

This weekend was quite a different weekend from last. Downstairs he could hear the loud voices of his brother-in-law, Donato, and Paolo, and in his mind's eye he could see Maria sitting on the sofa, her hands folded, her eyes looking down.

Agosto flushed the toilet and turned to look into the cracked bathroom mirror. He examined his image. His own face was certainly paler than it had been two months ago, but his pallor wasn't unhealthy like Philip's. It was the result of the change in his way of life; it was because he worked inside all day instead of out on the sidewalk like Paolo and Donato.

Agosto smiled at himself. Was he good-looking, as the bold Sarah Ainsley had suggested? He was certainly well enough built. His arms were muscular and his waist was trim. Yes, Agosto decided, he was reasonably attractive. And he complimented himself on having a certain European style of charm.

He decided he was flattered by Sarah Ainsley's behavior toward him. She flirted outrageously, but she seemed genuinely attracted to him. "But not for me," Agosto said to his image in the mirror. It wasn't that she wasn't pretty—she was. And she was both pleasant and bright. But a woman like Sarah Ainsley was not for him; he couldn't afford her either in the monetary sense or in the emotional sense. A relationship would take up too much time. And if he imagined her at Sunday dinner with his family, the thought was laughable. Yes, Sarah Ainsley came from another place, a world of elegance and money, a world of manners and affectations, a world far from the living room downstairs.

"Are you going to stay in there forever!" Donato's voice shouted from outside the bathroom door.

"I'm coming!" Agosto yelled back. He sighed. They were surely about to sit down at the table, and when they did, they would all start at once: "Where were you last weekend? Tell us about it. You were expected and didn't come!"

Agosto shrugged. The tiny bathroom was a refuge, the only place you could be alone in the entire house. He dreaded giving it up and reemerging to join the fray.

Abstractedly he touched the somewhat rusty nickel faucet on the basin. The faucets in the Ainsley house were gold and the basins marble. He smiled. His mother would like a marble basin. She wouldn't like a gold faucet, but she loved marble because it reminded her of Italy.

"About time," Donato roared as Agosto appeared. Donato hurried into the toilet, but obviously not to talk to his image in the mirror. Agosto made his way down the narrow staircase. The aroma of his father's stogies greeted him.

He went into the crowded kitchen and lit a stogie himself; its pungent smoke momentarily engulfed him.

"Dinner will be ready soon," his mother said as she stirred the contents of a large pot. It was Saturday and they would eat in the kitchen. The dining room, like the tablecloth, was reserved for Sunday.

Donato clambered down the stairs and stood in the doorway. He was dressed in a rumpled ill-fitting suit which was too tight for him. He was forty, eighteen years older than Maria, and, Agosto assumed, his lack of success was at least partly the cause of his sister's unhappiness. She had had few suitors, and when Salvatore's son, Sal, stopped seeing her, she married Donato. Donato was a good man, Agosto acknowledged. Not ambitious, but good. Still, they had been married for some time and there were no children. Maria, Agosto believed, didn't want to be a mother, but she did want children because Domenico wanted grandchildren and Maria believed that if there was a child, Domenico would give Donato more responsibility—perhaps even half the store when he retired.

"Maria has some news," Donato announced. "She wouldn't tell anyone, not even me, till we were all together."

"It's your fault," Maria said accusingly to Agosto. "I'd have been able to tell sooner if you'd come home as you should have."

"I told you, it was important business."

Maria didn't answer, but she looked sulky.

"You can tell now," Donato pressed.

"Not till we're all sitting down."

"Suspense," Domenico grumbled.

Agosto's mother began putting dishes of food on the table. "Sit down, sit down." She motioned with her hands impatiently and they all sat down in their usual places.

Domenico poured the wine and then turned to Maria. "Now," he pressed. "You have everyone's attention."

Maria looked at the table and fingered the bottom of her wineglass.

"I see this is going to be like a grand opera," Domenico intoned. "A long overture."

Maria looked up. "I'm pregnant," she announced abruptly. Her face flushed. "And I've had to keep it a secret for a whole week!"

"Pregnant!" Donato fairly leaped up. *"Glorioso!"* he shouted.

"It's about time!" He leaned over and hugged Maria, who remained somewhat stiff.

Agosto grinned. He got up and walked around the table and hugged his sister, leaning over to kiss her on the cheek. "It's wonderful news! I'm sorry I delayed its telling."

Maria blinked up at him. "Two months pregnant," she added.

"A grandchild! Hey, Mama, we're going to have our first grandchild!" Domenico hugged Gina, whose tears immediately began to flow. "I've waited so long," she wept.

"A toast!" Paolo offered. "To the next generation!"

"A toast to Maria," Agosto added. "And may she have many more."

"May she have a son!" Domenico bellowed.

They raised their glasses not once, but three times. Then Domenico set his down. "And when will you get married, Agosto? I want more grandchildren! I want some named Tonelli!"

Maria's face clouded over immediately and Agosto shifted uncomfortably in his chair. Domenico had unwittingly stolen Maria's moment of triumph by reminding her that her children would bear her husband's name.

"You should be thinking about marriage," Donato agreed quickly.

"I'm thinking about marriage," Paolo put in.

"To who?" Domenico asked, raising an eyebrow.

Paolo smiled. "Oh, I hardly know her. But I'm thinking of asking permission to call on her."

"Who?" Domenico persisted.

"Old Mrs. Solari's granddaughter, Cecilia. I see her in church. A very pretty girl."

Domenico grunted. "Very pretty," he agreed.

Agosto slapped his brother on the back. "I haven't seen this girl, where has she been?"

"Old Mrs. Solari has two sons. The one who gave her the telephone and another, Tomaso Solari, who only a few months ago moved here from New Haven with his family. Cecilia is Tomaso's daughter."

"And what does she look like?" Agosto prodded good-naturedly.

Paolo actually blushed. "Very pretty" was all he could say.

"And you, Agosto? You're older than Paolo and you have a good position now. When will you get married?"

"When the time is right," Agosto hedged. "But it won't be that long."

"Then you had better start looking," his mother said slyly.

"I always look," Agosto joked.

"You'll probably marry one of those women; who else will you meet working on Manhattan? Especially if you don't come home on the weekends."

"It was only one weekend," Agosto snapped with some irritation. He was doubly defensive, because he had been invited back to Westchester and he knew Maria was right, though he didn't want to admit it. He was certainly going to be away on future weekends.

"The dinner is getting cold," Gina said, picking up a large bowl of pasta. "And, Maria, you remember, you're eating for two now, so no more picking at your food. You're like Agosto, you're too skinny." She reached over and patted Paolo on the knee. "Now, Paolo knows how to eat!"

Paolo grinned. "I think I'll go and visit Mr. Solari tomorrow, I think I'll see if I can call on Cecilia."

Domenico grunted and wound the pasta around his fork. Agosto didn't want to look up. Clearly his father wanted his sons to marry in the order in which they were born. It was proper; it was expected.

4

Monday, December 24, 1900

BROOKLYN

A chilling wind blew off Sheepshead Bay, and hard, icy snow began to fall, making the steps that led to the church treacherous.

Donato held Maria's arm tightly and helped her up the steps; she was nearing her time and was heavy with child. She was small of stature, and now her girth appeared equal to her height.

Gina and Domenico were already inside. Midnight Mass was a special tradition on Christmas Eve, an event attended by the whole family. Agosto and Paolo paused outside to finish their stogies before entering. In spite of the cold, the night air was pleasant and invigorating, quite different from the warm, stuffy house that for days had seen the coming and going of distant family and neighbors. Christmas was for visiting, and families went from one home to another, eating, drinking, and talking about the past. The visiting continued till Twelfth Night, on January 6, when the children put out their shoes and stockings so that La Befana, the kindly old woman of Italian lore, would fill them with gifts.

Paolo nudged Agosto roughly in the ribs. "There," he indicated with his head. "Here comes Cecilia now!"

Agosto turned to catch a glimpse of a young woman bundled up in a great wool coat. On her right was Tomaso Solari, whom Agosto knew only by sight, and to her left was a woman of about forty—doubtless her mother. Behind them, two younger men, probably brothers. They helped old Mrs. Solari, Tomaso's mother, toward the church. Tonight, Agosto assumed, old Mrs. Solari had forgone praying into the telephone to confront God in person.

"Well, what do you think?"

Agosto smiled. "I can't see much of her with that coat and the scarf. It's much too dark to see her face."

"She's beautiful!" Paolo confirmed.

"I believe you," Agosto replied with a grin.

"Old Tomaso is strict," Paolo said with a shrug. "He says she's too young to be courted. I've called twice, though."

"And does she like you?" Agosto pressed.

Again Paolo shrugged. "Who can tell? She's only a girl—seventeen, and very shy."

"A girl like the ones from the old country?" Agosto joked.

"The best kind," Paolo replied, stamping out the butt of his stogie.

Agosto did the same, and together they went into church. Agosto inhaled. The scent of the incense filled his nostrils, and a wave of nostalgia swept over him as the priest began to chant the traditional Christmas prayers in Latin. In his whole life he had missed only two Christmas Eve Masses in this church—those two he had spent in Cuba. On one he had gone to the cathedral in Havana, but it was not the same, and only made him homesick. It was in this church he felt comfortable. He knew the names of the people for whom the votive candles flickered; he knew each of the statues that graced the church's tiny alcoves, and the small hand-carved figures of the Nativity scene that decorated a long table near the back of the church were nearly identical to his mother's Nativity set, which she had brought from Italy.

Agosto paused to look at it for a moment. The model thatched stable, the statue of the beautiful Virgin in her long blue robes, the miniature goats, sheep, and lambs, the proud Joseph and the three richly dressed Wise Men, their costumes painted with gold and their crowns bejeweled with dots of red to represent rubies . . . and the infant Jesus in the tiny makeshift crude crib lined with straw. Agosto stared at the manger scene and recalled how angry his mother was the day he took her set down from the mantel and rearranged it on the floor. "No, no, no!" she chided. "Those are special! They're to look at, not to touch! If you knew how I brought them all the way from Lecce! I wrapped them so carefully! I carried them in my satchel so they wouldn't be broken, so we could have a little bit of Italy in our home at Christmas! Those are not toys, Agosto! Those are holy objects!"

And Gina still had them. They were arranged on the sideboard in the parlor and augumented with cotton for snow, though Agosto didn't think it snowed in the Holy Land. And although the Virgin's blue robes were somewhat faded, the whole scene was now enhanced with a great glittering star that his mother had attached to the back of the stable with a wire. The manger set in the church didn't have a glittering star. And Agosto knew his mother was very pleased with her star because it was unique.

"Come on," Paolo whispered. "We have one of those at home."

Agosto smiled. "A moment," he whispered. He went to the alcove with the votive candles and deposited some coins in the box. He lit the candle and knelt down for a second. "For Philip Ainsley," he whispered. "May he recover from his illness completely, so he can go back to Harvard." Agosto crossed himself.

After Mass, they went to Salvatore's house. There they would remain till dawn, returning home to sleep until Christmas evening, when a huge feast would be served.

"Domenico! Agosto! Paolo!" Salvatore Giuliano greeted each of the Tonelli men like brothers. He boomed out their names and embraced them in turn, planting warm kisses on their cheeks. "I love Christmas!" he shouted loudly. "Everybody comes to Salvatore's house on Christmas! All the old friends!"

Maria waddled behind her husband, and Donato too embraced Salvatore. Gina took her daughter's arm and led her past the men in the parlor. The women congregated in the kitchen, apart.

"Tomaso Solari's here," Paolo whispered. "That means that Cecilia is in the kitchen. Oh, you must find an excuse to go in there and see her and tell me what you think." Paolo jabbed Agosto in the ribs and grinned.

"And how will I know her?"

"You'll know her." Paolo smiled. "Just look for the prettiest one."

"Hey, Agosto!" Sal, Salvatore's son, embraced Agosto. "We don't see you much now that you're working in the city. Good to see you, good you come home for Christmas!"

Agosto returned the embrace, a flood of childhood memories returning to him. He and Sal had been the terrible twosome, playing where they shouldn't, teasing old women, stealing buns from Como Gianelli's bakery and apples from his own father. "And when I'm home, you're not," Agosto replied.

Sal shrugged. "I travel some—up to Connecticut, over to Jersey. You know, around."

Agosto nodded and remembered Maria's not-so-veiled comments about Sal and his business. He decided not to ask. What Sal wanted known, he imparted freely; what he didn't want to discuss, he was silent about.

"You work in a bank," Sal said, arching an eyebrow.

"The Morgan Bank," Agosto confirmed. "On Wall and Broad streets."

"Across from the Federal Building," Sal observed, obviously

wishing to show he knew Manhattan too. "You going to be a banker for life?"

"I enjoy it."

"Good you branch out, get away from here. This place is going to die, the people in it are going to die. Look at my papa. He works all his life, hard. He takes his boat out, rain or shine, snow or sleet. And he fishes. There's no money in fishes anymore. He gets nowhere. The same with your papa. So he has a store? So what? Twenty, thirty years of hard work, and he's hardly any better off than he was when he started. No, you have to get out, do something new. Me, I want more than calluses. I want a big house and good things."

"I think my papa and yours are happy," Agosto replied.

"Sure they're happy, because they don't know why they shouldn't be. Me, I want a little more."

Agosto couldn't disagree with the sentiment, but neither could he show disrespect for his father's years of work.

"I appreciate you, Agosto, you work with your head instead of your hands! I work with my head too!"

"It's Christmas, Sal. Let's talk about old times."

Sal grinned as Agosto steered away from that which he didn't want to know about. He slapped Agosto on the back. "You understand," he said. "Let's go have a glass of wine."

Donato slumped in the corner of the sofa, trying to pretend he was part of a conversation between Tomaso Solari and old Salvatore. He concentrated on their words, his eyes moving from one to the other. But it was obvious his mind was wandering. He looked unhappy, left out.

"Hey, Donato! Maria's so big I thought she'd drop the baby in church, right at the altar rail during communion!" Sal guffawed.

Donato looked up, grateful to be spoken to. "Not till next week, the midwife says. Next week for sure."

"A new baby for the new year! That's good, that's a good omen."

Donato smiled weakly. But Sal poked him in the ribs playfully. "Now you discovered how to do it, you can have ten more!"

Donato turned beet red and tried to smile. He was not a man who took teasing well. Especially teasing about the fact that he and Maria had been married five years and this was their first child.

"Don't joke with Donato," Paolo interrupted. "He's sensitive." Paolo picked up an empty tray. "Here, Agosto, go out to the kitchen and see if Antonia has any more cheese."

"I'll go," Sal said.

Paolo held firmly to the tray. "No, let Agosto go. I have someone I want him to see."

Sal burst out laughing. "You don't stand a chance! Cecilia Solari is only seventeen and her father won't let anyone court her till she's eighteen. Then half of Sheepshead Bay is going to be standing at her door."

Paolo blushed.

"Then I really must see her," Agosto said, smiling. He took the tray and went to the kitchen. The women were in a huddle around Maria, who was basking in her pregnancy and the attention it created.

"It doesn't always hurt so much," old Salvatore's wife, Antonia, was saying, "but if you don't scream loud, your husband won't pay any attention to you!" The women all laughed, but they fell silent immediately when they looked up to see Agosto in the doorway.

"Shame! This is woman talk," his mother said, shaking her finger at him.

"I only came for more bread and cheese." Agosto smiled engagingly. "You would starve your men?"

His eyes perused the gathering and fell on the only one of the women he didn't know. She had long thick black hair and huge brown eyes. Her skin was flawless and the color of ivory, unlike many of the others, who had swarthy complexions. And she had the figure of an angel—rounded and full, without even a hint of overweight. She wore a long blue dress with a white collar, and Agosto could just see her trim black-stockinged ankles between the top of her shoes and the bottom of her skirt.

His mother smiled almost mischievously. "Ah, Cecilia. I don't believe you've met my oldest son, Agosto. Agosto is a banker."

Agosto leaned over and took Cecilia's small white hand. He lifted it to his lips and kissed it. "I'm pleased to meet you."

"Agosto's a hero," his mother added proudly. "And he got a letter from Mr. Theodore Roosevelt, the Vice-President elect of the whole United States of America!"

The women oohed and aahed. Cecilia smiled shyly. "I am glad to meet you, Agosto Tonelli."

"Aahhh!" Maria slumped into one of the wooden chairs, grasping her back. *"Madre di Dio!* The pain! The pains have started!"

Gina clapped her hands together with glee. "She's going to have the baby on Christmas Day! Oh, the saints be praised!"

Old Mrs. Solari crossed herself and seized the Giuliano

telephone. "Praise be to God! A miracle! Hail Mary!" she began reciting reverently in Latin into the receiver.

"Take her upstairs!" Antonia Giuliano said. "There's no time to take her home. Send for the midwife! Hurry, Agosto, and tell Donato to come in here and carry her up the stairs."

Agosto hurried back to the parlor. "Donato, Maria is going to have the baby! Carry her upstairs!"

"I'll go for the midwife," Paolo volunteered, scurrying toward the door.

Salvatore embraced Domenico. "A good Christmas, old friend! It's good your first grandchild should be born in the house of Salvatore Giuliano!"

Domenico grinned broadly. "Family," he said proudly.

Donato huffed as he carried the limp but loudly groaning Maria through the parlor and up the staircase.

"And now you all leave," Antonia said with unusual authority. "You take the wine, the cheese, and the bread to Domenico's. This is women's work! This is women's business!"

Maria shrieked from the bedroom and the men willingly donned their coats, arming themselves with the refreshments. "Nobody wants to stay anyway!" Salvatore joked. "Men have stomach for war, for work, for death—no stomach for birthing."

Donato returned white-faced and pale. "She's in terrible pain," he announced with grave concern.

Agosto took his brother-in-law's arm and smiled gently. He thought of the comment he had heard in the kitchen. "Don't worry too much," he advised. "It was all meant to be."

The hard, icy snow that fell at midnight turned soft and fluffy by noon on Christmas Day. But it was not a normal Christmas Day.

The men had stayed up most of the night, telling and retelling jokes and stories in order to distract a worried Donato Ferrante. Then, one by one they had fallen asleep where they sat, or struggled to an empty bed in the Tonelli house.

Domenico slept upstairs in his own room, having staggered up the stairs just before dawn lit the overcast sky. Old Salvatore and his son Sal slept in the room that Agosto and Paolo usually shared. And although there was a large double bed in the room normally shared by Donato and Maria, Agosto, Paolo, and poor distraught Donato sprawled out on the sofa and two easy chairs. When mother and child returned home, the room must be ready, just as it was left, Domenico proclaimed. Tomaso Solari, filled with wine and the spirit of the season, had retreated to the bathtub, where, with borrowed pillow and blanket, he curled like an embryo and snored noisily.

"What a mess! What did I tell you, they can't be left alone! Look at this clutter!" Gina's voice interrupted the uneven snoring as she swept into the room like an avenging angel, followed by Cecilia Solari and her mother, Concha, old Mrs. Solari, and Antonia Giuliano, Salvatore's wife.

Agosto's eyes snapped open and he jumped to his feet, rubbing his unshaven chin with his hand.

"Oh, it will take hours to clean this house! And with a new baby here and Christmas dinner to cook too! None of you are to be trusted! Look at this house! Just look at it!"

The beautiful Cecilia smiled knowingly at Agosto. She glowed with happiness. An angel on Christmas morning, Agosto thought. He could hardly take his eyes off her, and she somehow looked amused at the situation.

"This is no time for flirtations, Agosto," his mother said chidingly. "You and Donato go out to the cab and get your sister and the baby. You carry the baby, Agosto. You, Donato, carry Maria."

Donato stood dumbly, still rubbing the sleep from his eyes. He didn't even have the presence of mind to ask whether it was a boy or a girl.

"Domenico!" Gina called. "Salvatore! Tomaso!"

"I'll get them." Paolo bolted up the stairs.

Old Mrs. Solari shuffled over to a nearby chair and sat down. Cecilia began tidying up the room, emptying ashtrays and collecting dirty glasses. "It's a community birth," she said to Gina. "We'll all help to clean up."

"A lovely girl," Gina said to Concha. "You have a good daughter."

Donato came in with Maria, whose face was ashen and who clung to him, murmuring incoherently and weeping. Salvatore and Domenico came downstairs, Tomaso Solari emerged from the bathroom, and Sal stretched, smoothing out his clothes.

"Am I the grandfather of a boy or a girl?" Domenico shouted.

Gina looked down. "A lovely, beautiful baby girl."

"Healthy?" Domenico asked.

"Yes, of course she is healthy."

There was a round of applause. Salvatore raised one of the many empty wine bottles. "If there was any wine left, we could drink to a boy next time!"

"To a boy next time!" Sal drained a half-full glass that still sat on the table. There was another round of clapping.

Domenico rubbed his hands on his rumpled pants. "And now for the naming."

"If it were a boy, he could be named after you," Gina said. "But of course she could be called Domenica."

"But she was born in Salvatore's house," Domenico reminded his wife.

"We could call her Agostina after her eldest uncle," Gina suggested.

"Or Antonia after Salvatore's wife."

"I'd be so honored," Antonia said, blushing.

Donato stood in the midst of the group, having delivered Maria to her bed. Agosto paused in the doorway, his arms filled with his niece, who slept quietly.

"Or Maria for the Virgin Mother," Donato suddenly said. "She was born on Christmas morning."

"Then there would be two named Maria in the house," Gina complained. "What about Giuseppina for Joseph."

"Or Gina, after you," Agosto suggested. He looked at the sleeping baby in his arms and thought vaguely that he should like one. That thought caused him to look at Cecilia again. She was still cleaning off a table, emptying stogie butts into the trash and stacking dirty dishes to take to the kitchen. Paolo had good taste, he thought, reminding himself that Paolo had seen her first and was clearly smitten by her.

"Agostina Antonia Gina Tonelli!" Domenico suddenly said. "That is the name I choose! That is her name!"

"Tina for short." Gina looked at the infant Agosto held and smiled lovingly. "Tina," she repeated. "No one so small should have to be called by such a long name." Everyone laughed and applauded.

"Go! All of you go! I want all of the men out of here till four o'clock. Then you will all come back for a feast! A special Christmas feast to celebrate the birth of our first grandchild."

"Turned out again," Salvatore said. "Turned out on Christmas Day."

"Go!" Antonia added. Then she smiled softly. "It's been a special happening, a blessing. We've witnessed the birth of Domenico's first grandchild."

"But not the last," Domenico added. He looked at Agosto. "A natural father, yes?"

Salvatore grinned. "Yes," he answered.

BROOKLYN

Agosto slipped into his overcoat and pulled on his hat. The house was crowded, and as always, hot and stuffy. He admitted to himself that his weekends at home were growing more difficult. He attributed his discomfort to the fact that he'd been spending a great deal of time with the Ainsleys, visiting their town house on Park Avenue. He went to be with Philip, who had not returned to Harvard as planned, owing to his mysterious illness, and who appeared to grow weaker by the day.

But no one in his family understood his absences. When he didn't come home, his father seemed hurt, his mother curious, and his sister belligerent.

"Where are you going now?" Maria guarded the front door of the Tonelli house. Her wiry black hair framed her face and she wiped her hands on her stained apron even while she looked at Agosto with annoyance. In the living room Donato played checkers with Paolo while Domenico snored behind the Italian newspaper he pretended to be reading. Gina was in the kitchen, and upstairs two-month-old Tina bawled loudly, demanding to be taken up and fed.

"For a simple walk along the bay with Sal," Agosto answered. "It's hot in here."

"Half the time you don't come home at all on the weekends, and then when you're home, you wander off! And with Sal, of all people!" She scowled at him. "I told you, he's bad business." She lowered her voice so as not to wake Domenico, who would have silenced her. "They say he works with the Black Hand. Oh, Agosto, you mustn't get mixed up with them—it's bad enough you spend so much time at that place Westminster and in Manhattan with those people who put fancy ideas in your head!"

"Westchester," Agosto corrected.

"Fancy people," Maria muttered. "It's no good for you, Agosto! And Sal is no good for you either."

"I don't need a conscience, Maria."

She thrust her lip forward and glared at him. "Supper is at four!"

"I'll be back by then."

"Mama will be upset if you're not!"

"Maria, Tina is crying. Go see to your child."

"Bad," she reiterated.

Agosto held his temper and pushed past her, closing the front door behind him. She was growing worse each weekend. She asked questions and pried into his personal affairs; she harped on the fact that he was spending more time with the Ainsleys; she hinted that his friends were not honest; and she nagged, if not about one thing, then about another.

But Maria was not the sole cause of his discontent. There was no privacy and no place he could think. Moreover, Donato's lack of ambition and Paolo's passivity tended to make him angry. Their outlook was too restricted. But it is my fault too, he admitted. His father and mother heaped praise on him, and Paolo and Donato felt diminished by his accomplishments. And however small he considered those accomplishments, they loomed large for Donato and Paolo.

To top it all off, Cecilia Solari had rejected Paolo's courtship, and in order to regain his feeling of manhood, Paolo had taken to courting an overweight girl of twenty-two whose reputation was less than it might have been. Agosto sighed. He missed home terribly when he was in the city, and when he was home, he missed his life in the city.

And then there was work. . . .

"Hey, Agosto! You're going to walk right past me!" Sal grinned and slapped him on the back.

"I was thinking."

"So I see," Sal said with an amused grin.

The two of them fell in step and headed for the bay. The fishing vessels would all be in port because the sea was rough. But each ship was painted a different color, and they would give the bay a gaiety in spite of the dull sky. The bigger ones—old Salvatore's included—had statues of the Blessed Virgin on the bows. And some enterprising men would be selling freshly prepared calamari and squid cooked on tiny charcoal burners. Agosto's mouth watered at the thought, even though Gina was preparing her usual Sunday feast.

"So what have you got to think so hard about that you almost walked right past me?"

"Home, family, work."

"What else is there?" Sal laughed. "And what's wrong with work? I thought you liked it."

"I do, but I get sick of dealing with bluenoses. I get everyone else's work piled on my desk. I sit around making money for other people all day long. A couple of months ago I bought ten shares of stock for myself and advised one of our customers to

buy a hundred thousand shares. I made eighty dollars, he made
eight hundred thousand. Then I reinvested my eighty dollars and
lost it!''

Sal laughed. ''Your big finance sounds like a numbers game.''

Agosto shook his head. ''I usually do all right for myself. Not
big, but all right. No, it's the pressure at the bank. One false
move and I'd be out. Just another dumb dago!''

Sal nodded knowingly.

''I think I feel rotten about making so much money for people
who already have so much. The advantages of investment and
interest should be brought to the small investors. But hell, the
people at the Morgan Bank would all burst out laughing if a man
like my father came in to deposit ten dollars!''

''It used to be that way with stores—you wanted to start a
store, you had to start big.''

''My father started with a pushcart,'' Agosto said.

''That's it, Agosto. You should start a pushcart bank, going
door to door.''

Agosto smiled at the thought. It was rather appealing. ''Legally
you can't start any kind of bank without twenty-five thousand
dollars or so. But you're right, there's something needed for
people like my father—small business people, men whose only
collateral is their willingness to work.''

Sal nodded. ''You know how to do that? Could you run a
bank?''

''I know most of what it takes to run a bank. I need another
year, maybe two working in Manhattan. But there's another
thing stopping me.''

''And what's that?''

''Money. That's what stops most people from doing what they
want.''

Sal shrugged. ''Twenty-five thousand dollars—that's a lot.''

Agosto smiled. Sal was matter-of-fact. If he had talked about
twenty-five thousand dollars to Donato and Paolo, they would
have asked him if he was crazy, and Maria would surely have
said that his rich friends were putting impossible ideas in his
head. He could hear her saying, ''Twenty-five thousand! Are
you mad? Only thieves have that much money!'' No, Donato,
Maria, and Paolo could not even think in those terms. Probably
his father couldn't either. He wasn't certain about his mother.
She had a way of surprising him.

''It is a lot,'' Agosto agreed.

''I could help,'' Sal suddenly announced. ''It's a lot, but I
think I know where I could lay my hands on maybe twenty
thousand. It's a good idea, you know. I like it, I like the idea of

a bank for people like my father. Hey, Agosto, we could be partners! I'll raise the money and you provide the know-how. What do you say to that?''

Agosto stole a sideways glance at Sal Giuliano. His hat was flashy but out of style. His suit was rumpled and dark. His shirt was dark too, and his shoes . . . His shoes were too shiny. Agosto thought of a remark Ainsley had made, that he would like to buy his partner out. No, Agosto thought, partnership was a little like marriage. It had to be with the right person or not at all.

"Thanks, Sal. But if I decide to actually start a bank, it's something I'd have to do alone.''

"We'd be good partners, there's blood between us.''

"I know. But I would still want to do it alone.''

Sal laughed and slapped Agosto hard. "You're just like your papa! He used to own half my papa's boat, then one day he said, 'I want to do something alone'!''

"It seems to run in the family.''

"Stubbornness! That's what runs in your family.''

"And what runs in yours?''

"Stubbornness!'' Sal shouted.

Agosto paused by the sea wall. He squinted into the distance. "Sal, is that Mrs. Solari and her daughter?''

Sal looked off in the direction Agosto indicated. "Yes,'' he replied. "That's Cecilia, there's no missing her.''

"Should we go and say hello?''

Sal smiled knowingly. "You like her, don't you?''

"Yes, but it's a little difficult for me.''

"Why, because she rejected Paolo? He's already found someone else!''

"I know, but still . . .''

"Anyway, she might reject you too.''

"Maybe.''

"Well, come on, then. Saying hello isn't a proposal.''

Agosto nodded. "It isn't, is it?''

Friday, March 22, 1901

BROOKLYN

Fabiana Pucelli's long dark hair was divided and braided into two great thick ropes of hair which encircled her round olive-skinned face. Her eyes were too small, though they had an interesting hue, a golden brown. She was full of figure for one so young; her breasts were pendulous and fell to meet a rounded belly which in turn gave way to wide swinging hips. If she had one feature to commend her, it was her mouth, which was full and sensuous, and when she smiled, it was a warm friendly smile.

Paolo Tonelli drained the bottle of red wine he was drinking and set it on the sawdust-covered floor behind the turnip bin.

"I shouldn't be here," Fabiana whispered. "And I can't see, it's too dark."

"But it smells nice," Paolo slurred. "It always smells nice in here! It's the oranges and the tangerines." He inhaled deeply. "And where else can we be alone? I can't take you to my house to listen to a bawling brat!" He giggled. "Besides, Mama would disapprove."

"My papa would disapprove too," Fabiana reminded him.

"Come on, Fabiana, come on over to Paolo and give him a kiss."

"Can't we turn on a light? I don't like the dark."

"No! The neighbors will see the light and then someone will go back of the store to the house and tell Papa. Nosy, nobody around here can mind their own business!"

"You could call on me properly."

"But your papa wouldn't let me kiss you"—Paolo burped—"or put my hand down your dress either."

"I only let you do it once," she sniffed.

"Are you crying?"

"I'm scared, Paolo. Please take me home."

"Not now, it's the first time we've been alone."

"And you've had too much to drink."

Paolo pulled himself up off the olive barrel he had been sitting on. The damn store should have some purpose! "Come here, my little Fabiana, come give your Paolo a kiss." He lurched toward her unsteadily, and grabbing her arms, pulled her to him.

"Paolo, you're hurting me!" She wiggled in his arms, and Paolo kissed her neck roughly, rubbing his stubbey face on her skin. She relaxed somewhat, and he held her with only one hand, while he dipped the other into her blouse.

"Paolo! No! Its not right!"

He kneaded her voluptuous breasts. They were damp with perspiration and incredibly soft to the touch. He felt himself in the grip of desire as he touched her large nipple and felt it stiffen. "Fabiana *mia*," he gasped. "I must have you! I must possess your beautiful body! I can't stop, not now, I can't stop!"

"Oh, Paolo! Please! My papa will kill me!"

"I shall die of desire!"

"Say you love me, Paolo, say you love me!" She was panting as much as he, and had ceased resisting.

"I love you," he mumbled incoherently. He tumbled her robust form backward, but as she fell, she grasped the crate of cauliflower and the great white heads fell with her onto the floor, along with a crate of eggplant.

Paolo lifted her skirts and fumbled about the unfamiliar territory. He forced down her drawers while she wiggled beneath him. "I have such a fire for you!" He seized her thick black hair and then slid his hand between her plump thighs. "Oh, *Dio*," he groaned as he finally managed to push his swollen organ into her moist depths. In his drunken condition, Fabiana became a goddess.

She groaned loudly as he pumped into her, and Paolo felt himself on the verge, about to scream with joy, when Fabiana jerked beneath him and let out an ear-piercing shriek at exactly the same moment light flooded the store.

Paolo pulled away from her fear-frozen form, and his intended gift gushed out of him. "Shit!" he exclaimed loudly.

In the moment that followed, Fabiana struggled to her feet and smoothed her skirts. She covered her bare breasts with her large hands, and hanging her head, began to wail.

For his part, Paolo sat in disarray among the cauliflowers, looking dumbly into the infuriated face of Domenico, who towered over him, lantern in hand.

The silence was unbroken save for Fabiana's wailing. Then, after what seemed an eternity, Domenico cleared his throat.

"You have ruined the cauliflower," he said with disgust.

"Papa . . ." The color had drained from Paolo's face and he could feel the vomit rising in his throat. He turned abruptly and retched on the scattered eggplant.

"And now you have ruined the eggplant," Domenico said angrily. "I hear noises down here and I think I am being robbed. So I take the lantern and I come down, and what do I find? I find my son dishonoring the family!" Domenico was shouting now, but even though his voice was loud, it was even and filled with wrath. "You're drunk! You're a pig! Look at you!"

"Papa, I'm twenty-three years old!"

"And you act like sixteen! You're soft, Paolo, like this melon." Domenico kicked a melon with his foot. "Taking a woman! And in my store! Now a boy of sixteen can go to a whore if he wants, but he does not do what you have been doing with an Italian woman. I know this woman's father! He is my friend. She dishonors her papa and you dishonor me! This is not a woman for whoring!"

"He loves me, I love him!" Fabiana murmured, then ran to Domenico and dropped to her knees in front of him. "Please don't tell my papa! Please don't tell him! It will kill him, he's a sick man."

"And he would beat you," Domenico said, "and you would deserve it for bringing him dishonor."

"I didn't m-mean to," Paolo stuttered.

"That's worse!" Domenico shouted. "When you make love to a woman, you should mean it. But I'm glad you love her. You *do* love her, don't you?"

Paolo nodded stupidly.

"Good. I wouldn't want you marrying a woman you didn't love."

"Marry?"

"Next Saturday if possible. You'll speak to her father immediately, then I'll talk with him. The two of you will be married by the priest next Saturday, and that's the end of it!"

Fabiana sniffed and stared at the floor.

Paolo retched again.

"And now you'll take her home and then you'll come back and clean up this mess!"

"I'm sick," Paolo complained.

"Now!" Domenico shouted.

Saturday, March 30, 1901

"Paolo is getting married?" Agosto repeated his father's announcement in a stunned voice. He had spent the previous weekend in Manhattan, and had only just arrived in Brooklyn. "Today?" he questioned.

Domenico stood by the window looking out on the awning of the store. The house was unusually quiet. Paolo, the bridegroom-to-be, was still in his shopkeeper's green apron and was down working in the store with Donato. Maria was upstairs with Tina, and Gina was in the kitchen, discreetly remaining out of sight for the time being.

"Why didn't someone call me? I really don't understand. It's so sudden."

"I wouldn't bother a banker with this," Domenico replied. "You have an important job. As for the suddenness, it's a matter of honor. Your brother dishonored Fabiana and her father is my friend. They have to be married.'' Domenico's voice was steady and determined.

''Is Fabiana pregnant?'' Agosto queried. It was certainly all right to ask; his father's words begged the question, and clearly his father intended to confide in him. This was a meeting between the head of the household and his eldest son; it explained why it was so quiet and why neither Maria nor Gina was present.

''Not that I know of. But I found them together! I found them together in the store. Disgraceful!''

Agosto pressed his lips together. Poor Paolo. He was caught with his pants down, and by his own father. Still, Agosto's sympathy for his errant brother was short-lived. His father was quite right: there was no alternative. Paolo had to marry Fabiana, and that was quite clearly the end of it.

Domenico turned slowly to face Agosto. His face was like stone and he shook his head dejectedly. ''I don't know, I tried to raise my children to be good, to be independent, to work hard. Paolo is not like you, Agosto. He has no ambition, he drinks too much wine, and he has no discipline! I don't know.''

''He'll be all right, Papa. He'll marry Fabiana and he'll settle down. It's not your fault.''

''You're a good brother, but I tell you Paolo is weak. Still, I expect you to defend him, it's how you were raised.''

''It's not such a bad marriage,'' Agosto observed.

Domenico shrugged. ''I had to talk to her father. It was such a dishonor, what Paolo did, I was ashamed. But we agreed, we agreed the marriage should take place immediately.''

Agosto nodded. It would not be the usual joyous Italian wedding. Under the circumstances there would be no dowry and no great celebration. The two families would gather for an informal ceremony; there would be a quiet dinner and then Fabiana would simply come to live in the house, sharing Paolo's small room as Agosto had once shared it.

''I just don't understand,'' Domenico complained. It was as if he were talking to himself. ''Donato is no better than Paolo, except of course he doesn't drink so much. Maria didn't make the best of all choices.''

Agosto remained silent. Maria had not had all that many suitors in the first place. Her choices were certainly limited, and though Donato also lacked ambition, at least he worked hard in the store and he treated Maria well. That, Agosto decided, was not easy. His sister did have ambitions and they were unsuited to a woman. She was, he willingly admitted, a shrew.

''But you're a good son,'' Domenico confirmed with a tone of swelling pride. "You got a letter from the Vice-President of the United States and you have a fine job in a bank. You do us proud!"

Agosto looked at the floor. He wanted to say: Wait, Papa, maybe Donato and Paolo will do you proud too—give them a chance. But he didn't utter the words. Domenico was rooted in his traditions; he was a hard man, but just. If he had one fault, it was that his favoritism toward his eldest son was too open. And the more open it was, the more it stuck in the craw of Paolo, Maria, and Donato. It was a flaw Agosto had realized only on his return from Cuba; it was also a situation he felt powerless to correct, though he vowed that if he was successful he would employ Paolo, leaving the store for Donato, giving them the opportunity to break free and make something of themselves. But that was all in the future, Agosto thought. A future that might or might not materialize.

"Papa, a wedding should be happy even under these circumstances," Agosto pleaded. "Let me go out and buy a small gift and some wine. Let me tell Paolo to come up from the store and get ready."

"You're a good brother," Domenico said with tears in his eyes. "Loyal."

"Paolo would be loyal to me too. We are brothers."

"A family must stick together," Domenico concurred. "Go on, tell him to come upstairs. But don't tell him I forgive him for this dishonor!" Domenico looked up and met Agosto's eyes. "Yet," he added.

5

Saturday, June 1, 1901

WESTCHESTER

A gentle summer breeze caused the many colored paper lanterns to sway, casting waving shadows across the patio where some twenty young couples waltzed to a string orchestra. The older couples didn't dance; the women gathered together near the silver punch bowl and talked, and the men assembled in the salon and smoked while they talked business.

"That's it!" Sarah Ainsley's face was full of satisfaction as she looked up at Agosto. He held her stiffly, feeling incredibly uncomfortable in his borrowed tuxedo. It wasn't that he didn't enjoy dancing, it was more that this type of dancing was both formal and intimate, and he was obligated to hold Sarah Ainsley extraordinarily close. It was certainly not the kind of ruckus dancing Agosto did at home. He was accustomed to street dances, where there were no partners, but rather a twirling blur of grown-ups and children, of clapping hands and stomping feet. The tarantella was a folk dance and it was not for couples, but for families. The only other dance he had seen was a risqué performance by Little Egypt at Coney Island. She was an Oriental belly dancer who appeared at the World's Fair in 1893 and then moved her art to Coney Island. Agosto remembered the event fondly. He and Paolo had sneaked away to witness the wicked suggestive performance. Little Egypt's bare midriff had been a secret joke between them for years. "I wonder how she would look in tassels?" Paolo would say, eyeing a modestly dressed Italian beauty. Then, remembering Little Egypt, they would both blush and burst into laughter.

"Two to the side, and then one forward and one back. That's it! You're a good pupil, Agosto."

Agosto blushed as Sarah pressed against him. It wasn't proper.

75

It created desires, desires he shouldn't have for a well-bred young woman.

Sarah grinned up at him mischievously. "You don't really like to dance, do you?" She blinked her large blue eyes and brushed a wisp of blond hair from her forehead.

"I don't dislike it."

She slipped from his arms and took his hand. "Let's walk, then," she suggested. She sighed: "I love the garden at night. And spring is so short!"

Agosto obediently followed her lead. He ran his finger around his high collar. He had been to the Ainsley estate many times since he returned from Cuba, but this was his first party. That's what Sarah called it, a party. To Agosto it seemed more like a ball, a grand ball of the sort pictured on the newspaper society pages.

"You don't like me, do you?" Sarah said abruptly. She stopped and stood in front of him, looking up into his eyes.

"Of course I like you," Agosto protested.

"You don't act like it." She thrust out her lower lip and pouted. "You've never tried to kiss me."

Agosto looked at her in surprise. He shook his head dumbly.

"Then you must not like me."

"I like you, but not in that way."

"I like you in that way." She cocked her head and smiled flirtatiously. "You're the most different man I've ever met. Not at all like the others. They seem like boys."

She suddenly threw her arms around him and kissed him on the mouth. For an instant Agosto responded; then he pulled away and let out his breath. Why had he allowed himself to be led away from the crowd? This situation was awkward, and he wasn't at all sure how to disengage himself.

"We're very different," he began. "I like you, Sarah, but we're too different. We come from different places."

She giggled. "You mean you don't like me because I'm rich?" She suddenly turned in a circle, her dress rustling. She took both his hands in hers. "You're prejudiced," she said more seriously.

Agosto shook his head. "No. It's just not proper and I'm not ready. You're right, I have very little money. But it's more than that. Far more than that."

"I'm not Italian! That's it. You want a fat Italian girl. One with big hips!"

Agosto laughed in spite of himself. She made motions with her hands.

"I don't know what I want right now." That, Agosto admitted

to himself, was a lie. For over a month he had been thinking of calling on Cecilia Solari, and next weekend he intended to do just that.

Sarah's eyes searched the flower bed next to the pathway. It was laid out in symmetrical patterns. "My father likes you," she said, suddenly changing the tone of the conversation.

"I like him."

"And Philip adores you. Of course, he would never show it."

Agosto smiled. "I know that."

Her hands again flew to his shoulders. "And I like you, Agosto. You're so . . . so . . . well, strong."

Agosto shook his head. "I can only offer you friendship."

She looked at him intensely. "Just because you're not ready doesn't mean we couldn't—"

"Yes it does," Agosto interrupted. He leaned over closer to her face. "I'm a true Latin. When I start kissing, I won't stop with kissing."

Her full lips parted. "I wouldn't want you to," she said breathlessly.

"You're my friend's sister. No, Sarah, you're only pretending, and I know you're not the kind of woman you're trying to play."

She frowned. "You're horrid!"

Agosto laughed and took her arm. "Yes," he replied, feeling only a slight twinge of regret and thinking that there was some truth in her taunt. Her hips were much too slender. "Let's go back to the others."

"I've never been rejected before," Sarah confessed, tossing her head back.

"Be careful," Agosto whispered. "I don't think there are many men who would reject you."

He guided her toward the others. The orchestra had momentarily stopped playing and the guests gathered around a long table laden with delicacies: shrimp in silver dishes, lobster bisque, rare roast beef, breads and salads.

"Oh, there you are," Philip remarked. He had a girl on his arm, a raven-haired girl with large green eyes.

"We weren't long."

Philip nodded. "Did she seduce you yet?"

"Philip!" Sarah said in a tone of mock surprise.

Agosto shook his head.

Philip dropped the girl's arm. "You'll have to excuse me."

"Are you all right?" Agosto instinctively grasped Philip's shoulder.

Philip looked suddenly stricken, and though he was always

unnaturally pale, what little color he had had drained from his face.

"Let's go inside and have a smoke," Philip suggested. His voice seemed abnormal, quite different from only seconds before. He half-gasped out the words.

Agosto nodded and guided Philip toward the house.

"In the den, old man. Take me into the den. There's nobody there."

Agosto opened the great oak door and snapped on the light. The den was a room filled with soft leather with walls of highly polished wood. It was book-lined and smelled vaguely of pipe tobacco.

Philip slumped into one of the leather chairs. "There's some brandy over there. Will you get me some, old man."

Agosto did as he was bid. He returned with the brandy and sat down. "Philip, what is it?"

"A slight sudden attack," Philip answered, waving his hand in the air. He lifted the snifter and gulped down the brandy.

Agosto's face knit in a frown. Philip had been ill since he returned from Cuba, and he certainly wasn't getting better. "An attack of what?" Agosto prodded. "I sometimes get chills, but that's not what's wrong with you, is it?"

Philip swirled the brandy and shook his head. His colorless lips were pressed together; his pale blue eyes stared almost vacantly. "No . . . no, it's not just chills. And it's not something I acquired in Cuba."

"Then what?" Agosto questioned.

"Leukemia," Philip answered.

"I've never heard of it. What do you have to do to get over it?"

Philip shook his head. "There's no getting over it, there's no cure and no treatment." He looked up at Agosto, his blue eyes misty. "They used to call it 'wasting disease' twenty years ago because the victim just wastes away. That's what's going to happen to me, Agosto—I'm going to waste away." Philip lifted the glass to his lips and sipped the brandy. "But then, its only suitable! My whole life's been a waste!"

Agosto stared at Philip. He felt his mouth dry and his own eyes go moist. "There must be something," he started to say. He had known Philip was ill, he had even prayed for his friend's recovery, but this was a revelation he was unprepared for. The shock of Philip's words stunned him, and his first reaction was totally emotional.

"Nothing," Philip said. "And damn it, if you cry I'll never

forgive you, you sentimental dago!'' Momentarily Philip's eyes flashed.

"All Italian men cry.''

"Emotional bastards,'' Philip swore.

"I'm sorry,'' Agosto replied, only too aware that it was the first time he had ever apologized to Philip Ainsley for anything.

"I don't want your pity.'' Philip paused and flicked a strand of hair off his forehead. "But for some reason I need your friendship, Agosto. I need to know . . . to be with someone who isn't as empty as I feel.''

"How long?'' Agosto asked.

"I probably won't last the summer.'' Philip's voice strained against cracking.

Agosto's shoulders dropped. Hs feeling of shock had turned to anger. But with whom was he angry, or at what? Helplessness, that was it. For the first time in his life he felt helpless. "Shit,'' he muttered.

Philip forced a smile. "My sentiments exactly.''

"Does your father know?''

"He was told yesterday. But I can assure you he doesn't want to discuss it.''

Agosto's mind roamed over his trip up to Westchester with Barton Ainsley. He had seemed quite normal, though perhaps a little quieter than usual. At the time, Agosto had attributed Barton Ainsley's silence to fatigue.

"And your sister?''

Philip shook his head. "God no! She couldn't handle it. I'm not sure I can handle it, damn it!''

"You can,'' Agosto affirmed. "I know you, you can handle it.''

"I should have gone with you up San Juan Hill. Maybe I'd have gotten a bullet through my head. It would have been quicker.''

"That wasn't your time.''

"I never realized you were a fatalist.''

"Neither did I, but I guess I am.''

Agosto walked over to the side of the leather chair. He silently grasped Philip's shoulder and squeezed it to express his own feelings. There were no words to be spoken.

Saturday, June 8, 1901

BROOKLYN

As usual, the family assembled in the kitchen for Saturday-night supper. Domenico had built an extension for the table so that they could all be accommodated, and Agosto lamented that the house was now more crowded than ever. Fabiana and Paolo shared one bedroom, Donato, Maria, and Tina a second bedroom, and Gina and Domenico the third. On the weekends Agosto came home, he was obliged to sleep on the sofa.

"Do you want to play checkers after dinner?" Paolo queried.

"I'm going out," Agosto replied. "I'm going to visit Cecilia Solari." He had decided there could be no impediment. Cecilia had rejected Paolo months ago and Paolo was married to Fabiana.

Agosto watched for reactions. Paolo's eyes were glued on his soup. Maria's face visibly darkened, and Agosto knew she envisaged yet another competitor. But Domenico's face lit up and he grinned. "A beautiful, lovely woman!" he shouted.

Immediately after supper Agosto dressed in his best clothes, and carrying a bouquet of roses and violets, he went to call on Cecilia, whose father, Tomaso Solari, met him at the door.

"Agosto! Come in, come in!"

Agosto followed Tomaso into the parlor and sat down stiffly. He watched as the older man relaxed in a great overstuffed chair and lit a huge black cigar. His look was one of extraordinary amusement, Agosto realized. But then, when a man has a beautiful daughter and when a young man arrives, flowers in hand, the situation is painfully obvious.

"What brings you to my house?" Tomaso asked, grinning from ear to ear.

"I should like to call on your daughter Cecilia, if she is willing to allow me to do so."

Tomaso laughed heartily. "I didn't think the flowers were for me."

Agosto produced a package and handed it to Tomaso. "Not the flowers, but these."

Tomaso opened the box and let out a roar of approval. "Cuban cigars!"

"I've had them since I returned. I thought you might like them."

"I do, and it's very thoughtful of you. And something of a bribe, but I'm not opposed to bribery. Cecilia! Cecilia, come down here."

Cecilia came down the stairs almost immediately, and Agosto looked at her carefully. She was as beautiful as ever—a soft, feminine beauty. And her face was kind and cheerful. She wore a long brown dress with a high white collar, and her hair, which was uncovered, was hanging loose, held only with a single ribbon behind her head.

"Yes, Papa." Her lovely expressive eyes looked down modestly, but Agosto thought he caught a slight furtive glance toward him before she turned to her father.

"Agosto has come to call on you. I give him my permission to do so, if you wish."

"I would like that," Cecilia answered in a voice so low that Agosto could hardly hear her words.

"Good," Tomaso said, getting up out of his chair and grasping his cigars. "Now, this is a young man with a future," he admonished his daughter. "He has a fine job and I know he's ambitious." Tomaso then turned back to Agosto. "I like your mama and papa," he added, "and Cecilia is almost eighteen, old enough to be courted."

Agosto blushed. "I should like to court her," he replied.

Tomaso only nodded; then he waved his arm and left the room.

Agosto smiled and handed Cecilia the flowers. He suddenly felt tongue-tied and embarrassed. "I greatly admire you," he finally managed. "Please accept these."

Cecilia's heart-shaped face broke into a warm smile that sent Agosto's fear flying.

"They're lovely." She touched the violets lightly. "I love violets," she added, looking into Agosto's eyes.

"Do you like opera?" Agosto asked quickly.

"Yes, we have a phonograph machine"—she turned and pointed to the machine with its huge black horn—"and some recordings. Would you like me to play one?"

"Very much."

Cecilia's dark eyes seemed to grow even larger. "Do you like opera?"

"I love it. I sometimes go to the Met." Agosto inhaled deeply and on the spur of the moment he added, "I should like to take you there to see an opera—if your mother and father could accompany us, of course." Vaguely it crossed his mind that he might be able to borrow Barton Ainsley's box one evening if Sarah and Creighton Stearns were not using it.

"Oh, I should like that! I should like it very much!"

Agosto reached across the distance between them and took her small hand in his. "And you really do want me to call on you?"

Cecilia blushed deeply. "Yes," she answered. "I really do."

Saturday, October 5, 1901

Agosto leaned over the rail of Barton Ainsley's yacht and stared into the choppy waters of the Hudson River. The sun shone down on the water and the result was shimmering bands of dark water which the yacht cut through, leaving a trail of white foam in its wake.

It had been a month since Philip's death and it haunted Agosto in spite of preoccupation with work and his courtship of Cecilia. It was a depression that came and went; it came in the middle of the night, waking Agosto and causing him to lie thinking for hours. But during his work week at the bank or when he sat for hours with pad and paper working out his finances, the depression caused by Philip Ainsley's death left him and he retreated to happier thoughts of his future with Cecilia.

But now he was depressed anew because he had accepted an invitation from Barton Ainsley to visit the Ainsley estate in Westchester. "It's probably the last nice weekend we'll have," Ainsley had said, "and frankly, I can't stand to go up there alone." It will be terrible, Agosto thought. The billiards room would seem empty without Philip to offer a challenge, and there would be no bantering, no insults traded, no confidences shared.

No, Agosto could not forget, nor did he want to forget the last few weeks of Philip's life. During those two weeks Philip had nearly returned to normal. "I've outlived the doctor's predictions!" he said enthusiastically. "You know, I might make it . . . I might make it." Somehow God gave Philip those two weeks without pain; God gave him hope. Even Barton Ainsley had been hopeful. But it was premature hope and Philip died the last day of August. Mercifully, he passed away in his sleep.

"I almost wish he hadn't seemed better," Barton Ainsley told Agosto. "It makes it so much harder." Agosto had thought the same and said so. But there's a lesson in Philip's death, Agosto kept telling himself. A man can control his destiny; he can plan and he can know success. But there is always a facet of life that can't be controlled. The time of a man's passing is in the hands of God; therefore, he must always be at peace with God. He must live, ready to die. But part of the bargain was to live to the fullest, to make the most of your talents, to be disciplined.

"You're pensive," Barton Ainsley commented.

Agosto nodded.

"You're thinking about Philip."

"He's often on my mind."

"He was a good boy who would have been a better man with maturity. I had such plans for him."

"And for Sarah?"

"Daughters are not like sons. Sarah will marry rich, she'll have a good life."

"She's very depressed by Philip's death."

It was Barton Ainsley's turn to nod. Then, fighting his own emotions, he forced a half-smile. "You have other things on your mind."

"Yes."

"Are you going to be closemouthed, or are you going to give me pleasure and share your thoughts?"

"I've found a girl . . . I'm courting her."

Barton Ainsley grinned. "A pretty girl, I hope."

"Pretty, intelligent, and kind."

"I'm glad for you, but I sense you have something else on your mind as well."

"Yes, nothing personal in the family sense. It's business."

"Good. Tell me about it. Is the Morgan Bank boring?"

Agosto smiled. "Not boring, maddening. Certainly in another year it will have served its purpose in my apprenticeship. Frankly, I want to begin my own bank."

"That's rather ambitious," Barton Ainsley said.

"I want to start a bank for little people, for immigrants, for people who don't have access to the other banks."

"It's risky. Little people, as you call them, don't have many assets. They like to keep those assets at hand. What money they have, they keep under the bed. Good heavens, I don't have to tell you that. Just look at how Europeans save! They buy gold and diamonds when they have cash. How many people get off the boat with gems sewn in their clothing, only to discover that they haven't much resale value here? It's the European way. Europe has had so many wars that people don't trust institutions; they trust only material possessions, preferably portable possessions like gold and jewelry. And those are the people with a little extra cash. Most of them have only pennies of savings.''

"Boatloads and boatloads of immigrants every day, day after day, month after month, year after year. All those pennies of savings add up to a lot. No, I don't believe a man ought to need property or collateral in stocks and bonds to borrow; I think a man's collateral ought to be his willingness to work.''

"It's an interesting concept." Barton Ainsley laughed. "It would certainly turn banking as we know it on its ear.''

"Pennies from small investors add up. Loans to hardworking men are repaid in cash. I have some figures.''

"I'll bet you do.''

"I'm going to do it . . . one way or another.''

"And how much do you figure you need to get started?''

"Twenty-five thousand.''

Barton Ainsley didn't look surprised or shocked. "And how much have you got?''

"Three thousand," Agosto replied with a smile. "But I'll need some of that to get settled when I get married.''

"I'll lend you the rest," Barton Ainsley said dispassionately.

Agosto's mouth opened, then closed. "You believe in the idea that much?''

"No. I believe in you. Besides, I'd like to do it for Philip's memory. Damn it! I've lost my only son. I like you, always have. You once saved Philip's life, and I'd like to help. I can't do much for Philip now, so I suppose getting you started would make me feel better—to put it bluntly.''

Agosto inhaled. "It's tempting, but no.''

"No?''

"No. It's something I have to do on my own.''

Barton Ainsley took a sip of the drink he had in his hand. "Don't say no right now," he urged. "Go away, think about it, and investigate other possibilities. Then come back and talk to me. One lesson I could teach you now: don't make snap decisions.''

"I don't think I'll change my mind.''

"Just think about it.''

Agosto nodded. "All right, I'll think about it.''

"Good." Barton Ainsley drained his glass. "Stearns is coming over on Sunday. He's such a bore.''

"And a snob.''

"We are all, snobs." Ainsley said good-naturedly. He sighed. "You'll have your problems, starting your kind of bank. It's a threat, you know, an out-and-out threat to our traditions.''

"Pushcart banking," Agosto replied thoughtfully. "Well, Seligman started with a pushcart, and look how far he got."

"He's Jewish."

"A pushcart is a pushcart," Agosto answered.

Wednesday, January 1, 1902

BROOKLYN

Outside, a cold wind battered the Solari house, but inside, a warm fire burned in the hearth. Tomaso Solari was with his wife in the kitchen, tactfully leaving Agosto and Cecilia alone for a time in the parlor.

"It's much better when a holiday falls on Friday," Agosto commented as he leaned back against the chair and lit a stogie. "I spent two hours getting home last night; now I have to go back to Manhattan early in the morning."

"Do you like living there?" Cecilia asked.

Agosto shrugged. "I don't live there, I exist there. I'm not in my room often—only to sleep. But no, I don't like it. It's too crowded, families living on top of each other. You see signs in the window, 'Room for Italians.' One room, sometimes six or seven people live in it."

"I can't imagine living like that."

Agosto leaned forward. "We won't have to live that way, Cecilia. We'll live here in Sheepshead Bay. I've spoken to your father and he has given his permission. I want to marry you."

Cecilia blushed, then smiled shyly. "I want to marry you too," she said in almost a whisper. "And I'll come and live with you, wherever you choose."

"I'd like us to be married in the summer, August perhaps. It's my lucky month, you know. I'm named for it."

Cecilia frowned slightly. "You'll spend all your time going back and forth."

"It won't be for too long." He smiled. "Cecilia, I'm planning to work here. I don't know quite when, or even how at this moment, but I do know I want to start my own bank here in Sheepshead Bay."

"Your own bank?" Her large expressive dark eyes were wide.

"We'll have a hard time at first," Agosto told her. "We won't have much money." He butted out his stogie and came to sit next to her on the settee. He gently put his arm around her shoulders. "Will you take a chance with me, Cecilia?"

"Your mama took a chance with your papa. And when my papa married Mama, he had only just come to America." She smiled and covered his hand with hers. "Everyone starts out with nothing," she said. "But I know you, Agosto, I know you'll be successful and we'll have our own little business. I'll help you, we'll do it together, and we'll make it work together."

Agosto leaned over and kissed her on the cheek. "I love you, Cecila."

"Is the proposal over?" Tomaso roared. He burst into the parlor from the kitchen, his face round and red. And behind him his wife, Concha, carried a bottle of wine.

Agosto jumped to his feet. "It's over and Cecilia has accepted."

Tomaso grinned. "Then we'll have some wine to celebrate the new year as well as the forthcoming marriage!"

"I shall lose my daughter," Concha said, half sadly, but with resignation.

"Stop pouting, woman! You just don't want to be called grandmother!"

"I do!" Concha said, suddenly smiling.

Cecilia stood at Agosto's side and blushed deeply.

"I'll go to your papa tomorrow and discuss the dowry," Tomaso said authoritatively. "Of course, we're not rich people, but there will be something." he laughed heartily. "I hope Domenico doesn't drive too hard a bargain!"

Agosto shifted his weight from one foot to the other. He had chosen Cecilia not only because of her beauty and intelligence but also because she came from a family conscious of tradition. Yes, theirs would be a most traditional marriage, just as they were having a most traditional courtship. And Cecilia would have a dowry and it would be worked out by the two fathers and agreed upon ahead of time. Perhaps, Agosto thought, the only untraditional aspect was that he genuinely loved Cecilia and she loved him. In a sense, they had chosen one another, rather than having their marriage totally arranged, as was the case in their parents' generation.

"You'll be married at a high Mass," Concha said. "And we'll hold the reception at the Columbus Hall."

"With two bottles of wine for every guest!" Tomaso promised.

"We want to be married in August," Agosto told his future father-in-law.

"August! So soon!" Concha exclaimed.

"She thinks she has to start the cooking now!" Tomaso said

as he poured out the wine. "Here! A toast to my son-in-law-to-be . . . the banker!"

"We'll be starting small."

"You're a smart young man!" Tomaso slapped Agosto on the back. "You'll take care of my Cecilia, you'll take care of her good! I know that!"

Agosto pressed Cecilia's arm. "I will," he promised.

Tuesday, July 8, 1902

MANHATTAN

Agosto gulped down black coffee and shook his head as if to clear it. The weather was unbearably hot and sticky and he acknowledged the fact that he was approaching total exhaustion. Since February he'd been working at two jobs. Days at the Morgan Bank as usual and nights keeping the accounts of one Benjamin Cohen, who owned a garment factory. It was, Agosto thought, the perfect second job, since it could be done at night, but nevertheless, the pace of two full-time jobs was taking its toll.

But I need the money, he convinced himself each time he thought of leaving Cohen. His second job enabled him to invest more, and he would certainly soon need more. In a matter of weeks he would have Cecilia to support, and he vowed that they would live alone and not in the already overcrowded home of his parents, where Cecilia, the newest daughter-in-law, would come last in order of rank after Fabiana.

Agosto decided to rent a tiny two-room apartment from the Marcuccis, whose large rambling house, now virtually empty, except for Roberto and his prents, had been converted into several little apartments, which were rented out.

There was no more prominent Italian family in Sheepshead Bay than the Marcuccis. Joseph Marcucci, Domenico's age, was not only the local alderman, the president of the Columbus Society, but also the founder of Marcucci Concrete. Joe's son Roberto was one of Agosto's oldest friends, and Teresa Marcucci, Roberto's elder sister, had become a nun, which lent further prestige to the family. Agosto was satisfied with the arrangements, but now, with rent to pay, he would need more money. And paying the rent would, unfortunately, cut down on the amount he had to invest. Then too, there was the expense of the honeymoon to be taken into consideration.

"Tonelli!" William Fredericks' voice cut into his thoughts and Agosto looked up to see the grim-faced manager of the margins department.

"Yes?" Agosto responded. Fredericks had a way of pronouncing his name that aggravated him.

"You lost a bundle on that automotive stock!" Fredericks' face was set hard, his lips pressed together.

"I know that," Agosto replied. He squelched the temptation to rattle off the number of stocks he had made money on—for the Morgan Bank, of course. On balance, he was reasonably sure his record was better than anyone else's.

"I don't like to see those kinds of mistakes," Fredericks said evenly. "You're expendable, you know—especially on a personal level. But I know damn well if I tried to fire you, you'd probably go whining to Ainsley, who'd speak to J. P. Jr. I don't much like a junior like yourself kissing ass upstairs." His eyes narrowed.

"I don't kiss ass. I met them socially and by accident. And if you think I should be fired, then fire me."

Fredericks scowled. "No, I'm not going to fire you, as much as I'd like to. Frankly, I'd like to see you and your kind sent back where you came from."

Agosto didn't bother to answer. He simply looked at the papers on his desk.

"I hear you want some time off next month," Fredericks said.

Agosto looked up. "I'm getting married."

"You must think you're pretty secure," Fredericks sneered.

Agosto fought to control his temper. "I only asked for three days."

"You've been given them, but by God, you better not show up in here on Monday with a hangover from that dago red."

"I won't."

"And there better not be a repeat of that automotive-stock deal either, or all your friends put together can't save your job! You're on the line, Tonelli. I keep your balance sheet right in front of me all the time."

Fredericks turned around and stomped away. Agosto gradually unclenched his fist, aware that it felt cramped from holding himself in. "Shit," he muttered under his breath. "I want to get out of here as much as you want me out!"

6

Saturday, August 2, 1902

BROOKLYN

Nearly the whole Italian community of Sheepshead Bay attended the wedding reception at the Columbus Hall, including old Mrs. Solari, Cecilia's grandmother. With consideration for the financial situation of the bride's family, a great many brought their own huge bottles of homemade red wine, and all the women brought food.

Great long tables were covered with red-and-white-checkered cloths that were so stiff with starch they practically stood out and up by themselves. There were pastas galore, platters piled high with cheeses and sausages, long loaves of Italian bread, antipasta, and bowls of fruit. All around the hall, large pots filled with ferns gave the room a tropical atmosphere, and there were flowers everywhere.

The music was provided by the Italian Royal Band, whose drums, trumpets, and trombones were on this occasion augmented by three fiddlers and a pianist from Guido Gerardi's Music School and Shoe Repair Shop. "I teacha the musicians and they play and the people wear out their shoes dancing! I have a growth business," Guido proudly proclaimed.

And tonight Guido's proclamation seemed quite true. Everyone danced the old folk dances and swung their partners till they were all dizzy.

"This is a real wedding!" Domenico praised with joy. "A good Italian wedding! With luck it will last for three days and three nights!"

Agosto held Cecilia around her small waist. She was an angel in white, a vision of loveliness, and he felt overcome each time he whirled her around the floor, leading out an array of dancers. He thought briefly of Sarah Ainsley's party. No, elegance or not, they didn't compare. At the Ainsleys' a party was all show; the rich spent their money with élan rather than with sheer joy. But then, for the very rich bluenoses there could be no joy without money. That was not so here. The Columbus Hall was filled with people of all ages; some were poor, others had modest incomes. Men did not retire to the study, nor women to the powder room. The children were not put to bed. No, old Mrs. Solari, who was eighty if she was a day, sat with her family about her watching while her grown sons danced with their four- and five-year-old cousins, and older woman danced with young boys. It was a family affair with crying babies, women young and old, men who cursed quietly so as not to be heard, and nonstop eating. There was a happiness and completeness here that Agosto had not felt at the Ainsleys' in spite of Barton Ainsley's warmth and friendship. Nothing here was sheer glitter; it was all real and it had the continuance of tradition—from the length of the great sausages to the very dances the celebrants stomped out. It was a wedding much like his father's, and probably not unlike his grandfather's. Agosto realized that he suddenly felt at home, more at home than he had felt since his return from Cuba. He knew he could go into Barton Ainsley's world and return, that he could do business in that world and his own world. He smiled to himself. He had wanted to invite Ainsley to his wedding, but Ainsley had gone to spend part of the summer on the Riviera and wouldn't be back until the fifteenth of August. Still, Agosto wondered how Ainsley would have reacted.

He glanced at Cecilia. She was just right. He loved her with all his heart, not just because she was soft and beautiful, but because she was his past, his present, and his future . . . because they came from the same background, because she was part of this world which could never be forgotten or left behind.

"Work, work, work!" Domenico joked, slapping Agosto on the back lovingly. "When will you go into business for yourself? Soon Cecilia will be making babies! A man with a family should work for himself!"

Agosto smiled at his father. "I hope to be ready by next year."

"Another year!" Domenico sighed. "It takes more time than a greengrocery, I can tell you."

"But it will come," Salvatore put in. "And it will do a good business. Hey, Agosto, you going to loan Salvatore the money to buy another boat?"

"You come in when my bank is a reality, and we'll talk," Agosto said good-naturedly.

Salvatore drained his wineglass and shook his head up and down. "A good businessman. I can tell he's a good businessman."

"Are you and Cecilia really going to Atlantic City on your honeymoon?" Fabiana asked, her eyes wide. She had suffered a miscarriage in April, but was now once again pregnant.

"We are," Agosto answered.

Maria shook her head. "Such a frivolity! And when you're trying to save money to get started. Getting married and going into business. Agosto, you should be saving every cent!"

Agosto chose to ignore her chiding. Poor Donato, he could not afford to take his wife out for spumoni, never mind a three-day honeymoon in Atlantic City. Agosto leaned over and kissed Cecilia on the cheek. "Stay here for a moment," he whispered in her ear. "I'll be right back."

He eased away from the gathering and went over to Paolo, who was by himself and pouring yet another glass of wine. "Why don't you eat some more, Paolo?" Agosto suggested.

"I will," Paolo answered with mild irritation.

Agosto put his arm around his brother. "You mean a lot to me," he said, feeling both compassionate and sentimental.

Paolo looked up gratefully. "It's a wonderful wedding."

"I would have liked the same for you," Agosto said honestly.

Paolo looked at the floor and shrugged. "I was dishonorable," he mumbled.

"It's over. Are you happy? Is Fabiana a good wife?" It was dangerous territory. Agosto had seen his brother's eyes studying Cecilia. He might not still be in love with her, but the attraction was still there—the attraction, and no doubt a certain bitterness. Fabiana could not be compared to Cecilia.

"She's a good wife," Paolo finally said, leaving unsaid whatever else he was thinking.

"Paolo, when I go into business I will need help. I want you to come and work with me. You should get out of the store and leave Donato to help Papa."

Paolo looked stricken. "It's my life," he muttered. "If I work with you, Papa will leave the store to Donato."

"Papa will leave the store to whomever he pleases. I can give you a good job next year when I'm ready. You and Fabiana can move into your own place. Paolo, think about it."

Suddenly tears filled Paolo's eyes and he all but fell into Agosto's arms, not simply hugging him, but clinging to him. Agosto patted Paolo on the back. He felt at that moment more like a father than a brother. "Together," he whispered to Paolo. "We must stick together." They were the words his father so often spoke to him.

Without further conversation, Agosto guided his brother back to the family group. "Paolo," he suggested, "you dance with Cecilia and I'll dance with Fabiana."

Cecilia smiled and took Paolo's hand. Fabiana blushed and went off with Agosto, giggling girlishly. Agosto glanced over her shoulder and saw that Domenico had swept little Tina, who was just a year and a half old, into his arms and was dancing about, carrying her. It was a fine sight, and Agosto found himself longing to see Domenico hold the child he and Cecilia would have.

"Continuity," he said aloud.

"What?" Fabiana asked.

"Nothing." Agosto smiled. "Just a passing thought."

Sunday, August 3, 1902

ATLANTIC CITY

The wedding party lasted all night and when Agosto and Cecilia finally stole away it was nine in the morning. By the time they reached Atlantic City it was midafternoon.

"It's hot," Agosto acknowledged, though in fact New York City was hotter and much stickier.

"The weather's wonderful," Cecilia said with enthusiasm. "We can swim and sit in the sun for three entire days! And you'll finally get some rest."

Agosto hugged his bride. Her joyous mood was infectious. "I'd like to be able to bring you back here every summer," he said as they approached the hotel.

"It's wonderful," Cecilia replied. "And we'll come back one summer."

In front of the gray stone hotel which rose a full twelve stories, stretched the famous boardwalk. It was sixty feet wide and five miles long. Great piers jutted out from it into the Atlantic Ocean. The largest was Steel Pier, some two-thousand feet in length. And all along the boardwalk, vendors plied their wares in spite of the burning heat of the August sun. Hand-painted picture postcards were sold every few feet, and great bags of colored saltwater taffy were hawked with enthusiasm. There were brightly colored flags flying everywhere, and the dense crowds made for a carnival atmosphere.

"I want to see everything," Cecilia told him.

Agosto laughed. "Even after being up all night?"

She shook her head. "No, I want to sleep first."

Agosto looked at her longingly for a moment. He yearned to hold her in his arms and to make love to her, but such things should not be rushed. Cecilia gave every indication of being a woman whose sensual desires could be easily awakened, but she was also a virgin and the product of a strict upbringing. In all the months of their courting they had barely been alone. There had been kisses, and those kisses had grown more passionate, but beyond that there was only the promise of things to come.

The bellboy saw them to their room. It was not the plush bridal suite that Agosto knew existed, but it was what Agosto could afford and it was a pleasant, well-appointed room overlooking the boardwalk and the sea. Agosto tipped the bellboy and ordered champagne.

"Such an extravagance," Cecilia chided as she removed her fine black silk hat. It was a Corinne, and trimmed with ribbons with a fine rhinestone buckle and a large spray of velvet flowers. It cost five dollars at Macy's, where her mother had taken her to buy her trousseau.

Her rich dark hair tumbled down as she removed the pins that held the hat. "Aren't you tired?"

"Exhausted," Agosto willingly admitted. It was an honest enough reply, but it wasn't the whole truth. His exhaustion was augmented by a nervous energy and anticipation. Now, or when they had both rested, he would make love to Cecilia and consummate their marriage. But as great as his growing desire was, he felt a tinge of reserve, as a fear that he might not satisfy her, or that in some way he might hurt her. She had a rare delicacy and his desire was tempered by his protective feeling toward her and by what he perceived as her fragility. Somehow he felt that if he became lost in passion and lust she might shatter like a fine glass figurine.

The bellboy knocked again and brought in the small tea cart which held the champagne bucket with the cold bottle. And there were little sandwiches too, though Agosto did not feel hungry. Indeed, the night of eating and drinking had left him feeling quite full.

He tipped the bellboy again and closed the door after him. "Alone at last," he said under his breath. "I'll open the champagne." He hoped it might relax her. No, he hoped it would relax him.

"Point it the other way, it makes such noise!" Cecilia half-crouched behind the chair as Agosto pushed the cork out and it went flying through the air. She let out a little cry, and Agosto laughed and poured the foaming, bubbly liquid into two sparkling glasses. He handed one to her. The crystal glasses touched and made a tinkling sound.

"To a long happy marriage," he toasted, devouring her with his eyes. Thoughts of his parents crossed his mind. Gina had arrived not ever having seen Domenico, they could not have felt for each other what he and Cecilia felt. I'm fortunate among men, Agosto thought. I have found my woman, and I love and want her. He smiled warmly and leaned over to kiss Cecilia's throat. "I love you," he whispered.

Cecilia's huge eyes looked into his and spoke her response before she said the words. "And I love you, Agosto."

After a time, Cecilia disappeared into the tiny bathroom, and when she returned she was wearing a long white nightdress that clung to her fine figure and set off her skin and dark hair. She looked more like an angel than ever, and Agosto took her in his arms and they lay down together on the bed.

They kissed and caressed and Cecilia returned his kisses shyly at first, but more passionately as he continued. She sighed in his arms and shivered when he touched her swelling breasts.

Agosto relished her soft skin, and his hands explored carefully and lovingly. But even as his own passion grew, he was aware of his weariness and of the effect of the wine and champagne.

"I want you," he whispered. "But I'm not certain I can—"

Cecilia pressed her finger to his lips. "Then let us sleep and waken in one another's arms."

Agosto nodded and held her close. He could feel her pounding heart as it slowed, and still an innocent, she nestled against him, slipping into sleep.

Agosto's dream came only after some hours of needed sleep. It was a sentimental dream that engulfed him, and cast up images of the past. He seemed to be floating free through the air and looking down from some height. He saw the outlines of Manhattan as he had from the railing of the vessel that bore him home from his Cuban adventure, and briefly he saw Philip Ainsley's face. Then he saw Cecilia, a snow-white princess floating toward him. He reached out to her and drew her to him, and she stood at his side.

Agosto's eyes opened to find the room enveloped in darkness. Cecilia's warm form was pressed against him, as she lay curved in the outline of his body. He moved his hands softly, almost reverently across her bare breasts, exposed amid the ribbons and lace of her nightdress. She stirred in his arms and languorously turned to face him so that their noses nearly touched, and he could feel her breath on his face.

Agosto's hands traveled beneath her nightdress and felt the softness of her inner thighs. Cecilia moaned in pleasure and encircled his neck with her arms. As his eyes adjusted to the darkness, he could make out her face. She still looked angelic in spite of the sensuous movement of her body, and when he bent to kiss the dark tip of her breast, she quivered and kissed his neck in return. Agosto spoke words of love into her ears; then he gently felt her warm moisture and knew she shared his feeling of passion. He entered her slowly, as if the act were a part of the dream he had had only moments before. Cecilia let out a small muffled cry, but she clung to him and he knew that whatever pain she felt was combined with pleasure. He moved slowly, trying to think of the pounding surf below the room's window, trying to visualize the gay colored parasols . . . but the colors blended and merged in his mind and surged forward as he expelled all his passion, fully aware of Cecilia's response beneath him. It was as if they tumbled together into a sea of swirling, brilliant color and then lay once again peacefully in the cool shade, side by side.

After a time Cecilia kissed him gently on the cheek. It was a kiss that Agosto knew he would never forget—a tender, loving expression of her happiness.

"Did I hurt you?" he asked as he kissed her in return and tasted the salt of the tears on her cheek.

She shook her head and kissed him again. "I love you," she answered. "And I cry with joy, not pain."

It was unspoken, but Agosto understood. So many women married without love. And though they grew to love their husbands, he and Cecilia were different. They began their marriage with love.

"You are romantic," Cecilia told him after a time. "You have a tenderness and romantic nature you don't show to others."

Agosto smiled and stroked her hair. It was true that he tried to hide the sentimental side of his nature.

"But I knew you were romantic," Cecilia confessed.

"You'll be more than my wife," Agosto answered as he held her closely. "You are my lover and we will build together."

"Forever," she answered.

Agosto drew her into his arms, and together they fell asleep again, but this sleep was dreamless.

Monday, August 25, 1902

Agosto drained his coffee and set the china cup gently down in its saucer. It was his first visit to the Knickerbocker Club, that austere elite dominion founded by A. Hutton, J. J. Astor, and Philip Schuyler in 1871. He could not help stealing a furtive glance at the faces of the famous men who gathered in the secluded corners of the dining room. Nor could he feel quite comfortable knowing that had he owned the Morgan Bank, his wealth would do him no good here, he would have been barred solely on the basis of his name. But Barton Ainsley sat opposite him looking quite at home. He took out his pipe and lit it, leaning back casually. They had spent most of lunch discussing Ainsley's trip to Europe and Agosto wedding.

"Enjoy your lunch?"

"A little rich for me, I don't usually eat lunch." Agosto took out a stogie and lit it. The small black cigarettes were his favorite, but then, they were the favorite of most Italian men.

"You know, I'd still lend you the money you need to get started. Now that you're married, you should give that some thought."

"I have, but no, I can't borrow the money. Still, I want you to know I appreciate the offer. You've been a good friend . . . No, more than that . . . a kind of mentor."

Barton Ainsley flushed. "And you've helped to fill a void."

Agosto too was embarrassed.

Ainsley waved the smoke from Agosto's stogie away. "Vile things, those," he said with a grin. "I really don't know how you stand them."

"I'll put it out if it bothers you."

"Hell no! It's no worse than old Cornelius Vanderbilt's cigars!" Ainsley leaned forward. "If you won't take my offer, will you take some advice?—it's free."

"I'll try," Agosto replied.

"Buy those." Ainsley pointed to the stogie.

"I do buy them. I never smoke anything else."

Ainsley laughed and leaned even closer. "No, buy their stock. Buy as much as you can. Use all your cash and convert your other holdings, and buy as much stock as you can of the American Stogie Company."

Agosto took the little black cigarette out of his mouth and looked at it curiously. "I suppose it's a good investment," he allowed.

"Better than that I hope," Ainsley whispered. "There's a merger in the wind. Buy the stock, Agosto. Do it this afternoon."

"You seem awfully confident."

"I am. Will you do it?"

"You said I shouldn't make snap decisions."

"I take it back. You have to do it today. Tomorrow might be too late. Secrets aren't well kept on the Street, too many vultures circling.

"All right, I'll do it."

Ainsley leaned back and snapped his fingers. The waiter appeared instantly, tray in hand. "Some cognac, Giles!"

"I'll fall asleep at my desk," Agosto joked.

Ainsley shrugged. "You're going to resign anyway."

"Well, I was going to wait a bit."

"If I were you, I'd start looking for a location for that bank of yours."

"Is your tip that good?"

Ainsley nodded. "It's gilt-edged."

The waiter brought the cognac and Agosto sipped it. "I'd like to be able to give up at least one of my jobs."

"And you must. You look tired all the time. Is that work? Or just the normal effects of the first few weeks of marriage?"

"Work," Agosto replied.

Ainsley set his cognac down. "I really ought to thank you for spurning my daughter's advances. She can be quite shameless at times. I know you'll be much happier with your Cecilia."

"Sarah's very attractive. Spurning her advances, as you put it, wasn't easy."

Ainsley nodded. "She always wants what she can't have. You fascinated her, you know. You were out of her circle . . . intriguing because you were different."

"I suspected that. But Sarah and I have different destinies. We come from different traditions."

"She's still going out with Creighton Stearns. He's only distantly related to my brother-in-law and partner. He's in banking too, of course. In Boston."

"Is she happy?"

"Seems to be. It's always a little hard to tell with Sarah. But she appears to have adjusted to Philip's death. I suppose I regret that we kept his illness a secret from her. She might have been better prepared had she known.''

''I think she would have suffered more.''

''Maybe.''

Agosto drained his glass. ''I really have to get back to my desk. If I don't, I'll be fired before I have the opportunity to resign. I don't have the luxury of your long lunch hours.''

''That's because you don't own a bank . . . yet.''

Agosto picked up his pack of stogies and looked at them a second before putting them in his pocket. ''Yet,'' he replied.

Saturday, February 14, 1903

B R O O K L Y N

The icy February wind howled off the bay, whistled around the corners of even the smallest buildings, and propelled the falling ice pellets into an unpleasant swirling mass that stung the faces of those unwise enough to venture out. But for Agosto Tonelli, who hurried from the Marcucci house, where he resided, to his own family's home for supper, the weather could not have mattered less.

''Damn!'' he swore under his breath. Cecilia was already at his parents' house. He would dearly have liked to give her the news first, but now there was no avoiding an announcement to the whole family.

The fire of excitement and triumph that burned inside him was more than enough to offset the chilling effects of the inclement weather.

The stocks that Ainsley had suggested he buy had gone continually up, he had gotten in early and put every cent he had into the American Stogie Company. But today was the biggest day of his life. At three P.M., just minutes after he arrived from Manhattan, Agosto had been summoned from the tiny apartment where he and Cecilia lived, by Roberto Marcucci, who told him he had an urgent phone call from Manhattan. Agosto blessed the Marcuccis' success. They were one of three families in Sheepshead Bay to have a phone in their home. He also blessed the fact that he had come to the apartment first to change his clothes instead of going directly to his parents' house, where Cecilia was waiting.

The phone call was from an excited Barton Ainsley, who first asked, ''You did follow my advice, didn't you?'' Agosto replied that he had, and then he told Ainsley exactly how many shares he owned. He heard Ainsley breathe a sigh of relief on the other end of the phone, and then Ainsley said simply, "You've got your money, Agosto! The news is out: the American Stogie Company has merged with American Tobacco. Your stocks are, as of this moment, worth enough to pay back what you borrowed, and quite sufficient to open your bank!"

"My God," Agosto stammered. He had known the tip was good, but he had held himself in reserve, not allowing himself to think about the actual moment when his dream might have substance.

"I suggest you call your broker first thing Monday morning."

"Of course," Agosto replied. Then hesitatingly he thanked Barton Ainsley.

"Your risk entirely," Ainsley had answered. "And by the way, good luck."

Agosto had replaced the long receiver on its hook with a shaky hand.

"Bad news?" Roberto asked from across the room.

Agosto had shaken his head. "Hardly. I've got the funds now . . . or I will have on Monday."

Roberto grinned. "So, you will go into business for yourself now?"

Agosto had nearly burst out laughing. "And on Monday I'll resign from the Morgan Bank and kiss that bastard Fredericks good-bye!"

"And on Tuesday you will start looking for a location," Roberto predicted.

Agosto nodded.

"And what will you call this bank, Agosto? I want to be the first to know."

"The Italian Bank," Agosto answered without the slightest hesitation. He had named it in his head long ago. Now he allowed himself to see the sign above the bank in his mind.

"I like that," Roberto announced. "You know, I think I know just the place. Remember the dry-goods store on Emmons and Ocean avenues?"

Agosto nodded as he visualized the location in his mind. It was across the street from a large Catholic church, the Church of the Blessed Virgin. People would see the bank as they came in and out of Mass. Roberto was right, it was an ideal location.

"The Nelsons are moving to Minnesota to join their children. The store's empty now. You could either buy or rent it."

"Buy," Agosto replied. Renting implied a temporary status, and this bank was going to be permanent.

Roberto shrugged. "Of course, it would need some carpentry work. You'd have to build a big private office, hey?"

Agosto shook his head vigorously. "No office. I want no offices at all in my bank. I want people to see me working there like they see my father and brother and Donato at the store. This will be a bank people will have confidence in." Agosto thought of the Morgan Bank: it was like some sort of fort, and the men who ran it were unapproachable and distant, like feudal lords shut away in their castle. "No offices," he repeated firmly.

Roberto laughed. "Well, that will make renovations easier. And cheaper!"

Agosto grinned. "Good. I have to watch my money—I'm going to be a father in August."

"I thought Cecilia looked plumper." Roberto winked. "She was a good catch."

"The son of a fisherman should know a good catch," Agosto joked.

"You're a lucky man. You have a fine woman, you'll soon have a child, and you'll have your own business. All you need is customers!"

"I'm going to start the day I finish at the Morgan Bank, which, given the fact that Fredericks hates me so much, will probably be the same day I resign. I'll go door to door and tell everyone about the bank. I'm going to talk to them about losing their savings if there's a fire in the house, I'm going to explain interest, I'm going to go out and talk everyone in this neighborhood into putting their funds into the Italian Bank."

"I'll be your first customer," Roberto volunteered. "I'll talk to other businessmen and I'll even help you knock on doors."

"I could use your help," Agosto confessed.

"You'll have it," Roberto promised.

Then Agosto put on his heavy coat and boots, and wrapping his scarf around his neck, had started out for his parents' house. The moment has come, he thought as he climbed the steps that led to the house behind the store. He slipped on the ice and grasped the railing. "Nasty weather," he mumbled under his breath. "But one hell of a good day otherwise!"

Agosto requested that the whole Tonelli family gather in the parlor. Domenico sat in his chair, his feet up on the wood footstool. Gina sat in her chair primly, her long skirt folded about her. She looked a trifle agitated; she wasn't used to sitting, but rather to bustling about. Donato sat on one end of the sofa, with Maria at his side. Little Tina played on the floor with some wooden blocks Agosto had bought her for her birthday, which was of course Christmas Day. Paolo sat next to Maria, and on a stiff-backed wooden chair brought in from the dining room, Fabiana sprawled uncomfortably. She couldn't, in fact, sit in any other chair because she was great with child, and once down, could hardly stand again unless Paolo pulled her up. Cecilia sat next to Agosto, her eyes dancing with delight as if she had guessed his news already.

"I have enough money to open my bank," Agosto announced with pleasure. "I shall be purchasing the dry-goods store on Emmons and Ocean avenues. At least I think that's where I will locate."

"Purchase?" Domenico said. "You have so much money?"

Agosto nodded. He would discuss details with his father privately. But an inner sense of propriety told him not to discuss actual dollars and cents in front of Paolo, Maria, and Donato. To announce that in less than a year he had turned a few thousand dollars into more than forty thousand would invite both jealousy and questions, for by Maria and Paolo's standards it was a great fortune.

Domenico seemed to understand his reservations instinctively. "Glad your investments did well," he said flatly, closing the door on further financial discussion.

"We can live over the bank," Cecilia ventured. "If there's an apartment there."

Agosto took her hand and squeezed it. He wanted to shout: And as soon as I can, I shall buy you the finest house in Sheepshead Bay! But he didn't.

"Next I'll talk to the people in the neighborhood. They'll have to learn to trust a bank. How about you, Papa? Will you put the money from the store in my bank?"

Domenico frowned. "It's not much."

"It's a start," Agosto urged.

"I don't know. A bank . . . I've always been my own bank."

At that moment Gina got up and swept out of the room. She returned almost immediately with a small velvet bag held tightly closed with a drawstring. "I shall speak," she announced almost formally. "For years I've been saving pennies, money left over from this and that. Here, Agosto, you take this money. You take it and open a savings account for me when the time comes." She turned to Domenico with a broad, triumphant smile. "You count the money, Agosto, and tell how much it is. You see, Domenico, I trust my son and his bank. If Agosto's own family doesn't trust his bank, how will anyone else?"

Domenico looked almost sheepish. But he nodded his head in

agreement. "We must stick together," he finally said; then, looking up, asked, "Can I have it back whenever I want it?"

"Of course," Agosto said, dumping the contents of his mother's treasure into his lap. He counted silently, replacing the coins. "This is a lot more than pennies, Mama."

Gina shrugged. "When I get a hundred, I turn them in for a silver dollar, and when I have ten silver dollars, I turn it in for a gold piece."

Agosto grinned and stared at the solid gold 1857 Indian-head hundred-dollar gold coin. He turned it in his fingers.

"I got that because I thought it was pretty," Gina commented.

"You've nearly three hundred dollars here."

"Gina!" Domenico said in a shocked tone.

Gina leaned over to her husband and stroked his cheek. "For us, for a rainy day when things go badly, or for our trip to Puglia."

Domenico smiled and kissed her hands, mumbling an endearment in Italian.

"Your money will earn interest," Agosto told his mother.

"Interest?" Gina queried, arching one of her eyebrows.

Agosto explained, and she folded her hands in satisfaction. "See, Domenico? My money will work in Agosto's bank, and all by itself it will multiply. My money will earn money. I like that."

Agosto walked over and hugged his mother. Her eyes twinkled with her mysterious sense of adventure and he smiled across the room at Cecilia.

7

Monday, February 16, 1903

MANHATTAN

"What's that smell!" Fredericks' long nose crinkled with distaste and he stood back from the door of Agosto's cubicle as if in mortal danger of catching some disease.

Agosto looked up and smiled broadly. "Garlic," he answered, feeling pride in the admission.

"I think you were told when you started working here that you were never to come to work smelling of garlic! This is not some sweat shop, nor is it an extension of Little Italy! Our clients do not expect the odor of garlic."

Fredericks all but spit out the word, his eyes narrow. Agosto could see the man's prejudices rising to the surface like cream in a cup of coffee.

"From now on, Fredericks, I'm going to smell how I please, because I'm going to eat what I please." Agosto knew he sounded cheerful, which in fact he was.

"Not in the Morgan Bank!" Fredericks thundered.

Agosto smiled. "Precisely," he returned.

Fredericks' expression went from explosive anger to puzzlement. "What?"

"I'm resigning," Agosto told him, unable to suppress the grin on his face.

"What do you mean, you're resigning?"

"I mean you and Edwards and Smith—the whole lot of you—will have to do your own work from now on. I really hope that in the nearly three years I've been here you haven't forgotten how."

Fredericks paled slightly and Agosto felt considerable satisfaction. The man was a lazy, stupid son of a bitch, but he was just smart enough to know he was losing an employee with the best record in the office.

"Going back to work in your father's greengrocery?" Fredericks stumbled. "Or are you going to stay in Little Italy and become a—what do you call them?—*padrone*, finding work for foreigners and taking their pay?"

"No, I think I'll leave the exploitation of immigrants to you and your kind, Fredericks. I'm going to open my own bank."

"Your own bank!" Fredericks' face reddened all over again. "Your own bank! That takes money! It takes time. You haven't been making that kind of salary!"

"I've made some good investments," Agosto said as he stood up. I could almost feel sorry for him, Agosto thought. He's a little man, a man condemned to make money for men like Morgan for the rest of his life.

"You're taking a terrible chance," Fredericks blustered. "If you have that kind of money, you should reinvest it."

"I am reinvesting it—in myself. That's what really angers you, isn't it? You could never take a chance on yourself."

Fredericks snapped his head and looked across at Agosto. First anger, than disbelief, now the last tactic—belittlement. "There are documents to be filled out, papers to be filed. You don't just open a bank like you open a grocery store, you stupid dago! Even if you have the money, you could be stopped, and if you aren't stopped, it will still take you a year!"

"Are you going to stop me? You, Fredericks? You're a glorified office boy! No, Morgan could stop me, but he wouldn't bother. He'd at least take a decent capitalist view that I should have the chance to fail on my own. And, yes, I know what has to be done and how long it will take. But I intend not to waste that time. I have my own kind of preparations to make."

"You have a swelled head, Tonelli. It comes from having been invited to places you don't belong."

"Places you haven't been invited to at all," Agosto pointed out.

"Taking jobs from good Americans, causing the economy to go up and down like a yo-yo—that's what all you immigrants do. Tonelli, your a type—you're the type who wants to be what you can't be, and you're too stupid to see that."

Agosto sucked in his breath. On any other day, he would have wanted to flatten Fredericks for his remarks, but today he felt they were the remarks of a frightened man, a man who knew what he was and knew what he could never become. "Would you like me to leave now?" Agosto asked.

Fredericks' face hardened. "No. I expect you to work for the next two weeks. I expect you to work hard. No, Tonelli, I'll see that you don't leave without having given the proper notice."

Agosto smiled. "Then you'll have to put up with the garlic, Fredericks."

Fredericks turned and stomped away. "Get to work!" he shouted, betraying his total frustration.

Saturday, March 7, 1903

BROOKLYN

The building that formerly housed the Nelson dry-goods store was a large two-story brick building with big windows on the ground floor, and smaller windows on the top floor. A side entrance led to the apartment above the store.

"It needs painting," Agosto said as he looked around the four-room apartment with its cracked plaster walls.

"And new plumbing," Roberto commented as he stood near the yellowed sink.

"When I get through cleaning it, it will be lovely," Cecilia said dreamily. "Oh, Agosto, our very own place, our first home! See, it has two windows that overlook the street! I'll hang the white sheer curtains and it will be transformed!" Her eyes twinkled merrily and Agosto could not help wondering if Cecilia saw something he didn't. To his eyes the apartment was in need of major work, and repairs were needed downstairs too.

"I'll help you," Roberto offered. "And Paolo will help too. Sure there's plenty of work to be done, but there's plenty of time. You know how Albany is—it could take months to get your documents processed. When my father incorporated the concrete plant, it took six months! And he had political influence."

Agosto turned over his hands, examining them. "I've lost the calluses I once had," he said half-regretfully.

"That's what you get for working inside all day with your head. And two jobs, too! Are you telling me you can't hammer a nail anymore, or lay bricks?"

"I think I can still manage, but I'm going to be slow at first."

"Good thing you've got so many friends." Roberto kicked the floor symbolically. "You're going to have to lay a new floor."

Agosto laughed. "When I said I was going to build a bank, I didn't mean with hammer and nails."

"Look, the building was cheap. So it needs some work. When it's finished, it will make a fine bank, and when the apartment is repaired and painted, it'll be a good place for you, Cecilia, and the little one." He winked at Cecilia, who was four months pregnant.

"It'll be worth it," Agosto agreed. And he thought he'd be doubly proud. Not only had he made the money to back the bank, but he would also be actively involved in making the building ready. At the moment, he found the thought of wielding a hammer appealing.

"And you'll need a new sign for the front." Roberto's mind leaped ahead. "I think Guido the shoemaker has a brother who paints signs. Do you want it in English or Italian?"

"Both," Agosto answered.

"And look, if the building is ready before you get the go-ahead, you can open up and sell other things. I was up in Rome, New York, about a year ago, and I saw a little bank run by a guy name Rocco Gualtieri. He had the bank, a travel agency, an employment agency, and he sold tinned foods. It was like an Italian community center, crowds of people."

"Everything but a post office?" Agosto smiled.

"Probably got that too." Roberto laughed.

"Agosto, we should sell some dry goods too. It would be perfect for Fabiana. She's been so sad since she lost the baby, it would give her something to do." Cecilia looked up at him hopefully. "And she could be near Paolo," she added. "Working together is good." Unspoken was the tragedy that Fabiana had lost three babies, and been told she could not have children.

Agosto put his arm around Cecilia's shoulders. She liked Fabiana, and though she didn't say it, she feared Paolo would drift away, causing his wife even more torment. "I'll think about it," he agreed.

"It wouldn't be a mistake, Agosto. Fabiana has a lot of friends. They'd come to the bank to buy dry goods and they'd talk to her and stay to do their banking."

"Friends. . . . In Little Italy, the immigrants wouldn't trust an Italian banker. They've seen too many fraudulent ones," Agosto said.

"It's a bad business," Roberto agreed. "They're caught between bluenose prejudices and their own crooks. Sometimes it's hard to tell who the bloodsuckers really are."

"I want to help hardworking Italians prosper," Agosto added, looking out of the window and down on the busy street. "It's the way up, Roberto. It's the way to provide jobs and a future."

"Well, let's not just talk about it! If you and Cecilia are going to move in here, we had better get to work." Kicking the wall, he exclaimed, "*Cristo*, some of the masonry is rotten!"

Tuesday, August 4, 1903

BROOKLYN

Agosto paused momentarily and looked at his hands. If they had lacked calluses when he left the Morgan Bank four months ago, they had them now. The former site of the Nelson dry-goods store was transformed. Upstairs, the apartment was ready to move into. Its wall were repaired and painted. There were new plumbing and wiring. Downstairs, a new floor was laid, the brickwork and trim painstakingly repaired. Everything sparkled. On one side of the room there was a long counter with rows of shelves behind it. Here, it was decided, Fabiana would sell tinned goods and homemade candies. On the other side was a long counter divided into five wickets, and behind the counter were several big desks. This was to be the bank as soon as the documents were processed and the bank chartered. Agosto sighed. Probably Fredericks was right about one thing: it would take a year. But even so, he and Cecilia could move into the apartment soon, thus saving the rent now paid to the Marcuccis. Agosto stood up and wiped his hands on his overalls. The floor was now completely sanded and ready for varnishing. It had been slow work. He had worked nearly every day, and Paolo and Roberto came to help on the weekends, occasionally joined by Donato, whose greatest talent was painting. There had, of course, been days spent in Manhattan, and other days spent at the lawyer's office.

"Agosto! Agosto! You must come right away, you must come now!" Fabiana burst through the front door of the bank, waving her arms in the air. She had grown even rounder than before, and her face was the roundest of all. She was flushed with excitement and she exhibited a rare energy. "It's Cecilia!" Fabiana burst out. "She's in labor, she's having the baby. Come quickly, Agosto!"

"The midwife said it wasn't due till next week!" Agosto blurted out.

"She's never been right!" Fabiana said with mild condemnation. "Babies don't wait, Agosto. Hurry, your mama says you must come right away. Cecilia is at our house. She was helping your mama make bread, and then she started having the pains!"

"Why didn't you phone?" Agosto asked, glancing at the newly installed phone. "You could have called from the store."

"Mrs. Solari was praying," Fabiana replied with some annoyance. "I interrupted her, of course. I told her to stop praying and come right away because her granddaughter was having a baby and she would be a great-grandmother soon. But all she did was start another Hail Mary! Come on, Agosto. Hurry!"

"How long has she been in labor?"

"Nearly two hours," Fabiana replied. "But the midwife says the first is always harder. The second drops like a ripe orange from a tree."

"Why didn't you come sooner?"

"Because your mama said it might be false labor."

Agosto did not bother to change out of his overalls. He quickly put away his tools and locked the door, hurriedly heading home with Fabiana, who waddled rapidly at his side.

Agosto and Fabiana burst into the house in time to hear Cecilia scream. Agosto bolted for the stairs, but his mother barred the way. "No," she said simply. "Mrs. Rosario is with her. She's a good midwife, you stay down here."

Agosto paused and bit his lower lip. "She's in pain," he said earnestly. Cecilia was not like the other women. She wouldn't cry out to get attention, she would cry out only if she had to. He wanted to be with her.

"No," his mother repeated. She gently touched her son's cheek. "Go sit with your father in the parlor. I'll go back to Cecilia."

Agosto nodded silently. One did not break traditions. "Take care of her for me . . . tell her I'm here."

Gina smiled tenderly. "I will." She turned and hobbled up the stairs, leaving Agosto feeling empty, lonely, and excited all at once. He sat down next to his father, who only grinned and sucked on his cigar.

Cecilia screamed again, and Agosto leaned forward, his head in his hands. In the kitchen he could hear Fabiana fumbling about making tea. Had Donato been this worried when Tina was born? Agosto didn't think so. Briefly he wondered if Maria were upstairs with the other women. Somehow he hoped not. She would be like a dark cloud at an otherwise happy event. Her only child was a girl; she probably prayed constantly that Cecilia would not have the grandson that Domenico so dearly desired.

At that moment the silence was broken by the loud cry of a child. Domenico sat upright and grinned. "A new soul has arrived," he announced authoritatively. "And such a strong cry for one so young! It must be a boy!"

Agosto bolted to his feet. He seized on Domenico's words. Surely it was a son! He ran for the stairs and met his mother at the top. She beamed and carried in her arms a tiny bundle.

"My son!" Agosto shouted.

Gina laughed and pressed the child to her breast. "Your daughter," she corrected.

Agosto pushed the blanket away and looked into the tiny bright red face. "A girl," he said, aware of his disappointment.

"A fine healthy girl. And the next one will certainly be a boy."

"Cecilia?"

"She is resting. Come, I'll take you to her for a minute. But remember, Agosto, she needs to sleep now."

Agosto followed his mother, aware Domenico walked behind him.

In the bedroom Cecilia was propped up amid white pillows, her face nearly as white as the linens, and it seemed even paler because it was framed by her cascading black hair.

The midwife bundled bloodstained sheets, and Maria stood in the corner, her hands folded, a look of almost cheerful relief on her face. If she had failed her father by not producing a male heir, so had his favorite son.

Agosto went directly to Cecilia and kissed her tenderly on both cheeks and then on the lips. "She is a beautiful baby," he told her, though at the moment the reality was that the infant was not all that beautiful.

"A fine child," the midwife announced. "She had a hard struggle down the birth canal. She'll always be a fighter because she struggled so for life."

Domenico grunted. He too believed the superstition that the harder the birth, the stronger the child.

"Part of the cord was looped around her neck. That's why she's so red now. But she didn't allow herself to be choked. And I got it off in time. A strong child. It's good."

"I love you," Agosto whispered in Cecilia's ear. "She is beautiful."

Domenico strode across the room and took the infant from his wife. He walked to the bed carrying the child, whose tiny hand grasped onto his large callused thumb. "She likes me!" Domenico roared. "See, she knows her grandfather already!"

His admiration was so obvious that Agosto glanced at Maria, whose face had darkened and whose fingers clasped her skirts.

"And look at her eyes! They're blue!"

"All babies have blue eyes," Maria said quickly. "Tina had blue eyes too, but they turned brown."

"Not like these eyes," Domenico continued, oblivious of Maria's jealousy. "Ah, these are eyes the color of the sea—the calm blue sea. Clare Marina! That's what we'll call this angel, we'll call her Clare Marina. That's Latin—Clare for brilliance, Marina for the sea I once sailed!"

Agosto stepped to his father's side and looked at Cecilia, who nodded her approval of the name Domenico had chosen. "Clare Marina it will be," he confirmed.

"It's a stupid name for a child!" Maria said, no longer bothering to hide her envy over the attention her father bestowed on the little newcomer.

Domenico looked up and glared at her. "Clare Marina," he repeated firmly. "It is a beautiful name. It is the name I chose."

So powerful was his look that Maria fell utterly silent. She blinked and looked at the floor, not even daring to apologize for her outburst.

Domenico rocked the baby in his arms. "Little Clare Marina," he said over and over. Then: "You will be christened next week."

Monday, March 7, 1904

B R O O K L Y N

"If you clean off the counter one more time, you'll wear it out," Agosto said jokingly. He looked lovingly at his wife, who seemed more beautiful than ever. She wore a long brocade dress with a high, stiff, starched collar. Her hair was a mass of curls and her dark eyes were intent as she studied each and every corner of the bank. It was one hour before The Italian Bank would open its doors for the first time, and Cecilia wouldn't tolerate even the slightest flaw in its appearance.

"Besides," he added, "you should be resting and not working." He perused her figure. Her breasts seemed higher and fuller than before. Her stomach, which was well hidden by the fullness of her skirt, was just beginning to swell. Cecilia, much to Agosto's joy, was again pregnant.

"I feel wonderful." She smiled. "And there's no need to rest. Exercise is good for a pregnant woman."

"Most women go into confinement."

Cecilia shook her head vigorously. "My mother didn't, and neither did my grandmother. They worked side by side with their husbands till their babies dropped from their wombs. And I shall do the same."

Agosto leaned over and kissed her on the cheek. "I only want you to take care of yourself. Besides, Clare Marina is only seven months old. You already have her to care for."

"She's my bundle of joy," Cecilia said as she turned and glanced into the wicker basket sitting on the floor. In it, Clare Marina slept peacefully. "I'll take care to rest, Agosto, but I'll not miss the most important day in my husband's life!"

"The most important day in my life was our wedding day."

Cecilia blushed and went back to polishing the brass pots on the end of the counter. They were filled with flowers and gave the inside of the bank a feeling of warmth lacking in other such institutions. And as Agosto had ordained, there were no offices.

As for the other side of the bank, that too was ready. Fabiana had neatly stacked all her tinned goods and arranged her display of candies and sweets. She had gone upstairs for a moment to change her clothes, announcing that on this, the opening day of the bank, she would wear her very best dress.

"It's a good day for our opening," Cecilia observed, peeking out from the edge of the green shades that hung over the window. "The sun is shining, the sky is blue, and it's the seventh. That's a lucky number."

"That's why I chose it."

"We're going to be flooded with customers," Cecilia predicted. "Ever since Mr. and Mrs. Tersinni's house burned down and they lost all the cash they kept there, everyone has been saying, 'We can't wait for Agosto to open his bank so we can put our money somewhere safe.' It was such a tragedy, they lost everything."

Agosto nodded. "I intend to give him a loan to begin again. Personally, I think there's money in ice cream, and Tersinni makes the best ice cream in Brooklyn."

Cecilia smiled. "Even though he has no collateral?"

Agosto shook his head. Cecilia had been reading his books on banking in preparation for working with him. She insisted that if other women could work in their husbands' shops, she could work in the bank.

"He has his reputation," Agosto responded, "and I happen to think a reputation is pretty good collateral."

"And the calluses on his hands," Cecilia added, half-mimicking Agosto's favorite phrase. Then she giggled. "He doesn't really have calluses, but his hands are sticky from the strawberry ice. I guess in his case, the collateral is sticky fingers."

Agosto laughed in spite of his slight feeling of nervousness. Then, once again growing serious: "People are gathering outside. I wish Paolo would get here—I'm going to need his help. Anyway, brother or no brother, he shouldn't be late for his first day on the job. Especially since Fabiana has been here since eight."

"He'll be here," Cecilia said confidently. "And Maria too."

Agosto raised an eyebrow and Cecilia laughed. It was an unspoken joke between them. Maria had spent over a year complaining about the impracticalities of Agosto's endeavor; then, still complaining, she had insisted on coming to help on opening day. She mumbled about failure, but feared success would be too much for Agosto to handle without her. And she was good with sums, Agosto acknowledged. She was, in fact, a miser of the first class.

Domenico and Gina would come too, but not to help. They would come to deposit their money and show that they had faith in their son's idea. Donato was committed to working in the store, since everyone else would be at the bank for its opening.

"There's Paolo now," Cecilia said, looking up in response to a knock on the door.

Agosto went to the door and opened it a crack. It was not only Paolo, but the rest of his family as well. They were all dressed up in their Sunday best, as if they were going to Mass.

"It looks wonderful!" Gina said, embracing Agosto. "Just like a carnival or fair!" She referred to the outside of the bank, where Agosto flew both Italian and American flags and where Giuseppe had set up his pushcart to sell candied apples, popcorn, and nuts. His cart was covered with balloons and he had been instructed to give one to any child whose parents opened an account. It all caused Agosto much amusement. He wondered how the staid gray bankers of Wall Street would have reacted to the "carnival atmosphere." But, he reasoned, this was not Wall Street. For The Italian Bank to succeed, it had to appeal not to the people on Wall Street, but to the people of Sheepshead Bay. It had to be a part of their community and begin its life with a celebration just like the celebrations held to initiate any new place of business or to launch a new fishing vessel. What was familiar would be trusted; what was unfamiliar would be distrusted.

"It's nine o'clock," Cecilia said, pointing to the huge clock on the wall.

Agosto inhaled deeply and then walked around raising the green shades. As soon as they were all up, he unlocked the door and a flood of friends and neighbors trekked in, each one hugging him and congratulating him.

"Why did it take so long before you could open?" Mr. Romano, the baker, asked.

"All the documents had to be approved," Agosto answered matter-of-factly.

"That's because of your name," Romano commented with a frown. "Everything takes longer for Italians."

Agosto nodded his agreement. It was true that stumbling blocks seemed to have been placed in his way, stumbling blocks that wouldn't have existed if he'd had a name like Turner. But it certainly wasn't Fredericks making good his threat, it was only some government worker who failed to deal with the documents straightaway or who delayed because of some personal feelings about immigrants in banking. Agosto had found the waiting a source of great aggravation, but now he cast all of his ill feeling behind him.

"What will happen if I lose my bankbook?" Giuseppe's elderly wife asked as she deposited fifteen dollars.

"We'll give you another," Agosto promised. "An exact duplicate," he added for clarity.

She frowned. "Can I have two now? That way, if I lose one, I won't have to bother you."

Agosto grinned. "But if I give you both now and you lose them both, how can I give you a duplicate?" It was all possible, if she insisted, he decided.

Again she frowned. "Then I'll only take one now," she agreed.

Agosto made out the little bankbook and entered the fifteen-dollar deposit. Then he painstakingly explained the columns. "Your deposits will go in this column, your withdrawals in this column. And your interest in this column. You will earn three percent interest a year, but the entries will be made every six months."

"Then in six months I shall get two dollars and twenty-five cents?"

"More if you deposit more."

She smiled broadly and tucked her newest treasure down her blouse between ample breasts. Then she swept out of the bank to assist her husband in selling his wares and giving out the balloons to the new customers. Theirs too was a family business.

Agosto thought the day would never end. Hour after hour people poured into the bank, making deposits. Agosto thought of all the long hours he and Roberto had spent going door to door talking to neighbors and businessmen and explaining the concept of a bank. The work was not in vain; after the first five hours of its existence, the bank could be considered a success.

It was nearly six before all the paperwork was done. Domenico and Gina had left; Paolo and Maria remained to help.

"What do you say now, Maria?" Agosto asked his sister.

She shrugged and grunted. "I don't understand it all."

Agosto studied her. She did understand perfectly well; she simply did not want to admit defeat. According to Maria, he ought to have stayed in his father's business. She had been dead set against this venture from the start, and now she didn't know how to react. And, he suspected, she would react jealously, wishing that Donato had done something similar. Agosto felt he was beginning to understand his sister. She was chronically discontented.

For his part, Paolo worked steadily, if somewhat ploddingly. He seemed genuinely grateful for the opportunity to work in the bank rather than in the store with Donato and Maria. And he looked forward to next month, when he would move out of his parents' house and into a small rented flat with Fabiana.

Predictably, Maria, who so often lamented the fact that Paolo and Fabiana lived in the same house as she, now did nothing but complain about their plans to move out.

Cecilia collapsed onto a tall stool. "I shall have to clean it again." She sighed. "There are finger marks all over the counter!"

Agosto encircled her waist and squeezed her. "But not tonight," he whispered in her ear. "Tonight we'll rest and have a family celebration."

Cecilia took his arm and nodded wearily.

Agosto helped her down from the stool. He once again checked the gigantic safe in the rear of the bank. He and Roberto had laid its brick encasement themselves, an encasement built to house the heavy steel vault. Maria, Paolo, and Fabiana went on ahead home, where Gina was preparing a special Monday-night feast to celebrate the success of the day.

Cecilia and Agosto paused outside the bank after the front door was locked. Agosto touched the great brass plaque by the door almost reverently. "THE ITALIAN BANK," the sign read, *"Founded March 7, 1904."*

II

1904–1918

8

Sunday, May 8, 1904

BROOKLYN

Clare was dressed in a long stiff starched white baby dress, with white pantaloons, and because it was Sunday, Cecilia had pinned a huge white satin ribbon in her dark curls. The white outfit accentuated her round dark eyes, making her hair seem jet black, which in reality it wasn't.

Clare reached up with her tiny hands and played with Domenico's mustache. Her eyes glinted mischievously and she fluttered her long eyelashes.

"Give your grandpapa a kiss!" Domenico leaned over and swept little Clare Marina into his arms. She giggled with delight, shaking her curls. "Not yet two years old and so smart! Such a little flirt." Domenico laughed as he bounced Clare on his knee. "A real beauty! You'll have to watch this one, Agosto!"

Agosto grinned proudly and settled back in the easy chair opposite his father. Such moments were both rewarding and painful. Domenico's pride in little Clare was ever obvious, and in the process of lavishing her with attention, he often ignored three-year-old Tina, causing Maria's jealousy to grow like a tangled weed. At times, as a result of her mother's attitude, Tina became a sulking, unhappy child and little Clare reigned supreme in her grandfather's eyes.

Agosto glanced at Donato, Maria's husband. Unlike Maria, Donato seemed oblivious of Domenico's favoritism. Indeed, he was withdrawn and distant, as if in his mind he created a world apart where he did not have to live with the ferocity of Maria's envy or listen to her barbed comments and incessant nagging.

The women—Gina, Cecilia, Maria, and Fabiana—were all in the kitchen preparing Sunday dinner and talking together.

From the phonograph in the corner, Caruso's voice sang the

wrenching clown song from *Pagliacci* and great tears rolled down Domenico's cheeks, even as he cuddled Clare Marina.

The song came to an end and Agosto went to the phonograph and turned it off.

"Such a wonder!" Domenico announced. "To be able to capture the voice and bring it into the home!"

Agosto smiled. The phonograph and all the recordings issued by the Caruso Phonograph Company, located at Mulberry and Grand streets in New York, were a gift for his father's sixty-eighth birthday. They were a gift he enjoyed giving, but because neither Maria nor Paolo could afford such presents, it became a new source of dissension.

What more could he do that he wasn't doing? Agosto asked himself. He employed Paolo, thus giving him a valuable opportunity. He had set up a savings account for little Tina and he gave Maria clothes. She accepted his gifts, but she did not wear them. She was ever ungracious and complained that silk petticoats were not as practical as cotton. On Maria's birthday he had given her a dress. "I have nowhere to wear it," she complained, casting the gown aside with an air of contempt.

Agosto shook his head. No, he decided, there was no more he could do. Fate made him the eldest son; travel and natural ambition created his comparative affluence.

"Dinner's ready." Maria stood in the doorway. She was, as usual, clad in a dull, ill-fitting garment. "Come along, sit down. Come on, Tina!"

Tina left the two rag dolls she was playing with and came to the table, standing behind her chair. It was piled with cushions so she could reach her plate.

Fabiana emerged from the kitchen. Her hair was pulled back with a ribbon that gave her an absurdly girlish quality, matched by her plump face, which was as round as any plate on the table.

Cecilia, five months pregnant, helped Gina to the table. Agosto smiled fondly at his mother and his wife. They were inseparable; unlike many mothers and daughters-in-law, they clearly loved one another. Kindred spirits, Agosto thought. It was an irony that Cecilia was more of a daughter to Gina than Maria, her own child.

Donato and Paolo followed Domenico into the dining room, but no one sat until Domenico made himself comfortable. Then in a clamor of moving chairs, they all took their seats, Domenico at the head of the table, Agosto at the far end.

Domenico mumbled a prayer and they crossed themselves. Then plates of steaming food were passed and each member of the family took an ample helping. Domenico poured the deep red wine.

"To Agosto, who makes us all proud!" Domenico toasted. He set his glass down. "After only a year the bank is a great success! Everyone says it is a great success!"

Agosto smiled. "It's true, the number of accounts is growing, but it's still a struggle."

"You'll succeed and I'm proud," Gina concurred softly. Agosto smiled at his mother. His pleasure was marred only by the fact that she looked so frail. In addition to gout, her skin had taken on a sallow appearance and her usually bright eyes seemed to be sinking into her face, which grew thinner by the day. She didn't complain often, but he knew she was in pain. It isn't fair, he thought. She's only forty-eight years old. But, he admitted, she looked much older.

Agosto hesitated before he spoke. The others were all eating, but his mother's food remained untouched. "Mama, I think you should go to a doctor," he suggested after a moment.

"She only needs to rest," Maria countered. "She tries to do too much."

Agosto shook his head and glanced at his father for support. "I want to take her to a physician."

Gina looked up at her son. She bit her lower lip but remained silent.

"Agosto is right, you aren't looking well," Domenico agreed. "I think you should go to a physician. Perhaps all you need is a little tonic."

"Let me make an appointment, Mama."

Unconsciously Gina touched her bosom and nodded her consent. "If you want, Agosto," she whispered.

Monday, May 16, 1904

B R O O K L Y N

It was a perfect spring day. The sky was clear, the sun shone warmly, children played leapfrog in the streets, loudly calling out challenges, and old men sold candied apples from their pushcarts. On such spring days, Domenico and Donato were compelled to stand in front of the store guarding the fruit baskets, for there were always children whose desire for a ripe orange, apple, or juicy melon overcame honesty, and not having the pennies to pay for such treats, they made a game of trying to snatch them.

It was the kind of spring day that made childhood memories dance in Agosto's head; he remembered the day he and Paolo ran away to Coney Island to lie in the sun, even though it was too cold to swim. And there were memories of hot roasted potatoes and candy. "See, now you're too full to eat dinner," Gina would scold. When they were gone too long, she cried when they came home, "You should have told me where you were going! I was so worried!"

Agosto leaned back against the chair and closed his eyes against the gray walls of the gray hospital on Coney Island Avenue. He yearned for the carefree summers of youth, longed to see his mother's beautiful face as it had once been, and to hear her reprimanding him for his boyish misdemeanors.

"Cancer . . . a large tumor, very advanced. I don't know how she's stood the pain. There's nothing much we can do. She hasn't got more than a few months."

"Can the pain be eased?"

"We have morphine. . . ."

Agosto opened his eyes to make the vision of the doctor behind his lids disappear. He pressed his lips together and inhaled. The conversation had taken place an hour ago, and he repeated it over and over in his head as if it were a recording and the needle was stuck in the groove.

They took Gina away to prepare a room for her. He would go up and see her in a few minutes; then he'd go home and talk to his father. Agosto dreaded talking to his father; he was almost sorry he had insisted his mother see a doctor. Perhaps it would have been better if none of them knew . . . but then she would have to endure the pain.

"She's ready now, Mr. Tonelli."

Agosto looked up and into the angular face of the nun. She was solemn, and beckoned with her finger for him to follow. Agosto stood up and brushed off his suit. What was he to say? His mother didn't know; all the doctor had told her was, "You'll have to stay for further tests."

Gina was in a private room, as Agosto had requested. She was propped up in a high hospital bed that made her look even smaller than she was. She looked at him pleadingly. "Must I stay here, Agosto?"

He forced a smile. "Just a few tests, Mama."

Her eyes surveyed the room quickly and she patted the hard bed. "I won't sleep here, Agosto. I'll stay, but I won't sleep. I can only sleep in my own bed. I can only sleep with your papa snoring beside me. I can't sleep without that sound, Agosto. I've listened to it for over thirty years. It lulls me to sleep."

"It's only for a few days."

"And what will I do, Agosto? I can't lie here doing nothing."

"You need to rest, Mama."

"I'll rest at home, in my own bed."

"Only a few days, Mama. Till the doctor finishes the tests."

She nodded reluctantly. "Will you bring my sewing? I can't sit here and look at walls all day."

"I'll bring your sewing, Mama." He walked over to her and kissed her tenderly on the cheek.

"You're a good boy," she whispered, returning his kiss.

"I'll go home now and get your sewing. I'll be back tonight, and bring Papa."

Gina nodded again and grasped the tight white sheet on the bed. "Agosto, what did the doctor say?"

"He said he needed to do more tests."

"You're not lying to me, are you?"

Agosto had dreaded that question. He forced himself to look into her eyes steadily. He shook his head. "I wouldn't lie to you, Mama."

"Agosto, I want to die in my own bed, in my own house."

He blinked at her and shook his head vigorously. "You're not going to die!" He blurted out the hated words more firmly than he intended. She could read him like a book. She had always known his thoughts, since he was a boy.

"We're all going to die sometime, Agosto." She said the words calmly and with deep resignation. Her swollen fingers caressed the gold cross around her neck. "Agosto, I want to be at home in my own bed."

Agosto gulped and nodded silently.

"Go get your papa," she said finally. Then she added, "Be gentle with him. He acts like a bear, but underneath, he's a puppy."

Agosto fought the tears he felt forming in his eyes. He choked back a sob and he grasped her hand tightly. "I'll be back as soon as I can." He fled the room.

Across the busy streets—McDonald, Island, Nostrand. Then down the pleasant residential streets where the little houses were set back and where gardens blossomed in front yards behind picket fences. Agosto inhaled and smelled the sea breeze; wave after wave of nostalgia engulfed him. His gentle mother; her face filled his thoughts. He saw her as she had been years ago when he was a boy, he remembered her as she was when he was in his teens, he saw her tearstained face as she bid him farewell when he left for Cuba.

And his father. . . . Agosto fought back his anguish. His mother and father were like two vines, one tough and strong, the other blossoming with sweet flowers, but they were entangled and inseparable, grown together as one. But one would wither and die, and he feared that because of her death, Domenico too would perish.

Domenico wiped his large hairy hands on his green apron. His face was like a stone, but his eyes were filled with questions. "We'll go upstairs and talk," he said, studying Agosto's face.

Donato was unpacking vegetables; their wordless drama eluded him. Donato didn't see the stricken expression on Agosto's face, nor did he notice the tension in Domenico's shoulders or the questions in his eyes.

"Where's Maria?" Agosto asked as they climbed the stairs.

"Shopping," Domenico answered resolutely. He said it in a tone that meant: I'm glad we can be alone.

Agosto sat down at the kitchen table. His hands were spread out and he concentrated his eyes on them, studying the pores, looking at his clean nails. He could hear his father breathing, feel his father's eyes boring through him.

"She's very sick." Domenico's voice was low. It was half-statement, half-question.

Agosto nodded. "Very sick," he confirmed.

There was silence; then Domenico said, "Tell me."

"Cancer," Agosto uttered. He could hardly even say the word. "On the breast . . . under the arm, everywhere!" He fought back a sob.

"And the pain?" Domenico questioned.

"There's morphine . . ." Agosto didn't look at his father, but he knew that Domenico's hand covered his eyes; he knew his father was silently crying. "She wants to come home. She says she wants to die at home."

"Yes," was Domenico's choking answer.

In his mind Agosto saw the vines tangled together, the one had lost its flowers and leaves, but still it clung to the other, clutching for strength, struggling for life.

"They need permission for the tests." Agosto forced himself to look up and face his father. "They might have to cut the spinal cord to ease the pain."

"Will it make her more comfortable?" Domenico sobbed.

Agosto nodded. "For a time."

"Is it what she wants?"

"She doesn't know yet. She'll do as you wish."

Domenico groaned and nodded.

Agosto got up and walked around the table. He put his arm around his father's shoulders and hugged him. They said nothing further.

Sunday, September 18, 1904

BROOKLYN

Cecilia had never looked so beautiful to Agosto. Her rich dark hair cascaded over her shoulders, her eyes glowed with pride, and her full mouth curved in a half-smile, which spoke her pleasure and contentment. Neither of her pregnancies had ruined her fine figure, though her body now had a pleasant maturity. Cecilia was no longer a girl, but a woman in the full bloom of life.

But Cecilia's glowing good health was in sharp contrast to Gina's. She lay in the middle of her huge bed like a fragile china doll grown brittle and gray with illness. Her hair was snow white; her body had shrunk to a skeletal seventy-five pounds; her wedding rings were wrapped with tape to keep them on her fingers. Her eyes—those wonderful dancing eyes—were ringed with dark circles and had become morphine-muddied pools sunk into the angular face of a stranger.

On some days Gina's mind escaped into the past and she failed to recognize her children. On other days—days which haunted each family member in a different way—she cried out in endless pain, begging to be killed, and then turned on those who offered her medication, shrieking accusingly, "You are killing me! You are trying to murder me!"

On still other days—days which were even more painful because of the memories they stirred—Gina appeared to return to normal. But regardless of the ravages of her illness and her torments and tirades, Gina never raised her voice to Cecilia, who was the only one who could minister to her without threat or condemnation. Thus, through her pregnancy, Cecilia did double duty, nurturing her child from within while she cared for Gina.

Domenico stood by the great four-poster bed. In his muscular arms he cradled his newest grandchild. "A boy," he announced proudly.

Gina blinked up at the red-faced infant and nodded her head in wonder. "A miracle," she whispered.

Her eyes studied the baby for an instant and then roamed to search the room for Cecilia. "Cecilia . . ."

Cecilia stepped across the room and knelt by the bed, reaching for Gina's withered, bony hand. Watching her, it seemed to Agosto as if Cecilia was the only one unafraid of touching Gina. Maria fled from her mother and kept her distance—as if she might catch death, Agosto thought.

Gina tried to smile. "You have given me the greatest gift," she murmured. "Life. You have brought me a grandson and a wonderful granddaughter. "Clare Marina—where is she?"

"Napping," Cecilia replied. "Domenico has named the baby Anthony."

"Anthony," Cecilia repeated. There was then silence, and Gina momentarily struggled with her engagement ring. It slipped off easily and she held it up toward her daughter-in-law. "One should not be buried with such things," she said, pressing the ring into Cecilia's hand. "Take it . . . take it for Clare."

In the background Agosto dared not look at Maria's face. He knew it would be contorted with jealousy.

"Oh, Mama," Cecilia protested.

"Bury me with my wedding ring, but not this one."

"Do not talk of death," Domenico said firmly. "Look at your new grandson, look and rejoice."

Gina nodded and lifted a frail hand to caress the cheek of the baby.

"Beautiful, beautiful." Gina again tried to smile. "We are alike," she whispered to the baby. "We both have to eat baby food and people tell us what to do."

Cecilia smiled lovingly at Gina. Agosto mentally chastised himself for not spending more time at his mother's side. He tried . . . No, he confessed to himself, he did not try. The sight of his mother affected him so profoundly that he ran: he wanted her the way she was, he wanted to remember her as she had been. He did not want to live with the memory of her accusations and pain, with the memory of her drugged eyes, with the reality of her dying. And her lucid normal moments—moments like these—seemed somehow to make it all even harder to bear.

"Agosto?" She called his name as if to ask if he were present.

"Mama." Agosto went to his mother's side.

"He's a wonderful baby," Gina breathed. "A grandson. Your father has waited so long for a grandson."

"Haven't you?"

"Oh, I like little girls. It's easier to teach them to pee into the pot."

Maria gasped audibly, but Cecilia only smiled tolerantly. It was characteristic of Gina's disease that she often made strange statements. Sometimes she cursed loudly, something she had never done before. Once she asked in front of the whole family if Maria slept with Donato. The question sent Donato fleeing from the room and left Maria herself in a state of unparalleled agitation. But Cecilia patiently explained that it was the morphine. "She can't control her words anymore. You must try to understand that when she seems angry with you it is just the illness—it's not really her."

Gina groaned and moved restlessly.

"Do you want your medicine now?" Cecilia asked.

"Will you give it to me?"

Cecilia nodded.

"Tell them to go away," Gina said with a wave of her hand. "Tell them I want to sleep . . . that I never want to wake up."

"Gina . . ." Domenico's voice nearly broke.

"Go eat," Gina muttered. "New life . . . old life. New beginnings, old endings. Go eat, Domenico. Mourn when it is time."

Monday, January 8, 1906

B R O O K L Y N

Salvatore Giuliano's boat remained tied to its mooring. The Marcucci Cement Factory closed for two hours, and so did all the shops along Bedford Avenue. The green shades on the Italian Bank remained drawn and the sign on the door listed the number of Father Carollo in case of emergency. The sliding doors in front of Domenico's Greengrocery were also pulled shut, and in the house behind the store, the draperies hung over the windows, shutting out the sunlight and silently telling all who passed by that Gina Tonelli had died.

Domenico sat in his overstuffed chair and stared into space, reciting a litany of promises, even while tears tumbled down his cheeks. "Your mama, she always wanted to go back to Lecce," he sobbed. "I never took her . . . I never took the time." His swollen eyes searched out Agosto's face. "She'll be buried. Father Carollo says her body can be interred on the chapel

grounds. When I die, Agosto, you have us both taken to Lecce
for burial."

"Papa, you're not going to die for a long time," Agosto
promised.

"Never mind! I want you to know what I want. Promise me. I
want you to promise me!"

"I promise," Agosto replied.

Domenico pulled himself up out of the chair, and taking his
large white handkerchief out of his pocket, blew his nose loudly
and half-wiped the tears off his round cheeks. "Promise?" he
repeated.

Agosto nodded.

"Oh, Gina . . ." Domenico's eyes traveled to the stairs. "I'll
go back to Lecce with you. I will. I'm so sorry I didn't take you
sooner."

"Papa . . ." Agosto shook his head sadly.

Donato, Maria, and Paolo sat on the sofa silently. They were
all dressed in black, prepared to go to Mass. The house was
utterly silent. Gina was gone and Tina and Clare Marina had
been sent to neighbors for the day.

Cecilia walked over to Domenico and took his hands. "Papa,
you have your memories—she lives in your memories. Gina
went back to Lecce with you in her daydreams, but being with
you is what mattered to her." Cecilia stood on her tiptoes and
kissed his cheek. "It's time to go to Mass. Gina wouldn't want
you to be late."

Domenico embraced Cecilia and returned her kiss, nodding
silently.

Fabiana came to Domenico's side and took his arm gently.
"We all loved her," she said softly.

"She said she had three daughters," Domenico managed. He
allowed Cecilia and Fabiana to help him on with his coat and
hat, and they left the house, a sad procession on the way to the
chapel.

Fabiana and Cecilia walked with Domenico and Agosto. Maria,
Paolo, and Donato walked behind. As they proceeded toward the
chapel, they were joined by friends and neighbors, who silently
hugged Domenico and then fell in behind the family.

"I always loved her," Domenico said again and again. "She
was a good woman, a brave soul, a fine wife. Oh, God, forgive
me, I meant to take her home . . . I meant to keep my promise."

Wednesday, March 7, 1906

BROOKLYN

The Italian Bank was crowded with people who came to celebrate its second anniversary. They swarmed through the doors promptly at five o'clock, when the bank officially closed, and lined up to receive a free glass of wine from Fabiana and nibble from the trays laden with cheese and bread brought by Maria and Cecilia.

"You've done a lot!" Tomaso Solari praised. "My son-in-law has done well! You financed Guido's new shoe shop and the ice-cream maker, and I hear tell you've invested in Rocco's brick factory!"

Agosto gulped down some wine himself as he listened to Tomaso's energetic speech. He felt both satisfaction and pride. He had been right: his investments were paying off threefold. The neighborhood was prospering, and besides his local investments, Italians came from as far away as New Haven to seek loans. Moreover, he was able to make large investments outside the neighborhood, investments that were profitable and which fed funds back into the bank.

"Speech!" Salvatore shouted. "Get up on the counter, Agosto! Make a speech for us!"

Friends, businessmen, and depositors clapped loudly, joining in the acclamation.

Agosto climbed up on the counter, wondering if he looked as pleased as he felt. For weeks he'd been suppressing his excitement, waiting for this moment to make his announcement. It was, he reckoned, going to be a total surprise—a surprise for everyone, but for two people in particular.

He held out his arms, as if to embrace everyone. And for once he didn't try to hide his sentimental nature; it surged to the surface and he felt tears of joy in his eyes. "You've been good to me," he told the crowd. "A man can't succeed without family and friends. You're all my friends, and I have succeeded because of you."

"And we do good because of you!" Guido shouted.

Agosto grinned. "I have an important announcement to make. I'm opening a second bank!"

There was wild clapping and shouting.

127

"Do we need two?" Antonia, Salvatore's wife, asked. Everyone laughed.

"Perhaps the vault is full!" Guido shouted enthusiastically.

Agosto shook his head. "Not here. I'm opening the second branch at Brighton Beach Avenue and Coney Island!"

Everyone clapped. "A good location," Roberto agreed.

"And I'm putting Paolo in charge!" Agosto pointed to Paolo, who all but choked on his wine.

"Me? In charge!"

"A surprise!" Agosto laughed.

"But you'll supervise him, won't you?" Domenico asked.

Agosto nodded, wanting not to make much out of the question. He glanced at Paolo, his eyes filled with tears, and for once he embraced Fabiana. "You'll do a good job," Agosto told both Paolo and the crowd.

Domenico nodded his approval. "I raised good boys," he bragged.

Agosto glanced at Cecilia. She held Clare Marina by the hand, and little Anthony was on the counter, sleeping in his wicker basket. "And I have a surprise for my wife, too," Agosto told them.

"Tell us!" Tomaso shouted.

Cecilia's face had turned bright red, and she bit her lip and looked at him expectantly.

Agosto studied her for an instant. Domenico's unkept promise to Gina had made him conscious of what he owed Cecilia, and he'd vowed when his mother died to be certain that business didn't rob Cecilia of the life she deserved.

"When Cecilia married me, she took a chance," he said, grinning. "We were married before there was a bank, we had our first child before the plaque was hung. We invested everything—even Cecilia's dowry—to make the money to open the bank. There were some hard times, but there were no complaints." Agosto looked steadily at Cecilia. She had lowered her eyes, and she still blushed. "She's had to live not only *with* the bank"—he laughed—"but *over* it." At that, everyone else laughed. "It's a small place, but now that there are two children—"

"And, God willing, more!" Tomaso shouted.

Agosto nodded his agreement. "It's crowded up there." He pointed above, and there was more good-natured laughing. "My surprise for Cecilia is that I've purchased a house on Emmons and Twenty-sixth Street—a big house!"

Cecilia suddenly looked up and drew in her breath. "A house?" she murmured.

Agosto smiled, knowing that all that kept her from rushing to him was the inordinate number of people looking on. So he climbed down off the counter, and shaking everyone's hand, made his way toward her.

"Your mother would be proud," Domenico announced. "Two banks and a house! A grandson! You have done her proud!"

"I'll be managing a bank?" Paolo kept saying.

"And Agosto said we could have the apartment upstairs," Fabiana confided in a whisper. She was overcome with joy, and slyly finished an entire glass of wine, which made her round face red.

"Are you happy?" Agosto said when he reached Cecilia.

"I'll miss our little apartment," she whispered. "Oh, but, Agosto, Emmons Avenue! Those are big houses!"

He smiled and hugged her. "You'll find someone to help you," he whispered. "I won't have you doing all the work."

"It's nothing."

"Sh, we'll talk about that later." He hugged her again and kissed her warm cheek. When he did so, the onlookers all clapped.

"Has Fabiana run out of wine?" Tomaso asked loudly. "We should have a toast—a toast to the new bank and the new house."

Fabiana produced several more bottles from under the counter. "I wouldn't run out of wine today," she said proudly.

Saturday, August 4, 1906

BROOKLYN

Today, August 4, was a special day for Agosto and Cecilia. It was Clare's third birthday, but also the first time they entertained in their new home.

Agosto looked with pride on his new house. It had four large bedrooms, a bathroom, and two toilets. The dining room was long and narrow, the living room wide and spacious. And the kitchen, much to Cecilia's joy, was the largest room in the house.

Out front, there was a wide expanse of green lawn, and Cecilia had planted flowers in a neat little garden beneath the front windows. In the back, there was a giant oak, and from it Agosto had suspended a little swing for Clare. Behind the oak, Cecilia insisted on planting her own vegetable garden.

"I'm glad the sun stays up so late," Cecilia admitted as she looked into the backyard, where twelve of the neighborhood children romped noisily with Clare Marina.

"This is a strange custom," Agosto observed. He'd recently grown a mustache, and he toyed with it abstractedly. "When I was a boy, it was our name day that was celebrated, not the day of our birth. And it was only celebrated with the family." He shook his head. The gaggle of three- and four-year-olds in the backyard had been organized by Fabiana and Seraphina, the maid, into a circle, and they played drop the handkerchief and clapped their hands.

Cecilia smiled and wiped her hands on her apron. "They do things differently in America. Most people give presents on Christmas morning, not on Twelfth Night. Agosto, we're first-generation, and Clare is second-generation. She wants to do what the other children do, and I want her to. We can keep our traditions and have new ones too."

Agosto smiled. "Does that mean we'll have another party to celebrate her Christening and official naming?"

Cecilia laughed as she bent over to adjust one of the three candles in the large birthday cake. "You and I'll have our own little party on that day."

"It's a lovely cake," he allowed, looking at the clusters of pink-frosting roses that decorated it.

"I bought it from Causici the baker. He's doing a big business in these cakes. Everyone is having birthday parties for their children now."

"Circular money," Agosto joked. "I just made him a loan for new ovens four months ago."

"I could have baked the cake," Cecilia said, glancing at her new gas oven. "But I couldn't decorate it this way. Causici had this little tube—he invented it himself—and I tell you, Agosto, he uses it like Michelangelo! A genius! Just look at those roses!"

"I suspect they will soon be smeared on Clare's face," Agosto joked.

"You're right, but I want to save at least half the cake for the adults."

Agosto glanced at the clock on the wall. It was nearly seven-thirty, and in half an hour the grown-ups would arrive and the children would leave. Clare Marina was to have two birthday parties—the new kind for her little friends, and the traditional family dinner with Domenico, Paolo, Maria, Donato, Tomaso and Concha Solari, Roberto Marcucci, and all of Salvatore's family, as well as old Mrs. Solari.

The back door slammed and five-year-old Tina Ferrante, Clare

Marina's cousin, came into the house, tears in her eyes. "I won't play with those babies anymore!" she shouted angrily. "They won't let me be the cheese! And I'm the oldest! What do those babies know!"

Cecilia bent down and wiped off Tina's face with the corner of her apron. "You're quite right," she conceded. "You're much too old to play with them. Here, you sit down and have a glass of milk and a cookie. And when I go upstairs to feed Anthony, you can come with me."

Tina sat down at the table and smiled at Cecilia weakly. "I hate being the oldest," she pouted. "No one pays any attention to me! Everyone pays attention to Clare Marina!"

"That's because you're a good girl and Clare is always getting into mischief," Agosto said, patting his niece on the back. It wasn't altogether true, he thought as he said it. But Tina needed praise. Her statement that Clare Marina got all the attention was all too true.

Tina finished her cookie and slipped from the stool at the table. "Can I go upstairs and see if Anthony is awake?"

Cecilia nodded, and Tina scampered away.

"I wish Mama were alive," Agosto said, turning back to Cecilia, who was setting the kitchen table with plates for the children. "I think she'd like birthday parties."

"She's here in spirit," Cecilia replied.

Your spirit, Agosto thought without saying it. "Cecilia, do you need more help around the house?"

"Of course not. Seraphina is wonderful, so I don't have enough to do as it is."

"I don't want you 'doing' all the time. Cecilia, I don't want to be like my father. I want to travel with you while we're young, I want to take you places, I want you on my arm."

Cecilia smiled shyly. "I wouldn't know how to act around your important friends."

"You'll learn," he insisted. "Cecilia, my old friend Barton Ainsley is back from Europe. He's invited us to dinner, and I want you to come."

She looked at the floor for a moment, then lifted her head to look into his eyes. "Are you sure I won't embarrass you?"

Instinctively Agosto hugged her. "You could never do that," he assured her.

"The children want their cake now," Fabiana announced, opening the back door to a horde of shrieking youngsters.

Agosto threw up his arms and retreated into the parlor. "An interesting, but noisy custom!" he shouted above the din of squealing.

Saturday, September 1, 1906

MANHATTAN

The Ainsley home on Fifth Avenue was only slightly less grand than that of the Vanderbilts, who lived down the street at number 608.

It was a three-story brownstone surrounded by a black wrought-iron fence and its windows were heavily draped, hiding any glimpse of the interior of the house from passersby. A small sign posted on the outside of the great iron gate read: "Deliveries at the rear," though few, if any, of the deliverymen could read the sign.

The rosebushes which stood in the front garden were still in bloom, and the fading summer flowers were being replaced with heartier varieties that would last through the fall. The small gardens of Fifth Avenue, even the window boxes, were given professional care.

The carriage clattered to a halt in front of the house and the driver climbed down, opening the door for Cecilia and Agosto.

Cecilia Tonelli ran her finger around the collar of her dress. It was too high, much too high, and she felt a vague feeling of discomfort. But it's important that Agosto be proud of me, she reminded herself. Agosto told her a great deal about the Ainsleys, and sometimes he talked of Philip, whose youthful passing had spurred him on. "He died too young," Agosto once said. "Before he could accomplish much." And, Cecilia suspected, Agosto had secretly vowed to spend each day in accomplishment. He saw in his friend's death not only a lesson but also a warning. Agosto worked unceasingly to make his mark, lest life be snatched from him before he attained his goals.

"Cecilia?" Agosto alighted from the carriage and extended his hand to her. She withdrew it from her velvet muff and took his gloved hand.

Cecilia stood for a moment and adjusted her stole. Her skirts blew in the brisk September breeze.

She felt apprehensive. Agosto was so confident. He was at ease in all situations, like a chameleon. By contrast, she considered herself simply as the keeper of the home, and saw her main purpose as raising the children. But Agosto insisted she also be a social companion, that she attend parties with him and entertain.

It wasn't the traditional way, she thought. Oh, her mother cooked for her father's friends, but the women stayed in the kitchen. And when her father went out, it was to a male gathering, to the Columbus Society or the Garibaldi Club. She sighed inwardly. Tonight she and Agosto had been invited to dine with one of New York's wealthiest families and there'd be no retreat to the kitchen for her. The only other female present would be Sarah Ainsley, who, while close to Cecilia's age, was a college graduate and pursuing a career as a fashion designer. Cecilia shuddered at the thought. She suspected from comments Agosto made that Sarah Ainsley had once been attracted to him; and perhaps, she allowed, the attraction was mutual.

Agosto banged the brass knocker and Cecilia felt isolated even before the double doors were opened by a black servant.

"Oh, dear," Cecilia breathed.

Agosto paid her no mind. He helped her off with her fur stole and handed it to the servant, who also took his coat.

"This way, sir," the servant beckoned. Silently Cecilia allowed herself to be led down the corridor. More doors swung open and she and Agosto entered a warm, well-appointed room. The walls were soft leather, the rug deep and rich. There was a huge mahogany bar and a long billiard table covered in muted green. Cecilia's eyes fell on the multicolored billiard balls scattered in disarray on their green carpet.

She lifted her eyes to greet the tall gray-haired man who warmly took her hands. He smiled. "So this is your Cecilia, Agosto! I am delighted to meet you, my dear."

Cecilia searched for her voice. It seemed to have disappeared into her. She smiled nervously and nodded.

"Agosto told me you were beautiful. And you are."

"Thank you," she murmured. Had Barton Ainsley been Italian, he'd have given her a great bear hug and she would have felt at ease. But he did no such thing. He dropped her hands and stood looking at her. He smiled, but his emotions were imprisoned in precise sentences; his body movements remained distant and uninterpretable to her.

"You've been married four years," Barton Ainsley said. "I feel terrible not meeting you before this—no, not terrible, deprived."

"You've been away a lot," Agosto observed.

"Stearns has pretty much taken over here. I've been handling our European interests. Look, I'm getting older, Agosto. I enjoy winters on the Riviera."

"I ought to talk with you about European investments," Agosto suggested.

"And there are people you should meet. I have a business associate in Milan, about your age, Count Emiliano Sforza."

"Royalty? Sforza's an important name."

"He's not from the main line of the family. Interesting chap, like yourself, a builder. Rather an unusual personality for an Italian nobleman. He's a businessman, a budding industrialist, and a banker."

"I'd like to meet him."

"He's very handsome," Sarah Ainsley said from the doorway. "Our guests have arrived, and you're talking business already, Daddy! Shame on you."

Cecilia nearly gasped aloud. Sarah's hair was as blond as Cecilia's was dark. Her eyes were blue and her skin was white and flawless. But it was her dress that so shocked Cecilia. It was a soft blue and appeared to be almost transparent. It fell like veils on her slim figure. Cecilia peered at her. It was a most immodest gown, most immodest! Indeed, it was more immodest than Cecilia's own nightdress.

Sarah Ainsley glided across the room and right into Agosto's arms. She kissed him boldly on the lips, pressing herself to him. Then, like a bird on the edge of a birdbath, she darted back with fluttering arms. She stood and eyed Cecilia from head to toe.

"And you must be Cecilia," she said, smiling. But it was not a warm smile; it was cool and distant. If Barton Ainsley's emotional responses were limited to language, Sarah Ainsley's were nonexistent. She reminded Cecilia of a cake of ice—glittering and transparent, cold and untouchable.

Barton Ainsley moved to the bar. "Your usual?" He raised an eyebrow at Agosto.

Agosto nodded.

"Gin and tonic for me," Sarah said, turning toward her father.

Cecilia looked at Sarah in amazement. She drank hard liquor! No woman Cecilia knew drank such things. A little wine at dinner perhaps . . .

"For you, Cecilia?" Barton Ainsley again smiled warmly at her. He seemed to sense her shock.

Cecilia shook her head. "Nothing, thank you."

He didn't press her. He handed Agosto his drink. Sarah took her own, and Barton Ainsley gestured toward the sofa and the large leather chairs that surrounded it. Agosto sat down in one of the chairs, sinking back comfortably. Ainsley did the same. Cecilia perched uncomfortably on one end of the sofa, while Sarah sat opposite.

"It's been an age since I've seen you," Ainsley said. "You

don't come to Manhattan enough. And when you do come, you don't have time for lunch with me.''

Agosto grinned. ''My life has become more hectic.''

''I daresay, what with two banks and your personal investments.''

''I hear you sometimes work in the bank,'' Sarah said to Cecilia. ''I think a woman should have a career.''

Cecilia shook her head almost instinctively. ''No, no. I just clean them up . . . sometimes I do a few accounts. It's nothing, not really, it's nothing.''

Sarah frowned at the words. ''Clean them up?'' She delicately and pointedly raised one of her penciled brows.

''Don't let her tell you that! I couldn't manage without Cecilia! She's a fine accountant and she does much more than clean up.'' Agosto's eyes caressed her from afar, and Cecilia felt their warm comfort.

''It's a good time to expand,'' Ainsley said. ''Lots of growth, lots of confidence in the economy.''

''But for how long?'' Agosto questioned.

''Oh, people spend money like it was water!'' Sarah chimed in. ''You should see the crowds at Lord & Taylor! And my designs—mind you, they're very expensive—are selling like mad! Really, Agosto, you should bring Cecilia in. I have some gowns that would really suit her. Something with fine pleats, I think, just to cover the width of her hips a little. Really, Agosto, Cecilia should be prettied up.''

Cecilia blushed deeply and Barton Ainsley scowled at his daughter. Agosto looked warmly at her, as if begging her to ignore Sarah Ainsley's comments entirely.

''I'm not at all certain the economy is as healthy as it appears,'' Agosto countered, lighting a cigarette.

''Is that opinion based on some hidden indicator, or is it just the famous Tonelli intuition?''

''A little of both,'' Agosto replied. ''I believe we're at the top of a cycle. Unless there's a good deal of new money injected into the economy, it'll stagnate, people will lose faith, and there could be trouble.''

''The banks are issuing new banknotes all the time.''

''Precisely,'' Agosto said flatly. ''And if there's a sudden loss of confidence, there won't be sufficient specie to cover them.''

Barton Ainsley looked at his fingers. It was one of his habits. Whenever he was considering something, he always studied his well-manicured hands. ''I don't think that will happen,'' he finally said.

''It could start in Europe,'' Agosto elaborated. ''A lot of

banks have correspondence with European banks. They could be caught if there's a major bank closure on the Continent. It's like a house of cards, you know. One down, and there's a chain reaction."

"Sounds like you've been deep into the reports of some gloomy Harvard economist."

Agosto smiled. "Gloomy, but I think realistic. You know I have pretty strong feelings about the need for some sort of state bank to ensure the money supply. Seems to work pretty well in Scotland."

"What about the Bank of England?" Ainsley queried.

Agosto shook his head. "It's like the Bank of the United States—it's a banker to government, not a government bank. I'm talking about a federally controlled bank to manage the money supply. A bank that's not owned privately."

"Far be it from me to say the Scots don't know anything about money." Barton Ainsley laughed, lifting his arms in the air in a motion of surrender. "Do you really think we're overextended?" He used the royal "we," meaning the entire banking system.

"I think it's a good possibility. We don't control the world economy. Good Lord, there are a hundred things that could happen—and have happened in the past. Look at 1900! They say history repeats itself." Agosto offered.

"And there's an economic cycle. Except, of course, that nobody knows exactly what the cycle is, or why it dips and rises. It just can't be accurately predicted," Ainsley added.

"Personally, I think from our present pinnacle there's no place to go but down," Agosto concluded.

"Oh, Agosto, you are a gloomy old bear," Sarah winked at him flirtatiously.

Cecilia looked at her husband admiringly. He knew so much. Sometimes she felt he knew everything there was to know. Except about women. If he knew more about women, he would see right through Miss Sarah Ainsley. He'd see that she was jealous and bold. He'd know that while her father was kind and helpful, Miss Sarah Ainsley was not. She was spoiled, and now, Cecilia thought, she was inwardly angry because she had not gotten what she wanted. Clearly she had wanted Agosto, but Agosto had rejected her, preferring, Cecilia supposed, to marry a simple Italian woman who would bear him strong children, keep house, and keep her place.

And Agosto was not being gloomy, Cecilia decided. He just knew that a person should not spend more money than he had and that banks were no different from people. They too couldn't spend more than they had. After all, it was other people's money. And those people trusted Agosto. But Cecilia didn't say anything, because in truth she couldn't think of how to phrase her thoughts in a way that sounded intelligent.

"When are you going back to Europe?" Agosto questioned.

"Not for a while, even though I'll not enjoy the winter. I've affairs to take care of here. Young Creighton Stearns is taking over the European interests for the next little while."

"I'll be going to the Riviera," Sarah gushed.

"The social season in Cannes couldn't survive without her," Barton Ainsley jested.

"Dinner is served." The black butler stood in the doorway imperiously. Barton Ainsley stood up and walked over to Cecilia, helping her up. He took her arm, and Cecilia was vaguely aware that behind them, Agosto followed with Sarah Ainsley, who clung to him and cooed, "Don't always be looking for the worst to happen, darling. You're a great success! Everyone says so!"

9

Sunday, January 13, 1907

BROOKLYN

Agosto settled back in his overstuffed chair and lit a stogie. Paolo sat opposite, but he didn't lean back comfortably, rather he perched on the edge of the sofa, ready to engage in conversation with his brother.

In the kitchen Maria, Cecilia, and Fabiana cooked Sunday dinner; Domenico remained at church, as he had every Sunday since Gina's death. "It's where I talk to Gina," he told everyone.

Agosto watched the smoke from his stogie. Trying to explain the theory of economic cycles to his brother was difficult.

Paolo tried to study, but he didn't have a gift for economics; he had a gift for dealing with people and in that respect was an asset to the new bank branch. He brought in customers, and new customers were, in Agosto's mind, the best insurance a bank could have.

"Can you go over that again?" Paolo pressed.

"There was a recession in 1900. It was followed by our present period of growth—for example, pig-iron production has grown one hundred and fifty percent in the past six years."

Paolo shrugged. "I know, I know. Everything is fine." His face took on a slightly puzzled expression. "It seems fine," he corrected.

"Seems," Agosto repeated. His mind was filled with a hundred thoughts at once. The entire financial system appeared to be in jeopardy; a gut feeling told him a depression was on its way.

"The government prints a fixed number of greenbacks and produces a limited amount of gold and silver specie. We, of course, issue banknotes." He paused and exhaled smoke.

"During a financial panic, depositors flood banks to turn in their banknotes for specie or greenbacks. If the banks don't have

138

sufficient specie and greenbacks on hand, the run on the bank causes ruin.''

Paolo nodded. ''I remember that happening to a bank a few years back. It's what causes panic that I don't understand.''

Agosto smiled, ''If I knew for certain what causes a panic, I'd be able to predict the future, which would make me a very wealthy man. Some economists just believe there are cycles, that what goes up must eventually go down.'' He shrugged and motioned with his arms. ''But it seems to me that damn near anything can set off a panic—bad weather affecting a major crop, war somewhere in the world, the relationship between investment and consumption. Anything.''

''But everything is booming,'' Paolo returned.

Agosto lifted his eyes to meet Paolo's. ''Things are not always as they seem,'' he reiterated. ''To put it simply, I don't believe there's sufficient specie and greenbacks in circulation to go on feeding the present boom economy. If everyone begins demanding payment in specie and greenbacks, a great many banks couldn't meet the demands. That would lead to a run on banks, to lack of investment . . . well, to a great many things.''

''But what can we do?'' Paolo queried. ''We can't make the government print more money.''

Agosto smiled a half-smile. ''I want all payments made in banknotes, unless of course our customers specifically request specie or greenbacks. I want more accounts—that's very important. And I intend to convert all our assets into gold. If anything happens, Paolo—say, a rash of bank runs—I want our gold reserves put on display.''

''On display! That's dangerous!''

Agosto laughed. ''Well guarded. But on display. Our customers—all of them, from the smallest child to the oldest woman—must be convinced utterly and beyond all doubt that Tonelli banknotes are backed by real assets.''

''But are you so certain . . . ?''

''I'm not certain at all. But I hope to be.'' Agosto smiled confidently at his brother. ''New customers,'' he repeated. ''Paolo, I'm counting on you. Go out in the neighborhood. Go to every house and talk to people. Get them to invest their funds in our bank, Paolo. We have a lot of accounts, which you helped get, but we haven't fully tapped the possibilities at the Coney Island branch.

''I'll do my best.''

Agosto nodded pleasantly, though his mind had already raced ahead to other thoughts. His banks had relationships with several large Italian banks, which was to say that his banks cleared their checks when drawn in the United States. A run on the Bank of Naples, the Bank of Milan, or the Bank of Turin could cause added problems. Communications, Agosto thought, were the key, because instant information could prevent a disaster. He smiled to himself. Roberto was in Italy, visiting, but Agosto felt he could convince Roberto to remain for a time. Yes, that was a possibility. He'd write to Roberto immediately and back the letter with a telegram. He'd hire Roberto to report via telegram directly, so he'd receive news of runs on any Italian banks soon enough to take action.

"What are you thinking?" Paolo asked, breaking into Agosto's thoughts.

Agosto chuckled. "I was thinking how glad I am that Marconi invented the telegraph," he confided with a smile.

Paolo grinned too.

"Communication is important to Italians," Agosto mused. "You might say that it's central to our culture."

Friday, March 1, 1907

BROOKLYN

Agosto closed the ledger and looked up. Cecilia was polishing the brass lamp on the corner of the long counter. Her facial expression was intense as she studied her handiwork.

Three-year-old Clare Marina, following her mother's example, emptied all the wastebaskets. Little Anthony remained at home with Seraphina.

"You'll rub it away," Agosto warned teasingly.

Cecilia looked up, her expressive dark eyes serious. "I only want it to look neat in here."

"Neat? It's spotless!" Agosto laughed.

It was a far different bank than they had opened four years ago. The former apartment upstairs had been converted into office space when Fabiana and Paolo moved to a small house near the new bank on Coney Island Avenue. And tinned goods were no longer sold. The Italian Bank was strictly a bank, but Agosto still had no office, and the bank still retained a certain homey charm.

Agosto walked over to Cecilia and embraced her around the waist. "You don't have to come here every Friday night to clean up, you know. I could well afford cleaning staff."

Cecilia shook her head. "No, it's our bank and we should keep it clean and tidy." She wanted to add: And I want to be with you. But she kept silent.

She always came with Clare at closing time on Friday and cleaned the bank while Agosto worked on the books. But Agosto worked till eight o'clock on Fridays, and if she hadn't come to the bank on the pretext of cleaning, she'd have felt robbed of time with him. It was true that she also came in three days a week and worked behind the counter, but Agosto was not often there. When he was, he was busily engaged in meetings with merchants.

Cecilia considered their relationship. They were together, but they were apart. Her time with him was limited, and when he came home after long hours, he was exhausted. Not that she felt neglected. Agosto never forgot a birthday or an anniversary. He often brought her presents and made love to her regularly. But there was something . . . Cecilia could not express what it was, she was only aware of vague feelings of longing and, since they were seeing more of the Ainsleys, a strong feeling of inadequacy.

"You've been excessively quiet lately," Agosto commented, almost as if he had read her unformed thoughts.

"Have I?"

He kissed her cheek and looked down, feeling Clare Marina's button-bright eyes on them. She looked amused.

"Your papa's allowed to kiss your mama," Agosto said. "Have you finished your chores?" She nodded and tossed her black curls. "Well, go tidy up the other room, and in the bottom drawer of the big desk you'll find a candy." Clare turned and ran off like a squirrel in search of a prize nut.

"What do you say?" Cecilia called after her.

"Thank you, Papa," came the automatic answer.

Agosto kissed Cecilia's neck again, nuzzling her ear a little.

"Oh, Agosto. Someone will see in the window!"

"The shades are closed. Now, tell me why you've been so thoughtful."

Cecilia shrugged. "I didn't know I had been."

"I don't think you enjoy going to the Ainsleys'," he said after a moment.

"I enjoy it. It's a beautiful house. They have beautiful things." She frowned and her hands moved almost automatically to her full rounded hips. "Are my hips too wide?" she suddenly asked.

Agosto burst out laughing. "Not for me! Is that what's bothering you? Did Sarah tell you that again?"

Cecilia shook her head. "No," she answered softly. "I just wondered if they were too wide."

Agosto turned and faced her, pulling her into his arms. "You are just as I like you—you're the perfect wife and mother."

"I don't know what to say to people like the Ainsleys," Cecilia confessed. She felt incapable of explaining further. She didn't doubt Agosto's love; it was more that she felt she lacked learning and sophistication, and deep down, she feared she might lose him to someone like Sarah Ainsley.

"Are you happy?" Agosto asked, searching her face.

"Of course! Of course I am happy!"

"I love you as you are. You don't have to know what to say. Anyway, you're just shy. You know that banking is a man's world."

Cecilia nodded and wondered why it was a man's world for her, but not for Sarah Ainsley. Agosto seemed to listen to Sarah Ainsley's comments.

"Is there any more candy?" Clare stood before them, a smear of chocolate across her face.

"No, that's all."

Cecilia bent down, and taking a hankie from her pocket, wiped Clare's face. For a split second she almost envied her daughter. Clare asked for what she wanted. She sat on her father's knee and he talked to her about subjects she couldn't possibly understand. Clare would go to school, Clare would travel, Clare would grow up in a world similar to the world of Sarah Ainsley. Cecilia kissed her daughter's cheek. You won't be just another woman, she silently vowed, you'll be different.

Monday, March 11, 1907

BROOKLYN

Agosto ripped open the telegram, delivered by a breathless lad on a bicycle, whose cap had blown away in the brisk March wind. "When did this arrive?" he asked.

"It came into the terminal only fifteen minutes ago, sir."

Agosto smiled and gave the boy a large tip. "Good service pays," he told the young man, who hurried away with a satisfied grin.

"Not quite the ides of March," Agosto said aloud as he read the word "RUNS" on the telegram. Below that vital bit of information was a request from Roberto. "Can we make employment permanent? I don't like being stuck in cement!" Agosto couldn't help but laugh. The Marcucci Cement Factory bored Roberto completely; banking didn't.

Agosto crumpled it and reached for the phone on the corner of his desk. He gave the operator the number and listened as she dialed. Click, click . . . "Paolo?"

Paolo sounded almost dreamy, as if his mind were elsewhere. "Paolo, it's Agosto. Agosto!" He heard his voice rise and he automatically lowered it, lest one of the customers overhear. It was a slow morning, and for that he was grateful. Harry Boyle, an Irishman who owned a local pub, had just left, having negotiated a small loan. Mrs. Rubino was at the counter filling out a slip. But she was deaf in any case. The owner of a candy store was at a wicket, but he looked distracted and appeared not to be paying the slightest bit of attention.

"Paolo, you remember what I told you to do about my concerns?"

There was a pause on the other end of the phone. Agosto sighed. Then with relief he heard Paolo answer in the affirmative. "Start preparing to do it now," Agosto said flatly.

"Is there trouble?"

"Information. Do as I tell you and I'll explain everything tonight."

Agosto hung up the phone. He would have to call Ainsley, but of course that call would take considerable explanation. "I've got to leave for a few minutes," he told Marco, the young teller. "I'll be back within the hour."

The young man nodded and Agosto virtually ran from the bank. He glanced at his watch: it was nearly two o'clock. There was absolutely no way of knowing when the news would reach Wall Street. It could be later today . . . it could be tomorrow . . . it might even be Wednesday. But of course once it did, it would be all over the papers. Hearst would love it! Disasters sold papers, and Hearst printed all of them. But there was a little time. Communications were slow; it would take a while for the news to filter down and cause a panic among small investors. Loss of confidence might take place on one level overnight, but for the man on the street it would take time for the implications to be realized. The interlocking of trade, the interrelationship of nations, was not understood by average people, and after all, his customers were all average people.

Agosto reached home breathlessly.

"Papa!" Clare Marina was delighted. It was rare indeed to see him in the middle of the workday.

Cecilia, dressed in blue with her dark hair hidden beneath a kerchief, greeted him with a frown of concern. "What is it?" She wiped her hands on her crisp white apron.

Agosto pecked at her cheek perfunctorily. "Nothing for you to worry about," he said. "I simply have to make a phone call. A private phone call."

Cecilia watched perplexed as Agosto went to the phone. She bit her lip, wondering if "private" excluded her; then, deciding that it did, she went back to the kitchen. But Clare remained, curling up next to her father on the sofa even as he lifted the phone off the end table and placed the call to Barton Ainsley.

It rang only once on the other end, and surprisingly, Ainsley answered it himself. "Agosto Tonelli."

Ainsley replied warmly. "Coming into Manhattan?"

"I'm afraid that's not why I called."

"Oh?"

"Barton, I've just received word from my contact in Italy. There are serious runs on European banks. I thought you ought to know."

There was silence; then: "It's not on the wires yet."

"The information is reliable. It should be on the wires in a matter of hours."

"I see. Yes, I'll get right on it. Thanks."

Obviously Ainsley was not alone, Agosto thought. "You're welcome," he answered as he replaced the receiver on the hook.

Clare giggled and tugged at him. "How can a bank run, Papa? It doesn't have legs."

Agosto smiled in spite of himself. He ran his fingers through her hair. "It's not that kind of running," he said, wondering why he was even trying to explain.

"What kind is it?" she persisted. "Tell me."

Agosto studied her. She looked utterly intense and he searched for a way to satisfy her curiosity with a simple explanation. "People put money in banks," he began, "to keep it safe."

"I know that."

"Well, sometimes they get the idea that it's not safe, so they run to the bank and take it out. That's called a run on the bank."

She looked up at him earnestly. "Then you should put all the money where they can see it so they'll know it's safe. I keep all my pennies in Piggy, and I count them every night. I know they're safe because I can see them."

Agosto grinned. In her own wonderfully childish way, she'd just suggested exactly what he intended to do. "You're a smart little girl," he said. "Papa has to go back to work now." He kissed her on top of the head. "I'm leaving, Cecilia," he called out.

Cecilia appeared almost instantly. "What's happening?" she queried, a worried expression on her lovely face.

Agosto smiled. "It's not for you to worry about." He kissed her gently and whirled to leave the house.

"Papa's running to the bank too," Clare said, waving at Agosto's disappearing form.

Cecilia closed the door. He doesn't think I would understand, she thought sadly. She stood for a moment looking at the large oak door. It seemed to say: You don't belong to the world on the other side.

Wednesday, March 13, 1907

CONEY ISLAND

Since Paolo had taken over managing the Coney Island Bank, Maria had worked there keeping accounts. She insisted that Donato and Domenico could look after the store, and Agosto was glad to pay her for her time, since she was as meticulous as she was discontented.

It was eight-thirty in the morning and she had risen at six in order to be at the Coney Island branch before it opened at nine. She stood in the middle of the bank and her dark eyes followed her brother as he bustled about. Behind the long wooden counter that was divided into wickets, there was a table piled high with the gold bars that constituted the bank's assets.

"This is insane," Maria muttered. "It's dangerous."

Paolo stopped momentarily and looked at his sister in despair. "Agosto says it will give our customers confidence."

"Agosto says, Agosto says. What do *you* think, Paolo? Don't you have a mind of your own?"

"It's Agosto's bank. I do what he tells me."

"He'll lose everything. You'll both be right back working with Donato in the store."

Paolo shook his head. "This bank is a success and I'm a success. Agosto knows what he's doing. Besides, there are guards inside and out."

Maria hissed through her front teeth; it was the female equivalent of spitting. "You're no success! You are Agosto's shadow, Paolo. You're weak and stupid! When will you stop living in the image of your brother? When will you make something of yourself?"

Paolo didn't look at her, or answer.

"You don't answer because you know I am right! You know you're a failure and you know you and your fat, stupid wife live off Agosto's generosity."

"And I suppose your slow, dumb husband is more of an example!" Paolo shouted angrily.

Maria's face tightened. "Our father needs Donato. He's too old to run the store alone. Anyway, I'm not discussing Donato, I'm discussing you. You're doing everything Agosto tells you. What if he's wrong? He should do what he wants in Sheepshead Bay, and you should do what you think is right here. You are the manager here, aren't you? If you did one thing and he did another, at least one of the banks might survive."

On the surface her argument seemed to have some logic, but "manager" was the key word. It was Agosto's bank. Paolo shook his head. "I have to do what Agosto tells me. I may manage this bank, but I'm not the owner."

"It's not right, putting all that gold out! It's bad to let people know how much there is."

"You don't understand, Maria. It will give the customers confidence to accept our banknotes. If they don't have confidence, they'll demand to be paid in gold and take away all the assets."

"Such a big financier! What do you know about all this? And how does Agosto know there will be a panic? People know Agosto and should trust him without having to see all that gold."

Paolo sighed. "Well, you work here too! And you carry the ledgers home in a shopping bag, and what do you do with the money you earn?"

"That's none of your business!"

"I know what you do, you invest it. Are you a big financier?"

"I know what I'm doing," she said confidently.

"Well, then, do something besides bother me. It's what Agosto wants, Maria. Are you here to help or not?"

Paolo looked at her evenly, feeling somewhat stronger. What hurt was the truth in her words. He was Agosto's employee. But if he wasn't as insightful as Agosto, he at least had the satisfaction of knowing he'd brought in new customers. He'd joined local clubs to bring in still more new accounts, and he willingly admitted he found that aspect of banking fulfilling, since he truly enjoyed speaking in public. Then too, he always felt he was helping people when he made loans.

"There are different kinds of success," Paolo commented.

Maria turned away, and obviously feeling rebuked, busied herself filling the drawers with banknotes. The other two employees would arrive shortly, and things should be in order.

Monday, July 8, 1907

MANHATTAN

Whenever Agosto came to Manhattan, he lunched with Barton Ainsley, who had forsaken the Knickerbocker Club for the New York Yacht Club.

Agosto looked about and concluded that although he had not lunched here since March, when the downward economic cycle had begun, the decor was unchanged.

The thick red carpet and high ceilings still muted conversations, the walls were still decorated with nautical paraphernalia—ship's wheels, a great brass compass, life preservers painted with names of well-known vessels—and the china still bore a border of little blue anchors.

But Agosto noted a subtle change of mood among the diners. The conversations of the rich were less animated; the usual conservative optimism gave way to an inevitable gloom. Some faces were missing—men ruined by the current crisis. Others clearly felt the threat that loomed over the economy, which could, at any moment, snatch from them the accomplishment of a lifetime.

"They don't think of themselves as gamblers," Barton Ainsley said solemnly as his eyes roamed the quiet dining room. "They think they make the odds and when events prevent the predicted outcome, they crawl into a shell. I guess it's the shock of discovering that there are some elements they can't control."

Agosto smiled slightly. "And you?"

Ainsley shrugged. "Old money. Lots of land, lots of gold. Of course there are risky investments, but my personal fortune is balanced. God, I couldn't deal with poverty. I haven't the psychological makeup for it."

"Poverty is a state of mind," Agosto said plainly. "I've known poor men who made money and were still poor. They frittered it away because they lacked the imagination to make it work for them. Instead, they spent it on material objects of no substance."

"And you?" Barton queried.

"Money, for money's sake, doesn't interest me. I want money to build, to invest."

147

"This isn't the best possible time for investment," Ainsley observed.

"In a way it is. If new investment isn't made, it'll take longer for the nation to come out of the slump."

"You must have weathered this pretty well."

"Well enough. I bought a cement factory from a family in Sheepshead Bay—construction was down, so it wasn't doing well. I've hired the former manager—an old friend, Roberto Marcucci. We work well together. And I've purchased two more banks, one in Little Italy."

"Going after the savings of the new immigrants?"

Agosto nodded. "It's going to be rough at first. Most of those people have good reason for not trusting banks, since there've been a number of fraudulent operations."

"How do you intend to deal with that?"

"I'm going to put my brother in charge. His Italian's good, and he's a good talker. You don't sell vegetables in a storefront without learning how to talk to your neighbors. Paolo will do well."

"There's a big criminal element to deal with."

Agosto shrugged. "There are honest Sicilians, but only a few give them a bad name."

"Well, you've already proved your point about small investors adding up, but Little Italy is different. There's real poverty there."

"They send money home, so they need a bank that's in correspondence with the Bank of Palermo and the Bank of Naples. And they do save."

Ainsley smiled. "Needless to say, I wish you luck."

Agosto acknowledged Ainsley's good wishes.

"And thanks to your rapid tip, we've come out of this rather well too. "Your friend Marcucci made Creighton Stearns look bad, I'm afraid. He was off chasing Sarah in Cannes when the runs on the European banks started. He wired me three full days after your call—much to his embarrassment."

Agosto laughed. "Well, since he missed the economic news, did he at least catch Sarah?"

Ainsley nodded. "Sarah had been pursuing Count Sforza . . . I think I mentioned him to you once."

"You did."

"Well, the count, it turned out, was married and wouldn't give her a tumble."

"When did marriage over stop an Italian count?" Agosto asked, a bemused look on his face.

"Well, this young man—he's your age, actually—seems quite honorable. They didn't even have an affair."

"Is Sarah unhappy?"

"Hell, no. She's marrying Creighton! In fact, I have an invitation for you. You'll get one in the mail, of course—these things have to be properly done."

"That's wonderful!" Agosto exclaimed.

"I hope so," Ainsley returned. "I must say to me it seems more like a merger than a marriage, so I can't say I'm that enthusiastic. Then too, the kind of wedding Sarah wants will cost me more than this panic, I can tell you! It could wipe me out."

Agosto laughed. Ainsley was joking, of course, but no doubt it would be quite an affair. "Listen, it could become the social event of the season. God knows the denizens of Wall Street can use the diversion."

"Oh, a diversion it's bound to be. Three hundred guests, dancing, liquor, an orchestra. She wants the reception held in the St. Regis. The ceremony will be at St. Thomas."

"I wouldn't expect less of Sarah."

"You will come, won't you? You and Cecilia, of course."

Agosto nodded. "Certainly."

"You know, I can't honestly say how I feel about it. I always suspected you were Sarah's first choice, and I'm certain Emiliano Sforza was her second. But she's stubborn. Now she insists she loves Creighton, or more precisely that she's *grown* to love him."

Agosto blushed at Ainsley's openness. "Believe me, that was no more than a girlish crush. I'd have made her miserable, and I'm sure Count Sforza would have too, though I don't know him."

Ainsley nodded. "I didn't mean to embarrass you. I suppose most fathers want their daughters to marry their own kind, but down deep inside, I'm not that fond of my own kind."

Agosto laughed. "You're a rebel. And let me remind you, you were the one who said that Sarah always wanted what she couldn't have. If I'd ever responded to her, she'd have run like a frightened fawn. She'll marry Creighton Stearns and she'll have a house with servants in Westchester, a summer place in the Hamptons, an apartment in Boston on Beacon Hill. She'll vacation in Europe and her diamonds will weigh down her fingers. Sarah couldn't deal with less."

Ainsley nodded. "I rather imagine you're right. But their children will be Stearnses and they'll inherit the bank, and then it'll belong to them. If only . . ." His eyes misted over and his voice trailed off. He didn't need to finish his sentence; Agosto filled it in mentally: ". . . Philip had lived."

"They'll be your grandchildren too," Agosto stressed. "Continuity, Ainsley. You told me continuity was important."

"So it is."

Agosto sipped some more wine. His mind strayed to Cecilia and to his own children. They are my continuity, he thought. Anthony will grow into a strong, intelligent boy. He'll take up where I leave off.

Saturday, September 7, 1907

B. R O O K L Y N

Paolo watched Fabiana as she bustled about their small house packing. She still wore her hair in two long thick braids wrapped around her head, and although her face was still as round as a plate, she had lost some weight and now might be described as stout rather than fat. She's a good woman, he acknowledged, but I'm not the best husband.

Fabiana was wonderful with Agosto's children. Clare Marina and Anthony adored her. Even Tina, Maria's daughter, loved her. She was like a fairy godmother—the spiritual reincarnation of La Befana. Her love of children made Paolo sad, because Fabiana was barren. And in spite of how their relationship had begun, Domenico had adopted Fabiana as his own. More often than Maria, his own daughter, Fabiana was there to help him and work in the store with Donato. No, Paolo thought, it's not Fabiana's fault that I don't love her.

"It's best," Paolo said dejectedly, as she placed the statue of the Virgin on one of the boxes, "and I'll come home every single weekend, I promise."

Fabiana nodded, though he could see the large tears in her eyes.

"I could take you, we could move to Manhattan . . . Agosto wants me to take you."

Fabiana shook her head. "I don't want to live there. I don't want to leave the children and my friends."

"Then it's best that you live with my father. It won't be forever, only till I get the bank started."

"I know that, and I know it's a great opportunity for you. Oh, Paolo, I wouldn't try to stop you."

"Agosto says I'm the best person to get the new branch started. He was upset when he found out you didn't want to move there."

"I explained to him," Fabiana said softly. "I told him it was best. He worked in Manhattan after he married Cecilia, he commuted, so he understands."

"I know you wouldn't be happy there. No friends . . ."

"I agree with you, Paolo, you don't have to keep saying it." She was folding sheets now and piling them in another box.

"Every weekend," Paolo repeated. "I promise."

Saturday, November 16, 1907

MANHATTAN

Cecilia sat stiffly on the edge of the wooden pew, the skirts of her new prim brown suit folded neatly, her bonnet partially obscuring her face. St. Thomas, she decided, was a most peculiar-looking church.

Located on Fifth Avenue, it was less elegant than St. Patrick's on the outside, but inside it was comparable. St. Thomas was the church attended by the Morgans, the Astors, the Ainsleys, and the Stearnses. Indeed, even the Guggenheims had converted from Judaism and joined St. Thomas' Fifth Avenue.

It was certainly a far different church from the church in Sheepshead Bay where Cecilia attended Mass. Its walls were covered with paintings, rich tapestries, and there were treasures of European art everywhere, though as Agosto explained, the frescoes in the rear of the church had been destroyed in a fire two years ago.

By contrast, the church in Sheepshead Bay was painted sky blue inside and there were pictures, statues of the Virgin with her bleeding heart, and bright blazing colors everywhere. But here the rich art was subdued and not as colorful to Cecilia's eyes. She fingered the prayer book. Agosto had assured her that it was not a sin to attend this service. "The Episcopalians—Anglicans, they are called in England—are not heretics. They are in schism with our church. We cannot, of course, partake in the Mass, but it is quite all right to attend the service."

Cecilia frowned. It might be all right, but she felt ill-at-ease. Moreover, she decided, Episcopalians were dull.

The thundering pipe organ struck the wedding march and

Cecilia almost jumped. The pipes were on either side of the altar and the thundering noise filled the cavernous church with sound. Wagner, she thought. No subtlety. That was the trouble with German opera, it was all noise, and in this cave of a cathedral the Teutonic strains of the wedding march from *Lohengrin* were even heavier than when Agosto had taken her to see the opera at the Metropolitan. At least the performance had color and movement, and she especially remembered how the swan boats were magically transported across the stage.

Agosto craned his neck. "That's the groom," he whispered in Cecilia's ear. "The tall one in the dark suit."

"They've all got dark suits," Cecilia replied wistfully. A sea of dark suits. Still, the altar was pretty, flooded with cascades of flowers, more flowers than Cecilia had seen at any wedding, though in all honesty she felt it a pity that they were cut flowers, which would soon wilt and die. Flowers in great pots were much better. They continued to live, grow, and give forth life.

She looked about and vaguely felt like some sort of poor relation. The women who accompanied the men in dark suits were outfitted in furs—sables, mink, and white fox. They were bejeweled with diamonds, emeralds, and rubies. They wore hats trimmed in all manner of expensive materials. They were as elegant as their church, and this, Cecilia felt, was wrong. The house of God should be glittering; it should have a statue of the Virgin with rubies and emeralds, and all the statues of the saints should have an opulence greater than the dresses of those who came to Mass. Yes, the church in Sheepshead Bay had such statues; the rubies and emeralds weren't real, of course, nor was the gold trim on the altar, but the parishioners were plain and didn't try to compete with the Blessed Virgin.

Almost in unison the guests turned in their pews as the flower girls emerged from the bride's door at the rear of the church. It was then that Cecilia noted the design above the door. It was a dollar sign worked into the tracery. Cecilia poked Agosto. "Why are their dollar signs there?" Her eyes motioned upward.

"And there are three money bags over the choir stalls," Agosto replied, smirking. "Morgan practically built this church—it represents his twin roles of vestryman and wealthy banker. His nickname is 'Old Money Bags.' This is a very rich church with a very wealthy congregation."

Cecilia frowned and shook her head, but she said nothing further, because behind the flower girls, Sarah Ainsley emerged on her father's arm. She was resplendent in a long white satin dress with a train so long it had to be held by six small boys. Her voluminous white veils were held in place by a studded diamond tiara, and her long loose flaxen hair was visible beneath the veils. In her gloved hands she carried a pearl-studded prayer book, and from it, on long satin ribbons, fell tiny violets and rosebuds. So beautiful was Sarah Ainsley that the guests let out an audible ripple of approval. Never had Cecilia seen a bride so lovely. She glanced at Agosto and could see the clear look of admiration in his eyes. I was not such a bride, she thought, thinking of the bonnet she had bought at Macy's. She lowered her dark eyes. Agosto could have done better. He could have married Sarah Ainsley. "She's breathtaking," Cecilia said under her breath.

Agosto turned away from the spectacle of Sarah Ainsley, who now approached the altar in measured steps, clinging to her father's arm. "She's not as breathtaking as you were," Agosto whispered, squeezing Cecilia's arm.

Cecilia raised her eyes to her husband's face, and for a moment she glowed in the love she saw in his eyes. "I didn't compare," she said modestly.

"You did and do," Agosto insisted.

Cecilia felt for Agosto's hand, and in response he wrapped it around hers, holding it tightly.

"Weddings make me sentimental," he confessed in a whisper. "I think we should have a second honeymoon."

"But the children—"

"Will be taken care of," Agosto said firmly.

Cecilia admired the room in the St. Regis Hotel. It was high-ceilinged and, by her standards, immense. Paintings of European landscapes hung on the walls, and the furniture was expensive and covered in velvet. Agosto stretched out on a plush blue divan and puffed white smoke into the air.

"This was very extravagant of you." Cecilia looked at her image in the full-length gilt-edged mirror. "Our entire living room, dining room, and kitchen would fit into this suite."

"Not so extravagant. In any case, since the wedding was at noon and the reception is here tonight at eight, it's impractical to be running back and forth all day between Manhattan and Brooklyn."

Cecilia opened her mouth to protest again, but thought better of it. Agosto was right. He had insisted that they spend the weekend in Manhattan, and even if she felt it was an expense, she was enjoying it.

She walked across the room to the closet where her new gown hung. Agosto had made her buy it at Lord and Taylor. She lifted it down and held it up to her, posing in front of the mirror.

"You'll be the most beautiful woman at the reception."

"I won't be, the bride will be."

"You're too modest," Agosto said, smiling. "Sarah's a good-looking woman, but you're more beautiful in my eyes. And, my darling, you're going to stop living like a lovely canary in a cage. I meant it about a second honeymoon."

Cecilia bit her lip. "Oh, Agosto, I don't know if I could leave my babies."

He smiled at her. "You can if they are in good hands."

Cecilia stared at the carpet. Agosto *did* love her; of that she was absolutely certain. "Would we be gone long?"

"I hope so . . . but it won't be for a while. I can't leave immediately. I'm talking about the future, but not too far in the future. I want to travel with you, Cecilia, but of course travel will be intertwined with business."

A wave of contradictory emotions overcame her. She wanted to travel with Agosto, to be with him. She was overjoyed that he wanted her at his side. But she felt a lingering doubt. She feared she could not be the kind of woman he needed, that one social situation after another would reveal her shortcomings.

"You're supposed to look a bit happier than that!" Agosto bounded from the divan and came to her side, embracing her. "Do you know where we're going to go?" He whirled her about, forcing her to smile at his unusually impetuous actions.

"To Atlantic City?"

Agosto laughed. "No, my darling. I want to go to South America."

Cecilia looked at him wide-eyed. "That's half the earth away!" she gasped.

Agosto bent over and kissed the tip of her nose. "And I shall buy you Brazilian emeralds for your neck and ears." He touched her tiny curved ears with his fingers, then kissed them.

Cecilia shivered in his arms. "Oh, Agosto. I want to be what you want me to be, but I'm afraid," she confessed in a whisper.

He laughed and hugged her. "You *are* what I want," he replied.

She leaned against him. He was so confident, so different, so unlike anyone she knew or had ever known. But he didn't understand. So great was Agosto's faith in himself that he failed to grasp the depth of her misgivings.

Agosto held her tighter and then lifted her into his arms. "We have a long time before the reception," he said mischievously.

Cecilia flushed, but didn't resist. She leaned her head against her husband's broad chest and gave way to the feelings he always aroused in her. He would carry her to the bed and make love to her, surrounding her and holding her till they melded into one. He would overpower her with his love, and she would gladly yield to him, giving everything, though in her heart she was afraid she had little to give save her body.

"You don't mind that I'll have to combine business and pleasure?"

Agosto laid her on the huge bed. He caressed her gently, removing her clothes carefully.

Cecilia shook her head in answer. "Of course not," she murmured as she felt his soft lips on her flesh. She sighed. "Oh, Agosto, I don't mind anything you do . . . ever."

"Mr. and Mrs. Agosto Tonelli!" The man at the head of the reception line called out their names, and Agosto led Cecilia down the long formal line, shaking hands as he went and introducing her.

When they reached Barton Ainsley, Ainsley reached over and hugged Agosto. He kissed Cecilia and held her hand warmly. "I told you this would cost a fortune," he whispered.

Agosto smiled knowingly, and they were pressed onward. Creighton Stearns shook hands coldly. "Nice to see you, old chap," he muttered. Agosto grinned and then kissed Sarah, who stood at Creighton's side looking like an ice princess. "May your marriage be as happy as mine," Agosto told her.

Sarah blinked at him and smiled enigmatically. But she held his hand tightly, and then, leaning toward him, said, "I shall save a dance for you, Agosto."

He shook his head and whispered back into her ear, "A woman shouldn't flirt with other men at her wedding."

Sarah stiffened, but the smile did not leave her face. "Later," she said quietly.

Agosto and Cecilia shook hands with the groom's family, then were seated at a small round table with another couple. As soon as they sat down, champagne was placed on the table and their glasses filled.

Agosto watched Cecilia. Her eyes took in everything. The high ceiling, the ornate woodwork, the long blue velvet draperies that hung from the huge windows. The room had several crystal chandeliers, a stage, and a twelve-piece orchestra ready to play. "The blue room is full of blue bloods," Agosto joked to her. "There are the Morgans." He used his chin to indicate the table.

Cecilia tried to smile at him. "Am I dressed all right?"

"You look beautiful," he replied.

She was wearing a soft blue gown with puffed sleeves and ivory lace trim. Around her neck she wore a cameo on a gold chain, and her rich dark hair was combed up in a massive cluster of thick curls. Compared with the overdressed glittery women in the room, Cecilia had a wonderful understated elegance. Her long white neck seemed even longer with her hair swept up, and her profile was not unlike the beautiful Roman lady on the cameo.

"Are you in finance?" the woman across the table asked. She was as richly clad as any woman in the room, and she spoke her words precisely. She reminded Agosto of a great plumed parrot.

"Banking," Agosto replied. "Agosto Tonelli." He leaned over to shake hands with the parrot's mate, a poor plain pigeon in his late fifties, outfitted in tie and tails and sporting diamond cufflinks that paled next to his wife's tiara, necklace, earrings, and bracelet.

"Astor, John Astor," the man replied.

Agosto nodded. The gentleman had left off the numeral behind his name. "I am pleased to meet a relative—grandson—of the great founder of the New York Public Library, where, I might add, I've spent many happy and useful hours." Silently Agosto wondered who had made the seating arrangements. Surely the Stearns family wouldn't have placed him at the same table with the Astors. They would have put him with the Italian ambassador, where, for reasons all his own, he would have preferred to be.

Astor lifted his glass of champagne. "I'm certain we shall be doing this all evening, but shall we toast the bride?"

Agosto lifted his glass. "A bride can't be toasted too often."

"Are you one of the Italian bankers from Milan?" Astor asked stiffly.

Agosto grinned. "No, one of the Italian bankers from Brooklyn."

"Brooklyn?" Mrs. Astor echoed, stifling a nervous giggle which would have been unbecoming in such an amply proportioned middle-aged woman.

"Across the bridge, my dear," Astor replied.

"Oh," Mrs. Astor said, unconsciously touching her diamond necklace.

Astor grinned. He seemed to enjoy his wife's discomfort. "My grandfather made his fortune in furs. Smelly furs. He was truly an old German skinflint. Practically sold out the U.S. to the British during the War of 1812."

"John! Really! What will these people think?"

"They'll think they met an honest man. What investments interest you these days?"

"Many," Agosto replied. "But recently I've bought into rubber."

Astor nodded. "Fine dinner companions, I say. The grandson of a robber baron meets an Italian rubber baron."

"Not a baron, just minor nobility at the moment." Agosto sipped some more champagne.

"Well, God knows there's money in it. High growth potential, I say. Telephones are made of hard rubber, and more and more people have telephones. And records, of course, they're hard rubber too. Heaven knows there'll be more and more vehicles that need tires. Rubber is a commodity with a future."

Agosto nodded. The orchestra suddenly struck up a dance tune and Creighton Stearns led Sarah onto the floor. There was a round of good-natured applause as they danced the first dance together under the watchful eyes of New York's elite.

When the first dance was over, the guests began dancing.

Agosto led Cecilia to the floor.

"I doubt I can dance this way," she murmured.

"Of course you can! Come along, I'll show you."

"Oh, Agosto, I feel everyone is staring at me."

"Of course they are. People always stare at beautiful women. Come, come . . . we'll dance the night away."

"I saved this dance for you, Agosto." Sarah Ainsley touched his arm lightly. "Creighton is dying to dance with Cecilia," she announced.

Agosto bowed slightly. "It's always an honor to dance with the bride, and a pleasure too." He took her in his arms and glanced away as Creighton obediently glided away with Cecilia. "White becomes you," he said, turning back to Sarah, who pressed herself against him.

"You should have married me, Agosto." Sarah looked up into his eyes. She was intense, her mouth slightly parted, and she almost seemed to be breathing her words rather than speaking them.

Agosto flushed. "I'm really very happy, and you will be too."

"Maybe . . . but you and I could have been happy together."

Agosto shook his head. She was still such a child. "Sarah, you married the man you were destined to marry. He'll give you the kind of life you want. I married the woman I was destined to marry. We come from the same place, like you and Creighton."

"On and on and on . . ." Sarah murmured. "I'm an adornment for Creighton, a feather in his social cap."

"If you feel that way, why did you marry him?"

"Because you wouldn't marry me," she said plainly.

Agosto whirled her around, feeling distinctly uncomfortable. "Sarah, be happy. I know I wouldn't have made you happy."

"And of course you're never wrong," she said somewhat sarcastically.

Agosto leaned down and kissed her forehead in a fatherly manner. "I'm not often wrong," he corrected. " 'Never' is too strong a word."

10

Saturday, February 29, 1908

BROOKLYN

Agosto felt wonderful in spite of the wretched February weather. The recovery he had anticipated in the economy was well under way, Paolo was blissfully happy working at the bank on Mulberry Street, Fabiana seemed more than content living with Domenico, Maria, and Donato. In all, he thought, things could not be going better. And, God and business willing, he planned to take Cecilia to South America next year, a short eleven months from now. This winter was impossible, and summer would be unbearable, so he planned to go next January.

And to top off all of Agosto's good feelings, he and Paolo were at this moment talking to a charming and most enthusiastic man.

"There won't be another day like this for four years!" George Tilyou joked. "Leap year! I love it. February 29 is a unique day for unique transactions."

Agosto smiled. Tilyou's vigor was infectious; his sea-blue eyes gleamed as he ran his hand nervously through his thin flaxen hair. He was a bundle of Nordic energy, a short good-natured Viking out to conquer uncertain shores.

"You're Norwegian?" Agosto ventured. There were a lot of Norwegians in Brooklyn.

"Danish! A bit stickier!" Tilyou roared at his own pun. "I'm at home here . . . very much at home. Copenhagen—all Denmark—is nothing but islands joined by giant causeways! It is like that here, islands and rivers . . . some rivers that aren't really rivers, like the East River . . . bridges and more bridges, landfill. I too come from a country that has conquered the sea."

Agosto smiled. Tilyou was a builder, an entrepreneur, a risk taker who knew his risks would pay off. Agosto bit into his hot dog and inhaled. Nathan's had a different aroma, but an aroma

159

that blended so well with the sea air that it made a man's mouth water. It was hardly an Italian meal—a cold foaming beer and Nathan's famous hot dog drowning in Nathan's special relish and hot mustard. But Agosto liked it, it brought back memories. Nathan's was already a landmark in Coney Island.

Tilyou leaned over conspiratorially. "This is the perfect location. People come here anyway. Look, try to envisage it. A huge park like the Tivoli Gardens in my Copenhagen—except for refugees from Manhattan, people trying to escape the summer heat. "I want a roller coaster—the biggest roller coaster in the world. And a steeplechase—wooden horses on a wooden track! I have it all in my mind. Houses with mirrors that distort the body! A mirror, Agosto Tonelli, that would make you seven feet tall! You'd pay to see yourself seven feet tall, wouldn't you?"

"I suppose I would," Agosto agreed. He thought of Atlantic City and its boardwalk—not that it had anything like what Tilyou was talking about, but it did have its entertainments and it certainly did draw thousands and thousands of tourists who paid to be pushed along the boardwalk, ride in little boats, play miniature golf, and eat saltwater taffy. He thought of his honeymoon.

"And you'd bring your children to ride on the roller coaster! I know you would, and so would millions of others. I tell you, my Steeplechase Park—that's what I want to call it—would be a fine investment."

"Have you the plans—I mean, on paper?"

Tilyou grinned. "Of course. I don't expect you or any other investor to put money into a dream—though of course that's what it comes down to, with or without plans. But when you're out trying to find money, you make your plans look concrete, solid."

Agosto laughed. "You're admitting it's a dream."

Tilyou nodded. "Only to the two of you. I'd deny it with any Wall Street banker. But I hear the Tonellis have a sense of humor and a humanness, are men who aren't afraid of dreams or ideas, men who know that all investments are dreams and all good investments are made in dreamers."

"My first investment was in motion pictures."

"The very substance and essence of dreams, my friend. What was your second investment?"

"Stogies . . . cigarettes."

Tilyou roared again. "People spend their money to watch it go up in smoke, and you profited from it."

"It merged with American Tobacco."

"I can't promise a merger, only a place where people will come again and again for amusement."

"To eat Nathan's food and throw up on your roller coaster and then come back and eat again. Nathan will make as much as you," Paolo put in.

"It's a good location, this. Think of it on Saturdays . . . so close to the city. It'll be a mecca! Fun and amusement, sun, and good food."

"It is seasonal."

Tilyou shrugged. "Life is seasonal. Oh, the first sunny weekend of the summer will make up the winter's loss. Think of it, Tonelli, a permanent fair, a carnival that stays put—a circus, if you like. A family place."

Agosto raised his hands in surrender. "I'll look at the plans . . . listen in detail to the dreams of a dreamer. And I like you, so I think I'll invest in your dream after all is said and done."

Tilyou grinned. "You won't be sorry," he said with conviction. "And your children, what are their names?"

"I have two, Clare Marina, who is four and a half, and Anthony, who's two and a half."

"Well, Anthony is a bit small, but Clare Marina will take the first ride on my roller coaster," Tilyou promised.

"I'll look forward to it," Agosto replied as he drained his stein of beer. "But I'll look forward even more to seeing myself seven feet tall."

Paolo glanced at the clock on the wall. "We should be going," he suggested.

Agosto nodded, and the three of them stood up. Agosto reached across the table and shook hands with George Tilyou. "Call me next week," he urged.

Paolo and Agosto walked along toward the streetcar stop. "It's cold," Agosto complained.

"You really going to invest in an amusement park?" Paolo questioned.

"I think so. I like him, that's why I brought you along. He's imaginative, and I wanted you to meet him. What do you think?"

Paolo shrugged. "I think there are better ways to spend money."

Agosto half-smiled. Paolo had become quite serious lately. "Like what?"

"In Little Italy. Our people live badly there, and the working conditions are terrible. I don't know how you stood living there. I feel guilty every time I eat a good meal."

"I thought you liked working there."

"I do! I feel like I'm helping. But I can't close my eyes to the living and working conditions. Didn't it bother you?"

"I didn't think about it much. I wasn't working there, and I was only in my room to sleep."

"It's terrible."

"But that's how it always is. It takes time for people to get started. The first generation always has a bad time of it."

"I'm not just talking about 'rough.' I'm talking about exploitation. Kids working fourteen hours a day in sweat shops."

"We worked when we were kids."

"Out in the fresh air," Paolo said glumly.

"Well, obviously it's not that way for everyone. You've got a lot of accounts."

Paolo concurred with a motion of his hands, then thrust his hands in his pockets. "The streetcar's coming," he said, deciding Agosto just hadn't noticed much of anything in Little Italy.

Wednesday, December 30, 1908

Paolo Tonelli studied his image in the mirror over the washbasin. He had celebrated his thirtieth birthday on the first of December, and he decided that his face, while still round, was taking on a new maturity. Agosto gave him full responsibility for the new bank in Little Italy, and he was basking in his success. Agosto praised him, and even his father seemed pleased. He smiled at himself, admitting that he liked living in Manhattan, even if he did have to go home on weekends. It gave him a new independence, a feeling of being on his own, a belief that for the first time in his life he was his own master.

Like Agosto, he rented a room on Sullivan Street. But it was a nicer room than Agosto had rented so many years ago. And it was much nicer than the people he lived among could afford.

Paolo put on his hat, coat, and scarf. Snow had fallen the night before, and though it had melted away under the feet of the throngs of people who were on their way to work, it was still wet, damp, and cold outside. However, he comforted himself, it was not a long walk to the bank on Mulberry Street next door to the offices of *Il Progresso*, the Italian newspaper.

Paolo trudged along, but when he reached Mulberry, he found large crowds of people standing in front of the newspaper office and indeed all along the sidewalk, even in front of the Italian Bank.

He hurried toward the crowd, but stopped dead when a woman began to wail loudly and was joined by yet another. He hurried forward, pushing past people lined up in front of the newspaper's office. Their faces were grim, many were crying, and some appeared angry.

"What is it, what's happened?" Paolo asked as he pushed his way toward the bank.

"You can't crowd in here!" someone shouted in Italian. "We're all waiting!"

"Waiting for what?" Paolo shouted back in irritation.

"Dispatches! The newspaper has a teletype machine! They're the only ones with news!"

"You can't shove in!" another woman warned.

"I am not shoving in," Paolo shouted back, "I am trying to get to The Italian Bank!"

"Yes, he's the banker, I've seen him there," a woman in the crowd confirmed.

"A banker! We could use a banker! Our people need help!" a man shouted.

Puzzled and still irritated, Paolo stopped. "Tell me what's happened," he demanded of a younger man. "I can't read minds!"

"A tragedy! The end of the world, the biggest tragedy you can imagine! Messina . . . It happened on the twenty-eighth, but the reports only began to come in last night. A tragedy."

"Messina? What happened in Messina?"

"An earthquake," a woman wailed. "It killed everyone in the city! And those not killed by the shaking earth were killed in a tidal wave! They're dead! All dead! My sister, her brother, my mother . . ." The woman dissolved in shaking, wrenching screams, and another standing next to her comforted her.

"They may not all be dead—we're waiting here for news," a man said, somewhat more rationally.

Paolo bit his lip. "I'm certain there are survivors," he said, trying to offer comfort. Then, wanting to know more: "You must let me into the newspaper. I must speak with them. The survivors will need help."

"He's right, the whole city will have to be rebuilt," a man shouted. "Let him through, he owns the bank!"

The crowd melted before him, and Paolo hurried inside the newspaper office. The stairs were guarded by a young man. "You can't go up there!" he said authoritatively. "We have a paper to get out. When there's news, it's brought down to me and I announce it to the crowd.''

Paolo studied him. "I'm Paolo Tonelli, the banker.'' He extended his hand. "And what's your name?''

"Vince . . . Vincent Pedroni.''

Paolo could see the young man was pale and that his eyes were misty. "Do you have family in Messina?''

"Who doesn't? My whole family is there, except for my sister.''

Paolo gripped his shoulder. "Be strong. I'm sure there are many survivors. Look, you must let me upstairs. I have an idea. I think many people will want to help their relatives. I run the bank next door, and there are ways to send money to Messina.''

"You're not Sicilian," the young man observed suspiciously.

I'm not, Paolo thought, but my customers are, and certainly Agosto wouldn't disapprove of the bank spearheading a drive to help the victims of a disaster. Two years ago, after the San Francisco earthquake, Agosto had helped families send money to relatives there.

"I'm Italian," Paolo proclaimed proudly. "Garibaldi united Italy, and a tragedy in one part of Italy is a tragedy for all Italians.''

"You talk good," Vince said in English.

Only then did Paolo realize that he had lapsed into English. He did that when he got emotional, because his parents had always made him speak English. It was just the opposite with Domenico. He spoke English, but lapsed into Italian when he was emotional or angry.

"I was born here," Paolo admitted. "My father is from Puglia.''

Vince only nodded. "I could get in trouble if I let you upstairs.''

"You won't. And I'll come back and take you to lunch." That, Paolo decided, would be the clincher. Vince didn't look as if he ate all that often.

Vince didn't say anything more; he simply stepped aside and Paolo climbed the stairs hurriedly. Once in the office, he found the editor with little difficulty, and he explained how he might be helpful.

"You are the answer to a prayer!" the editor shouted enthusiastically. "All morning people come and ask how they can help . . . it'll ease the pain if they can help. We intend to raise money, but for now we must concentrate on what is happening.''

"I'd like all the details," Paolo suggested.

The editor led him into a tiny office piled high with papers and books. "There are the latest dispatches," he said. "You can sit down and read them. I've got work to do."

Paolo made his way to the desk and sat down.

The first reports told of at least 100,000 dead in the city itself and perhaps as many as 200,000 in the region. There was, he noted, no mention of a tidal wave. And even if these first reports were exaggerated, there was no question that it was a disaster of major proportions. More alarming were the reports of the aftershocks, which continued unabated, destroying the remaining buildings.

Paolo read the reports and felt increasingly sick thinking of the people in the streets who had no way of knowing about their relatives. In Sicily, even more than in the rest of Italy, the family was the most important institution. Paolo's heart genuinely went out to the throngs in the street, but he was not beyond realizing that if he could help them, he could also help the bank.

He put down the dispatches and lifted the receiver on the phone which sat on the corner of the desk. He asked for the number and in a moment heard Agosto's voice.

"I'm in the offices of *Il Progresso*. You've heard about Messina?"

"Half an hour ago," Agosto replied.

"I want to have the bank spearhead a drive for funds," Paolo announced. "The newspaper will help. What do you think?"

"Paolo, that's a wonderful idea! But I don't know about the newspaper. *Il Progresso* is . . . well, radical."

"I expect it'll bring in new customers," Paolo added, wanting to emphasize his newfound business acumen. He ignored his brother's comments about the newspaper's radicalism. For a man living in Little Italy, *Il Progresso*'s radicalism wasn't all that difficult to understand.

"I suspect you're right, but in any case it's the right thing to do. I'm proud you thought of it so quickly."

"I try to stay on top of things," Paolo replied. And he thought to himself: I'll yet make Maria be quiet—I've something to offer. His mind strayed to Vince's comment: "You talk good." Yes, he thought, a spokesman for a charity drive ought to "talk good."

New Year's Day, 1909

BROOKLYN

The entire family was gathered at Domenico's house for the New Year's Day feast. Maria, Fabiana, and Cecilia outdid themselves in the kitchen, and the table was filled with delicacies and special dishes. Cecilia prepared *ricci di Donna*, a specialty of the Abruzzi region from which her grandmother, old Mrs. Solari, came. It was a spiral pasta over which a stew of delicately roasted crabs smothered in tomatoes and garlic was poured. Fabiana made a fish dish of squid cooked in a special sauce, and Maria made the antipastas, the bread, and more ordinary pastas. And as usual on New Year's Day, there was extra wine.

"I am proud!" Domenico roared. "Salvatore shows me the Italian newspaper from Little Italy and I read Paolo's name in this *Il Progresso* and I'm proud! Your mama should have lived to see her second son do such good things! I never say it before, Paolo, but I say it today! You are a success!"

Paolo's eyes were filled with tears he couldn't hold back. And Agosto felt his eyes misty too. Paolo had waited too long to hear Domenico praise him, and to Agosto's way of thinking, the praise was long overdue, even if he did regard *Il Progresso* as a somewhat dubious newspaper.

"So much money," Fabiana said in awe. "I think of all the little children, the orphans in Messina who'll be helped. Paolo, you are a good man and a good husband."

"It's wonderful," Cecilia acknowledged. "Thousands of dollars for Messina, to help the people rebuild."

"The first reports were exaggerated," Paolo said knowledgeably, "but it was a terrible tragedy nevertheless—a hundred and fifty thousand people killed in the region, eighty-five thousand in the city."

"And so poor to start with," Fabiana lamented.

"Well, I'm proud! I'm proud of my two sons!" Domenico said again.

Maria stared into her pasta. Her father was proud of everyone but Donato, who worked all day for him.

"Where is Messina?" Clare Marina asked.

"In Sicily, an island off the Italian boot. I'll show you on the map after dinner," Agosto answered. Not yet six, Clare Marina was a question box, but he always tried to answer her.

"Mama says this is a special dinner because next week you and Zia Cecilia are going away," Tina put in.

"To South America," Agosto answered.

"Don't let's talk about it," Cecilia said quickly. Her eyes rested on Clare and Anthony.

Agosto patted her hand. "They'll be fine. Seraphina will take good care of them, and so will Fabiana."

"It's my chance to be a mother," Fabiana declared. "You wouldn't deny me that, would you, Cecilia?"

Cecilia shook her head. "Of course not. It's just that I'll miss them so."

"Well, Paolo, that means the rest of the transfers to Messina will be in your hands. You and Roberto will have to look after everything else, too. I'll be in touch."

"Three months is a long time," Domenico observed.

"Roberto and Paolo know what they're doing." For once Domenico didn't say anything contradictory or diminishing. Today, Agosto concluded, was truly Paolo's day.

"Paolo's the hero of the whole Sicilian community," Domenico bragged.

Maria could take no more. She hissed through her teeth and muttered, "Sicilians!"

"Close your mouth, woman!" Domenico shouted in irritation.

"They're all in the Black Hand like Sal!" she countered in spite of her father's warning.

"Quiet!" he roared back at her, pounding his fork on the table. "You know nothing of men of tradition! Their ways are not our ways, but they've their own traditions, and not everyone adheres to them. You're a woman and you know nothing of these matters."

Maria fell silent.

"How do people get black hands?" Clare asked. "Do they play in the mud?"

Cecilia smiled and Agosto actually laughed.

But Domenico turned to Clare solemnly. "It is just a name," he said patiently. "Eat your pasta."

Clare smiled at her grandfather, and Agosto smiled at Cecilia. It was certainly not going to be the end of it, Agosto thought. Later, when they were alone, Clare Marina would ask to see Sicily on the map and she would ask what "black hand" really meant.

Friday, January 8, 1909

Agosto swung open the door of the stateroom, and lifting a surprised Cecilia in his arms, carried her over the threshold and inside.

"Oh, put me down, Agosto!" She moved in his arms in mock protest.

"It's our second honeymoon! I intend to play the bridegroom one more time."

He set her down gently on the edge of the large double bed. Cecilia's eyes were huge as she looked around. Baskets of yellow roses and bunches of deep purple violets decorated every table, and next to the bed was a round table bedecked in a white tablecloth which held a bottle of champagne chilling in a silver bucket.

"This room is like a suite in a grand hotel. Oh, Agosto, you're frivolous."

He grinned mischievously. "I want you to travel in grand style! Should I take you to Brazil on a cattle boat?"

She smiled at him shyly. "You made the family say their farewells on deck . . . you didn't want them to see this room, did you?"

Agosto shrugged. "I didn't want a lecture from Maria, nor did I want to see her turn green with envy."

Cecilia nodded knowingly. "I miss my babies already," she said wistfully as she ran her hand over the blue brocade bed cover.

"Seraphina is quite competent. You said so yourself. And they have Fabiana too. So little in their lives will change . . . and it's not for so long in any case."

"Are you trying to convince me my babies won't miss me?"

He leaned over and kissed her cheek. "They'll miss you, but not as much as I would if I made this trip alone. Cecilia, when the children are older, we'll travel with them. This is almost our last chance to travel alone together . . . for you to have what I couldn't give you when we were first married."

"You gave me all I ever wanted."

"But not as much as I wanted to give." He sat down beside

her. "I'd planned to go earlier, but there was no way last winter, nor could I have left in the spring."

"It makes no difference. In Brazil it's always summer," Cecilia observed.

"Are you excited?"

Cecilia looked across at him solemnly. "Yes, but I'll still miss my babies. I keep thinking even now that there is something I must do."

"First of all, they're not such babies. Clare will be six in August and Anthony four in September."

"They'll always be babies to me," Cecilia said, trying to smile. "It's just that I'm so used to doing things for them."

"There's nothing you must do but be my wife. Mind you, I have work to do in Rio and I'm afraid the trip to Manaus won't be luxurious. It's rough, wild country, hot and humid."

"Like Cuba?" Agosto had told her many stories about Cuba, and she was certain the Amazon must be similar.

"I think the Sierra Maestra must be a paradise compared to the Amazon. But Manaus is wealthy, a boom town. Still, I think it has elements like our West. All kinds have come to make their fortune. There are robbers, royalty, adventurers, and just plain hardworking men. And Indians. Still, it will be an experience, one which we will share."

"Oh, Agosto, I don't want you to think I didn't want to come. I did."

"I know. Do you think I won't miss them too? Clare is the joy of my life, and Anthony is growing so fast I can't believe it. Sometimes when I go away for a few days, it seems they've grown visibly just while I've been away."

"And what'll they be like after three months!"

"It'll be wonderful to see them again, that's what it will be." He kissed her cheek, "Don't worry."

Two weeks of placid waters and shipboard routine. Breakfast at nine, lunch at one, dinner at nine. And in the evenings, cocktails and dancing in the lounge, gambling at the casino tables, and long walks on moonlit decks. The routine of the ship was broken only by long days spent ashore in Havana, Trinidad, Caracas, and Recife.

On the fifth of February, four weeks after leaving New York City in a lightly falling snow, their ship, the Maria Christina, sailed into the majestic harbor of Rio de Janeiro.

"I've never seen the sky and water so blue!" Cecilia enthused.

"It seems more blue because of the vegetation," Agosto pointed out. Sugar Loaf Mountain jutted out into the water, its distinctive shape a green mass of tropical life. Behind it, the Baia de Guanabara; islands strung like a chain of emeralds in the placid blue waters, islands heavy with tropical trees, lush and beautiful, extending as far as the eye could see into a blue mist. And before them an alabaster white city trapped between sea and mountains and teeming with life.

"It looks mysterious," Cecilia announced. "Oh, I do wish Clare could see it! You know, Agosto, this trip would have been very educational for her."

"She's a bit young yet. Besides, the trip down the Amazon would be too difficult for a child."

Cecilia sighed. "It is beautiful."

"Not as beautiful as it looks from afar. There's immense wealth here, and great poverty. It's a strange country. Only the coastal areas are developed, save for the rubber plantations on the Amazon. The rest is mountains and jungle. The whole population is by the sea, clinging to it as if they were afraid to venture into the interior."

"If you really wanted to go to the Amazon, why did we come here first? It's so far from the mouth of the river."

"I told you, I came here to buy you emeralds," he joked.

"Agosto Tonelli, I know you better than that!"

He circled her shoulders with his arm and hugged her. "Yes, you do. There's a meeting here. Exciting things are happening in this country. The new President, Alfonso Pena, is taking a major step to stabilize the nation's currency. He is setting up a state bank, the Caixa de Conversao. Its function is to redeem inconvertible paper currency by issuing convertible paper currency through the deposit of gold."

Cecilia frowned.

"I don't expect you to understand the ins and outs." He laughed softly. "It's all rather complicated. But what it essentially means is that the currency used in the country could be converted to gold at any time. It's a function now served by every bank in America, but here it'll be served by a national, federally operated bank. There are some important Italian bankers coming here, and some influential men from England and America as well."

"And you could have seen them all in New York."

"Quite true. But then I couldn't buy you emeralds, bring you on this trip, go down the Amazon, or be able to study the details of such a plan on the spot."

Cecilia smiled. "But you'll have to put up with my lack of knowledge."

"I don't expect you to partake in discussions with bankers,

only to be on my arm at parties and receptions. Only to be your beautiful and gracious self.''

Cecilia's eyes drank in the beauty of the harbor. Yes, she thought. She could do what Agosto wanted and she could be what he wanted, but she wished she understood, she wished she could be his confidante and know his business as well as Gina had known Domenico's business. But then, she admitted, there was much more to banking than to selling fruits and vegetables.

"I don't understand Portuguese,'' she protested.

"I daresay many Brazilians speak Italian. Don't worry, you'll be perfect.''

The perfect what? Cecilia wondered. Poor Agosto, he might just as well have a mannequin on his arm.

Saturday, February 20, 1909

MANHATTAN

Paolo Tonelli climbed the narrow staircase of the tenement. Young Vince Pedroni, the office boy at *Il Progresso*, had given himself entirely over to the task of helping him raise money for the earthquake victims, and in the process, Paolo had come to like and admire him. Now that the fund drive was over, Paolo determined to hire Vince and pay him a somewhat higher wage than he received at the newspaper. His English was improving, he appeared ambitious, and certainly he could be trained, Paolo reasoned. In any case, having him work at the bank would help appearances in the community. Not that he needed much help now. Accounts were growing by the day, since he himself had become a hero. But Vince was a good boy, and Paolo felt nothing short of fatherly toward him.

Short of breath, Paolo reached the fifth floor and searched the doors for numbers. The hall was dimly lit, and much to Paolo's fright, a rat skittered past him in the near-darkness. It was truly a disgusting place, filthy, cold, cockroach-ridden, and overrun with vermin.

Paolo paused in front of the door. The number was scrawled on it in fading paint. He took a deep breath and knocked. In all the weeks he had been working with Vince, he'd never been to the tenement where he lived.

"Paolo!'' Vince exclaimed. "You should'na come here. I could have met you.''

"I wanted to see you . . . see where you live."

Vince opened the door and Paolo went in.

"Cristo," he muttered under his breath. The room was no more than nine by twelve. Along the walls were bed rolls, seven of them. On one a middle-aged woman nursed a tiny, frail baby. On another a young girl sat trying to pull her long dull wool skirt over her worn shoes.

"This is my sister, Angelica."

Vince pointed to the girl, who, Paolo thonght, must be seventeen. She was a tiny little creature with delicate features, large eyes, and a tangled mass of black hair. She was quite breathtaking in spite of her clothes. "How do you do," Paolo said in Italian. She smiled, a warm radiant smile. Paolo took her hand, and immediately noticed that it was rough and red.

"She works on a sewing machine," Vince explained. "This is Mrs. Marcos. Her husband's out, and so are the rest of the men who live here."

Paolo paid his respects to Mrs. Marcos, who acknowledged him with a nod. She had the listless facial expression of one who doesn't eat well, and it crossed Paolo's mind that the leftovers on New Year's Day could have fed her for a month.

Paolo's eyes took in the half-loaf of bread on the rickety table, the yellowed chamber pot, the lack of water. It was a hole, but he knew it was no worse than the way many lived. "I've come to offer you a job," Paolo announced. "As a teller trainee."

Vince's face lit up, but he was cautious. "I don't want no charity," he said firmly, pulling himself up to his full five feet, three inches.

"I'm not offering you any," Paolo returned. "Only a job, and you'll have to work hard."

"Okay. But why me?"

"Because I've seen you work. I know you'll do well. Now, look, a teller in training can't live here. I know a place on Sullivan Street. You'll be able to afford it. It's only one room, but it's better than this. At least there are no rats."

"I'll have to save first. You gotta have a deposit."

"I'll advance you some money," Paolo offered.

"I said no charity. I got my pride. I gotta take care of Angelica, but I got my pride."

"Yes, that's why you should move." Paolo glanced at her again. Clearly she couldn't understand them, since they were speaking English. She looked so frail. "I promise you you'll work for it," Paolo reiterated. "Come on, gather up your things and let's go now."

Vince inhaled and glanced at his sister. "All right," he agreed. He turned to Angelica and spoke to her in Italian.

She stood up, and Paolo could see just how tiny and delicate she was—not even five feet tall. She reminded him of one of Clare Marina's dolls.

"She's going to have a baby," Vince confided. "That's what happens when you bring a dumb Sicilian woman to live in a place like this. She got raped. So I gotta take care of her."

Paolo bit his lip and felt tears forming in his eyes. She was only a child. He inhaled deeply and felt like a hero all over again as silently he vowed to help Vince take care of his sister.

Monday, March 1, 1909

M A N A U S

It was their last night in Manaus, and Cecilia stood on the terrace of the Moravias' home. Dano Moravia was a wealthy Italian rubber baron, and his wife, Greta, like many women in Manaus, was German.

Greta was large-boned, tall, and had pale blond hair. She wore eight jeweled rings, and necklaces that sparkled with diamonds and emeralds. She always dressed in white and she spoke in English in short halting sentences which Cecilia had difficulty understanding. She also drank to excess, beginning before lunch and insisting that she drank for medicinal purposes. "It's ugly here," she often said. "So ugly that it's unbearable without gin."

Cecilia inhaled the night air. Back in the Moravia mansion their farewell party was in progress, and the strains of a Strauss waltz could be heard above the loud laughter and the clinking of glasses. Alone for a rare moment, Cecilia thought about their trip; it was an excursion into a world she had never dreamed existed.

The steamship on which Cecilia and Agosto had traveled down the Amazon was dirty white and manned by a mixed crew composed of a British captain, three Italian seamen, two Peruvians, and four Spaniards. Their cramped cabin was far from luxurious—in fact it barely met the standards of second-class travel on a ship crossing the Atlantic. The tiny bed on which they slept was covered by thick netting, and the bathroom facilities, such as they were, were shared with other passengers.

It was, Cecilia thought, in marked contrast to their voyage to Rio and the time they spent there. In Rio they were invited to a ball at the palace of the President of Brazil, Alfonso Pena. It was an elegant evening, but one Cecilia remembered with some discomfort. The Vice-President, Nilo Picanha, had repeatedly requested she dance with him, and had made bold advances, begging her to remain in Rio for Carnival and allow Agosto to go to Manaus alone. He admired the emerald earrings Agosto had given her, and he had caressed her ear. She had virtually fled from him, and finally discovered Agosto talking business with a group of bankers. When she told Agosto what had happened, he had taken it as a joke. Cecilia remembered how perplexed she had felt. I really *am* unsophisticated, she now told herself.

When they left Rio, they traveled up the coast of South America to the mouth of the Amazon, then transferred to the steamer. "Not a relaxing trip," Agosto admitted, but an adventure.

Cecilia agreed. Never in her entire life had she imagined a world like this one. The insects were unbearable, so unbearable that she was obliged to wear a hat with a long veil that fell to her shoulders. The heat too was oppressive. It was still, without even a breeze on the great river to relieve the constant humidity.

Yet the discomfort was bearable because the sights and sounds of the deep jungle were compelling and the contrasts of color, sound, and smell were as great as the visible social contrasts. The jungle met the river, and the river brought dabs of civilization to a landscape and a people who were wild and primitive. Great steamers navigated the Amazon's waters, as did bark canoes paddled by half-naked Indians; an opera house graced the city of Manaus, while only a short distance away deadly crocodiles sunned on the banks of the Amazon, which was as dangerous as it was beautiful.

"They call this the land God forgot to finish," Agosto told her. It was a phrase that stuck in Cecilia's mind. In the early morning the sounds of the jungle were everywhere: wild birds that both sang and shrieked, insects, prowling animals that came to the water's edge to drink. Once they had glimpsed a great anaconda, a snake fully twenty feet long that moved through the water with a speed greater than any powered vessel. At midday the jungle slept, wrapped in heat and lulled by the effects of the sun as it beat on the tops of the tall umbrella trees and created nature's own greenhouse. In the afternoon, dark clouds gathered and it rained for two hours, a penetrating, drenching, blinding rain. At eventide the jungle once again seemed to come to life, the skies cleared, and spectacular sunsets painted everything orange and pink.

"As an oasis is to the desert, Manaus is to the jungle," Agosto told her. It was a sprawling city hacked out of the tangled weeds and giant trees. She had the feeling that if neglected, the jungle would close in on it immediately and devour its streets, covering its buildings with thick green mold. It was, Agosto admitted, even more exotic than he had been led to believe, but to Cecilia's eyes it was a study in decay.

Well-dressed women wearing fine Italian shoes and dainty dresses picked their way through mud-strewn streets. Planks served as sidewalks. Tumble-down shacks lined the riverfront, and from them half-breeds emerged to tend the steamboats that docked, or to fish from canoes on the river. Beyond the tumble-down shacks were houses so magnificent that they rivaled the palaces of Rio and the homes of Westchester. They rose in the wilderness like overdecorated wedding cakes. Within those homes were telephones that didn't reach the outside world, and electricity that powered colored lights imported from Europe.

But what sparkled more than the lights were the diamonds. Manaus was the world's largest diamond market, and in many cases they were used instead of money. The children of the wealthy played with gold toys, and Cecilia felt that everyone she met was involved in a game to see who could spend the most.

But, Cecilia thought, it was all a struggle against nature. Indian laborers scrubbed marble statuary daily to keep it from being overgrown with fungus, while the wealthier inhabitants played at the game of civilization by attending the opera, going to the theater, dressing in all the latest European fashions, and eating the most expensive of imported foods. But they lived side by side with the Indians—men, women, and children who only a short time ago had lived a Stone Age existence and who now appeared to serve in slavery, bound over not so much by law as by the need to survive in a world that had taken a leap of centuries in a few short years.

And even the wealthy were a strange collection of the human species. The wealthiest woman in Manaus was a prostitute who read Boccaccio and who dressed like Mrs. Vanderbilt. There was a smattering of European nobility, and they mingled uneasily with illiterate rubber barons who came in all nationalities and personalities to rape the jungle and milk the precious trees for wealth. "In Manaus," Agosto told her, "there are saints and murderers, sophisticates and primitive Indians, money and poverty, and it's all here in this desolate place where rubber is king."

At first the sight of the Indians had shocked Cecilia. More ofen than not, the women were bare-breasted, nursing their babies as they worked. The men, too, dressed scantily, their red-brown bodies glimmering with sweat as they toiled in the miserable heat. At first they had looked ferocious. They were a short people, square of face and stony of expression. But soon Cecilia learned that they were truly shy; afraid of the Europeans, they shrank from all contact with them.

"Not only are they practically enslaved," Agosto explained, "but they die in large numbers from diseases carried by Europeans." Cecilia tried to understand, but she found the way of life in Manaus more distressing than interesting.

Each morning, Agosto met with a variety of people; in the afternoons both he and Cecilia slept; and in the evenings they attended parties or the theater. It was at night that Manaus came to life; the temperature dropped slightly, and occasionally a breeze came up to cross the patios of the fine homes that overlooked the river.

Cecilia counted the days in spite of the opera and the parties. They had been here two weeks, two weeks which included tours of various rubber plantations, inspections of dock and warehouse facilities, interminable discussions on the transfer of gold for payments, politics, and all that did or might threaten the future of the commodity that created the city and its wealthy citizens.

Cecilia took a last look at the view from the terrace. She had come out alone in search of cool air and solitude. She strolled back to the doors of the grand reception room and stood for a few minutes watching Agosto. He was speaking with an English plantation owner, but she noticed that Agosto spoke little, and he kept wiping his brow. After a time she intruded on them, moving to her husband's side protectively.

"You need some air," she said softly. "Come onto the patio with me."

Agosto took her arm and willingly allowed her to lead him to the patio. Again he wiped his brow, but this time he shivered.

"You're not well," Cecilia said with concern. "Agosto, don't you tell me an untruth. I know you're not well—I've been watching you all evening."

"I have a fever," he admitted.

Cecilia looked at the tile floor. She herself had suffered stomach upset, but she'd recovered. "Agosto, we can't leave tomorrow if you are ill."

He tried to smile. "And I know you're anxious to leave."

She nodded, and saw that he shivered again. Instinctively she reached up and felt his brow. He was burning hot.

"Dear heaven! You have a very high fever. Agosto, you must go to bed immediately!"

He gave her a look of defeat. "I think I'm having a malaria attack," he said quietly.

"Then you must go to bed, and we cannot go tomorrow!" She took his arm and guided him back inside and up the winding staircase to their room. She could feel tears forming: she wanted to go home. There wouldn't be another steamer for a week, they'd be delayed getting back to New York. She felt trapped. Agosto was terribly ill, even if he wouldn't admit it, and sadly, another week—or perhaps even more—seemed like an eternity.

Agosto sprawled out on the bed and grasped the covers about him in spite of the heat. He began to shake and shiver even as beads of sweat broke out on his forehead. Cecilia covered him with netting and took his hand. "I'm going to find a doctor," she said firmly. Agosto only nodded.

"Cecilia!" He called her name through a pitch-black haze. His arms grappled for her, but they touched only air. His teeth chattered uncontrollably, and everything before his eyes was darkness, though he felt certain his eyes were open. No shadows, no forms. "I'm going blind!" His voice pierced the silence. He saw the image of Philip Ainsley standing in front of him with outstretched hands. He heard the distant sound of a military band as it played on the road to the San Juan hills.

Philip Ainsley grew closer. "Come along, Agosto . . . come along. . . ."

"No! No!" Agosto shouted. He withdrew his hands and flailed his arms around. "I won't die! I'm not ready to die!" He felt soft hands on his face, damp wet cloths, and he shivered again, fighting away the cold. "Get away from me! For God's sake, give me a blanket! I'm freezing! I'm freezing to death!"

11

Friday, March 12, 1909

BROOKLYN

Donato Ferrante slumped on the sofa, having dropped off into a weary, troubled sleep. He had awakened in the morning with a terrible headache, and during his hours of work in the store, it had not gone away.

The newspaper behind which he hid was unfolded and untidy, having slipped to the floor.

Maria came into the room, and hands on hips, looked at him, exasperation and disgust visible on her face. "Donato!" she shouted loudly, and stamped her foot. His sleepy eyes opened and he looked at her questioningly. "You're asleep again! You're sleeping your whole life away! Wake up, you lazy self-centered pig!"

He jolted up and shook his head. "Don't talk to me like that! Tina will hear, your papa will hear! A woman shouldn't talk to her husband that way!"

Maria scowled at him. "Tina's asleep, Domenico and Fabiana have gone for a walk! Who do you think you're fooling!" She knew his tone of voice well. He tried to sound angry, but in reality he was intimidated. "No one will hear me, Donato! Of course they don't need to hear me call you a pig. It's true! Everyone knows you're a pig. Everyone knows you can't make a living except from my father, everyone in Brooklyn knows what a failure you are! Look at my brother, Donato. Look at Agosto. Agosto owns banks, Agosto has a fine new house. Agosto has servants and he takes his wife on trips and lavishes her with gifts. He even gives Paolo a decent job. And now Paolo is a big hero. But you, not even my brother would hire you! You're lazy and stupid and dull! And while Agosto's children will grow up to have everything, Tina will have nothing because her father is a lazy pig!"

Donato jumped to his feet. "Shut your mouth! I'm sick, I don't want to listen to you!" His face had gone beet red and he stepped toward her menacingly.

"That's the trouble. That's just the trouble! For years I've kept my mouth shut while you've lived off my father . . . while we lived in my father's house. For years I've kept silent! I have kept silent knowing that the only things in life that Tina will ever have will come from my brother—charity. That's what you have done, and you sleep in the chair like a king!"

"Silence! You haven't been silent a day since we've been married!" He glared at her, but in return met a look of pure hatred. He recoiled before her expression, and his eyes dropped as he muttered a curse.

"Have you nothing to say?" she demanded.

"I don't feel well—that's why I fell asleep."

"You don't feel well . . . you don't feel well! Where don't you feel well? Has your brain become active and given you a headache?"

"It's my arm—it aches . . . and so does my head." He reached upward and touched his brow. Who could feel healthy married to such a woman? But it was true, his arm did ache and he felt ill, even sicker than he'd felt in the morning.

"Your arm! Your head! Your arm is weak from lack of use, and your head is empty! You don't feel well? It is I who am slaving in this house from morning to night taking care of two men and a child. It is I who don't have a maid like Cecilia. I have to do everything. I even have to work in Agosto's bank to make extra money."

"You have Fabiana," Donato said defensively. His breath felt short, and a sudden sharp pain ripped through him.

"Little good she is! And why do I need extra money? Because you make nothing, because we are charity cases. I hate you! I hate this house! I . . ." She stopped short at the sound of Donato's deep guttural groan. His knees suddenly buckled beneath him like an accordion and he gripped the chair as he fell to the carpet gasping.

"Donato! What foolishness is this! You're trying to frighten me!" She moved toward him, and he suddenly fell backward, limp and grasping his chest. He screamed one long agonized scream, panted again, groaned, and his head seemed to go loose, falling to one side even as his great brown eyes stared vacantly upward.

"Donato?" Maria advanced on his crumpled form. She bent over and examined him. "Donato!" She screamed his name and shook him. Then, in a whisper: "Donato . . ." She shivered and crossed herself. Then she stood up quickly and backed away. She stared at his body and let out a long wail. "Papa! Fabiana!" Maria fell to her knees and shrieked again and again.

Saturday, March 13, 1909

M A N A U S

Cecilia's nightmare lasted two weeks. As helpful as their hosts, the Moravias, tried to be, nothing would ever blot out her experiences during Agosto's illness.

The doctor who was summoned spoke only German and thus Cecilia had to consult him through Mrs. Moravia, who was, more often than not, drunk. The doctor gave her instructions to keep Agosto cool, to rub his body with alcohol, and to keep him under the netting. He gave her quinine powder to administer. But he was German, and dour. He seemed to hold out little hope for Agosto, and his attitude made Cecilia even more fearful.

She stayed by Agosto's side night and day. He woke now and again, and she bathed him in cool cloths. Sometimes he talked to her rationally; other times he didn't seem to know her. At last, after twelve days, his fever broke.

Cecilia watched him with pleading eyes. "You're not well enough yet. Please, Agosto, please stay in bed another week till you regain your strength."

Agosto half-leaned against the bed as he buttoned his shirt. "You don't understand malaria or the tropics," he told her. "The longer you stay in bed, the weaker you get. I can rest on the voyage." He tried to smile. "After all, I don't have to run the ship, do I?"

Cecilia bit her lip. "I still think you should rest longer."

"Come, come. It's you who want to get back home. Don't tell me you want to be delayed another week? The steamer leaves in two hours, and we'll be on it."

"I don't want to stay, but if it's necessary for your health, I'd gladly be delayed."

"It's not. Are you fully packed?"

Cecilia pressed her lips together and nodded. "Let me help you." She stepped toward him.

"I think I can manage," he said stubbornly. She let out her breath in exasperation. "You lead the way."

Cecilia picked up her tapestry satchel and opened the door. Together they descended the winding staircase.

"Determined to leave in spite of your illness," Mr. Moravia said as he walked across the black-and-white tile floor to greet them. "Jungle curse—it gets everyone, you know. Mind you, if you live here long enough, you become immune."

"I've had it before," Agosto confided. "In Cuba."

"It's bad, but one recovers. I must say, you gave us a scare."

"I'm fine."

"Well, the carriage is outside to take you to the dock. What can I say? . . . Have a good voyage, keep healthy." He reached out and shook Agosto's hand. Then he bowed deeply and kissed Cecilia's.

Agosto responded with a pat on the back. "You've been an excellent host. And in spite of everything, I'd say we accomplished a great deal."

Moravia beamed. "We'll be in touch."

Agosto took Cecilia's arm, and they left.

"I did enjoy the opera," Agosto said as their carriage passed the magnificent Teatro Amazonas. He hearkened back to the performance they had witnessed. Not only was it a fine company imported from Italy, but the opera house itself was a masterpiece of old-world charm. It had 632 red-velvet-cushioned seats, which were occupied by rich but often illiterate men and women. It cost ten million dollars to build in 1896 and was a scaled-down version of Milan's La Scala. The iron frame was fabricated in Scotland and shipped to Manaus. The pure silk panels along the walls were imported from China, the marble floors from Portugal, the chandeliers from Venice. The finest artists in Europe were hired to paint masks of famous composers and murals to decorate the hall. Outside, the dome of the opera house glistened in the sunlight. It was made of over sixty-six thousand hand-painted French tiles. All the surrounding streets were paved with rubber to muffle the sound of traffic inside the building, so that outside noise would not mar the performance.

"I enjoyed it too," Cecilia said, taking a last glance at the glittering dome. "But one day the jungle will take it back . . . it will take this whole place back."

Agosto laughed. "You may be right."

She sighed again. "I just feel it. There's something temporary about it. It's new, but it's decaying."

He smiled at her. Sometimes she was wonderfully intuitive. She managed to put his half-formed thoughts into words. But that was always when they were alone. Among strangers she was quiet and withdrawn.

"You're right," he said, patting her knee. "There is an essence of decay."

The carriage came to a clattering halt, and the driver, a coal-black man, helped them down onto the wooden plank that led to the steamer.

The English captain, dressed in spotless white, greeted them.

Agosto smiled at him. "We'll go aboard now," he said as Cecilia helped him up the rickety gangplank.

"Your luggage is already stowed away," the captain informed them with a wave. "We sail in one hour."

"Not a moment too soon," Cecilia whispered. "Oh, Agosto, I will be glad to get home!"

"But it's been an adventure," Agosto said, winking.

Cecilia shook her head. "An age of parties, you so sick I thought you would die . . . I think I can live without adventures."

Agosto leaned over and kissed her forehead. "You'll feel better when we catch our ship in Macapá."

"I'll feel better when there's a cool ocean breeze," she replied honestly.

Wednesday, March 17, 1909

MANHATTAN

Paolo felt good, even though Luigi's was a tiny, relatively unimpressive restaurant. The food was tasty enough, he decided, and watching Vince and Angelica eat and drink gave him immense pleasure. I certainly need distractions, he admitted.

Donato's sudden death had truly shaken him, but Donato was forty-nine, fully nineteen years his senior. Still, it made him think. It was true that he was happier working here in Little Italy, and it was true that he was well known and liked in the community. It was also a fact that he had made a great success of the bank. On the one hand, Paolo felt he had accomplished a great deal. But on the other, he admitted how unhappy he was married to Fabiana, how miserable he was not to have a son, and how much he truly hated going home on the weekends.

Paolo wrapped the pasta around his fork and glanced at Angelica. She was four months pregnant, and although her stomach had begun to swell slightly, she still looked frail and delicate. Her large eyes expressed her fondness for him, and he in turn fantasized about holding her, making love to her, and being a father to her child. He had seen her often since hiring her brother, and each time he felt a greater longing for her as his sexual desires mixed with feelings of protectiveness toward her.

"Where do you go every weekend?" Vince asked, taking a gulp of wine.

"To visit my aging father," Paolo answered, neglecting to mention his wife. "I'd invite you, but my father is feeble and very strict. He wouldn't understand Angelica's condition . . . I mean, the fact she isn't married. You understand how it can be, hey?"

Vince nodded, and ignoring the fact that his sister was sitting next to him, shook his head dejectedly. "I don't know what to do with her. Who will marry her? No dowry, another man's kid to support."

Angelica must have understood, though Vince spoke in English. She blushed, lowered her eyes, and Paolo thought he saw tears forming. "I would!" he blurted out.

Vince looked at him steadily. "She's pregnant," he reiterated.

"I know that. I don't care." A thousand thoughts ran through Paolo's mind. He could get a small apartment and use his aging father as an excuse to go home on weekends . . . eventually he would leave Fabiana . . . but in the meantime, who would know? He only saw Agosto at business meetings. No one came to visit him in Manhattan.

Vince's eyes seemed to bore through him. "You mean marry her properly?" he questioned.

"Of course!" Paolo said. "At City Hall . . . properly." Visions of Angelica wrapped in his arms at night sped through his head. Visions of holding the child he would make his. Perhaps he could eventually get a church annulment, since Fabiana was barren. But it would be necessary to keep it all a secret for a while. Neither Domenico nor Agosto would countenance his leaving Fabiana, not to mention bigamy. He couldn't risk losing his job, not at least till he had something else.

"You sure?" Vince prodded. "Most men, especially one in your position, wouldn't want her now."

"I'm sure," Paolo answered.

Angelica lifted her eyes. She certainly had understood part of the conversation. Big tears of gratitude streamed down her lovely face, and she looked at him longingly.

"Yes, I want to marry her," Paolo pledged.

Thursday, March 18, 1909

MACAPÁ

Cecilia sat in the luxurious cabin on the *Maria Christina*, which they had boarded only twenty minutes ago, having journeyed up the Amazon and spent one night in Macapá waiting for the ocean liner that would take them back to New York. Agosto went immediately to the communications room of the ship. There was no telegraph service to Manaus from Macapá on the coast, so he'd been out of touch for nearly three weeks.

Cecilia leaned back on the bed and relished the cool sea breeze that swept into the room through the open porthole. "I never want to go to the tropics again!" she said aloud. "I never want to leave home again," she added. The sudden opening of the cabin door caused her to jump, and she sat up, immediately seeing the look of distress on Agosto's face.

"What is it? Are the children all right?" Certainly there was bad news—Agosto held a sheaf of wires in his hand.

"It's not the children. They're fine."

"What, then? Is something wrong at the banks?"

Agosto shook his head and sat down on the edge of the bed. "It's Donato. He died of a heart attack."

Cecilia's face clouded over. "Oh, poor Donato . . . poor Tina and Maria."

"I sent a wire back."

"It's terrible." Cecilia closed her eyes and leaned back against the pillows. "He was such a good man. Not talkative, but a good father."

Agosto nodded. Certainly Donato was a better father than Maria was a mother. And, Agosto thought sadly, he'd certainly been forbearing with Maria. "Tina will miss him."

"Oh, Agosto, you must try to make it up to her. You must be a father to her. She's such a lonely child. Maria's harsh with her, and I know she longs for affection."

"I'll do my best," Agosto promised. "God, what will become of Maria now? I suppose she'll put on black and never take it off."

"Your sister is a bitter woman," Cecilia observed.

"I think that's an understatement. She was reclusive before, but now she'll be even more so."

"Oh, Agosto, we must do more to make Maria and Tina part of our lives." Cecilia took his hand, and her expressive eyes pleaded with him. "They're family, Agosto."

He leaned over and kissed her, feeling a rising passion born of her beauty and goodness. No man could ask for a better wife. Her love was unshakable, and she reached out, loving and drawing the family to her. "I adore you," Agosto said, kissing her neck. "I need you, Cecilia, I'll always need you."

Wednesday, March 31, 1909

NEW YORK

"Mama! Papa!" Clare broke away from Seraphina and ran across the crowded platform. Agosto held out his arms, and she leapt into them, hugging him and giggling. "Don't go away again!" She kissed his cheek, and Agosto could feel her soft skin against the rough stubble on his face.

"Clare Marina!" Cecilia held out her arms and took Clare from Agosto. "Oh, I've missed you!"

"Did you bring me a present? What is South America like, Mama? Grandpapa says it's down under the earth, so Anthony thinks it's in our basement! He cried to go to the basement so he could see you! He's a baby. Fabiana showed me South America on the map and read me a story about it!"

"You're a babbling brook!" Agosto laughed as he turned to greet the others. "Anthony!" Three-year-old Anthony wrapped himself around his father's legs, and Agosto and Cecilia bent down to kiss and hug him.

"Oh, my babies," Cecilia breathed.

Anthony shoved at Clare and screamed.

"Sh!" Clare said to her brother. "Stop being a baby!"

Agosto grinned. "He *is* a baby!"

Clare straightened up. "But he shouldn't act like one."

Agosto smiled in spite of himself. He turned to hug Maria. "I wasn't here when you needed me," he said, searching her eyes, which were obscured by her dark widow's veil of mourning. She didn't reply, but only nodded.

Cecilia hugged Fabiana. She was dressed in a blue woolen suit that like all her clothes was too tight. But in the light of Cecilia's warmth, her round face beamed.

"You've been good to the children while I was gone," Cecilia whispered. "Thank you."

"I love them," Fabiana replied shyly. She refrained from adding that since she did not have children, Clare Marina and Anthony were a special joy in her empty life.

Agosto looked around. "Where's Papa?"

"He's not well," Maria answered quickly.

A look of concern came over Agosto's face. "Is it serious?"

Maria shook her head. "Only a cold, but the doctor said he should stay in bed for a few days."

He didn't bother to ask after Paolo. It was a weekday and Paolo was obviously at the bank and had sent Fabiana in his place to welcome them back. "Who's managing the store?" Agosto asked.

"We hired someone for a few weeks, and I check every day," Maria answered. The unspoken hung between them. Agosto had wanted to say that some arrangements must be made now that Donato was gone, but he held the comment. This was a homecoming. They were all standing on Pier 43 of the docks, with hundreds of people milling about. Questions as well as answers would have to wait. There was plenty of time for family business. And now that he had stepped ashore, he felt the pressure of his own responsibilities. For weeks he had had only telegraph contact with his banks. Business went on, but there were many things to do. His working holiday and adventure were over.

"What did you bring me?" Clare persisted. She tugged on his pants leg and searched his face with her huge brown eyes.

Agosto smiled. He remembered his return from Cuba and all the gifts he'd brought. Those gifts were simple; now his luggage overflowed with expensive presents.

"Everything is packed away and I'm afraid you will have to wait until we get home. You can't have your presents till everyone else has theirs."

Clare thrust out her lower lip and pouted. "Will I have to wait long?"

"Only till we get home."

She sighed with impatience. Cecilia took her hand. "I think we should go home now." They moved as a group, Agosto leading the way, with Maria at his side, Clare and her mother behind, Fabiana and Anthony bringing up the rear.

"It's good to be home." Agosto looked straight ahead. He and Maria would have to talk, but he pushed it out of his mind. He wasn't certain he wanted to talk to her. Widow's black veil or no, he could sense her lack of emotion over Donato's sudden death. Her face bore no unhappiness, her eyes revealed no sign of tears, indeed she looked more placid than she'd looked for a long time, and he found that distressing.

Seraphina opened the door and hugged Cecilia, who bounded into the house with uncharacteristic enthusiasm. She twirled about, dropping her satchel on a nearby chair. "I feel like dancing!" she sang out. "It's so good to be home!" She moved around the room drinking in its warm familiarity. She smiled. "Look how clean it is! Just as I left it. And the children are happy and healthy. Oh, I never want to leave again!"

Agosto laughed. "I told you everything would be fine."

Cecilia sighed. "I'm glad it is, but a little disappointed that everyone seems to get on so well without me." Her expression was happy, and Agosto squeezed her shoulders gently. "I could never get on without you," he whispered.

Maria had been let off at home, and Agosto had promised to come within the hour to see his father. But for the moment he dropped lazily into one of the comfortable chairs in the living room while Clare and Anthony swarmed over him.

Cecilia took Fabiana's plump arm. "Let's have a cup of nice hot tea," she suggested. Fabiana nodded gratefully and followed Cecilia into the kitchen.

"Oh, I've missed you," Fabiana said, sitting down. "Maria doesn't talk to me, and Paolo . . . Paolo is never home."

Cecilia put on the kettle and sat down. She reached across the table and took Fabiana's hand. "I'm glad to be back," she said sincerely, "and very glad to see you."

"I came all the time to be with the children. Seraphina is good, but she's not family."

Cecilia nodded. "I know."

Fabiana bit her lip and looked down. Her face was clouded with unhappiness, with words unspoken.

"It's been a sad time," Cecilia concluded. "Donato's death . . . it's terrible that we weren't here."

Fabiana nodded. "He was kind," she said, almost in a whisper.

"Is something the matter, Fabiana?"

Again Fabiana nodded. "I won't trouble you now."

"Please, tell me."

Fabiana shrugged helplessly. "It's Paolo," she said, leaning over and continuing to whisper. "Please don't tell Agosto . . ."

"Don't tell him what?"

"Oh, I don't know. It's just that Paolo has been acting so strange lately. I don't know what's wrong . . . I don't know if anything *is* wrong."

"Do you think something's wrong at the bank?" Cecilia pressed.

Fabiana shook her head. "I don't know. I only know he's not himself."

No, it can't be the bank, Cecilia thought. Agosto had been in touch with both Roberto and Paolo. He would know if something were wrong. "Perhaps he's just tired and overworked, Fabiana."

Cecilia studied Fabiana's expression. She was a sad, sweet woman, and it was no secret that she and Paolo had a loveless marriage. But she wasn't bitter like Maria. She worked hard and made the most of her life. She loved to be with Clare most of all, and accepted her role in the family without complaint, tried to be a good wife to Paolo, who rewarded her by ignoring her. But Paolo had always ignored her, so Cecilia assumed that Fabiana's distress was based on more than the usual problems that existed between them.

"In what way is he strange?" Cecilia prodded.

"He seems . . . well, completely distracted." Fabiana leaned over, and her face turned a deep red as she whispered, "He doesn't sleep with me anymore."

"When did this begin?" Cecilia asked, trying not to sound shocked. A loveless marriage was one thing, but men had physical needs, and Fabiana's confession was troubling indeed.

"Soon after you left."

"Perhaps it's just overwork. Now that Agosto has had his vacation, Paolo should have his. He should take you on a trip, Fabiana."

"He wouldn't take me anywhere," she murmured.

"May I suggest to Agosto that Paolo needs a vacation?"

Fabiana nodded silently and reached across the table and took Cecilia's hand. "It is so good to have you home, so good to have a woman to talk to . . ." Her words trailed off and tears formed in her eyes. "I'm so lonely," she confessed.

Friday, April 2, 1909

MANHATTAN

Vince and Paolo agreed that the marriage should take place as soon as possible because of Angelica's condition. But Paolo, fearing discovery, insisted they travel by train and be married in New Haven. "My father would never understand," he told them, knowing there was no chance a civil ceremony in Connecticut would ever get in any paper his father read. And what legal authority cared about Italian bigamists? To Paolo's way of thinking, no one outside of Italians cared what Italians did.

Paolo felt lighthearted in spite of everything. It was as if Fabiana didn't exist, as if there was no family in Sheepshead Bay.

He propped himself up and gazed on Angelica. Her small brown nipples were relaxed now, and she slept peacefully next to him like a child. He bent over and kissed her smooth skin. She was indescribable! When he held her, she pressed herself to him, and she had moaned with pleasure beneath him. For his part, he had tried to be gentle—she was so tiny, so vulnerable, so lovely. Her skin smelled sweet and her hair was thick and rich, a mass of curls. He lightly ran his finger across her stomach. "Our child," he whispered. It didn't matter that someone else was the father, nothing mattered but holding her, caressing her, and protecting her. His eyes grew misty, and he thought that for the first time he understood what Agosto had with Cecilia. "My little doll," he murmured, again kissing her neck.

She opened her eyes and automatically put her arms around his neck. "Mio Paolo," she whispered, following his name with words of endearment.

"I have to go to see my father tomorrow," he told her.

"I know," she whispered back.

"And you understand why I can't take you?"

"Yes," she replied, pressing her small naked body against him.

Paolo groaned and again kissed her dark nipple, which hardened beneath his lips. "I love you," he murmured, and he moved his hands across her smooth skin. "I have never loved anyone or anything so much as you." He lifted her hands to his lips. They were still red and sore from the long hours she spent working in the garment factory. Paolo kissed them, envisaging her labor and thinking about the evil employers who hired such young girls. He kissed her hands again and again, and he wept, murmuring, "I'll protect you, I'll take care of you."

Saturday, April 3, 1909

BROOKLYN

Agosto sat on the edge of his father's bed. "You're still not feeling well," he suggested, holding Domenico's hand.

"It's nothing!" Domenico protested. He withdrew his hand and doubled it into a fist. "I'm as strong as an ox! I've nothing but a cold! Everyone is making a hill out of an ant mountain!"

Agosto smiled. His father's English was quite good, but whenever he used an idiom, it was never quite right. "You'll stay in bed till you are well. Then you'll get permanent help with the store. Not that you need to work there at all. You should retire, travel, rest."

"No! Work keeps me alive. I'll work until I drop. I'll work until they close the lid on my coffin."

"That's foolish. You should sell the store, go back to Italy on a trip."

Domenico shook his head. "I'll never sell the store that your mother and I built together. It's my life, Agosto."

"Don't you want to go back to Italy?"

"Next year, but just for a vacation."

"You've been saying 'next year' for ten years, Papa."

"Well, this time I mean it. Now, stop nattering at me as if you were Gina. Tell me about Brazil. Tell me everything!"

"You're a stubborn man, Papa."

"Good," Domenico said with satisfaction.

"He does need help in the store," Paolo said from the far side of the room.

Agosto looked up. "All things in good time." Cecilia was right, Agosto thought. Paolo did look tired, and he kept talking about going back to Manhattan on Sunday night instead of Monday morning.

"Well, if I can't get Papa to take a vacation, I can get you to take one, Paolo."

Paolo's hands tensed and he shook his head vigorously. "No!" he said too suddenly.

Agosto laughed. "What do you mean, no? You should take Fabiana on a trip. I've had my adventure, you should have yours. Come on, I'm not a slave driver, and besides, travel will be good for you."

Paolo shook his head. "It's too busy, I couldn't leave now."

Agosto scowled at him. "Are you hiding some big deal from me?"

Paolo shook his head again, though he could feel the blood draining from his face. "Of course not," he stuttered, fully aware of his sudden nervousness and of his damp palms.

"Then you'll go. I absolutely insist. You'll take Fabiana to Europe. Go see Italy. I have business you could see to in Naples."

"I can't."

"You can!" Agosto walked across the room and put his arm around his brother's shoulders. "You will," he repeated.

Paolo felt the weight of Agosto's arm; it was like lead. He searched the pattern on the flowered rug with his eyes, unable to look Agosto in the eyes. "I'm not going!" he shouted. "I'm not leaving!"

Agosto stared at him. "I was suggesting a vacation, not a punishment."

"No," Paolo said, turning away. He ran out of the room, and in a moment Agosto heard the front door close with a slam.

"My God," he said in surprise.

Domenico frowned. "There's something the matter with him."

Agosto twisted his mustache and pulled at it in agitation. Fabiana's concern, relayed to him through Cecilia, and Domenico's comment both seemed understated.

Friday, May 21, 1909

MANHATTAN

Luigi Antonini was with the International Ladies Garment Workers and Frank Bellanca belonged to the Amalgamated Clothing Workers of America.

"We have to stick together!" Antonini shouted at the gathering. "Unions are the future! They're all that'll protect the workers from the exploitation of capitalists, who don't think of people, but only of workers! Workers, an anonymous horde who represent profits for industry! And where are those profits? Are they put into your housing?"

The small crowd shouted, "No! No! No!" in unison and stamped their feet.

"Do you see those profits on your dinner tables?"

"No! No! No!" the gathering again shouted.

"Do you see them in the weary faces of your daughters? Thirteen-, fourteen-year-olds working in their sweat shops! Working long hours, working without protection! Working without decent wages! I'll tell you where you can see those profits! You can see them in the mansions of Westchester! You can see them in the tall buildings being erected for their benefit! You can see them in the roads being built for their fine cars! You can see them in the big stores! Stores you can't afford to shop in! But who makes all this money? Do their daughters work in the shops for a few pennies an hour?"

"No!" the people shouted, and Paolo shouted too.

"We make the money! They reap the benefits! This isn't justice! And their women—their women, like Mrs. Catt—say, 'Give us the vote! If you give us the vote, we'll have enough numbers to keep the dagos out of office!' Well, we come to America and we work hard! And we want our share! We want justice!"

"Yes!" they shouted.

"We want better wages and decent conditions to work and live! We want enough food for our children! You gotta join the union! You can't be afraid because they want you to be afraid!"

Paolo took Angelica's hand and wrapped it in his as Luigi Antonini continued to speak. He knew, as he listened, he couldn't stay with the bank. It was part of the exploitation, part of the injustice. How many garment factories did Agosto have investments in? How many big companies that exploited workers used Agosto's banks? He bit his lip and looked at the ground even as Antonini's words burned in his ears. "I have to help," he said under his breath. And in his heart he knew he'd found his niche. He spoke both Italian and English. He'd go to work for one of the unions and help protect girls like Angelica from long hours, poor pay, and intolerable working conditions. He'd seen those factories, he'd seen what they did to people.

Friday, June 4, 1909

B R O O K L Y N

Lines of workers stood at the wickets of the Italian Bank waiting to deposit their weekly earnings. Behind the counter five tellers worked busily, updating savings-account books and taking payments on loans. Behind the counter Agosto worked quietly at his desk, looking up now and again to acknowledge one of his many personal friends who came into the bank.

"Hey, Agosto!"

Agosto looked up and waved a friendly greeting to old Salvatore Giuliano.

"How's your papa? Is that old man back in his shop yet?"

"He is," Agosto replied, getting up from his desk. He walked over to the counter and shook Salvatore's hand. "You should go see him, he needs old friends."

Salvatore grinned a toothless smile. "It's his turn to come to me. I don't go out much anymore."

"Oh," Agosto answered. "I'll remind him."

"Hey, when you going to have the annual bank picnic on Staten Island? Last year I heard it was quite a celebration. Marco, your teller, he took Rosa, my wife's niece, and she had some stories!"

Agosto laughed. Only a few years ago, all the employees of the Italian Bank could get onto one ferry. Now, with over ten banks and a hundred and fifty employees, they had to go in waves. "Fourth of July like always!" Agosto answered. Then he leaned over. "I think Marco will ask Rosa again."

The large door of the bank swung open and Agosto looked up to see his sister. As always she was dressed in black from head to toe, but much to his relief he saw she'd given up her widow's veils. She walked over and stood silently.

"Ah, Maria!" Salvatore bowed to her formally.

Maria smiled her tight-lipped smile. "Good day," she said coolly.

Agosto had only to look at her to know her unexpected visit was not a friendly call. Her face was unusually tense and she clutched her bag tightly.

"What brings you here?" he asked, trying to sound casual.

"We must talk."

Agosto glanced around uneasily. "It's Friday. You know how busy Fridays are."

"We must talk," she insisted.

"A little secret business," Salvatore said with a wave of his hand.

Maria neither replied nor smiled.

Agosto grasped Salvatore's shoulder and squeezed it. "Can you excuse me, my friend?"

Salvatore looked only bemused. "One must never keep a lady waiting—not even one's dear sister."

Agosto gripped Maria's arm and led her away. "We can sit at my desk," he suggested.

"No! We must be alone. I told you, you should have an office!" She sighed in exasperation. "There is nowhere here to talk privately."

"And what's such a big secret and why are you here? I thought you were at the Coney Island branch."

"I took part of the afternoon off, and it's a good thing I did! It's a good thing I was home!"

"What is it? Is Papa all right?"

"Yes, yes . . . it is not Papa. We can't talk here, Agosto. Not about this."

Agosto glanced at his watch. "We'll walk, then, but only for a few minutes. It's really busy today, and I've got to make a number of calls to Manhattan."

Maria turned and headed out the door, Agosto following in her wake. She looks like a thunder cloud, he thought. And the damn woman is going to rain all over this beautiful June day.

"Down by the bay," Maria said flatly. She led and Agosto followed. She walked with surprising briskness, looking purposeful and strong. He caught up and walked alongside her in silence.

"I thought we were supposed to talk," he ventured.

"At the sea wall," Maria said vaguely.

They stopped at the sea wall and Maria sat down and patted the hard stone beside her. Agosto sat down too, his nose sniffing the familiar aroma of fish and the sea, his eyes drinking in the colorful boats that filled the harbor.

"We used to come here as children," Maria said.

Agosto looked at her in surprise. Her tone was almost wistful and her voice seemed to have softened slightly. Her eyes too were different; they held a faraway look, as if she were remembering happier times, times when she was less brittle, times when she too had laughed and played, climbing on and off the boats.

"I remember," Agosto said, surrendering to her mood.

"And do you remember the day we sat here, you and I and Paolo? Remember, we pledged always to be loyal to one another?"

Agosto smiled. "I remember. But we're loyal with or without that pledge, we're family."

She turned suddenly; the wistful expression had disappeared as if it were a fluffy cloud dissipated by the north wind. Her face was again hard and tight, her lips pressed. Instantly she had gone from young again to old. "Something terrible has happened."

"What?" Agosto asked with irritation.

"Paolo is gone. I came home and he was packing everything. Fabiana was crying and sobbing and Papa was in a rage."

"Gone? Maria, what are you talking about?"

"Paolo, he's left Fabiana. He says she's barren, he says he will divorce her. He left this for you!" She thrust a note at him. "It's his resignation from the bank. He told me he has a job, something about being an organizer for something. Agosto, he says his marriage to Fabiana was only a church marriage. Only! He says he's found a woman he loves. He's gone mad, Agosto! He's disgraced us! Papa says if Paolo ever comes back he'll kill him!"

Agosto opened his mouth and tried to make sense of her words.

"I'll never be able to face any of my friends again!" Maria shouted. "How could he do this to me! To Papa! To Tina! What will people say? He's godless! He's given up the church, he's run off with some Sicilian woman . . . I think Fabiana will die. How can she ever hold up her head again?"

Agosto shook his head. "She hasn't done anything," he said weakly. Maria's tirade was incredibly self-centered, but there was no question of Paolo's disgrace. "I better go see Papa," Agosto concluded.

"He's still in a rage—he's so furious I'm afraid he'll have an attack. He was throwing things of Paolo's out the door after him. He went on screaming and crying for an hour!"

Agosto took his sister's arm. "I'll stop at the bank and tell them I have to go home," he said, still feeling in a bit of a daze. Paolo was doing so well. What could possess him to do such a thing?

12

Saturday, March 25, 1911

MANHATTAN

"You can talk good" was what they always told him, and Paolo knew it was true. He was employed by the Industrial Workers of the World and he talked not only to workers but also to management on their behalf. Management. He spit if he thought about them. How could Agosto have lived in Little Italy so long and not seen anything! Well, Agosto with his fine banks and his growing wealth thought he was doing something! And maybe Agosto wasn't as bad as some, but Paolo knew that Agosto made plenty of money investing in factories, and those factories were practically using slave labor. The American system! In the past two years Paolo had learned something about the American system: it bled immigrants, got them lined up row after row— "like sardines in a can," Vince would say. Don't pay them much, overwork them, use children, do anything, but make sure there's profit. That was the American system, and it was the system that had made Agosto rich.

Paolo bit his lip and watched as Angelica dressed. It was five A.M. and little Mario was still asleep. Paolo looked about; the apartment was untidy from the night before—there had been a meeting. He sighed. It wasn't a large apartment, nor was his salary large, but they had enough, and for the first time in his life, Paolo knew he had a purpose.

"I hate to have you working in that place," he said as Angelica pinned on her hat.

She turned and smiled at him. She had the sweetest smile in the world. No matter what, the last two years had been the happiest of his life.

"If I don't work there, how can we know about the conditions?" she answered. "Anyway, I get twelve dollars a week!"

"For slaving at a sewing machine for ten hours. For having to work on Saturday without extra pay."

"There's a big order to fill," Angelica answered. She went to the crib and looked at Mario. "You take him to Mrs. Battaglia when he wakes up."

"I will, and I'll feed him and dress him and kiss him good-bye."

She came over to him and took his hands. "You're such a good father, Paolo. You're such a good man, and I'm so lucky."

Her eyes danced and he pulled her into his arms and kissed her passionately. She was three months pregnant, and this time he was the father, though in fact he thought of himself as Mario's father too. "I love you," he said. "Angelica, I've never known such happiness." Then he looked at her sternly. "Information or not, I won't have you working there for more than another week."

She nodded and smiled. "You'll come and get me at closing?"

"I'll be there, and we'll go have dinner at Luigi's."

He kissed her again and watched her hurry out the door. He hated it when she worked on Saturday—he hated having her work at all.

The Triangle Shirtwaist Factory was housed in three large rooms on the eighth, ninth, and tenth floors of the Asch Building on the corner of Washington Place and Greene Street. Some eight hundred and fifty girls worked there, tightly packed in rows and rows in front of their sewing machines. Paolo knew most of the girls were fourteen or fifteen. They earned ten dollars a week for working six days a week, thirteen hours a day. Angelica got a little more, because she was older and had more experience and spoke English now, which most of the other girls didn't.

Paolo comforted himself: Angelica wouldn't be working there much longer. Her work had a purpose, though in fact the Triangle Shirtwaist Factory was no worse than many others. But it and four sweat shops on Elizabeth Street had been singled out for special scrutiny. Information was needed to press demands, and more often than not, the girls who worked in such places were too frightened to talk, fearing they might lose their jobs or be deported.

Paolo shook his head; it was discouraging trying to organize workers. They had to be made to realize their value. Instead, they saw their salaries as valuable, and feared losing them, even if they were underpaid.

He thrust his hands in his pockets and headed down the street. He stopped suddenly as he heard the sound of fire engines. They turned, and with a sudden chill he realized they were heading in the same direction as he. Paolo quickened his step, then in sheer panic began to run.

By the time he was in sight of the factory, flames were jutting from the windows, and dark black smoke poured from the building. Still a block away, he could hear the shrill screams of women.

The police held a line in front of the building. A huge crowd gathered; some had tense tight faces, and others screamed, matching the shrieks of fear and agony of the women who stood at the windows, their backs to the flames, their eyes on the sheer drop below.

Paolo pushed and shoved through the crowd. "My wife's in there!" he shouted. His eyes were already filled with tears, but he stopped dead as a flaming woman leapt through a tenth-floor window and fell straight through the fireman's net to death on the sidewalk below. Paolo's mouth opened, but it was dry and he couldn't even shout. Four more women jumped, then more— skirts and shrieks in the wind—and from inside the building he could hear the pitiful cries of women and girls being burned alive.

Paolo could see the interior of the building in his mind's eye: there were heavy locked steel doors to the main entrance. There was only one long narrow corridor of escape; that was because the owners checked each girl as she left to see that she wasn't stealing anything. No more than one person at a time could squeeze through that corridor.

"The fire escape out back has collapsed," someone shouted. "It had too many people on it!"

Paolo pushed his way to the police line. "Let me through," he wailed, "let me go in there! My wife! My wife's in there!"

The large Irish policeman seized his shoulders roughly. "Stand back! Get back, you dirty dago!"

Paolo doubled his fist and struck the policeman, who without hesitation brought his nightstick down on Paolo's head, causing him to stagger backward, blood running into his eyes. He looked upward and let out a long agonized wail. The blood was blinding him, but he saw Angelica on the ledge, her hair blowing in the wind. "No!" he screamed, and it was as if he was alone and there was no crowd. She jumped, her checkered skirts billowing around her, and fell like a tiny broken doll on the sidewalk.

Paolo sank to his knees. "Angelica!" he wailed like a wounded animal. Tears flowed from his eyes and mixed with the blood on his cheeks. "You'll pay!" he shouted to no one and everyone. "Someone will pay for this! God in heaven! They're murderers! Filthy pigs! Dirty capitalist murderers!"

Paolo didn't even feel the nightstick when it came down the second time. He was numb, and he collapsed in a puddle of his own blood, sobbing even as he lost consciousness.

Sunday, March 26, 1911

MANHATTAN

Agosto stood in the waiting room of police headquarters at 100 Centre Street. He felt ill-at-ease and shifted his weight restlessly from one foot to the other. It was a dismal place, all black and white tile, with dim light bulbs and perfunctory personnel. He lifted his hand to his mustache and pulled on it with irritation. For God's sake, he'd paid the fine, where was Paolo?

Agosto stared at the floor. It was Cecilia who'd taken the call, and Cecilia who had convinced him to come, even though he hadn't seen Paolo for nearly two years. Not that he didn't know what Paolo was doing. A labor organizer indeed! Well, this was what came of organizing labor—you ended up in jail with your head cracked open. Paolo was a disgrace! Leaving Fabiana, running off with another woman, making speeches and getting into trouble.

"He's all yours," the burly policeman said, shoving Paolo toward Agosto with disgust.

Paolo's head was swathed in bandages. He looked at Agosto defiantly in spite of his condition.

"Come on," Agosto said, taking his arm. "I'll take you home, wherever that is."

Paolo didn't answer, but he followed Agosto out into the daylight. It must have been four or five in the afternoon, but he wasn't certain.

Agosto led his brother to his waiting car. "Where to?"

"Sullivan Street," Paolo answered.

Agosto climbed in and sat tense behind the steering wheel. His mind wandered back to the call from police headquarters and to his conversation with Cecilia. "You have to go and get him out," Cecilia had said. "It's only right, Agosto, he's your brother."

"He's a bastard," Agosto had replied. But she had prevailed upon him. "You don't have to make up with him, just go and get him out. Agosto, do it for me, do it because he's family."

So, reluctantly, he had come. Now, sitting in stony silence, he was almost sorry. Whatever the reason for his being in jail, Paolo seemed totally unrepentant.

"Here," Paolo said as the car came to a halt in front of the building where he lived. Agosto watched as Paolo climbed out; then, out of sheer curiosity, he parked and followed Paolo up the narrow staircase of the decaying building.

"Why are you following me?" Paolo asked accusingly.

"I thought you might offer me a drink," Agosto replied tersely. "I did come all the way over here to get you out, and it's a long trip back."

Paolo opened the door and Agosto followed him in.

"This where you keep her?" Agosto asked meanly.

Paolo turned on him, his face ashen and angry. "She's dead!" he shouted. "Dead in that fire yesterday! I was trying to get to her . . . the police wouldn't let me . . ." His voice trailed off for a minute. "She was my wife, she was pregnant! I know you don't understand, I don't expect you to understand how much I loved her. But think about Cecilia working in a place like that, think about her being trapped by the flames and screaming for you! Think about that, Agosto Tonelli, Mr. Banker! Think about girls hardly older than Clare Marina working thirteen hours a day, six days a week! That's what Italians do! You know how many of those little girls were Italians?" Tears were running down Paolo's face, and it was distorted with pain and emotion.

Agosto steadied himself, holding on to the chair. He had never seen Paolo this way, never heard him speak so passionately, never seen him filled with such emotion. "I didn't know she was dead," he managed. "I read about the fire, Paolo. It was a terrible tragedy."

"Read about it! That's you, read, read, read! Do you know anything from living? That tragedy could have been prevented!"

"I don't deny that. You can't think I approve of sweat shops or those kinds of working conditions!"

"You just *think* you don't approve. What the hell do you invest in, anyway! Well, god damn it, I'm going to do something about it!"

"Strikes and violence are not the way to—"

"What the hell do you know about it? What should the workers do, Agosto, invite the bloodsuckers to a tea party?"

"Paolo—"

"Don't Paolo me! Two years ago I was disowned! Well, now I disown you, you upper-class dago bastard! I thank you for getting me out of jail—I'll never bother you again on that score!

Now, get the hell out of here!" Paolo's tears were flowing down his face. He looked around the apartment, thinking that Mario was still with Mrs. Battaglia. "Get out of here! Dammit, I've got a kid to raise!"

Friday, August 4, 1911

BROOKLYN

"Eight years old, Clare Marina! You're growing up so fast!" Domenico kissed his granddaughter. Clare was dressed in a long white dress, her dark curls pulled back and held with a white satin ribbon. "You're pretty like your mama," Domenico observed. "Isn't she, Agosto?"

"You'll make her vain," Agosto scolded his father gently, though in fact he agreed with him. Clare was beautiful, and as bright as a newly minted penny.

Fabiana, Maria, and Cecilia had collaborated on Clare's birthday dinner. Anthony, who was almost seven, remained outside riding his new tricycle, under the watchful eye of his ten-year-old cousin Tina.

Domenico squinted at the clock on the wall. Cataracts clouded his brown eyes, and he was stooped and stiff as he approached his seventy-fifth birthday. "What time is it?" he asked.

"Six-thirty. We'll be eating at eight."

Domenico nodded and sipped some wine. He smiled at Clare Marina. "As young as I am old," he mumbled wistfully.

Domenico was growing more sentimental with age. He wept more and he often spoke of Gina as if she were still alive. He spent little time in the shop now, leaving its care to Maria and Fabiana. But it was Fabiana who meant the most to him. She cared for him and read to him. She took him for walks along the bay and didn't complain when he talked for hours about the past.

"I'm going to join your mother soon," Domenico muttered.

"Papa, you're still healthy," Agosto protested. He hated it when his father spoke of death. But he had only to look at his father to know that the prediction would soon become a reality.

"Papa, you should see Paolo," Agosto ventured. "It's been a long while, and you should see him."

Domenico's face turned red immediately and he shook his head angrily, causing his white hair to fly. "Never. Paolo is dead to me," he replied evenly. "I will never forgive him. Never!"

Agosto shook his head sadly. He had not seen Paolo himself since the day after the fire, but he knew where he was and what he was involved in. He had mixed emotions toward his brother. There was love simply because Paolo was his brother, and anger because Paolo had left Fabiana. That was an irony, Agosto thought. Of all the family members, Fabiana was the first to forgive her errant husband in her heart, even though he did not return to her. Emotion filled Agosto as he recalled his last meeting with Paolo, reluctantly admitting that there was some truth in Paolo's harsh words, but still he believed that Paolo's way was wrong, that violence was wrong.

"I miss Uncle Paolo," Clare Marina said, looking up from her book.

Domenico turned to her and said firmly, "You have no Uncle Paolo. He disgraced the family, he is dead to us."

Clare bit her lip and stared at her grandfather. Seldom did he speak to her without smiling.

Agosto saw the look of puzzlement on his daughter's face and quickly tried to change the subject. "Do you like your birthday present, Clarissima?"

Clare looked up from the ten-volume set of Wonder Books her parents had given her. "Oh, yes," she answered enthusiastically. "They have fairy stories, geography, history, and science! They're wonderful! Look, Papa, here's a picture of the elves who live in the sky and make rain, thunder, and lightning."

"I didn't learn to read until I was twenty-five," Domenico informed them. "It's not always good for women to read, Agosto. They learn too much, and become discontented, like Maria."

Agosto stroked his mustache and tried not to laugh. He seriously doubted that Maria's ability to read had had much of anything to do with her discontent. "Fabiana reads," he pointed out. "And so does Cecilia. In fact, Cecilia reads to Clare and Anthony all the time."

"Cecilia's a good wife. She's a good mother and she works hard raising money for the church. Those are the things a woman should do." He nodded to himself. "Fabiana and Cecilia know their place," he concluded.

"Well, I'm sure Clare will know her place too."

Clare looked up, her eyes large and round. "I'm going to be a banker like Papa," she said flatly.

Domenico roared, "See, Agosto! See what I mean?"

Agosto laughed. "She's only a child," he whispered to his

father. "But don't worry, she'll learn to cook and sew. She'll make some man a fine wife."

"You'll have to find a good match for her," Domenico said, staring off across the room. "A man must honor and respect his wife, take care of her and shelter her."

Masking his thoughts, Agosto leaned back in the chair, glancing only once at his daughter. He didn't believe in arranged marriages, but his father was too old to argue with. A man should die happy, believing he left the world as he'd found it.

Friday, October 18, 1912

B R O O K L Y N

When Cecilia opened the door for Agosto, she was already wearing her coat and hat. Her expressive face revealed consternation as she reached for Agosto's arm. "Oh, I thought you'd never get here! I called the bank and they said you'd left."

"What is it?" Agosto did not step into the house, but paused apprehensively on the doorstep.

"Fabiana called. It's your father. Agosto, he's had a terrible fall. He's in the hospital. Fabiana said to come right away."

"Oh, God." Agosto pressed his lips together and whirled around. Their new Packard was parked in front of the house, its sleek lines shining in the late-afternoon sun. He took Cecilia's arm and they hurried down the steps.

Agosto started up the car while Cecilia fidgeted in the front seat. At last the rumbling motor caught.

"Horses were less trouble," Cecilia murmured.

Agosto drove to St. Mary's as fast as the car would go. They drove in silence, and vaguely he wondered how his father had fallen, though in fact he knew Domenico had been growing progressively weaker over the past year.

He brought the car to a clattering halt in front of the gray stone building and paused only to help Cecilia out of the car.

Domenico was in a large high-ceilinged room with dim lights that cast shadows across the floor. Maria stood by the bed like a sentinel while Fabiana knelt by Domenico, her bulk hidden under a tentlike coat.

Agosto reached out and touched Fabiana's shoulder affectionately. He leaned over his father.

"Agosto?"

Agosto took his father's hands. "Papa . . ."

"Agosto, listen to me. Listen to me. I haven't much time."

"You have time, Papa. You have time, you'll be fine."

Domenico shook his head. "No . . . listen to me."

"I am listening."

"Remember what I always told you. Remember: *Senti tutti i consigli, ma il tuo non lo lasciare*. Listen to all counsel, but keep your own. Agosto, you must look after Fabiana . . . take care of her. She is not to blame for Paolo. Fabiana, come here."

Fabiana stood up and leaned over.

"I have business," Domenico said slowly. "I leave everything I have to you, Agosto, except two things. You listen, you all listen! Agosto, you take the store, but let Fabiana run it. You take everything else except for the shares in your bank that you gave me. I give half of those shares to Maria and half to Fabiana, who's been a daughter to me."

"Papa!" Maria's voice broke in, and Agosto heard the hardness in it. He stared at her and she fell instantly silent, though her expression did not change.

"Half to Fabiana," Domenico repeated, "so she'll have some security. Paolo should have taken care of her, but he broke his vows. We take care of our women . . . but he isn't honorable."

Fabiana knelt over and kissed Domenico's hand. She cried silently.

Domenico touched the gold St. Christopher's medal that hung around his neck. "And this for my little Clare Marina. It protects the fishermen, and it will protect her. And you, Agosto, will see that Anthony is given all the money I've saved."

Agosto nodded.

"Keep it in the bank till he is old enough."

"Papa, you're not—"

"I am, I want to, I'm ready." He inhaled and they could hear his heavy breathing across the large room.

Agosto took a deep breath. "Papa, you must let me get Paolo. You must."

Domenico turned his face to the wall. "Get the children," he ordered. "Bring them to me. I want to hold them once more if I am given time. Don't get Paolo. Paolo is dead."

"Papa, you're too hard."

"I'm a man of honor. I have one son. My other son is dead."

Fabiana, tears in her eyes, stood up. "I'll get the children," she volunteered.

Domenico uttered an unintelligible reply and clutched the

blanket around his neck. He began saying the rosary in Latin from rote; over and over he repeated it. Then he looked up into Agosto's eyes. "Take me to Lecce," he breathed. "Agosto, take your mother and me home."

Friday, November 22, 1912

L E C C E

The two caskets were lowered into adjoining graves, and the priest recited the prayers rapidly, crossing himself as he did so.

The first fistful of moist earth was sprinkled on the coffins, and Agosto crossed himself. He let out his breath and stared for a moment as the two workers began to cover the graves. He had fulfilled his father's last wish. His parents' were side by side, interred in the cemetery behind the church where they had been baptized, in the town of Lecce, where they had been born.

Agosto had offered to bring the entire family, but Maria had refused the trip, preferring to remain reclusive, though at last she gave in and allowed Tina to come. Fabiana came too, and helped with the children.

They turned and walked silently away. Agosto held Cecilia's hand. Fabiana followed with the children, who were for once silent.

"It's beautiful here," Cecilia said after a time. "And it's good, Agosto. It was your father's wish."

Agosto nodded, thinking of how often his father had spoken of returning to Italy to visit but postponed trip after trip. But there was no postponing this trip. This was the final voyage.

Clare Marina broke step with Tina and Anthony and skipped to her father's side, taking his hand. He smiled down at her, noting that in the warm Adriatic sunshine her dark hair glistened with reddish streaks of fire and that her skin had browned slightly.

"This is our ancestral home," he said to her, knowing he sounded a bit like a teacher. "Puglia is a large region, and Lecce is a province and also a city. Your grandfather and grandmother were born here."

Clare nodded. "Grandpapa used to tell me stories."

"Did he?"

"I want you to tell me some stories too."

"Your father is tired," Cecilia said protectively.

Agosto shook his head. "I feel like walking. Why don't you take Tina and Anthony back to the hotel. I'll walk with Clare for a while."

Cecilia smiled at Agosto. "All right," she agreed. "But not for too long."

Agosto looked down at Clare. Her bright eyes shone and she smiled conspiratorially at her father, happy to have the opportunity to spirit him away.

"Come along," Agosto said, leading her away from the others and down a narrow winding street. "The houses are all yellow," he said, touching the side of one of the buildings. "They're made of *pietra leccese*—it's a limestone that's taken from the ground of Lecce. For a time, in his youth, your grandfather worked in a quarry."

"I thought he was a fisherman."

"Later he was, and he always loved the sea. Ah, here we are. Do you know what this is?" Agosto's arm swept the scene in a grand gesture.

Clare's face knit into a frown. "A crumbled-down theater?" she replied.

Agosto laughed. "Yes, a crumbled-down theater, a Roman amphitheater built in the fourth century. That was more than fifteen hundred years ago."

"I know about the Romans. They fed Christians to the lions, that's what Sister told us in history."

Agosto smiled. He sat down on the rough stone step of the highest tier of the theater and pulled Clare down beside him. "I'll give you a history lesson," he told her. "This town, Lecce, was built on the ruins of the ancient Roman town of Lupiae. It was fought over by the Byzantines, the Lombards, and the Saracens after the fall of the Roman Empire. Then in the eleventh century the Normans conquered it, and in 1463 it went to the Aragonese kings of Naples. Wave after wave of people came to conquer us. That's how the family grew strong, Clare. Armies can conquer land, but they can't take away the spirit of freedom. And when it came time for Italy to become one nation, the people of Lecce took part in the Carbonari uprisings. Lecce founded its own provisional government in 1848—when your grandfather was only twelve years old. But the outsiders came again, and your great-grandparents were imprisoned along with hundreds of others. After that, there was suppression, and many who were not imprisoned were exiled. That, I suppose, is why your grandfather left here as soon as he was old enough. He had good memories and bad memories, but he never forgot that this was where he was born. We're a proud people, Clarissima; the blood of a thousand conquerors flows in our veins, but our spirit belongs to freedom and to this land.''

Agosto finished and then smiled at her. "I know you don't understand all that," he said, laughing at himself. She was only nine. And, he thought somewhat guiltily, he ought to be explaining these things to his son rather than his daughter. But Anthony was only seven, and somehow he didn't seem as curious as Clare.

Clare ran her finger across the stone. "I understand." Then she looked up at him. "But there's something I don't understand."

"And what is that?"

"I don't understand why you invest your money in buildings in New York. If you love Lecce and if this is our ancestral home, why don't you invest in buildings here?"

Agosto frowned. Clare was a deceptive child. Sometimes when she spoke, she sounded much older and wiser than she was. He always felt he had to be careful to remember that she was a child, because often, as now, she caught him off guard with a comment that was both grown-up and insightful.

"I intend to invest some money here in port facilities for Lecce and Brindisi. But that's very complicated, and you're only a little girl." He stood up and stretched. "I feel like some wine and cheese. Will you come with me to the wine cellar, Clarissima, or should I take you to the hotel first?"

Clare seized her father's hand. She had him to herself for a rare moment, and she decided not to relinquish him so easily. "No, I want to come with you," she said, tossing her long hair. "Papa, I want to see more . . . I want to see all of Italy."

Agosto smiled. "You're too young to appreciate it now."

She pressed her lips together. "When will I be old enough?"

"When you're confirmed, Clarissima"

"Will you bring me to Italy then? Just you and me, Papa. Will you?"

"As a confirmation present?"

"And a graduation present . . . before I go to high school."

"Are you going to high school?"

"Sister says I am."

"For confirmation," Agosto agreed, thinking that he might bring Anthony and Tina as well. "Travel is educational."

Clare beamed. "I want to go to Rome and to Genoa. I want to go to Florence and to Milan. I want to—"

"I want some red wine and cheese," he said, interrupting her and taking her hand. "All things in good time, Clarissima. All things in good time."

Tuesday, November 26, 1912

NAPLES

"We've only three days before our ship sails," Agosto said, unfolding the map of Naples. "We must see all we can."

Cecilia stood at the white-curtained window and stared out on the city and the Bay of Naples. It was a magnificent panorama that curved gently around the harbor. On the far side of the bay she could see Vesuvius. It spouted smoke like a dragon and periodically rumbled ominously.

Their hotel was a five-story stone building near the Piazza Vittoria and Pausillipo. Directly below the window the well-kept lawns of the park stretched out like a green velvet bolt of cloth and the graceful palm trees swayed in the ocean breezes while gaily colored flowers bent to the wind.

"It's hard to believe it's November," Cecilia commented.

"It's always summer here," Agosto returned, looking up from his map and guidebook. "We must take the children to the Donn' Anna Palace and to the National Museum on Via Foria. And to the Piazza Plebiscito and the Royal Palace, and of course to the New Castel and the Arch of Aragona."

Cecilia smiled. "You'll wear them out . . . especially since we are going to the opera tonight."

"And the fortress of Nisisa too," Agosto added.

"I want to climb Mount Vesuvius," Clare declared, edging beside her mother at the window.

"We could do that, but it takes a whole day," Agosto put in.

"Climb that?" Cecilia shook her head. "You'll be killed—it's dangerous!"

"The pathways are quite safe. Did you know it last erupted only four years ago?"

"It makes me nervous."

"A volcano is one of nature's great shows."

"It's a show I'd rather miss," Fabiana confessed. She was sitting in a great overstuffed chair mending one of Anthony's shirts. She looked less bloated and seemed to have lost a little weight. It was not a subject they discussed, but Cecilia urged Fabiana to eat less, and she had taken her shopping for some attractive clothes. Even Agosto had to admit that the transformation was something of a miracle. Her color was better and she seemed to be enjoying herself tremendously. She'd been wonderful on this trip. She often stayed with the children in the evenings so he and Cecilia could go out. But tonight would be the exception. He deemed the children old enough to sit through the opera, and he insisted they all go because the famous Teatro San Carlo was not to be missed and there was plenty of room for everyone in the box he had purchased.

"I think it should be the Royal Palace this afternoon," Agosto announced. "The lions that guard it were brought by Napoleon from Corsica. The piazza's magnificent. Then we can walk a bit and see Via Litoranea. It's got the best view of Vesuvius."

Fabiana set down her sewing. "There, Anthony, there is your shirt."

Anthony walked drowsily to Fabiana and took the shirt she extended to him. His hair was all rumpled, and he ran his fingers through it.

"Say thank you," Agosto told him. "Your aunt is not your maid."

"Thank you, Zia Fabiana," Anthony said rather formally. "May I wear it now? It's cooler than the one I have."

Fabiana nodded and ran her hand through his thick hair. "I think Anthony is tired."

"There's too much to see to take time for naps. Anthony must learn his history," Agosto said.

"I don't like history," Anthony grumbled. "But I don't want to take a nap either. Anyway, we can't go anywhere till Tina's out of the bathtub."

"If you're not going to nap, you'll come with us, because like it or not, history is important and you learn more when you see things than when you read about them in books."

Agosto's words were punctuated by one of Vesuvius' frequent booms. The chandelier in the room swung from the ceiling in a wide arc, as it did every time the mountain spoke.

"It goes off every twenty minutes," Clare announced triumphantly. "I've been timing it."

"So that's why you borrowed my watch."

Clare smiled and handed Agosto back his handsome gold pocket watch. "If it doesn't go off regularly, pressure builds up and then there would be a big explosion."

"I didn't know you were an expert on volcanoes."

"I read it in my book. When it exploded in 1906, the sky turned black for two weeks and lava and mud slides killed three thousand people."

"Gracious," Fabiana murmured.

Agosto stood up. "We should be off. Clare, go tell Tina to

hurry. I have two hours to see the sights, then I have a meeting with the president of the Bank of Naples, and after that we must all get ready for the opera.''

"The children can nap while you are at your meeting," Cecilia suggested.

"I'm not tired," Clare pouted. "I want to meet the president of the Bank of Naples."

"You'll be tired after our walk," Agosto promised.

"If I'm not, can I come?"

Agosto shrugged. "It's a business meeting."

"I want to come."

He smiled at her tolerantly. "If you're not tired, I suppose you can come. It's an informal meeting. But you have to be good. I don't know why you want to come anyway—he's just an old man."

"I want to see the president of the Bank of Naples," Clare said matter-of-factly.

They walked for nearly two hours, and Agosto pointed out the sights and explained everything from his guidebook. Anthony climbed the great stone lions outside the Royal Palace and sat astride the dormant concrete statues while the soldiers who guarded the palace laughed.

Fabiana had her picture taken with her back to the stone sea wall so that the thundering volcano would be in the background, and Cecilia bought a lovely lace shawl from a street vendor. Tina complained of weariness and constantly grumbled that everything looked alike. In the end, Agosto sent them back to the hotel in a carriage and he and Clare set out to meet the president of the Bank of Naples.

"Oh, Clare Marina! What a lovely name!" Mr. Concello leaned over her and pinched her cheeks. He was almost as round as he was tall, and his teeth were yellowed from the cigars he smoked. He sat in a swivel chair behind a great desk and stretched his plump short arms in front of him. "Sometimes I think that half of Naples has moved to New York," he said cheerfully. Then added, "And the other half has moved to San Francisco."

"There are a lot still here," Clare said, thinking of the crowded winding streets and the wash hanging from the windows. Brooklyn was not like this. Here everyone seemed to live on top of one another, and the women sat in front of their narrow houses and rocked on old chairs while they gossiped and talked rapidly, waving their hands about expressively.

Mr. Concello laughed loudly and pounded the desk with his

fist. "Yes, no matter how many leave, there are always more left!" He turned to Agosto. "Do you know the Italian banker Giannini? He's in California."

Agosto nodded. "We've met. But it is a long way from New York to California."

"I need a bank in New York," Mr. Concello confided. "To handle transfers. You know how many Neapolitans send money back home!"

"We could handle that," Agosto replied. Currently many of those transactions went through small local banks, banks Agosto considered somewhat unstable because they were often over-extended. The banking system in Italy was so much more advanced than it was in the United States.

"We'll have to talk at some length," Mr. Concello suggested. "When do you sail?"

"In three days."

"Perhaps if we met all day tomorrow," Concello suggested.

Agosto fiddled with his mustache and considered the suggestion. It would mean giving up a day of sightseeing, but he supposed that Cecilia could take the children if he hired a guide. "All right . . . yes, tomorrow."

Mr. Concello grinned, displaying his yellowed teeth. "Good, good! I dislike discussing business so late in the day. Now, let me see . . . right around the corner is a wonderful toy store. I think I should buy the little one a fine stuffed leopard, something to remember Naples by. Then, my friend, you and I will sip a little Cinzano together, and tomorrow we'll settle everything."

"A stuffed leopard?" Clare said, her dark eyes sparkling.

Mr. Concello leaned over. "A large stuffed leopard, with long white whiskers and a button that makes him growl."

Clare flushed. "That would be lovely," she said politely.

"Lovely little girls deserve lovely presents," Mr. Concello said. "And with your eyes, the presents will get lovelier and lovelier as you get older. I'm a fortunate man to have met you now. Presents for big girls are much more expensive than presents for little girls."

That evening, Cecilia, Agosto, Fabiana, and the children went to the San Carlo theater. Fabiana gasped as they went in. "Oh, I've never seen such magnificence," she said in a whisper as they were shown to their box.

"A true old-world opera house," Agosto said proudly. The ceiling displayed a great painting full of cherubs and angels in a swirl of blue and pink clouds. The painting was in a gilded oval, and around the edge of the oval were great gold leaves that culminated in an ornate gold structure that held a chandelier just over the stage, which had such great depth that it seemed to extend backward for an entire city block. At the far back of the stage were endless columns, and from the ceiling of the stage one could see four velvet curtains which hung in tiers and could be lowered as backdrops for various scenes. On each side of the theater, six rows of boxes divided by columns rose to the ceiling, and below, rows and rows of seats filled the orchestra. The boxes were all decorated with gilt paint and boasted ornate curlicues, candelabra, and chairs with red plush cushions.

"It's rather like the opera house in Manaus," Cecilia said, "but cooler, and there are no insects."

Agosto settled back and unfolded his libretto. "*Madama Butterfly* is a very sad opera, but one of Puccini's best." He glanced at Clare. She looked beautiful. Her long dark hair was pulled back with a bright red ribbon, and Cecilia had dressed her in a long red taffeta dress—her very first long dress. It rustled when she walked, and she lifted it daintily as her mother had taught her to. On her lap she held the stuffed leopard, which she stroked lovingly now and again.

"Shere Khan would have preferred *Aïda*," Clare said solemnly, looking at her leopard. "Then he could have growled at the elephants."

"Shere Khan? Is that what you have named him?" He smiled, remembering that Clare had been reading *The Jungle Book* on the ship. "I thought Shere Khan was a tiger."

Clare petted her toy. "He is, but it's a good name for a leopard too."

"Well, I hope Shere Khan will enjoy the opera."

"He will." She turned her eyes to the orchestra pit. The conductor had just taken his place, and applause filled the theater.

So smart, Agosto thought silently. And pretty too. He shook his head and glanced at Anthony, who squirmed uneasily in his seat, and at Tina, who, though almost three years older than Clare, seemed less mature. Well, Anthony would change, he thought to himself. He was, Agosto reminded himself, only in the second grade.

BROOKLYN

Agosto stood uneasily in the office of the mother superior of Our Lady of Mercy Convent School. It was a cluttered office filled with books and papers and reeking of incense that did not overcome what he thought of as "the odor of schools." A smell caused by milling bodies, assorted paints, glues, and heaven knew what else.

He shifted his weight from one foot to the other. He disliked waiting, but on the other hand, he thanked God that his interview was with Sister Mary rather than with the mother superior, who was, by any standards, a stiff cheerless woman totally lacking in humor. She was Irish to the core, hard and strict. All the nuns in the school were Irish; small wonder they were having difficulty with Clare Marina, who expressed her Italian heritage at every opportunity. He sighed again. He had been summoned to the school as if he himself were an errant child rather than one of New York's most important bankers.

"Mr. Tonelli?"

Agosto turned around to greet the piercing green eyes of an alarmingly young nun.

"Yes," he answered. "Clare Marina's father."

Sister Mary looked no more than twenty and she had freckles. Agosto wondered if nuns should have freckles. Somehow it didn't seem right, but she did serve to destroy his stereotype that all the Irish nuns were crinkled-up old prunes. Her smile was, he decided, rather engaging.

Sister Mary straightened up. "I've asked you to come because Clare Marina is giving me some difficulty."

"Is she naughty? I won't have that. She has to be respectful," Agosto said solemnly.

Sister Mary shook her head. "Not naughty. Naughtiness, I could deal with, I assure you. No, Mr. Tonelli, we have quite another problem with Clare Marina."

"And the nature of the problem?"

"She refuses to sew properly. In fact, Mr. Tonelli, I doubt that young lady will ever be able to sew a straight seam. And if one thing is worse than her sewing, it's her cooking. She's quite,

quite hopeless at mastering the skills that will enable her to lead a useful life.''

"She is only ten.''

"I assure you she'll be just as hopeless at sixteen. She's simply not interested, and she's very stubborn.''

"I'll have a talk with her, and my wife could help her. I'm sure she'll improve.''

Sister Mary shook her head. "No. I want your permission to transfer her into a strictly academic program. It's rather unusual, but we do have a few students like her.''

Agosto frowned. "I don't understand.''

"Well, I've given her the A-level mathematics tests and she has passed them all. She's excellent in geography and history, and she even writes quite well. These, of course, are the same subjects young men at St. Bartholomew take, but usually the girls are educated in . . . in things more useful for women. Still, we did start this program last year, and I think Clare should take it. Frankly, Mr. Tonelli, Clare is extraordinarily bright.''

"Women aren't supposed to be doing geography and history and mathematics,'' Agosto protested. "They're supposed to learn those other skills. If she didn't go to school at all, she'd learn them at home.''

"I know, Mr. Tonelli, but the world is changing.'' Sister Mary tossed back her head and looked him straight in the eye. "I've fought for this program, Mr. Tonelli. I believe there are many young women who should be studying these subjects. There are certainly plenty of young women in the Eastern universities. Our young immigrant women should be able to compete. I had quite enough trouble making the bishop understand. Now I have to fight to get students. Please, Mr. Tonelli, your Clare is exceptional. Don't suppress her intelligence because she's female. I believe that she'll finish advanced studies young. She could then go on to Saint Elizabeth's College in New Jersey—it's the closest we Catholics have to a school like Smith. After all, she could always become a nun and teach others.''

Agosto almost smiled. The very thought of Clare Marina becoming a nun was enough to make him laugh. Even at ten, one could clearly see the spark of an adventurous personality. He thought of Sarah Ainsley. She was educated, but she was hardly his model woman. He then thought of Cecilia. Cecilia certainly was his model woman. She was innately bright and self-educated. Still, she was painfully shy, and that, he quickly decided, was because she felt inferior to those who were educated in school. He certainly didn't want Clare to be that shy.

"Are you really certain she has the talent for these subjects?''

"Oh, Mr. Tonelli! Her mathematical ability is superb! It's her sewing that's a disgrace."

Agosto smiled. In spite of his minor prejudices, he found Sister Mary's lilting Irish accent rather cheerful, and he decided he liked her freckles too. "All right," he agreed. "Put her in this program of yours, but remember, I'm a banker and I'll know if she's not learning her sums properly."

Sister Mary laughed. "Oh, I know you're a banker, Mr. Tonelli, and I've wanted to speak to you about that too. You see, we desperately need to expand this school. Our classrooms are terribly overcrowded, and—"

Agosto laughed and leaned over. "I know what you want," he said good-naturedly. "When it comes to fund-raising for the church, you Irish are not a subtle people."

"Subtlety does not do the work of the Lord, Mr. Tonelli."

13

Wednesday, May 5, 1915

GENOA

Since his father's death, Agosto had journeyed to Europe each year. He always combined business with pleasure, and though he usually traveled alone, this year Clare Marina accompanied him. He glanced indulgently at her. As a companion she was both interesting and interested. Her dark eyes seemed to see everything, she asked questions, and her conversation was thoughtful. "I considered this trip for a long while before I decided to bring you, Clarissima."

Clare pinned on her bonnet, whirled around, and smiled at him engagingly. "Because of the war, Papa? But Italy's not at war, and neither is America."

Agosto nodded. "We've docked, Clarissima. Are you excited?"

"Very excited. Will we go visit the birthplace of Columbus?"

"Of course." Agosto led her out onto the deck; then, looking at the deserted docks below, he shook his head at the abnormality of the scene.

"Is something the matter, Papa?"

"No . . . well, maybe yes. There should be more people about."

"Perhaps they all went somewhere."

Agosto grumbled slightly. "We'll ask as soon as we're ashore."

Agosto watched as Clare Marina walked down the gangplank, grasping her own little satchel and holding on to her bonnet so it wouldn't blow off in the brisk sea breeze. Three months short of her twelfth birthday, she seemed much older to him. Not in appearance, he contemplated, but in attitude. She still wore her hair long in heavy ringlets, her angular face and large round brown eyes still held a childish innocence, but when she spoke, she sounded like an adult, choosing her words carefully and always using large words to express herself.

The low dismal buildings of the dock area were gray, and steam rose from the stacks of the many smaller vessels in port. In the far background he could see the rising hills above Genoa.

"It's not a beautiful city," he commented. "It's a major port, and all ports look alike. We'll stay at the Hotel Terminus Milan tonight. It's near the railroad terminal. Tomorrow we'll go to Milan, and after that to Florence—you'll like Florence. Then we'll go on to Rome, and I promise you'll love Rome."

"I'll like everything," Clare promised.

At the bottom of the gangplank, those workers who were about milled around. Agosto stopped to speak to one of the men. Clare listened as her father spoke Italian rapidly. There were gestures and frowns, and then Agosto turned to her. "He says that the entire city has gone to hear the poet Gabriele D'Annunzio dedicate a statue to Garibaldi."

"Can we go too?"

Agosto looked about for a taxi. "I suppose I could have our luggage sent on to the hotel," he agreed. "Though I doubt you'll find it interesting."

"I still want to go," Clare replied.

Agosto agreed, and signaled the driver. He decided he was glad Clare was so curious, for while he had no desire to bore her with a long political speech in a language she wasn't fluent in, he himself wanted to know why such an affair would draw virtually the entire city. It was true that D'Annunzio was a famous man, but not that famous, and certainly not that well known to illiterate dockhands.

Agosto spoke to the driver at length; then he and Clare climbed in and were whisked away along the wide streets and avenues of Genoa. As they got closer to the square, they passed large groups of people walking rapidly. The traffic became congested, and contingents of youth passed them waving Italian flags and singing patriotic songs. At last, exasperated and bogged down, the driver suggested they walk, since they were within blocks of the square and could make better time on foot. Agosto helped Clare down and instructed the driver to take their luggage on to the hotel.

"Who is this man D'Annunzio?" Clare asked.

Agosto smiled, wondering how to describe D'Annunzio to an eleven-year-old.

Gabriele D'Annunzio was a poet, novelist, short-story writer, and journalist. He also dabbled in politics, but given the subject matter of his novels and poems, that was not surprising. Agosto had read *Canto Novo*—"New Song"—and he'd read *San Pantaleone*, which detailed the life of the peasants in D'Annunzio's native Abruzzi. But after reading *The Child of Pleasure*, a novel with a passionate Nietzschean hero whom Agosto found amoral, vicious, and self-seeking, he'd read no more of D'Annunzio's novels. But he continued to read the man's poetry, and liked *Alcyone*, a lyrical recreation of the sights, smells, tastes, sounds, and experiences of a Tuscan summer.

"He's a poet," Agosto replied. "A fine poet, but a bad novelist."

They crowded into the square. D'Annunzio was perched on a high platform, ready to rouse and to entertain. He was a narrow-faced man with a small goatee and sharp flashing eyes. He began his speech and a hush fell over the crowd. Agosto strained to hear him. Somehow, D'Annunzio's appearance belied his reputation. The poet had once had an affair with the beautiful Italian actress Eleonora Duse. He'd written play after play for her, but when she left him, he wrote a novel called *The Flame of Life*, which exposed their erotic relationship. It created a major scandal, and one critic called it "the most swinish novel ever written."

D'Annunzio leaned forward and waved his arms in the air. Agosto thought he had a charismatic quality, and the crowd reacted to him with cheers as he spoke of Garibaldi. Then the speech took a sudden turn, and Agosto strained to hear above the shouting. D'Annunzio was urging Italy to join the war, to re-nounce the Triple Alliance.

"The people of Trentino are Italians! But they suffer under the yoke of the Austro-Hungarian Empire! Trieste could be ours! We must fight for Italy! For Italians!" D'Annunzio proclaimed.

Clare stood on her tiptoes in order to be able to see. "Why is everyone cheering? Is he saying good things about Garibaldi?"

"He's saying Italy should go to war," Agosto replied grimly. Renouncing the Triple Alliance would certainly bring Italy into the growing conflict and add to the list of combatants. There was talk in America too, talk that America wouldn't be able to remain aloof, safe across the ocean. Agosto grasped Clare's hand more tightly as D'Annunzio's speech reached a fever pitch and the crowd broke into pandemonium.

If Italy joined the war, his investments would be threatened; it could bring America in, and he'd certainly have to divest himself of investments in Austria and Germany. But most important, there would be much to do at home. America would have to expand industrially—wartime industries would be grow-ing quickly. D'Annunzio finished, and a roar of approval greeted his proposals. Instinctively Agosto began guiding Clare out of the crowd.

"Is it over?" she queried, trying to catch one last glimpse of the poet.

Agosto pulled her along. "No," he said softly, "it's just beginning."

The Hotel Terminus Milan was not Genoa's most elegant hotel, but its location across from the railroad station made it ideal for the short time Agosto and Clare planned to stay in the city. They would, he determined, sightsee for the rest of the day, have a good night's sleep, and catch the early-morning train to Milan.

The main salon of the hotel had an inlaid oak floor scattered with rich Persian rugs, dark massive mahogany furniture, and a central lighting fixture made of brass. Inlaid panels on the walls had hand-painted murals in the neo-Renaissance style. The high ceilings, so characteristic of all European hotels, gave the lobby a feeling of spaciousness.

Agosto stood at the oval-shaped desk and wrote his name in the registry book, then turned over their passports.

"American?" the clerk asked, pondering the pale-blue passports. "What do you think? Will America go to war now?"

Agosto frowned. "Why?"

"Because of the ship," the concierge replied.

"What ship? I've been out of touch."

The concierge shrugged. "The *Lusitania*, the American ship. She was sunk by the Germans two days ago in Irish waters. There were hundreds killed."

Agosto felt a tinge of resentment. Certainly the captain of their vessel had received this news while they were at sea. But no announcement was made, though, he acknowledged, such an announcement would only have caused panic among the passengers.

"Have you a newspaper?" Agosto inquired.

The concierge bent down, searching beneath the desk. "I've this Italian one. Do you read Italian as well as you speak it?"

Agosto nodded.

"And I have yesterday's *News of the World*."

Agosto took them both. "Come, Clarissima, we'll go to our rooms. I'm afraid I must send some cables." Agosto turned back to the clerk. "I must wire New York immediately," he said solemnly. "Can it be done from here?"

The concierge scratched his head. "Normally, but if it's urgent, you should go to the post office or to the cable exchange. When the lines are busy, we've trouble getting through."

Agosto envisaged lines of people waiting to send cables.

Every businessman and tourist in Genoa would be sending messages to the United States.

"Italy will soon be at war too," the concierge said matter-of-factly. "Only today D'Annunzio called for war, and all over Italy other men of influence do the same."

"I heard him," Agosto said dejectedly. Being isolated from his banks and his investments was troubling, but in the back of his mind was the fact that he and Clare would most certainly have to cut their visit short and leave Italy as soon as his meeting with Count Sforza, the prominent banker and industrialist in Milan, was concluded. But what would be the safest route home? To leave from an allied port could be extremely dangerous now. Especially in light of the fate of the *Lusitania*.

He turned to Clare, but she had wandered off to inspect the lobby. "Come, Clarissima," he called out.

She skipped to his side, smiling. Agosto took her hand gratefully and thought how wonderful it would be to have the untroubled mind of a child.

After Agosto sent his wires, he took Clare to the birthplace of Columbus. It was a round stone building, and rapidly jabbering guides showed tourists through it, singing out the praises of the explorer.

"Why didn't Columbus sail for Italy?" Clare asked.

"Italy wasn't united then, you know that. The city-states couldn't afford to mount a voyage, so seamen sailed under the flags of other countries. Giovanni Caboto was Italian too. He sailed for England, but changed his name to John Cabot. Italy wasn't united till Garibaldi, who was a great man."

"Because he was a general?"

"No, because he refused power when his job was done. The test of leadership, Clarissima, is to know your own strength, but to resist using it to enslave others. But you're a young lady and I don't expect you to understand war or politics."

Clare stopped short and looked defiantly at her father. "Papa, Garibaldi's wife fought at his side. She was as brave as he—he said so himself. She understood war and politics."

Clare had made a rather firm point and one he could hardly deny. "I see you have been reading up on Garibaldi."

"I read the book you gave me, *The Gadfly*. And I found a picture, too, in another book. It was a picture of Garibaldi's wife."

"Well, she was unusual."

"I'll be unusual too," Clare announced resolutely.

His daughter's pride amused him. "I suppose you will be," he replied somewhat patronizingly.

"Explain this war to me," Clare persisted.

"You're much too young to understand."

"Tell me anyway," she insisted. "Papa, how can this war hurt your banks and your investments?"

Agosto laughed. She was such a little question machine. But a child, most especially a girl, couldn't possibly understand. "It's very complicated."

Clare studied the tile floor. "Have you investments in the wrong countries, Papa?"

"I suppose I do," Agosto replied, raising a bushy eyebrow. Then he added, "But I won't have them long."

Monday, May 24, 1915

M I L A N

Trying to leave Italy was a nightmare in which patience was more an ally than money, Agosto discovered. The ports were filled with tourists fleeing the country, visitors terrified of being passengers on any vessel that might meet the same fate as the *Lusitania*.

Agosto considered going back to Genoa and sailing from there, but he quickly changed his mind when Italy declared war on May 22.

"We can't sail from an allied port," he said aloud. "So we'll travel by train through southern France to Spain, and sail from Bilbao."

"Is it a long journey?" Clare was dressed in a crisp clean skirt and blouse and wore a broad-brimmed hat with two ribbons streaming down the back. They blew about in the light spring breeze that provided a welcome breath of fresh air on the crowded railroad platform.

"Not so long as we ever get on the train," Agosto grumbled. The station was packed with troops who had been called up; with wives and lovers; with screaming children being dragged along by impatient parents. It was a sweating, swearing mass of humanity, all struggling to cram their bodies onto the train that somehow reminded Agosto of a toy train, the sort he had bought Anthony for his birthday. He held Clare's hand tightly. "Don't let go of me," he cautioned.

They pushed forward in a surge from the rear, up against a hastily erected four-foot iron guardrail. There, on either side of the opening, two burly soldiers stood and repeated over and over, "Passport control . . . Passport control," in Italian. Their faces were stern and weary, and they stared at the surging crowd as if they were cattle being let into a pen. And, Agosto admitted to himself, he felt like a cow being herded along.

"I haven't felt like this in a long time. When there is an emergency, Clarissima, people have no faces, money is of no importance, position and status don't matter. War is terrible, Clarissima. When I was in Cuba I saw lines of homeless people, forced from their homes by the fighting. They picked up all they had and marched along the pathways. They didn't know where to go. It's a scourge, that's what it is, a scourge. And so useless, killing, death, and disease! It's all Europe has ever known. That's what's so wonderful about America, Clarissima: it's behind the sea, and the sea protects it from invasion."

"But you said America would go to war," Clare reminded him.

"She might. If she does, it'll be to keep the European war from coming to her. Americans will come to Europe to fight, but there won't be fighting in America. It's a blessed land. You remember that, Clarissima. America is blessed. I want you always to remember your Italian heritage; I don't ever want you to forget what Italy has given the world, but, Clarissima, you and I, we're Americans first."

"What about Uncle Paolo?" Clare asked suddenly.

"What makes you ask about him?" Agosto scowled.

"You said once to Mama, I heard you, that Uncle Paolo was causing trouble in America."

Agosto turned to her. "He and his kind are bringing to America the sort of ideas that ruined Europe. I don't approve of violence. But never mind, what's between me and your Uncle Paolo is men's business. Have you got your satchel?" He pulled her, seeing a slight break in the crowd as they edged toward the opening in the gate that would allow them onto the restricted portion of the platform and thus onto the train. He pressed his lips together; the train already looked packed.

They reached the opening and Clare smiled at the guard. It was a warm, friendly, little-girl smile and his hard features melted as he motioned them forward and through the opening, holding the crowd behind them at bay.

"Passport control," he said, bending over and touching Clare's long dark curls.

"Ah, American. Tonelli. You're from Brooklyn, I see. I have

a brother in New York, a lucky man. He won't have to go to fight the Huns! And rich, too. Everyone in America is rich, yes?'' He grinned at Agosto and in return Agosto handed him an American five-dollar bill. He motioned them on with a wide smile. ''Your daughter will be a real beauty in a few years!'' he called after them.

Clutching his suitcase in one hand and holding Clare with the other hand, Agosto guided her across the platform toward the train.

''It was a good idea to send the heavy luggage by sea. We could never have managed it. And who cares if it's lost? It's not human. One suitcase is bad enough, especially if it's filled with paper. I'm sorry about your clothes. I'll buy you new ones in Bilbao. You have to understand that it's important that I have these papers with me—they're more important than our clothes. And it's very important that we get out of Europe and leave from a port that's in the hands of neither side.'' He lifted Clare up and scrambled on behind her. ''Don't pay any attention to me, I'm talking to myself.''

The railway carriage was packed and people were crowded in the aisles. ''I think we'll have to sit on our suitcases.'' Clare sighed with resignation.

''Not quite the way you're used to traveling.''

Clare smiled and laughed. She put down her satchel and sat on it. Agosto did the same and the train lurched backward, sending the passengers who were standing staggering, as it backed out of the terminal. ''This will be a long night,'' Agosto predicted.

The overburdened train crawled along, winding its way down to Genoa and the sea. There it stopped for what seemed an eternity, stalled on the tracks while bundles of cargo were unloaded, while soldiers climbed off and more soldiers climbed on, and while passport patrols went up and down the train three times checking and rechecking the papers of the imprisoned passengers. Clare sat on her satchel, her bonnet lopsided, its gay ribbons wilted. Her head rested against the side of the train, and miraculously, she slept.

Finally the train jolted forward into the starless night. It stopped again at Savona, and Agosto pried open one of the sooty windows and bribed an official on the platform to buy him some wine, bread, and cheese. He was surprised when the man returned, but he supposed the promise to double the money was more the motive than kindness.

He opened the wine and glanced at Clare, hoping that if he drank a bit, he too might enjoy sleep. But logic told him that his need to protect her from the surging crowds that invaded the train, plus the constant chattering of his fellow passengers in the corridor, would not allow for more than a furtive cat nap.

The train skirted the tiny principality of Monaco as it descended the foothills of the Maritime Alps and finally came to a clattering halt with half its snakelike steel body at rest in Italy and the other half in France.

In the early dawn Agosto could see the craggy landscape through the dirty windows of the train. Great rocks jutted up on one side, and from them wild bouquets of pink- and orange-flowered bushes sprang as if carefully hung to decorate the barren stone.

"Menton!" a male voice called out. Then: "Franco-Italienne Frontière! Have your passports ready!"

Clare blinked open her eyes and stretched. "Is it morning?" she asked drowsily.

Agosto nodded. "We're at the French-Italian border."

She looked mildly disappointed. "I was hoping it was the Spanish border," she admitted.

"I'm afraid there's nothing to eat on this train, Clarissima. But I bought some bread and cheese last night. Have some." Poor Clare, he thought. She must be terribly uncomfortable and unhappy. She'd always traveled with all the comforts money provided. Now he was dragging her out of Europe with thousands of others, and the circumstances of their flight were bound to be hard on her. "There's nothing to drink but wine," he said guiltily.

"Can I have a sip? The bread is dry."

Agosto passed the bottle. "Just a little to wash it all down. You're used to having it with water, but there isn't any water."

Clare smiled. "I don't mind." She took a sip and ate some of the bread and cheese, then took a few more gulps. When she had finished, she stood up and stretched and looked out the window. "The sun is coming up," she observed. "It's beautiful here! The flowers look as if they grow right out of the mountain rocks."

Agosto sighed. "I'm sorry this is not the fine sightseeing trip I'd planned."

She turned to him in surprise. "I'm having fun, Papa. This is a real adventure."

Agosto put his arm around her. "You're a good girl, Clarissima. And I'm glad you're not frightened."

She looked up at him adoringly. "I couldn't be frightened with you, Papa."

He sighed. "I wish I had your faith in me."

"You've been in a war before," she said. "You know just what to do."

"Passports, papers!" The French border patrol soldiers entered the car. They wore brown boots and long dark green stockings and green knickers and belted green jackets with gold buttons down the front and on their pockets. Their hats were round on top and bore a gold *fleur de lys*. The Italian soldiers followed them, dressed in light brown and wearing flat brown hats. All of the soldiers were armed.

Agosto produced their papers, and they mumbled among themselves on seeing the American passports. Then, in the peculiar French dialect of the district, the French soldier announced, "America should join the war. Tell them all that when you get home! We need America!"

Agosto nodded wearily. He almost complained that he wasn't the President and had no control over what America did, but he was well aware of people's attitudes. One American was all Americans in their minds.

"Destination?" the French soldier demanded.

"Spain," Agosto replied. He hated borders; he supposed they made everyone feel like a criminal.

"What's in your suitcase?" the Frenchman inquired. And the Italian beside him scowled, seeming ashamed that he hadn't asked first.

"My clothes and some papers," Agosto replied. There was no point in lying. They'd open it if they wanted; then they would be delayed, and heaven knew what would happen.

"What kind of papers?" the French soldier asked suspiciously.

"My pàpa is an important banker," Clare interrupted as she adjusted her bonnet. "He's carrying important business papers to America, and if you want America to enter the war and you want my papa's help, you should hurry up. Besides, i'm thirsty and there's no water on this train!" She flashed her round dark eyes, but she smiled too.

Agosto flushed and started to apologize, but the two soldiers were laughing. The French one bowed to her. *"Oui, mademoiselle,"* he said solicitously. Then he took her hand and kissed it rather gallantly. "I'd like to chat," he told her, "but we have many people to check."

The soldiers pressed on, and Agosto watched as they made their way down the aisle, inspecting documents. When they finally left the carriage, he turned to Clare. "You must be more careful," he warned. "You don't understand soldiers."

Clare giggled. "But I *am* thirsty," she said innocently.

*   *   *

Again the train jolted forward, and in a short time it crossed the high white stone railway bridge at Point San Luigi and began its descent into Nice, which lay twelve miles inside the French border and was the gateway to the golden sandy beaches and clear blue waters of the Côte d'Azur.

The train stopped in Nice for some time and passengers scrambled off to get food and water, hurrying back with their precious hoard.

Agosto sent someone rather than risk leaving the train or somehow getting separated from Clare in the crowds. Certainly he was not the only one to fear leaving Europe from an allied port; Nice had a large English population, and many English crowded onto the train.

Forward again, and the train wound its way through the trees up onto the high track from which they could see the landscape below as clearly as if it were a painting. The blue sea stretched out to meet an even bluer sky, and the buildings of Nice disappeared and gave way to the spectacular old fortress of Eze, the guardian of the Côte d'Azur which had been destroyed in the 1700's but whose ruins still stood like a sentinel looking down on the sea. Next came the mountainside village of Saint Jeannet and after more than two hours, the creeping train reached Cannes.

"Did you finish your business in Milan?" Clare asked after a time. Her father had sent her on a tour while he met with Count Sforza. He'd originally met the count through Barton Ainsley.

"Yes, but it will all have to wait now. This is no time to invest in Italy."

"You already have investments," Clare replied, remembering the port facilities at Brindisi.

"I meant new investments."

Clare nodded knowingly and returned to looking out the window.

In late afternoon the train rumbled into Marseilles, where, Agosto happily noted, more people got off than got on. Certainly there were ships leaving from Marseilles, but he stubbornly decided to stick with his original plan and leave from Bilbao.

"A family got off!" Clare announced proudly. "Papa, I have found us two real seats."

"You're a good girl," Agosto praised. He stood up and stretched, lifting his somewhat flattened suitcase, and followed her to the fifth compartment, where, as promised, there were two seats.

Clare immediately took the one by the window and Agosto hoisted his suitcase to the shelf above, glad to be rid of it for a while. He sank into the seat, blessing its comfort. "This is more like it," he said, patting his daughter's knee.

There were three seats on each side of the carriage. On the end by the folding door that led to the narrow corridor, an old man snored peacefully. Opposite them three well-dressed prim-and-proper ladies sat looking distressed. All three stared at Clare as if she was from a distant star.

"Whatever are you doing traveling in Europe with a child?" one of them finally asked in a crisp British accent. "Surely she should be away at boarding school!"

Agosto pulled his mustache. The English were a difficult people. Perhaps more so for Italians, he mused. Italians took their children everywhere; the British took theirs nowhere. "We're American," he answered, as if the information were enough to satisfy their curiosity.

"Oh," the woman uttered. She obviously held the conviction that she was speaking to an inferior. "Still, this is no time to be traveling with a child."

Clare scowled. "I'm on my vacation from school. Travel is educational."

The woman sniffed. "I suppose it is," she allowed, then without further conversation opened a magazine and began to read.

Darkness enveloped the sea and the mountains. The train curved inland to Nîmes and then to Béziers, where it returned to the sea. It crept along till it reached Perpignan, and then once again it halted at a border, this time the French-Spanish border.

"We've got to change trains here," Agosto told Clare. "The track gauge isn't the same as in France."

The passengers all got off the train and walked to the border station. Here the soldiers were stricter and even more disorganized. They studied each document and passport forever, as if trying to make out the words and memorize the contents. They scrutinized each passenger and haphazardly looked through luggage. To Clare's delight, they inspected the luggage of the Englishwomen and even unpacked their undies, much to the ladies' discomfort. But they didn't look into Agosto's suitcase. Instead, Clare and Agosto were motioned forward and allowed to board the train on the other side of the border.

"Papa!" Clare Marina tugged at her father's coat sleeve. "Papa, we're in Bilbao!"

Agosto's eyes snapped open and he shook his head groggily. It was the first time he'd taken more than a short nap. He stood and stretched; then, taking the suitcase, they both climbed off the train and were suddenly out in the warm Spanish sun.

Clare Marina sighed happily. "Will we get on a ship right away?" she queried.

"I don't think so. I think we'll go to a first-class hotel, have a good big breakfast, and sleep until after the siesta. Then I'll see to our passage."

"Papa, will we be here long enough to go to a bullfight?" Her eyes glistened as they passed a poster advertising the event.

Agosto shook his head impatiently. "No," he answered. "I don't think so. Clare, it's very important for me to get home as soon as possible."

"Whatever is best for the banks," she answered contentedly. Then added, "But I'll come back one day and see a bullfight."

14

Monday, April 9, 1917

BROOKLYN

Clare left school at three-thirty when her classes ended and walked to her father's bank. It was her routine, and when she arrived, he gave her some job to do while she waited to walk home with him. Sometimes she counted coins, and other times he allowed her to work on the account books, because, as he admitted, her math was as good as the tellers'. At first he had always had her work checked, but finding no errors, he allowed her to work alone.

"American Federal Banks," Agosto said aloud. "Our banks are no longer going to court only Italian customers! We're Americans, and now that America has entered the war, we must show our patriotism. Ah, Clarissima, there is so much to do, there will be so much growth!"

Clare Marina smiled brightly. Moments when her father confided in her made her especially happy. He did it often, though he usually also added, "I'm just thinking out loud."

"I dislike war," her father intoned. "But I have a great opportunity to serve America, Clarissima. The country is building new industries to help the allies, and large sums of money will be needed for loans too." He beamed at her. "I've been invited to Washington, Clarissma. I've been asked to meet with other important bankers."

"But you won't have to go and fight, will you?" A look of concern clouded her face.

"No, Clarissima. This time I'll do my fighting from behind a desk. But others will go, many others." He shook his head sadly. "Young men," he added.

Clare frowned. "Some already went. One of my friends at school has a brother who left almost as soon as we came home from Italy. I've seen pictures of others in the papers."

"They went to join the Italian Army. Now Italians will join the American Army. It'll take a little time, but America is going to send soldiers to Europe. Germany mustn't win this war, Clarissima. And the countries fighting against Germany need supplies that they can no longer pay for. That's why they'll need loans."

"Why did America wait so long?"

Agosto shrugged. "The President is an intellectual, a man of peace who believes in compromise. But there's no compromise with injustice. War, as I've told you many times, is dreadful. But sometimes there's no other way. You can't allow someone to walk over you. When you have tried everything else, then you must fight. Clarissima, we've lost many ships to German submarines. We lost them even though we tried to stay neutral."

Clare nodded. "Can I go to Washington with you, Papa? I'd like to see the White House, the Washington Monument, and most of all, the Smithsonian Institution."

"But you have to go to school, Clarissima. And besides, I'll be in meetings. You'd be bored."

"I could miss a few days of school."

Agosto shook his head. "No, I'll be too busy to go sightseeing with you. Besides, it would be unfair to Anthony."

"I don't think he wants to go to Washington. Anthony doesn't care about history. All he cares about is playing baseball. Please, Papa, you could ask Fabiana to come. She could look after me, and while you are in your meetings, we could see everything."

Agosto looked at his thirteen-year-old daughter. Her dark eyes were filled with joyous anticipation. "I spoil you," he reflected. "You know how to get around your papa, don't you?"

She smiled impishly. "You always say travel is educational."

He nodded. "You can only come if Fabiana agrees to come too."

Clare smiled and sprang down from the high stool on which she was perched. She jumped up and down and clapped her hands. "She'll come! I know she will!" Clare sang out gleefully.

As soon as she got home, Clare ran directly upstairs to her brother's room. He sat at his desk, homework spread out in front of him, but he wasn't studying, he was gazing out the window dreamily.

"Tony?" Clare poked her head in the door and whispered his name. "Guess what? Guess what?" She danced merrily into his room, twirling about.

He turned to her and ran a pudgy finger through his hair. Clare always imagined that Tony looked like her father when he was a child. He had square shoulders and a square face and mops of thick dark wavy hair. But although she thought he looked like their father, she also thought him less intelligent.

"What?" he said with some annoyance.

"Papa is taking me to Washington with him. I'm going to see all the historic places there."

Anthony scowled at her. "I hate history, and Washington is too hot."

"You're just jealous," Clare taunted, affecting a slight pout. "You're jealous that Papa's taking me and not you."

Anthony shook his head. "I don't want to go." He looked back at his pile of books, then with large eyes looked at her pleadingly. "Clare, I think I'm failing math and history. Father O'Hare says if I don't pass I might not be able to go on to high school. Papa will kill me!" Tears filled his eyes and he wiped them away with the back of his hand.

"Stop crying, you're acting like a baby." She raised a dark eyebrow at him. He was two years younger than she, but she knew that two years ago when she had been in Europe with her father, she'd not been such a baby. "You're like a squishy pastry," she teased.

"I am not!" He put his head down on his arm. "I'll never be an important banker! I'll never get into high school! Papa will kill me!"

"I'll be an important banker," Clare said, taking a step toward him.

He glared up at her, then stuck out his tongue and said, "You can't be a banker because you're only a girl. You can't do anything but have babies! That's what girls are for, to have babies and clean the house and sew and cook!"

"I'm not going to do that! I'm going to be a banker like Papa. I don't care if I am a girl. You can't stop me! Nobody can stop me!" She looked at him angrily. "And you *are* a squishy pastry!"

"Not!"

"Are!"

"Go away, go away, you silly girl!"

But Clare did not go away. Instead she walked over to him and yanked on his hair. "If I go away, I can't show you how to do your math, and then you will fail."

He looked up at her questioningly and sucked on his lower lip. "Would you help me?" he asked more softly.

Clare lifted her head. "If you say I can be a banker."

"You can be a banker," he said without conviction.

"Louder," Clare demanded.

Tears welled in Anthony's eyes. "You can be a banker, dammit!"

She smiled and sat down beside him. "Which problems can't you do?" she asked sweetly.

"All of them," he admitted in a defeated tone.

Clare turned the book around and looked at them. "They're easy, Tony. Baby problems, that's what they are."

Friday, September 7, 1917

BROOKLYN

Clare Marina sat on the park bench and lifted her legs out straight so she could examine her oxfords. They were quite ugly, she decided, and so was her school uniform, which hung on her body like an old heavy blue sack. She looked much better in the dresses her father bought her, but those couldn't be worn to school.

She sighed and looked around. The late-afternoon sun filtered through the trees. In the playground little children played on the swings and slides, squealing with pleasure and running about. Clare sighed. It didn't seem so long ago that she was doing the same, but now for some reason she had lost all interest in such things and found herself wandering about dreamily and seeking out places where she could be alone. Her mother kept telling her that soon she'd be a woman . . . but she never exactly explained what that meant or how Clare would know when she was.

Normally Clare went to the bank on Fridays after school. But today her father, who was the head of the Brooklyn draft board, was at a meeting and she decided to walk in the park and watch the ducks down by the water. Summer was fading, and Clare felt sad to see it pass.

"Hello." The young man's voice startled her, and Clare spun around to face Johnny McKenna. He was Irish and attended the boys' school next to her school.

"Hello," she replied. He was two years older than she, and for sixteen he was quite tall, much taller than any of the Italian boys she knew.

"You're Clare Marina," he said, sitting down next to her.

She nodded. He had thick sandy hair and blue eyes. When he smiled he had two dimples, and, she noted, he had strong broad shoulders.

"I play football," he said matter-of-factly.

"I've seen you."

He smiled and his dimples came into clear view. "You're pretty," he said suddenly.

Clare blushed. "You're very bold," she said, trying to sound sophisticated. She was certain it was what her mother would say.

But he didn't apologize. "I might join the army. I might go to fight."

Clare smiled. "You're too young," she told him. "My father's head of the draft board. You can't join the army till you are seventeen."

"I could lie. I look older."

She tilted her head and it crossed her mind that she was sorry she was dressed in her school uniform and that her hair was pulled back. "I suppose you do," she conceded.

His eyes seemed to be studying her, but it was not just her face. They traveled from her ankles upward and settled on her breasts, which had only just begun to swell and were now almost as full as her mother's. She flushed again and was aware of the strange warm feeling that swept through her.

"You're only fourteen?" It was half-question, half-statement.

"I'm just fouteen. My birthday was last month."

"Italian girls mature faster," he said somewhat appreciatively. "You know, if I join the army and go away, I ought to have a girl to write to."

Clare stood up and looked at him in surprise. "I'm not supposed to talk to strangers," she said, as if she'd only just remembered her father's instruction.

"I'm not a stranger. I go to St. Bartholomew—you said you'd seen me! Besides, I want you to be my girl."

She shook her head. "My father would never allow it! My cousin Tina is almost three years older than me, and she's not allowed to have a boyfriend. It's not at all proper to be with a boy alone." She lifted her head and in one motion pulled on the ribbon that held her hair, allowing it to fall over her shoulders.

He winked at her impishly. "Do you have to be like all the other girls?"

"I'm not," she protested.

"You act like it. I'll bet you've never even held hands with a boy, and I'll bet you never kissed one either."

Clare took a step away from the bench. "Of course not!" she said, trying to sound as shocked as possible at the suggestion.

He stood up too and grabbed her hand and squeezed it. He smiled, and Clare went slightly limp, unable to withdraw her hand from him. "See?" he said, winking again. "It's nice."

Clare nodded and looked at the ground. "But I won't kiss you," she said firmly.

"Okay. Let's just go for a walk, then."

Clare nodded again and he fell in step beside her, still holding her hand. "Every soldier should have a girl," he said. "I want you to be my girl."

Tuesday, September 18, 1917

BROOKLYN

"Clare! Clare Marina!" Agosto's voice roared through the house. Upstairs in her room Clare looked up from her books. Her father's voice sounded angry, and he called her full name rather than "Clarissima," the endearment he normally used.

She closed her algebra book and left her room, calling out, "I'm coming, Papa."

As she hurried down the hall, Anthony opened his door. "You're in trouble," he hissed through the crack in the door. "Papa sounds mad."

Clare ignored him, but she was glad that Tina, who was staying with them, wasn't home. "Why can't you be like Tina?" was a constant question of late. Tina was becoming a fine cook, Tina had made a dress by herself, Tina did this and that. No, Clare thought. It was bad enough Anthony was home.

Clare braced herself as she reached the bottom of the stairs. "Papa?"

"I'm in the study," Agosto answered harshly.

Clare walked in and stood before him. No, he didn't look happy with her. His face was knit into a scowl.

"Do you know what a busy man I am?" Agosto questioned, his dark eyes flashing.

"Yes, Papa."

"I own over a hundred banks. I'm an economic adviser to the President of the United States. I have worldwide investments and I spend three nights a week chairing the draft board. Do you think it's easy deciding who will go and fight? Do you know what kind of responsibility that is?"

Clare nodded.

"Don't just nod at me! Answer me! Do you know what kind of responsibility that is?"

"Yes, Papa."

"And of course I have to keep making trips to Washington, I have meetings, meetings, meetings! I have responsibility for other people's money, for lives, for so much!" He wiped his brow angrily. "And what do I expect at home, Clare? You tell me, what do I expect?" He leaned over and crossly shook his finger in her face.

Clare looked into his dark eyes unflinchingly. "I don't know," she answered.

"You don't know! You don't know!" His face was growing red now. "Well, let me tell you. I expect both you children to do your chores. I expect you to study hard and make me proud of you."

"I study hard," Clare protested. "I got straight A's."

"Not in a subject that would help you make some man a good wife!" he thundered.

Clare's eyes were large and steady. "I'm going to be a banker," she said proudly.

"Girls do not become bankers," he shouted.

"The work I do at the bank is always correct," Clare said, lifting her chin.

"Simple sums," Agosto mumbled. "And this has nothing to do with why I'm talking to you." He was growing even more annoyed.

"Yes, Papa."

"I also expect you to behave in a certain way; I expect *you* to be a lady!"

Clare looked at him, her eyes wide and innocent.

He lifted his finger and shook it in her face again. "I expect you to be a lady like your mother! I expect you to be a lady like your cousin! Look at you! You're just fourteen years old. Fourteen years old and I get a phone call from the Mother Superior telling me you've been holding hands with a boy! Clare Marina, that's not proper. You're too young to be with a boy and much too young to be holding hands. Proper girls do not go out until they are seventeen, and they do not go out unescorted until they are engaged. I'm ashamed!"

Clare did not hang her head; instead she looked at her father steadily. "I like him," she answered simply.

Agosto glared at her. "You're a child! I've made a mistake with you! I've spoiled you, Clare. I've taken you on trips to Europe and Washington. I've let you work in the bank after school. Obviously you think you are much more grown-up than you are. And, I might add, even if you were older, your behavior is unacceptable."

His voice was now low and menacing, but Clare sensed that much of his real anger had been expressed.

"I'm sorry, Papa. I didn't mean to upset you."

Agosto looked at her and shook his head. "I don't ever want to receive such a phone call again," he said flatly. "I forbid you to see this boy again. I forbid you to hold hands with any boy! When you're old enough, and that will be many years from now, you'll be courted properly and you will have a chaperon."

"He's a nice boy and we didn't do anything but walk," she protested.

Agosto scowled. "No more walks! No more! Do you understand?"

"Yes, Papa."

"I should take you out of that school," Agosto threatened. "You're too young to be learning all the things you're learning. And now Mother Superior says you will graduate two years early! They want to send you to Saint Elizabeth's College. But I'm not certain I agree with all this learning, not when I see how you behave."

Clare shook her head. "Papa, you believe in education."

"Girls don't need that much education. College indeed!"

"Agosto . . ." Cecilia stood in the doorway of the study. Over her modest housedress she wore a crisp white apron.

Agosto looked beyond Clare, who did not turn around. "I'm having a talk with Clare about the phone call I received."

"I know," Cecilia said softly. "Clare, go to your room."

Clare hesitated only a moment, then darted past her mother and up the stairs. Only then did the hot tears fill her eyes. "Papa had better not take me out of school," she whispered to herself. "If he does," she vowed, "I'll run away! I'll let Tony fail his courses! And I'll rip Tina's dumb homemade dress to shreds!" She ran into her room, slammed the door, and stamped her foot.

"We were talking," Agosto said, facing Cecilia. "That child must be disciplined, Cecilia. I know what you're thinking . . . I know it is unjust because I'm the one who spoiled her so, taking her to Europe and on business trips . . . but she must learn. I won't have her behaving this way!"

Cecilia ran her delicate hands across her apron. "Have I been a good wife, Agosto?" She looked at him steadily.

He was taken aback by her question. "Of course. Cecilia, I love you, you are the perfect wife—never have you been anything else. How could you ask?"

Cecilia turned and quietly closed the door to the study; then she turned back to Agosto. "Agosto, you've made me go places where I was uncomfortable. You've drawn me into conversations when I was too frightened to open my mouth for fear of disgracing you and making a fool of myself. You made me travel with you, you kept saying I was intelligent . . ."

"You are." He looked into her beautiful troubled face, unable to understand the pain he saw there and genuinely shocked by her tone as well as her words.

"Agosto, I was always afraid because I had no book learning and you and your friends did. No, don't say anything, just listen. Agosto, the world is changing and women are different. Clare is a bright child. You were so proud of her when you came back from Europe—it was you yourself who said how smart she was and how she did just the right things at the right time. Agosto, you must allow Clare to finish her education so she won't have my doubts and my fears. She's not growing up in the world I grew up in, or the world your mother grew up in." Cecilia shook her head. "You always loved your mother because you said she had the spark of life, Agosto. Your daughter has it too. Truth be known, Clare is more like you than Anthony is. Don't deny her an education, Agosto. Don't make her afraid as I am. I want Clare to be different, I want her to be strong and confident."

Agosto sank back down in his chair and looked in amazement at Cecilia. Hadn't he always tried to bring her into his life? Hadn't he always told her how he admired her good sense and intelligence? He felt suddenly at a loss for words.

She bent over and kissed his forehead tenderly. "I love you, Agosto. You've made me happy, but many times you have also made me feel inadequate. Don't send Clare out into the world of the Sarah Ainsleys without the education she needs and deserves."

"Sarah Ainsley?"

"That's the world Clare is growing up in, Agosto. You made the break with tradition, and Clare is only following your example."

"She's a woman," he protested.

"Then she has different traditions to break with," Cecilia said firmly. "Agosto, in all the years we've been married, I've never asked you for anything. You've given me everything, but I have never asked. Now I'm asking you: don't try to punish Clare by threatening to take her out of school. Try to appreciate her intelligence, please."

"I wouldn't really have taken her out of school," Agosto replied. "I was just trying to—"

"I know what you were trying to do. But let me handle this, Agosto. Please."

Agosto bit his lip and then silently nodded. After a moment he reached for Cecilia's hand. "I do love you," he said sincerely.

"I know that," she said, kissing him.

After a time Cecilia went upstairs and knocked on Clare's door.

"Go away!" Clare sobbed.

"It's Mama." Cecilia opened the door and walked in. Clare was on the bed, sitting cross-legged and toying with the bedspread. "You don't have to be angry," Cecilia said softly as she sat down and put her arm around her daughter's shoulders.

"I'll run away if I'm taken out of school!" Clare said defiantly, thrusting her lower lip forward.

"You won't be taken out of school. Clare, I love you and I trust you. I know you have a special future ahead of you, and I know you have a good mind. I want you to finish your education, but you must try to understand your papa. He knows you're different, and in his own way, he's proud of you. But your papa also believes in traditions, Clare. He wants you to wait till you're older, and then, when you go out with boys, you'll be chaperoned. He wants to protect you from gossip, and he doesn't want you to make bad decisions. When people get married, they have children. Marriage is a family matter." Cecilia blushed a little.

"Mama, we were only holding hands!"

Cecilia pressed her lips together. "Clare, women have to be very careful. It starts with holding hands, but one thing leads to another. Girls get into trouble when they're not chaperoned."

Clare frowned. Her mother was blushing and looked uncomfortable.

Cecilia hugged her daughter again. "Don't do that again, Clare. For me?"

Clare snuggled up against her mother. "All right," she agreed, still uncertain of what the danger was in holding hands with a boy.

Monday, November 11, 1918

MANHATTAN

As soon as the ticker tapes clicked out the news that the long-awaited armistice was signed, Agosto called Cecilia and told her to come and bring the children to Manhattan. "We'll all go out to dinner to celebrate," he promised. "And we'll spend the night at the Waldorf. This is a historic moment, an exciting moment! The war is over, Cecilia, and now all the brave young men can come home."

The celebration was spontaneous, and it seemed as if the entire population of the city and its surrounding bouroughs had flooded into Times Square to celebrate.

Times Square was a sight to behold. Colored lights blinked on and off, the traffic was so heavy that no one could move a vehicle, and crowds streamed into the square and spilled over onto the surroundings streets. There were at least ten bands playing on various corners, and periodically a would-be orator tried to mount a makeshift stand to give a speech. But it was no use; a speaker couldn't be heard above the din of the merrymakers.

Strangers danced together in the street, and men in uniform were mobbed by women who kissed and hugged them. The Irish carried beer in buckets and drank right out of them, singing and dancing. Italians danced too, and they sang just as loudly. There were, at any given moment, as many as ten languages being spoken. It was, Agosto said, "an emotional, happy expression of relief."

Cecilia talked Maria into letting Tina come along. She was like a daughter, Cecilia often said. And she always reminded Agosto of his responsibility toward Tina. "Her father's dead, Agosto. You must be her father."

Tina was almost eighteen, but she looked younger because her hair was still worn in braids and because her face had a pleasant roundness.

She danced with Anthony, who was thirteen and nearly as tall as she. They held hands and whirled about in circles, shouting. Agosto held on to Cecilia, and Clare stood by her father's side taking in the scene, a serious expression on her face.

"I hardly think we'll find a place to eat in Manhattan tonight," Agosto said cheerfully. "I think I underestimated the crowds."

"It's a big party!" Tina said enthusiastically. "Like a giant birthday party!"

"I want some cake!" Anthony called out.

Cecilia clung to Agosto. "It's really very crowded here," she said a little breathlessly.

"Would you have wanted to miss it?"

Cecilia shook her head. "I didn't say it wasn't exciting."

Clare stood silently, hardly aware of the throngs of people, but very conscious that she felt awful. Her stomach ached with cramps as if she had eaten something rotten, and she felt weak in the legs and dizzy as the crowds pushed in around them. Her breasts hurt and felt swollen and huge.

"Clarissima, why aren't you dancing?" Agosto asked.

"I don't feel well," she admitted.

She was not often ill. Agosto turned to her. "You do look a bit pale."

"My stomach hurts," she complained.

Cecilia moved over to Clare's side. "Agosto, I think we should take Clare to the hotel—she doesn't look at all well."

"Anthony! Tina! We're going to the hotel," Agosto shouted.

"I want to stay here," Anthony called back as he clung to his older cousin.

"Your sister isn't well."

"She spoils everything," Anthony complained.

"Hush!" Cecilia said, giving him an annoyed look.

Agosto took Clare's arm as well as Cecilia's. He propelled them through the crowd, glancing back now and again to make certain Anthony and Tina were behind them. They walked over to Fifth Avenue and down to the Warldorf at Thirty-third. Agosto led them into the lobby and went immediately to the desk.

"Are you all right, Clare?" Cecilia asked.

"I still feel faint." She crouched on the arm of a green leather chair, Tina sat primly opposite, while Anthony giggled. "Sh!" Clare said harsly. "This is a hotel, not a nursery!"

"You think you're so smart," Anthony hissed through his teeth. "See, you've ruined everyone's night!"

"Everyone's!" Tina added for emphasis.

Clare glared at her brother, then leaned over and whispered, "I am smart, smarter than you will ever be, you little baby!"

Anthony lurched toward her menacingly, but Cecilia glared at him and he fell back into the chair grumbling.

"It's all arranged," Agosto said "Let's go up and order tea from room service. You'll feel better when you are out of the crowd, Clarissima. And later we can order dinner from the dining room. Oscar of the Waldorf is New York's most famous chef!"

Clare smiled weakly; the very thought of food made her stomach turn.

They took the elevator to the fifth floor and the bellboy showed them into their suite. It was deadly quiet inside compared with the hallways, where people were partying. Agosto tipped the young man and ordered tea.

"You should lie down, Clarissima," he suggested.

Clare did not answer, but instead darted into the bathroom.

"Perhaps she's sick to her stomach," Agosto said with some concern.

"Mama! Mama!" Clare's voice called out from the toilet.

Cecilia ran across the room and went into the toilet, closing the door behind her.

Clare stood by the toilet bowl biting her lip. She was pale and shaking.

"Are you sick to your stomach?" Cecilia asked.

Clare shook her head. "Mama, I'm bleeding." She whispered the words.

Cecilia looked at her fifteen-year-old daughter. She had been expecting this for some time, given Clare's mature body and dreamy attitude. "I should have guessed," she said, smiling. "Clarissima, you are now a woman. I did tell you about this."

"You didn't tell me I would bleed! You didn't tell me I'd feel so terrible!"

Cecilia leaned over and kissed Clare's forehead. "That will pass in a few hours. But I'm afraid you'll bleed for at least four or five days. It's the curse of womanhood, Clare. And it will happen every month—unless you are pregnant, of course."

"Five days? Every month!" Clare said in disbelief.

Cecilia smiled tolerantly. "You'll feel better soon. It's not so bad."

"I don't want to be a woman!" Clare wailed, as rare tears filled her eyes. "I hate it! I want to be a boy!"

Cecilia took her daughter in her arms. "Sh," she said, rocking her comfortingly. "There are compensations, I promise you. And, Clare . . . you'll be the kind of woman you want—I promise you that too."

For a time Clare sobbed against her mother's breast; then Cecilia pulled away. "Let me go talk to your father," she whispered.

"Don't you tell Tony," Clare whispered back. "Please."

"I won't. You stay here for a while and wash your face. I'll have to get you some pads—you wear them till it stops. In the meantime, fold over some toilet paper and put it between your legs inside your bloomers. "

Clare nodded.

Cecilia emerged from the toilet.

"Is she all right?" Agosto asked.

"Quite. Anthony and Tina, I want you to go into the other room for a while and close the door. I have to talk to your father."

"I want some tea!" Anthony persisted.

"When it comes you'll be called. Go now, please," Cecilia insisted.

Dejectedly Anthony allowed himself to be led away by Tina. When the door closed behind them, Cecilia told Agosto about Clare.

"And I think you should order some wine," she suggested. "It'll help her sleep. In a little while we'll go out to the pharmacy."

"You can come out now, Clarissima," Agosto called out.

Clare opened the door and crept into the room. Her face was still pale and Agosto could see that her eyes were swollen from crying. She went to the bed and curled up on it, and her father came to her side.

"It's nothing so terrible," he said kindly.

Clare blinked at him. "I don't want to be a girl," she declared.

Agosto leaned over and kissed her cheek. "You'll change your mind."

"Only if I can be a banker," Clare said, looking into her father's eyes.

He sighed. "We'll see."

III

1922–1924

15

Friday, December 15, 1922

B R O O K L Y N

"It's the best we can do," Cecilia told Agosto nervously as she looked around the Tonelli living room, which was filled with vases of red roses from Mike Falvo's hothouse. "If only I'd had more warning. Agosto, two cardinals! Princes of the Church! A count! What can I say to two cardinals? What could I say to even one cardinal?" She fretted all afternoon, and finally retreated to the kitchen in a fluster to supervise Seraphina. "Everything must be perfect," she mumbled again and again.

Agosto ushered his important and unexpected guests into the living room. Cardinal Tanuto, Cardinal Mundelein, and the two black-clad priests who served as their secretaries. Count Emiliano Sforza followed in their wake, a bemused smile on his face.

"I'd have made more appropriate preparations, had I more warning of your visit," Agosto apologized. He'd expected Count Emiliano Sforza, but the representatives of the Holy See were a total surprise.

"Our schedule in America is tightly planned," Cardinal Tanuto explained in Italian. "We weren't certain we could come till the last minute."

"I'm honored you found time," Agosto replied.

Cardinal Tanuto smiled a restrained, polite smile. "Your business with Count Sforza is of the utmost importance to us, for as you know, the land on which the proposed dam is to be built is owned by the Church."

"I'm aware of your concern, your Eminence."

"And the Church must protect its assets," Emiliano Sforza added with a wry smile.

Agosto pressed his lips together. The cardinals surveyed the room, its furniture, and its decor with jaded eyes. Emiliano was casual and at ease with the princes of the Church; Agosto felt less comfortable. Doing business with the Vatican required at least as much skill as dealing with J. P. Morgan.

"You're a wealthy man," Cardinal Tanuto stated. He said it in a questioning tone, as if he couldn't quite believe that a man with several hundred banks and vast international investments would live in such a modest house.

"He's extraordinarily wealthy," Count Sforza added on Agosto's behalf. "Don't be deceived, my friends. In America life is quite different. Equality is a virtue, so Americans desire their elite to disguise themselves." He laughed gently. "I love America—you can't tell anything about a man from outward appearances."

The two cardinals nodded and mumbled something unintelligible.

"Will you be staying for dinner?" Agosto queried.

"I'm afraid their Eminences have a reception tonight at Saint Patrick's," one of the secretaries answered.

"But I'll stay," Count Sforza said with a smile. "Ah, Agosto, on this trip I've had enough of hotel food to last a lifetime."

Agosto laughed in spite of his ill ease. "I must speak to my wife, if you'll excuse me for one moment."

"They're not staying for dinner," he whispered as he opened the door to the kitchen a crack. "Only Emiliano is staying."

Cecilia leaned against the counter. "That's a relief," she whispered back.

Agosto winked at her. "Give us an hour, then come in so I can present you."

"Must I? Agosto, two cardinals . . . What will I say?"

"You can't be the invisible woman," he joked.

She shrugged and nodded. "Go back to them. . . . Having a count to dinner is almost as bad as two cardinals!"

Agosto returned to the living room and pulled the oak doors closed. "May I offer you some wine?"

"That would be pleasant," Cardinal Mundelein said stiffly.

"Do you have children?" Cardinal Tanuto inquired.

"Two, a son and a daughter."

"Only two?" Cardinal Tanuto raised an eyebrow.

Agosto nodded, somewhat annoyed at the personal questions and with the cardinal's tone.

"I do hope we'll have the opportunity to meet them," Cardinal Mundelein put in. "To put it delicately, when the Church does business, it likes to think ahead. Long-term arrangements such as this could conceivably involve heirs."

"You'll have the opportunity to meet my daughter," Agosto informed them. "She's nineteen and will graduate from Saint Elizabeth's Convent College in New Jersey in June. She's home for Christmas recess now. I'm afraid my son—he's seventeen—is visiting friends in Manhattan.''

"A daughter in college!" Cardinal Tanuto uttered in a shocked tone.

"It's a Catholic college," Agosto reiterated.

"And a very good one," Count Sforza put in, only too aware that Cardinal Tanuto came from Calabria and didn't approve of educating women, unlike Cardinal Mundelein, a northern Italian, who was considerably more sophisticated.

"Naturally it would be better if we could meet your son and heir," Cardinal Tanuto suggested.

"I rather hope it'll be a long while before I have to think of heirs," Agosto replied tersely.

Emiliano Sforza laughed. "He's only forty-six, two years older than I."

Cardinal Tanuto nodded and grumbled something about the "liberalism" of the Church in America.

A cold December wind swirled through the treetops, shaking the bare branches. Ominous snow-laden clouds moved rapidly across the early-evening sky, indicating that the season's first blizzard might soon be on the way.

Clare Marina hurried down the street toward home. Her heavy navy-blue coat fell to her ankles and her hat and scarf completely covered her brown hair and part of her angular face.

She inhaled deeply and smiled to herself. In her purse were her first-term marks, and they were all in the high nineties. In June she would graduate, the youngest graduate in her class, and as the letter which came with marks announced, she had been chosen valedictorian. Six months, Clare thought. Six months and she could enter the world of banking.

She hastily climbed the steps of the house, seeking the shelter of the enclosed porch just as a gust of wind carried the first snowflakes.

The door opened before she knocked, and Clare saw the frowning face of Seraphina, the maid. Her finger was lifted to her lips, indicating silence, while her head motioned toward the living room. "Your father has important company," she confided in a low whisper. "Very important company."

Clare squeezed past Seraphina into the hall and took off her coat, scarf, hat, and boots. Silently Seraphina handed Clare her shoes, and Clare slipped into them.

"Your father wants you to go into the living room to meet his guests, but you aren't to stay."

Business, Clare thought to herself. Why not stay? No, she

decided, she would stay. Her career as a student was nearly over, and it was time her father grew used to her presence in business meetings. She studied her image in the hall mirror. Her cheeks were all rosy from the cold, and her curly dark brown hair clung to her head, matted by her hat. She quickly ran her fingers through it, fluffing it up.

"Now," Seraphina urged in her nagging whisper.

Clare gave her a disparaging glance and cautiously opened the double oak doors to the living room. "Oh, my," she said under her breath.

The living room was bedecked in roses, a large vase of bright red roses on virtually every table. They exploded in color, transforming the entire room and filling it with the instant aroma of spring.

"Clare Marina . . ." Her father's voice broke into her vision of having suddenly entered a garden.

"Come in, Clare, and meet our guests."

Clare glanced around the room. Amid the roses sat five men: two black-clad priests, two cardinals of the Church dressed in their bright red robes, and an extremely handsome man wearing a stylish dark suit.

Agosto took Clare's arm and led her to the cardinal who perched on the end of the sofa. It wasn't the custom for cardinals to stand. He remained sitting and looked up at her indulgently with large brown cowlike eyes.

"Your Eminence, Ignacio Cardinal Tanuto, I should like to present my daugther, Clare Marina."

Clare knelt just as she had knelt years ago at her confirmation. She took the cardinal's extended hand and kissed his ruby ring. His short fat fingers were covered with hair and they tickled her nose.

"Your Eminence," she whispered.

Cardinal Tanuto smiled benevolently with his uneven yellowed teeth. His face was perfectly round and marked by deep wrinkles. His short neck virtually disappeared into his robes, and his heavy gold cross, encrusted with rubies, was partially hidden by the folds of his belly.

"My daughter," he intoned. "You should be marrying soon and bearing children for Mother Church."

Clare neither nodded nor answered. She feigned a smile and studied the tips of her shoes, thinking that one had to expect such an attitude from a cardinal.

Again her father took her arm, leading her to the second cardinal. "Your Eminence, Joseph Cardinal Mundelein, may I present my daughter, Clare Marina."

Cardinal Mundelein was thinner than Cardinal Tanuto. His facial features were sharp, his teeth whiter and straighter.

Clare dropped to her knees again and kissed the ruby ring. "Your Eminence." His fingers were long and graceful, and his hand, Clare noted, smelled of lavender.

"You're as fresh as a lovely flower in the Vatican garden," the cardinal mused, moving his head and hands as he spoke.

Agosto held out his hand and Clare stood up. "And this is Father Cuestra, Cardinal Tanuto's personal secretary, and Father Civitello, Cardinal Mundelein's personal secretary." Clare politely shook hands with each of them. They were young men and they smiled warmly—far more warmly than the stiff, dour Irish priests who taught her classes.

"And, Clare, this is my European business associate, Count Emiliano Sforza of Milan."

Count Sforza stood up. He was tall and had wide shoulders. His hair was thick, wavy, and just beginning to gray around the temples, his face remarkably young-looking, and his eyes were blue and framed by long lashes.

He bowed from the waist and kissed her hand, then, turning to Agosto, raised his eyebrow. "You've been hiding her from me all these years!" Clare felt the heat in her face and knew it was flushed.

"A woman in college," Cardinal Tanuto complained again. "What, pray, do you study?"

"History, geography, mathematics, the same subjects men study," Clare replied, aware of the cardinal's disapproving stare.

"Well, this *is* America," Cardinal Mundelein intoned with resignation. "After all, women are allowed to vote here."

"Those are excellent subjects for study, and no doubt required, but what are you truly interested in?" Count Sforza asked.

"Banking," Clare answered without hesitation. Then, for good measure she added, "And politics."

"Excuse me, Clare." Her father's hand gently touched her shoulder.

"Yes, Papa?" Clare smiled innocently at her father, knowing full well that her answer to Count Sforza's question had annoyed him. Whenever she expressed her all-consuming interest in business, he became annoyed.

"We've business to discuss."

Clare smiled again and sat down on the sofa near Cardinal Tanuto. "Then I'd like to listen," she announced.

Agosto's face clouded instantly, but before he could speak, Count Sforza interjected, "A woman's presence would be a great help." He winked at Agosto. "Women are very insightful, my friend."

Woman . . . not girl. Clare looked warmly at the count, and in return he nodded toward her, an expression of amusement on his face. Her father sat down, still looking annoyed.

"So you see the Church's position, Agosto." Count Sforza turned to Agosto immediately. As he spoke, he reached into his vest pocket and removed a gold cigarette case.

Count Sforza was an elegant man, ruggedly handsome, and dressed in the very best of taste, Clare thought as she observed him.

Cardinal Tanuto protested that roses wilted in smoke. But the count paid no attention, and went on speaking in his deep baritone voice. "As soon as a dam can be built on the Ticino River, Torino and Milano will have the hydroelectric power they so desperately need," he explained.

"Ah, this is such a fortunate country! So much coal, so much oil! We have coal in southwest Sardinia, of course, but the quality is poor and the mines are inefficient," Cardinal Tanuto lamented.

"We use far more than we produce," the count added. "And of course, importing foreign coal causes further drains on our foreign reserves. The lira isn't the strong currency it once was. I'm afraid we won the war but lost the peace, my friend." He lifted his arms in the air in a gesture that indicated the irony of Italy's dilemma. "We believed that by fighting with the allies we would be rewarded, that the peace treaty would recognize our contribution to the victory. Instead, the war drained our economy and the peace treaty gave us none of the land we were promised."

"War seldom has glorious results," Agosto observed. "But I agree Italy was treated unfairly in the peace negotiations."

"Not receiving the coal mines in Slovenia destroyed our ability to recover. The French got what they wanted when they recovered Alsace and began to work the coal mines there. As a result, they can boast of 'national honor.' But we were told by our allies that if Slovenia were given to Italy, it would upset the newly declared Kingdom of the Serbs, Croats, and Slovenes." The count sounded mildly disgusted.

"Our allies didn't fulfill their promises," Father Civitello agreed.

"The policy of irredentism is as old as European politics," Cardinal Mundelein stressed, shaking his head. "Those areas Italy claimed have large Italian populations. They should have been restored to Italy."

Irredentism, Clare thought to herself. It was irredentism that D'Annunzio used to fire the people of Genoa that day in the square when she and her father listened to him dedicate the statue of Garibaldi. She hadn't understood it then, but she understood it now. It was the policy that sought to recover a linguistically or historically related area from foreign rule. Italy had been promised the Austrian provinces of Trentino, South Tyrol, Gorizia and Istria, and the Dalmatian coast. Slovenia was in the Dalmatian area. Italy had succeeded in taking control of South Tyrol and the Istrian peninsula, but not Slovenia. The Italian irredentists, those nationalists who believed that Italians living under foreign rule should be reunited with Italy, were furious with the terms of the peace treaty. And there was no denying that the terms of the treaty had seriously affected the Italian economy.

"But our main concern is man's soul," Cardinal Mundelein said loftily, "and honest labor feeds the soul. Hydroelectric power is needed to get men back to work. There are godless forces at work in Italy." He shook his head. "Some speak of the glorification of the worker, yet they deny God. Just two years ago, I believe, those same evil forces wreaked havoc in the very shadow of Wall Street."

Clare's eyes studied her father's face and she wondered what his reaction would be to the cardinal's comment. It would certainly stir him. Barton Ainsley, his friend and mentor, had been one of the thirty people killed in the blast that ripped open the wall of the Morgan Bank.

At the time, Agosto had been torn between mourning his friend, and almost total irrationality, shouting that the blast was caused by people like Paolo who were constantly stirring up trouble. But the explosives were planted by anarchists, and Paolo was not an anarchist, he was a socialist. Clare knew her father didn't differentiate between anarchists, socialists, and communists. Rather he believed they were all part of one godless force bent on destroying the United States. And certainly even if her father had reservations about the church hierarchy and their business dealings, he would agree with the cardinal that anarchists, communists, and socialists were a danger.

Months after the blast, he had taken her to Wall Street and shown her exactly where the horrible explosion had ripped through the front of the Morgan Bank. He had ranted on about communism, issuing grim warnings about the future if such people were not put away.

The mention of the Wall Street blast caused Agosto's features to harden. But much to her relief, he didn't begin his frequent tirade, though judging from the cardinal's comments, Agosto's views would have fallen on sympathetic ears.

"In any case, we don't have the coal mines," Cardinal Tanuto summed up. "Therefore, we need the dam."

"Which will benefit the Church in two ways," Count Sforza said bluntly. "It's a project that will employ people, and therefore may be construed as accomplishing social good, and the rents paid on the land will provide the Vatican with added income."

"Which will be used to feed the poor," Cardinal Mundelein quickly explained.

Count Sforza leaned forward. "I'll personally be contributing one-fourth of the total sum required, the government of Italy will contribute an additional forty percent, and we seek the remainder from your bank."

"It's not charity we seek," Cardinal Tanuto stressed, "but your considered assistance, which will naturally result in large profits for you too."

Agosto's face took on a neutral expression. "Your Eminences, Emiliano, allow me to ask just why you have come to me. Surely the Bank of Milan is interested in this project."

"The Bank of Milan is interested, but it's also desperately short of foreign reserves. Italy has been dutifully paying her war debts to America, France, and England. And naturally the change in American immigration laws has meant fewer Italians are coming here, and as a result, less American money is being sent to Italy. It can all be summed up quite neatly: a variety of circumstances causes us to seek help in America. You played a vital role in the Italian economy when you funded the modernization of the port of Brindisi, you're of Italian heritage. It's quite natural that you'd be our first choice."

"Brindisi . . ." Agosto said the name almost longingly. "A family debt owed to the province. My father and mother were born in Lecce, only a few miles away. They're buried there."

Count Sforza laughed gently. He had a nice voice, Clare thought. "A debt, perhaps. But certainly you made money on the transaction, and I feel certain that even greater profits will accrue from an investment in the Ticino dam project," he stressed.

Agosto nodded, and Clare thought that he and the count understood each other. It was difficult to talk pure business with cardinals and priests, who preferred, even in knowledgeable company, to play down the vast holdings of the Church, even though, she thought, they were quite willing to reveal their political concerns.

"When do you envisage the dam operational?" Agosto asked.

"With your backing, we could begin construction immediately.

I would imagine the first generators could be started, say, by the end of twenty-four.''

"The end of twenty-four," Agosto repeated thoughtfully. "I must confess to giving this some thought before your arrival." He smiled. "In fact, I paid for a rather extensive investigation and analysis after receiving Emiliano's original proposal. I've got some reservations. The most serious involve Italy's labor problems, which I know the new government is trying to rectify. But the new government isn't yet stable, it's unproven. Most American bankers, and I'm no exception, have taken a wait-and-see attitude toward investment. Mussolini has been prime minister only since October, and the situation prior to his appointment was absolutely chaotic.''

"We were in a fight for our lives," Cardinal Tanuto admitted. "But you'll see changes. The communists and socialists won't win now.''

"Papa, labor problems don't keep you from investing here," Clare pointed out.

Agosto frowned at her sudden interruption. He turned to Count Sforza. "I've always believed investment offers economic progress and is the best tool for fighting social evil. I haven't said no, I'm simply explaining my hesitation.''

"Your daughter's right, Agosto. Labor problems here don't stop you from investing, nor would a change of government. And you of all people should know that the press exaggerates. It's quite true that in certain regions of the country there were communist organizers playing on economic discontent. But they're being dealt with . . . the heroes who returned from the war have no patience with these imported troublemakers, these Bolsheviks. Believe me, the troublemakers are being put down, but we too have an obligation, Agosto. We have the means to change the economic climate, create an environment that isn't favorable to these disrupters. They grow and blossom with unemployment and discontent, so until there are more jobs, their seeds will grow in fertile ground. Agosto, come to Italy this summer. Bring your family and we'll have a summer of work and relaxation. You'll see firsthand what's happening, and you can evaluate the progress made by the new government for yourself. If possible, I'll introduce you to our new prime minister. He's a young man, the youngest prime minister in Italian history. But he's a genius, and he's going to unite the country economically. As you know, the lira is already gaining in value.''

"A great man," Cardinal Tanuto intoned. "He'll solve the Church's problems as well.''

"Some of his critics say he has no respect for the parliamentary system," Agosto suggested.

"He had no respect for the weakness displayed by Parliament under the former prime minister. But you'll see: Il Duce will lead Italy to stability and will restore national pride and increase international respect."

"Do you know him well?" Agosto asked.

"Very well. His headquarters were in Milan."

"Now, there's a man who knows how to handle the socialist threat!" Cardinal Tanuto's eyes flashed with admiration.

"We must go," Father Civitello announced with some agitation. "The Italian ambassador, Romano Avezzana, is hosting a banquet at the Italy America Society tonight, and after that there's the reception at Saint Patrick's for the American clergy."

"We'll talk at dinner," Agosto said to Emiliano. Then, turning to the cardinals, who were putting on their heavy black capes: "I think you can count on my support."

They mumbled their thanks and hurried to the waiting car that had come for them.

Saturday, December 16, 1922

B R O O K L Y N

Billows of steam floated up, coating the bathroom walls, mirrow, and windowpanes. The air was heavy with the scent of lilacs as Clare lay in the bathtub, idly playing with masses of bubbles.

The night before recreated itself in her mind over and over; images floated before her closed eyes, bits of conversation ran through her thoughts. The evening had been bittersweet. Emiliano Sforza filled her daydreams, but the argument she'd had with her father lingered and the recollection of his angry words and belittling attitude still brought tears of defiance to her eyes. Sometimes she felt as if her father were two different people. He indulged her with one hand and denied her with the other.

Her mother's dinner had been a masterpiece. The first course was an appetizer, *sarde beccafico*—small filled sardines individually stuffed with bread crumbs and pine nuts and flavored with a dash of lemon juice. Then there were three pastas; two were specialties of the Abruzzi region, one a delicacy from Puglia. And certainly during dinner the conversation had been as good as the food. Emiliano Sforza turned to her often and asked, "Clare, what do you think of that?" She'd sensed her father's irritation, but did he expect her to reply "I have no thoughts"? So she had answered, expressing herself freely and fully taking part in the political-economic conversation.

After dinner, Count Sforza extended an invitation, an invitation that meant she would see him again.

"Will you be my guests at the opera tomorrow night?" he asked. And then, turning to Clare, said, "I'll tell you about *Nabucco*, I'll explain why it's the favorite opera of all those who come from Milan."

"Tomorrow is Saturday," her father replied. And for a moment Clare was afraid he'd reject the count's invitation. But instead, he only explained that Anthony would be home.

"But of course your son is welcome to join us," Count Sforza replied. "I'm looking forward to meeting him."

Count Sforza had been the sweet part of the evening; the bitter part came after his departure, when Agosto and Clare were alone and Cecilia had gone upstairs.

"You were impertinent!" her father had stormed. "Women do not partake in business discussions. You knew—I *know* you knew—I didn't want you to stay while I was discussing business with the cardinals!"

"Count Sforza didn't seem to mind," she retorted.

"You're my daughter, not his! And then at dinner you went on and on about the gold standard, of all things! Clare Marina, you were most unfeminine! And what do you know of these matters?"

"Papa, I just received all nineties! I'm going to be valedictorian of my graduating class in June. I must know something!"

"Not as much as you seem to think. And don't you realize the competition isn't as stiff in a girls' school as it is in a real university?"

Tears had begun to form in her eyes, tears born of anger and frustration. "Why can't you ever be proud of me?" she had shouted in return. "It *is* a real university! And I'm not only the highest-ranking student, I'm the youngest."

"Just the point," her father had answered. "You're young and you're a woman! You don't know about business."

"I'm going into business! And I do know about it!" She hadn't waited for his answer. Instead she had whirled around and fled to her room before the tears began to tumble down her cheeks.

* * *

"Clare!" Anthony bellowed, loudly pounding on the door. "Clare, have you drowned in there? I have to use the toilet!"

"Go away, Tony! Go find a tree. Boys are always using trees."

"Clare, let me in. I have to . . . Well, I can't use a tree."

"Use Mama's bathroom!" she called out with irritation.

"Mama's in there!"

Clare sighed. "Oh, all right, but you'll have to wait a minute."

With little urgency, Clare reluctantly climbed out of the tub and dried herself. Wrapped in a robe, she unlocked the bathroom door. Poor Tony, he was dancing about.

He stormed into the bathroom, waving at the steam. "Christ, what are you doing, growing mold in here?" He then sneezed at the overpowering smell of lilacs.

"You're a bore," she said, brushing past him, allowing him to lock the door. "One day," she called out, "one day I'll have a house with five bathrooms. And two of them will be only for me."

"Then you better marry a rich man!"

"I'll have my own money!" Clare stormed as she hurried toward her room. At least she'd have the dressing table to herself!

On the bed Clare laid out her finest clothes. A pure silk envelope chemise, over which she'd wear her sophisticated rose organdy dress. It was a wonderful dress. Huge deep ruffles bedecked its V neck and a mock apron of ruffles went around her hips below the deeper rose satin sash that pulled in her waist. And tonight she chose to wear silk hose and her best satin slippers. Her gown fell nearly to her ankles, but didn't quite cover them, she thought happily.

She pictured herself: My hair will fall in masses of curls. . . . All day she'd worn rag knots in her hair to set it properly for evening. Count Sforza cared about her views. He was suave, handsome, and he listened to her. Clare looked at her image in the mirror. "I'm a woman," she said aloud. "And I'll show Papa that a woman can be both feminine and intelligent."

"Quite the two most beautiful women at the opera," Count Sforza said admiringly as he kissed first Cecilia's hand and then Clare's. He turned to Agosto. "It's easy to see where Clare Marina gets her good looks."

Agosto held Cecilia's arm protectively. She was paler and thinner than she had once been, but she was still a stunning woman. Her dark hair was attractively peppered with silver, and at thirty-nine her face was unlined. Her large expressive eyes were absolutely beautiful. She wore a pale blue dress, a single-strand gold necklace, long gold earrings, and a bracelet.

They settled into the box Count Sforza had taken. Clare arranged her dress around her and studied the libretto, aware that Emiliano Sforza had taken the chair next to her and, indeed, had moved it a bit closer.

"You see," he said, leaning over, "*Nabucco* is ostensibly about the Hebrews and King Nebuchadnezzar II. When it was produced in Milan at La Scala in 1847, the chorus—the mournful chorus of the captive Hebrews—sparked a dormant wave of true Italian nationalism because, as you probably know from your history, Milan was dominated by the Austrians at the time. The prayer of the Hebrews for deliverance from domination matched Italian aspirations, but the opera dealt with the Hebrews and the parallel was overlooked by Austrian censors."

"I'd like to see Milan now that I'm older," Clare declared.

Count Sforza smiled. "Ah, yes, I remember. You were there with your father just as war broke out."

"Yes, when I was eleven—well, almost twelve—Papa took me, but we had to leave because of the war and I only had a short tour of Milan while he was with you."

"When you come this summer, I'll arrange for you to see everything."

"I'm looking forward to it."

"And after Milan, we'll spend a few weeks at our villa overlooking Lake Como."

Our, Clare thought. "Are you married?" she whispered.

Count Sforza smiled. "A widower. But my sister lives with me."

Clare leaned back in her chair, a wave of satisfaction sweeping over her.

The low, sad strains of the overture began, and the house lights dimmed. "As you listen, Clare, remember that a man can be held prisoner in many ways," Count Sforza whispered. "Try to feel *Nabucco*, as well as hear and see it."

He touched her hand, and Clare felt a slight chill of anticipation.

"There's a reception for Giulio Gatti-Casazza, the director of the Metropolitan, at the Waldorf," Emiliano Sforza told them as they filed out of the opera house and into the cold December air. "I've been invited, and I think you should all join me."

Cecilia audibly sighed. She knew just who would be there: the Stearnses, the Auchinclosses, the Harrimans, the Whitneys, the Lamonts, and possibly the Morgans. It would be a long evening of business conversations among the men, the occasional dance around the floor, and the barbed comments of bored wealthy wives.

"Let's go!" she heard Clare say enthusiastically.

"I love the opera, but receptions make me uncomfortable," Cecilia whispered to Agosto.

He squeezed her arm. "I haven't seen Lamont in ages, and there are matters I should take up with him."

"You're all business," Emiliano Sforza said with a wink as he overheard Agosto. "Americans don't know how to simply enjoy themselves. They feel sinful if they don't combine business with pleasure."

Agosto agreed. "I know my weaknesses. But I promise not to spend the whole evening talking to Lamont. Should we go, Cecilia?"

Cecilia nodded and thought silently: I mustn't let my own ill ease spoil Clare's evening.

The reception was held on the roof garden, where an orchestra played dance tunes, alternating between waltzes for the elderly and the tango and black bottom for the younger set.

Near the punch bowl, Giulio Gatti-Casazza held court. He was flamboyantly dressed in a flowing black cape and a wide-brimmed floppy hat that would have better suited one of the society matrons.

Clare and her mother stood discreetly by while Agosto and Emiliano talked with J. P. Morgan Jr., Thomas Lamont, and Dwight Morrow, who were better known as the financial trinity of the Morgan Bank.

Cecilia knew all three gentlemen from innumerable events Agosto had taken her to, but Clare knew only Thomas Lamont; the others she recognized from their pictures in the financial press. They were, she mused, even more wooden than they appeared in print, and the conversation revolved around the need to reupholster the seats at the Metropolitan. And as was the usual case, the trinity of bankers was more interested in speaking with Tony, the heir apparent to the Tonelli banks, than with her.

"These affairs make me uncomfortable," Cecilia confessed to her daughter.

"Mama, you look beautiful! You've no reason to be uncomfortable."

"I have nothing to say to these people. I'm not educated as they are." Cecilia looked at the floor.

Instinctively Clare hugged her mother. "Mama, you are too educated. You read to me, you told me stories, you always talked to me about everything! Mama, don't be so shy. I wouldn't know anything if it weren't for you.''

Cecilia didn't answer. Clare was so different, so full of self-confidence. She felt proud of her daughter, yet awed by her at the same time. I can't explain, she thought. I can't describe the fear that takes hold of me, that ties my tongue in knots, that makes me want to run home, where I feel sheltered and protected. She felt suddenly like talking to Clare about the argument she'd overheard last night, but her opportunity was short-lived. Count Sforza broke away from the men and joined them.

''You look restless,'' he said to Clare, taking her arm. ''Come, come, let's circulate. I've more than ample opportunity to be with bankers in Milan.''

The band began to play, and he swept Clare onto the dance floor, embracing her around the waist while Cecilia watched. A handsome man, she admitted. She frowned slightly. Was she imagining it, or was Emiliano Sforza really taken with Clare? On the dance floor, Clare relished her moment. Count Sforza took three long steps backward and then dipped her downward.

''Oh, I've never done the tango.'' Clare laughed.

''Quite the most popular dance in Italy last year.''

''It's fun,'' Clare whispered, aware of the pressure of his fingers on her back.

''I think we look like professional partners, almost as good as Fred and Adele Astaire,'' he said mischievously. ''There, you see, I go to American movies, I keep up.''

Clare allowed him to hold her closer, and she thought: He's flirting with me. She glanced over her shoulder at Tony, who was surrounded by bankers. On another night, she reflected, she'd have felt put out that her father's banking associates sought Tony out. It made her want to scream that she too would go into the family business, that she too would one day have power. But tonight it hardly fazed her to see Tony being courted. Emiliano was one of the most important men in the room, and he *listened* to her even as he looked at her as if she were a woman.

''You're very beautiful, Clare Marina,'' he said, looking into her eyes. ''And you're intelligent too. I'm looking forward to the spring, to showing you Milan. You'll find that in Italy a new day is dawning. Yes, I'm looking forward to the talks we'll have; one always sees things best through younger eyes.''

Clare leaned against his chest. The promise of his words and the look in his eyes filled her with pleasure. So much pleasure that the argument she had had with her father momentarily faded from her mind.

Sunday, December 17, 1922

BROOKLYN

Clare sat at her desk, books piled in one corner, papers scattered about. "Nobody with a neat desk can be accomplishing anything," her father often joked. If he was right, she fully expected to get a high grade on her essay. Her desk was a mess.

"Clare . . ." Cecilia whispered her name and tapped lightly on the bedroom door.

"Yes, Mama. Come in."

"Am I disturbing you? I know you're studying."

Clare closed her book. "I have plenty of time. My essay isn't due till January 15, and my primary research is already done."

Cecilia came into Clare Marina's room, closing the door behind her. She looked around, then sat on the edge of the bed. "What's it about?" she inquired.

"Trade barriers," Clare replied.

Cecilia frowned.

"You know, taxes on imported goods . . . things like that. America taxes certain imports to protect our own industry—that's one kind of trade barrier. Another is a restriction on certain items. That is, not allowing them in the country at all. Like shoes—without protection, our own shoe industry would suffer."

Cecilia nodded. "I understand. . . . Clare, I want to talk with you."

"And not about trade barriers," Clare guessed.

Cecilia paused as if searching for the right words; then she sighed. "I heard you and your father arguing the other night."

"Oh, I'd hoped you hadn't."

"Clare, you mustn't think your father isn't proud of you. I know he is. He just can't show it, and he's convinced you shouldn't go into banking."

"Mama, he has to let me go into the family business, and if he won't, I'll find a way to go into banking on my own."

Cecilia looked indulgently at her daughter and shook her head. "Your father's a good man—he's fair and he's honest. You challenge him, Clare. You challenge him, and he gets stubborn."

"How can I make him understand, Mama? I've worked hard to get good grades. I studied hard and I want to put my studies to use. Now he acts like I've done nothing!" She could feel the tears beginning to form again. Her father's lack of recognition was like a stabbing pain, and talking about it brought it all back.

"Don't cry, Clare." Cecilia reached out and touched her hand. "Your papa will come around, I know he will. But, Clare, you have to be patient, you have to avoid challenging him and making him angry."

"If he could just say once that he was proud of me, that he knew I could succeed. . . ." Clare fought back her desire to cry.

"He will say it one day, Clare. I know he thinks it . . . I know that he wants to say it, but he can't."

Clare nodded and squeezed her mother's hand. "I love you," she whispered.

Cecilia stood up and kissed her daughter on the cheek. "You write your essay," she said. "You write the very best essay in the class. Don't let your father upset you. He loves you . . . he doesn't mean it."

Clare watched as her mother left her room. She shook her head sadly. He won't change, she thought to herself. He won't change, and I can't.

Friday, January 12, 1923

NEW YORK

Creighton Stearns, who had married Sarah Ainsley, was the same age as Agosto Tonelli. He was a man of medium stature with stone-blue eyes and a pale complexion; he was also a man of considerable wealth. When his father-in-law, Barton Ainsley, had died, Creighton had inherited Barton's share in the banks once held in partnership between the Stearns family and the Ainsley family. Having already inherited the Stearns shares, he now had total control.

It was twelve-thirty-five and Creighton Stearns sat at his table in the Knickerbocker Club and poked at his luncheon salad, though his mind was still firmly on breakfast.

"I hear Agosto Tonelli is trying to put together a consortium to make a major investment in Italy," Sarah had announced. The look on his wife's face was one of challenge; she might as well have added: What are you going to do about it? But Sarah was a trifle more subtle; she waited for him to bite.

"Really?" had been his only answer.

"But why am I telling you?" she asked. "You're the banker, you have all the connections. I supposed you knew."

"I had heard something about it," he lied. "I don't think Tonelli has it off the ground, though."

She set her coffee cup down somewhat forcefully. "More international prestige for the Tonelli empire, nothing for you. Honestly, Creighton, you never do anything with flair! You never do anything to bring the family name into the limelight."

"Bankers don't seek publicity," he had answered defensively.

"No, they seek power. Agosto has power."

"I have it too."

"Not as much," she said, needling him. "And you inherited it. Agosto built it from the ground up."

"With your father's help."

"Precisely," Sarah said coolly.

"Well, my dear, American Federal Banks is strictly a family corporation. I can't buy into it and attempt a traditional takeover bid, you know."

"You could do something to stop Agosto from making more money, though. You could put barriers in his way, if you wanted to."

He had only shrugged. But Sarah's words had stayed with him throughout the morning. He had made phone calls, he'd checked to see whom Agosto Tonelli was approaching. Lamont was solid. He respected Agosto, he trusted his instincts, and that meant that the Morgan Bank would be in on the consortium. But there were others. . . . Impatiently he checked his watch. As he looked up, he saw Willard Harrison approaching.

"I hope I didn't keep you waiting." Willard smiled and sat down.

"I only just arrived," Creighton replied. He and Willard Harrison went back a long way. They were both Back Bay Bostonians, both had attended Harvard, both had been members of the Hasty Pudding Club. They understood each other.

The waiter came and Willard ordered. They made small talk about the market and about a mutual real-estate deal they had going in Florida. Finally Willard leaned back and lit a cigar. "You seemed anxious to have lunch. I thought you had something serious to discuss."

"I do rather." Creighton lit a cigarette. "It's about Tonelli."

Harrison laughed. "I hear the dago banker is about to become a big-time Italian financier."

"It's damn unpatriotic if you ask me. He's pulling in banker after banker to form a consortium to build some dam in Italy . . .

just so their industry can compete with ours. Hell, aren't there enough Americans who need loans?''

"I guess not," Harrison answered, raising an eyebrow. "But the investment will be lucrative, you know.''

Creighton moved in for the kill. "Sure, and Tonelli will end up with a bigger share of the American investment market as a result.''

"You have something in mind?''

"Yes, but we'll have to be discreet. I wouldn't want it to get around. I think if we could actively discourage participation in the consortium, it would put Tonelli on the spot. He'd feel duty-bound to stick by his deal with Sforza, so he might overextend himself.''

Harrison laughed. "To the extent that he wouldn't have the assets to move in on your control of Ashby Steel?''

Creighton nodded. He wondered if Sarah knew about Ashby. Probably not. If she had, she would have mentioned it; she wasn't one to ignore a weapon in her arsenal when it came to her jealousy over the Tonelli fortune. And even Creighton had to admit there was nothing underhanded in Agosto's move. Ashby needed the extra capital, Agosto had made an offer, and he'd even called Creighton to explain that he had no intention of interfering with the company's management. But it gnawed at his soul. The fucking dago was going to do him a favor.

"Well, I don't much like the way American Federal Banks is spreading its wings either. I think it's time we did something.''

"At best, he won't be able to get together with anyone but Morgan. At worst, he'll have to use a lot of his own money to keep his deal.''

Harrison smiled. "Count me in. I'll start making contacts tomorrow.''

Creighton butted out his cigarette. "Brandy?" he asked.

16

Sunday, April 22, 1923

BROOKLYN

Agosto sat at the cluttered desk in his study. It hadn't been a good week. Three of the banks he'd thought were in on the consortium had suddenly backed out. "And we'd shaken on the deal," Agosto muttered to himself. And he himself had shaken hands with Emiliano Sforza. That meant the funds had to be provided by American Federal. His honor was at stake.

"You're just in a bad mood because those deals to form a consortium fell through," Tony muttered from the chair.

"Damn right I am! When I do business, my handshake is my word, it's as good as a written contract. I don't like dealing with men who go back on their word. But you don't have to worry, the deal will go through because I gave my word to Emiliano Sforza that it would. And none of this has anything to do with why you're here, young man!"

"You're mad and you're going to take it out on me," Tony declared, a self-righteous tone in his voice.

Agosto's face was distorted with anger. "No, but I am going to take this out on you, as you put it. I can't believe this!" he shouted, throwing down the report from the prestigious Newman School in New Jersey. "Not only will you fail to get into Villanova! You may fail your senior year entirely!"

Tony crouched in the green leather chair and thought about Clare Marina. Supposedly she was in the kitchen, but he was sure she could hear. God, the way his father was shouting, the whole neighborhood could hear.

"The priests don't like me," he complained. "They're all Irish! They hate Italians!"

"Don't give me that! Clare has Irish priests for teachers, and she never failed to get an A! You, you can't even pass!"

"I tried!"

"You didn't try! You spend all your time going to baseball games with Joe Giuliano. It's all right for him. It's not all right for you! I expect more of you than knowing the inside of Ebbets Field and the batting averages of Babe Ruth and Rogers Hornsby!"

"I know all the batting averages," Tony countered defensively.

"You should know the Dow Jones industrial averages so well!"

"I study!"

"And so you're telling me that you're not as smart as your sister? You're admitting that?"

Tony shook his head. "Of course not! She's a girl!"

"Well, she does much better than you! I think you'd better give that some thought."

Tony grumbled, wishing he could disappear into the chair. "I'm only fifteen!"

"And in September you'll be only seventeen! What do you think you're going to have, perpetual childhood? When I was your age I was getting straight A's in school and working thirty hours a week—fifteen in my father's store, fifteen in the cement factory. And no smart cars to drive around in either, Tony. We had to walk in the snow, back and forth, back and forth. I must have walked three miles a day. And in the summers I worked all day in the cement factory to make more money. I had to lift bricks and blocks. You, you couldn't even lift a pebble!"

"I'll try harder," Tony promised.

"Damn right you'll try harder! My father expected us all to work *and* go to school. He expected respect. I thought you'd do better than I did. I thought if you didn't have to work, you'd get better grades. What I learned, I learned the hard way, but I thought: Anthony will be smarter because he's going to have a better education. Well, let me tell you, you *are* going to have a better education. I was going to take you to Europe this summer, but not now, my boy. Now I've arranged for you to stay at the Newman School and be tutored by Father Murray. A good Jesuit, I hope he works you till you drop!"

"All summer! Christ, I'll miss the whole baseball season!"

"Damn right you will! No weekends off. Not one! And if you don't pass your entrance exams to Villanova at the end of the summer, you'll be spending next summer the same way."

"Papa . . . all summer?"

"You heard me!" Agosto roared. "Now, get upstairs and begin right now!"

Tony grimaced and pulled himself up out of the chair, barely managing to hold the tears back. He fled the room.

*　　*　　*

"Is he all right?" Cecilia asked timidly. "Is Tony all right?"

"He'll be fine, he just needs a firmer hand," Agosto stressed as he lit a stogie and leaned back in his chair.

"I could hear every word, Agosto. It's a pity he'll miss the trip."

"It's necessary."

"Agosto, I've been thinking. I've been thinking that you and Clare Marina should go to Europe alone."

"Cecilia, the three of us would have a wonderful time."

She studied the floor and avoided looking into her husband's eyes. "Agosto, I love you, but I really wouldn't enjoy it. Let me stay here with Fabiana, where I belong."

"You belong with me," he said, searching her face.

"I know, but you'll be busy, and Clare is a fine companion. She'll get so much out of the trip, Agosto. Please, please try to understand that I just don't enjoy traveling very much."

Agosto reached out and touched her shoulder gently. "Are you sure?"

She lifted her eyes and smiled at him. "Yes. Agosto, I love you and I'll miss you. But it is only for a few months, and I really want to stay home."

Agosto cupped her chin in his hand and kissed her on the cheek. "If that's the way you want it," he agreed. "But I'll miss you."

Cecilia kissed him in return. "Agosto, tell Clare Marina the trip is a graduation gift. Tell her you're proud of her. I know you are, but she needs to know it too."

"I am proud of her. I just want her to fulfill her natural role."

"I'm sure she will," Cecilia replied. "I suppose the real question is, what's natural for a girl as talented as Clare."

"It's impossible, Cecilia. I'm not the only one who couldn't accept a woman in banking."

Cecilia smiled. "Nothing is really impossible, Agosto." With that she turned away and went back to the kitchen.

Monday, April 23, 1923

NEW JERSEY

Clare Marina looked around her room at Saint Elizabeth's. In keeping with the austere quality of the institution, it was little more than a cell furnished with a bed, a dresser, and a small desk. "Soon," she said aloud. "Soon I'll be gone from here. No more cafeteria food, no more curfews, no more scratchy woolen uniforms." She flopped down on the bed. "And no more nuns!"

She reached in her pocket and took out the letter she'd received that morning from Emiliano Sforza. Again she carefully unfolded it and reread it—she had already read it four times.

> Milan
> April 1, 1923
>
> My Dear Clare Marina,
>
> I hope you will not think it forward of me to write to you. I remembered the name of your college and looked up the address.
>
> I attended La Scala last night, and the experience vividly brought back our meeting. But then, I must confess that from the moment I met you, you have remained in my thoughts. I am greatly looking forward to your visit this summer. I look forward to showing you Milan and Lake Como, to long walks with you along the shore, and to the talks we will share.
>
> You are an enchanting young woman, the kind of woman who lingers in a man's mind. Your father tells me that the two of you will be sailing on June 15 and that you will first visit Paris, then arrive in Milan on the twenty-ninth. I shall of course meet you. Have a safe journey, Clare Marina, and remember: I am looking forward to being with you, so don't fall in love on the ship.
>
> Affectionately,
> Emiliano Sforza

Clare sniffed the letter, which smelled slightly of musk. She rolled over, putting the letter on her heart, and sighed deeply, allowing her imagination to conjure up images of Lake Como, of the Sforza villa, of her and Emiliano dancing. . . .

Saturday, June 9, 1923

NEW JERSEY

Clare Marina stared out at the assembled guests. They were dressed impeccably. But then, she thought, since she had gone to school with their daughters, the parents should come as no surprise. They were the cream of American Catholic society. Only the wealthy Catholic families of New York, Philadelphia, San Francisco, Boston, and New Haven and the old established families of Maryland, the first Catholic colony, sent their daughters to college. Few of the girls were from families that had recently immigrated. Most were fourth- or fifth-generation, and only five girls in the entire school were of Italian heritage. But daughters were sent to college with one thought in mind: intelligent women made intelligent mothers. Daughters, Clare thought, were secondary; sons were the main concern.

Father Murphy had requested she rewrite her valedictory speech. She objected, and finally he gave in with a grunt. "It's your speech, but I don't approve."

Clare stood behind the podium, her long black graduation gown fluttering in the breeze. Before her, the audience sat in portable chairs on the green lawn. Women held their hats lest the wind blow them away; the men looked generally uncomfortable.

In the third row, Clare saw her father, sitting straight and tall. Her mother sat next to him, wearing a beige straw hat and brown dress. Tony sat next to Cecilia, eyeing her classmates, and Fabiana and Maria sat next to him. Maria wore her traditional black. Fabiana wore green, and her wide hips spilled over the chair.

Clare cleared her throat and addressed the guests. Father Murphy had introduced her, paying homage to her academic record and then carefully explaining that the valedictory speech was prepared by the student and did not necessarily reflect the views of the school.

"I wish to speak to you on the economic role of women in the United States," Clare began.

Agosto cringed. He was glad women already had the vote; if they didn't, Clare would have doubtless joined Carrie Catt in chaining herself to the White House.

"During the last war, women were called upon to work in factories, to fill the vacancies left by our fighting men in Europe. . . ." Her voice rang clear across the open space. Agosto shifted uncomfortably in his chair.

"And they worked the same hours, did the same work, and received half the pay. Women filled those jobs, but the experience they gained, the work they did, went unnoticed, and when men returned from Europe, women went back to their kitchens. . . .

"Nor are immigrant women to be overlooked. Wave after wave have worked in American factories for low wages. Generations of women have worked beside their men to help them achieve economic success. . . ."

Fabiana nodded her agreement silently. Agosto wiped his brow and commented in a whisper that the sun was hot.

"And as they earned, women also spent. Few people realize that women are an economic force in America. They buy food and clothing for their famillies, they are responsible, in a sense, for the circulation of nearly two-thirds of the money in this country. My father began his banking career by providing banking services for Italian immigrants. He did so because he recognized that the banking establishment was essentially elitist and ignored immigrants. I suggest to you that women are ignored in the same way. . . ."

There was a ripple of comment through the audience. Clare took a sip of the water from the glass in one corner of the podium.

"Today Saint Elizabeth's is graduating a class of well-educated young women, women who could have careers and perform useful and needed tasks. All over this country other universities—Smith, Vassar, Radcliffe—are graduating women with the same knowledge and the same skills. We are a fortunate generation to have been so educated, but the question remains: where are women in American politics? in industry? in banking?" She looked directly at her father, whose expression was utterly stony. She turned to the graduating class behind her. "I say to my fellow students that we have an opportunity . . . no, we have a *challenge* to use our education, to strive to break the barriers that keep us out of the mainstream of America's economy. I am certain we will take up that challenge. I know we can do the job!"

There was a ripple of applause and Clare sat down. She could see her father scowling at her, but she only smiled back. This, she decided, was one day he would not make her cry.

Friday, June 15, 1923

NEW YORK

The *Leviathan* flew banners and ribbons from her smokestacks and halyards, her lights blazed a path through the murky waters of New York harbor as dozens of tugboats escorted her out of the harbor with toots of farewell. Along the dock from which the huge white ship departed, hundreds of well-wishers waved good-bye and threw confetti.

"Not the family adventure I'd hoped for," Agosto lamented as he looked over the rail and studied the waves lapping against the side of the ship. He had not talked to her about her valedictory speech yet, though he certainly intended to. On the one hand, he felt a certain pride; on the other hand, her speech had embarrassed and angered him. Clare had taken their private battle public, had used his own philosophy to strengthen her arguments. He had wanted to reprimand her immediately, but Cecilia prevailed upon him to wait, to think about what he wanted to say, to consider his own position carefully. So he had said nothing, and now he found his anger had faded.

"I'll miss Mama," Clare said, breaking into his thoughts. She pointedly ignored the absence of her brother, whom she happily admitted she wouldn't miss. "It's really coming true," Clare added dreamily. "This is our first trip to Europe together since I was eleven."

"I hope that doesn't mean there'll be another war," Agosto said somewhat sarcastically, remembering their frantic flight from Europe.

"The boat looks beautiful." Clare could still hear the sound of the band on the dock, playing a marching tune.

"As this isn't your first voyage, you should be careful of your terminology," Agosto reminded her in his professional tone. "The captain won't like it if you call the *Leviathan* a boat. A boat is something you float in the bathtub, and a vessel is something you put under the bed. This, Clare, is a ship."

She laughed. "Oh, Papa."

"I'm quite serious. That's what Teddy Roosevelt told me, and since he was once Assistant Secretary of the Navy, he should know."

"I suppose," Clare said, hardly paying attention. Her mind was filled with thoughts of the trip and of her reunion with Emiliano Sforza.

"We've been assigned to the captain's table tomorrow night and on Monday," Agosto told her. He cleared his throat. "These shipboard affairs tend to be rather formal," he added.

"I'll dress up," Clare promised.

"And will you also be a lady? Will you refrain from discussing business and economics?"

Clare turned to her father. "Will you?"

He scowled at her. "That's not the point."

Clare turned and looked over the rail. "What is the point? I know you didn't like my speech . . . I know you're still angry. But, Papa, how can you disagree?"

Agosto's face flushed. "I don't entirely disagree with your arguments. Women are an economic force. But women couldn't operate in the boardrooms of the nation. Clare, you're young. You don't understand."

"Papa, what is it that I don't understand?"

Agosto grumbled, "Women are too emotional. What would you do in a meeting if you didn't get your own way, cry? And you'd be shocked at the language, at the bargaining, you couldn't stand up to the long hours of negotiations. Clare, I don't consider women inferior. I believe that men and women are given different natures so they could each perform their roles. Men should earn the living, women should nurture the family."

"Unless there's a war or unless the family needs more money. Then it's all right for women to work in factories."

"If there's an emergency—"

"Papa, there's no logic in your argument."

"There is complete logic in my argument! And what's more, I'm not going to discuss this with you further! Clare Marina, men were born men and women were born women. They each have a role in life. I am going to Europe on business and to enjoy myself. You are being taken on this trip as a graduation present. We are not going to spend the next few months having this argument. I want you to use the time to think. I want you to consider your future."

Clare pressed her lips together and nodded. Her father wasn't happy with her, but this was the first discussion of this sort they'd ever had without fighting. Perhaps, she decided, he was, as her mother predicted, "coming around." "All right, Papa," Clare said thoughtfully. "We'll call a truce."

Agosto looked at her for a long moment and then half-smiled. "And enjoy ourselves, Clarissima?"

Clare hugged her father, "Yes, Papa."

After two days on the Atlantic, Clare felt quite a part of the shipboard routine. A leisurely continental breakfast was served promptly at nine, although first-class passengers could eat in their cabins if they desired. Following breakfast she took a brisk walk along the promenade deck. Her father spent the mornings in the communications room reading ticker tapes from New York and cabling orders to his office.

Sometimes Clare sat in her assigned deck chair relaxing in the sun. Then later she read F. Scott Fitzgerald's newest book, *The Beautiful and the Damned*. She had begun with Booth Tarkington's *The Magnificent Ambersons*, but found it far too dreary and depressing. A story about a family that lost its money held little appeal.

"You enjoying that?"

Clare looked up from her book into the gray-blue eyes of a tall sandy-haired young man. He was, she surmised, in his late twenties.

"Not really," she confessed. "I liked his other books, but this one's turning out to be something of a gloomy satire. There's not much in it except descriptions of parties, petting, and anxiety over money."

"Too much reality?" he asked.

"That's not reality." Clare frowned. "I suppose the descriptions are good enough, but the characters have absolutely no sense of purpose in life."

The young man's expression turned serious. "Believe me when I tell you, there are millions of such people."

Clare closed the book. "Well, I don't have to read about them." She studied the young man, who sounded older than he looked, and she felt a trifle annoyed because he seemed to be treating her like a child. Like her father, he had that professorial tone—"let me tell you about life, my dear." It was an attitude she could accept from her father, but certainly not from a young man who couldn't be more than eight years older than she. "I prefer the classics," she added loftily.

He nodded, and without further conversation thrust his hands in his pockets and continued his walk around the deck.

Clare followed him with her eyes, shrugged, then checked her watch, deciding to go back to the library and find a more suitable book. Well, she thought, there was dinner at the captain's table to look forward to.

"Mr. Tonelli and his daughter, Clare Marina," Captain Sanderson said, bowing. "May I present my other dinner guests, Mr. Mark Lyons and his associate Mr. Levinson, from California, and Mr. Nelson Winston-Jones from the Argentine."

Clare glanced at Mark Lyons—he was the young man who'd spoken to her about F. Scott Fitzgerald. He had a pleasant face when he smiled, but as soon as his smile faded, he looked distracted and, she assumed, annoyed. His companion, Mr. Levinson, was short and stout and wore thick glasses. Mr. Winston-Jones was also heavyset, but he was older—perhaps sixty.

They all took their seats. Clare was placed between Captain Sanderson and Mr. Levinson. Agosto was seated between Mr. Winston-Jones and Mr. Lyons.

Captain Sanderson looked every inch a seagoing man to Clare. He was six feet tall, walked as straight as a rod, and sported a salt-and-pepper beard.

Mr. Winston-Jones, who turned out to be a rancher from the Argentine pampas, engaged her father in a long, tedious, one-sided discussion punctuated with a variety of grunts and other guttural noises. "Plenty of market for our beef in Europe, what?" he kept saying. "Good thing the whole pampas is controlled by ten good solid British families, what? That's why our production is so high, good firm English management."

Clare gave up listening and talked to the captain.

"I first started sailing over forty years ago," he told her. "I've been with the *Leviathan* since the first day she flew the Stars and Stripes. Government seized her in 1917 from the Germans. She was called *Das Vaterland* then, the pride of the German fleet. She was built in Hamburg as a rival to the *Titanic*, but she was bigger, faster, and considerably safer. The Germans know a lot about technology—not much about people, but their technology is definitely superior."

"Then what happened?" Clare asked, ignoring his comment about Germans.

"Well, she was refitted and used to send our boys to Europe. That's when I was made captain. I loved it! I loved the thought of the Jerries seeing their biggest, fastest ship carrying our boys. 'Course, you probably don't remember much about the war— you couldn't have been more than ten or eleven."

"Eleven," Clare confirmed. She glanced at Mark Lyons, hoping that he now realized she was not fifteen, but nineteen— nearly twenty. But to her disappointment, he wasn't listening. Instead, he picked at his food while feigning an interest in her father's banter with Mr. Winston-Jones.

"Well, anyway, after the war all the furnishings were put back and the *Leviathan* resumed her life as a luxury liner. I like being her captain more now because I don't have to worry about U-boats." He laughed heartily.

At that moment a white-uniformed steward handed the captain a note, which he quickly opened and read. Then he stood up, and using his fork, tapped authoritatively on his water glass until all conversation ceased and there was silence.

"I've just been informed by the bridge that the *Leviathan* has established a new water-speed record. For the last twenty-five hours we've maintained an average speed of 27.5 knots. That's roughly thirty-two miles an hour. No ship has ever traveled faster for this length of time. Ladies and gentlemen, you are part of maritime history."

There was polite clapping and Clare smiled and clapped too.

After his announcement, the captain left to congratulate his crew.

"How very exciting," Winston-Jones intoned.

Mark Lyons continued eating. "It can't go fast enough for me," he said without looking up.

He definitely seemed annoyed with life, she decided. But Mr. Levinson, his business associate, was full of humor. He and Agosto were happily engaged in telling jokes about Jews and Italians, for as it turned out, Mr. Levinson came originally from Brooklyn.

When they finished dinner Clare and her father strolled back toward their staterooms.

"There's a party tomorrow night," Clare told him.

"I'll escort you," Agosto volunteered. "Are you going to wear your new evening gown and dance with me?"

Clare smiled and kissed her father good night on the cheek. He was beginning to relax and to enjoy himself. I love him when he's like this, she thought. "Of course, Papa. You're certainly the handsomest man on the ship."

Agosto laughed and squeezed her arm gently. "You must want something to be so flattering. There are certainly young men on this ship. Don't waste your wiles on me."

"Oh, Papa . . ." Clare blushed. "There's no one I'd rather dance with."

"Not even Mr. Lyons?"

Clare shook her head. "I think he's too stuck-up," she answered playfully.

"Perhaps he has things on his mind."

"Perhaps," Clare conceded. "Good night, Papa. Sleep well."

"You have the perfect face," the hairdresser in the ship's salon said. There was a tone of envy in her voice. "Such sculptured high cheekbones, a fine nose, full sensuous lips! But your hair . . . Oh, my! Your hair is a challenge! It's all curly and girlish."

She handed Clare the mirror and directed her to study her image from various angles.

"This style you're wearing . . . well, it's no style at all, really. It's woefully outdated and makes you look like a child. No sophistication. No sophistication at all!"

Clare sighed. The woman was quite right. "How should I wear it?"

"Here, let me get some pins and give you an idea. Here, see this picture in *Box Office*? It's Barbara La Marr, Douglas Fairbanks' leading lady. It's called a flapper cut, but of course it's really a bob. Yes, no question about it, you'd look stunning with your hair bobbed."

Clare stared in the mirror intently as the woman used hairpins to illustrate how her hair would look short. "I've been thinking about getting it cut." It wasn't true; cutting her hair had not, until this moment, crossed her mind. But as she studied the picture in *Box Office* and looked at her pinned-up hair, she made her decision.

"Well, what do you think?"

Clare smiled. "I like it. Go ahead and cut it."

When Clare returned to her stateroom, she went directly to the door that separated her room from her father's. He was napping and she could hear his snoring.

She carefully laid out her clothes on the bed and began to get ready for the party.

"Clare, Clare Marina! Are you in there?" It was her father's voice through the door. Almost an hour had passed and he was up and dressed.

"I'm not dressed yet, Papa."

"Don't be too much longer."

Clare stood up and smoothed out her dress. She looked into the mirror and to her delight saw a totally changed reflection. She took a deep breath. "You can come in, Papa!"

Agosto Tonelli opened the door and his mouth fell open. "Clare! What have you done to your hair! You've cut off your beautiful curls!"

Clare nodded. He looked angry.

"You look like . . . like . . . like one of those women!" His face had gone red.

"What women?"

"Those immoral women," Agosto stumbled.

Clare burst out laughing. "You sound like Aunt Maria!"

"It's terrible! I hate it! You look too old."

"I like it, Papa. It's the way everyone wears their hair. Even Sarah Ainsley wears her hair this way. Is she immoral?"

Agosto scowled. "You don't have to be like everybody else."

"Papa, I want to be stylish. I don't want to look like a child when in fact I'm a woman. I'll be twenty in August, older than Mama was when you were married."

Agosto stood for a moment. The scowl faded from his face and he shifted his weight from one foot to the other. "Papas don't like to think of their little girls becoming women," he finally admitted.

Clare flew into his arms and kissed him. "Oh, Papa . . . I love you."

Agosto nodded and hugged her in return.

Morty Levinson adjusted the red satin cummerbund around his ample midsection. Then, running his hand through his hair, he admired himself in the mirror. "Look at you!" Morty turned to Mark, who sat on the edge of his bed, still wearing his robe. "I've known you for five years, and I've never seen you this preoccupied."

Mark stared at the carpet. "I apologize, but dammit, this isn't a pleasure trip."

"I'm well aware of that, but you aren't accomplishing anything staying holed up in your cabin. Why the hell don't you get dressed and come along to the party?"

"I hate ship's parties. Anyway, I don't feel like talking to all those people, and I certainly don't feel like dancing."

Morty shrugged. He'd known Mark long enough to be aware of his single-mindedness. If it was a business deal, Mark thought of nothing else. If it was a woman, he pursued her till he lost interest. And when it was family, it troubled him deeply. Mark became overwhelmingly distressed, brooded, and more often than not blamed himself. And of course this was no ordinary family problem. This problem involved his sister, and Morty well knew that a strong love-hate relationship existed between them. Mark could condemn Louisa and chastise her, but if anyone else criticized her or hurt her, he was like an avenging angel, ready to do battle. Now Louisa had done the unforgivable. She had voluntarily vanished, refusing to communicate with her mother, who was seriously ill. And beneath Mark's anger, Morty knew he was afraid for Louisa. "You'll find Louisa," Morty said, knowing it was an inadequate comment.

"I have to find her," Mark replied. "Look, don't let my family problems spoil your fun. Go on . . . go dance the night away."

"That Tonelli girl is really a looker," Morty announced with appreciation. Perhaps a change of subject or a distraction would help.

"Girl," Mark repeated. "She's young and not for you."

Morty laughed. "I was planning on dancing with her, not seducing her."

"Good thing. Can't you see the look in her eyes when her father is talking? She's like all young girls—her father's still her big hero. She'll probably end up marrying a man twice her age in an effort to find someone like her father. She won't be interesting till she gets over her daddy worship.''

"You're really very jaded for a man of twenty-nine.''

"Comes from having a sister.''

"Not all women are like Louisa.''

Mark nodded. "That's a blessing.''

"Well, if I can't talk you out of your depression, I'm just going to leave you here.''

"Good, I'll read myself to sleep.''

Morty closed the door of the cabin after him. Poor Mark, he thought. His father was dead, his mother was dying, and his only sister—whose personality was akin to that of the beautiful and unstable Zelda Fitzgerald—was missing somewhere in Italy. He was embroiled in family concerns. But then Morty supposed that was the curse of small families: they were tight and dependent on one another. He had five sisters and two brothers, and frankly, if one of his sisters was missing, he would count it a blessing rather than a hardship. As it was, his weekly mail from New York usually brought five letters from his sisters, plus one from his mother. They all pleaded, "Why don't you ever write, Morty?''

Saturday, June 23, 1923

R O M E

Emiliano Sforza, dressed in his robe, stood and gazed out the window of Louisa's apartment. Rome, the Eternal City—he felt enormous pride as he looked at the skyline in the distance, and he believed that soon Rome would be restored to its position of historic leadership. The new, disciplined government of Benito Mussolini would succeed; the world would recognize Italy's strength, her leadership, her potential. And I, he thought proudly, have been instrumental in bringing this government to power.

Emiliano closed his eyes and remembered that fateful night in Milan almost a year ago. Thirty-nine-year-old Benito Mussolini stood with his feet wide apart, his hands on his hips, and his chin thrust forward defiantly. His large dark, piercing eyes surveyed the scene and his nostrils twitched like an animal sorting out scents that humans couldn't detect. "I love the smell of smoke!" he roared. "And flames. I love to watch them dance! Watch them consume the socialist propaganda presses as they will tonight!''

The crowd was mixed, hundreds of black-shirted, uniformed *squadristi*, and those who fell in with them and marched beside them, shouting and cheering. Emiliano, with several other Milanese industrialists, stood near Mussolini.

Mussolini spoke to all. He raised his fist in a symbolic salute and shouted in a strong hard voice, ''From today onward, we are all Italians and nothing but Italians!''

The crowd roared its approval, and General Italo Balbo, who stood nearby listening to his leader, smiled proudly.

Mussolini's cry never failed to bring a thunderous applause, Emiliano thought, though in fact those exact words had been Mussolini's rallying call since 1915.

''Viva Italia!'' Mussolini bellowed.

''Viva Italia!'' the crowd shouted back in unison.

They had poured out of Milan's Fascist headquarters, had marched into Milan from the countryside, streamed out of their houses like ants to follow their leader, the great orator and publisher of *Il Popolo d'Italia*, Benito Mussolini.

''No to this general strike!'' Mussolini roared. ''The Bolshevik pigs will not destroy Italy! They will not destroy or lay idle the factories of Milan! No!''

''No! No! No! No!'' the crowd shouted, stamping their feet as one, in a thunderous motion that shook the ground beneath them. Mussolini raised his arm and pointed it forward. From within the crowd, well-trained martials led off, and the group of shouting, screaming followers fell in behind. A chorus of ''No! No! Bolsheviks!'' was punctuated with periodic, *''Viva Italia!''*

Torches appeared and dispelled darkness. The scene had resembled a religious procession, Emiliano thought. Had the demonstrators been silent, they might have been wending their way to Jerusalem to offer up their souls to God in a midnight Mass.

But instead these worshipers sought a new Rome, and envisaged themselves as the born-again legions who within hours would light the skies of Milan with the flames of the Socialist newspaper and the inferno of the burning headquarters of the Christian Democrats, the left-wing Socialists, the Communists, and the Anarchists. ''Bolsheviks all!'' Mussolini proclaimed. ''Treat them as one! Let them taste the vengeance of real Italians!''

The *squadristi* guard of honor surrounded the hastily erected platform in the shadow of Il Duce, the leader. Emiliano watched as they marched off.

''Aren't you going?'' Emiliano had asked General Balbo.

''I watched Ravenna burn only last month,'' Balbo answered

dryly. "And one Socialist headquarters burning is much like another!"

Balbo was like Mark Anthony playing to a new Caesar. And as the sound of the marching horde of legionnaires faded in his ears, Emiliano had walked away with General Balbo.

"I wonder if Il Duce will be able to halt them as easily as he rouses and excites them?" Balbo asked.

"Do you doubt our new leader?"

Balbo had shaken his head. "No, I have faith in Fascism."

"Are you going to look out the window forever?" Louisa's plaintive voice broke into his reminiscences and he turned to look at her. A delightful creature with no thought of politics. Her eyes begged him to return to their bed; her long white arms were outstretched, waiting.

Emiliano Sforza lay back on the wrinkled sheets, his eyes closed as Louisa gently caressed his hairy chest. She was leaning over him like a child and he could feel her long flaxen hair on his flesh. She was wanton and beautiful, all pink and white with golden fleece and huge brown eyes.

"You don't come to Rome often enough," she whispered.

He opened his eyes. "I'm sure you find other entertainments."

Her brown eyes blinked as she shook her blond hair.

"I keep you well," he said. "And look at you. How long has it been since you went to the hairdresser?"

She let out her breath and didn't answer. He smiled at his own quite blatant cruelty. Louisa was a true masochist; she believed it was her destiny to be treated badly, and he found it exciting to oblige. In point of fact she was quite ravishing and he had few complaints. Indeed, he well knew she was faithful to him. But if he treated her lovingly, she wouldn't have been; a woman who demanded to be wounded would turn away from a kind man; every masochist should find a sadist.

He reached up and touched her small white breast. "How many men have you been with this month?" He squeezed her nipple.

"None, Emiliano, none." She shook her head and he thought she looked like a small bird with a broken wing as she moved her arm gracefully in a motion of silent denial.

He released her breast and ran his hand over her white skin; it was like fine marble, milky and cool. He loved blondes, especially blondes with long thighs, graceful hairless legs, and lovely slender arms—they were like a different species. But Louisa was a foundling, one of thousands of American women who came to Italy to live the bohemian life. She wasn't a woman he would consider marrying. Marriage he deemed to be an important merger. Marriage offered nothing save a strong new business alliance. Of course if the bride were a beautiful young woman such as Clare Marina Tonelli, it would be far from unpleasant. He smiled to himself. Yes, Clare Marina was an obvious choice, and the truth was, he had been considering it from almost the first minute he'd laid eyes on her.

Louisa reached out and encircled his manhood with her soft white hands, and he felt himself respond instantly to her touch.

"You know I can't stay longer," he said, looking at her fingers. They danced on his flesh and he knew he wouldn't pull away, because when she came to him this way she was irresistible. He could look down on her flaxen hair and conjure up a thousand fantasies. Sometimes he imagined the youthful Clare Marina, but just as often he thought of the coal-black, dark-nippled women he had possessed while visiting the Somali sultanates some years ago, and now and again he thought of the sultry Spanish dancer he'd spent a week with in Pamplona when he'd last gone to watch the bulls running during the fiesta.

"A little longer," Louisa whispered. He lay back and watched her, feeling the ecstasy of her slow experienced movements, which combined the soft delicate motions of her fingers with the glories of her full red-lipped mouth. He allowed his mind to roam free, and in a few seconds he burst forth, satisfied.

"You don't really like to do that, do you?" he asked.

"I do it for you."

"You do it to make me stay longer, and I really must go."

"When will you be back?" Her lovely mouth glistened with his gift.

"I'm not sure. I'm having house guests." He began to dress, and his mind raced over his itinerary. This was an important trip to Rome. He had much to do, many influential men to see before the arrival of Agosto Tonelli. First he had to see Il Duce, then a man Il Duce had suggested might be of help settling a labor dispute in one of his factories. And of course he had to be back in Milan when Agosto and Clare Marina arrived.

Monday, June 25, 1923

ROME

Amerigo Dumini was a small dark man whose language was as disgusting as his demeanor. "You won't like him," Mussolini warned. "Actually, I don't like him, but he's a useful man. Utterly ruthless. Frankly, if I were you, Count Sforza, I'd deal with him through an intermediary. No, you won't like him at all."

But Emiliano had insisted that he didn't hire people without first speaking with them, no matter what form of low-life they might be. "You'll have to arrange for his payment," Mussolini went on to explain. And Emiliano had readily agreed. Regardless of Dumini's manners and morals, both of which were nonexistent, he had a reputation of doing jobs quickly and efficiently.

Dumini was credited with a number of violent attacks and murders. He was the unofficial head of the *ceka*, a special squad used now and again to intimidate labor organizers and any member of the opposition parties who became a nuisance. His credentials for this "position" were excellent. Born in Italy, he'd moved to the United States, where he plied his talents as a professional gangster in St. Louis for some ten years. He returned to Italy a wanted man, and the Fascists soon found a niche for him.

Doubtless, Emiliano thought, Dumini made a pretty penny. Rumor had it that Mussolini paid him a handsome salary, and then too, he worked free-lance, so to speak.

It seemed to Emiliano that Dumini was the perfect choice to carry out the assignment he had in mind. One of the factories owned by Sforza Industries in Turin had special labor difficulties. The workers were led by a group of Socialist organizers, men who continued their activities in spite of all warnings and in spite of what Emiliano felt were more-than-generous terms for the workers. His own personal production quotas had fallen behind and with his new responsibilities as an economic consultant to the government, he'd have to find a solution to his labor problems. Dumini came highly recommended.

Amerigo Dumini quartered himself and some twenty of his "associates" in a small hotel near the Parliament buildings. And Emiliano noticed that he seemed to live rather well.

"Whada'ya want to drink?" Dumini asked, standing by the private bar in the living room of his spacious, expensively furnished apartment.

"Whiskey, I think."

"Do ya think, or do ya know?" Dumini laughed and displayed his uneven pointed teeth. He reminded Emiliano of a shark.

"Whiskey."

Dumini poured the drinks and handed Emiliano his. "Can't drink in the States," he swore under his breath. "Ya know, when they passed that law, I wanted to go right into that women's temperance organization and blast all those old bitches to kingdom come! But then I said: Whoa! Amerigo, there's a lot of money to be made on this! People ain't going to give up booze just because of some lousy law. So I ran booze and heroin for a while. Had a good thing going in East St. Louis—the cops are real nice there, real cooperative."

"So why did you come back to Italy?" An idle question, Emiliano thought. Actually, he wanted to get on with the arrangements, but Dumini wasn't the sort of man you insulted. A little harmless banter never hurt, he convinced himself.

" 'Cause the mobs all moved in on the action. They don't like free-lancers, and I ain't paying no respects to some 'family.' I ain't cutting with them, either."

"Oh," Emiliano replied. "Well, I have this little job for you. I think it suits a man of your talents."

"How many?"

"How many what?"

"How many people? I price according to the number."

"Oh . . . ah, three."

"Well, I'm not a fucking Gypsy, you know. I don't got a crystal ball. Whada'ya want done? You want them roughed up, made unrecognizable, or just taken out entirely?"

"You put it rather bluntly."

"Yeah, so what'll it be?"

"Entirely," Emiliano answered, feeling rather dispassionate. "Here are their names, addresses, and photos. Don't make any mistakes."

"I don't make mistakes."

"How much?"

"A thousand American dollars each."

"That's a rather high price."

"You're a rather rich man."

Emiliano shrugged. "All right," he answered.

"Cash—I don't take no checks."

"I'll have to come back with it."

"Okay." Dumini smiled. "It's a pleasure to do business with you. You got more business, you just call Amerigo."

17

Wednesday, June 27, 1923

PARIS

Clare Marina remained at the Hotel Ritz, taking a short rest before dinner. Restless, Agosto had gone to the newsstand to buy the American papers.

"Agosto! Agosto Tonelli!"

Agosto looked up from the array of international papers and into the face of Sarah Ainsley Stearns. She was resplendent in a gold print dress, a shawl, and a quite remarkable hat that tilted rakishly to one side. "Sarah, what a surprise!" He held out his arms warmly and she floated into them, pressing herself to him in what was more than a friendly greeting.

"Darling, it's wonderful to see you. Where's Cecilia?"

"In Brooklyn," Agosto answered.

Sarah ran her cool hand over his face, kissed him on the mouth, then stepped back. "She and Creighton are stay-at-homes," she declared. "But, Agosto, this is fantastic, we're alone in Paris! Take me to dinner. We'll have a marvelous evening." She smiled coquettishly. "This is such a coincidence. You know, I'm usually in Cannes for the season, but I came up to Paris on impulse, sheer impulse, to view the new fashion line."

Agosto smiled at her. In twenty years she hadn't changed one iota. Even motherhood failed to alter her gadabout style and relentless pursuit of the unobtainable. "I hardly think it would be proper for us to be seen dining alone together," he replied.

Sarah held his hands and squeezed them. "You're right. We could dine in my suite." She leaned over closer and whispered, "Everyone needs a change now and again, Agosto."

He laughed. She was so blatant, there wasn't any other possible response. Then, summoning his most sober expression, he said, "I don't think the beautiful young woman I'm traveling with would approve."

But Sarah's reaction wasn't what he'd expected. She visibly paled and stepped back with a shocked, hurt expression. "What?"

"Oh, Sarah! I'm talking about Clare. She's with me, she's upstairs resting before dinner. I was only joking. Please join us for dinner, please."

Sarah's expression took a moment to return to normal; then, almost in relief, she laughed. "Clare Marina! Agosto, you're a terrible tease."

He winked at her. "No, it's you who are the tease."

Sarah didn't blush. "I'd never tease you, Agosto. I meant it."

He flushed and pulled on his mustache. "Well, will you join us for dinner?"

She nodded. "If Clare wouldn't mind."

"Of course she wouldn't."

Sarah took his arm. "Naturally I'll have to change. Walk me to the lift, will you?"

Obligingly Agosto led her across the elegant lobby toward the brass-enclosed elevator.

"I certainly didn't expect to see you!" Sarah gushed. "I heard you'd gone to Italy . . . that you are, in fact, going ahead with the dam project."

"Of course I am. I gave my word."

Sarah smiled sweetly. "Creighton said it was all quite terrible. He said you had to invest in the project heavily because two of the consortium partners backed out."

"That's true, but I think I'll survive."

"Creighton says that's no way to do business. He says it was most unethical of them after they'd agreed to it and all."

Agosto shrugged. He decided against agreeing with her—even if he *did* agree. Comments, even casual comments, had a way of getting back. "I'd hoped for their participation, but they changed their minds. So there will be more profit for American Federal Banks, of that I'm certain. As for the future . . . well, I expect I'll have continued business dealings with them. I simply chalk it up to their natural conservatism." He smiled. "Like Creighton. I didn't approach him in the first place because I knew he was too conservative to take on a foreign venture."

"Very wise of you, darling. He would have said no. But I daresay if he'd said yes, he wouldn't have backed out later."

Agosto nodded his agreement. Creighton Stearns was what Agosto thought of as "the typical gray banker." But he conceded that Creighton had a good reputation.

"Ah, here comes the lift. What time shall I ring you? How about nine?"

"A good Continental hour for dining. Nine it is."

Sarah got into the elevator and waved to him as it jolted upward.

Clare and Agosto dropped Sarah Ainsley Stearns off at the hotel, then walked to a small sidewalk café on the Champs-Elysées. It was after midnight, but the street was just coming alive.

"Tired?" Agosto queried.

"A little," she admitted.

"Well, tell me, have you enjoyed Paris?"

"Yes . . . and I've seen and done everything I wanted to see and do."

"Since your forty-six-year-old father has been your guide, your dancing partner, and your walking companion, that hardly seems possible. Now, admit it, wouldn't you rather have been in Paris with a man who wasn't your father?" He smiled at her. She is truly beautiful, he thought to himself. Even more beautiful than her mother at this age. Her soft brown hair caressed her high cheekbones; her brown eyes were large, luminous, and fringed with long lashes. Her lips were full and she wore a hint of lipstick. And her figure! Agosto felt ill-at-ease thinking about it. She was taller than Cecilia—all Italian-American children seemed to grow taller with each successive generation. Her legs were long, her waist small, her hips gently rounded. When they walked together, men stared at her and Agosto knew it was more than fatherly pride that made him think her exceptionally attractive. But when had she grown up so? Where had he been? It was as if she were a butterfly that emerged whole in full flight before his very eyes. He felt he'd boarded the ship with a schoolgirl, albeit one possessed of definite opinions with which he didn't agree, and disembarked with a woman. But of course, he reminded himself, she was not as sheltered as many Italian daughters. Indeed, that was the problem. She wasn't sheltered at all.

But, he silently acknowledged, she did have a mind and she was excessively intelligent. She was like a sponge; it was as if for years she'd been soaking up every conversation. He was amazed at her knowledge; she knew things he had no idea she knew. And that troubled him. I want her to be happy, he thought. But banking is no place for women, even talented women.

"No, I'm glad I was with you," Clare answered, interrupting his thoughts.

"I know it's our last night in Paris, Clarissima, but we do have to catch the train to Milan at ten in the morning."

Clare sipped her Campari. "I'm looking forward to it. I like trains. It should be an interesting trip."

"And a tiring one. May I suggest we go back to the Ritz and get a good night's sleep."

"I'll give in," Clare replied. "In any case, I really don't think I could stay awake much longer. Sarah all but put me to sleep at dinner, going on and on about fashions," Clare smiled. "Papa, I think she's interested in you."

Agosto inhaled in sheer surprise. This wasn't the kind of conversation to have with your daughter. "Clarissima! Where did you get such an idea?"

Clare giggled. "I'm not blind, Papa."

He cleared his throat. "She's just pretending. Flirtations are just a joke to Sarah."

"Oh, Papa, you're a handsome man! I don't think she's joking."

"Well, never mind," he said, looking flustered. "Anyway, I'm proud to have worn you out in Paris. Perhaps I'm not as old as I thought."

"Oh, you're not old at all!"

He took her arm as they left the café, and thought how mature she'd become; then he wondered vaguely how many of the people they passed thought they were man and wife or man and mistress—he had noted more than a few long, knowing looks, and they embarrassed him. But of course older men and younger women were a common sight in Europe.

Thursday, June 28, 1923

R O M E

Mark Lyons shifted uneasily in his chair, thinking that he'd be glad to return to his hotel. He found this meeting with the Italian parliamentarian Giacomo Matteotti a little strained and uncomfortable.

"Tell me about your family," Matteotti requested. He ran his hand across his thinning dark hair.

It was a friendly and reasonable request. Matteotti was Mark's ailing mother's second cousin, and apart from that remote connection Matteotti knew nothing of his long-lost relatives.

It was, however, an awkward question. Mark's father's family—and he as well—were certainly what Matteotti, a dedicated Socialist, would consider capitalists. Under ordinary circumstances Mark wouldn't have felt defensive about either his money or his philosophy, but in the last half-hour he'd been charmed by the thirty-eight-year-old Italian Socialist's hospitality. Then too he needed Matteotti's help.

"I come from the midwestern United States," Mark Lyons answered. He swirled the whiskey in his glass and thanked heaven that Socialists drank. "My father was in the auto industry." He didn't bother to mention his father's millions. And he was relieved when Matteotti didn't ask about labor conditions.

"After my father died, I went west," Mark continued. "I'm afraid I made rather a lot of money in the California oil fields."

Matteotti grinned. "You don't have to be ashamed of making money. There are rich people who believe in social justice." He laughed. "Not many, but a few."

Mark took a sip and found himself relaxing a bit. He really didn't want to have an ideological conversation with this man. "In any case, I suppose I'm what you'd call a member of the new western establishment in the States."

"Old money and new money," Matteotti said, steepling his long fingers.

"I suppose I've an unusual family," Mark admitted. "My father, as you know, married an Italian-American. As I wrote you, your second cousin."

Matteotti smiled warmly again. "I doubt there are any Italians without cousins in America. Tell me, isn't it unusual for a member of the establishment—as you Americans say—to marry the daughter of an Italian immigrant?"

"Probably," Mark admitted. "My mother is very gifted. She used to sing like an angel and she studied opera. My father met her when she was singing with the Chicago Symphony. They fell in love and married—over the objections of both families.

"And how's your mother now?"

"Ill," he replied softly.

"You should be with her," Matteotti suggested.

Mark Lyons took another swallow of his drink and shook his head. "My mother sent me here to find my sister. She left home some months ago to come to Rome. She's written only once, and then we heard no more."

"The American embassy can't help you?"

Again Mark shook his head.

"And what can I do?"

"I had hoped . . . thought perhaps she might have contacted you. She knew you were related to our mother, she had your address when she left."

"I'm afraid you're the first member of my cousin Alfredo's family I've heard from in years. I'm terribly sorry."

Mark knew he looked dejected, but certainly Matteotti looked both concerned and sympathetic. He seemed a genuinely nice man.

"I don't know Rome at all," Mark confessed. "I don't speak Italian well either. I keep mixing it up with Spanish."

"That won't inhibit your being understood. Do many people speak Spanish in America?"

Mark shook his head. "Only in southern California. All the street names are Spanish, and there's a large Spanish-speaking population."

Matteotti nodded, as if storing away the knowledge.

"I know you're a busy man," Mark told him. "It was good of you to see me."

Matteotti stood up. "Not at all, not at all! No, please, you mustn't leave. Share a simple meal with my wife and me and we'll talk. Did you bring pictures of your sister? I'll make inquiries."

Mark nodded. "I suppose I should go to the police."

"If you do, don't mention you know me," Matteotti advised. "And I must warn you, the police are most uncooperative and inefficient."

Mark thought vaguely of the morning spent at customs and immigration. Never had he seen so many papers stamped so many times. If the police were like the officials he'd already encountered, Matteotti's assessment was probably quite correct.

"I'd be grateful for any inquiries you might make." He opened his briefcase and handed Matteotti some photos.

"Which is the most recent?"

"This one," Mark answered, handing him a photo of Louisa. It was a lovely photo, taken at a party in his own home near Pasadena. She'd visited him there and been the toast of every party of the season. She had blond hair like their father, and dark, heavily lashed brown eyes like their mother. She was dressed all in white, and while the black-and-white photo didn't reveal it, she was wonderfully tanned. "The great American beauty," someone had once said of her. "Blond hair and brown eyes, the most striking of all combinations."

"I've seen this woman," Matteotti said, holding the photo up to the lamp. "Yes, yes, I'm certain it is she."

Mark felt his heart leap. "Where?"

Matteotti frowned. "I am afraid you'll be distressed."

"I'll only be distressed if I don't find her," Mark replied.

Matteotti took in a deep breath. "She's seen often in the company of Count Emiliano Sforza of Milan . . when he's in Rome. It's said she's the count's mistress."

Mark pressed his lips together. Matteotti's revelation didn't shock him. But there was no time to explain Louisa. And even if he'd bothered, he wasn't certain Matteotti would have understood. "I suppose this means that Count Sforza will know her whereabouts."

Matteotti nodded. "I imagine he's in Milan now, although sometimes he summers at Lake Como."

Mark hesitated, then decided to ask, "What kind of man is this Count Sforza?"

Matteotti shrugged. "He belongs to a cadet branch of the famous Sforza family of Milan, not the mainline Sforzas. But he's extraordinarily wealthy, he's the sole head of Sforza Industries and is tied to banking as well as manufacturing. I am afraid, however, that he's anything but a friend of mine. You understand, Italian politics is in turmoil. . . . I'm a man whose life is constantly threatened."

At the moment the intricacies of Italian politics didn't interest Mark. "I won't mention you when I speak with him."

"Good," Matteotti answered. "Now, might I ask my wife to serve our dinner?"

Mark nodded and smiled.

Friday, June 29, 1923

M I L A N

"Milan has certainly improved," Agosto commented as they stood waiting for Count Sforza's car. "The last time I was here, in the spring last year, the whole city was on strike. The phones didn't work, the banks were closed, and even the hotels were running on skeleton staff. I tell you, Clarissima, I see a big difference already. I see that this Il Duce is bringing order to the country!"

"I'm sure the workers had some legitimate complaints," Clare countered. "Even in the United States they have reason to complain."

"I didn't say they didn't! But strikes are no way to redress grievances!"

Clare didn't respond. Her father's bitterness toward organized labor and what he called "social agitators" was deep-rooted and personal. In all the years since 1911, he had seen his brother Paolo only once, and then by accident when Paolo led a demonstration in New York's Union Square in 1913. Agosto's recounting of the incident was emblazoned in her memory because she'd never seen her father in such a fury. "He said I wasn't Italian! He said 'our' people suffered in the sweat shops! He asked me, 'How could you live in Little Italy, Agosto, and not know or care?' " Clare remembered her father slumping into his chair and shaking his head sadly. "Cecilia, I tried to help our people by giving them the opportunity to invest, to start their own businesses. Have I been wrong?" Cecilia had shaken her head. "Of course not," she replied, kissing him on the forehead. Yes, Clare thought, she remembered that incident clearly. And she knew that a good deal of her father's emotional reaction to organized labor grew out of his relationship with Paolo.

"Mr. Agosto Tonelli?" A tall, lean, uniformed chauffeur approached them.

Clare looked around and felt a surge of disappointment. She had hoped Emiliano Sforza would meet them personally.

"I've been sent to drive you to Count Sforza's home," the chauffeur explained. He took their bags and Clare and her father followed him out of the station, where at the curb a long black sleek Fiat awaited.

"What a grand house," Clare said as the car came to a halt in front of the iron gates that surrounded the huge two-story stone mansion. With a wave from the driver, the gates swung open.

The maid ushered them in. The entry hall was long, its floors marble, and the lighting was still provided by gas lamps. Paintings and tapestries hung on the walls, reminding Clare of pictures of medieval castles.

The maid left them in a large high-ceilinged reception room. In a few moments they were joined by a thin, sharp-featured woman who looked to be in her forties and wore her hair piled high on her head. She was dressed entirely in black, but it was not the kind of black garb worn by elderly Italian women in the United States. It was an elegant, highly styled dress, discreetly trimmed with black lace. Around her neck she wore a gold cross. "I am Constanza Sforza, Emiliano's sister," she said without smiling.

"Agosto Tonelli, and this is my daughter, Clare Marina Tonelli." Agosto graciously kissed her extended hand.

"Ah, Mr. Tonelli . . . I know Emiliano is expecting you. He asked me to meet you and explain."

She motioned them to the tapestried sofa and they sat down, as did Constanza Sforza. "Some brandy," she offered.

"Yes, thank you."

Constanza Sforza rang a small silver bell; a stony-faced butler arrived, took her request, and disappeared.

"Emiliano asked me to greet you, to welcome you to our home. He phoned last night. I'm afraid he was delayed in Rome, but he will return on the late afternoon train and he'll be here for dinner, of course."

The butler returned carrying three crystal brandy snifters. He served the three of them, then disappeared.

"I do hope you understand. Sometimes business delays can't be helped."

"Of course I understand," Agosto assured her.

"Let me show you to your rooms," Constanza offered, standing and smoothing out her dress. "Dinner will be formal," she informed them.

Clare's room was immense. It had floor-to-ceiling windows that overlooked an enclosed formal garden. The small adjoining bathroom had the largest tub she'd ever seen. There were gold faucets on the sink, and the mirror was gilt-edged. But the bedroom, like the rest of the house, seemed somber and strict. Its colors were subdued, its furniture massive with intricate carvings—the credenza alone was more than ten feet long and took up nearly half the wall it was set against.

For much of the afternoon Clare read and walked in the garden, which seemed like a magical place with its marble statuary and carefully laid-out flowerbeds and beautifully pruned shrubbery. Walking through it and sitting for a time on the marble bench before the five-tiered marble fountain, she felt as if she had suddenly been removed from the modern world and transported back in history to the garden of the Medici.

ROME

"This has been the most frustrating goddamned two days of my entire life! First I call Milan and they tell me Sforza's in Rome. Then I find out where his Rome office is, and they tell me he's gone to Milan! Now I keep calling and nobody tells me anything! Shit!" Mark punctuated his tirade with the sound of ice cubes as he plopped them into a glass. "You want something?"

"Why not? If you're going to get drunk, you should have company." Morty settled back in his chair. The Hotel Pension Liverpool on the Via Sicilia wasn't Rome's ranking tourist hotel, but it had private baths and well-appointed rooms. Morty felt at home largely because the concierge was so nosy.

"Am I going to get drunk?" Mark asked, raising one eyebrow.

"I expect so. Can't say I blame you. Christ, dealing with the Italian system is enough to make anybody want to get drunk. I always thought Jewish time was bad. Italian time runs even slower."

"Jewish time?"

"Yeah, you know, if synagogue starts at eleven, that's eleven-forty-five Jewish time."

Mark laughed in spite of himself, but then he shook his head. "What's so damned frustrating is the thought that she could be next door and I wouldn't know it. I keep looking for her in sidewalk cafés, I keep thinking I'll run into her in a restaurant."

Morty nodded sympathetically. "You never talked much about your sister. Want to tell me about her?"

Mark drained his glass and poured another double. "She's different, very different from me. She's beautiful and high-strung as hell. She's an artist, a painter. She disavows money and lives like Van Gogh on a bad day . . . says it's the only way to 'create.' And she's got a talent of finding men who make her feel like nothing."

"But she hasn't cut off her ear yet?"

Mark shook his head. "Not yet, but she probably would if she thought it would help. I don't know, I don't understand her. When Father died, I left Indianapolis and went west. My challenge has always been using my money to make more. Louisa went to New York and lived down in the Village on bread and wine, supporting all her friends, living like a pauper.''

"How good are her paintings?"

"Competent. She says she can't create a masterpiece till she's suffered.''

"They call that artist's disease."

"It's more than that. She's really unstable."

"So what are you going to do when you find her? Get angry because she's some count's mistress?''

"No. She's slept with more men than I even know. No, I don't want to burst in on them. What the hell do I care about that? What I do care about is getting her to come home before Mother dies and trying to get her to behave herself for a few months so Mother can at least die feeling a little contentment.''

"You don't like her much, do you?"

"It's hard to explain. I don't hate her. In one way I love her. Morty, she's mad . . . her madness takes turns and twists, she does unexpected things. She makes me angrier than anyone I know, but then I feel terrible because I know she's not really responsible. But shit! It's really hard to live with madness." He gulped down his drink and poured another. "She's ruined my mother's life. Maybe all mad people are selfish. . . .''

"I would think being self-centered was a symptom of madness," Morty observed. "So now what? Your only link is this count, and this is a hell of a big city.''

Mark let out his breath. "I want you to stay here . . . handle any business decisions that might have to be made. I'm going to Milan. Since I can't get this bastard on the phone, I'll have to confront him in person.''

Morty sucked in his lower lip. "If we get a cable that the Huntington Beach properties are available, do you want me to buy?''

"You bet. There's lots of oil under that ground."

"What's your ceiling?"

"I'll leave that up to you."

"I don't want you overextended on leases—doesn't leave enough cash to develop.''

"You've never done that yet," Mark answered, feeling the full effect of the Scotch. "Come on, Morty, you know more about my business than I do.''

Morty smiled. "I'd be a lousy manager if I didn't." He watched as Mark poured himself another drink. Good for him to open up a little, he thought. Yes, Mark's feelings toward Louisa were just what he'd expected. "Love-hate " was just the right word for their relationship.

MILAN

Clare put her book of poems down and once again looked around the garden. It was twilight, and the setting sun cast long shadows on the patterned pathways. She sighed. The sky was magnificent, a deep blue with streaks of orange light on the eastern horizon.

"Ah, there you are, Clare Marina!" She looked up to see the figure of Emiliano Sforza etched in the doorway that led from the study into the garden. He strode toward her, and when he reached her, kissed her hand. "Where is your father?"

"Napping," Clare replied with a smile.

"Then we're alone." He laid some emphasis on his words as he looped her arm through his. "Come walk with me. I need to stretch—the train ride from Rome is long and tedious."

"You must be tired."

"I was, but seeing you has fully awakened my senses. You look ravishing." He gazed at her with hungry eyes.

Clare shivered.

"Are you cold?"

She shook her head.

"I can't tell you how sorry I am not to have met you at the station personally." He squeezed her arm meaningfully. "But I must confess, finding you in my garden is much nicer than seeing you for the first time on a crowded train platform."

"It's wonderful to be here," Clare said, pausing before a cluster of rosebushes.

Emiliano bent over and picked a full red rose. He ran his fingers around the petals and then handed it to her. "Wear this at dinner," he said.

"It's beautiful."

He stood looking at her for a moment. "Clare, I've thought about you a great deal. I've looked forward to seeing you. Is that wrong? Do you think of me as an old man?"

"Of course not! You're not old!"

He smiled and touched her throat with his finger, tracing small circles under her chin. "I don't like to think of myself as old, and I assure you, when I stand next to you I feel very young indeed. I feel . . . drawn to you."

Clare blushed.

295

"Oh, I'm embarrassing you. That's enchanting in a woman. You're as red as the rose"—he touched her cheek—"and your skin is as soft as its petals."

"Emiliano . . ."

He lifted his finger to his lips. "Say no more. We have time, Clare Marina, we have the whole summer to get to know one another." He looked at his watch. "Time to dress for dinner."

Clare nodded and allowed him to guide her back toward the house.

"Remember," he said as they stood by the winding staircase, "wear the rose over your heart."

The dining room was formal, and Clare could not help but think that Emiliano must entertain a great deal. But tonight the long table that could easily have seated twenty-six was set for five: Emiliano and Constanza, Clare and her father, and Luigi Catelli, the amiable managing director of Sforza Industries.

"First on our agenda, Agosto, is a tour of the dam site, then the steel mill. After that, a general introduction to Milan's industrial community." Emiliano held his wineglass while he spoke.

"I can't get over the change since I was last here," Agosto replied.

Emiliano laughed. "We've survived the storm before the calm, my friend, if I may appropriate a phrase. Yes, as we all hoped he would, Mussolini is well on the road to bringing order out of chaos."

"I'm impressed. Mind you, I always thought Mussolini displayed unusual leadership, even in the early days. When I was in Puglia in 1912, the year after the great drought, I read one of his articles in *La Lotta di Classe* that said, 'Before conquering Tripoli, let Italians conquer Italy! Bring water to parched Puglia, justice to the South, and education everywhere.' I liked the sentiment."

The count smiled. "He understands, and I hope you understand. We northerners have always been blamed for the difficulties in the south. It's the old story—the industrial heartland versus what should be the breadbasket. I believe that even in the rich and ordered United States there are strong feelings in your Midwest about the Eastern establishment."

"There are indeed," Agosto agreed.

"Mussolini will bring social justice to Italy without socialism—he knows the importance of both regions historically and economically. It is industry that will change the south, my friend. Mussolini will achieve full employment, and the unrest will cease. Tradition and progress are the two cornerstones of growth. Look what's happened in Russia!'' The count's face reddened. "The aristocracy has been destroyed and thus traditions have been shattered. The Socialists wallow in a mess of their own making. They can't produce sufficient food or industrialize without leadership—a leadership they destroyed when they murdered the aristocracy and educated elite. Oh, I admit that to survive we of the aristocracy must change—I'm quite different from the mainline of my own family. Most of them are content with their decaying fortunes and titles, whereas I've turned to industry to make a new fortune and a place for myself in what I believe will be Italy's new order. And you, my friend, have done the same. You've carved out an investment empire in America. You're part of the country's growth, a major factor in its expansion.''

"Well, as I said, I'm impressed. The strikes seem to have ended. I won't say that I don't have some reservations about the way Mussolini came to power, however.''

Emiliano smiled broadly. "Ah, my friend, you wouldn't have, had you been here in October last year when it all materialized. Certainly Il Duce had a plan. At a mass meeting of Fascists in Naples, he made a stirring address from the stage of the San Carlo Theater.'' Emiliano chuckled. "He spoke with his back to the scenery of *Madame Butterfly*, he laid out the plan then, and he returned to Milan. He spoke to all of us involved in industry individually. He laid out a program for a balanced budget, another to reduce the bureaucracy, and a third to stop inflation. Now, mind you, while all this was going on, Prime Minister Facta was fiddling. There were insurrections right across the length and breadth of Italy, the people were speaking, and speaking loudly. But we all knew. The king knew too, in spite of the fact that at the last moment he signed a decree of national emergency. Believe me when I tell you everyone in government was reconciled to Mussolini's takeover. We went to the king, a large delegation of industrialists, and we persuaded him not to sign a decree declaring martial law. We persuaded him to appoint Mussolini prime minister, to allow him to form a government.''

"But there was no election,'' Clare put in.

Emiliano smiled at her. "Not of the traditional kind, no. But if you had been in Rome, you'd have had no doubt! Mussolini crossed the Rubicon with his legions . . . the people poured into the streets and tossed flowers at him. 'Il Duce! Il Duce!' filled the air. He's popular—he's what the people wanted and he has their support.''

"I have no trouble believing that," Agosto said, laying down his fork and sipping some wine.

Emiliano turned to Clare. "While we're touring factories, Constanza will take you shopping at La Galleria where you can buy almost anything you desire. By the way, have I mentioned how much lovelier you look with short hair "

Clare glanced at her father. "Thank you," she replied softly. "Papa was upset when I had it cut."

The count turned to Agosto and pressed his arm. "Your father was upset because you've grown into a woman and he's lost his little girl."

Monday, July 2, 1923

MILAN

It was seven o'clock and Mark Lyons stood restlessly in the reception room of the Sforza mansion. He was tired of waiting and he felt impatient and angry, though he reminded himself not to be angry, but to behave in a civilized manner. He couldn't, in all honesty, blame this man for the relationship he had with Louisa, since all her adult life Louisa had sought out such relationships.

He walked restlessly to the window and moved the heavy draperies with his hand to look out into the garden. There on a marble bench sat a lovely young woman. She was staring intently at the fountain and was quite clearly lost in a daydream. Then he recognized her from the ship. She had had her hair cut, and now he remembered that Morty had mentioned that the morning after the ship's party. He wondered what she was doing in the count's garden, though he supposed her father, Agosto Tonelli, the banker, was somewhere around. Not so much of a coincidence, he concluded. After all, Sforza had banking interests.

The door opened and he turned to face a well-dressed man in his forties. He was handsome, Mark allowed. "Suave" was the word.

"Mr. Lyons," he said formally, extending his hand. "I'm sorry to have kept you waiting. I'm afriad you've come at a very bad time. I'm simply not entertaining any entrepreneurs who come to me with projects."

Mark stood rooted to the spot. The man didn't seem to recognize his last name.

"I'm not an entrepreneur, as you put it."

Sforza frowned. "I'm sorry, I don't understand. You told my servant you were an American businessman who had urgent business with me. Have I misunderstood?"

"My business is personal, and I thought it best to be discreet."

The count raised an eyebrow. "Discreet?"

"I'm Louisa's brother and I'm trying to find her. I know she's in Rome. I want her address."

"Louisa . . ." He said the name slowly and walked to the small bar. "Would you like a drink?"

Mark shook his head.

"Well, I'm sure you won't mind if I have one."

"I only want my sister's address."

"I really don't know why you think I know it."

"Because I'm told she's your mistress."

Sforza turned around suddenly. His face was hard. "I don't know a Louisa by the last name of Lyons."

Mark inhaled sharply. How like his sister, the artist who affected poverty, to use another name. "Then give me the address of the Louisa you know," he said firmly. He withdrew a picture from his pocket. "*This* Louisa," he said, hardly managing to conceal his temper.

Count Sforza glanced at it and handed it back. "104 Via Montebello, Pension Primrose."

"Thank you," Mark said, putting the picture away.

Sforza put his glass down and stared at Mark. "I want no scandal," he said rather firmly. "There are many crimes in Italy . . . people are set upon. We live in unsettling times."

Mark stared Sforza in the eye. "Are you threatening me?"

"I'm merely telling you that it pays to be careful."

"And you're a man of influence," Mark observed coolly. "Well, Count, rest assured I didn't come to cause a scandal. I came to take my sister home to America because our mother is extremely ill."

Sforza looked at him for a long moment, then said, "I'm sorry if I assumed wrongly."

A hundred possible retorts ran through Mark's mind. He wanted to tell this pompous bastard how much he disliked him, but instead he forced himself to turn toward the door. "I'll be going back to Rome," he said calmly.

Sforza nodded. "Good."

Tuesday, July 3, 1923

ROME

"Mark!" Louisa flung open the door with her usual exuberance. "What are you doing here, how did you find me?"

Mark came into the apartment, which, he noted, looked like every place Louisa had ever lived. The dull furniture was covered with gaudy throws and there were huge pillows tossed about with abandon.

Masses of half-finished canvases were piled in one corner, and on a table, half-open tubes of oils, brushes sitting in jars of linseed oil, and messy rags stained with innumerable colors gave the impression of a bleeding rainbow. The bed was unmade, a rumpled mass of sheets piled in one corner. On the table there were dishes left from at least three meals. On the tiny gas burner the perpetual coffeepot sat in a pool of congealed brown liquid left from its overboiling.

"If I'd known you were coming, I'd have cleaned up," she said apologetically. "But you know how I am, don't you, darling? The life of an artist. I don't do the dishes till they're all dirty, and it's utterly pointless making the bed because you just mess it up again when you sleep in it."

He let out his breath. He'd heard it all before. "Have you got any Scotch?"

"In the cupboard under the sink. I think there might be a clean glass left on the shelf . . . no ice, I'm afraid."

He retrieved the Scotch and poured some, then added bottled water. "This will do," he said as he began to remove her discarded clothing from one of the chairs so he could sit down.

"Sorry," she pouted. "I almost never get around to cleaning. I have to spend my time creatively."

"You've time to drink, time to smoke, and time to entertain your count. Presumably if you strained yourself you'd have time to wash your clothes. You don't have to live like this. Why the hell don't you move into a proper studio? And for Christ's sake, why don't you hire a maid!"

"I'm making my own way in the world now. I don't have money for things like that."

"Making your own way, shit! The rent here is paid by Count Sforza. I presume he provides you with the other necessities of life too. Making your own way! Call it 'being a mistress' if you like. I call it prostitution.'' He instantly hated himself. It was not the way he had intended to begin. And he was arguing logically with her, when in fact he knew logic didn't apply to her condition.

Tears welled in her great brown eyes. ''Don't talk that way. I know what I am.'' She picked up a glass of wine and gulped some down. Certainly she'd been drinking before his arrival. ''Don't you see, don't you understand? I have to do this, I have to be on my own, I have to create, and to create I have to know love and to suffer.''

''Does Count Sforza make you suffer?''

Her face took on a strange expression. It was an expression he'd seen before, but he didn't know what it meant. It was a faraway look, a vacant look.

''I'm going to marry him,'' she announced.

''What makes you think so? Has he proposed?''

Louisa shook her head. ''No, but he always comes back. Emiliano and I belong together. He knows how to treat me, he understands my needs.''

He treats you like a whore, he thought to himself. He probably treats you like shit, which is what you believe you are and why you like him. But he didn't say it. ''Why are you living under the name Louisa Louis?''

''I don't want him to find out who I am. I want him to love me for what I am.''

He didn't ask what she was. ''Can you possibly imagine that a man of his means is a fortune-hunter?''

''It's not that,'' she protested. ''I just didn't want him to know.''

''Well, he met me and didn't recognize the name—hell, why should he?''

''He has many business connections in the States.''

''All in the East,'' Mark answered. They were off on a tangent. It was impossible to talk to Louisa and not go off on tangents.

''You went to him?'' Her eyes were still moist, but now they were wide.

''You need not worry, my dear. I didn't reveal that you're not a slut by heritage and breeding—far be it from me to tell him you live this way by choice.''

''I *am* a slut!'' Again her eyes filled with tears and she began to cry into her wine, sobbing violently. ''A useless, worthless slut! I can't even finish my paintings, I can't do anything.''

He resisted the heartless desire to agree. He'd done that too many times before. She was sick. He'd decided that long ago:

she was sick and she needed help, though he didn't know how to give it. He silently prayed for patience. Don't let me lose my temper again, he thought. But God in heaven, it was so difficult. She kept shifting the ground, pulling the rug. Marry Count Sforza indeed!

He walked over to her and patted her shoulder. "Stop crying, Louisa, I'm sorry, it's just that I've spent days trying to find you. It's my fault, my frustration."

"Why?" she said between sobs, lifting her wide eyes to look at him.

"Mother's ill, and wants to see you. Louisa, come home with me."

She shook her head. "I can't leave. I won't."

"Mother's dying." He hated even saying it, but it was true, and denying it made it no easier.

"I'll die if I go home," she replied. "No, I can't come, not now . . . not ever."

"Louisa, I've never asked much of you, but Mother wants to see you. Please come home." He tried desperately not to reveal his anger.

But she continued to shake her head. "No, no, no. I won't leave, I can't leave."

It was no use. He was as angry as he had ever been. But if he stood here and cajoled and shouted for a lifetime, he knew it wouldn't do any good. "Well, I can't stay longer," he said, thinking that the whole trip had been an utter waste of time and energy. "If you won't come, I insist that at least you sit down right now and write her a letter for me to take home."

"I can't do that."

He pressed her arm. "You can and will."

"I don't know what to say."

He was aware he was pressing harder. "I'll dictate it," he said firmly. "Damn you, I won't let her die without some comfort."

18

Tuesday, July 24, 1923

BROOKLYN

Milan
July 17, 1923

Dear Mama,

Milan is a very exciting city. The pace is like New York, fast and furious, and not at all like Rome, which seems to be dedicated to its history and to life's pleasures. That's one of Italy's most interesting aspects: each city has a distinct personality. Emiliano says Italian cities are like women: some are reserved and ladylike, some are just for fun, while others concentrate on their age. Milan is a banker's city, an industrial giant! No wonder Papa loves it so; it suits him. He's busy all the time going from one meeting to another. I'd like to go with him, of course, but no such luck. I have to spend most of my time shopping with Constanza Sforza, Emiliano's sister—I wrote about her last week. But I must tell you one thing. I'm taking your advice. I'm trying not to challenge Papa (so much) and we're getting along much better. You know, I believe you're right. I believe he might come around and finally accept the idea of my going into banking. Anyway, the three of us discuss politics all the time, and Papa's given up scowling at me when I have an opinion.

Constanza Sforza is very sophisticated, but her only interest in life seems to be spending money. I can't tell her, but shopping day in and day out bores me.

In spite of it all, I am enjoying myself. Emiliano is the perfect host and he spends a great deal of time with me, mostly in the evenings when Papa has gone to bed. We discuss art, literature, and even business. He's not like any other man I've ever known; he seems to know everything and everybody. We'll be at Lake Como by the time you get this letter. I can hardly wait! Emiliano says the mountains are awesome and the lake is as clear as crystal. He promised me we could go riding along the shore. He's not only mature and knowledgeable, he's also very athletic.

I am babbling on—I miss having you and Fabiana to talk to, and it's hard to discuss personal matters with Constanza. I bought a beautiful leather purse for Fabiana, by the way. I would have bought one for Maria, but I know she'd still carry all her things in that dreadful shopping bag.

I'm going to beg off shopping tomorrow and visit the Pinacoteca Ambrosiana again. Not only is it a magnificent museum—it has over a thousand drawings by Leonardo—but its architecture is glorious. And tomorrow night Emiliano promised to take me to the theater. At this rate, the summer will pass very quickly. I'll write again in a few days, Mama, and I do miss you.

Love,
Clare

Having read the letter to Fabiana, Cecilia put it down dejectedly. "I don't know, perhaps I'm imagining things."

"What do you mean, Cecilia?"

"It was my idea for her to go on this trip with Agosto. I didn't want to go, but you know how I feel about Clare. I don't want her to be like me. I want her to be worldly and able to get along. Clare's always been different. Agosto senses it, but won't acknowledge it because she's a woman. But a mother knows, Fabiana, I know. Clare is different."

"And won't the trip make her more worldly? What are you worried about, Cecilia?"

Cecilia shrugged. "I've seen Emiliano Sforza. He's a few years younger than Agosto. At least twenty-four years older than Clare. Fabiana, Clare's letter is full of Emiliano. Emiliano this, Emiliano that."

Fabiana burst out laughing. "And?" she asked. "Are they betrothed? Clare only said he was nice to her, and perhaps she does have a girlish adoration for him, but there's no harm in that."

Cecilia nodded. "When he was here, I saw the way he looked at her. A woman knows those looks. And Clare is entranced with him. She's so smart and so mature for her age, and she's naturally attracted to a sophisticated older man."

"I don't think you have to worry. Clare isn't so anxious to get married and have babies. And she'll be less so if Agosto agrees to let her work."

"But Count Sforza's a charmer."

"She's very smart, Cecilia."

Cecilia smiled. "Oh, I know. And very special, too."

"A mama shouldn't play favorites," Fabiana chided.

"I love my children equally, but Clare is my firstborn and I've always known how bright she was. Ah, Fabiana, I remember everything she did as a child. She was always so purposeful, as if she were walking straight down a path and knew exactly where she was headed."

"That's why I think you have no cause for concern."

"When you are growing up, the path twists and turns. It's harder to follow, Fabiana."

"Of all people, you don't have to tell me that."

Cecilia leaned over and kissed her sister-in-law on the cheek. "You're a good woman and you've always been a great comfort to me; you're a second mother to my children."

Tears filled Fabiana's dark eyes. "You're my family, Cecilia. And it's family that matters."

Wednesday, July 25, 1923

C O M O, I T A L Y

Emiliano, Clare, and Agosto traveled twenty-five miles by train from Milan to the city of Como, located on the lake, and the capital of the Lombardy region. They waited outside the terminal, standing in the warm sunshine.

"A magnificent fluke of nature," Emiliano explained with an expansive wave of his hand. "Tropical . . . divine . . . yet completely surrounded by mountains. Those to the north are more than eight thousand feet, while the ones we just came over by rail are two thousand. It's a very deep lake, more than a thousand feet. And the mountains are all limestone and granite. You'll see, the shore of Como is in miraculous contrast to the snow-covered mountains. It's warm, and you'll see that this haven in the Alps has palm trees, grape vines, figs, pomegranates, olives, chestnuts, and flourishing oleander trees. Yes, a paradise!"

Clare smiled. Clearly Emiliano relished playing the tour guide. "I understand now why it's called the jewel of the Alps," she said, taking in the view.

"As soon as the car arrives, I suggest we motor around the city, then in a few hours we'll take the steamer to Villa Sforza, which is near Lecco."

"The steamer?" Clare exclaimed in delight. "I've never been on a lake this large in my entire life. I've only been on a tiny little lake in Prospect Park. I've never been on a lake steamer."

"It's far more comfortable than driving. All the larger villas are linked by steamer. The road is long, tiring, rugged, and mostly unpaved. It's straight up on one side and straight down on the other. I'm afraid there are frequent landslides."

"I think a steamer sounds good," Agosto put in.

Emiliano shrugged. "I doubt it will be long before there's a proper road. Mussolini motors to Lake Como frequently from Milan, and I shouldn't think that now he's come to power he'd allow his favorite resort to go without a good road!"

"I wouldn't think so," Agosto agreed.

"I think we should go first to the Piazza Cavour. It opens directly onto the lake and there's a fine promenade. Ah, and you will see such architecture! The Church of Sant Abbonidio is ancient. It was consecrated in 1065 and it's the oldest church in the area. It is surrounded by buildings in the Gothic style, and nearby, many built during the Renaissance. Como has been a refuge and playground for centuries, and there's an architectural contribution from almost every period."

"I'm looking forward to an exploratory tour," Agosto said. He wandered off, moving to a newsstand, where he began looking at some foreign newspapers.

"That's just like Papa," Clare said, smiling. "He doesn't like waiting, and if there's anything to read, he finds it."

"He should learn to take it easy. Your father works constantly."

"I know. That's why he's so successful."

"Ah, Clare, there's something special for you in Como."

"For me? It's enough to be here, the air is wonderful!"

"Ah, but there's more than fine mountain air. This is the home of the silk industry and there are shops filled with lovely silk dresses and . . . ah, more intimate garments."

Clare turned her head away and wiped her brow. The sun was hot, and she hoped Emiliano would mistake her blush for the effect of the heat. He'd emphasized the word "intimate" and given her a penetrating, meaningful look.

"You didn't buy much in Milan, only a few dresses."

"I must confess that I'm not really fond of shopping," Clare admitted.

Emiliano smiled broadly. "A refreshing confession from a woman. Had my late wife felt that way, I would today be even wealthier."

"If one has nothing special to purchase, shopping seems like a waste of time."

"And you don't like to waste time."

Clare shook her head. "Only now and again, when I'm on holiday."

He feigned a stern expression. "And that's time earned by hard work, yes?"

"Yes."

"I like you, Clare Marina . . . I like you very much indeed."

Again she blushed. "You embarrass me, Emiliano."

"Oh, I shouldn't want that. Do you think you could bring yourself to stop calling me Emiliano and call me Emil? 'Emiliano' makes me feel like a relic."

"Emil," she repeated.

"Ah, the car is here!" Emil announced. "Come, Agosto . . . come, my friend! Come! Wine and cheese and an unsurpassed view of the lake await us at the piazza!"

Thursday, July 26, 1923

N E W   Y O R K

A whirlwind trip, Morty Levinson thought. They'd sailed on June 15, arrived in Rome on the twenty-fifth, and sailed from Le Havre on July 15, twelve days after Mark's meeting with his sister. Mark would have left immediately, but it was summer and it hadn't been all that easy to book passage.

"Let's grab a coffee at Fred Harvey's," Morty suggested. "The train doesn't leave for half an hour."

"Sometimes it seems like the whole population of the country is on the move." Mark looked around Grand Central. It was a cavern with ornate lighting suspended from the faraway ceiling, but its design muted the noise of the thousands of people who were constantly milling about.

Grand Central was larger than Dearborn in Chicago, where they would change trains. Morty was heading directly back to the Coast to see to business. He was planning to take the Monad Line to Indianapolis to visit his mother.

They ordered a quick coffee from the pert little waitress who wore the standard uniform of the Harvey Girls, a long black ruffled dress with a crisp white apron and tiny white cap. Morty followed her with his eyes, but Mark stared at the table, a sure sign he was still absorbed in his own thoughts. "You're not noticing much these days," Morty ventured.

"I guess not." Unconsciously Mark felt the letter in his breast pocket. At least the letter would soothe his mother. She would know Louisa was safe. He leaned back and closed his eyes for a moment; it seemed as if they had been traveling nonstop for an eternity.

"You're still depressed," Morty observed. "Did you talk to that guy again—what was his name?

"Matteotti. Yes, I talked to him. He helped me to arrange to have her watched. I told them not to follow or harass her, just keep an eye on her so that I'll know she's all right—you know, in case she gets sick."

"How often has she been sick before?"

"Twice," Mark admitted. "Once when she was sixteen, again when she was twenty-three. Both times she spent six months in a rest home."

"You mean a mental institution."

Mark nodded. "A mental institution for the wealthy."

"I really think you've done all you could." Small comfort, Morty thought. Mark couldn't handle it. He was a tough, talented, ambitious young guy—everything he touched turned to gold. He had it easy, too easy, and that fact fitted into Morty's own personal philosophy of life: if everything went right in one part of your life, everything went wrong in another part. If you had a happy childhood, you got slammed as an adult. If you had a miserable childhood, you might be lucky when you got older. Mark was a business natural, but his personal life was marred by loneliness. Not that women weren't attracted to Mark, but he didn't know how to treat them. He was too abrupt, too honest, and too busy. As soon as they discovered he didn't want to devote himself to endless flattery, they left him. Usually they left about the time they discovered he was married to Lyons Oil and had no intention of giving up twelve-hour workdays.

"I suppose her Count Sforza might marry her, but somehow I doubt it. If he doesn't she'll be vulnerable to another breakdown," Mark said, breaking into Morty's thoughts.

"You can't worry about something that hasn't happened."

Mark gulped down the coffee. "I know."

"How long you plan to stay in Indianapolis?"

"Two weeks . . . three at the most."

"Well, I guess Lyons Oil won't fall apart in three weeks."

Mark laughed. "I trust you to see that it doesn't."

LAKE COMO

Villa Sforza reminded Clare of the pictures she'd seen of Spanish haciendas. Carefully built around a series of small patios, it was a rambling white stucco house with a red tile roof. The marble-floored corridors that connected the rooms were filled with potted plants and freshly cut multicolored flowers. Outside, lush purple blossoms seemingly climbed the side of the house, their vines sprawling out over the roof.

The vast reception room with its floor-to-ceiling windows looked out on a magnificent terrace and formal gardens that were enclosed by a tall iron fence. Beyond the garden, a lawn stretched out to meet a rugged rock wall, which gave way to a long stretch of private beach on the shore of the lake. On one side of Villa Sforza there were acres of olive trees, and on the other, cultivated vineyards. The estate was approachable from two directions—by steamer from the lake, where guests disembarked onto a private dock, or from the road that wound past the estate. The latter entrance was walled off, and armed guards stood duty at a gatehouse, barring entry to all but those specially invited.

They finished dinner, and one of the dozens of servants that lived on the estate cleared away the fine china and crystal, leaving only the brandy snifters.

"The mountain air makes me sleepy." Agosto yawned.

"I was thinking of a walk in the garden," Emiliano suggested.

"Not for me," Agosto replied. "I swam this morning, and judging from my stiffness, I'd say I stretched something that hasn't been stretched for some time."

"That's the trouble with Americans—all work and no play. The body is a temple in which the mind is lodged, and must be kept fit." Emiliano turned to Clare. "Will you join me? I'm dedicated to after-dinner walks through the gardens and along the shore."

"I'd love to go for a walk."

"Better bring your shawl. No matter how warm the days, the nights are cool."

Clare wrapped her embroidered shawl around her shoulders and followed Emiliano through the great glass doors and across the expansive terrazzo terrace that led to the steps and into the garden.

"It's beautiful here," Clare said. "And so peaceful."

"An illusion," Emil replied. Then, almost wistfully: "But we can't live without illusion; it's the sustenance of our class."

Clare stopped and looked at the roses. Their delicate soft pink petals were closed.

Emiliano stopped too, and lifted his fingers to her lips, running one around the outline of her mouth lightly, so lightly that a chill ran through Clare Marina. "Emil . . ." she whispered in slight but meaningless protest.

"Ah, my roses . . . they're the most sensual of all flowers. That's why I asked you to wear one that first night when we were reunited in Milan. Poets have likened roses to women for centuries, you know. The opening and closing of their blossoms, the soft velvet feel of their petals." He ran his finger around her lips again. "Have these lips known kisses? You have a beautiful mouth, full and sensuous."

Clare's face burned red, but in the shadows he couldn't see her flush. "Childish ones," she answered in a murmur.

"Ah . . ." He moved his finger once more in a full circle and then let his hand drop away. "You know I was married for many years, until Donna Anna died four years ago. But Donna Anna and I were never lovers. I think it would be more appropriate to describe our marriage as a merger of two supremely important families and businesses. It was an arranged marriage, a marriage without passion. Of course, there's no divorce. But I shouldn't like to leave the impression that our union was entirely unpleasant. We grew used to one another, learned the art of accommodation. A very wise man once wrote that real happiness doesn't exist, that the best one can hope for is a modicum of contentment."

"No, there's love," Clare said, looking into his face. "I shouldn't want a loveless marriage."

He brushed her hair with his hand. "You're stunningly beautiful, clever, and wise beyond your years, Clare Marina Tonelli. I can't imagine you in a loveless union."

"You flatter me, Emil." They were standing close together and Clare felt drawn to him. His eyes held a hungry look, a look of wild longing. On impulse Clare threw her arms around his neck and kissed him. He bent down and his arms encircled her, turning her warm girlish kiss into a passionate one, moving his mouth on hers till he felt her yield and go limp in his arms.

"Has anyone ever kissed you like that, Clare Marina?"

She shook her head, and her eyes studied him.

"What do you see, Clare Marina? Do you see lust in my eyes?"

"Is it only lust?"

"No, it's more. But I'm much older than you."

"Age is unimportant. I see a warm, compassionate man. To me you're youthful."

"And I see a young woman who is mature, an irresistible woman who enchants me."

"Emil, I don't know what to say."

He laughed. "Ah, Clare, now you're being coy. You've seen my feelings for you in my eyes since the first night we met, and I, my dear, have seen your response. You have young, healthy animal instincts. I could make you burn with desire." He touched her ear, running his finger around it, then down her long neck.

"Emil . . ." He kissed her again, holding her so closely she felt she would faint in his arms.

When he released her lips, he held her with his eyes. "When the time comes for words, you'll have them."

Clare nodded, though both desire and apprehension flooded over her.

Wednesday, August 8, 1923

LAKE COMO

Two weeks. They had been at the Lake for two weeks and tomorrow Emil and her father were returning to Milan for two weeks to sign contracts. She would have to talk to her father tonight. *If only I weren't so confused,* she thought. Each night she and Emil walked in the garden and exchanged wild romantic embraces. Her lips burned with the memory of his kisses, and her mind was filled with his promises of passionate moments to come. And they talked too, sometimes long into the night. He sought her opinion, he encouraged her to discuss her views. Clare bit her lip. *Love.* Was she in love with Emil?

"Papa?" Clare knocked softly at the door. "Papa, are you awake?"

"Yes, come in, Clare."

Clare opened the door. Her father, in a blue silk dressing gown, sprawled out on the lounge, newspapers and folios surrounding him. "Is this how you rest?" she asked, laughing. "Shame on you, Papa, you're working!"

"Sh! You mustn't tell Emiliano. He's a dedicated believer in holidays without work."

"I'll keep your secret," she promised. "How's the stock market? I've lost track of everything."

"You came here to discuss the stock market?" He raised his eyebrow.

"No."

"But you do have something to discuss?"

"Yes, I just don't know how to begin."

"When I read a book, I like it if it goes from beginning to end. Flashbacks confuse me. So why don't you begin at the beginning."

Clare pressed her lips together. "I'm not sure where the beginning is. It's Emiliano."

Agosto put his paper down and looked at her. "I'm not blind, I see the way you look at each other. Of course it's not hard to understand. He's a handsome, brilliant, and wealthy man and you're a beautiful woman."

"Money doesn't enter into it," Clare said.

"Well, it should. Poverty isn't as noble as it's cracked up to be."

"Papa, I think I'm . . . well, I feel very attracted to him and I believe it's mutual."

"He's older than you."

"Grandpapa was older than Grandmama, you're older than Mama. Age doesn't matter."

"What does matter to you, Clare?"

"Papa, Emiliano hasn't known happiness in marriage. He hasn't known love. I feel . . . well, that I could give him love."

"Sympathy isn't a good basis for marriage."

"It's not sympathy."

"He hasn't proposed, has he?"

"Not yet."

"But you feel it coming."

Again she nodded, and then seemed to fall into thought.

Agosto leaned back against the arm of the lounge. "Frankly, if I looked for a long while I couldn't find a better husband for you than Emiliano Sforza. But I don't believe in arranged marriages, so when the time comes, *if* it comes, I think you'll have to decide for yourself, Clare. Now, let me say this: Emiliano is a man of honor, but he is human. There won't be any lovemaking without marriage.''

"Papa!" Clare frowned at her father. She felt relieved that he didn't object to her growing relationship with Emil, but angry that he thought she might give in to immorality. At the same time, she felt a contradictory surge of emotion. She'd always had to fight to make her own decisions, and now when she might face the most important decision of her life, her father had seemingly thrust independence on her. Reluctantly she admitted that she wasn't sure she wanted to be that independent.

"I think I can control myself," she replied coolly,

Agosto suddenly winked at her, catching her off guard completely. "I should hope so," he replied. Then, more seriously: "Clare, nothing would delight me more than seeing you married."

"Papa, I wanted . . . No, I still *want* to go into banking."

Agosto frowned. "Clare we've been through this. I don't approve, and you wouldn't be accepted. Personally, I'm relieved that you're attracted to Emiliano. You're twenty—you should be married."

"Why can't a married woman be in business?"

"Women and business do not mix!" Agosto scowled at her.

"I don't think Emiliano feels the same way," Clare said defiantly.

"And what if he does?"

"I think I love him, I think I can convince him I have a role to play. I think he knows I wouldn't be happy living the idle life of a society wife."

"I want you to be realistic, Clare."

"I am realistic!" She was fighting back tears now. What did her father know of Emiliano?

Agosta shook his head. "If Emiliano loves you and you love him, I would bless such a union. What you do after your marriage—what Emiliano allows you do—well, that's out of my hands."

"You would never have let me go into banking, would you?" Clare felt betrayed. In spite of his stubbornness, there had always been a half-promise.

"I doubt it."

Clare pressed her lips together. There it was, the half-carrot dangling in front of her, as if she were a starved rabbit. She could take a chance—perhaps attain all her desires with Emil—or she could refuse him and pray that her father would mellow and give in eventually. But then, even if he did, it might be an empty life, a life without the love Emil seemed to offer.

"I want you to be sure," Agosto said firmly. "Marriage is a big step."

Clare turned away from her father. "I'll be sure," she replied.

Friday, August 10, 1923

MILAN

Constanza Sforza stood by the window looking out on the patterned paths of the formal gardens.

Her hands grasped the heavy green velvet draperies, squeezing them between her fingers so hard that the color drained from her hands. Her aristocratic face was knit in a scowl and she desperately tried to compose herself before turning about to face her brother. She arched her brows and shook her head. "Marry her! Really, Emiliano, I think you've lost your mind."

"Hardly. She's young, she's lovely, I'm sure she'll get pregnant almost immediately, and her father is one of America's wealthiest bankers. Ah, Constanza, you should be pleased."

"She's a peasant!" Constanza said meanly. "A simple peasant!"

Emiliano laughed. "Hardly that."

"Money! Money doesn't change breeding. It doesn't alter generations of genes! It's really of no importance to me how much money a peasant has, a peasant is still a peasant and no one can change that!"

"I think she's rather well-bred and quite intelligent."

"You're taken with her youthful body, not her mind. Emiliano, I know you. Don't try to be so clever with me!"

"I certainly won't deny I'm attracted to her nubile charms, my dear. Firm youthful flesh, rounded buttocks, high breasts, are all, to say the least, alluring. And I must confess she has lovely feet—tiny delicate feet. But all that aside, I need her father's continued investment and support. Frankly, I can't think that being married to an American citizen has any disadvantages, either. It's true that I have faith in the future of Fascism, but an intelligent gambler hedges his bets."

"I hate the Fascists—they'll destroy our class. And you are utterly absurd! Imagine, a Sforza marrying into a family that comes from Puglia! Disgusting! I tell you, Emiliano, heredity will tell. It always does. Money can't buy our lineage. Oh, I entertain them because you ask me, and I am pleasant because I know it's good for Sforza Industries, but marriage? Emiliano, the nouveau riche make me retch! They don't understand power, they don't understand manners, they don't really understand money. You yourself have told me that in spite of their money they live in Brooklyn in a house which is above average but simple. You yourself have told me they have only two servants! How can a person of this background adjust to our way of life? It's always the mistake of such people to believe that money is power, when of course it is not. Money is simply an enabler—it enables us to live as we were born to live. What do you want, Emiliano? Should the queen mother come to visit, and find your Clare running about chasing her own babies while preparing pasta in the kitchen? I warn you, Emiliano, you can't dress her up, put her in a setting like a doll, and expect anything. Money doesn't take the peasant out of peasants.''

"Rant all you like, Constanza. I intend to marry her.''

"If all you want is an American, why don't you marry your mistress in Rome?''

Emiliano smiled and ran his hand through his hair. ''There are women you sleep with and women you marry. Clare is a woman you marry. Her father's an important man. Louisa is nothing, she's one of thousands of American bohemians, very pleasant in bed, but she offers no real financial benefits.''

"I presume you'll keep on seeing her.''

"As long as she amuses me, yes. I'll certainly keep her until the marriage.''

"How very like you. You'll ruin that girl's life. You're making a mistake, and I think it's the most serious mistake of your life.''

"Oh, Constanza! You're wonderfully inconsistent. First she's a peasant unworthy of the Sforza name, then you're worried that I'll ruin her life.''

"I don't hate her, I just don't want you to marry her—as much for her own good as for yours. She's young, Emiliano. She's young and she's blind to what you are.''

"And I'm the master of this house and you shall do as I tell you and hold your tongue. Now, I have a task for you, Constanza, one that is suited to your gifts. The queen mother will be in Como on August 20, and I should like you to arrange a reception for her, an extravaganza. I want you to invite everyone, and I do mean everyone. I want you to go to Como while Agosto and I are busy here in Milan. I want you to prepare Clare for presentation to the queen. You will instruct her in protocol and see to it that she is dressed properly.''

"I think you've lost your mind. And August 20? That's only ten days away!''

"I have faith in you. Now, let me remind you of my main concern. I will yet have an heir, Constanza, and that heir will link Sforza Industries and a vast network of banks in North America. He will link them in a way that no contract ever could. And I shouldn't think that siring heirs will be unpleasant. Yes, Constanza, I shall at last have what I want, and I will enjoy getting it."

"You're a ruthless man, Emiliano. You always get what you want." Constanza fought to hold back angry tears as she stared at her brother.

"You of all people know just how ruthless I am, my dear. Don't cry, it's unbecoming."

Monday, August 13, 1923

LAKE COMO

"Do I really need a new gown?" Clare whispered to Constanza.

"Of course you do, my dear. And I went to a great deal of trouble to bring Milan's three foremost couturiers and their models with me so that we might choose just the right gown to suit the occasion. After all, we haven't a world of time. The queen mother will be here in seven days!"

"I could've gone to Milan," Clare protested.

"No, no, I wouldn't dream of it. Besides, with your father and Emiliano away, it's the perfect opportunity to view the new fashions in seclusion. I do love private showings."

Constanza clapped her hands regally and the butler showed three men into the room. "Clare, may I present Signori Renaldo, Puchelli, and Lorenzo." She nodded toward them and in turn they each bowed back.

"Knowing each of you as I do, I'm certain you've been fighting all the way from Milan. So we won't see all of one collection first or last. You'll rotate. First a gown from you, Signor Lorenzo, then one from you, Signor Puchelli, then one from you, Signor Renaldo. You see, you're in alphabetical order." She nodded toward them and whispered to Clare, "They have dreadful temperaments, my dear. You must learn to treat them correctly."

Clare leaned back in the chair as the three nodded and disappeared. "I'm used to trying dresses on," she said.

"Well, you aren't looking at dresses, my dear, you're looking at designs—high fashion. Whatever you choose will be made to fit just you. Naturally, it'll be one of a kind. I know you're not used to that sort of thing, I understand that in America clothes are mass-produced and that women buy them off racks. But such a dress simply wouldn't do for a Sforza gathering. The guests will each be uniquely dressed. Oh, my dear, it would be the end of the world if two women turned up in the same gown!''

The parade of specially designed garments began with another clap from Constanza, and one after another the models came for two hours. There were Grecian-style gowns, long straight gowns with layered hemlines, gowns with a Turkish motif worn by models in ornate turbans, slinkily revealing gowns, and ruffled organdy gowns that made the models look like overdressed cherubs.

And, Clare thought, suppressing a smile, if some of the dresses amused her, the poses assumed by the models were somewhere between hilarious and ludicrous. They draped themselves over the grand piano, slithered from the staircase banister, hung limply across chairs as if embracing them, and generally stood with their feet wide apart and their hands on their hips, as if to challenge the world. They turned slowly and rapidly to illustrate the fullness of a skirt or a slit that daringly revealed a bit of leg. Their facial expressions ranged from vacant and empty to purposefully pouty as they went through their absurd patterned routine.

"I can't tell them apart anymore," Clare complained.

"Perhaps you're right, this is a bit tedious." Constanza got up and left the room. But she returned almost instantly. "I've told them to hold off while we talk. Have you seen anything that strikes your fancy?"

Clare glanced at her notes. "I think I like the one that Signor Lorenzo described as having the Turkish hemline."

"Ah, a wise choice. It's in perfect vogue!"

Constanza left again, but this time she walked only to the door. "Bring back number seventeen, Signor Lorenzo!"

Within moments a flushed, excited Signor Lorenzo burst into the room carrying the dress, a pad of paper, and a tape measure. "Such a lovely gown, made from pure silk, very fashionable, very chic indeed!" His arms flew in all directions.

"Are you certain, Clare?"

"Yes . . . yes, it's very nice."

"Nice! It's a masterpiece! My clothes are never simply 'nice.' " He held the dress protectively to his chest and pouted like a small child.

Constanza touched him tenderly. "My dear Lorenzo, she

didn't mean to insult you, darling. Americans use 'nice' in a different way than we. Do be a darling and measure her.''

"I'm sorry," Clare said coolly, not knowing how to treat this foppish, petulant little man.

"Oh, very well," Lorenzo relented as he began to measure. "And what color would you like it in?"

"Green," Clare said without hesitation.

Constanza was displeased. "Oh, no, my dear. No, no, no! Green does not suit you at all! It should be either peach or blue."

Clare inhaled. How to be polite and still firm? "I want green," she insisted.

"I quite agree, my dear. Green is not your color." Lorenzo made a face, and his hand fluttered in the air.

Clare glared at him. "I want green," she reiterated.

Constanza shrugged and waved her arms in a gesture of surrender. "Green, Signor Lorenzo . . . for me."

MILAN

"Brandy?" Emiliano offered. "Or would you prefer a Campari on ice? I must say the last few days the weather's been oppressive!"

"Not as bad as Manhattan in August, but I think I'll have the Campari all the same," Agosto answered, settling back in the leather chair and lighting a cigar. The study in the Sforzas' Milan mansion was the smallest room in the house and it vaguely reminded him of his own study.

Emiliano handed Agosto his drink. "Prohibition must be a bore," he joked.

"I think it's why I'm doing more business in Europe."

"We have much to do in the next few days. I've a pile of bids for us to examine. Then we'll return to Como. I have a little surprise. I've arranged a reception for the queen mother." He leaned over toward Agosto. "You'll like her and you'll see that she adores Mussolini."

Agosto thought for a moment. "I suppose you're anxious to return to Como—to be with Clare," he said cautiously.

Emiliano nodded. "Agosto, I want to talk to you about Clare, and as you've brought her up, there's no time like the present."

Agosto nodded.

"I know you must have reservations—I'm older, I'm a widower. But, Agosto, I must confess, I love your daughter."

Agosto shifted uneasily in his chair. "I've known you for several years, Emiliano. I find this conversation . . . well, a little difficult."

"I too. Should I play the traditional suitor? Should I tell you I'll provide for her, honor her, cherish her?"

"No, none of those are in question."

"Be honest with me."

"Emiliano, my only reservations involve Clare herself. She's headstrong and, I'm afraid, not a traditional woman. She's well-educated, she has a flair for business, but more, she has an ambition for it."

Emiliano smiled. "I think I can keep her amused, and believe it or not, I appreciate her mind."

"I only wanted you to know that she might grow restless. Oh, she wouldn't want another man, Emiliano, but she might want to involve herself in Sforza Industries. I don't approve myself, of course. Women don't belong in the business world, certainly not in banking."

"A woman could not involve herself in business in Italy, but there are certain charity endeavors in which she could become active. As I told you, I can keep her amused. Then too, if she thinks she's involved, I think she'll be contented. Few men are able to come home and seek their wife's advice. I don't think Clare will take long to come to the conclusion that our marriage will be a partnership—even if she has to remain behind the scenes."

Agosto smiled. "I thought you'd understand. But I did feel it only fair to warn you. Now, let me say this: if I'd been asked to pick a suitor for Clare Marina, I couldn't have chosen a man I respect more than you. Yes, Emiliano, you have my blessing."

"I'd like to drink to that," Emiliano replied. "More Campari?"

Agosto accepted the Campari. "When do you wish to marry?"

Emiliano sipped his drink. "I intend to propose when we return to Como. Agosto, I don't want to wait. I thought toward the end of September. You could cable your family, have them come here for the wedding."

"That's very soon," Agosto said with some apprehension. Cecilia, he thought, would be shocked.

"Shall we leave it up to Clare?" Emiliano suggested. "After all, she might not accept my proposal."

Agosto nodded silently. It would be best for her to be married, he thought. Marriage would change her; she would forget her desire to go into banking.

19

Monday, August 20, 1923

L A K E   C O M O

Villa Sforza hummed with activity. Delivery after delivery arrived from Como: pastries from Modena Pasticceria, cartons of liquor and liqueurs, breads of all kinds, imported delicacies, and the fresh ingredients for local dishes. The orchestra and their tempestuous leader also arrived in a red-white-and-green bus.

The terrace was transformed into what looked like the setting for a Roman bacchanal. Long tables that would hold the food were draped in flowing cloths, bowls of grapes in silver vessels were placed on each of forty small tables, and leafy vines covered two white-painted wooden Roman columns that Constanza had borrowed from the set director at La Scala.

At the far end of the terrace a dais was constructed for the queen mother, who was obliged to sit at a higher elevation than the other guests. All other tables were arranged in precise groupings that Constanza assigned with all the ingenuity of a diplomat. So-and-so could not sit with so-and-so; others of course simply had to be together; and naturally, everyone had to be able to see the queen mother.

"I must say you do this sort of thing well," Emiliano said, pouring himself a drink. "Where is Clare?"

"I sent her to rest. Since she'll be meeting the cream of Italian nobility, I supposed she should look her best."

"I'm sure she will," Emiliano replied without concern. "Have you instructed her in protocol?"

Constanza turned slightly away and suppressed her smile. "As well as possible. Personally, I don't feel much can be done with Americans. They simply don't understand royalty."

"If she accepts my proposal, Constanza, we'll be married at the end of September, before her father returns to America."

"You're mad! She only came here in June!"

320

"And we've been together almost every day. Besides, my dear, I have my reasons. I want the Tonelli banks married to Sforza Industries as soon as possible."

"I don't understand."

"You couldn't possibly. Let me just say that the health of Sforza Industries is not as it appears. You will stop your infernal complaining, and you will begin to make the arrangements for the wedding."

Constanza straightened up and turned. "All my life I've done as you told me, Emiliano. I've regretted it, but I've always obeyed you."

He looked at her scornfully. "You didn't really have a choice," he answered.

Clare stood before the floor-length mirror and turned this way and that. Her dress shimmered in the subdued light and her hair was expertly coiffed by a hairdresser brought to the villa from Milan.

"Clare?"

"Come in, Papa," she answered.

Agosto opened the door and stood looking at her admiringly. She reminded him of Cecilia the night they had attended the President's reception in Brazil. But Clare was even more lovely than her mother, and clearly she was more at ease.

"You look stunning."

She smiled radiantly. "Thank you, Papa. Should we go downstairs now?"

Agosto shook his head. "Not just yet. I'm told that the queen mother should arrive first and be seated. Then we'll be presented to her. Formality and all that."

"Formality is hard to get used to."

"Should you marry Emiliano Sforza, you'll have to get used to it, Clare."

"I'll manage. Papa, Emiliano loves me, I love him. He respects me . . . he understands . . ."

Agosto was about to reply, but the butler tapped lightly on the door. "We have to go," he said instead of what was on his mind.

Emiliano stood at the bottom of the stairs, but he didn't smile when he saw Clare, he simply took her arm and led her aside into a tiny alcove.

"People are staring at me," Clare observed in a distressed tone. She could hear muffled whispers, and she sensed eyes on her even though she was still preoccupied with her thoughts about her father.

"I should think so," Emiliano confirmed.

"Are you angry, Emiliano? What is it?"

"It's your dress, Clare. Why in the name of heaven are you wearing that color?"

"I like this color," she said defensively. "I really don't understand—Constanza kept objecting too."

Emiliano's expression softened. "But she didn't tell you why she objected?"

Clare shook her head.

"*Dio,*" he muttered. "This isn't your fault."

"What's not my fault?"

"Green is the color of the House of Savoy. The queen mother is wearing green, her royal color, and no other woman wears it."

Clare frowned. "I should change my dress."

"No, you should not. Everyone has seen you now. You'll come along and make the best of it."

Clare took a deep breath. Constanza had done this on purpose, and Emiliano knew it, she thought. Clare pressed her lips together defiantly. I'll show her, and Papa too, she thought.

"When you're presented to the queen mother, you must curtsy and extend your hand to her. Don't speak until she does. And you must always address her as 'your Royal Highness.' "

Clare nodded and allowed Emiliano to lead her away. The queen mother, Margherite, sat at a small table on her dais.

"Your Royal Highness, may I present my house guest from New York, Miss Clare Marina Tonelli."

Clare curtsied and extended her hand. The queen mother shook it lightly and Clare straightened up.

"What a lovely dress," Margherite said, eyeing her.

"I wore it in honor of the House of Savoy," Clare said as clearly as she could. "I hope I haven't offended your majesty."

Margherite laughed. "Offended? Not at all, my dear. It's a pleasure to see the royal color worn by so beautiful a young woman from abroad."

Behind her Clare could feel the disapproving eyes turn away and she could all but hear Emiliano sigh with relief. But she knew long before she saw her face that Constanza wasn't pleased.

On a signal from Emiliano the orchestra played "The Hymn of Mameli," the Italian anthem, and the guests, all of whom had previously paid their respects to the queen mother, stood and now faced her. At the end of the anthem the men bowed and the women curtsied.

"Will you sit with me, my dear," the queen mother requested.

"Thank you, your Royal Highness."

"And you too, Emiliano, and Mr. Tonelli as well. I'm an old lady, and it's an old lady's privilege to be surrounded by handsome men. Will Benito Mussolini be here?"

"I'm afraid not, your Royal Highness."

"Oh, how very disappointing. Have you met Benito Mussolini, Mr. Tonelli?"

"I haven't yet had the pleasure," Agosto replied.

"He's very impressive. He's all that stands between Italy and the Bolshevik hordes."

After a few moments Emiliano stood up. "If I could be excused for just a moment, your Royal Highness."

She smiled and waved him away. Emiliano headed directly for Constanza, who was chatting with the French ambassador. He joined them and after a decent moment introduced the ambassador to someone else and led Constanza away.

"Why did you let her wear that dress?" he demanded angrily as soon as they were out of earshot of the other guests.

Constanza's face was stony. "I objected, I told her to wear another color. She's a stubborn girl. I told you, Emiliano, you can't change a peasant."

"But she outwitted you, Constanza. And you didn't tell her why she couldn't wear green, and now, dear sister, you are furious because Clare was quick enough to cover the gaffe." He shook his finger at her. "Don't ever do anything like that again, Constanza. Ever!"

Constanza didn't answer her brother. But he could see that although she was angry, she was also shaken.

Across the room, Clare searched for Emiliano with her eyes. She finally saw him and his sister talking. She smiled to herself.

"Your commitment to Italy's future is greatly appreciated," the queen mother was praising Agosto.

"It's a good investment," Agosto said honestly.

"We are such a poor country," the queen mother lamented. "Not like the United States. I was there once, you know."

"I didn't know that, your Royal Highness."

"Yes, it was in 1893. We went to Chicago for the Exposition honoring Columbus. My goodness, the Queen of Spain was a terrible bore. I had to point out to your President—Mr. Cleveland, was it?—that while Spain may have paid for Columbus' exploratory voyage, it was Italy that was his inspiration!"

Agosto smiled; he wasn't sure if he should laugh or not. He finally decided not, because she looked altogether too serious.

Emiliano returned. "May I steal Miss Tonelli for a dance?" he asked, bowing again to the queen mother, who nodded her approval.

"I'm truly sorry about the dress," Clare said when they were dancing. "And I had an argument with my father, too."

Emiliano smiled. "You handled the dress affair well, my dear. Not another word about it. But tell me, why did you have an argument with your father?"

"He's stubborn," Clare answered. "He's so opposed to women in banking."

Emiliano nodded knowingly. "You need someone who understands you, Clare Marina." His arms encircled her protectively and he waltzed her around the floor again and again. "I suppose you want to dance with others," he said after a time.

Clare looked up at him dreamily. "No," she replied.

"Come, Clare Marina," Emiliano said, leading her into a secluded part of the garden.

She looked up into his handsome face and felt the pressure of his hand on the small of her back.

"I want to marry you, Clare."

"Oh, Emil, I expected this, but I'm unprepared for the reality of it."

He leaned over her, and moving his hands across her back, kissed her passionately. She could feel his strong muscular body pressed to her, and a chill ran through her as she returned his kiss with equal desire.

"I feel the fire within you, my Clare."

"I love you, Emil."

He kissed her ear, moved his hands over her hips, and pressed her so close she could hardly breathe. His touch was sensuous, and one of his hands brushed her breast ever so lightly. The sensation excited her.

"I dream of you, I see visions of your alabaster flesh, of your firm breasts. I yearn to feel you, Clare Marina, to awaken you, to make love to you for endless hours."

Clare felt warm all over. His tone, his seductive language, his confession of desire enraptured her, and momentarily she forgot her father.

"Will you marry me, Clare?"

"Yes," Clare murmured. "Yes, Emil, I'll marry you."

"I want it to be soon . . . September. Clare, I can't wait."

Clare leaned against him and murmured her agreement. Emiliano loved her—he would give her the opportunity to prove herself.

Monday, September 3, 1923

BROOKLYN

Cecilia put down the letter from Agosto and wiped the tears from her face. The two letters—Agosto's and Clare's—sat on the coffee table, and Fabiana, who had read them too, looked at Cecilia with concern.

"She'll have a wonderful life, Cecilia, she'll be a countess. Cecilia, you'll have grandchildren."

Cecilia looked up. Fabiana always tried to look on the bright side of everything. "They'll live in Italy—they might as well be on the moon. Oh, I so wanted Agosto to relent, I wanted her to go into banking with her father, because since she was a little girl she always said that was what she wanted."

"But now she's met a handsome man and changed her mind, Cecilia."

"He's so much older . . . Oh, Fabiana, it doesn't seem right, it's too soon, too sudden."

"You could write to Agosto. You could insist she come home."

Cecilia shook her head. "No, Fabiana. This isn't what I wanted for my Clare, but I can tell from her letters that it's what she wants. I wanted her to have what we didn't have. I wanted her to break the pattern, to have different kinds of opportunities. I really wanted that. Perhaps I even wanted it selfishly for myself. But, Fabiana, I can't live Clare's life for her, and I can't live mine through her."

Fabiana sat next to Cecilia and put her arm around her. "Cecilia, think of what you've given Clare. You bought her books and you read to her, you saw to it that she traveled, you made Agosto see that it was important for Clare to have an education. Clare is a fine, intelligent young woman, Cecilia, and she's that way because of you. But perhaps you did want too much for her."

Cecilia nodded. "Too much. . . . You're right. I wanted everything for her. I wanted her to have her career, to eventually find a man who would accept that, to have fine children."

Fabiana smiled. "Cecilia, Clare's life isn't over, it's only beginning. Don't be unhappy. Wait, give Clare a chance."

LAKE COMO

A soft breeze blew off the lake, rustling the leaves on the olive trees and sending a shiver of movement through the flowerbeds. Clare and Emiliano sat on an iron bench looking out on the placid waters as the sun sank behind the majestic peaks of the Alps.

"The end of summer," Emiliano said, putting his arm around her. "Constanza's doing well. She's already mailed the invitations." He laughed under his breath. "The news of our coming marriage is all over the society pages."

"Papa's arranged for my family to sail on the fifteenth. They'll be here in plenty of time. I'll be glad to see my mother," Clare admitted.

"Did I tell you we're going to Spain on our honeymoon? First to the coast, then to Madrid, and then on to a ranch near Aranjuez—it's a beautiful place, Clare, it was once the royal summer residence."

"It sounds very romantic." She leaned against him.

"You have something on your mind, I can tell."

"Emil, I always wanted to go into banking, you know that."

"I know and I understand. Now, mind you, I want children."

"I want children too, but I couldn't stand being just a wife. I've been investing since I was a child, and I've done very well."

"I didn't know you had money of your own."

Clare laughed. "Oh, it's a secret, though it's in my father's bank. It's not much by his standards, or by yours. But it's money I made myself."

"I'll have to watch you—you'll be running Sforza Industries."

"Would you let me be involved?"

He hugged her. "I intend to make you happy, Clare Marina." It was a good evasive answer, he decided as he kissed her, running his hands over her long neck, down her back, and then touching her breast lightly. "I've bought you a gown, a Turkish gown to wear on our wedding night. Layers and layers of veils, my darling, so I can remove them slowly, one by one, till you are naked and begging to make love." He felt her shiver in his arms and he caressed her ears, breathing into one gently while he toyed with the other.

"Oh, Emil . . ."

Her cheeks were warm, and again he let his hand run across the curvature of her high, firm breast. He could feel her growing excitement. "You tempt me," he whispered. Then, knowing that she was aroused, he withdrew and kissed her cheek. "We must wait," he told her. "But you're always on my mind, Clare. I never think of another woman—for me there *are* no other women."

"I wish you didn't have to go away."

"My little trip to Rome? I'll be back in Milan in three days. And on the twenty-fifth we'll be married."

"I do love you," Clare murmured.

CANNES

Sarah Ainsley Stearns sat in the garden of her summer villa. Coffee, croissants, and marmalade had been placed in front of her, together with the morning papers. Cannes, she reflected, was not nearly as interesting now that Creighton had arrived for a brief two weeks. His presence cast a pall over her social life, not to mention the social life of Jenny, their daughter.

"Good morning," Creighton said from the doorway of their bedroom, which faced the garden. He walked toward her, tying his robe together. "You're up early."

Sarah nodded at him and opened the paper, turning immediately to the society section. "Good heavens!" She set the paper down dramatically.

"A new scandal to whet your appetite?" Creighton said sarcastically.

Sarah glared at him. "Clare Marina Tonelli is marrying Count Emiliano Sforza. Their pictures are right here, big as life!"

Creighton sniffed. "And? What's so interesting about two dagos getting married?"

"You're a fool!" Sarah stormed. "She'll be a countess! Their marriage means the amalgamation of two fortunes!"

"You're turning green around the gills, my dear."

Sarah's face was hard. "It's you who should be turning green. You and your little schemes, Creighton. You make me sick. Well, you succeeded in making Agosto use more of his own money to fund the dam project, but you know as well as I do that he's already made it all back! The next time you want to break him, maybe you should *join* him! With you around, he couldn't possibly succeed," she said meanly.

"I don't like him. I don't like his kind, but you, my dear, are the one who wants to break him."

Sarah stared at her husband. "No," she said suddenly. "I think our purpose might be better served by joining him. Clare Marina's not the only one who can make a good marriage."

"What are you talking about?"

"I'm talking about having it all, Creighton." With that, Sarah put down her coffee cup with some force and stood up, smoothing out her silk dressing gown. "We shall go to the wedding," she announced imperiously. "Creighton, sometimes patience pays."

Wednesday, September 5, 1923

R O M E

Emiliano ran his hand across Louisa's hip, down her long white thigh, and then back across her stomach. She moaned slightly, and he studied her facial expression. Her eyes were closed, her lips open. She was tense, like a cat before springing. He always aroused her slowly, because he derived a good deal of delight from watching her wait for her pleasure. She was a welcome break from his meetings in Rome, and while he waited for his marriage to take place, she was an outlet for his sexual desires.

For a time, he'd considered keeping Louisa after his marriage, but now he reconsidered. The possibility of scandal was too great, and he believed he could be faithful to Clare for a few years in any case. So, he decided, this would be his last visit with Louisa, and he planned to tell her he was to be married. Fortunately, he thought, she didn't read the papers. He watched her face, her intensity. In a way, he felt almost benevolent. The pain his announcement would cause her, in a perverse way, would give her pleasure, since she derived pleasure from suffering and attempted to convert her emotions onto canvas.

But it was only kind to make love to her one more time. He moved slowly, teasing her till she writhed beneath him, whispering, "Now . . . oh, please, now." Then he took her, and he took her as roughly as he ever had taken anyone, so roughly that hot tears streamed down her cheeks even as she shook convulsively beneath him.

He waited a moment, and looking at her steadily, told her, "I won't be coming here anymore."

Her huge watery brown eyes grew larger and she sat up suddenly. "What do you mean?" Her little-girl voice trembled.

"I'm getting married."

"Emiliano, I thought we . . . I thought you . . . Married to whom?" Her words poured out of her mouth in a long anguished cry.

"To a very beautiful young woman, a lovely virginal twenty-year-old, a woman from a very influential American family, Clare Marina Tonelli."

Louisa's lovely mouth opened. "I thought you'd marry me," she sobbed.

He looked at her harshly. "There are women men sleep with and women men marry. You are a woman to sleep with."

She visibly shuddered, then in an instant seemed to recover. "I am not who you think I am," she said, wiping her cheek. "I am not as powerless and as stupid as you think!"

He frowned. She was acting out of character. "No matter," he commented with a wave of his hand. "I won't be seeing you anymore."

"My real last name is Lyons," Louisa said, staring at him.

"I know that, I met your brother."

"*The* Louisa Lyons. My brother owns Lyons Oil of California; my father was Charles Lyons of Detroit."

Emiliano stared at her, and his throat felt more than a little dry. It was a common name; he hadn't made the connection.

"I'll go to your Clare Marina and I'll tell her about you. I'll tell her that while you've courted her, you've been with me! I'll tell her what sort of man you are, Emiliano. I doubt she knows what she is getting into!"

It was with supreme effort that Emiliano kept from striking her. And it was with equal effort that he kept from revealing his own fears. She'd never acted like this before. She was always subservient and totally lacked self-esteem. He couldn't comprehend what she was saying, but Lyons Oil did exist and her threat seemed suddenly quite real, more so since the marriage announcement was front-page society news.

"Do as you wish," he said, standing up. "It doesn't matter, I won't be back." He took small comfort in the fact that Louisa didn't know where to look for Clare—she could easily go to the newspaper, the *Herald Tribune*. Gossip traveled quickly.

He glanced at his watch as he hurriedly dressed. It was only four P.M. His mind strayed to Amerigo Dumini. The *ceka* had been disbanded for a few months; then it was reformed and installed in new offices next to the Parliament, largely so that its members could inhibit the opposition party. Yes, Emiliano thought, with a little luck he would find Amerigo Dumini this afternoon, and Amerigo could guarantee Louisa's silence.

Saturday, September 22, 1923

MILAN

Cecilia, Anthony, Tina, Fabiana, and Maria arrived in Milan on September 22 for the wedding, which was to be held on the twenty-fifth.

"I thought someone would be here to meet us," Anthony complained.

"This is Italy, the traffic is terrible! No one is ever on time," Cecilia said, looking around anxiously.

Twenty-two-year-old Tina stood flanked by Maria and Fabiana, who warded off would-be lotharios attracted by Tina's buxom figure.

"Cecilia!" Agosto pushed through the crowd, followed by Clare Marina and Emiliano. They all embraced, and Emiliano kissed each of the women's hands and shook Anthony's.

"Clare talks of you endlessly," Emiliano said. "How is school?"

"Fine, but I hate New Jersey. Too far from Ebbets Field."

Emiliano smiled. Clearly he had never heard of Ebbets Field.

"Clare!" Cecilia hugged her daughter and wished they were alone.

"We'll talk at home, Mama." Cecilia smiled and turned her eyes to Count Sforza. She wasn't altogether pleased with what she saw. Well-mannered, suave, good-looking, cultured . . . but there was something, something she could not put into words.

Clare and Cecilia stole away to Clare's bedroom upstairs, a large airy room decorated in subdued blues and greens.

Cecilia hugged Clare and kissed her. "I've missed you so," she wept. "We should have had this wedding in New York!"

"I've missed you too, Mama."

"This is so sudden . . . oh, Clare, it's so sudden."

Clare smiled and led her mother to the giant four-poster bed.

"Sit down and talk to me, Mama." She patted the side of the bed.

Cecilia sat down, and taking Clare's hand in hers, squeezed it. "I can't believe you're getting married. Clare, are you certain this is what you want?"

Clare nodded. "Yes, Mama, I'm sure."

"I always thought you wanted more. I thought you wanted to go into banking. Whenever your father mentioned marriage, you laughed."

"Mama, Emiliano respects my mind. He's not as stubborn as Papa about women staying home and having babies. Emiliano promised we'd find a way . . . suggested I may be able to work with him. I know I can convince him. Sforza Industries is huge. Mama, I'm not giving up my dreams. I'll make Emiliano happy and he'll make me happy. He's a wonderful man, and he's had a lonely, unhappy life."

Cecilia blinked back tears and hugged and held Clare in her arms. "All my life, Clare, I've been shy and afraid. Your Papa's a wonderful man too. He always took me places and bought me beautiful clothes and jewels, but he never talked business with me, and he's always working. My mama worked with my papa, and your grandmother Gina worked with Domenico—they shared everything." She shook her head. "Don't misunderstand, Clare. I love your papa more than anything in the world except you and Anthony. But so often I've felt left out, and I always felt stupid and out of place with your papa's friends. I don't want you to be that way, Clare. Be different, Clare Marina. Don't be like me. You dare to be different, do you understand?"

Clare kissed her mother tenderly. "I understand, Mama."

Tuesday, September 25, 1923

MILAN

Emiliano adjusted his bright red sash, then smiled at his image in the mirror.

"Peasants," Constanza complained, looking at her brother. "And what do you think of that person Maria, your dear Agosto's sister? She looks like a fishmonger's daughter!"

"She *is* a fishmonger's daughter," he said dryly, then added, "Well, almost."

"I realize that by tradition the bride's family pays for the wedding, and I realize they did hire Signor Puzio to organize everything for them, and of course I did recommend him, but, Emiliano, that woman alone will make us the laughingstock of the Italian aristocracy!''

"Good Lord, Constanza, people in this country have more important things to occupy their minds.''

"She's dreadful! She's impossible! She had the audacity to tell me what to do! She actually argued with me over the food to be served at the reception. In two days she's managed to drive Signor Puzio mad. He's beside himself. She keeps insisting on this vile pasta, this . . . this southern Italian garbage that is fit only for pigs—and southern Italians, of course.''

"Your ability to adjust amazes me,'' he replied. "You know, Clare has spoken often of her Aunt Maria, the family piranha. I tend to think you have met your match, my dear.''

"My match! My match! She is a simple-minded idiot! A selfish, stupid woman, and I shouldn't even be obligated to be in the same room with her!''

"But you are. Constanza, go do what you must and don't bother me. I don't ask you to do these things, I simply tell you to do them. Endure, Constanza. They'll be gone soon and you'll forget this entire experience. Take my word for it, my dear, your world is changing, and like the dinosaur I know you to be, you will either learn to adapt or you will die.''

Constanza glared at him. He was incredibly selfish.

"So Agosto's peasant sister causes a mild twitter. It's not as serious as the scandal that would develop if the wedding were canceled.''

"You have doubts!''

"Not at all. I've never spent a second reconsidering. I think this is a perfect match, no matter what you think. If you were a man, you'd understand! Unfortunately you are a woman. But I think you've learned your place, so please, Constanza, let's have no more complaints.''

"You'll be sorry,'' she mumbled. "And Clare Marina will be sorry too. She's not as compliant as you think, Emiliano. She's not like I am!''

Count Emiliano Sforza, dressed in black tails, his bright red sash across his chest, emerged from the vestry and stood next to young Anthony Tonelli.

The organ of Milan's Duomo boomed out the traditional wedding march as a procession of young girls sprinkled flowers in the path of the bride. Clare Marina wore a full-length white silk wedding dress trimmed in handmade laces that had over a hundred tiny pearls sewn into them. Agosto Tonelli walked proudly with his daughter on his arm.

Behind them walked Clare's cousin Tina dressed in pale blue, followed by Fabiana in gold, Maria in a russet gown, and Constanza Sforza in green.

The pews in the cathedral were nearly full and the guests included Italy's most important political, industrial, and military elite, including young General Balbo, who was easily the most important man in Italy after Benito Mussolini. All of Agosto Tonelli's European associates came, as did Sarah Ainsley Stearns, who was vacationing on the Riviera with Creighton, her daughter Jennifer, and her son Barton.

Clare, whose face was covered with a white net veil, shivered when she saw the large number of guests. She felt her father squeeze her arm to give her support and comfort. There had been two wedding rehearsals on Friday, but Clare found the reality terrifying. She felt as if she were onstage and the whole world was watching her every step.

It was an endless walk down the long red-carpeted center aisle and up the steps to the foot of the altar. It was to be a solemn high wedding Mass sung by Cardinal Tanuto himself, and, as Clare well knew, a solemn high wedding Mass took well over an hour even when the bride and groom were the only recipients of the Blessed Sacrament.

At last Clare reached Emiliano, and together they knelt at the altar as the cardinal began to sing the Mass in his fine deep baritone voice.

"*Asperges me, Domine, hyssop, et mundabor: lavabis me, et super nivem dealbabor!*" he sang out the first *Asperges*.

Clare's father's words came back to her: "It's not everyone who has the opportunity to marry in the world's largest church. This wedding will be truly blessed because a cardinal is performing the Mass."

Clare looked about. The Duomo was magnificent. So intricate was its exterior that it looked like fine lace. Yet the inside had an austere quality.

Next the prayers were said, and then Cardinal Tanuto went to the foot of the altar and sang. "*In nomine Patris, et Filii, et Spiritus Sancti, Amen.*"

This began the ordinary of the Mass, and as the cardinal chanted out, "I will go to the altar of God," the choir sang back, "To God who giveth joy to my youth." And so went the psalm, first the cardinal singing, then the answers from the choir. This was followed by the general confession and the absolution, then the *Kyrie eleison*, the *Gloria in excelsis* and the *Agnus Dei*.

Clare knelt next to Emiliano, her eyes fastened on the high altar, where the sun streaming through the slit windows cast an eerie light.

The cardinal stood before them and they recited their vows on their knees before the altar. Then together they received the Blessed Sacrament. When they finished Communion, the cardinal in the magnificent white-and-gold robes of the season returned to the altar to finish the Mass. That done, he returned to them, and blessed them. *"In nomine Patris, et Filii, et Spiritus Sancti, Amen.*

The music burst forth once again, and Emiliano lifted Clare's veil and bent to kiss her softly on the lips. Then, taking her arm, he hurried her down the aisle as the guests tossed flowers at them.

They went directly to the reception in the grand ballroom of the Milan Palace Hotel. There, as tradition demanded, they stood in the center of a long reception line that consisted of Cecilia, Agosto, Maria, Fabiana, Tina, Anthony, Constanza, and a host of Sforza relatives. Not till each of the two hundred guests had shaken the groom's hand and kissed Clare were they allowed to mingle with the guests.

"You *would* marry a count," Tina pouted when she finally succeeded in cornering her cousin in the private powder room, which was also to be used when Clare changed from her wedding dress into the dress she'd wear on her honeymoon. "How does it feel, Clare? How does it feel to be married?"

Clare slumped onto the velvet stool in front of the gilt mirror that covered the wall. "I don't know," she confessed, feeling almost on the verge of tears. "I'm exhausted and I was in a trance during the whole ceremony. It's as if it happened to someone else. And I was so nervous! All those eyes . . ." She covered her eyes with her hands and fought to hold back her tears.

"You're not going to cry! Don't *you* cry. I've been drying your mama's tears for hours!"

"Just nerves," Clare confessed. "I'm happy, really happy."

Tina shrugged. "You don't have to convince me. You've captured a count!"

Clare studied her older cousin. She was small, only a little over five feet, and heavy-busted, though her waist was small and her hips were rounded without being fat. She had exceptionally dark hair and pretty brown eyes. She worked at the original

Tonelli bank on Ocean Avenue, and Clare knew she led a reasonably sheltered life. "Why haven't you married, Tina? I always thought you'd marry before me."

Tina shrugged and shook her brown curls. "I just haven't found the right man yet."

"You will," Clare promised her. She turned and looked in the mirror, wiping her eyes. Then she dabbed powder on her face. "This day will never end, never, never, never!"

"I shouldn't think you'd want it to. I think it's grand! Clare, I've never seen such a house as Emiliano's. I've never seen such wealth! I want to marry a rich famous man too!" Tina began dancing about. "I'm going to ask the orchestra to play some decent music! I want them to play 'I'm Just Wild About Harry.' I want to kick up my heels!"

Clare frowned at Tina. "Not here," she cautioned. "You don't know Constanza, and you don't understand the Italian nobility. I think you'll have to suffer through waltzing."

"You're becoming stuffy," Tina returned. "You and Anthony! Is being a countess going to change you, Clare?"

"There's a time and place for everything."

"Don't you and Emiliano dance to popular tunes?"

"Of course we do, but not when he's around his relatives." It was a lie, in fact, she and Emiliano had never danced to anything popular save the tango in New York. But she supposed they would, and she supposed that Emiliano was quite capable of kicking up his heels too.

Clare stood up. "Back to the fray," she said bravely.

Tina smiled. "I saw a handsome general. I think I'll go and flirt with him."

Clare laughed. "Really!" she said. "Well, don't let your mother see you."

"Please accept my warmest wish for happiness." A bearded man in a white uniform took Clare's hand and kissed it.

Clare smiled. She didn't remember seeing him come through the reception line, but perhaps he had arrived late. "Thank you," she murmured.

He clicked his heels. "General Italo Balbo, at your service."

Clare started to say: I've read so much about you. But she didn't. He seemed shorter in person than in the press photos, and young for a general, hardly thirty. "I've heard my husband speak of you," she said politely.

"I should congratulate him," General Balbo replied; then, winking at her: "I'll never find a wife if old codgers like

Emiliano keep marrying all the eligible young women. I really don't know if I want to congratulate him.''

Clare blushed deeply. It seemed like a very rude comment and she felt flustered by it. But it was Constanza who came to her rescue, floating up to them and smiling radiantly at the general.

"Madam," he said taking her hand and kissing it. "It's been too long, far too long." Constanza smiled a courtly, restrained smile.

Anthony came up behind Clare and squeezed her around the waist. "Congratulations!" he said brightly. "My own sister, a countess!"

Clare started to introduce him to the general, but her father beckoned her from across the room and she quickly excused herself and went with Anthony.

"Congratulations indeed!" Constanza hissed to General Balbo. "No one, but no one with even a modicum of breeding and manners would dare congratulate a bride! It's so boorish. Doesn't that young man know that only the groom is given congratulations!"

Balbo grinned. "Come, my dear Constanza, come and dance with me. I'll try to explain to you how the world is changing. I know it won't comfort you, but perhaps my arms around you will."

"You're really terribly conceited."

He gave her his most devastating smile. "Not without good cause, my dear lady."

Sarah Ainsley Stearns stood near the silver punch bowl, dressed elegantly in a long blue silk gown. Her eyes followed Clare and Emiliano Sforza as they danced together and her lips pressed tight. Creighton was off talking business. He was always working, and unless she nagged him, he wouldn't even have joined her for a few weeks. He hadn't taken her to South America as Agosto had taken Cecilia. In fact, although he allowed her to travel wherever she wished, he never came with her. Sarah smiled and allowed the gentleman on her left to refill her cup. She sipped it, and gave way to feelings of jealousy and ill-ease. This could all have been mine, she thought. It wasn't humiliating enough that Agosto had rejected her and married Cecilia. Now Clare, a mere twenty-year-old, had married Emiliano Sforza.

"Whatever is the matter, Mother?"

Sarah turned and looked into the eyes of her daughter Jennifer. They were beautiful eyes, and Jennifer was a most attractive young woman. "Nothing, really," Sarah answered. She reached out and touched her daughter's hair. "I was just thinking."

"You look dismal."

"Not at all! My, this really is the season's best wedding, isn't it?"

Jennifer nodded.

"There, there, darling. When the time comes, yours will be just as nice."

Jennifer looked at her mother, a puzzled expression on her face. "Are you sure you're all right?"

"Of course, darling. Say, I have an idea. Why don't you go and dance with Anthony? He looks so lonesome."

Jennifer smiled. "You don't mind?"

"Of course not. In fact, I rather think I'd enjoy watching."

At four o'clock Clare made her way to the dressing room and with Tina's help changed into a lovely yellow linen traveling suit.

"Are you excited?" Tina asked. "I think it's terribly exciting to spend three weeks in Spain and then go to a castle!"

"I think it's more of a ranch—it was a castle in the 1700's—and yes, I'm excited."

"You're so lucky! I wish I were you, Clare. Oh, I wish I were you."

Clare kissed Tina on the cheek. "Be yourself and be happy to be yourself," she told her.

"Cecilia's going to miss you," Tina said.

"I hope Emiliano will take me home for Christmas," Clare answered.

Tina smiled. "Cecilia would like that."

Clare hugged her cousin again. "You be a daughter to her, Tina. Take care of Mama for me."

20

September 25, 1923

MILAN

The train left at six P.M. and Clare's last image as it pulled out of the station was her mother waving to her from the platform.

"I really think a private railway carriage is a bit extravagant," Clare chided as she gazed dreamily at the lavish decor. The carriage was paneled dark wood, had gas lights, and the furniture was plush velvet. It was like a cabin on a ship, but longer and narrower. A dining table was set up at one end of the car, and in the corner there was a bed. Each and every one of the small tables was covered with baskets of flowers.

"Some champagne?" Emil asked as he dipped into the silver ice bucket on the table. "I hardly got one sip at the reception. Every time I tried to have a drink, I had to stop and talk to someone."

"I'd love some," Clare answered, hoping that the champagne would help her feel less tense.

Emil forced up the cork and it went flying across the car. Then he poured two glasses and handed Clare one. "To a long and happy marriage," he said, raising his glass and studying her.

"To a long loving marriage," Clare replied.

Emil sipped his wine. She was truly lovely, young and innocent. Her skin had a soft ivory hue, her hair was dark and luxuriant, and her face had a sculptured elegance that sang the praises of the Arab bands who had once swept across southern Italy, depositing their mideastern genes to mingle with genes of conquerors past.

"I want children badly," he said, looking into her dark eyes. "I want an heir."

Clare smiled. "I know." She curled on the red plush sofa like a child and closed her eyes. "I want them too, but you know I don't want to lead an aimless life either. I love the parties, Emil,

I love to travel, I think I even love the power that money brings . . . but luxury, manners, form, and endless rounds of drinks and idle conversation—I couldn't lead a life with such emptiness, Emil. We'll have lots of children, but I don't think they'll fulfill my own aspirations.''

He leaned down and kissed her forehead. This was no time to tell her how foolish her aspirations were, no time to tell her he had no intention of letting her be involved with his business. That would come later—after their honeymoon. He stepped quickly to her, and taking her hands, pulled her up and kissed her hard on the mouth. "You think too much, Clare. This is not a night for thinking. Go put on your Turkish nightdress, then come back and sip champagne in bed with me."

Clare went to the tiny dressing room in the rear of their private carriage. She slipped into the nightdress, a many-layered gown of veils, each layer more transparent than its overlay. She brushed out her hair and studied herself in the mirror. Emil did love her, and he'd let her become involved in some aspect of his business. She'd convince him that a woman could be accepted.

She returned and stood by the side of the bed. Emil had turned the gas lights down low, and he lay beneath the snow-white sheet, leaving his bare chest exposed.

He patted the bed and Clare sat down. He proffered a second glass of champagne. "I'll soon kiss your breasts," he said, gazing at her. "I'll awaken you, my little Clare, I'll teach you the meaning of pleasure."

Clare felt her hand shaking as she sipped her champagne. His words, his tone, his lingering looks, aroused her.

He sat up and the sheet fell away as he moved to the bottom of the bed, where he took one of her feet in his hand. He kissed it, spreading her toes one by one. "I'll buy you a fine pair of sandals in Spain," he told her. "You have lovely, perfect feet, magnificent feet." His lips caressed her legs; then he removed the first layer of her gown. His hands stroked every part of her body through the sheer layers of material, but he returned again and again to her breasts, watching as her nipples hardened beneath the flimsy gauze. She moaned in his arms, yielding to her sensations.

"Young men have so little patience," he breathed in her ear. "I have infinite patience. . . ." His hands seemed everywhere, sometimes soft, barely skimming over her, other times grasping her firmly. Before she opened her eyes, the second and third layers of her gown were removed, leaving only the last, a totally transparent covering.

"Lovely," he whispered as he put his hand over her mound

momentarily. She expelled her breath. "Oh, Emil . . ." He massaged her gently, watching as she moved her lovely hips. Then he returned to her legs, which he kissed until again he reached her feet, once more kissing her toes. He kissed and caressed her body through the netting, then parted it and kissed her breasts while he fondled her intimately with his hand.

"Now," she breathed. "Oh, Emil . . . please. . . ."

"A little longer . . ." His hand slipped between her legs and opened them as she moaned softly. He returned to her breasts, kissed her stomach, moved against her till she was sighing and clinging to him like a child.

He hovered over her writhing body for an instant, then entered her slowly.

She let out a little gasp of pain, but he ignored her. She was moist and filled with fire, her arms encircled him, and he moved slowly until he felt her reach full satisfaction, then allowed himself the same pleasure.

Wednesday, September 26, 1923

Clare Marina watched out the window as their carriage sat on the siding near the border between Spain and France. They had just transferred into another private car attached to a Spanish train because, as Emil explained, the Spanish and French had a different gauge of railway track.

"I expect we'll be here for a while," he told her.

"They're inefficient. I've been here before, in 1915 with my father. It took them nearly two hours to check everyone's passport. But at least we can wait in our carriage." She smiled. It was nearly identical to the car they'd just left.

"I doubt we'll have that problem," Emil said with a laugh.

Clare smiled at him. She felt a strange mixture of emotions, a combination of exhilaration and weariness. They'd made love, talked, and made love again. She would have thought him insatiable, but in truth she herself was no less desirous. He could arouse her as easily with looks or words as with caresses.

There was a loud pounding on the door of their private car. "I suppose that's the border patrol," Clare said resolutely.

Emiliano opened the door.

"Emiliano! I had this train delayed just because I knew you

were on it!'' A blustering portly man in a general's uniform burst into the carriage. He turned to Clare and shouted, ''You're under arrest!''

She blinked up at him uncomprehendingly. ''What?''

He roared with laughter. ''I should like to arrest you! You are most arresting!'' He bowed and kissed her hand.

Emiliano hugged him. Then, turning to Clare: ''Clare, may I present General Miguel Primo de Rivera, Spain's new leader.''

''How do you do.'' Clare extended her hand and the general kissed it—though in fact she thought it more of a slurp. He was a bear of a man, and his demeanor reminded her of Mussolini.

''I came to personally greet you at the border!'' he roared.

''You're looking well,'' Emiliano observed.

''Part of rigorous army training!''

Emiliano ushered the general to a chair and poured brandy. ''How's the situation in Morocco?''

General de Rivera shook his head, a look of sadness flooding his face. ''Every day the sons of Spain die in the desert. But I intend to stop it. Spain must right itself. Forgive me, Emiliano, but I must say the Spanish aristocracy has been fiddling while Spain burns.''

Emiliano's facial expression didn't change. ''I know you'll make favorable changes, and I certainly hope you'll do more to encourage foreign investment than the former Parliament.''

''They didn't even make it easy for Spanish investment! Blunderheads!''

''You sound like Il Duce,'' Clare commented.

''An interesting man. But I've reservations about some of his followers. I've always believed the army to be the repository of a nation's strength and character. I fear that Il Duce will stumble because he's chosen to rebuild national character on the shoulders of rabble!''

Clare frowned. ''He has the true support of the Italian people.''

''Who are fickle. You sound like my lawyer son. He has a sublime faith in *intuicísimo*—the theory that people's intuition will show them what is right. People haven't the slightest idea what's good for them. Mussolini will realize that soon enough, and he'll remember I told him that!''

''I think his greatest fear is what you call the 'rabble' within his own movement. Knowing that, I must disagree with you,'' Emiliano countered. ''I believe the rabble has served a certain purpose, but now that power has been seized, Mussolini courts more moderate factions, both in the army and in Parliament.''

''You approved of the *squadristi*?'' Clare asked. She could scarcely believe her ears. To her knowledge, even Mussolini had condemned their violence.

Emiliano smiled at her patronizingly and turned to General de Rivera. "American women have the vote, and they're all obsessed with politics." His tone was apologetic, as if he were excusing her interest to the general.

Clare pressed her lips together, determined not to be ignored. "Emiliano, are you saying that the end justifies the means?"

Emiliano shrugged. "Sometimes," he allowed. Then, turning to General de Rivera: "More brandy?"

"Of course! Tell me, Emiliano, what's your itinerary in Spain?"

Emiliano filled the snifter. "The Costa Brava for a few days, Barcelona, Madrid, and then we'll go to Aranjuez—Juan de Carlo Herrera has extended an invitation to us to visit his ranch."

General Primo de Rivera roared. "And doubtless having missed Fiesta in Pamplona and the running of the bulls, you will play the matador at the ranch! Ah, my friend, I remember you at Pamplona two years ago!"

"It makes the blood run," Emiliano replied with a grin.

"You intend to bullfight?" Clare said in amazement.

Emiliano patted her on the knee. "Ah, yes, my dear. It's fine sport . . . man against beast, it tests the nerve."

"Magnificent!" General de Rivera bellowed. "If only I had time for such pleasures!"

"You have a country to run, my friend."

"And endless problems in Catalonia. Democracy! Rubbish! I've dismissed Parliament, as you know."

"I believe in democracy," Clare said firmly and with some irritation. "You're critical of Mussolini, but at least he is working with the Parliament and he hasn't suspended constitutional guarantees as you have."

"What is this, Emiliano, my friend? You've married a beautiful woman full of democratic idealism! But I forgive her because I can see that she's young and inexperienced. Women know nothing of the real world. 'Country . . . Religion . . . Monarchy' —that is my motto, the motto of a new Spain. The Spanish need their army—we know how to run the country. You will see, my dear, that democracy is a failing notion. It will one day fail even in America—probably sooner than expected, now that women can vote!" He laughed and slapped Emiliano on the back. "A stunning woman, Emiliano. I trust you will educate her to reality."

Emiliano laughed too. "She will see," he replied.

Clare felt her anger rising. They spoke of her as if she weren't there; they were treating her like a naive child. "I will never give up my belief in democracy," she said coolly. But neither the general nor Emiliano reacted.

"The train will be here for an hour, Emiliano. Come to my carriage so we can talk."

Emiliano turned to Clare. "I'll be back soon," he told her.

Clare opened her mouth to protest. Why was he treating her this way? He seemed totally different with General Primo de Rivera than he had been when they were alone. But perhaps there was some reason, she told herself. They were in Spain, the general had seized power in a *coup d'état,* there were soldiers everywhere . . . Perhaps Emiliano was only humoring the general. She forced herself to hold her temper and nodded her acquiescence. The general, she decided, was a moral vacuum.

Emiliano returned just as their car was attached to the train to begin its onward journey.

"I suppose you're angry with me?" he said, smiling and holding out his hands.

"You didn't pay any attention to me, you were patronizing." Clare looked at him evenly.

"Clare, come and kiss me. Try to understand that while I may feel one way about you, there are many men—certainly the majority of men in Europe—who resent a woman talking politics, more so if she's going to lecture them on democracy. General de Rivera's an important man. He won't change his views, and alienating him is, frankly, bad for business. It's important for me to appear to agree with him. He's going to be expansive, he's certainly going to want to build new roads, and frankly, I'm hoping that he'll come to Sforza Industries." He touched her cheeks with his hands. "Clare, General Primo de Rivera isn't a young man—he comes out of a Spanish military tradition, he's a member of the aristocracy, of the old guard."

Clare looked into Emiliano's eyes. "You were trying to humor him?"

"Of course, my pet." Emiliano kissed her forehead. He would have to teach her to keep her views to herself . . . and he would, but later. Nothing, he decided, should inhibit their loving relations at the moment.

Thursday, September 27, 1923

SAN MARINO, CALIFORNIA

Rome
September 18, 1923

My dear friend,

This is a difficult letter for me to write because it bears bad news and I have not the words in English to express myself so well in writing.

Those whom you left to watch your sister report to me that she has been killed. It happened on the night of September 7 when she was walking on the street and was run over by a car. Because she was living under an assumed name, she was not identified, and not knowing what to do, I acted through intermediaries to have her remains interred in a mausoleum here. You could of course come to Rome and arrange through your embassy to bring her ashes home. But since I had no way of knowing your wishes, I did what I thought best.

There are many things about your sister's death that are suspicious, but I cannot chance to put these things in writing. I hope you will come to Rome so we might speak. I also took the liberty of removing your sister's personal belongings from her rooms. There are many paintings she has made, and I am sure you will want these.

I wait to hear from you and I am most sorry to be the messenger who delivers such terrible news.

Yours,
G. Matteotti

Mark Lyons put down the letter and blinked back his tears. A sudden feeling of supreme loneliness filled him. His mother had died last month, and now Louisa, his only sibling, was also dead. He silently cursed himself for not forcing her to come home with him in June. "It's my fault," he muttered. And in his mind, he focused on one word in Matteotti's letter: "suspicious." He conjured up the image of Count Sforza. Had he had something to do with Louisa's death? He shook his head. There were too many unanswered questions, and clearly Matteotti, an opposition Socialist-party leader, was a man who had to take great caution. "I'll have to go back to Italy," he said aloud. Then, under his breath: "Damn!"

Saturday, October 6, 1923

ARANJUEZ, SPAIN

They spent three glorious sun-drenched days on the Costa Brava—"the wild coast"—near Blanes. It was appropriately named, Clare thought. The shore was rugged, and the great jagged rocks were arranged by nature in such a way that it looked like a giant's playground. But the rocks were deceiving, for they hid small sandy bays with gentle white-crested waves and turquoise water. On the shore, in and around the rocks, and farther away on cliffs, the wind sculptured misshapen trees, which Clare learned were cork trees. The Costa Brava was idyllic, the days long, the sunsets magnificent, and they were alone in the small inn where they stayed. Clare couldn't count the times they made love—more than once on the moonlit sandy beach, sheltered only by a huge gaunt rock . . . once at sunset while the waves washed over them . . . and always at night in the seclusion of their room.

After the Costa Brava, they went on to Barcelona for three days. Barcelona, Clare thought, was not idyllic. Emiliano attended countless business meetings, returning to her only late in the evening. And on two of the three nights they were there, they attended lavish parties. Lavish, boring parties where the men congregated to discuss business and the women were relegated to a reception room to discuss fashion. "Spanish custom," Emiliano explained offhandedly.

And Madrid was no better. There he left her to tour the city alone while he met with various leaders in the new government. And at night, there were still more parties and more formal receptions. Emiliano, Clare lamented, was like a different person when they were among others. He was all too willing to exclude her from the exciting aspects of his life. But he assured her things would change when they returned to Italy. "Be patient, my Clare Marina," he told her. "This is Spain, we must adhere to custom."

Clare gave in. It will be different when we're home, she told herself. And how could she complain when she longed for him so? He had only to touch her and she wanted to make love again. He had a thousand ways of seducing her, and he always succeeded in making her happy.

Clare felt relieved when they arrived at the *rancho* of Juan de Carlo Herrera. No more parties, no more receptions, no more business, she thought happily. It was a magnificent *rancho*. The house was in the Spanish design, twenty-two rooms of sprawling luxury built around an enclosed flower-filled patio. The pungent fragrance of oleander flooded their room at night and lingered till noon each day. In the main room, a huge stone fireplace provided heat and a warm friendly atmosphere for conversations with their host, the elderly former general who now bred prize bulls and grew strawberries, the latter being the specialty of the region.

Juan de Carlo sat in a great leather chair before the fireplace. He was a short, squat man with thin gray hair and watery blue eyes which spoke of his Castilian ancestry. The lines in his face were deep, and he seemed to sink into silent thought often.

Emiliano sat opposite him, Clare sat on the stone hearth, listening as the dry wood crackled in the flames. They had arrived two days ago, and both mornings they had ridden horseback. Her legs felt a bit stiff, but she loved riding. One could ride in New York, of course. But there you rode along narrow paths in the park and you were never far from the sound of traffic or the sight of buildings. Here you could ride into the sunrise and encounter nothing save the natural landscape.

"I am terribly sorry to tell you this, my friends, but tomorrow I must leave. Urgent business calls, or I wouldn't dream of deserting you." He laughed heartily. "Oh, Emiliano, don't hide your feelings! You two are newlyweds—I rather imagine you're delighted at the thought of being in this paradise alone!"

Clare blushed and Emiliano responded only with a smile.

"No need to worry! My servants will see to your every need. Stay as long as you wish. Regrettably, my trip will be a long one. The owner of a fine *rancho* in the Argentine wants to buy some of my bulls. And then too, I have never been to the pampas, so I'm looking forward to my adventure."

"It's an interesting country," Emiliano said. "But don't expect Spain! It's very different."

"So I've been told, so I've been told."

"But you do disappoint me. I had looked forward to being in the bull ring with you!"

Juan de Carlo laughed. "You don't need an old man like me!

José will see to your desires, but be careful, my friend. Juan de Carlo breeds the fiercest bulls in all Spain!''

"Emiliano . . . isn't it dangerous?"

"Dangerous! Of course it is! Why else would I want to do it? Ah, my Clare, to face the bull is exhilarating! It makes my blood run. And when I return to you, I'll make love to you as we have never made love before!''

Clare blushed deeply and avoided looking at Juan de Carlo, who roared out his approval.

"Machismo! There is nothing like facing the bull to make a man feel his virility, eh? A young wife is good, Emiliano. She makes you young. You face the bull, you win, and you return . . . certainly you will be in the mood to plant your seed!''

Clare stared into the fire. Machismo indeed. She felt a wave of deep resentment. Why was Emiliano always talking about her as if she weren't there? She frowned and thought she was glad Juan de Carlo was leaving. At least they would be alone as they had been on the Costa Brava.

Monday, October 8, 1923

Clare dressed in full tan culottes, a long-sleeved brown silk blouse, Spanish boots that came to her knees, and a wide-brimmed dark Spanish hat. She and Emiliano toured the pens where the bulls were kept with José, the overseer of Juan de Carlo's *rancho*.

"I want the most ferocious!" Emiliano said with determination.

José eyed him but said nothing. "They are all ill-tempered," he replied.

"Show me the best! I want to play the matador in style."

José pointed to a giant animal that pawed the earth and snorted in the corner of his pen. "That one señor, he is our El Diablo.''

"Emiliano, he looks dangerous."

"Clare Marina, danger is what I seek. In any case, I am only going into the ring with him for a short time . . . enough to taunt him and know the pleasure of eluding him." Emiliano turned to José. "Yes, El Diablo will do nicely. Tomorrow at dawn?"

José bowed from the waist. "At your pleasure, señor."

Emiliano took her arm and they strode back toward the house.

"I doubt it will be as exciting as Pamplona during Fiesta, but I shall enjoy it."

Clare sighed. "I'm not sure why you need to do it. It seems terribly dangerous to me."

He put his arm around her shoulders. "Men need danger. They can face it; they have to face it. Oh, my darling, how can I explain it to you? In the ring a man is alone with his adversary, he is alone with the beady-eyed beast, he must face life as well as death; it's delicious, it's a moment to savor."

Emiliano dropped his hand to the small of her back and she could feel the pressure in his hand. "Come, let us lie before the fire and make love . . . let me feel you beneath me. And tomorrow, tomorrow when I have faced the bull, I'll return to you. You'll see the difference. I'll be renewed."

They went into the house, where the evening fire was already laid. Emiliano locked the doors to ensure privacy, then slowly undressed her, laying her on the great fur rug before the hearth.

He taunted her with his caresses, and she grew weak with his intimate kisses. His skilled hands made her feel warm inside, his low, soft-spoken words inflamed her as he breathed in her ear, kissed her breasts, carried her into a world dominated by sensations. Clare clung to him, her misgivings swept aside by his powerful presence.

Tuesday, October 9, 1923

At five-thirty, just before sunrise, the maid knocked at the door and Clare stirred in Emiliano's arms.

He jostled her. "Clare! Wake up! It's time for me to go and face the bull."

Sleepily she stretched, watching as he bounded from the bed. He slipped into his shorts, and then, breathing deeply, exercised for a few moments, moving his body this way and that while inhaling deeply.

Clare pulled herself from the bed and yawned. She hurriedly dressed. By noon the temperature outside would be warm, but now, in the hour before dawn, she felt goose pimples on her flesh. She put on her undergarments, then her culottes, her blouse, and her boots. Over her blouse she wore a heavy shawl.

Emiliano dressed in black from head to toe.

"You look like a matador," Clare observed.

Emiliano laughed. "As a child, I dreamed of being one."

Clare looked at him seriously. "I do want you to be careful."

He laughed. "Come, come, it's not as if I'm not experienced."

Clare pressed her lips together. Emiliano was well-muscled, in good physical condition, he looked younger than he was, but the men who fought bulls publicly were all in their twenties and were agile and fast as well as graceful. "I worry about you," she confessed.

"Ah, you will love me more when you see me face the bull!" He kissed her and took her hand.

They left the house and walked across the field toward Juan de Carlo's own bull ring. In the eastern sky, stripes of gold light broke the darkness of the night sky, even though in the western sky stars were still visible, as was the waning moon. The shrill call of a lone bird greeted them.

How beautiful is the Jarama Valley, Clare thought. And how rich the soil. Beyond the bull ring, vast fields of strawberry plants spread for miles, and nearby were the acres of grazing land on which the ferocious bulls fattened themselves, turning their huge muscular bodies into powerful, dangerous objects of sport.

"It's the sheer excitement," Emiliano told her as they looked at El Diablo, the pride of Juan de Carlo's herd.

"*Buenos días,* Conde Sforza." José greeted them with a sweeping bow. "Condesa." He kissed Clare Marina's hand. "Condesa, if you will just sit here, you can see everything. I, señor, will go and prepare the bull. You enter the ring from there." He pointed off to the gate which gave access to the ring in which Juan de Carlo tested his bulls, preparing them for sale to great rings in Barcelona and Madrid.

Emiliano kissed her on the cheek, gave a jaunty wave of his hand, and was gone.

Clare decided not to sit. Rather, she stood against the rail and peered into the empty ring. Emiliano entered it and waved again to her. Clare waved back and tried to smile.

Then José swung open the great wooden doors of the paddock and the huge black bull came rushing out. It ran to the center of the ring, kicking up dust, then paused and pawed the ground, snorting and moving its head.

Emiliano moved cautiously away from the side of the ring; the bull stood stock-still, its ears twitching, its eyes following the lone figure in black. Emiliano swirled his red cape and the bull looked at it a long moment, then charged toward it.

Clare covered her mouth with her hand, her dark eyes wide,

and she shivered. But Emiliano sidestepped and the bull thundered on, halting with a loud snort at the far side of the ring.

"Toro! Toro!" Emiliano shouted. He moved across the ring toward the center and again held out the cape, this time stomping his foot and shouting.

"Oh, dear God, I wish he'd stop," Clare said under her breath. She could hear herself breathing, and she was afraid she would scream and startle the bull.

But this time the bull stood still, sizing up his adversary. His nose flicked as he strained to pick up the scent of the man who challenged him. He pawed the ground again, his strong muscles tensed, but still he didn't move.

"Toro!" Emiliano moved closer.

"Dear heaven," Clare murmured.

The bull still didn't move, even though Emiliano flicked his cape. Emiliano took another step forward. Clare felt she'd stopped breathing. It was as if time were standing still. Bull and man were stock-still; even the early-morning breeze had stopped blowing.

Then the bull charged, a wild snorting charge, his head down, his hooves beating across the dusty ring. Emiliano moved to sidestep, to finesse the bull once again. But the animal's huge head veered, as if he anticipated the move, as if he knew exactly where Emiliano planned to go. Clare let out a long shriek as Emiliano's body was flung over the length of the bull, landing with a thud on the hard ground. She heard voices in Spanish— José's and the other men's.

"Emiliano! My God!" She clung to the rail and fought the urge to climb over.

"Don't move, Condesa!" It was José's voice. He was in the ring. The bull charged toward him, and José leapt to safety as the mad beast rushed through the open doors leading to his pen. Clare heard the doors close.

"Emiliano!" Tears ran down her cheeks as she stumbled over the rail and ran to her husband's still form. José had come running too. He stood behind her, crossing himself and muttering in Spanish.

Clare touched his shoulder and he rolled over on his back, displaying a huge gaping wound where the bull had gored him. His black shirt was covered in blood. His eyes looked vacantly up at her, his mouth open. Clare let out a long wailing cry and fell across him.

She felt José's hands pulling her away. He wrenched her from Emiliano and pulled her to her feet. "He's dead," she heard José say. "I'm sorry, Condesa. The bulls are a sport for . . . younger men. . . ."

Friday, October 12, 1923

ARANJUEZ

Clare's sides ached from being sick to her stomach, her head pounded from the medication given her by the doctor, and her eyes were red and swollen from crying. She sat in a straight-backed chair before the cluttered desk of Captain Armando Garcia, the chief of police in Aranjuez. It was unbearably hot, a stifling room aired by an inefficient squeaking overhead fan.

Beside her stood Elia Riggio, the Italian consul, who had come from Madrid. He was immaculately dressed and looked surprisingly cool.

Clare's memory of the last twenty-four hours was vague because shortly after Emiliano's death, a doctor had given her sleeping powders and she had slept fitfully on and off for twelve hours. In her troubled dreams fantasy mingled with reality. She reenacted her wedding, the trip to Italy with her father in June, the talks she had had with her mother, the talks she imagined she had had with her mother, and finally, the horrible sight of the mad bull and the vacant expression on her dead husband's face as he lay on the cold table in what served as the town's morgue.

"And the name?" Captain Garcia asked.

"Clare Marina Sforza-Tonelli."

"The Countess Clare Marina Sforza-Tonelli," the Italian consul, Mr. Riggio, said officiously.

"But that's the name of a woman." Captain Garcia, shook his head. "The body is that of a man."

"No, no, that's my name," Clare said impatiently.

"Thank you, Condesa, but it's not your name I require. What is the name of the body?"

"Count Emiliano Sforza," she replied.

He wrote it down. "And your nationality?"

"American," she replied.

Captain Garcia looked up and frowned. "You're taking the body to America?" He laughed, a high silly laugh. "They don't even let in live people from Spain. No, no, it is very difficult to take a body to America."

"I'm not taking the body to America!" Clare felt like screaming. Her nerves were taut, and she cursed the fact that Señor Juan de Carlo Herrera was on his way to the Argentine and General de

Rivera, her only influential acquaintance in Spain, was away reviewing his troops.

"And why isn't the American consul here? Why is the Italian consul here?"

"Because my husband, Count Emiliano Sforza, is . . . was Italian. I want to take the body to Italy."

"Yes," the consul confirmed. "Yes, that is correct. I have the papers here. Do you want to see them?"

Captain Garcia giggled. "No, no, I have quite enough papers of my own, thank you." He looked up at Clare. "Excuse me, Condesa."

He summarily stamped the paper he had been filling out with no less than six stamps. "This is the death certificate," he confided.

"Is that all I need?" Clare asked.

"No, no, no, of course not. First someone must sign for the body."

"I'll sign for it," she said, leaning over.

"But you can't. You're a woman. Women cannot sign legal papers in Spain."

Clare sank back.

"That's why I am here. I will sign them," the consul put in.

"Good, good. Right here, right here on the dotted line."

The consul signed and Captain Garcia again went to his stamping. One blue stamp, one red stamp, two black stamps, and a special black seal.

"Now, who will pay?"

"Pay?" Clare repeated.

"Oh, yes. When a person of foreign citizenship dies, there are certain charges. There is the charge for the time in the morgue, the examination by the doctor, the fee for all these papers, and of course the fee for a temporary coffin for shipment, and the special fee for the transport across Spain, and of course the body must have all the regular visas and so on."

Clare felt she was close to hysteria. She stood up and turned to the timid, idiotic consul. "Pay him," she demanded.

"I must have some guarantee that the Italian government will be reimbursed, Countess."

"I guarantee it," she said wearily.

"But you are a woman, and a woman cannot give such a guarantee against her husband's estate."

Clare stomped her foot. "I have money of my own!" she shrieked hysterically. "Pay him!"

The consul shook his head and mumbled. Clare turned and fled from the room.

21

Wednesday, October 17, 1923

MILAN

"A widow of eight days does not meet with lawyers," Constanza complained. "A decent, well-bred woman would know that. You remain in absolute and complete seclusion for a period of not less than three months."

"There were arrangements to make," Clare replied. She felt numb. First the horrible trip back from Spain, the interment and requiem Mass, and then this morning's meeting with Emiliano's four lawyers. And through it all, Constanza was at her side, not as a helpmate, but as a hindrance. More disturbing still, Constanza appeared emotionally unmoved by her brother's death.

"The lawyers could have waited," Constanza said bitterly. "What you did isn't proper."

"I really don't care," Clare declared, remembering her nightmare in Spain. All her own money was in New York; she didn't have a lira to call her own. She had had to borrow funds from the consulate to pay all the costs, then borrow more to purchase her railway ticket. And though she'd wired her bank in the United States to transfer funds, the money hadn't arrived yet. She would be without money for some time, since every penny of Emiliano's estate was frozen until the reading of the will and the property settlement. And as she had just learned, that couldn't be done for three months, because, as the lawyers pointed out, she might be pregnant and that would legally affect the disposition of property, since women could not, in and for themselves, inherit property in Italy. Instead, they inherited only in the name of their sons, if there were sons, and acted as a kind of regent till the male heirs came of age.

"Are you in need?" Constanza said sarcastically. "You've a roof over your head—quite an elegant roof, and better than you are used to, I'm sure. You have food, and you can go if you

353

wish to the villa at Lake Como. I don't understand your concern with Emiliano's business matters, with your so-called need for funds. Surely you don't think you are entitled to anything save the allowance the estate would pay you after things are settled. You were, after all, married to him for only a matter of weeks.''

Clare sat down in the chair and stared past the stony-faced Constanza. I'll never be without my own money again, she silently vowed. Never. She'd felt utterly helpless in Spain, and she felt so now in spite of Constanza's assurances that she would be provided with the necessities of life for the next three months.

''You can't inherit Sforza Industries either,'' Clare countered. ''You too are a woman.''

''It'll go to a consortium of Emiliano's closest male relatives, and both you and I shall receive a generous allowance.''

''I've met those relatives,'' Clare replied. ''Constanza, they're all dilettantes who haven't the vaguest notion how to run a business. Emiliano was different—it's a rare member of the Italian nobility who enters the world of business and builds such an empire. Oh, Emiliano was aware of his nobility, but he was also a shrewd businessman.''

''And of course you, a young widowed bride, a girl who isn't yet twenty-one, know better than all those gentlemen Emiliano hired over the years to assist him.''

''I know enough to know that such assistants grow careless when left to their own ends.''

Constanza examined her hands, moving her fingers in agitation. ''Business is crass, hardly an occupation for a countess.''

''You never wanted Emiliano to marry me, did you?''

Constanza looked up and arched her perfectly plucked brow. ''That question is also crass.''

''Stop playing so noble, Constanza! Be blunt, reveal your true colors. The last week has been hell for me. I'm numb now, and I think you and I'd better settle a few matters.''

Constanza's dark eyes glared at her. ''All right, I never wanted Emiliano to marry you. You may have a rich father, but you're common! And now, practically before my brother's body is cold, you are proving just how common you are!''

In a different time and place Clare thought she might have laughed. Constanza, who hadn't shed a tear, was accusing her of being unfeeling.

''What meant the most to Emiliano?'' Clare asked, meeting Constanza's eyes.

Constanza's expression darkened, and Clare thought it was because she felt trapped. ''Be honest, if you can,'' Clare challenged.

"Sforza Industries," Constanza finally said in a low, hesitant voice.

"If you honor his memory, you should want to see Sforza Industries stay intact. To accomplish that, certain steps must be taken now, Constanza. Regardless of whether or not I'm pregnant, you and I must make a temporary truce and go to the board of directors as one. We must insist on obtaining all necessary documents and information and we must let it be known that we'll not countenance mistakes during the next three months."

"Why? So that if God has blessed you with a son, you can take all my brother's fortune in his name?"

Clare shook her head. In all truth, she didn't feel pregnant. She inhaled deeply. "No, Constanza. Now, listen, and listen carefully. If I'm with child and that child is a son, then I'll inherit in the child's name regardless of what happens. That's what the lawyers just said. If I'm not pregnant, or if I give birth to a daughter, we're equals, since we'll both receive an allowance. Let me make you a bargain, Constanza."

"A bargain?"

"If I'm not pregnant, or if I have a girl, I promise you I'll return to America and thus rid you of what you obviously consider a millstone around your regal neck. But either way, I want your help now. You owe it to your brother's memory to join forces with me. If you don't, you'll see his life's work destroyed, because the people left in charge will feel they have total control and they'll grow careless."

Constanza frowned. "Do you promise you'll go away if you aren't pregnant or if you have a daughter?"

Clare nodded. "I give you my word."

Constanza nodded her agreement and watched as Clare left the room. "Emiliano's memory . . ." she whispered. Then she shook her head dejectedly. "Not for your memory," she whispered. "But to give the whole affair with Eduardo some meaning."

ROME

Mark Lyons sipped his Campari with lime and watched the passersby on Via Veneto. The tourist season was over, but the small sidewalk café was still crowded. He wiped his brow. Even though it was mid-October, it was hot and sticky and he felt like ripping his shirt open and tossing away his tie.

"Hello, my friend." Matteotti sat down and signaled the waiter. "A Campari with lime for me too."

Matteotti had insisted they meet here in the crowded café. He wore a wide-brimmed hat and dark glasses so as not to be recognized. As he explained, it wouldn't do for him to be seen with an American oil man, and conversely, it would be better for Mark if their relationship remained unknown.

"I wouldn't have known you," Mark confessed. "But why all the subterfuge? Surely we couldn't ruin each other's reputations that easily."

Matteotti pressed his lips together. "My house is watched, and I'm followed." He half-smiled. "No need to worry, I've eluded them."

"But you're a member of Parliament."

Matteotti's smile was full of irony. "It's a name-only Parliament. Mussolini will soon stamp out all opposition, and if he can't get rid of us at the ballot box, he'll dispose of us with bludgeons, knives, and pistols."

"Can't you go to the police?"

"No, my friend. But let's not concern ourselves with my little problems. This is a luggage check," he said, handing Mark a receipt. "Your sister's belongings are packaged and waiting for you at the railway station."

"Thank you, you've been kind."

"It's nothing. But we must talk, and I have little time."

"Tell me everything," Mark requested.

" 'Everything' is not much. Your sister was run over by a car on the sidewalk. Hit-and-run, as you say in America." He leaned over and whispered, "It's the traditional Italian way of assassination."

"But why?" Mark's face was knit in a frown. "Why in the name of heaven would anyone assassinate Louisa?"

"There's no evidence, merely a story that I've heard."

"Tell me," Mark persisted.

"I've heard she was killed by a man named Dumini, a criminal who is for hire. But he's not loyal to those who hire him. He's a blackmailer. I've heard he was hired to kill your sister by Count Sforza because the count was about to marry a wealthy young woman and your sister threatened to tell all."

Mark's face reddened and his mind flashed back to his brief meeting with the count and to his memory of Clare Marina Tonelli in the garden. They had married; he'd read about the wedding in the papers.

Matteotti patted Mark's arm affectionately. "If you plan revenge, I must tell you that fate has taken that from you."

Mark looked at him questioningly.

"Count Sforza was killed on his honeymoon—gored by a mad bull. That's why Dumini's so talkative. He's angry because now he has no one to blackmail."

Mark leaned back in his chair. Revenge had not really entered his mind—justice was what he wanted; but as Matteotti reiterated, there was no evidence of any kind, only a rumor that seemed borne out by scant facts.

"And this killer, this Dumini?"

"Impossible," Matteotti answered. "He's in the employ of the government and responsible for acts of terrorism against the opposition."

"Against you?"

"I've been threatened by his thugs. He doesn't act alone. No, you must not attempt to find him. He's a hired killer, he's well-protected, and there's no way to bring him to justice in this matter." Matteotti shook his head sadly. "I am sorry."

"No way at all?"

Matteotti smiled. "None unless the government is brought down. As long as Mussolini is in power, Dumini will be safe."

Mark nodded. "I appreciate all you have done."

"I must ask that this meeting terminate our relationship. Both for my sake and yours. I'm afraid I'm in a rather delicate position, since I've been investigating the existence of some most unfavorable contracts between large American oil firms and the Italian government. Naturally, I find knowing you and liking you something of an embarrassment. But you and your sister are relatives, and"—he smiled and nodded—"in Italy family transcends politics."

"You're a good man," Mark acknowledged. "I don't share your political views, but I don't like what's going on in this country either. What the hell kind of government hires a man like this Dumini?"

"One that's morally corrupt and dangerous," Matteotti answered.

Mark nodded silently. "I'll not be staying in Italy, though I may be back next year for a short time." He paused momentarily. "You said you are investigating oil leases between American firms and the Italian government?"

Matteotti nodded.

"If I learn anything interesting, I'll let you know."

Matteotti smiled. "For such information, I will gladly be seen with you again."

Monday, October 22, 1923

MILAN

Clare had wired her family from Spain directly after Emiliano's death, and when she returned to Milan she found a wire from her parents. Again she wired for money from her personal account, and wrote a long letter after her meeting with the lawyers. Now, after what seemed an eternity, she received a long letter from home:

My dearest Clare,

I cannot express my feelings in words. I know this is a terribly difficult time for you. I would turn right around and come back to Italy to be at your side, but it's impossible. Truly impossible. First, your mother became quite ill on the voyage home, and second, there are matters of great urgency I must see to here. Anthony wanted to come in my place, but of course he can't miss his classes.

I've sent the money, as you requested—it's probably arrived by now. I carefully read your letter—the one sent after your meeting with the lawyers. You're quite right, of course, a business without a head decays quickly. It's true that I too don't believe women should be involved in these matters, but in your case there's no choice, and I must confess I have a certain amount of faith in your ability. So in addition to sending you the money, I've notified my Italian lawyers that you should be given my power of attorney in all matters concerning the dam and related projects that Emiliano and I were involved in. This for two reasons: (1) I can't come and deal with this matter myself and I have a large investment at stake, which should be protected by a member of the family; and (2) it will give you some real clout in dealing with Sforza Industries. Also, blood (ours) is thicker than water (business and my feelings toward women in business). Your mother, who will write in a few days when she is feeling better, says I have done the right thing.

And your Aunt Maria says you must watch Constanza
Sforza because she is a snake in the grass!

I, my darling daughter, give you the advice my
father gave me: *Senti tutti i consigli, ma il tuo non lo
lasciare.* Now, for the first counsel: don't allow any
liquidation of Sforza Industries. This is a bad time to
sell. Mussolini is still consolidating his power, and
when that consolidation is complete, the economy will
stabilize and all the Sforza holdings will become more
valuable. Pick out those managers who are the best
and make it known to them that their salaries will be
raised if you take charge. Don't hesitate to let it be
known who will go if they're uncooperative. Feel free
to consult my Italian lawyers; they are independent of
the Sforza family. I am afraid this is the most I can do
for you at the moment, Clare.

Your mother sends her love, and Fabiana says she
will write immediately.

All my love,
Agosto

Clare put down the letter. She could not believe it was from
her father! It was wonderfully supportive, and for the first time
since Emiliano's sudden death, she felt as if a weight had been
lifted from her shoulders. All that kept her from feeling complete
relief was her mother's illness. But, she told herself, if it were
serious, her father would have told her.

Saturday, November 3, 1923

M I L A N

Clare sat at one end of the long table and Constanza at the other.
Their truce was holding, she thought. Constanza was only mildly
hostile now, and sometimes they even managed to have semi-
pleasant conversations. Clare motioned to the servant and he
poured her some more wine.

"You haven't eaten much," Constanza commented.

"I haven't been feeling well since this morning."

Constanza's face clouded over. "What's the matter?" she
queried.

Clare shrugged. "Nothing, really." And it was nothing, just a little nausea. But there was more. Her period was late, and it crossed her mind that she might actually be pregnant. Women should know more about these things, she thought.

"The dinner's excellent," Clare said, trying to eat a little more to please Constanza.

"Do you think you could tell me what was going on at that dreadful meeting yesterday?" Constanza leaned forward.

Clare kept herself from smiling. Constanza had invited three of the board members from Sforza Industries to tea and then had hated every second of it. It was clear why, too. She hadn't the faintest idea what was being discussed.

"Cash flow," Clare said.

"What does that mean?" Constanza said with annoyance.

"Essentially that more money is going out than coming in."

"But there are so many undertakings . . ."

"Yes, that's the problem. The projects initiated by Emiliano are going ahead, and they must be paid for, but it'll be a long time before the cost of initiating them is returned to the company in profits. There's an immediate need to find new sources of revenue." That was as simply as Clare could put it.

Constanza frowned. "Well, I thought that's what Signor Sangallo wanted when he suggested those sales of those things."

Clare smiled. "They're not *things,* Constanza, they're subsidiary holdings of Sforza Industries. They're the very heart of the empire Emiliano built. Selling them isn't a satisfactory solution to what I see as a quite simple problem."

"If it's so simple, why did Signor Sangallo not suggest the solution?"

"Signor Sangallo is, if I am not mistaken, married to Eleonora Gaspari, a niece of Raza, Fiat's fiercest competitor. Raza is the most likely purchaser of any Sforza holdings, so I don't consider Signor Sangallo to be acting entirely in our interests, Constanza. That's why I asked Signor Catelli, the managing director, and the others to come back in a few days. There's to be a board meeting, and that gives me the excuse that I must consult my father, who has a large investment in the dam."

"What can you do in two days?"

Clare smiled. "You'll see, Constanza. And I promise you, not one subsidiary will be sold."

Constanza pressed her lips together. "I wish I understood all this better."

Clara smiled. "You do have a terrible problem," she allowed.

"What's that?" Constanza raised her eyebrow as usual.

"You don't trust me, and you're not sure about Signor Sangallo either."

Constanza put down her fork. "Well, I do know he is married to Raza's niece."

Monday, November 5, 1923

MILAN

Signor Luigi Catelli, the managing director, sat perched on the edge of his chair in the living room of the Sforza mansion. Signor Sangallo leaned back against the sofa, trying to pretend this was a social visit and not the meeting it obviously was. Signori Fantasia and Ferroni sat near the coffee table and munched on olives and cheese.

No one in the room was used to having women present when business was discussed, and each looked duly uncomfortable and inhibited by the unusual situation.

Signor Catelli cleared his throat. "This is . . . ah, an informal meeting held for the benefit of the Countess Clare Marina Sforza-Tonelli and the Countess Constanza Sforza. Signor Sángallo, will you make your presentation, the one you were about to make before the . . . the delay requested by the Countess Sforza?"

Signor Sangallo stood up. He opened a portfolio of papers and officiously spread them out on the coffee table. "We are out of options," he began glumly. "Unless we declare bankruptcy, a course I would never advocate, there's no way out of the hydro-electric project on the Ticino." He turned and bowed slightly toward Clare Marina. Then, turning: "Nor can we forsake our contracts with the state for the building of an autostrada through Liguria to the French border. The state is depending on our fulfillment of those contracts. The problem is our short-term ability to meet our weekly payrolls as well as our regular obligations to subcontractors."

Sangallo paused and took a lengthy sip of Campari. "Now, we do own a concrete plant in Abruzzi, and several hotels in Calabria and Sicily. None of these is essential to the future of Sforza Industries. I think we should sell them, and sell them quickly."

"But to whom?" asked the bespeckled Signor Fantasia.

Sangallo smiled and opened yet another folder. "Last week I was contacted by a Swiss firm, Gerlach und Sohne, who seek to purchase these very properties. Here's the offer, and in my opinion it's quite fair and reasonable." He paused and handed a copy of the offer to each of the board members; then, as an afterthought, he turned around and handed copies to Clare Marina and Constanza.

"As you can see, it's a fair price. It will solve our immediate problems, and I can't think we'll get a better price."

Signor Fantasia and Signor Ferroni grumbled slightly. Signor Catelli turned to Clare Marina. His expression was both benevolent and patronizing. "You wished to say a few words on this subject?"

Clare smiled and nodded. "Please," she said, standing up. "You'll excuse me, gentlemen, if I'm wrong, but I hold the belief that when a company begins to liquidate its holdings and drastically cut back because it is suffering from a temporary cash-flow problem, an irreversible process is initiated. And before you know it, the company ceases to exist. The strength of Sforza Industries is based on real property and on solid contracts for projects which, over the years, will make a handsome return. If we are seen to be cutting back, a negative momentum will be created. The market value of our stock will decline and that will make many hundreds of shareholders uneasy. So uneasy that mass selling might well occur. Confidence, gentlemen, is everything." There was a certain mumbled agreement. "I know this, gentlemen, because when I was a little girl, during the panic of 1907, my father had all the gold in the vaults of our bank put on display in order to create confidence. Ours was a bank that survived."

The reference to the 1907 crash caused Signor Fantasia to sit up and stare at her, as if suddenly she'd become older.

"I've been told by others, and by you gentlemen, that Italy has undergone a major social revolution. I believe you, and I believe that Italy's entering a period of unparalleled economic growth. Signor Mussolini has imposed order where there was once chaos. He's made the lira sound and he's given Italians reason to anticipate tomorrow. Signor Sangallo has requested that you sell off the concrete plants in Abruzzi. . . . I think that would be most unwise. Our construction companies build the finest highways in Europe. Must they buy their concrete from a competitor? Or should the profits remain with Sforza Industries and the shareholders?" She paused a moment and noted that they were all paying attention. "Further, Signor Sangallo suggests we sell off our hotels and resorts in Calabria and Sicily. It's true that those hotels haven't been showing a profit for the last few years—who wanted to come to Italy in the aftermath of war and during the so-called civil war? If my father hadn't already had holdings here, I for one wouldn't be here. But Italy is recovering. There are over twenty-five million Italian-Americans, almost a third of them from Calabria and Sicily. There's bound to be a new boom in travel, so why should we sell off our hotels? That would be foolish indeed.''

Signor Sangallo stood up. He looked, Clare thought, like an old rooster about to go for a strut in his barnyard.

"May I speak for a moment, Signor?'' he addressed the chair. Signor Catelli nodded.

"The countess is quite learned for a young woman, and I quite agree that the future is bright, but I must ask, Countess Sforza, what do we do in the immediate short term?'' He sat down with a self-satisfied smile on his face.

Clare smiled too, then stood up and walked to the writing desk, returning with a folder. "Through my father's lawyers, I spoke with Signor Forlanini. His company, Forlanini e Figlio, is known to all of you, I believe.'' There was a mumbling and nodding.

"His firm has agreed to draw up papers for the issuance of four-percent bonds that will mature in twenty years. I realize the interest is slightly higher than is being paid currently, but that only ensures their quick sale and an end to the problems of Sforza Industries.'' Clare passed copies of her papers around the room.

"As you see, we can authorize the issue in whatever sum we deem fit. I for one would feel quite comfortable with a two-hundred-million-lira issuance. It would, according to my calculations, and based on the documents I have studied, provide us with sufficient liquidity to cover almost any conceivable contingency for the next three years. At the same time, with the increased capital flow, we can expand several operations. The autostrada in Liguria is only a small beginning. We can look forward to building roads all over Italy. No one can match the expertise or experience of this firm.''

Sangallo stood by his chair, and Clare could see his white fingers clutching the edge of it. The gentlemen of the board clapped, and Signor Catelli clapped too. It was at that moment that Constanza stood up and, stony-faced, looked at the four important board members, who together represented the votes necessary to swing the board one way or the other. "I support my sister-in-law fully,'' she said imperiously, then added: ". . . in her effort to keep my late brother's empire intact. In the event that Clare Marina gives birth to an heir, I shall become her legal guardian until she reaches the age of twenty-one in August.''

There was utter, complete silence because every man at the table knew that meant that Constanza Sforza would be completely in control of Emiliano's staggering forty percent of the shares of Sforza Industries for two months.

Constanza turned toward Sangallo with rigid meanness. "Signor," she said, taking a step closer to him, "I suggest you either leave your wife or resign from this board."

Sangallo didn't answer her, but merely muttered, "Women and girls!" as he slammed shut his briefcase and stormed out of the living room.

"I suppose that's a resignation," Signor Catelli said.

Constanza smiled. "You gentlemen will make our wishes clear to the remaining board members, won't you?"

Signor Catelli nodded.

Constanza ran her hand over her dress. "I do love entertaining," she commented. "Would anyone like more Campari?"

When they left, Clare turned to Constanza, laughing. "You were magnificent!"

"I regard business as crude," she said, "but you were correct."

"Thank you," Clare said.

Constanza paused. "Your blood has not yet come, has it?"

Clare shook her head. "But that doesn't mean I'm pregnant."

"It doesn't mean you aren't, either," Constanza replied.

Monday, January 7, 1924

MILAN

December 24, 1923

My Dear Clare,

As you know from my previous letters, I am much better, so you mustn't worry about me at all. The doctor said the fluid I had on my lungs was just the result of a weakness I was left with after I had the flu in 1917. But really I'm quite all right except for missing you so very much on this Christmas Eve. But what a Christmas present you have given me! To know that you are pregnant and that I will have a grandchild is the very best gift I could have, my darling.

Anthony is home for the holidays. And Tina is here too, so the house isn't quiet. She never turns off the gramophone—she may be "Wild About Harry," but I'm not. I don't suppose you hear much popular music in Italy. Tina wants to send you some records.

Your father says his lawyers in Italy say you are doing very well indeed, even if you are shocking everyone. Good for you! Your father is surprised, but I'm not. He is even more surprised that the bonds issued for Sforza Industries are selling so well in America.

Keep well, my Clarissima. Write to your mama as often as you can.

Love,
Mama

Clare put the letter away and went downstairs. The house was as silent as a tomb. She paused before the full-length mirror in the hallway. Black, black, black! She hated wearing black and despaired at the thought that she'd have to wear it till next October.

She turned sideways and viewed her swelling stomach. Obviously she had become pregnant during her honeymoon—the baby was due in mid-June.

22

Thursday, May 1, 1924

L O S A N G E L E S

"You're a real bastard!" Morty Levinson announced cheerfully.

"Is that in anticipation of something I've done, or something I'm about to do?" Mark replied, looking up from his desk in the executive suite of Lyons Oil.

"Something you're about to do. I've got your documentation. But let me warn you, releasing this stuff isn't going to make you any friends."

Mark pressed his lips together. "No one will know who it came from."

"I should hope not. Old Morty could go to jail."

"That good, huh?"

"Take a look for yourself." He thrust a file in front of Mark, who opened it and began flipping the pages.

He whistled through his teeth. "Shit! This is dynamite! Those stupid pricks are paying out a hundred and fifty million dollars in bribes!"

"To the Minister of Works, Gabriele Carnazza, the Minister of Economics, Mario Orso Corbino, Undersecretary for Home Affairs Aldo Finzi—he's Mussolini's own press secretary—Cesare Rossi and Filippo Filipelli, and the editor of *Corriere Italiano*. They're practically paying off the entire Italian Cabinet."

Mark smiled. "Could bring down the whole damn Italian government. Imagine a big American oil company doing this!"

"Imagine," Morty replied dryly. "Hey, it was only last month we slipped ten grand to the son of that Diego Manuel Chamorro in Nicaragua. You're getting awfully holier-than-thou."

"So I've a personal vendetta. If I can't bring that murdering Fascist pig Dumini to justice, I'd at least like to get the sons-of-bitches that pay him. And maybe, just maybe, if the government falls and there's a new government, he could be brought to justice.''

"Okay, okay. Look, you want me to send this stuff to that guy Matteotti or what?''

Mark smiled. "No. Last time I was in Italy I missed St. Peter's. I think I'll take it myself.''

"That's dangerous. You're being cavalier.''

Mark smiled. "Probably. Look, while I'm at it, no more bribes out of this company.''

Morty frowned. "That sort of honesty and upright attitude could hurt our expansion program in Latin America.''

"Sorry, I've had a taste of these people personally. I don't care if it's a Mr. Big like Il Duce or a two-bit Central American dictator. No more bribes.''

Morty nodded. "You were always a good guy in this business. Now I see you're going to be a *really* good guy.''

Mark flushed. "No, I just think I'll put my money where my mouth is.''

Thursday, June 5, 1924

M I L A N

"Emiliano Romano Gregorio Sforza the Third!" Constanza said proudly as she held the tiny infant.

Clare edged up in her bed. "The other names can go on the birth certificate, but I think we'll just call him Emil.''

"It was a perfect birth. You're in excellent health, Countess,'' Dr. Contini advised her.

The birth had occurred some ten hours earlier and the doctor had returned to check on mother and son.

Clare watched as Constanza returned Emil to his crib. "I only wish that Fabiana had arrived in time for the birth.''

"She'll be here for the christening, and so will your father's friend. He wired this morning.''

"Roberto! Oh, I'll be glad to see him. He's more than a friend, Constanza, he's my father's right-hand man and the vice-president of American Federal Banks.'' Clare suddenly grinned wickedly. "You'll like him. He's good-looking, unmarried, and just a few years older than you.''

"I'm past that sort of thing.''

"I doubt it!''

"I'll come tomorrow," Dr. Contini informed her. He fidgeted and fussed, stuffing his stethoscope into his bag.

"Let me see you to the door," Constanza said pointedly. The doctor frowned slightly, but followed her. She closed the door behind him.

"You really shouldn't discuss personal matters in front of inferiors. Now it'll be all over Milan that you are trying to marry me off to this Roberto person."

Clare giggled.

"You certainly seem in a good mood," Constanza commented. "I trust you won't forget that I'm your legal guardian till you turn twenty-one in August."

Clare sat up fully. "I feel wonderful! I hope no one ever tells me again how glowing pregnant women look. They aren't pretty, and they don't glow. They're fat, awkward, and absurd-looking!" She glanced over at Emil. "But you were worth it, and in spite of your aunt over there, you're going to be rich and powerful and like your papa."

"What do you mean 'in spite of' me?"

"Well, if you act the guardian too much, it will be in spite of you. Constanza, you must trust me to make the business decisions."

"I've lost anyway," she said, looking at Emil. "Now you'll inherit everything. My power over you is short in duration—too short to matter. Obviously I'll let you make the business decisions. I hate those meetings, I hate it all. It's all crude, but you're good at it."

Clare laughed. "Oh, Constanza . . . you'll never give up. The business may be crude, but you enjoy the money."

"It has advantages," she admitted. "But I don't like to discuss those things."

"I know you don't. So let's discuss fashion. You like that topic. Why don't you call Signor Lorenzo, the designer of my famous green gown. Constanza, I've decided to give up wearing black. A new mother shouldn't be in mourning," Clare announced.

"But it's nowhere near a year. What will people say?"

"They will say nothing . . . except perhaps that I look better in white."

Constanza nodded. "I suppose white is better for a christening," she conceded. She walked again to Emil's crib and looked at him thoughtfully. I hope you're not like your papa, she wished silently, and then said, "You did love Emiliano, didn't you?"

"Of course I did, I adored him!"

"I always wanted a baby."

Clare frowned. "Constanza, why didn't you ever marry?"

Constanza turned around, and her face was no longer hard. She bit her lip and rubbed her hand against her dress in agitation. "I was married. I'm a widow."

"A widow? Constanza, you never mentioned it, and Emiliano never mentioned it. Why is your last name Sforza?"

"I married a second cousin with the same name."

"Oh, Constanza. I'm sorry. No one ever told me."

Constanza shook her head. "It was a long time ago," she said ruefully. "It was an arranged marriage . . . you know how those can be."

"You weren't happy?"

"He wasn't the one I loved."

Tuesday, June 10, 1924

ROME

Mark Lyons and Giacomo Matteotti sat at the table in Matteotti's kitchen. Spread out before them were documents which each studied as they drank black Italian coffee.

"You've brought me the missing puzzle pieces," Matteotti confided. "And these documents confirm my own research."

"I thought you'd find them useful."

Matteotti licked his thin lips. "You've gone to considerable trouble, and placed yourself in danger."

"I have a personal interest."

Matteotti nodded. "Nevertheless, don't grow careless. The *ceka* doesn't examine passports before striking. Italian or American, it wouldn't matter. My Socialist colleague Gonzales was badly beaten, and even a Fascist, one who opposed the policies of Il Duce was attacked. Foreign journalists who have tried to report these atrocities have been set upon and have suffered injuries."

"I'll be careful."

"Forni, the Fascist who tried to break party discipline, was beaten in broad daylight outside Milan station, my friend. You must be more than careful, you must be wary."

Mark studied Matteotti's face. It was tense, and across his forehead there was a thin white line, a scar. "Have you been attacked?"

Matteotti folded his hands and looked at his long thin fingers. "Twice, and tortured."

"Tortured?"

"In a special way. A friend, a journalist who writes for *Corriere della Sera,* tried to report it, but his editor said it was too vulgar to be printed."

Mark bit his lip. The man across from him seemed gentle and somewhat frail. He didn't look the sort to hold up under torture, especially the sort he hinted at.

"You're pale—don't be so shocked. They could have killed me, and I confess at the time I wish they had."

"What did they do?" Mark could hear the sense of outrage in his own voice .

"Let's just say I won't father a child. You don't want to hear the details. I only told you so you'll take care, so you'll get out of Italy now that you've given me these documents."

"I will."

"And you must go immediately. In fact, when you leave this building, I want you to leave by the back entrance. When you get to the ground floor, continue into the basement. You'll find a door at the far end which leads out into the alley."

"This house is watched?"

"I'm not sure. It's only a precaution. I'm a public figure, so I can be seized at any time or attacked in any one of a dozen places I must go to daily. But this is an apartment house. When you came in, anyone who was watching from outside would not know which apartment you came to. Still, I want you to leave by the other entrance, just in case."

"All right."

"I'll leave first. You stay, and when I'm away from the front of the house—you can see through the front window—you leave."

Matteotti gulped down the rest of his coffee. He stuffed the documents into his briefcase. "You have done me a great service—indeed, you have done Italy a great service. I won't see you again, my friend. And remember, when you leave here, go directly to the train station. Get out of this country."

Mark stood up uneasily and extended his hand to the Socialist leader. "Take care," he told him.

Matteotti half-smiled. "Remember, if anything happens to me, I personally won't regret it. I've lived in the shadow of death for two years, and I'm reconciled to the fact that if I'm killed, my death could become more important than my life." He laughed lightly, squeezed Mark's hand, and added, "See, I have quite an ego."

Matteotti put on his jacket and picked up his briefcase. He waved once again, and left.

Mark sipped his coffee, waited a few seconds, and then went to the window. Matteotti's slim figure emerged from the front of the building, and he strode across the street, the afternoon sun-light reflecting off the shiny leather of his briefcase.

Mark saw the long black car as it sped around the corner, skidding to a stop directly beside Matteotti. He opened his mouth in an instinctive gesture to give a cry of warning.

Three men jumped out of the car and seized Matteotti, who struggled fiercely. Then one delivered a vicious blow to Matteotti's head with a bludgeon. They pulled him into the car, and it quickly sped off.

Mark whirled around, and paying no attention to Matteotti's instructions, ran down the stairs and out the front of the building onto the street. On the curb an old woman and four men stood shaking their heads.

"Call the police!" Mark yelled.

One of the men grinned stupidly and pointed to a piece of paper he held in one hand. "I have the license number," he said proudly in Italian.

Mark leaned against the side of the building and bit his lip. They had Matteotti, and from the vicious blow he'd seen delivered, he had no reason to believe his friend was still alive. They also had the briefcase with the documents, and though the documents couldn't be traced to Lyons Oil or to him, certain connections would be made if his relationship with Matteotti were discovered. He turned quickly and hurried away, even as the sound of police sirens could be heard in the distance. The police would ask questions, seize passports, and certainly the police couldn't be trusted either. Someone would ask what an American oil man was doing outside Matteotti's building in a suburb of Rome, and someone who opened the briefcase would be able to surmise the answer. Mark darted down a back alley, then up another street. Then he climbed aboard a crowded tram and headed back into the city.

June 12, 1924

M I L A N

Tears tumbled down Fabiana's plate-round face. "My baby, my little Clare! You're a mama. I can hardly believe it!"

"Zia Fabiana! It's so good to see you—you're a breath of home!"

"Your mama said I should kiss and hug you for her."

Clare pulled Fabiana to the side of the bed and motioned her to sit down. "How is Mama? I mean, how is she really?"

Fabiana wet her lips and frowned. "She's had fluid on the lungs. She seems better. When your papa comes in August to open the dam, he's sending your mama and Maria to Arizona so she can get lots of sunshine and dry air. You mustn't worry—the doctors say she'll be fine."

"I'll miss not having her here. I so wanted her to see Emil."

Fabiana nodded and reached into her gigantic satchel. "I brought the Brownie your papa gave me for my birthday. I'm to take lots of pictures of Emil so Cecilia can put them on her mantel."

Clare smiled. "You can start this afternoon at the christening."

"Will there be many people? I hope not as many as were at your wedding."

"No, just family and a few friends. Constanza and Roberto. Luigi Catelli, the managing director of Sforza Industries, and his wife, General Balbo, who seems to have invited himself, you, and the cardinal of course."

"Oh, dear, a cardinal?"

"Well, he's not coming for dinner afterward." Clara smiled. "He says the food Constanza serves is too rich."

"Is that woman treating you all right?" Fabiana asked suspiciously.

"We get on just fine now," Clare confided. "You know, I was teasing her about Roberto being single, and I think she took me seriously. She's flirting with him outrageously."

Fabiana hugged her. "You're too young to be a matchmaker."

Clare leaned against her aunt's soft shoulder. It was good to have a woman to talk to. Constanza was all right, but talking to her wasn't the same. She was close-mouthed about personal things; there were few confidences shared. She never spoke of her own marriage or of the love affair she had alluded to once. In a sudden rush of emotion, Clare realized how much she missed the unique company of the Italian women she'd grown up around, who were always close and supported one another so. "Oh, Fabiana, stay till Papa comes, please stay till August."

At four o'clock they assembled at the rear of the cathedral, the vast Duomo. She had wanted to have Emil's christening in a smaller church, but Cardinal Tanuto reigned over the Duomo, and he insisted on officiating. The little group was dwarfed by the emptiness of the huge church as they huddled near the baptismal font while Cardinal Tanuto chanted out the blessings, his voice lost in the vast chamber.

Little Emil was dressed in a long white christening robe fashioned of silk and trimmed in handmade lace. Clare passed her son to the cardinal, who dipped the infant's tiny head into the holy water, then gave the final blessing: "In the name of the Father, the Son, and the Holy Ghost, I christen thee Emiliano Romano Gregorio Sforza the Third!"

Clare held out her arms and Emiliano was returned to her. She kissed him lightly on the cheek while Cardinal Tanuto blessed Fabiana and gave her the necessary instructions on her responsibilities as official godmother. Then the cardinal gave the final blessing, and as a group they left the cathedral and headed out into the warm afternoon.

Clare walked with General Balbo. He was pleasant enough, she conceded, but he seemed to be overly concerned with her personal life. But he had been a friend of Emiliano's, she told herself, so it was only natural that he wanted to be at little Emil's christening.

"I have a fine dinner prepared," Constanza announced, taking Roberto Marcucci's proffered arm.

"Good, I'm starved!"

Constanza smiled devastatingly at Roberto. "You'll love what I've had prepared," she cooed flirtatiously.

Friday, August 1, 1924

MILAN

Clare's heart pounded as she searched every face emerging from the crowded train. "Your grandpapa's coming," she whispered to Emil. He was all wrapped up in a light summer sleeping sack and only his round face and dark curly hair could be seen. "I hope the train's not late. Emil will miss his feeding," she said to the nurse, who stood nearby.

"He's going to be a big boy," the nurse observed. "He eats well."

Clare nodded, but all she could think of was seeing her father. A week ago she had received a letter from Rome, a letter written by Il Duce's secretary. It politely but all too firmly requested a meeting with her father and it made clear that Il Duce would make a speech at the opening of the dam. The letter, Clare admitted to herself, troubled her. Il Duce was under attack in both the Italian and the foreign press. It was said that the opposition leader, Giacomo Matteotti, who had been abducted in June—witnesses claimed he was killed on the spot—was dead and that the thug Dumini, who had been arrested, was actually in the pay of the government. And there was no question in Clare's mind that Mussolini was moving to stamp out all opposition in Italy. The opening of the dam would now be turned into a political event, but what's more, Mussolini clearly wanted to meet her father in order to arrange for foreign loans.

Clare craned her neck and stood on tiptoes. "Papa!" she cried out. "Papa! Over here!"

Agosto made his way through the crowd. Tears filled his eyes as he wrapped his arms around Clare and Emil, and for a moment there was nothing but hugs and kisses.

"Oh, Papa, you don't know how glad I am to see you!" Clare wiped the tears off her own cheeks, and Agosto took Emil from her arms.

"My first grandson," he said proudly. But Emil began to cry.

Clare took him back and hushed him. "That's no way to greet your grandpapa," she chided. "It's the crowd, and it's almost time for his feeding." Clare handed Emil to the nurse and linked arms with her father. "Oh, Papa, tell me everything. . . ."

They climbed into the back of the long Alfa Romeo while the nurse and Emil rode in the front seat with the chauffeur.

"Your mother wanted to come," Agosto said. "She's not well, Clare. It's fluid on the lungs again."

Clare pressed her lips together. "What does the doctor say?"

"Only that she must rest. I sent her to Arizona with Tina and Maria. The doctor said the warm dry air will do her good. And of course Fabiana can come back with me—she's a great help."

"Oh, Papa, I miss you all so much."

He hugged her. "Anthony sends his love. He's doing well. He'll learn, you know. A while back he came to me and suggested we invest in those Florida land deals. But I explained to him that it wasn't our kind of investment. It's all speculative, I told him. They buy only to sell at a higher price, and that's not building, it's just taking. It's more like stealing than like investing. I think he understood."

Clare only smiled.

"It's crazy, Clarissima. America has a new game. Everybody wants to get rich quick. They try everything except hard work. The stock market is going mad. It's just like the craziness in Florida. Everyone is buying just to sell."

The car stopped in front of the house, and Clare, her father, and the nurse carrying Emil got out. In the front hall Clare kissed

Emil again. "You'd better feed him and put him to bed," she advised the nurse. "He looks very tired."

Agosto kissed him again too. "I want to hold him when he wakes up. He has to learn not to cry at his grandpapa."

Clare led her father into the study and poured him a drink. She poured herself a glass of red wine. In a few days they would go to Pavia for the opening ceremonies at the dam. Between now and then she and her father had much to discuss. Clare smiled to herself. In a sense, this was the first time' they had approached each other as business equals.

Agosto pulled on his mustache. "You've done a fine job, Clare. The dam's been completed three months ahead of schedule, and that means revenues will be coming in sooner."

"And that will take the strain off American Federal Banks. Papa, you should have told me sooner about the consortium. I didn't realize you were carrying such a heavy load."

Agosto shrugged. "Two banks backed out at the last minute." He shook his head. "No way to do business."

Clare studied her father. No, that wasn't the way he would do business. "Do you know why they backed out?"

"Pressure from somewhere."

Clare frowned. "It couldn't have come from Creighton Stearns, could it?"

Agosto laughed. "I don't think so. He's always been very friendly. Actually, he wants to get in on some Italian investments himself."

"With you?"

Agosto nodded.

"Papa, I don't think that's a good idea. Creighton represents . . . well, the stodgiest of banking interests."

"Creighton's an honorable man. No, I think he's just beginning to expand, take an interest in international investments. I don't know why you would object to him as an associate."

Clare sighed. This was something she couldn't argue about. Her feeling was based on intuition, not hard fact. "You got my wire?" she said, changing the subject.

"Yes. Tell me about Mussolini," Agosto requested. "When will I meet him?"

"He'll be here tomorrow and we'll be his guests for the day. I expect you'll be with him most of time in Pavia as well."

"And what does he want?"

Clare shrugged. "He's been using the Morgan Bank as a corresponding bank in the United States. General Balbo gives me the impression that Mussolini's not happy with them. I suspect he might want to change banks. Then too, the government is short of foreign exchange. I think he may want a hefty line of credit. I know there's talk in the Finance Ministry of taking a loan of five hundred million.''

Agosto threw up his arms in a typical Italian gesture that silently asked: Why not the moon?

"It's a lot, isn't it?'' she said, sipping her wine.

"Too much for me alone, but then, it's too much for Morgan too. I could put together a syndicate—we could probably make a tidy penny.''

Clare nodded.

"You have reservations? I can see that look in your eyes, Clare.''

"Political, not financial,'' Clare answered.

"I read the papers,'' Agosto said. "I know about the Matteotti thing. But he has arrested that man . . . Dumini.''

"Yes, but there are ugly rumors, some demonstrations, and they're all put down with force.''

"Matteotti was a Socialist, I know. The Socialist hordes in the United States are objecting too. But Mussolini still has the backing of the Italian people—do you deny that?''

"Oh, Mussolini has the backing of the people. The cries of 'Il Duce! Il Duce!' drown out all criticism.''

"And you're a critic?''

"I don't know,'' Clare answered honestly. "I haven't met him.''

"He's praised by world leaders and greatly respected by influential people in the United States.''

"I know, but I don't like to see Parliament suppressed, and if he is responsible for eliminating the opposition . . .''

Agosto leaned back and played with his mustache again, a sure sign of his agitation. "This isn't America. Democracy is a very difficult form of government.''

"You believe in it.''

"Of course I do, but it's easier to believe in it if you live in a country where it works. One has to be pragmatic. It's a question of growth and readiness. America is more democratic now than it started out to be. In any case, I'll make my decision after I make a personal assessment.''

"I wouldn't expect anything less,'' Clare replied thoughtfully. I won't challenge him, she vowed. Mama's right: Papa's stubborn, he has to see for himself.

Sunday, August 3, 1924

MILAN

"It's impressive in a cold, sterile way," Clare commented in a whisper as they approached the newly built Fascist headquarters. As Milan was the birthplace of the Fascist movement, the building was more monumental than utilitarian. It was rectangular, eight stories high, and the facade was made entirely of marble. A lengthy row of arches was placed in front of the edifice, and all were square. Surrounding the entire structure were scores of statues, massive modern works, every hero from Caesar to Garibaldi depicted in a toga, his right arm extended in a Fascist salute.

"The statues are in atrocious taste," Clare whispered to her father. She was aware that she was using exactly the same words to describe them as Constanza had.

On the steps a crowd of local Fascist and military dignitaries milled about. They were all uniformed and fairly dripped with medals. But is was General Italo Balbo who met them at the entrance and led them down the marble hall.

"We met at your daughter's wedding reception," he reminded Agosto.

"I remember," Agosto replied.

As they rounded the corner and walked up a wide marble staircase, photographers snapped pictures.

"Why the press?" Agosto asked.

"You're an important man, and when important men visit Il Duce, there are always photographers."

"Bankers don't have high public visibility," Agosto replied, but nonetheless he smiled and waved for the photographers.

A uniformed Benito Mussolini appeared at the top of the stairs. But he wore no medals, save for two war ribbons earned in combat in 1916. He had a distinct military bearing, standing absolutely straight with his arms folded boldly across his chest.

"Countess Sforza-Tonelli!" Mussolini embraced her in a great squashing bear hug. Then he turned to Agosto and did the same. The cameras clicked and the bright lights were nearly blinding on the white marble. Mussolini led them into a reception room. General Balbo followed, but then the great doors were slammed shut and the press was excluded.

"A necessary inconvenience of power," Mussolini said to no one in particular. He turned to Agosto and for a long moment stared into his eyes. "I like you," he announced. "You have strong eyes. I can trust a man with strong eyes."

"Shall I remain, Il Duce?" Balbo asked.

Mussolini shook his head. "I want to talk to Signor Tonelli in private. Why don't you give the Countess Sforza-Tonelli a private tour? Your husband was a good friend," Mussolini confided. "I feel bad that this is the first time we've met."

"Thank you for the flowers and condolences."

"Very sad, terrible to lose a man of Emiliano's competence." He smiled and bowed. "We'll have more than enough time to talk at lunch. Go along with Italo—he can be quite interesting when he tries. . . . Before we begin, Agosto . . . May I call you Agosto?"

"Please do, Signor President."

"I consider myself a man of action. I make decisions, they are carried out. Also, I am not one for cat-and-mouse, as you Americans say. One does not invite a banker to a private lunch-eon unless one wants something. So, to get it out of the way, I want money to help rebuild the Italian economy."

"That's refreshingly frank," Agosto said, grinning.

Mussolini threw up his arms. "But you are not an idiot! A smart man will ask, 'Who is this Benito Mussolini who calls himself Il Duce—the leader! Who is this man who has seized power?' You will ask about the violence and about the parliamen-tary system, you will ask, 'What is this Fascism, and where is Il Duce leading Italy?' I know what's on your mind." Mussolini paused and smiled at Agosto.

"I will answer those questions. I come from the Romagna district, I had humble beginnings, my father was the local blacksmith. We ate little, we lived in poor surroundings. I'm a man of the people, who understands the cries of the workers. But I believe those cries are best answered with good jobs, with opportunities, and with self-discipline. I believe in values and morals—in a man having only one woman. I believe in tradition and I believe in leading Italy back to the glories of the Roman Empire! And I do not countenance the violence, my friend. I know that the mass movement I have formed has factions—that there are evil men who carry out acts in the name of Fascism, but who do not understand the meaning of Fascism. To lead a country like Italy is not an easy task." Mussolini shook his head sadly and thrust out his lower lip. "Garibaldi united the city-states. I must take up where he left off, I must unite the spirit of Italians! No, no, it is not easy." He shook his finger for emphasis.

Mussolini's dark flashing eyes fascinated Agosto. The man cast his charismatic spell like the cloak of night cast darkness. His voice rose and lowered with the nuance of his words. "Italy is factionalized," Agosto agreed. "So are Italian-Americans."

"We are an emotional people—we feel our politics in our guts. Oh, make no mistake, I believe in freedom, but I believe that we must right ourselves first, that we must grow strong physically and morally. Then and only then can we have the fiber to deal with freedom, which offers too many temptations when we are weak and greedy." Mussolini smiled. "Have I answered the questions in your mind, Agosto Tonelli?"

"You answered all, before I asked, and I can think of no more," Agosto admitted.

Mussolini pressed his lips together. "I would like you to consider setting up a five-hundred-million-dollar credit line—I know it's a great deal, but the resources of American banks are great."

"I'd have to put together a syndicate, but I'm certain it can be done."

"Ah! I love men of action. You are certain it can be done! I like that!" Mussolini got up and walked over to Agosto. He slapped him on the back. "We'll join the others for lunch now!"

"There's an exhibition of gymnastics I want you to see," Mussolini said proudly after lunch. "You see, Agosto, we're building a new Italy . . . not just with our souls, but with our bodies. Bravery and fearlessness shall be the hallmark of the new Italian man. With men fashioned of steel, our factories can run twenty-four hours a day, producing goods for the world market. No country will ever insult Italy again, my friend. Our army will be invincible, and the more the world is made aware of that invincibility, the less likelihood that we'll have to enter the field of combat. It might be necessary from time to time to teach the odd lesson—nothing serious, mind you, just a little test of strength and resolve. Don't you agree?"

Agosto thought of the "splendid little war" he'd been in, and for the first time in a long while he thought of Philip Ainsley. "No, I can't agree," he replied.

Mussolini roared with laughter. "Few people disagree with me! At least to my face!"

A dais had been erected in the Parco Sempione and Mussolini, General Balbo, Clare Marina, and her father sat on the platform. In front of the dais was a contingent of more than one hundred young soldiers, standing smartly at attention.

Clare thought the first hour of the exhibition had been an incredible bore. For the most part, it consisted of soldiers running around the track. And at one stage Mussolini himself had joined in, completing three laps. When he returned to his seat, he was not even out of breath.

"I run a longer distance each morning, Contessa Sforza. Running gets the blood circulating. More people should run for health and fitness!"

As the soldiers finished their running, a group broke off from the rest. Some carried hurdles and others carried large numbers of rifles with bayonets in place. The rifles were fixed to the hurdles, bayonets pointing toward the sky.

A captain came to Mussolini. "With your permission, Il Duce, the jumping will begin."

Mussolini gave a wave of his hand, and then, turning to Clare, said, "This is both exciting and inspiring."

To shouts of "*Viva Il Duce!*" the men, now stripped to their shorts, ran toward the post of bayonets. One after another they leapt over them, ran around the field, then leapt again.

Clare watched, her mouth partially open in horror. One slip and any one of the jumpers could be impaled. She thought of little Emil as a young man engaged in this insanity. She felt nauseated and more than a little angry.

At last the mad jumping ceased and the runners came to the platform in close order and raised their right arms in the Fascist salute, and again shouted, "*Viva Il Duce! Viva Il Duce!*" The sound rang in Clare's ears.

Monday, August 4, 1924

PAVIA

The late-afternoon sun shone over the dam site near Pavia. Huge crowds of people sat row on row in hastily erected stands. There were soldiers galore, and schoolchildren summoned to attend, as well as Fascist leaders and their followers from all over the province. The hierarchy of the Catholic Church was also present, and they were clearly delighted not only with the dam but also with Il Duce's presence. This Clare attributed to the strong rumors that Mussolini had begun negotiations with the Vatican to restore lands confiscated in 1870.

Agosto hugged his daughter. "Happy birthday, Clare! Opening the dam today makes it very special."

Clare smiled. "I didn't plan it that way," she replied. Still, she felt strong satisfaction. The dam was three months ahead of schedule, she had floated the bond issue, and Sforza Industries not only had sufficient capital, but she had turned more than half the companies around, placing them in a profit position. From this day forward she would attend the board meetings instead of acting through Signor Catelli. Her head was filled with plans. She would streamline the organization of the twenty-two diverse companies she now controlled, and place them under one major holding company. She had jointly arranged a scheme with American Dollar Lines to bring tourists to southern Italy, having them fill the Sforza-owned hotels there, thus proving the wisdom of not having sold the hotels as Signor Sangallo had suggested. Two major highways had been completed. And today . . . today, she thought, would make it possible for new industries to begin operation, industries which would run on the power supplied by the dam. Two of those industries—a large shoe factory and a textile mill—were funded by the Sforza banking interests. "Yes, Papa," Clare said aloud, "I'm having a good birthday." Her only worry, she conceded to herself, was the government.

The ceremonies began with scores of soldiers marching in long lines, singing while a military band played the Fascist anthem, "Giovanezza." It culminated with cries of "Il Duce! Il Duce!", the Fascist salute, and wild enthusiastic cheers.

Cameras clicked and lights glared. At last the military pageantry subsided and Cardinal Tanuto came forward, followed by a group of priests. He sprinkled holy water ceremoniously into the dam and blessed it. Then, amid a great fanfare, Mussolini led Clare to the main switch, and with his hand atop hers, it was pulled down. In a second the coughing and spitting of huge turbines could be heard, then the rhythm of the machine. The great sluice gates of the dam opened and the river surged through, turning the turbines faster and faster.

A string of light bulbs fashioned in Il Duce's profile lit up as the electricity surged through the wires. The crowd was ecstatic and Mussolini basked in his moment of triumph. "Glorious! Glorious!" he shouted.

The opening of the dam was followed by yet another reception. It was, for Clare, a long, exhausting day that extended late into the night.

*   *   *

"You look rested now," Agosto told her at dinner the next evening.

"And why not? I slept all day."

Agosto sipped his wine. "This is the first time we've been alone since the day I arrived."

"Pomp and more pomp," Clare said in irritation. "Papa, what do you really think?"

"I think Benito Mussolini will lead Italy to glory! I think he's fantastic!"

"Papa! What did he say to you?" Clare was floored by her father's reaction. She had been certain that he wouldn't like Mussolini.

"He answered my questions before I asked them." Agosto lit a cigarette and told Clare of his conversation with Mussolini.

"Oh, Papa. The man is an egotist, he's erratic, he's an actor with a stupid, silly militaristic show! How could you promise such a huge loan? How could you?"

Agosto scowled at her. "You weren't so against it when I arrived."

"That was before I saw that insane gymnastic exhibition. Imagine jumping over bayonets! It was before I saw the hypnotized crowds mindlessly screaming, 'Il Duce! Il Duce!' I hated it. It was all terrible."

"He's right: this country needs discipline. What do you know? You're a woman! Politics is not for women—they're too soft!"

"I know a fake when I see one. This week for the first time I realized how isolated I've been from what's going on in this country. Papa, Mussolini is a dangerous man. So he answered your questions before you asked. He's clever. He knew you wanted to hear those things, and he held a mirror to your thoughts. He said the things you believe, the things you wanted to hear about freedom and workers, and hard work and discipline."

Agosto's face flushed bright red. "You're wrong! You're still a girl and you know nothing of the world of men. I like Mussolini. He's right for this country. I'm not as stupid as you think."

Clare stared into her wine. Tears welled in her eyes. She loved her father more than any person in world except her son. But he was wrong and she wanted to scream and shriek like a child in the face of his stubbornness. She stood up abruptly. "I'm going to bed, Papa! But you think carefully . . . you ask yourself if Mussolini flattered you or if you really believe. You ask yourself, Papa, because I think you're making a mistake."

23

Thursday, August 7, 1924

MILAN

Agosto and Fabiana returned to New York two days after the opening of the dam. Constanza left the same day to close her villa in Venice; she, much to Clare's amusement, had decided to accept Roberto's invitation to visit New York in November. Their attraction to one another was evident, and Clare took great pleasure in her matchmaking.

Clare approached the reception room wondering who would call without notice so early in the morning. "Two men to see you," the butler had announced. Of course he didn't know many of the regular visitors to Villa Sforza—he worked only on Thursdays as a replacement for Giorgio, the regular butler, who had the day off.

"General Balbo," Clare said in surprise, but her eyes did not linger on the general. Instead, she looked at his companion, a tall dashing man with warm brown eyes and a slightly crooked smile that gave him a mischievous expression. He was dressed casually in tan knickers and a tweed jacket, a jaunty silk ascot tied around his neck.

"I hope I won't wear out my welcome at the Sforza home," General Balbo said, bowing from the waist.

"Of course not. It's very nice to see you."

General Balbo straightened. "I come on business. And I assure you I would have called if my business had not arisen so suddenly. Please, let me introduce Signor Alessandro Palma, the former vice-president of Savoia-Marchetti and the first man to pilot the SM-55T, the finest clipper yet to be flown." General Balbo virtually beamed. "Alessandro's an old friend. We flew together in the war, and he's the only man in Italy who has more medals than I do! A genuine daredevil and hero, but also a designer of planes, not merely a pilot."

Clare smiled and gestured for them to sit down. "May I offer you something?" she inquired, hardly able to take her eyes off Signor Palma, who in turn gazed at her warmly.

"A cup of espresso would be welcome," General Balbo answered.

Clare summoned the butler and asked him to bring the espresso.

"Let me explain." General Balbo leaned forward in his chair. "Alessandro is exploring the possibility of beginning his own commercial airline. I'm sure you know such an airline exists between London and Paris, as well as between other important European cities."

Clare nodded, though in fact she knew little of air transport.

"Alessandro flew into Milan yesterday from Rome. For many months he's been in England studying. I can assure you, his qualifications in this area are excellent."

"I'm sure they are," Clare replied.

Alessandro Palma gave General Balbo an amused look. "He's too kind in his praise, Countess. The truth of the matter is, I left Savoia-Marchetti because they weren't moving quickly enough and because I'm an individualist and don't like working for others."

"That's a sentiment I'm familiar with."

Alessandro leaned forward. General Balbo had made his introduction, and now he began to speak for himself. Clare could sense his excitement; his whole body appeared tense, and as he began talking, he warmed to his subject, projecting his own enthusiasm.

"Countess, air travel is going to revolutionize transportation. It'll change the way people live, how they think. How can I describe it's importance? . . . I think it will change the world the way Columbus' voyage did, I think there will come a time when man will be able to fly high enough to see the earth's curvature, when he'll be able to go from Rome to New York in a matter of hours, when, like signals on a telegraph, he'll be able to travel vast distances, circle the planet in the high atmosphere in minutes. It's the wave of the future, Countess, and we who are involved now know we can ride that wave to success." He stared into her eyes. "I know I'm being forward, but I hope you'll forgive me. General Balbo tells me you're young and adventurous, that you have a fine-tuned business sense, and that he thinks you might be a gambler. To be blunt, I have the plans for a highly successful commercial venture. I have some money, but not enough to finance the construction of airports and purchase the necessary planes. And there's still some research to do. I need additional financing."

"Surely the government is interested—it sounds to me like the kind of project Il Duce would jump at."

General Balbo shook his head. "Perhaps in a few years, but not now. He's primarily interested in military aircraft—and not as interested in that as I'd like him to be. No, the development of commercial aviation will have to be done privately, though I imagine the government could be convinced of a need for airfields."

Alessandro Palma watched General Balbo carefully, then turned to Clare. "And there are other problems, Countess. I'm not convinced the Fascists are good for this country. On that point Italo and I disagree. Frankly, even if it were available, I wouldn't want government financing."

"I see," Clare murmured. She felt a surge of admiration for Alessandro Palma. He was very blunt about his views, and he didn't let General Balbo inhibit him one iota. "Of course I'll look at your proposal," she promised.

"Countess, I have to leave Milan tonight and I'll be gone for several weeks. I know this is a terrible imposition, but could you spare me a few hours of your time this morning?"

"The espresso," the butler announced.

General Balbo stood up abruptly. "Even though I'm the one who requested it, I'm afraid I don't have time to drink it." He bowed again and kissed Clare's hand. "I have an important meeting. Can I leave Alessandro in your capable hands?"

"Of course." She turned to Alessandro Palma. "I'll have to cancel my noon meeting with Signor Catelli, but I'm sure he'll understand."

"You won't regret it," Palma replied confidently.

General Balbo smiled. "If he weren't such an old friend, I'd be upset about his political views, but I have faith we'll prove him wrong." With those words and a nod of the head, General Balbo left.

"The military does strange things to men. Look at General Balbo. He never stops running. I can assure you that three years ago he would not have left me alone in the company of such a beautiful woman!"

Clare blushed but did not reply.

Alessandro Palma smiled engagingly. "Indeed, he told me he would take me to an influential widow—a woman who could help me. He certainly did not mention he was taking me to an angel, the most beautiful woman in all Milan."

"Please . . ." Clare could feel the warmth in her face. His eyes all but devoured her and she felt a pleasure she hadn't felt since before Emiliano's death. How lonely she'd been, and even if he was simply flirting, she was enjoying it.

"I'm embarrassing you." He winked at her. "All Italian men are devils," he confessed disarmingly. "Please, let me discuss some of my plans—as an introduction. As I mentioned, I'll be going back to Paris tonight, but I'll be returning to Milan in a month—sooner if you show the slightest interest."

"In your proposal," Clare added mischievously.

He gave her a long, lecherous look. "Or in me," he teased.

Unconsciously Clare ran her hand through her hair. How long had it been since she'd had it seen to? And her dress was quite plain. I'm starting to look like a housewife, she silently lamented. "Let's go into my study," she suggested.

He held out his hand to help her out of her chair. "Let's," he agreed, picking up his briefcase.

Alessandro spread his papers out on Clare's desk. There were plans for planes, for airports, for schedules. There were endless projection figures, advertising budgets, staffing needs. He talked seriously, interspersing his presentation with jokes, with stories, and with talk of the future.

"Business—you can't imagine what it will do for business! Imagine, because flying takes so little time, a man with far-flung interests can visit all his operations, can make a personal impact on his staff. And mail . . . Countess, do you realize what air transport will do for mail?"

"You don't have to call me Countess," Clare told him. "It makes me feel old."

"That you are certainly not!" He smiled at her. "Tell me what to call you."

"Clare Marina."

"For the clear sea. What a beautiful name. But then, it's a name that suits a warm, beautiful woman. Have you ever flown, Clare Marina?"

Clare shook her head.

"It's unbelievable, it's liberating, it's the most exquisite feeling imaginable to be soaring like a bird, diving in the wind, skimming the treetops and soaring above the clouds. You can't imagine how it looks. The land is a panorama, a relief map, it's as if the world is a toy, as if you were the master . . . and then you cut the engines and float on the wind drafts like a gull. There's this incredible silence up there, this feeling of being one with the universe. . . ."

Clare watched him. He was in love with flying and he spoke of it with the fervor of a fanatic. His feeling was contagious, and simply listening to him, she found she wanted to fly, to experience what he had experienced.

He studied her and glanced at his watch. "Will you let me take you out to an early supper? Regrettably I have to leave at seven."

"My heavens, what time is it?"

"Nearly four."

Six hours? They'd been in the study since just after ten. The hours had passed so quickly, and Clare didn't want to say good-bye. "I'd love to go for an early supper, but you must let me change."

He nodded. "I know a special place. We won't know it's afternoon there. It's always alive, always dimly lit, and there's always music. We can drink a little wine, Clare Marina, and have a light pasta. We'll pretend it's a midnight supper . . . we'll pretend I'm not leaving."

Antonio's was just as Alessandro described it—a tiny cellar restaurant with small tables discreetly hidden in alcoves. "It's a place for lovers," he said, squeezing her arm.

They ordered wine and fettuccine, and then, when the Gypsy musicians began to play, Alessandro took her to the middle of the restaurant and danced with her, whirling her about, holding her close. Then he held her by the hands and they twirled in wide circles, as her full skirt billowed and the musicians played a wild Romany tune. "You have the fire of a Gypsy," he told her, laughing, "and the thick luxuriant hair and flashing eyes!"

Alessandro's teasing smile enchanted Clare Marina, and his arms around her waist awakened sensations that had slept since Emiliano's death. His intensity, his love of flying, fascinated her. He drew her close and kissed her hair. "It's time for me to go," he told her. "But, Clare Marina, I'll be back."

Friday, August 22, 1924

NEW YORK

" *Criminalità Fascista! Criminalità Fascista!*" the chanting, angry crowd outside American Federal's branch on Mulberry Street shouted in unison.

"*Il Libro!*" other voices called out. They carried the placards of the Italian Socialist Party of America and they roundly condemned the abduction of Giacomo Matteotti. "He was Italy's Lincoln!" Paolo Tonelli shouted as he stood on the steps of the bank.

"This bank! This bank and all its branches support the murdering Fascist criminals! They lend vast sums of money to the dictator Mussolini! They lend money to buy guns to kill Italian workers! They lend money to pay criminals who murder the leaders of Italian workers!" Paolo raised his arms over his head, and the crowd grew momentarily silent. "The capitalists and Fascists are one and the same animal! Pigs! Matteotti was about to reveal huge bribes paid by an American oil company—bribes paid to Mussolini and his henchmen. That's why Matteotti was abducted. And now his beaten body has been found! This was a planned criminal act. An act instigated by Mussolini!" The crowd roared and was only slightly distracted by the sound of the approaching police sirens.

"Destroy this bank!" Paolo shouted. "Destroy it economically! Don't invest in the future of Fascism!"

The police poured from their cars, firemen attached their hoses to nearby hydrants.

"Break it up!" came the shout from the bullhorns. "Go home! Break it up!"

Paolo, from his vantage point on the steps of the bank, looked across the heads of the crowd. Agosto was standing near one of the police cars, his face tight, tense, and angry.

"That man!" Paolo shouted, pointing toward his brother. "That man supports the Fascists! That's the man whose picture you've seen with Il Duce!" Paolo's voice dropped. "That man . . . my brother."

The fire hoses sprayed into the crowd, and women screamed as the steady, hard stream of cold water battered them, stinging their skin. The police waded into the crowd with their clubs, swinging wildly and indiscriminately.

"You're not a real Italian, Agosto Tonelli! You're one of them! Just because you haven't changed your name to Morgan doesn't mean a thing! Exploiter!"

Those who stood near Paolo took up the chant of "Fascist Criminal! Fascist Criminal!"

But the police moved into the melee, and Paolo was seized as the bitter struggle developed. The sounds of bludgeons on bare heads and cries of anguish filled the summer air. The crowd scattered and men were dragged fighting to nearby paddy wagons.

"My brother!" Paolo shouted as he was dragged past Agosto. Paolo spit on the ground, but one of the police kicked him viciously in the gut, and Paolo doubled over in pain.

Agosto winced and held out his hand in an automatic gesture of momentary conciliation. But Paolo's pain-filled face lifted only momentarily, and Agosto heard him mutter, "I have no brother."

M I L A N

My dear Clare Marina,
I confess immediately to being an incurable romantic. I've always loved Paris, but on this trip I find it empty and boring. I pass flower stalls and think how I would like to surround you with carnations and violets; I hear the mournful love songs of *les chanteuses* and I am filled with desire to see you. I walk along the Seine and think of you. Paris was meant for lovers, not for lonely men on business trips.
Am I wrong to think of you night and day after so brief a meeting three weeks ago? Am I too forward, too quick in my hope that we will see each other again—not on business? I hope not. I have ordered flowers delivered with this note. Regrettably I am detained and will not return to Milan for another week. If I were writing to a lesser woman I could not hope for her to understand my delay, but I know you will because you understand the importance of planning. My research of the commercial flights between Paris and London and between Paris and Berlin is both exciting and necessary. I confess my dreams alternate between you and the realization of Air Italia, a commercial airline that would link Rome and Paris, then Rome and Milan. I envisage the use of twelve-seater aircraft such as those in operation now on Paris–London flights. Have I succeeded in infecting you with my dream, Clare Marina? Did I tell you that flying became my dream when I was a small boy and I first looked at Leonardo da Vinci's sketches of aircraft? Flying is the future, Clare Marina, and your encouragement stays with me as well as the vision of your beauty. I will call you immediately when I return.

Affectionately,
Alessandro Palma

Clare smiled to herself and folded Alessandro's letter. In spite of her distraction with business, she had found herself thinking of him often. The morning they spent together, he had presented his proposal for the building of two small airports and the purchase of two planes. His excitement was indeed infectious, his boyish smile captivated her, yet she was aware of his intensity. Alessandro Palma seemed warm and protective, flirtatious, yet honest. That something between them had clicked immediately was evident, and Clare found herself anxiously awaiting his return so they could get to know each other better.

Wednesday, August 27, 1924

MILAN

"You said you'd phone . . ." Clare stood awkwardly on the threshold of the reception room. Alessandro waited by the settee, looking equally awkward, she thought. There was a moment of silence. It was strange, Clare thought. They'd spent only a day together, but they were looking at each other like two lovers who'd been separated for months.

We've woven fantasies about each other, and now, here we are face to face, not quite certain what to say or how to behave, she thought.

"I loved the flowers . . ." They both burst into laughter simultaneously.

"I have to get to know you . . ." He took a step toward her.

Clare lifted her hands to her head. "You're moving too quickly."

"You don't want to slow down. I think it's called chemistry."

Clare met his eyes as he walked toward her, then closed them as he took her in his arms and kissed her deeply. She felt weak and helpless, just as she had always felt when Emiliano kissed her. But there had been few kisses from Emiliano—there had been so little time.

"Don't fight your feelings, your desires. I wanted to kiss you the first moment I laid eyes on you. Poor Italo! He wouldn't have understood. Too much military discipline. Tell me you didn't feel the same."

Clare remained silent, letting the waves of pleasure roll gently over her. Part of her argued that it was all too sudden, too much pure physical desire, but another voice seemed to draw her to him, saying: Who cares? Enjoy it, give in to it, don't question it or it will be snatched away as Emiliano was.

"I feel like a girl instead of a widow and a mother."

"Do you? You are a girl, too young, too beautiful, and too filled with life to be in perpetual mourning." He suddenly laughed and hugged her. "I'm taking you to dinner," he announced.

"And where are we having dinner?" Clare felt totally disarmed, ready for any adventure of his choosing.

"I have reservations at Passetto."

"That's in Rome!"

"I'm a flier, remember? My plane is only a short ride away. Clare, if we're to know each other, we must know each other's passions. You have to see Italy as I've seen it, to feel the sensation of flight and love it as I do."

"No! Oh, Alessandro, I don't know if I can!"

"It's an extremely safe plane, and I'm one of Italy's better pilots."

"You're not modest, though," she joked.

"Come, come with me now, this moment. Tonight I'll show you all Italy, and it'll be a view few others have ever seen. I know you, Clare Marina. If you'd lived in the fifteenth century you'd have been sailing to the New World! Let me show you a new world, let me show you man's last frontier."

Clare followed him to his waiting car. It was a short drive to Malpensa, where his plane waited.

"Isn't she beautiful!" Alessandro asked as he helped Clare Marina into the cockpit.

Her heart beat wildly as Alessandro pulled on his leather flight jacket and goggles. He tied a long white silk scarf around his neck.

"This is insane," Clare said above the whistling wind that blew through the trees that lined the makeshift runway. "I can't believe I'm here!"

Two members of Alessandro's ground crew spun the propellers and the entire plane shook as the engines caught. Alessandro took it down the long straight runway till its wheels lifted off the ground and they were flying above the treetops.

"How does it feel, Clare Marina? What do you think?" he shouted over the noise of the engines.

"My eyes are closed! And I'm going to freeze!"

"There's a flight jacket behind your seat. And open your eyes—you'll miss the view of the Duomo! I'm going to fly you right over Pisa so you can see the Leaning Tower from the top."

Clare cautiously opened her eyes. "It's exhilarating! I feel like a bird!" She sighed. "It's much higher than George Tilyou's Ferris wheel!"

"Who's George Tilyou? Is he a suitor? Should I be jealous?" Alessandro asked loudly.

"He's a friend of my father's. He owns an amusement park."

"You didn't answer my question. Should I be jealous?"

Clare laughed. "No," she answered. Alessandro was a tease.

"Let me show you what my bird can do! Here we go, my woman!" He pulled back the throttle and they began a vertical climb. Clare fell back against her seat, clutching her seat belt. Above, all she could see was the golden sky of dusk. She felt like Icarus on his flight into the sun. Then, just as suddenly as they had started to climb, the plane went into a tailspin, its nose pointed to the ground, which loomed larger and larger. Clare let out a cry and clutched Alessandro's arm just as he pulled out of the dive and banked the plane on a steadier course.

"Ah, I frightened you! But I like the feel of your clinging to me. Hold on, Clare! Pisa is coming up!"

Alessandro completed an intricate loop, swooping the plane down like a bird of prey coming in for the kill. Again Clare felt as if she would fall through the windshield as the ground came hurtling toward her and they missed a barn roof by what seemed only inches. Then they were aloft again. "You're crazy!" she shouted.

"And you love it!" They whooshed down over the Leaning Tower and circled it. Clare could actually see startled tourists covering their heads, the plane skimmed so close. Again they climbed quickly, and Alessandro banked sharply to the left. He turned to her and winked confidently. "How about another pass at the tower?"

"Oh, dear!" were the only words to escape Clare's lips. The plane was actually sideways, one wingtip pointing to the ground, the other to the heavens. They skimmed between the tower and the baptistry.

"Even Galileo would have been shocked," Alessandro proclaimed.

He again pulled the throttle, and the plane climbed; then he turned it over and Clare hung to her seat for dear life, laughing half in panic, half at the sensation. "No! Not again!"

He laughed. "Only a demonstration! I'll show you Rome right-side-up."

The plane leveled out and below them in the twilight the landscape stretched like a carpet. The villages below them reminded her of the toy miniatures she had played with as a child.

She remembered arranging the little wooden houses and trees on the green lawn and pretending she was a giant.

As they circled Rome, darkness enveloped the sprawling city, and as Rome's inhabitants lit their lamps, lanterns, and candles, it turned into a fairyland, a sea of twinkling light.

During dinner, Alessandro held her hand. "Flying is going to revolutionize travel, and warfare too. But we're slow and stupid, and no one has had the sense to expand. We Italians were the first to use aircraft in war, you know. One of our young pilots made a one-hour reconnaissance flight over enemy positions between Tripoli and al-Aziziyah in 1911 during the Italo-Turkish War. And only nine days later we made the first air bombing raid, dropping grenades on 'Ayn Arah and Tajura. Our Caproni bombers were the finest planes in the last war. But now we're falling behind."

"I'd prefer to think of the possibilities for civilian transport."

Alessandro shrugged. "You don't give war enough credit. We owe a lot to war—advances in technology, medicine . . . What is it you Americans always say, 'Necessity is the mother of invention'? War makes invention necessary."

"War is destructive. But I can't deny the advances."

"Not, alas, in aircraft. Italy had nearly twenty thousand Caproni bombers left over at the end of the war, but there's been a depression in the industry because the powers that be are content to rest on their laurels and fly leftovers instead of experimenting with new models. I want to change that . . . I want to build new planes and train more pilots. And of course I agree, the civilian use of air is all-important. Commercial airlines are going to change everything—how we think about time and distance, where we go, how we plan our lives, even what we eat. I could fly fresh oranges to Russia in the winter, Clare!"

"I'm glad you're not in the air force," Clare said, studying his handsome profile.

"I'm not fond of the Fascists," he confessed.

"You're a close friend of Italo's."

"We go back a long way. We trained together and fought together in the war. Fascism in Italy has even split families, so it's not unusual for two friends to have political differences."

"I hope you enjoyed dinner," Alessandro said, taking her shawl. "And I apologize for my apartment. It's Spartan, but then, I'm seldom here."

Clare looked around. "I didn't know you had an apartment in Rome." The walls were white and the furniture was utilitarian rather than decorative. There were no paintings, but everywhere there were model airplanes.

"My hobby," he explained with a sweep of his hand. "I've had them all made according to the original designs. I have a complete collection of models, from the very first aircraft to the most recent."

"They're impressive."

"I didn't bring you here to examine my toys. I brought you here to drink champagne."

Clare leaned back on his sofa. He returned from another room with a silver ice bucket and a magnum of champagne.

"Are you going to stay in Italy?" he asked suddenly. "I know you don't like Fascism."

"I don't know," Clare answered honestly.

"The future is always a mystery, Clare. We know what Italy is like only today, not what it will be like tomorrow."

"It could be worse," she said, looking into his eyes, which had gone from dancing humor to solemn consideration.

"Or it could be better. Politicians come and go in Italy, but things never change as radically as they appear to on the surface. You have a fortune invested here, and you have the influence and the power to help improve the economy, to build."

He touched her hair and ran his hand over her cheek. He leaned over her and kissed her mouth, beginning softly and increasing the pressure till he felt her lips move beneath his. He ran his hand over her throat. "You're beautiful," he breathed in her ear. "I feel as if I've known you and loved you for a lifetime. I don't want to talk about the economy or about Fascism. I want to take this moment and make love to you."

Clare looked at him and inexplicably felt her eyes fill with tears. His lips were warm and passionate, and she felt the flame Emiliano had once kindled start to burn. Instinctively she put her arms around him, wanting to feel again the comfort she had lost in Pamplona.

Alessandro said no more. He kissed her passionately and touched her intimately. Clare was hardly aware when he unbuttoned her blouse and removed her chemise. His lips on her breasts were soft, arousing, and she quivered with excitement.

He carried her to the bedroom and laid her on the bed, covering her with his own young strong body. He toyed with her hair, ran his finger around her full lips, and kissed her ears.

"You're an exquisite creature, Clare Marina. A treasure."

She moaned as he caressed her, running his hand across her mound and between her legs. His hands were everywhere, and as he touched her, pressing himself to her, it was as if they were again climbing to the heights and floating through the clouds toward the sun. She put her arms around him and lifted herself to him, but he was a slow and deliberate lover. He teased her flesh till she groaned in his arms, and when he entered her, she moved against him, murmuring words of passion.

They were climbing, climbing, and she whispered, "Now," but still he waited. Then it was as if they were diving again, plunging together into the depths of ultimate pleasure.

Saturday, August 30, 1924

MILAN

All morning Clare lay in bed daydreaming. When she closed her eyes she could feel Alessandro's hands on her, could relive the ecstasy he brought her, savor the memory of his soft lips, his words of love, his quiet promises. They had spent two glorious days together and he'd flown her back to Milan, going on to Turin himself for a business meeting.

When she finally climbed out of bed, she stood before the mirror for a long while looking at her face; she felt renewed, suddenly alive, she felt like singing and dancing about. "I'm shameful," she announced, whirling about. "I allowed myself to go on a spur-of-the-moment flight to Rome . . . I did it knowing full well I'd allow Alessandro to seduce me, and I loved it!"

The knock on the door startled Clare. But then, she reminded herself, it was noon. "Come in," she sang out, wrapping herself in her fluffy negligee.

"There's a phone call, signora. It's General Italo Balbo. He says it's most important."

Clare smiled. This morning she felt so good she might even have spoken to Mussolini himself. "I'll be right there," she replied.

"Good morning, Clare Marina." General Balbo's voice crackled over the phone line. Somehow Clare could picture him sitting in Fascist headquarters surrounded by the poor taste and sterility of that marble cave. Still, she reminded herself, she owed him one thing: he had introduced her to Alessandro.

"There's an important dinner tonight," General Balbo told her. "It's for the British consul and several visiting industrialists. Would you attend?"

Clare frowned into the phone. "Would you attend" sounded

somehow like a command, and she toyed for a moment with the idea of saying no. But then, Alessandro had flown to Turin and there was no particular reason not to attend. "Yes, I'm free," she replied.

"May I pick you up at seven-thirty, then?"

"All right," she gave in.

Dinner for fifty guests began exactly at eight. Clare sat next to General Balbo, and on her right was the British consul, Mr. Lionel Wylie-Jones. During the seven-course meal the conversation was light, but as after-dinner brandy was served, it grew more serious in nature.

"Beastly business, this Matteotti affair," the consul intoned, shaking his head in disapproval. "It'll cost Mussolini dearly." The consul spoke near-perfect Italian, but he spoke with a distinctive Oxbridge accent, translating English words such as "dearly" literally.

"What are you implying?" Balbo asked.

"Well, that he was set upon by those who . . . well, needed to get rid of him. Mind you, that's been said since June, but now that they've found the body . . . well, there can be no doubt."

"It's terrible," Clare put in. She'd been unnerved by the incident, though not surprised. She had, in fact, decided to discuss the whole affair with Balbo later.

"Isn't it a fact, General," the consul persisted, "that there exists within your Ministry of Justice something called the *ceka*, organized for the sole purpose of taking punitive measures against those who oppose the government?"

Balbo laughed lightly, his facial expression displaying nothing short of total amusement. "The *ceka*? That's something that exists in Russia. I wouldn't deny that there are a few young Fascists who might give government opponents a strong dose of castor oil, but no, there is no organized group such as you suggest."

"Then you deny your government was involved in any way?"

Balbo didn't even looked distressed. "I know it wasn't," he said with absolute confidence. "After all, the thug Dumini is already in jail, and he wasn't even a Fascist-party member."

Clare listened to General Balbo intently.

"There are hoodlums everywhere, my friend," Balbo said to the consul. "Even in England."

After dinner General Balbo drove Clare home.

"You seem troubled, Clare Marina."

Clare pulled her shawl around her and settled back against the leather seat of the car. "I'm distressed with the continuing violence," she said pointedly, aware that she used the word "distressed" when she meant "disgusted." But Italo Balbo was an important man, close to Mussolini, and Clare deemed it wise not to be entirely forthright.

"I'd like to be able to explain Italian politics to you," he said quietly. "You're American, and you're a romantic, as are all Americans. They believe in the parliamentary system—in that elusive word 'democracy.' Democracy is a luxury, Clare. Mussolini hates the violence within his own party, as I hate it. I'm a soldier, Clare. I'd fight on a battlefield with honor, but I don't approve of kidnappings and beatings. That kind of thing results in rule by thugs and criminals. I can assure you that Mussolini doesn't want that kind of government, but there are those who do evil deeds in his name. But he'll root them out. When he's consolidated his power, he'll be able to run this country properly and return full powers to the Parliament."

"I wish I could believe that."

"I must confess I told a half-truth tonight."

"To the British consul?"

"Yes. The Matteotti affair is very serious. There'll be resignations in the government, and the scandal will reach Il Duce himself."

"There was government involvement?"

Italo shrugged. "Not in unison, I assure you. Il Duce has always said that the right wing of the party was as much a danger as the left-wing opposition. But the Matteotti affair will affect our foreign image and it'll reach high places."

"Why do you tell me this?"

"I'll be completely honest. You're an influential woman, you inherited your late husband's fortune. Sforza Industries, Sforza banking interests—they're very important to the economy, and thus very important to the government."

"In a dictatorship they could be confiscated," Clare said plainly.

"Il Duce would never do that. It would deeply affect Italian relations with banking interests in America and Britain and would inhibit foreign investment that's desperately needed. Frankly, such a move would create more problems than it would solve."

"So the remaining choice is to convince me to remain in Italy and to accept what's going on."

"I would simply prefer to ask you to be patient and wait for the return to normalcy."

Clare didn't answer. Balbo's Fiat turned into the circular drive and hummed to a stop.

"Are you going to remain in Italy?" he pressed.

"I couldn't leave immediately in any case," she hedged, realizing with clarity, for the first time, that her position was obviously a matter of real concern in certain government circles.

"What does that mean?" General Balbo asked, a hint of near-panic in his tone.

"It means I have no choice other than patience," Clare said wearily. Let him report to his superiors, she thought, let him think what he wants to think. Everything about this conversation required thinking out.

"Be as wise as I know you to be," Balbo said, kissing her hand.

Clare nodded and uneasily glanced up to the bedroom window where she knew her infant son was sleeping peacefully. Whatever decisions I make, she thought, must be made with Emil's future in mind. As she walked toward the front door, General Balbo at her side, she thought of Alessandro. She wanted the comfort of his arms, the distraction of the pleasure they gave each other, and she desperately wanted to talk to him, to confess her fears and discuss the future with someone who wasn't a Fascist.

Monday, September 1, 1924

ROME

General Italo Balbo's dark eyes flashed with amusement and that knowing look that men give one another when they share tales of female conquests.

"Another brandy, Alessandro?"

Alessandro slumped on the sofa and fingered his empty glass as if asked to make a weighty decision.

"It's certainly not the most unpleasant assignment you ever had," Italo Balbo said somewhat sarcastically.

"Not at all," Alessandro replied thoughtfully. "That, of course, is the difficulty. She's not only beautiful and intelligent but also very vulnerable."

"Precisely why you were chosen. I suspected you'd be able to put your heart into your work." Balbo grinned.

"I'm a pilot. I don't enjoy the role I'm playing."

"From your attitude I'd say it was less of a role every day. I'd say you were thoroughly enjoying the charms of our lovely

American resident. Tell me, does she excite easily? Are her breasts as lovely as they look beneath her clothes?''

"Shut up! I may have to do this, but I won't discuss her with you!" Alessandro scowled and held out his glass, which Balbo refilled.

"Ah, you see, you're perfect! I knew she'd fall for sober intensity, your fine wit, and your ever-handsome face. I personally told Il Duce you'd have her in bed the second time you saw her and that within months she'd agree to marry you."

"We haven't discussed marriage."

"But you will. Indeed, you will discuss it quite soon. Once the two of you are wed, you become the child's guardian, and Sforza Industries will be safely returned to Italian control."

Alessandro sipped his brandy. "I'd never have done this willingly, It's low and vile."

Balbo lifted his hands in a gesture of surprise. "Low and vile! I find you a rich, beautiful wife who's obviously good in bed, and you call it low and vile?"

"I want to see my family."

"I've told you time and time again. They're perfectly happy and contented. They're living in style at the state's expense. Once you're married, you can have a family reunion. Look on the bright side. You'll build and control Italy's first commercial airline, you'll have a stunning and loving woman, and you'll have your family around you."

"You took my family, and you know I wouldn't do this otherwise."

"Insurance for your continued cooperation, my friend. You'll have a life of comfort and happiness, the realization of a dream, and the government will not have to run the risk of seeing vast quantities of capital taken out of the country."

"What if she doesn't want to marry me?"

"Don't be absurd. I saw her the day after you slept with her. Ha! I know that look on a woman's face and in her eyes. She's in love, she radiates it. Women are always more attractive in the first bloom of sexual satisfaction, you know. There's a kind of animalism about them, an aura of sexuality. I myself found her more attractive. I could feel it when I was with her."

"Why, then, aren't you doing this?"

"Oh, she would never accept me. She knows how close I am to the government. I'm a military man, and she knows I'm a dedicated Fascist. No, I come with too much political baggage, whereas you come with none at all."

"She may be interested in me only sexually."

Balbo shook his head. "I chose you because you're real,

because you do have a passion for flying, because you do want your airline. She's attracted to dreamers, to men who want to do things. She's not the type to have mere sexual dalliances. No, no, I congratulate myself on my selection. You two will have a long, happy, and loving marriage. And much to my relief, the Italian government will be spared the choice of losing much money or doing something highly undiplomatic."

"Which would they have chosen?"

"Losing the money, I suspect." Balbo smiled and raised his glass. "But then, we don't have to think about that anymore, do we?"

24

Saturday, September 6, 1924

MILAN

The sun filtered through the crack in the heavy brocade draperies of Clare Marina's bedroom. She lay on the bed, her transparent nightdress half off her shoulder, her hair damp wih perspiration from lovemaking.

Alessandro leaned over her, his eyes intent. "I love watching you. I love the expression on your face."

She smiled and stroked his cheek, rough and bristly since he hadn't shaved. "It's good to have you back, good to know that from now on you'll be staying in Milan."

He collapsed back on the bed, his arm still beneath her. "It's good for me too. I'm tired of traveling, tired of having no roots. Besides, when I'm away I can't concentrate on anything but coming back to you. I can't get enough of you, Clare."

She smiled and turned toward him, running her hand over his hairy chest. "You make me happy, because I feel secure with you. I need you to make love to me, I need you to talk with. . . . Sometimes I feel I can't trust anyone. Oh, Alessandro, I don't know what to make of it all, it's so unsettling. I can't stand the violence and the constant marching of the Black Shirts. Some of them are only children. What's the point of it all?"

"They say it's discipline. You know the Fascist philosophy: strong bodies, strong minds."

"I *don't* know the Fascist philosophy. I can't find *any* philosophy in Fascism, save militarism. I've seen that so-called discipline. They're training people to die without giving it a second thought—jumping over bayonets, saluting and shouting mindless phrases. And what about killing the parliamentary opposition? Matteotti was no Communist, he was no danger to Italy."

"I hate it as much as you do. But I have to concede that there is more employment."

"For party members," Clare replied tersely. "God, I'm so glad you're here—sometimes it seems to me you're the only one I know who isn't a Fascist or a soldier. Even the Church has fallen in line. They believe Mussolini will return their confiscated property and declare the Vatican independent."

"Everyone makes compromises with themselves, it's a basic human weakness."

"I'm making them," Clare said dejectedly. "Every shop steward in Sforza Industries is now a party member. There's nothing I can do about it."

"I have to believe that once things improve, people will demand a return to the parliamentary system, that the Fascists will lose control."

"You want to believe it," she replied.

"Yes, I want to believe it, just as I want to believe you truly love me."

Clare looked at him, a sadness in his eyes. "I do," she quickly said. "Oh, I do love you."

"Enough to become my wife?"

Clare sighed and moved even closer to him. "I think so," she answered honestly. "It's only that we've known each other such a short time."

"Are you still in love with Emiliano Sforza?"

"I don't know. . . . I can't explain how I feel. I still think of him. I did love him, I admired him . . . but in all truth, I'm not sure that if he'd lived we would have been happy. He always promised he'd involve me in the business, but I'm not certain now he really would have."

"And business and banking are your first love."

Clare nodded. "But not my only love."

"Will you marry me?"

"I love you, but you must give me some time, Alessandro. Now that you're back in Milan for good, we can see each other more often. We must be sure, very sure."

"I suppose I shall have to find an apartment, now that your sister-in-law is coming back to Milan. We can't go on being together here."

Clare frowned. "Did I tell you Constanza was coming back?" When? she thought to herself. He'd arrived late last night, and she'd only just received Constanza's cable that she was returning to Milan to stay until she went to New York at Christmas.

"You mentioned it last night."

"Oh." Clare thought, but could not remember.

Sunday, September 7, 1924

MILAN

Constanza descended the stairs like a princess, paused in the hall and looked around, then turned to Clare Marina. "I'm all unpacked. It's wonderful to be back here. Venice is so confining."

"Did you look in on Emil?"

"Of course! My heavens, he's growing by the day. Nurse is feeding him just now and his face is all covered in cereal, so I'll wait to hug and kiss him."

Clare laughed lightly. "Mealtime is a bit messy."

"Well, come, sit down with me and tell me everything," Constanza urged.

"Are you going to tell me everything?"

"Naturally. Roberto's been writing almost daily."

"You could go to New York before Christmas, you know."

Constanza's expression feigned disdain. "One mustn't appear overanxious, though I have decided to sail the first of November. Now, you tell me about this young man."

"Alessandro. . . . He's . . . he's turned out to be everything I'd hoped he'd be."

"You're blushing. But then, you should. You're grist for the gossip mill. Rumors of your romance have even reached Venice. I've even heard he proposed."

"What?" Clare studied Constanza. Was she fishing, or had she actually heard such a rumor?

"Constanza, I don't know where you heard such a thing. I realize the aristocracy has little else to do but entertain itself with gossip, but—"

"Oh, my! I didn't hear it at a cocktail party. I heard it from General Balbo. He was in Venice and he called on me. Frankly, he was rather strange. He seemed to think I'd be overjoyed at the prospect. Either that or shocked that you would consider marriage so soon. He actually delivered this little lecture to me about the fact that you were young and alone and needed a husband."

Clare sank into the chair and stared at Constanza. "General Balbo hasn't been in Milan since August 10th! How on earth does he know so much about my personal life?" She felt her irritation rising.

403

Constanza shrugged. "Is it all that important? After all, he did introduce you two. Perhaps your Alessandro spoke with him."

Clare shook her head. "Oh, I don't think so. Besides, I haven't said yes, though admittedly I wanted to."

Constanza too sat down and leaned over toward Clare Marina. "Good. You should give marriage a lot of thought. I hope you won't mind my giving you some advice."

"No, I don't mind. I might not take it, but I don't mind your giving it."

"It's hard to say these things, but you do have to consider Emil's future and your own. You're a very wealthy woman, Clare. Your Alessandro isn't wealthy. He may be everything you believe him to be, but he isn't wealthy."

"Oh, Constanza! Are you suggesting Alessandro is a fortune-hunter?"

Constanza shook her head vigorously. "I'd be the last to say true love couldn't be the only motive, but, Clare, you're vulnerable. Under Italian law Alessandro would take charge of the estate—you know women have no rights in this country. I just want you to be sure, to be certain. There's too much at stake."

"I'm certain I love him, certain he loves me."

"That's not enough. For Emil's sake, you have to know."

"How can I know? I can only feel it's right."

"You can test him."

"Oh, Constanza. This is life, not a Shakespearean comedy."

Constanza sighed. "It wouldn't hurt to tell him you've signed over the estate and made your father Emil's legal guardian. If he truly loves you, it won't make a bit of difference."

"I couldn't lie to him."

"Look at you! You're hard as nails in the boardroom, but not when you're in love. All right, I won't say any more."

"I appreciate your concern."

"I know that. I just want you to be careful."

Clare smiled. "I always am."

B R O O K L Y N

"Paolo's dead." Agosto spoke the words as if he didn't believe them. He sat on the edge of Cecilia's bed and she held his hand. "I should have intervened, I should have stopped them!'' His voice rose and he stared at the coverlet on the bed, his face a mask of pure anguish.

"Agosto, it's not your fault." Cecilia's breathing was labored, but she squeezed his hand.

"It *is* my fault. I should never have called the police."

"They'd have come anyway—you know that. The police don't tolerate lawlessness."

"They beat him." Agosto shook his head. "I saw them beat him." He ran his hand through his hair and bit his lower lip so hard Cecilia thought he would draw blood. "He died of internal injuries to his liver caused by that beating. I might as well have killed him myself!"

"That's not true. Agosto, you always tried to help Paolo. You gave him a job."

"I failed him."

"You didn't. Agosto, you're a good man."

Agosto shook his head. "I don't know . . . I don't know why I didn't intervene, Cecilia. I'm responsible. I don't know, maybe Paolo was right for the wrong reasons, maybe I've forgotten what I set out to do. Cecilia, help me!" Great tears fell out of Agosto's eyes and he collapsed against her, sobbing incoherently. "He was family. I should have stopped them! God will punish me, Cecilia, God will punish me!"

Monday, September 22, 1924

MILAN

Alessandro's apartment on the Corso Verselli was both more spacious and warmer than his previous apartment in Rome. Though his original furniture was still in use, colored cushions and two chairs had been added. Print draperies gave it brightness, and some paintings now augmented his model-plane collection.

Clare sat in front of the mirror and brushed her hair. "It's all tangled from the wind," she complained.

"It's beautiful. I love to watch you brush your hair. I want to watch you brush it every day for the rest of my life."

"You're always flattering me. Sometimes I think you're just a tease."

"At least you smiled. I haven't been able to coax a smile out of you for days. But I know you must still be upset about your uncle's death."

Clare inhaled deeply. "Not in the way you think. The last time I saw my uncle I was very young. I'm worried about how it happened and I'm worried about my father's reaction. Paolo and my father were deeply estranged, but my father still loved him. They were, after all, brothers."

"Your father's a strong man—at least he has the reputation of being a strong man."

Clare turned away from the mirror to face Alessandro. He seemed troubled and preoccupied. "There's more," she said hesitantly.

He gently touched her shoulder. "Tell me. I want to share everything with you . . . I want to know all about your family."

"It's not about my family. I've wanted to talk with you for days, but you seemed depressed yourself."

He smiled. "It was nothing, just creative block. I was having some trouble with my plane design. Tell me what's bothering you."

"My mail—I'm sure it's being opened. And I'm sure I'm followed."

"Oh, Clare! You can't be serious!"

He looked at her steadily with his brown eyes, and for the first time in their relationship Clare suddenly felt he wasn't being genuine. He didn't sound surprised and he didn't sound shocked.

"I *am* serious," she insisted. "And angry. Last night Italo Balbo phoned from Rome and told me—didn't invite me, *told* me—to attend a state reception for General Primo de Rivera next month."

"Why does he want you there?"

"Presumably to impress the dear general. He was a friend of Emiliano's. And I am sure about my mail. Sometimes I feel they know everything about me, and you too."

"I think you're letting the political situation affect you too much. Still, it is troubling."

"Alessandro, tell me how General Balbo knew you'd asked me to marry you the day after you proposed." Clare looked steadily at him, and for a single instant she thought she saw real surprise, but then he laughed. "I suppose he knew because I called him the week before to thank him for introducing us and I told him I was going to propose."

Clare turned back to the mirror. "I'm sorry, I'm behaving like a child. Don't misunderstand. I love you and trust you. I'm just being made a little nervous."

Alessandro leaned over and kissed her hair. "Come let me make love to you," he whispered. "I want you . . . I need you, Clare Marina."

Friday, October 10, 1924

MILAN

October 1, 1924

Dear Clare,

Your papa and I miss you a great deal, and how I wish I could see little Emil! His pictures are adorable. I think he looks like your father.

I am supposed to tell you that your father is divesting himself of his Italian investments and has backed out of the syndicate arranging the loan. He only mumbles that he doesn't like what is going on in Italy, but I think it has a lot to do with Paolo's death. He has not forgiven himself. I do not pretend to understand these matters, but I know you do. Clare, is it so bad there? I do read the papers and I know there's lots of trouble, and your father says you are opposed to the regime. I worry about you all the time. I wish you could come home for Christmas, but I know you have many responsibilities now that you have fully inherited Sforza Industries.

Roberto told me that Constanza Sforza is coming to New York in November. Clare, could she bring Emil for a short visit? It's terrible to have a grandson you haven't seen. I know he's still tiny, but Fabiana will take good care of him, and so will I.

Your brother is fine. He is doing better at college now. Tina goes out a great deal, and Maria doesn't like that at all. I'm afraid I don't have any other news, but please do consider sending Emil.

Love,
Mama

Clare put her mother's letter down. Clearly it too had been opened. They were certainly inefficient: the envelope flap had been slightly ripped and glue applied rather sloppily. "Oh, Papa," Clare said out loud. "You're such a stubborn man, you couldn't write yourself and tell me about your decision." She half-smiled. It was because of the argument they'd had after the dam opening. "Stubborn," Clare mumbled. She shook her head.

Paolo was family, and the reality of his death had clearly affected her father, who now saw the dangers of Fascism and probably understood her feelings better as a result. Fascism was evil—beatings, kidnappings, and murder—and the long arm of Mussolini's Italy was reaching into the United States, dividing Italians and causing them to turn on one another just as they did in Italy. It was a terrible irony: Paolo and Matteotti had died the same way, and the ocean her father had once told her isolated America now seemed small indeed. And they know, she thought. They know you've divested yourself of your Italian holdings and they know I'll probably follow suit.

Tuesday, November 18, 1924

MILAN

"I'll miss you when you're in Rome." Alessandro kissed her neck hungrily and nuzzled her ear.

"Believe me when I tell you I don't want to go."

"I know you don't. Clare, it's been months—I need to know. When will you marry me? I want to be living with you, not having you sneak away to my apartment like this."

His hands touched her intimately, and again, as always, she was filled with conflicting desires. His fondling set her nerve endings on fire; he was gentle, yet firm, a slow, deliberate lover who sensed her needs and then satisfied them. It was so easy to lose herself in him, but she fought for control, telling herself that the very strength of the physical attraction made it imperative that she be doubly cautious.

I wasn't hesitant when Constanza left, she thought. "Take Emil to New York with you, and don't bring him back unless I personally write," she had instructed her sister-in-law. Nor had she lacked clarity of mind yesterday when she transferred all her liquid assets to New York and instructed Signor Catelli to find a buyer for Sforza Industries. And then there was the letter she'd given to the American consul, the letter that was being sent to New York and which was to be turned over to the New York *Times* if anything unusual happened. The letter was deliberate and well-thought-out, the culmination of weeks and months of suspicion. Unquestionably those who followed her and opened her mail knew she had transferred her liquid assets; they knew she had visited Senior Catelli too, but then, she often visited him.

"I think I'm insulted. Usually when I caress you, you moan and move closer . . ." Alessandro's voice broke into her thoughts.

"I'm sorry, Alessandro, there is something you should know."

"Yes, my darling."

Even as he answered her she could feel the pressure of his hands, the weight of his body as he half-leaned across her. She looked past his handsome face at the ceiling . . . the room, his room was so familiar. I love him, she thought. But Constanza is right, I have to know, I have to be sure. "I've transferred the ownership of Sforza Industries to my father," she said slowly, listening to her own lie and wondering just how convincing it was. If he was in any way connected with those who followed her, he would know it was a lie. . . . She hadn't been to her father's lawyers, and transfers took weeks. Alessandro's reaction was not immediate, it was in slow motion. He seemed to lift up and away from her, his face pained, surprised, and confused all at once.

"You couldn't have!" he finally blurted out in a shocked tone. He didn't say it doesn't matter, or even ask why. Clare closed her eyes at the sight of his face, the allure of his strong shoulders, the strength of his tan broad chest. His tone, his expression . . . they revealed too much. There had been a need to know, a need to test, but now suspicion flooded over her.

"Why couldn't I?" she asked, struggling with the words. "Tell me, Alessandro, why couldn't I have transferred Sforza Industries to my father? Do you know what I do every day, whom I see, how I run the business?" She could feel the tears forming in her eyes, as an overwhelming sense of betrayal overcame her. "I trusted you . . ." she wailed.

There was absolute silence. Then: "You don't know what you've done!" His voice was half-angry, half-agonized. She heard him dressing and she didn't open her eyes. Then she heard him stomp across the floor and slam the door.

Wednesday, November 19, 1924

B R O O K L Y N

Cecilia cradled Emil in her arms and softly hummed a lullaby to him. Then, seeing that he was fast asleep, she kissed him on the cheek. *"Mi molto poco bambino,"* she whispered.

Constanza smiled. "He's adorable, and he was so good on the trip."

Cecilia turned. "You've brought me the best Christmas present I could have." She wiped a tear from her eye. "I only wish Clare were here too."

"I'm sure she'll be home soon." Constanza fought to hide her feelings. Cecilia wasn't well, but she'd promised not to tell anyone about Clare's situation in Italy.

Cecilia closed the door to the bedroom and took Constanza's arm. "Has Roberto proposed? Have you set the date?"

Constanza blushed. "In the spring," she confirmed. "I feel like a schoolgirl. I'm so old to be getting married."

Impulsively Cecilia hugged her. "You're never too old to get married."

"I feel as if my life's been given back to me," Constanza confessed. "I'm about to have a husband, and I seem to have acquired a family."

"You've changed," Cecilia told her.

Constanza shook her head. "No, I've returned to what I once was, and I owe that to Clare Marina."

Cecilia sighed. "I'll be glad when she comes home. Agosto doesn't realize it, but he needs her."

"You need her too," Constanza suggested.

"Oh, you mustn't tell her, Constanza. Promise me you won't tell her how sick I am. She'd worry too much."

Constanza studied Cecilia. She was terribly frail and clearly had difficulty breathing. But seeing Emil had temporarily revived her, and sometimes she spent hours by his little crib just talking to him. "I won't tell her," Constanza promised. "But you should."

Thursday, November 20, 1924

R O M E

The reception for General Primo de Rivera and the Spanish monarchs was a glittering state dinner held at Quirinale Palace. Dressed elegantly in white, Clare Marina thought she could feel the hostile stares of Mussolini's inner circle of confidants when she entered the room with her escort, General Balbo. Balbo himself exuded a strange mixture of Italian charm and cold restraint. Clearly he had spoken to Alessandro. Just as clearly, he and the others knew she had transferred her liquid assets and ordered Sforza Industries sold.

"It was good of you to come," Balbo said, pressing her arm a bit too tightly. "Especially given your views."

"I was ordered to attend," Clare said coolly.

"Because Emiliano Sforza was a good friend of General de Rivera, the general asked personally for you to be here."

"Well, I am here," Clare said, "against my better judgment." General Balbo retorted only with a stony stare that as much as said: Hold your tongue and be careful.

Clare and General Balbo were placed at the head table with General de Rivera, his son, José Antonio, King Alfonso, the queen, King Victor Emmanuel of Italy, and of course Il Duce.

Clare was seated between General de Rivera and his son, who was the very antithesis of his blustering father. The general was boisterous and gregarious, while José Antonio appeared to be a serious young man with a dark and brooding personality.

General de Rivera loved women, and Clare fought her apprehensions, trying desperately to make pleasant conversation. What was it Roberto Marcucci always said? "Business and politics are like poker—hold your cards close to your chest."

The moment she was seated, General de Rivera poured her some wine and began talking about their previous meeting, about the coup d'état he'd engineered almost a year ago in Spain, and about his plans for Spain's glorious future. Clare Marina was grateful for his monologue, since it allowed her to ignore General Balbo's carefully tempered antagonism.

General de Rivera quickly drained his glass of wine. "My sincere condolences," he said seriously; then, leaning over: "What do you think of my lawyer son?"

Clare didn't know how to answer, since José Antonio was seated next to her. "You must be proud of him," she finally murmured.

"A lawyer! Proud of a lawyer? Spain is a nation of warriors, not lawyers. It wasn't lawyers who drove the Moors from our shores. It wasn't lawyers who conquered Mexico and Peru."

Clare frowned. "I think if you look into your history books, General, you'll discover that Hernán Cortés was in fact a lawyer and that he studied at Salamanca."

But the general was too drunk to be concerned. "An exception!" he shouted. He pointed to the Spanish king, who sat with the Italian king and queen at the center of the guests. "He calls me 'his Mussolini' and I call him 'my Victor Emmanuel'!" Primo de Rivera roared at his own humor while the two monarchs seemed to share a silent embarrassment.

Clare felt uncomfortable. General de Rivera was a bore, and in spite of his earlier comments about Mussolini and the Fascists being "rabble," he was now openly courting a close relationship with Il Duce. Nonetheless, she thought, his adoration of Emiliano, his insistence that I be here, may be a protection. Certainly, she thought, the evening would not go by without a conversation with Il Duce, and that conversation she had prepared for well. She drank slowly and carefully. I need all my mental faculties, she reminded herself. I need to be calm and deliberate. Above all, I need to make it clear that I hold the cards.

Toward the end of the evening, General Balbo took her arm and whispered, "As you might have suspected, Il Duce wants to speak with you."

"We do have things to say to each other," she said, refusing to become flustered. Cat-and-mouse, Clare thought as they approached Mussolini. He looked almost benevolent as he kissed her hand. "How is your son?"

"Very well," Clare answered.

Mussolini eyed her up and down slowly, and Clare felt a rush of apprehension. His eyes were dark, penetrating.

"And how is your good father?"

"Well," Clare replied, feeling even more edgy. But smiling, she added, "You should know as well as I."

Il Duce pressed his lips together and his fat cheeks seemed to puff out like a cobra before the strike. "We have our loan, but I hear that Agosto Tonelli no longer heads the syndicate that arranged it. Il Duce doesn't like to lose friends, and your father's backing out seems to have something to do with the slanderous accusations made about my involvement in Matteotti's death."

"I know nothing about it," she replied unflinchingly.

Mussolini expelled the air in his cheeks and put his hands on his hips. "Italy might want further loans, so I shouldn't like to think a door is closed. I should remind the Countess Sforza that she has interests in Italy, many interests. I'm personally taking the trouble to tell you that Matteotti was a fool who didn't have the best interests of this country at heart, as I do. I know best, Countess. Il Duce is never wrong."

"I know very little of the whole affair," she lied. "But, Mr. President, I do not like being threatened and harassed. I'm liquidating my interests in Italy and taking my money home. My son is already in New York, Mr. President, and should anything happen to me, or if attempts should be made to restrain me from taking what is rightfully mine out of the country, a letter will be delivered to my father and to the New York newspapers. In the event of its publication, I can easily predict that a great many doors will be closed to Il Duce. Perhaps all of them.''

Mussolini's reaction was immediate. His face clouded over, his square jaw thrust forward in anger, and his dark eyes bore through her. But he kept his voice under control. Rather than shouting, he hissed at her, an ominous low insult. "You are a mere girl. You have no right to speak to Il Duce this way. I could—''

"Do many things,'' Clare said evenly. "But you're smart enough to know I'm not worth the scandal . . . especially now,'' she stressed.

Mussolini almost seemed to quiver, as if he were fighting for control; then his expression changed. It was as if he were a chameleon suddenly moved from a dark background onto a gray slab.

"You could have married and stayed in Italy, you could have been part of a new Italy, part of our glorious new beginning.''

Clare shook her head. "No,'' she whispered. "It's not new. There's nothing new in terror, force, and murder.''

Il Duce's moods were many, and she felt as if she'd seen at least three in a matter of minutes. Now a strange sadness filled his face—sadness and shock. "You don't like me,'' he muttered.

"I'm leaving,'' Clare said, feeling suddenly weak and tired. Ego. She'd actually wounded his ego. He needed adoration, he fed on the shouts of "Il Duce!'' But he needed more than the shouting masses; he needed the undying loyalty and adoration of every person he encountered.

"Go home to America,'' Mussolini said, pulling himself up straight. "Go home and tell them I'm generous, that I even let women insult me.''

Clare looked at the tile floor. "I wish Italy well,'' she said, turning. Sadness filled her. God knew where this man would take the country; she could only pray it would survive, for Mussolini appeared to be in a battle with Italy's history. His ego demanded he supersede it, bury past glories, and enshrine his own deeds.

IV

1926–1932

25

Friday, March 12, 1926

NEW YORK

A collage of memories flooded Clare Marina's thoughts. For the most part the last sixteen months had been filled with anxiety, work, and loneliness. It had taken her six months to close her house in Milan, another three to close Villa Sforza on Lake Como. And during all that time, she was compelled to attend meeting after meeting in her efforts to divest herself of Sforza Industries. She dared not leave Italy before the money had all been safely transferred, and she dared not have Emil brought back. And each day the atmosphere in Italy grew worse. Political parties were banned, public meetings were forbidden, individual freedoms were denied. Then, in the midst of her final negotiations to sell Sforza Industries, her mother died. Clare couldn't go home and she mourned alone, grateful only that Emil was there and that her mother had had the final comfort of being with him.

Then at last the final business papers were signed, and Clare, tired and strained, fled to the French Riviera to recuperate. Constanza and Roberto brought Emil, there was a tearful reunion, and Clare settled down for seven months, basking in the warmth of the Côte d'Azur, getting to know Emil, and enjoying the social life of Cannes. But as her strength returned, Clare grew bored with the endless parties, the gossip, and the reporters who seemed to follow her everywhere. Anthony came in April and begged her to come home. "Papa's not the same since Mama died," he pleaded. "Clare, you have to come home. He's ignoring business, and he's depressed all the time." It was the excuse she needed, and, she acknowledged, for the first time she felt her father might give in, might accept her as a full working partner in the management of the vast Tonelli holdings. I'm older, she told herself. I'm a widow, I'm wealthy in my own right, and he needs me.

Emil, who was nearly two, clutched the side of Clare's deep blue woolen skirt. His tugging jolted her back to reality, the reality that she was coming home.

She bent over and touched her son's tousled hair. "You're not wearing your cap," she chided. "You must wear it. This isn't the south of France, and you're going to catch your death of cold."

He frowned up at her, his eyes wide. Then he shook his head defiantly. He was just beginning to talk, but even without words he could be stubborn.

"Do as Mama tells you." Clare firmly wrenched his cap from his hands and put it on his head, pulling down the flaps over his ears. "It's cold," she repeated.

Emil grimaced, but he made no move to remove the cap again.

"If you don't do as Mama says, you'll have to wait in the cabin while the ship docks; then you'll miss seeing the great lady who guards the harbor. You don't want to miss her, do you?"

Emil shook his head and Clare sighed inwardly. Emil paid more attention to Sylvia, his nurse, than he did to her. Of course, Sylvia spent more time with him, Clare admitted to herself a trifle guiltily.

Two, Clare decided, was a difficult age. She loved Emil deeply, but something in her wished he were older so she could talk to him. What did one say to a two-year-old?

Her eyes searched the harbor, and her ears were assaulted by the sound of piping foghorns, some low, some deep, some shrill. They played a discordant kind of tune that suited her mood.

Clare Marina inhaled the odors of New York harbor: fog and smoke intermingled. "There!" She blinked into the fog and quickly wiped her eyes with her hand. "There's the lady—that's the Statue of Liberty!" Liberty, Clare thought. God, after Italy the word had new meaning.

Emil leaned over and peered through the mesh rail. "Can't see," he complained.

"We'll be closer soon," Clare promised, though she was unsure if that would make a great difference.

"Pity to miss her," a deep male voice said. "When I don't see her, I don't feel I've come home."

Clare turned. The gentleman was tall, perhaps six-foot-one. He had sandy hair and blue-gray eyes. His face was square and he smiled warmly. She'd seen him many times at dinner since they boarded the ship at Le Havre, but they had never spoken.

"You're not from New York," she said, returning his smile. He spoke his words clearly and slowly, but he didn't have a southern drawl; instead, there was a kind of twang to his speech pattern.

"I was born and raised in Indianapolis," he answered. "Biggest city in the United States not located on any body of navigable water. Home of the Five Hundred, Notre Dame, and, I'm proud to say, the home town of Booth Tarkington, that seer of a critic George Jean Nathan who writes for *Vanity Fair*, and a great number of other luminaries, including myself. However, I now live in California." He raised his eyebrow. "You don't remember me, do you?"

Clare looked at him intently. "I thought you looked familiar when I first saw you board."

"I met you three years ago on the *Leviathan*. You were traveling with your father."

Clare smiled faintly. Three years—it seemed like half a lifetime. "I vaguely remember, but I'm sorry, I don't recall your name."

"Mark Lyons." He turned to Emil. "Come on, son, let me lift you up. You can't see the Statue of Liberty from down there."

Clare watched as Mark Lyons hoisted Emil up and perched him high on his shoulder. Emil giggled with delight.

"For heaven's sake, don't drop him!" Clare said nervously.

He laughed. "I never drop anything."

She turned away, content that his grip was strong enough and that Emil would only cause a scene if she insisted on removing him from his perch.

"I've watched you at dinner every night for the seven days of this voyage," Mark Lyons admitted.

Clare didn't turn to face him. He seemed so *American*. European men had a kind of slow charm; American men made advances like bull elephants.

She stared into the gray water as it lapped against the side of the ship. Sometimes she felt as if she had emerged whole from those waters, like a mermaid marooned on a rock. Even her name meant "clear water." And there was no doubt she felt as if her home were mid-Atlantic; it hadn't been America for three years. It had never been Italy. She'd gone from her father's house into marriage, from marriage to a short but heartbreaking affair.

"You're a very attractive woman," Mark Lyons observed.

Clare still didn't turn. He had a nice smile and seemed warm and friendly, but she was used to men being forward with her, and her experience with Alessandro made her cautious.

"I enjoy knowing beautiful women."

"We don't really know each other," Clare replied. She was

well satisfied with her own icy tone of voice; it definitely had a regal ring to it.

But he only laughed; he didn't seem an easy man to put off. "I know you're now the Countess Clare Marina Sforza-Tonelli. I know Count Sforza was killed three years ago."

Clare nodded silently and cursed the fact that although she enjoyed having her picture taken, she was now a public figure, the papers wrote about her often, and that resulted in little privacy.

"She's a big lady," Emil said in awe as the Statue of Liberty came into closer view.

"She was a gift from France," Mark Lyons told him.

Clare ran her gloved hand over her fur stole. "I'm sorry, Emil, we have to go below now and get ready to leave the ship. We'll be docking soon."

Emil groaned, but Mark Lyons set him down.

"It's been interesting meeting you." His eyes traveled her body, and Clare turned away. He was very attractive, but attractive men could be emotionally dangerous, and she had vowed to protect herself against another Alessandro.

Anthony slumped onto the bench in the waiting room. He eyed the huddle of photographers in the corner and shook his head. He was the son of Agosto Tonelli, and as far as the press was concerned, totally anonymous.

But Clare! Dear Clare could not open the front door of her summer villa in Cannes without appearing on the pages of *Vanity Fair*, the *Herald Tribune*, or *Paris-Match*. The press is a bother, he told himself, though in fact he felt a bit miffed by their neglect. If his picture showed up anywhere, it would be because he was with Clare, and with their usual lack of accuracy, the reporters never captioned the picture properly. Such captions read: "Countess Sforza with unknown man."

That's the way it had been in France. He had made a rush trip in January to urge Clare to come home, and when she agreed, he had left immediately. But during his two-week stay with her they had been dogged by the paparazzi, and nine times out of ten his name was never mentioned.

Now it would all start in New York. He would patter around in his sister's shadow just as he usually pattered around in his father's shadow. Nonetheless, he admitted he was glad Clare was coming home. God, he needed her! Since their mother's death, Agosto had not been himself. He stayed away from the office, slipping into deep depressions which Anthony hadn't the faintest idea how to handle. And business was a nightmare! There were over three hundred and fifty banks in the Tonelli empire and literally hundreds of investments and firms under the control of the corporate structure. Roberto Marcucci was in charge, of course, but he lacked Agosto's flair and there were decisions to be made that had vast implications.

Anthony felt that those decisions had to be made by a member of the family, because the Tonelli empire was still very much a family business, even though Agosto often spoke of the need for it to "go public." His father had expanded rapidly in the boom years following World War I. And now, just when he was needed most to effect a consolidation, he had for the first time in his life retreated from his all-consuming interest. And who else was there?

Maria, Agosto's sister, was the strongest of the women. Anthony could always count on her, but although she had often worked in the banks in the early days, she had no understanding of what the Tonelli empire had become.

And then there was Fabiana. She had inherited Domenico's shares in the bank, but she was a homebody and knew nothing of business.

"Women," Anthony muttered. He lived in a family dominated by women since his father had abdicated his major role. Of course Clare was a woman too, but she knew more than he and she was now wealthy in her own right. Not that she didn't have shares: Agosto had given her shares at birth, and for some reason no one understood, Cecilia had left everything to Clare.

But in the final analysis, Clare's shares wouldn't matter. Anthony knew he had the majority of shares either in hand or coming to him. There was no question of his father's wishes on that matter. Sons inherited, not daughters. Agosto was, however, still quite healthy, but it wasn't his health that made Anthony think of the future, it was Agosto's mental state, his depression, his unstated retirement.

A garbled announcement proclaimed the disembarkment of passengers. Anthony struggled to his feet. It would be an ordeal, he decided. The press had scattered and clearly it was Clare they watched for as the passengers, gaily dressed and carrying baskets of fruit and bouquets of flowers, began to stream into the room from the customs area beyond.

"There she is!" a reporter called out gleefully.

Clare stopped and smiled. She waved an almost queenly wave as the cameras flashed and clicked.

"How about one holding your son?"

Clare obliged.

"Side view?"

Clare obliged.

"Now looking at the American flag!"

Clare obliged.

Anthony shoved his way through the crowd and Emil broke away from his mother to run into his arms. But it was not until Clare was kissing Anthony that the cameras again flashed. Then, Anthony noted, her hat obscured his face.

"What a ruckus." Clare smiled brilliantly and squeezed his arm as they settled back on the leather seats of the grand touring car which eased away and purred toward the Brooklyn Bridge. Emit sat in the front seat with the chauffeur.

"He loves cars," Clare Marina said, nodding toward her young son. "How's Papa?" she asked after a moment.

"The same as when I saw you last. He goes for long walks, he ignores business, and I'm worried about him."

Clare didn't comment. "And Fabiana?"

"She's fine. She takes care of Papa. I don't know what he'd do without her."

The big black car turned onto the bridge and Clare looked out the window, watching as the steel girders seemed to whiz past, each one bringing her closer to home.

"I expected Papa to come to meet me," she said quietly.

"He said he can't stand waiting rooms and he gets annoyed at the press. He said it would be better at home, because he'd be more relaxed."

Clare nodded, then in a sudden change of mood asked, "What are you up to these days? Have you got a girl? You didn't mention one when you were in France."

Anthony flushed. Clare always made him feel like a child. "I've been dating Jenny Stearns," he answered.

"Jenny! Good grief, she's only seventeen!" Clare turned to her brother seriously. "You ought to be careful, Tony. I think Sarah's been pushing Jenny at you for years."

"Nobody pushes anything on me," Anthony replied. "I like her."

The car passed down residential streets and halted in front of the Tonelli house on Emmons Avenue.

"We're home!"

Emil climbed out of the front seat and stood on the sidewalk looking up at the neat three-story house. He looked puzzled. "Where horses?"

Clare smiled. The villa at Cannes had stables, and Emil loved animals and was going to miss them. "There are no horses here," she said.

Emil pouted. "I want horses!"

*   *   *

"Papa!" Clare ran into her father's arms while Emil stood back shyly.

Tears ran down Clare's face; then she sniffed and murmured something about her makeup.

"I'll be back in a while," Anthony said, deciding to leave them alone. "Hey, Emil, come on, I'll show you the park."

Agosto bent down and kissed his grandson. Then he whispered hoarsely, "Go with Anthony. Later on I'll tell you a long story."

Obediently Emil followed Anthony, and Agosto took Clare's hand, leading her to the couch. She looked around, drinking in the room. The furniture was the same, though a little more worn. There was certainly a fresh coat of paint, but other than that everything was the same, including the mantel, where lines of yellowed tintypes and photographs depicted Domenico and Gina, Agosto in his uniform, Cecilia and Agosto on their wedding day, Paolo, Maria and Agosto in their youth, and finally, the picture of Emil that Clare had sent her mother.

"I should have been here, Papa. I knew she wasn't well, but I didn't know she was that ill."

Tears flooded Agosto's eyes. "No one knew. She kept it a secret. I knew she had fluid on the lungs, but I didn't know she'd been left with a permanent weakness. It left her vulnerable to infection. She got a staphylococcus infection, and there's no cure."

Clare looked at him steadily. Cecilia, her mother, had been the love of his life. They had shared everything.

"I miss her," Agosto half-sobbed. "I miss her more when I see you, you look so much like her."

"Papa, I know you loved Mama, but she wouldn't want you to spend your life mourning her."

"I have an emptiness."

Clare reached out and took his hands. He looked much older than his forty-nine years. There were rings under his eyes and he seemed to be in a trance. She squeezed his hands. "Papa, you've spent your life building, you can't let go now. Anthony is too young. Papa, this is a family business, no matter how large it has grown. It needs you. You need it."

"My other wife." Agosto sighed. "That's what the bank is, you know. It took me away from her. I tried to make time, but I couldn't make enough. I always thought we'd retire together and travel. I swore I wouldn't make the same mistake my father did, but I have. I didn't take the time when I had it . . . when *we* had it."

"Mama understood."

Agosto shook his head. "She always believed she didn't fit in; she always felt awkward with my friends. She put up with everything for me."

"She loved you," Clare said simply. Her mind wandered back to a long-ago conversation, the conversation she'd had with her mother the night before her wedding. "I want you to be different," Cecilia had told her. "I want you to be sophisticated and worldly. I want you to be what I'm not."

"She did love you, Papa," Clare said again. "Stop torturing yourself. Mama wouldn't like that."

"What would she like?"

"She'd like you to go back to work. Papa, I was thinking on the ship—I think the banks, the investments, and the various companies should be consolidated, perhaps by creating a holding company and selling shares on the market."

"I was considering that before." Tears flooded his eyes again. "Before your mother died," he finished.

"Papa, let me help you. Sforza Industries was a holding company, so I know about the kind of organization that's needed."

"Oh, Clarissima!" Agosto laughed and blinked back tears simultaneously. "It's good to have you home! But you shouldn't be acting like a corporate mogul. You should be looking for another husband. Emil needs a father."

Clare quite suddenly stomped her foot. "No! Absolutely not, no, no, no!"

The smile faded from Agosto's face. "Clare, what is it?"

"Don't put me off," she said, trying to control her voice. "I'm going to work. I want to work with American Federal. I'm not going husband hunting, Papa. I'm quite content single."

"Well, I didn't mean right away."

"You meant a woman shouldn't be doing what *you* do. Papa, that's just foolish." She reached across to the coffee table and picked up *Time* magazine. "There!" she said triumphantly, passing it to her father. "Who is that on the cover?"

"Mrs. Scripps-Howard," Agosto responded, hardly bothering to look at the elegant woman.

"Exactly," Clare said. "Mrs. Scripps-Howard, a woman who's been working on her father's newspapers for ages, a woman who's risen to control a fortune and who has made a place for herself in the world of journalism, which, I might remind you, is also a man's world."

"She does charity work."

"She's a corporate giant. Papa, you come back to the bank and you keep an eye on me. But don't tell me I can't do what I intend to do. I have managed quite well in Italy on my own. If you don't let me get involved, I will use my own money and start my own banking system. What's more, I'll yank every bit of my late husband's investments and U.S. assets out of our bank."

Agosto leaned back and actually laughed. He slapped his knee. "Ah, Clarissima, at least you get my blood flowing," He studied his daughter's intent expression. He didn't approve; a woman's place was in the home, not on Wall Street. And, God, not only did he disapprove, the banking establishment would be shocked. But he reluctantly admitted that Clare Marina did have a gift: she understood the world of banking and investment well, and she was a widow. *Just as I mourn Cecilia, Clare must mourn Emiliano Sforza. Clare needs to keep busy,* he thought, *at least until she remarries.*

"Would you be content to work in the background?" Agosto said after a long moment.

Clare bit her lip and nodded. "As long as the responsibility is real."

Agosto pressed his lips together. "All right, Clare. We'll try it out for a while. You come, you help your papa turn American Federal Banks into a holding company."

Clare smiled cautiously. "And you'll come back too."

"I suppose I have no choice, otherwise everyone on Wall Street will say I have turned over my banks to a woman."

Impulsively she leaned over and hugged her father. "I love you," she said.

"We'll fight like cats and dogs all day at the office and all evening at home!"

Clare shook her head. "I'm not going to live here, Papa."

"Clarissima, not live here?"

"I'll stay for a while, till to find a place. No, Papa, I want an apartment in Manhattan."

"Manhattan! Clarissima, you can't live alone in Manhattan. It's not proper."

"Alone? I have Emil and Sylvia. That's hardly alone."

Agosto started to complain, but his words reminded him of a conversation long ago that had taken place the night he told his family he was moving out to work in the Morgan Bank. He decided he would sound too much like Maria had sounded if he said anything further. "I suppose it's best," he allowed. "You'd drive me crazy, and I'll see you at work."

Clare waited a moment, wondering if she should fully explain why she'd sold Sforza Industries after fighting so hard to keep it together following Emiliano's death. She'd kept much from her family because she hadn't wanted to worry them. "Papa, I sold

Sforza Industries because of the Fascists, and I think you ought to divest yourself of your interests in Puglia. Luigi Catelli put together a consortium to buy me out, and I'm certain he can do the same for American Federal Banks."

"It's a profitable investment," Agosto argued, staring at the rug.

"Papa, Mussolini is a tyrant. After Uncle Paolo's death I know you eased out of the syndicate that had backed the loan to Mussolini and that you divested yourself of your interest in the dam. But I think it's wrong to have any money invested in that country."

Agosto's face flushed, and Clare could see him tense at the very mention of Paolo. "I made a good business decision as far as Italy was concerned. I wasn't wrong."

"Papa, you made a bad moral decision, and you *were* wrong."

"You sound like Paolo!" His voice rose.

"Paolo was a socialist, and the socialists were Mussolini's opposition. I'm not a socialist, Papa, but you can't eliminate the opposition by murdering them, and now there's general repression, and not just against the communists, socialists and anarchists."

"We fought about the Fascists the last time we were together," Agosto remembered. He shook his head. "I'll think about divestment."

Clare smiled faintly. He was an obstinate man.

Saturday, March 27, 1926

The Italian consul, Nicola Cerri, was tall and thin and had a receding chin and the nose of a bird of prey. He had a long neck, short curly dark hair, and a tendency to walk with the top half of his body leaning forward. He was also exceptionally nervous and had a habit of always clenching his fist while trying desperately to project the warm friendly smile his diplomatic position demanded.

Only last year his ability at public relations had been strained to the hilt when he was forced to escort the famous Italian general Armando Díaz on an official tour of the United States. The tour was followed avidly not only by the American and international press but also by the Italian-American press, particularly *Columbus Revista*.

Alas, he'd been forced to smile nonstop for weeks. Yes, he contemplated, it was a trial being sent to America. Nearly a third of Italian-Americans were from the south, while most of the diplomatic corps was from Milan, Florence, or Turin. The Italian diplomatic corps boasted many members of the aristocracy, to which, of course, he belonged. And on any other posting, he might have enjoyed the delights of royalty, the familiarity of form and tradition. But not so in America. Not only were the immigrants with whom he had nearly constant daily contact all peasants to his way of thinking, but the American government was distastefully egalitarian and its officials completely lacked any kind of charm.

But tonight was different. Tonight he was invited to a wonderful party to honor the return of the famous Italian conductor Arturo Toscanini to America. Toscanini was well known in America; he had been musical director of the Metropolitan from 1908 to 1915 and had returned to Italy in 1920 to conduct at La Scala during its season. But now he had been appointed conductor of the New York Philharmonic.

Cerri did have a minor problem. Toscanini absolutely abhorred Benito Mussolini, and when Il Duce went to La Scala to hear the maestro conduct, Toscanini, broke his baton and stormed offstage, refusing to play for the Fascist leader. And he continued to refuse. As a result, tonight the room was devoid of portraits of Mussolini.

Nonetheless Cerri had been commanded to attend. Mussolini wished to illustrate the fact that he held no ill feelings toward Toscanini, and he instructed the diplomatic corps to use the occasion to promote the aims of the Italian government with the cream of New York society, which was represented by the Symphony Association and the Metropolitan Opera Association. The Vanderbilts, the Astors, and, much to Cerri's delight, the beautiful widow Clare Marina Sforza-Tonelli were among the guests.

The doors to the elegant ballroom were open, and Cerri extended his hand and warm diplomatic smile to the entering partygoers. "Charmed," he said, kissing Mrs. Vanderbilt's hand. She smiled and adjusted her fur.

Two hundred hands to be kissed, an equal number of handshakes, and always the smile.

The Countess Clare Marina Sforza-Tonelli swept into the room accompanied by her brother and her cousin Tina.

She was even more stunning than her pictures, Cerri thought. She wore a shimmering, clinging silver gown, her long lovely neck was wrapped in a diamond-and-emerald necklace, and her short bobbed hair was waved stylishly. She wore diamond-and-emerald-stud earrings, a matching bracelet, and on her long fingers, two rings, one a huge perfect diamond and the other her wedding band, which had been moved to the right hand to indicate her widowhood.

Her brother was dressed in tails. He was a good-looking young man, Cerri conceded, and walked proudly. But why not? On one arm he had his sister, the countess, and on the other his cousin, who, though she decidedly lacked the glamour of the countess, was a well-dressed, petite, but heavy-busted woman in her mid-twenties, with brown eyes, thick long hair, and a heart-shaped face.

Cerri bowed deeply and kissed Clare's hand. He held it a bit too long, and he smiled sincerely for the first time all evening. After all, few of the wealthy women he was compelled to kiss were good-looking. Most of them were prunes bedecked in jewels. "I'm charmed that you could attend," he said, blinking his eyelashes.

Clare smiled. "I'm looking forward to meeting the maestro. I saw him once at La Scala."

Tina leaned over, her face in sudden animation. "Look, Clare! There's Alessandro Palma, the flying ace. I saw him last summer at the air show. He's a daredevil, and so handsome!"

Alessandro Palma. Clare all but froze at the sound of his name. Why was he in the United States? Her family knew nothing of her and Alessandro; only the tight-lipped Constanza knew of her relationship with Alessandro. Clare fought to control her facial expression.

Cerri looked around the room, craning his neck. So many people had passed by him, he wasn't at all certain Palma was there. Flying stunt men, however much publicity they created, were not his main interest in life. Daredevil antics were crass as far as Cerri was concerned. Hardly as exciting as fencing.

Cerri spotted Alessandro's profile and nodded. "He's over there. Would you like to be introduced?"

Tina smiled. "Oh, yes," she whispered.

Anything for the Countess Sforza-Tonelli's cousin, he decided, taking her arm. "Please come, I can even arrange for him to be seated at your table if you like."

"Oh, please," Tina cooed.

Clare felt Anthony take her arm, and she walked mechanically across the room, not knowing what to say or how to act. I don't want to see him, she thought to herself, but it was all unavoidable.

"No portraits of Il Duce," Tony whispered. "Of course, if there had been, Toscanini wouldn't have agreed to come."

The guests were primarily from the Eastern elite, and so the room was decorated with the portraits of Italian musicians, opera stars, writers, and artists. This was ostensibly a cultural event rather than a political one. A little something to remind the upper class that those they were so prejudiced against were a people with a brilliant cultural past and present. Clare passed the carefully arranged tables with the red-and-white tablecloths, the proliferation of flowers, the little Italian flags. What will I say to him? What will he say to me? She could hardly bring herself to look up for fear of being confronted by him, even as Anthony led her toward that confrontation.

Cerri was introducing Tina to her hero, Alessandro Palma.

Cerri turned. "And I should also like to introduce the Countess Sforza-Tonelli and her brother, Mr. Anthony Tonelli." Clare looked into Alessandro's handsome face and shivered with apprehension.

"I'm honored to see the countess again," he said, bowing. "We met once in Milan."

As he lifted Clare's hand to kiss it, she stood like a statue trying to compose herself. He was still handsome, but he looked worn and tired. He didn't smile at her, didn't squeeze her hand in a meaningful way. His eyes revealed nothing of his inner thoughts at this unexpected and, for Clare, unwelcome reunion.

"I'll look forward to a dance with you," he said, still holding her hand.

Clare nodded, not wanting to say: I don't want to dance with you.

"And with you too, Miss Ferrante," he said to Tina, who looked too impressed.

"Shall we sit down?" Anthony suggested.

Alessandro bowed. "I have to see a friend. May I join you later?"

"Of course," Anthony replied.

Alessandro turned and half-waved as he walked across the room. Clare all but collapsed into the chair Anthony pulled out for her.

The evening wore on and Alessandro returned to claim his dance with Clare Marina while Tina sat dejectedly at the table plucking the petals from one of the carnations. "It's not fair, Tony!" Tina's face was clouded by an expression that was half-anger, half-pout. Her dark eyes followed Clare and Alessandro Palma as they danced. "She has everything! She's going to be married twice before I get married once!"

Anthony remained expressionless. "You're only twenty-five."

"And Clare is only twenty-two, the rich widow of a count!"

"You have money."

"It's not really mine, but Clare's money is hers. She's a widow, a merry widow! Look at her! The only man in this room I want to dance with, and she's run off with him. It's not fair!"

Anthony looked away. He felt that Tina was about to cry, and he didn't want to see the tears welling in her eyes. He hated it when she cried.

She suddenly stood up. "Tony, take me home."

He turned to her dejectedly, knowing that he'd take her home despite the fact that he himself wanted to remain. "We shouldn't leave without Clare," he suggested.

"I'm sure Clare will find someone to take her to her apartment!"

Tina's tone was icy. Anthony stood up and followed her as she walked across the room. He tried to smile and nod at people, but Tina didn't slow down. Without seeing it, he knew her face was set and hard. He glanced back once and waved at Clare. But she didn't seem to notice. "Women," he muttered under his breath.

Clare danced stiffly with Alessandro. She was waiting for a surge of emotion, for some sensation to sweep over her. They'd been lovers, they'd touched each other intimately, yet now he seemed like a stranger, and his hand on the small of her back caused no sensation.

"You're silent," he finally said. "Did you think I'm such a cad that I'd run up and shout, 'I've missed sleeping with you'?"

Clare shook her head. "It's a shock to see you," she admitted.

"You don't understand, Clare Marina. You never let me explain."

"Was there anything to explain, save the fact that you courted me at the behest of General Balbo and Il Duce? It would have been convenient, wouldn't it? You'd have had control of the Sforza fortune, and they would have had control of you." Clare shook her head sadly. She wouldn't cry; she'd already cried.

"You don't have to believe it, but I truly loved you. They were holding my family, you know, I was made to do it. Then I fell in love with you, Clare. I suppose that's why I confessed so easily—it was harder and harder to live a lie."

Clare lifted her face to his for the first time and looked into his eyes. "I didn't know about your family," she said softly. "Are they safe?"

"There was no point in holding them any longer. I, of course, lost everything and now I'm in exile."

A dreamer without a dream, Clare thought. He'd really wanted to build an airline—of that much she was certain. "Oh, Alessandro, if what you say is true, you should have trusted me, you should have told me. If you'd really loved me, you would have.''

"I was a coward. . . . Strange, in a plane I'm fearless, but with you . . . with the government, I was a coward.''

"I'm sorry," Clare heard herself saying. "I'm sorry for both of us.''

"Clare Marina, I still love you. I want to see you, I want to be with you.''

Clare shook her head slowly. "No, it wouldn't work.''

"Don't you remember how it was? Clare, I want to feel your breasts, I want to know the warm response of your body against mine.''

Clare avoided his eyes. Her attraction to him had been so physical, and now it no longer existed. It was a relationship born of loneliness and need, a relationship destroyed by external forces. "No, Alessandro. No.''

"You don't still care?''

He seemed shocked, and Clare again shook her head.

"You've changed," he said.

"I've grown up," Clare answered.

26

Sunday, April 4, 1926

BROOKLYN

Fabiana supervised the Sunday feast, a meal that was traditional in the Tonelli home, a weekly dinner that Clare had missed now for nearly a month.

"You're late," Maria said sharply as Clare stood in the hall taking off her spring coat. She was careful not to wear her most expensive clothes home on Sunday because they elicited sarcastic comments from Maria.

"Are we late?" Emil asked with apprehension. He adored Sunday dinner with his grandfather, his great-aunts Maria and Fabiana, Tina, and Uncle Anthony. He was doted on and spoiled. If he thought he was late and missed one minute, he would be disappointed.

"No," Clare whispered. "Not really. Emil, go off to the kitchen and give Fabiana a kiss. Go on, shoo!" She patted him on the rear and he was off running through the house, shouting for Fabiana and Agosto's cat, Vanderbilt, simultaneously.

Maria watched him as he raced by, then stood in the hall grimacing at Clare. "You should get him a pet. Of course, I don't suppose you can keep pets in your Manhattan apartment." She emphasized the words "Manhattan apartment" and might as well have said, "In your disreputable apartment."

"I suppose I can have anything I want," Clare replied icily.

Maria hissed through her teeth, "It's not decent, living alone! Not decent!"

Clare's dark eyes flashed. Maria's comment was the sum total of why she hadn't been home for nearly a month. Her aunt's venom angered her, but what angered her more was her father's sullen, if silent agreement with his sister's observations.

But Maria wasn't finished. Her eyes traveled up and down

Clare and silently cast aspersions on her dress, which was, even Clare had to admit, a little shorter than her others.

"You're disgracing this family," Maria said in a lower voice. "Disgracing it! What kind of a home are you providing for your son? Men running in and out at all hours of the night! Living alone, going out dancing in public! A fine example, a fine example! A mother who is a . . . a . . ."

Clare stood rigidly and fought the urge to put her coat back on and leave. Maria wouldn't do this in the living room in front of the others. Instead she trapped Clare in the hall and poured out her disapproval in a whisper.

"I'm perfectly decent," Clare said defensively. "And you know nothing about my life, nothing!"

Maria's eyes narrowed. "I know what I read! I read about you in the New York *Evening Mail* . . . that Cholly Knickerbocker! The Countess Clare Marina Sforza-Tonelli was seen here and there, with first this man and that. She's having an affair with a flier, with an industrialist, with a musician . . . with half the men in New York! And now you're corrupting my Tina!"

Clare stared at Maria. She half-wanted to cry and half-wanted to laugh. Maria had that effect on her. What she said was so absurdly stupid it was funny, but she said it so meanly it hurt and angered her too.

"It's a gossip column! None of it's true! You can't believe all that garbage. As for Tina, she's twenty-five years old, and I've taken her to only a few parties—with Anthony!" Clare bit her lip. It was unfortunate that someone had caught her picture on the dance floor with Alessandro, whom she hadn't seen since the night of the reception. It was doubly unfortunate that there had been a photographer in the restaurant the night she'd dined with the vice-president of General Motors. But her male companions were little more than escorts, there was no relationship. As for Maria's accusation about Tina, it was patently absurd.

"Well, thanks to you, she's been going out with that flier, Alessandro Palma!" Maria grimaced.

Clare stared at Maria. Was this true? Was Tina seeing Alessandro?

"Oh, you needn't worry. I've sent her away to Virginia Beach with her own friends. I told her I wanted her going out with *her* friends, not yours. As for the columns, if they're not true, you should sue! Besides, if you got married, as you should for Emil's sake, and gave up working and behaved like a decent woman, they wouldn't write about you at all! Next . . . next I'll get up one morning and find your picture on *Time* magazine!"

Clare shook her head. "People write about countesses. I can't help that." She pushed thoughts of Tina and Alessandro out of her mind. Clearly Maria had taken care of it, in any case.

"It's wicked, what you're doing to that boy! And you're killing your father. He is utterly disgraced!"

"Fiddlesticks," Clare replied. She lifted her head and edged past Maria, who stood like a giant stone in her path, but who at the last moment moved aside, allowing her pass.

"Clare!" Anthony got up and hugged her warmly. She kissed him. At least Tony never said anything to her about living alone, and if he was distressed by the items in the magazines and papers, he never mentioned it.

"Where's Papa?"

"He went for a walk, probably to the church. He should be back soon."

Clare nodded and went to the kitchen to see Fabiana, who, she decided, would always be her favorite even if they were no blood relation. From Fabiana there was never even a hint of condemnation, never a word or a question about what she was doing or whom she was seeing. If only Maria really knew! she thought bitterly. There were no affairs, and even if she did seem to lead an unconventional life, appearances were deceiving.

"Fabiana . . ." Clare embraced her aunt, who hugged her back.

"Clarissima, I missed you!"

"Fabiana got me a coloring book," Emil announced, holding it up. He was sitting at the table coloring in the outlines of a dog surrounded by puppies. Vanderbilt, the cat, was placidly sitting on the chair next to Emil, allowing himself to be stroked now and again.

"Thank you," Clare said, kissing Fabiana on the cheek. It was a simple but thoughtful gift. It was always that way with Fabiana. She didn't buy Emil expensive toys as Agosto did, as Clare herself did. Fabiana bought plain gifts, but they were always just right.

"Your papa's here," Fabiana said in response to the sound of the front door slamming. "He always slams the door." She shook her head good-naturedly. "Always. That man has never learned to close a door without slamming it."

"Can I help you with something?" Clare looked around. Seraphina was actually doing the cooking, and the question was rhetorical, but it was also more than that, Clare realized: it was asked in hopes of finding a way to avoid the living room and the dual criticism of her father and aunt.

Not that she didn't see her father often. She saw him at meetings, and at least three times a week they had lunch. But Agosto Tonelli was a different man during the work week. Then they discussed the proposed holding company, to be known as American Federal; they talked investments; and more often than not, Roberto Marcucci joined them. During the week, Agosto made scant reference to her personal life. But at home it was another matter. In his castle, he was like his own father, Domenico. He was consumed with the opinions of family and neighbors, was the consummate Italian father, in sharp contrast to Agosto Tonelli, the consummate banker, or so it seemed to Clare Marina.

"No, there's really nothing to be done," Fabiana answered. She said it regretfully, as if she understood why Clare had asked in the first place.

"I'll go see Papa," Clare said. "Come on, Emil . . . come see Grandpapa."

Emil scrambled down off the high stool and ran out of the kitchen ahead of her. Clare followed, thinking that Emil was a distraction on the one hand, and the excuse for the criticism on the other.

"Clarissima . . ." Agosto came into the kitchen and hugged his daughter even as Emil hugged his grandfather's legs. "And my little Emil!" He stooped to pick up his grandson. "And what have you been coloring?"

"Dogs," Emil answered, pointing to the coloring book.

Agosto kissed him and sat him down again on the stool by the table. "Clarissima, I want to talk with you."

Agosto led his daughter out onto the back porch rather than into the living room. "That boy loves animals," he began. "He misses the open spaces."

It was another version of Maria's earlier speech. "I am not moving back here, Papa."

"Well, you could let Emil move here. Manhattan is no place for a young boy."

Clare shook her head. "No, Papa, Emil and I will stay together."

Agosto frowned at her. "I don't like the way you live," he said sternly.

"It's my business," Clare replied defiantly. "I've already heard this once today!" She brushed past him and through the kitchen. Silently she vowed it would be at least another month before she came home again.

Monday, April 5, 1926

VIRGINIA BEACH

Tina stretched out on the bed languorously. Her pink satin nightdress, trimmed in ivory lace, slipped over her shoulder, revealing the curve of her heavy breast. Her dark eyes looked around the room as the morning sunlight streamed through the window. It was certainly Virginia Beach's finest seaside hotel, and this room, with its luxurious furnishings, seemed to have a special magic about it.

At the window, silently looking out on the beach and the ocean beyond, was Alessandro Palma. He wore only his underwear, and Tina dreamily studied his tanned, well-muscled back, narrow hips, and strong hairy legs. He was a gorgeous man!

He turned toward her as if he felt her eyes on him. "Ah, mia Tina, you are awake, my little darling."

Tina turned over, and propping her head up with her hand, nodded silently. I shall never, never, never forget last night, she thought, nor this room. It was like a dream, a long pleasurable dream.

Alessandro had begun taking her out a few weeks ago, declaring that Clare was not the woman he had thought her to be. "And you, my darling, are nothing like your cousin," he had told her. "You are soft and beautiful, full of life, charming and daring." His kisses were deep, his arms strong, and Tina had melted in them, thinking only that Alessandro had given up Clare for her.

He walked over to the bed and sat down. With his index finger he circled her mouth, then traced the outline of an ear and ran his finger lightly down her neck. Tina shivered.

"How does it feel, my little virgin? How does it feel to be a woman?"

Tina circled his neck with her arms. "Wicked," she answered, fluttering her eyelashes and vaguely thinking how shocked her mother would be. She'd lied, of course, had told her mother she was staying with friends.

He dropped his hand and brushed her nightdress away, cupping her breast in his hand, then bent and kissed its tip, pushing her backward on the bed as he did so. "You are an adventure," he whispered in her ear. "I was stupid not to find you in the first place . . . to have overlooked you, my precious little flower."

Tina sank down, squirming beneath him until she felt his hands on her thighs and her nightdress lifted above her waist. He is mine, she thought. Mine, and not Clare's! I have finally taken something away from Clare! Thoughts of the famous Alessandro Palma filled her. He was an idol; thousands of women were thrilled by his barnstorming. He's mine, she thought.

"Oh, I love you so," Tina whispered.

Alessandro didn't answer. He continued to caress her till he felt her ready. "You are so sweet," he whispered, closing his eyes. Tina Ferrante was not Clare Marina, but Tina Ferrante could help him fulfill his last dream. Air Italy might never come to pass, but there were opportunities galore in the United States, and with the backing of the Tonelli empire everything was possible. I lost Clare, he contemplated, but there's no need to lose everything.

Thursday, July 15, 1926

NEWPORT

At forty-seven, Sarah Ainsley Stearns was still an attractive woman. Her blond hair was turning silver, but her blue eyes were youthful and piercing. Tall and slender, always perfectly dressed, she ruled over her society kingdom, relishing her role as a prominent hostess.

Sarah's daughter Jenny was eighteen and the mirror of Sarah's lost youth. Sarah watched as Jenny brushed out her flaxen hair, preparing to put it on top of her head.

"I hope you're going to wear it down tomorrow," Sarah said. She was perched on Jenny's bed, while Jenny herself sat at the dressing table.

"Why? It's cooler up."

"It's more seductive down," Sarah said authoritatively.

Jenny smiled and tilted her head. "Did you come in here to tell me how to wear my hair?"

Sarah shook her head. "No, I just thought the time was right for a little mother-daughter talk. You've been seeing a lot of Anthony Tonelli, haven't you?"

"You know I have. You said you liked him. I know Daddy

isn't crazy about him . . . well, about his name, anyway. But you've known his father for an age. I certainly didn't think you'd care.''

"I haven't been alive 'for an age,' my dear. But I certainly have known his father for a long time, and of course it was your grandfather who gave Agosto Tonelli his start.''

"Are we taking credit for the Tonelli millions, Mother? The way I heard it, Grandfather only gave him a stock tip. He did the rest. And according to Anthony, it was a rough journey. He told me his father lost a lot when rubber prices collapsed in 1910 . . . but he made it back on steel. Anthony has lots of interesting stories.''

"All about poor boys getting rich?''

"Mother, I really don't understand. I thought you liked the Tonellis. You invited Clare and her brother to your party tomorrow.''

"Of course I did! What's a party at Newport without the Countess Clare Marina! Though I do wish she weren't bringing her cousin Tina. For a woman of twenty-five, she's positively childish.''

"Mother, do you object to my seeing Anthony?''

"Oh, I don't object. I want you to see him. I even want you to marry him.''

"Mother!''

Sarah smiled and walked over to her daughter. She ran her hand over Jenny's smooth, silky hair. "He likes you a lot. I can see it in his eyes, Jenny. Anthony Tonelli is going to be a very wealthy young man, very wealthy indeed. You'd make a fine match.''

Jenny studied her mother's reflection in the mirror. "Well, I do like him.''

"That's good, dear. It's even convenient.''

"I hardly think we have to fortune-hunt,'' Jenny said defensively.

Sarah stared at herself and ran a hand through her own, short hair. Agosto had rejected her when she was young, and she'd loved him. She'd tried again in Paris, had actually offered herself, but again Agosto had turned his back on her. Even after Cecilia's death . . . Sarah's features hardened. Agosto had left her trapped in a passionless marriage with Creighton Stearns. "He should have been mine,'' Sarah said aloud.

"What should have been yours?''

Sarah smiled. "Nothing, darling. I was just thinking aloud. And do wear your hair down, and be especially nice to Anthony.''

"I intended to be."

"You'll get what you want, Jenny. What you go after."

Jenny glanced up at her mother. "I suspect I'll be getting what *you* want," she replied.

Sarah turned away, masking her expression. She'd have a certain revenge. She'd see to it that Jenny married Anthony. Anthony would inherit, and then Creighton could take over. And I rule Creighton, she thought triumphantly.

Friday, July 16, 1926

N E W P O R T

The Stearns mansion in Newport rivaled Count Sforza's estate on Lake Como in size—a great, rambling three-story brick house with a wide portico, a long private drive, and an expanse of manicured lawn that could have held an eighteen-hole golf course. The rooms on the lower floor were massive and could easily hold several hundred guests. And there were sufficient bedrooms and small surrounding guest houses to accommodate weekend visitors. One room was decorated in Louis XIV, another in Early American, still another in Italian Renaissance. But it was never the style that mattered; rather it was the expense of the furnishings— marble slabs from Italy, gold faucets in the bathrooms, hand-painted tiles, crystal chandeliers, carved ivory from the East, handmade furniture, velvet draperies. It was all a game, a game to see which of the luxurious Newport homes was the most lavish.

Each weekend was planned to outdo the one before. Orchestras were imported from New York, theatrical acts, whole plays, and the mix of guests was carefully gone over to make sure it included a certain number of well-known writers in vogue, entertainers of note, wealthy industrialists, Wall Street luminaries, and European royalty.

This weekend gathering included F. Scott Fitzgerald, whose book *The Great Gatsby* was still the rage a year after publication, assorted members of Newport society, and the usual mix of bankers, stockbrokers, investors, and entertainers.

Mark Lyons sat back in the blue velvet chair and sipped his drink. Such occasions were, he contemplated, rather like visiting a high-class zoo, and Sarah Ainsley Stearns was a master of putting together just the right establishment animals and imported exotics from the world of art, literature, and theater.

Mark considered himself a West Coaster, in spite of having been born in the Midwest. And like other wealthy well-known Californians—the Stanfords, the Huntington Hartfords, and the Scrippses—he was perfectly welcome in Eastern society when business brought him East. Welcome, but not entirely comfortable.

Still, an occasional sortie into the world of Newport could be entertaining, and there were reasons why he had accepted Sarah's invitation.

His first reason was the fact that he had learned that the Countess Clare Marina Sforza-Tonelli would be attending; his second was to meet Fitzgerald; and his third was the simple fact that he hated New York and the necessity of being there for a prolonged period. Any respite from the city was welcome, especially in July, when the heat and humidity turned it into a steamy concrete jungle.

And parties at Newport had one compensation: the very best of good imported liquor. The Treasury Department would never raid the home of Sarah Ainsley Stearns. Prohibition denied alcohol only to the poor; the rich were merely inconvenienced by the law.

Mark sipped his Haig and Haig gratefully, mentally thanked Joe Kennedy for smuggling it into the country, and continued with detachment to watch the other guests and wait for the arrival of the Countess Sforza-Tonelli.

The long circular drive was filled with parked cars when Clare's Daimler turned into it.

"Oh, there are a lot of people here," Tina moaned.

"There always are," Clare said.

"I don't feel like seeing all these people."

"Are you still feeling ill?" Anthony asked, leaning over toward her as the car came to a stop.

Tina nodded. "Just a little carsick. The road was so winding."

"You've never been carsick before. Are you coming down with something?" Anthony peered at her. "You look awfully pale."

"I'll be all right. But I don't want to party, not right away anyway. I want to go to my room and lie down."

"That's all you've done for the last month. I think you ought to go to a doctor."

"I told you I'm fine!" Tina snapped with irritation. "Anyway, why do you care? You're going to spend the whole weekend

vith your Jenny Stearns, and Clare will be the toast of the party.
don't even know why you both insisted I come.''

"It'll be fun," Clare said cheerfully as the car stopped.
"Besides, your mother always accuses me of corrupting you.
he hates to be wrong, and I can't corrupt you if you stay home
ll the time.''

Tina didn't answer. The very mention of her mother made her
▌.

The chauffeur opened the door and the three of them climbed
ut.

"I think all of Newport is here," Clare announced, looking at
e array of cars.

Anthony took Clare on one arm and Tina on the other. "It's
▐t every man who's lucky enough to escort two beautiful
omen.''

"Especially when he intends to spend the entire weekend
ourting a third," Clare joked. She glanced at her brother. He
as terribly handsome and one day he would be terribly rich too.
e'll control the banks, she thought. That's why Sarah Ainsley
earns would like to see Anthony and Jenny married. Inwardly
▌are wondered if Jenny was as much like Sarah as she seemed—
t she vowed not to say anything. Anthony liked Jenny, and
ere was no point in irritating him.

The great double doors swung open and the hum of voices
▐m the reception room and far patio could be heard even above
▐ music being played outside. The butler took their coats and
▌hered them into the main reception room. "There's dancing on
▐ patio," he announced in his cool British accent. "Drinks in
▐ billiards room, and Miss Molly, the housekeeper, will show
▐u to your bedrooms if you would like to freshen up.''

A half-hour later Clare descended the stairs alone. Anthony
▐d gone directly to find Jenny; Tina had remained in their
▐m, pleading an upset stomach and a headache.

At the door of the reception room Clare was greeted by Sarah,
plendent in a long muted blue chiffon gown that set off her
vy gray hair and made her blue eyes seem even larger. Gray
▐r became Sarah Ainsley Stearns because she still had a young
▐e, a face carefully sculptured with the finest makeup, makeup
subtle it seemed almost nonexistent.

'Clare darling! Oh, why didn't Agosto come with you?''

Clare smiled. "Too busy, or at least that's what he said.''

'Yes . . . yes. Agosto is always too busy. But of course you
setting up things, aren't you? What is it going to be called?''

'The American Federal Corporation—AmFed," Clare an-

swered. Sarah always sounded as though she only half-understoo
the corporate world, when in fact she was quite knowledgeable

"I have someone I want you to meet," Sarah cooed. She too
Clare's arm and led her across the room. "He's terribly nic
terribly rich, and terribly quiet. I thought perhaps you coul
bring him out a little. You're so . . . so outspoken."

Sarah stopped. "Ah, Mr. Lyons . . . I'd like to introduce th
Countess Clare Marina Sforza-Tonelli. Of course, I've know
her since she was this big"—Sarah held out her hands—"so
just call her Clare."

Clare flushed, wondering why Sarah always made it a point
mention how long she had known her. She turned and looked
Mr. Lyons. "We've met," Clare said, remembering how flirtatio
he'd been on the ship.

"How nice! Well, let me leave you two together. There a
just hundreds of people outside, and some of them I haven't ev
said hello to yet." She whirled away in a rustle of chiffon.

"A guardian of upper-class society," Mark observed.

"She's a very old friend of my father's."

"Can I get you a drink?"

Clare nodded and watched him as he walked to the bar. H
was back in an instant. "I hope you like Scotch?"

"That's fine."

"Now that we've been properly introduced, do I have to c
you all those names? May I call you Clare?"

She looked down at the floor. "I suppose so."

He grinned. "Please call me Mark."

"Sarah said you were shy. You certainly weren't shy on t
ship, and you don't seem shy now."

"Not shy, just bored. It's hard to start a conversation in
place like this. They're all the same, you know: 'I'm so-and-s
What are you into, old man? I'm into oil myself. Where's yo
house? Do you have a place in Newport? Oh, how terrib
Everyone who is anyone has a place in Newport.' "

Clare laughed in spite of herself. He kept a very straight fa
even while perfectly mimicking the typical conversation.
don't have a place in Newport," she said, sitting down on t
sofa.

"Oh, I know. And your father still lives in Brooklyn. F
middle-class pretensions for one of America's wealthier men.

Clare looked into her drink. "My grandfather was a gre
grocer."

"So was Giannini's—another fantastically wealthy Itali
American banker."

"My father opened his first bank before Giannini—not long before, but first. He broke ground, because apart from a few small local banks in Italian communities, there weren't any Italians in banking."

"It's always good to be first. He was the first to make large investments in Italy too."

Clare frowned. She liked his humor, he had a certain charm, but something in his last comment bothered her. "He's divested himself of his Italian holdings," she replied. "And so have I."

It was his turn to frown. "I didn't know that," he responded. "Why?"

"Why? Because Italy is a repressive country, because Mussolini has done away with the parliamentary system."

Mark Lyons sloshed his Scotch about in the glass, watching the amber liquid foam slightly. "Somehow I thought you supported Fascism."

"You're wrong. I don't, and neither does my father. I lived here, I know what it's like." Clare shook her head. "Mussolini's a dangerous egotist. He stopped at nothing to gain power, and he'd stop at nothing to retain it."

Mark studied her lovely intense face. "Your late husband was an arch supporter of Il Duce, and after your husband's death you were reportedly involved with General Balbo. Of Course Balbo never was a socialist and Mussolini turned away from socialism early in his career—didn't just turn away, mind you, but stamped it out with utter and complete brutality. A brutality I'm quite certain your late husband condoned."

Clare stiffened and stared at him. "I was never involved, as you put it, with General Balbo. Indeed, he tried in every way possible to see to it that I didn't sell Sforza Industries and take the money out of the country. As for my husband, he was an industrialist, and most of the Milan industrialists supported Mussolini and still do. Thomas Edison calls him the greatest genius of our age . . . world leaders flock to support him. I grant you that time and his actions have changed a lot opinions. But you can't go back and blame people for decisions made in good faith at a different point in history. If Emiliano had lived, I know he would have turned against the Fascists." Clare paused to compose herself. "My husband was a fine man."

"What you say about going back in history is true," Mark agreed. Then he shook his head. "I'm sure you loved your husband, but I know he wouldn't have turned against Fascism, and he wasn't a fine man. Your husband went along with violence, encouraged it, and would have continued to do so."

"You seem to think you know a great deal about my late husband," Clare said coldly.

"I met him once."

"Once? You seem rather quick to make judgments." Clare scowled at him. She'd liked him at first, but just as she was beginning to enjoy the conversation, he'd become strangely antagonistic, or so it seemed to her.

"Perhaps, but perhaps I knew a side of your husband you didn't know."

Clare stood up. "That I doubt," she replied defensively. " must ask you to excuse me, Mr. Lyons." She turned and walked toward the staircase.

Mark set his glass down on the coffee table with irritation and watched as she flounced across the room. I'm not too bright, he admonished himself. What woman wants to be told her husband wasn't the person she thought she loved? He shook his head at his own stupidity. Clare Marina wasn't what he'd expected. She was intriguing as well as attractive, and, he thought, very intelligent and perceptive.

Clare opened the door of the room she was sharing with Tina. The memory of her short conversation with Mark Lyons lingered and she found it both angered and puzzled her that he seemed to dislike Emiliano so. Perhaps, she rationalized, Emiliano had beaten him out on some business deal.

"Tina?" Clare looked into the dark room, and as she did so she heard the clear sounds of Tina being sick in the adjoining bathroom.

Clare tapped on the bathroom door. "Tina?" There was no voiced objection, so Clare opened the door. "Oh, dear," she said, looking at her cousin, who was leaning against the sink looking ghastly pale and shaken.

"Tina, you really are sick. I think I should find Sarah and have her call a doctor."

"No!"

"But you look terribly ill."

"No!" Tina backed away from the sink, holding her hand against the wall for support. "I have to lie down," she said, pushing past Clare into the bedroom.

Clare followed. "Why are you so stubborn? It's probably only stomach flu, but it wouldn't hurt to have the doctor—"

"It's not flu!" Tina sat on the edge of the bed, her hand covering her face. "I'm not sick! I'm pregnant!"

Clare looked across the dark room, unable to see Tina's face and not even certain she wanted to. "Pregnant? Oh, God, Tina! Pregnant?"

"I took him away from you," Tina said defiantly. "I took him away from you, Clare, and now I'm going to have his child."

"Who? What in heaven's name are you talking about?"

"Don't pretend with me," Tina replied. Her voice suddenly seemed stronger. "He told me how upset you were when he left."

Clare stood stiffly. She felt suddenly cold, and time seemed to stand absolutely still. "Who?" she repeated.

"Alessandro, of course!"

"What? I left him!" Clare blurted out angrily, but she stopped short as the horror of the situation sank in. Tina was jealous, Alessandro was hurt and angry—doubtless he still had ambitions. He was, she acknowledged, more than a victim of circumstances, he was bitter enough to try to fulfill his ambitions at Tina's expense.

"Don't lie to me!" Tina shouted. "He said you cried! But he loves me, Clare, and I won't listen to your lies!"

Clare couldn't answer. She gripped the doorjamb and stared into the darkness. Poor Tina. How could she insist on telling her the truth? What could she say?—We were lovers. I found out he was forced to try to marry me to keep the Sforza fortune in Italy. He lost everything, and now he's bitter and wants to salvage something. . . . Tina wouldn't and couldn't understand.

"I have to go to him," Tina said with determination. "As soon as he finds out I'm pregnant, we'll be married. It'll be all right."

Clare wanted to scream: He's no good! He only wants to marry into this family. But she didn't. She fought the urge to shriek: Your mother will kill you! But she didn't say that either. Slowly she walked across the room toward her cousin. Quietly she sat down on the bed and thought that although she was younger, she felt older. I grew up so much faster, I've had so much more experience. Clare let out her breath and put her arm around Tina's slim shoulders. "Where is he?" she asked calmly.

Tina sniffled. "In Florida. He's doing an air exhibition there before he goes West. He said something about getting a job as a stunt pilot in films. He hasn't answered my letters, Clare. But I know he loves me, I know he does."

Clare nodded in the darkness. "I'll get in touch with him, Tina. As soon as I've spoken with him, you'll go to join him. Then you'll write to your mother and tell her you were secretly married."

"You forgive me for taking him away?" Tina spoke in a little-girl voice.

It all sounded so childish, it was all so wrong. "Yes, I forgive you," Clare said, hugging her cousin. He'll want the backing for his airline, she thought. Yes, that was it, that's what he'd want.

"I'm sorry," the woman-child beside her sobbed.

Clare put both arms around her cousin and hugged her. Tina sobbed against her as the tension of keeping her secret poured out of her. "It's all right," Clare said over and over as she rubbed her cousin's back to comfort her. "It will be all right, Tina . . . everything will be all right."

27

Saturday, July 24, 1926

MIAMI BEACH

Alessandro stood framed in the doorway. He was dressed entirely in white, and his brown eyes were soft, almost sad as he looked at her. "Clare, it's good to see you." The words were innocuous, but he looked her up and down, a pleading, searching, sexual look, a look that spoke volumes.

Clare brushed a wisp of hair off her forehead. The heat and humidity were oppressive, and the ceiling fan in her hotel room was of little use. She shook her head, "Oh, Alessandro, how could you have done this?"

"If it's any compensation, I regret it."

"It's too late for regrets! Alessandro, Tina's pregnant."

Alessandro's face contorted slightly, "I didn't know," he said slowly.

"Abortion is out of the question, and if she had an illegitimate child, her mother would disown her. Alessandro, you have to marry her." Clare watched as the look of confidence faded from his face. He sat down on the chair by the table and avoided looking into her eyes.

"I'm hardly in a financial position to marry."

"I think you made love to Tina just so you *could* marry her. You did it to ensure funding for your airline, didn't you?"

He nodded. "But I changed my mind. I told you, I regret it."

"Regretful or not, you'll have to marry her. I'll see that you get the money."

He lifted his eyes to look into hers. "Clare, I have the plans. Could we look at them together? We could work together, you know . . ." He got up out of the chair and was by her side instantly. "It could be like it was, darling. We could share it, we could—" He reached out for her, and Clare moved away.

"No we couldn't! Alessandro, you're weak! I don't know how

447

you could imagine I'd come back to you! I'm here to see that you make Tina happy—I don't want to see you *or* your plans!''

"You're paying me to marry your cousin!"

"That's what you had in mind, and that's what you're getting!"

He stood, his lower lip quivering with pent-up emotion, his arms stretched out toward her. "You're cruel," he said accusingly.

Clare closed her eyes. "Marry Tina, go out to the Coast. I'll see to it you have the seed money and an income. Do it, Alessandro, before I change my mind."

"Are you sure that's what you want?"

Clare took a deep breath and nodded. She felt empty, more empty than when she'd fled him in Italy. How could I have thought I loved him? He doesn't even have the courage to be a real fortune hunter. He's torn between a moral code he can't adhere to and his ambition. But being with him, talking with him, gave her a feeling of strength. My wounds are healed, she thought, but his are still festering. "It's what I want," she said firmly. "And take care of her, Alessandro. I warn you, take care of her."

Monday, August 16, 1926

M A N H A T T A N

"This is your fault, Clarissima!" Agosto's face was bright red and his hand was clenched into a fist that he brought down on the coffee table with a resounding slam. "You introduced them! You were seeing him! Now she's run off to California, and Maria is beside herself!"

Clare stood by the table listening to her father's angry voice echo through the rooms of her apartment. Silently she thanked God that Emil wasn't home and that the servants were gone as well.

"Papa . . ." She didn't know what to say.

"Maria was worried about your influence on Tina. Ever since Donato died, Tina's been like a daughter to me. I love her, I have a responsibility toward her, and I have one to Maria."

Clare blinked back hot tears and fought the temptation to tell her father the truth. But the truth wasn't simple. "She's just a romantic and fell in love," Clare said, trying to sound calmer than she felt. "She's married and—"

"Married to some no-good daredevil pilot!"

"Tina's twenty-five years old! She has a right to marry whom she pleases. I was much younger, and you let me choose to marry Emiliano."

"He didn't marry you for your money!"

"And I didn't marry him for his," Clare said defensively.

"It's not right, her running off! She should have had a proper church wedding."

"Are you mad about that, or because you think he married her for her money? Or are you mad at me, Papa?"

Agosto shook his head. "I'm mad because I can't believe you didn't know about this. I'm mad because you introduced them and because I think he's no good!"

Clare didn't reply. Alessandro wasn't evil; he was simply weak.

Agosto picked up the telegram from Tina and read it again. "Pregnant," he muttered. "That man has dishonored me. He's dishonored this family! This is the telegram Tina sent to her mother!" He shook his head. "Maria says she'll never speak to you again, Clare."

"Honor! Papa, will you try to think of Tina's happiness? What is honor compared to her happiness, Papa? And she *is* married! It's not as if the child will be illegitimate!"

"I would give him credit for that, except that I suspect his decision was made a little easier because of Tonelli money."

"Has he asked for any?" Clare retorted. She bit her lip. It wasn't easy to lie to her father. Alessandro didn't have to ask for money—she'd already paid him.

"Not yet." Agosto sneered.

"Oh, Papa, I'm sure Alessandro will be good to her. He's very charming." It was a stupid comment.

"Charming! What a criterion! Clare, I expect more from you!"

Clare closed her eyes and thought: And you *get* more from me, so much more than you realize at this moment. What should she have done? How else could the problem have been solved?

"She says she won't be home for a while. She says he has a commitment to appear in several air shows and that he's making plans to open a commercial airline between Los Angeles and San Francisco. Big plans, no money!"

Clare nodded. "I'm sorry," she said quietly. "Papa, I never dreamed—"

"You always dream—that's the trouble. For a woman so practical in business, why are you so impractical in other matters?"

"I'm not."

"You are. It's you who should be married, not Tina. Emil

needs a father, and you have been a widow too long. You have got to stop living this way!''

"No! Papa, I spent my youth in convents and my adolescence pregnant and in mourning! I'm a young woman, Papa, and I won't live like Zia Maria. I won't!''

Agosto closed his eyes. "I'm going home," he said pointedly. "I'm going home to try to forget what you've done."

Clare let out a long-held breath. "Tell Maria to write and wish Tina well, Papa. Don't let Maria make her miserable."

Agosto grunted and opened the front door.

"Please," Clare said, fighting back her own tears.

"I'll think about it," he allowed. "But not right away."

"Papa, don't be that way! Tina will suffer till she knows her mother accepts the marriage. Please don't be stubborn."

"I'm not the stubborn one—you are!"

Clare shook her head. "Then I guess I inherited it," she replied as her father closed the door.

Saturday, December 25, 1926

CALIFORNIA

Tina and Alessandro took off at five A.M. The sky was golden over the San Bernardino Mountains as the sun hovered behind their jagged peaks. To the west, a dark velvet sky hung over the Pacific, and the morning star shone brightly.

Tina was wrapped in a blanket; Alessandro was dressed in his flight knickers, his jacket, his helmet cap, and his ever-present long white silk scarf. He had a jaunty air about him. He always did when he was flying.

"Warm enough?" he queried.

Tina nodded; the roar of the engines made much conversation impossible.

The little plane followed the coast; as the sun rose, the ocean looked like glass and the white-tipped waves appeared to roll onto the sandy beach in slow motion. And behind the sea, the mountains rose majestically. The plane bounced one or two times on the wind drafts.

"Are you sure you'll be okay?"

"The doctor says I'm fine. Anyway, it's not due for two weeks."

He laughed lightheartedly, and Tina thought he was a different person when he was flying. It was as if nothing else existed.

Over the jagged solitude of Morro Rock the fog bank began to roll in. Heavy dark gray clouds hung out over the ocean, and it was daylight on one side of the plane, night on the other.

"It's getting foggy," Tina pouted. She pulled the blanket tighter around her as the dampness penetrated the small plane. She strained to look out the window. The coastline here was beautiful; the mountains met the sea, and the waves crashed against huge jagged rocks.

"We'll have to head inland and try to land," Alessandro said, turning the plane slightly. "The fog's getting too thick."

Tina leaned back. Over the mountaintops the Salinas Valley would be hot, dry, and clear. The fog would evaporate as they climbed, and there would be a sudden burst of sunlight and blue sky.

The plane suddenly sank, and Tina let out a little scream.

"Wind draft," Alessandro cursed. But it didn't stop. The plane sank and rose again, a sickening jolt like a toy boat caught in a maelstrom. Alessandro muttered and Tina clung to her seat as the engines vibrated. Fog totally surrounded them, looking soft and harmless.

"*Cristo!*" Alessandro yelled as jagged rock appeared out of the dense fog. Tina let out a long shrill scream. Alessandro pulled back on the stick, veering up and to the left, skimming a jagged rock face, only to be confronted by another.

The plane shuddered as he pulled on the throttle to veer off again, but his right wingtip hit a rock, sending the light plane down through the fog into the treetops. The small plane was a ball of roaring fire that shattered the silence with a muffled boom and momentarily burned a hole in the fog. Then there was nothing but silence and the wind rushing through the scrub of the mountains.

Friday, January 14, 1927

B R O O K L Y N

December 24, 1926

Dear Mama,

It's Christmas Eve, but it doesn't seem like Christmas because it's hot and sunny out here. Mama, I thought for weeks and weeks before I sat down to write this letter, because I know that when you receive it, it will make you unhappy. Try to understand, I have to tell you the truth because I cannot live a lie any longer, and I can't have you blaming Clare for something that's my fault.

Alessandro didn't leave Clare for me. She left him, and she tried to warn me about him. But I was so jealous of her and I was so much in love. I was pregnant before we were married; the baby is due in two weeks. Clare knew it, and she only tried to help me. But Alessandro doesn't love me. I know that now. He's good to me, though, Mama, he really is. He's been honest with me and he's told me everything. It's hurtful, but I'd rather know. Mama, you mustn't be angry with Clare Marina.

Alessandro is taking me with him to San Francisco tomorrow. He takes me flying a lot, Mama. It's wonderful. I love the feeling—that's one thing we do share, and when the baby's born, we'll share that too. I think he might learn to love me after a time. That can happen, can't it?

Have a good Christmas, Mama.

> Love,
> Tina

Agosto put down Tina's letter to Maria and wiped his eyes. He bit his lower lip hard, fighting the thoughts that had flooded his mind since the arrival of the wire telling of the plane crash.

"Clarissima, I blamed you wrongly."

Clare nodded.

"I wanted to see you . . . to let you see Tina's letter. You tried to do the right thing, Clarissima, I know that. Maria knows it too, but she's still in shock."

Clare let her tears flow. "It's all right, Papa," she said quietly.

Agosto stood up and walked over to her. He bent and kissed her damp cheeks. "It's not your fault, Clarissima—you did what you thought was right."

Clare touched her father's hand. Tina's death was an emotional assault on the family that left each of them overwhelmed and isolated, feeling both responsibility and guilt.

"If you have good, you have bad," Agosto said. "Barton Ainsley once told me that tragedy stalks the wealthy." He pressed his lips together. "First Paolo, now Tina."

Clare looked into her father's face. It was a mask of misery. And it was a misery she and her father shared completely. A misery heightened by irony: the American Federal Corporation was born just as Tina died, and AmFed—the holding company under which all the banks, businesses, and investments were organized—was the hottest new public corporation on the ticker tapes. A hard-won business success offset by family tragedy.

"Papa, stay here for dinner. Emil will be home soon, and he's missed you."

"Will you come Sunday?" Agosto asked.

"Yes, Papa." She hadn't been home in a long while—the rift over Tina had been too deep—but now they needed each other. "I'll come home," Clare promised.

"I don't know if Maria will come," Agosto told her. "But Clare, you be there."

Saturday, June 4, 1927

M A N H A T T A N

More than five months had passed since Tina's death, and during those months Anthony and Jenny Stearns had courted. Clare sat in the front pew at St. Thomas; it scarcely seemed possible to her, but Anthony and Jenny were getting married.

Jenny stood at Anthony's side in her white satin wedding dress, a lace veil covering her face. Her long blond hair fell over her shoulders; her blue eyes were fixed straight ahead.

Beside Jenny, Anthony looked tall and handsome in his formal attire, but he looked young too, much too young to be getting married. To Clare, Jenny and Anthony looked like two little statues sitting atop a wedding cake—perfect, stiff, and almost expressionless. This was, Sarah Ainsley Stearns proclaimed, the wedding of the year, much as her own had been. The guests were an odd mixture, Clare thought. One side of the church was filled with the familiar names of New York society, while the other side was filled with the Tonelli family and their friends.

"Their children won't be Catholics," Fabiana whispered.

Clare nodded. Fabiana was only mildly upset by the Protestant union, but Maria had almost refused to attend the wedding, giving in only at the last moment.

Clare, flanked by her two aunts, wore her most chic outfit, a gold silk dress and a lovely picture hat with a long feather in its wide gold satin band.

"You should have dressed more simply," Maria hissed. "You look better than the bride."

Clare didn't answer; she was lost in thought. Jenny was certainly attractive, and there was no denying Anthony's adoration. They're in love, Clare told herself. Still, the union troubled her. She had heard rumors that Creighton Stearns was less than enthusiastic, but that wasn't all. Moments before, when the guests had mingled on the steps outside St. Thomas, she had overheard an odd conversation. "I couldn't have been more surprised when I got my invitation," a distinguished gray-haired banker from New England had muttered to his companion. "Fancy Creighton's daughter marrying a Tonelli! And after all Creighton did to stop other bankers from investing in that consortium Tonelli set up a few years back!" And then there was Sarah. She reacted to the marriage as if it were a business merger. Clare reminded herself that the powerful Stearns family had absorbed the Ainsley fortune and was now uniting with the Tonelli empire. Marriage, Clare thought, can make alliances that money can't. Silently she hoped the comment she had heard outside was only idle talk, and she sought comfort in the fact that the Tonelli banks, their investments, and their real-estate interests were now all united under the giant public AmFed Corporation. The controlling interest in AmFed was securely held by Agosto, though she herself had vast amounts of stock, as did Anthony.

"You may kiss the bride!" The priest's words broke into Clare's thoughts as she watched Anthony lift Jenny's veil and plant a long, passionate kiss on her lips. A slight hum broke through the church: apparently Episcopalians were not much on passionate kisses, or more to the point, they frowned on public passion.

The reception that followed the wedding was held at the Knickerbocker Club, which looked especially elegant filled with the hundreds of bouquets of spring flowers that Sarah used for decoration. The usual small dining tables were replaced by long white-covered trestles laden with platters of caviar, lobster, crab, and shrimp. The official drink of the afternoon was ginger ale served in delicate crystal wineglasses, but for those who wished it, imported champagne was served surreptitiously in the same glasses.

"I should have insisted that we hold an evening reception in the Waldorf-Astoria, but Jenny wouldn't hear of it!" Sarah burbled. "She wanted to keep it simple, you know. Well, I daresay it is simple. I've had more elegant house parties in Newport.''

Clare was quite tempted to comment that Mrs. Vanderbilt had been known to have more elegant house parties for her pets; her dog's dinner was considered the most "divine" way of wasting money yet found. But the antics of the idle rich aside, the wedding reception would be considered "simple" only by Sarah Ainsley Stearns, who, Clare contemplated, had not the faintest idea of what real simplicity was.

"We meet again," a smooth male voice said to Clare.

She whirled around, champagne glass in hand, to see Mark Lyons.

"What are you doing here?" she asked, knowing that her voice was tinged with just the right amount of annoyance to make him feel thoroughly unwelcome.

"I believe it's the bride's family that sends out the invitations," he replied hesitantly. "Clare Marina, I owe you an apology. I came to the reception primarily to make it.''

Clare looked up into his face. His expression was one of genuine concern. His blue-gray eyes looked a little sad and had a pleading quality. He was an extraordinarily good-looking young man, she thought. He was tall and muscular, his sandy hair a little unruly, his eyes the color of the sea. Clare's expression softened, and she nodded silently.

His face broke into an infectious smile. "I'd hoped you'd forgive me. I'd like to make you understand, but I'm not sure I can.''

"I assume you had some difficulty with my late husband," Clare said carefully. "I loved and respected my husband—you have to understand that.''

"And you don't want to hear anything against him.''

"No. He's dead, and I cherish my memories, more so because experience has taught me that I'm unlikely to find another man like Emiliano Sforza.''

Mark forced himself not to say any more. It certainly wasn't her fault; she couldn't have known about Louisa of about Sforza's connection with the *ceka*. Sforza was a smooth operator who'd succeeded in deceiving a great many people, including his wife. Still, Clare's image of Sforza troubled him. Clearly she still loved Emiliano Sforza—or at least the memory she'd created of him. And that, Mark knew, was an illusion. "We won't talk about your husband," he finally said.

Clare smiled. "Agreed.''

"I only get East about twice a year," he said, changing the subject.

"Oh, yes, I remember, you live in California. My cousin lived there for a while . . ." Clare stopped mid-sentence; the wound hadn't healed in spite of all her efforts.

"I read about the plane crash. I'm sorry. I take it you were very close."

"We were like sisters. It was a terrible shock."

Mark waited and then after a moment changed the subject again. "Have you ever been to the Coast?"

Clare sipped her champagne. "No, but I'd like to go."

"You'd love it," he told her. "There's a mood of expansion, and California's a fantastic place, not like any other. It's got the contrast of the mountains, the desert, and the sea. It's got millions of acres of natural resources, of farmland, and there's building going on everywhere." His eyes flickered with enthusiasm. "Doesn't AmFed have West Coast investments?"

"We have a few banks and some investments in Hollywood." Clare smiled. "My father had a passing love affair with film. When I was born, he gave me some stock in a film company."

Mark grinned broadly. "You ought to come West and take over the AmFed interests. The Bank of America's really expanding; it could use the competition. Let me tell you, with a little personal management, AmFed could really do well in California. Right now it's considered the poor cousin of the Eastern establishment. There's a lot of regionalism in this country, and the West wants its own managers and its own companies."

Clare watched Mark Lyons' expressive face. Go West and take over the management of AmFed? This was the first man she'd ever met who would even suggest such a thing. And what's more, he said it almost offhandedly, seemingly taking for granted her ability. "Do you think a woman would be accepted?" she asked, fascinated with the idea.

Mark looked amused. "I think you'd be accepted," he replied. "You may be working in the back room, but you've built a reputation. Tell me, are you satisfied in the back room?"

Clare shook her head. "No," she said emphatically.

He leaned over conspiratorially. "There's only one rule for success," he whispered. "It's the same rule for men and women. Know what you want, and go after it."

Clare felt herself blush slightly. "And what do you want, Mark Lyons?"

"I want to dance with you." He glanced at his watch. "Now, because I have to leave for California within the hour."

Clare allowed him to take her arm, feeling suddenly alive.

She danced for nearly an hour with Mark Lyons. He was a good dancer, and made her laugh besides. But the time passed quickly, and he had to leave. "Come to California, Clare Marina," he said as he bid her good-bye.

"I'll think about it," she allowed, admitting to herself that the idea was, in fact, a very agreeable one.

"Are you happy?" Anthony finally broke away from a crush of people. His face was flushed from champagne, and Clare decided he had the look of the apprehensive bridegroom.

"Are you?" she asked, winking.

"Of course . . . but a little tired. I think we had a hundred rehearsals. I wanted you to be a bridesmaid, you know."

"Jenny has her own friends, and besides, I've been too busy for rehearsals." Clare studied her brother's face, then impulsively hugged him tightly. "I love you," she told him. "Be happy, Anthony. Be really happy."

Sarah took Agosto's arm. "You must dance with me," she persisted. "We were never lovers, but now we're practically related."

"We're growing old," Agosto answered, trying to make light of her comment. "Old enough to see our children marry one another."

"Oh, Agosto! You're not old, and neither am I. This is a glorious day, darling. We've united two important families."

"I trust they married for love, not ambition."

"Oh, of course! But it works out well."

He didn't answer, but took advantage of the faster tempo of the music to hold her back a little. "I'm happy Tony has found a woman he loves," he said after a time.

"May I dance with my wife?" Creighton Stearns stood near them. He was smiling and he reached out and shook Agosto's hand.

Agosto bowed from the waist. "Certainly," he replied. "It's been a pleasure, Sarah."

She smiled, and Agosto moved away, heading toward Clare.

"I suppose you're happy now," Creighton said, holding her tightly.

"Of course I am."

"It does give you an excuse to be with Agosto Tonelli more, doesn't it?"

Sarah lifted her head and looked into her husband's eyes. "I really don't understand that comment."

"Yes you do, Sarah. You might as well have arranged the marriage. For years I've watched you with Agosto. I'm not

458————————————————Joyce Carlow

blind, you know. And since Cecilia's death you've become more brazen, though I think more frustrated as well.''

Sarah stopped dead. "This is hardly the time or place for this discussion, Creighton.''

He smiled and pulled her back into his arms. "It's quite all right, my dear,'' he whispered into her ear. "I'll get you the revenge you've always wanted, but don't think I'll be doing it for you.''

Sarah's face hardened. "I don't love you,'' she said meanly.

Creighton's expression remained impassive. "I've long grown used to that. Bear in mind, I take rejection better than you.''

28

Tuesday, January 1, 1929

MANHATTAN

Clare Marina curled up in the big white chair opposite the sofa where her father sat smoking his traditional after-dinner stogie and sipping brandy. Constanza and Robert Marcucci were together on the love seat. It was impossible to look at Constanza and not realize how much she had changed. New York suited her, and she was obviously happy and content in her role as the wife of the vice-president of AmFed.

"I'm glad you came," Clare said, looking across at her father.

Agosto shrugged. "The house is empty. When I stay there alone, I hear too many voices and have too many memories."

Life for her father was no longer the same, Clare thought. She still lived on Park Avenue, and Anthony and Jenny lived on Fifth. Only Fabiana and Maria remained at home, but Fabiana had convinced Maria they should go to Florida for the holidays, and Tony and Jenny had gone to the Caribbean.

Since her father was alone, Clare held the New Year's Day dinner. And, she thought, having him in her apartment suited her purposes. She deemed it necessary to draw her father away from his lair in order to discuss what she wanted to discuss. Since her lighthearted conversation with Mark Lyons more than a year ago, the idea of going to California had been much on her mind. She'd done a considerable amount of reading, familiarized herself with the California business scene, and prepared her arguments.

Clare studied her father's face; he was just fifty-two, but the increased responsibilities of managing AmFed showed. The corporation's interests included far-flung European investments, banks from coast to coast, and now meanderings into the lucrative Asian markets. On top of that, the economy showed signs of instability—in simple terms, it was as "upsy-downsy" as a roller coaster. "You look tired," Clare observed.

"He doesn't let me do enough," Roberto lamented. "He thinks he's a one-man show."

"You do need a rest," Clare persisted. "You don't travel enough."

Agosto shook his head. "I can't travel. You know as well as I do what's happening, Clarissima. I don't like it, and among bankers, I stand alone. There's no support for sanity."

"I gather that means you had no success last week." She referred to a meeting of the country's leading bankers. Her father had tried vainly to get them to support limited controls—if not controls brought about by the Federal Reserve Bank, then self-imposed controls.

"None whatsoever, Clarissima. All I see around me is money madness. I've said it before, and I say it now: buying only to sell at a higher price is not true investment, it's folly."

"Look at what the other banks are doing," Roberto added. "They're making foreign loans in Latin America, to little German municipalities, to anyone who asks. And there's no stability in those governments and no collateral for those loans. The bond market is a nightmare! Once foreign loans went only to competent foreign borrowers, but now even the big houses are lending to dishonest borrowers. I sometimes can't believe what's happening."

"Look at National City Company and J. & W. Seligman— they used to be conservative investors," Agosto put in. "Now they pay half a million dollars to a Peruvian dictator for his so-called services in promoting a fifty-million-dollar loan to Peru—naturally, marketed by themselves! And what happens? The Americans lost and the Peruvians didn't benefit at all. No, that's not investment, it's stupidity."

"What's happening here isn't any better. Papa, corporations are creating more corporations to hold stock in their own corporations. They're paper companies that don't employ anyone and therefore don't contribute to real growth. They're pyramids and they're secure only as long as the company at the bottom is secured, but insolvency could bring disaster."

"I'm glad you see that. I haven't had any success making other people see. I've talked and talked till I'm blue in the face. The bull market can't go on day after day, year after year. There are too many people buying stocks with nonexistent money in companies that are nonexistent." He shook his head. "God knows I don't believe in government controls, but I do believe the financial community has to control itself! I feel as if everyone has gone mad.''

Clare leaned forward. ''We can't control the other bankers, but we have to make sure that as much AmFed stock as possible is in our hands.'' She smiled to herself. Her father was leaning forward in his chair; the discussion had brought him to life.

''I've always had one philosophy,'' Agosto reiterated. ''Investments should build and provide new jobs. When I first started, they said I was bringing a pushcart philosophy to banking, that I was going into the neighborhood and selling banking to immigrants the way the old Italian immigrants sold cloth, shoes, and food. But I still believe that a man's investments should be like a great river that runs mighty because of its millions of tiny tributaries.''

Her father had given her the opening she'd been waiting for. ''Papa, our tributaries on the West Coast are not very strong. I want to go to California and take over AmFed's interests there. Papa, I believe in the future of the West.''

Agosto laughed. ''Giannini has it sewed up!''

''Nonsense!'' Clare said defiantly. ''The population is doubling almost every year . . . talking pictures are going to mean a revolution in film and in the film industry . . . California is the single biggest oil-producing state . . . their agriculture is growing by leaps and bounds. Papa, there's room for competition, and the truth is, I feel useless here.''

Roberto laughed. ''I think she's researched this.''

Constanza smiled brightly. ''If Clare goes West, I'll be the only countess in New York, apart from exiled Russian nobility. If there's one thing nicer than being nobility, it's being the *only* nobility.''

Clare giggled. Constanza was a rare social asset for Roberto, but quite clearly he had changed her whole pattern of thinking. She still joked about nobility and peasants, but she was the shrew who'd been tamed.

''You've been working hard. What do you mean, useless?'' Agosto said, ignoring Constanza.

''I'm not initiating anything. Papa, I work, but not on my own, and I'm tired of living this way. I've fallen into a pattern I despise. Parties and more parties.''

Agosto raised an eyebrow. ''I thought you liked them. Every time I suggest you settle down, I get an argument.''

Clare looked away. Certainly her father had stopped preaching at her since Tina's death. If he disapproved of the gossip about her reported flings with various men, about the social life she led after her workday, then he said very little. And she knew that he relied on her insofar as AmFed was concerned. He not only used her as a sounding board for his own ideas but also listened to her more and more. "My life differs a lot from the way it's pictured," she confessed. What she left out was her own feeling of emptiness, her fear of falling into the trap of living a life without aim or direction. "Papa, I need a new challenge. I want to go to California and open a West Coast headquarters. I want to expand and control our operations."

Agosto half-smiled, and Clare was certain he was going to seize the opportunity to tell her that marriage would be a new challenge. But for once he didn't.

"Clarissima, I've let you work with me here. But manage the West Coast? You're a woman—you wouldn't be accepted in that role."

Clare felt her anger rising, but she fought to control it, to be firm. "Papa, I'm capable and you know it. You're using me here. I'll be accepted because I know what I'm doing. I want to go West. Papa, I'm not just your daughter. AmFed's a public company and I'm a major stockholder. I have a right to be in management."

"She'd be a real asset on the Coast," Roberto said supportively. He rubbed his chin and watched Agosto. "She's a genius, Agosto." Roberto laughed. "Fate dealt you a blow, my friend, because your daughter is a financial wizard."

"She almost drove me mad in Italy," Constanza said dryly.

Clare took a deep breath. "Papa, let me do this . . . let me do it, or I'll sell my AmFed shares and go West on my own."

Agosto grimaced and Clare could see his stubbornness coming to the forefront. "You're threatening me," he said harshly.

"It's not a threat, Papa, it's a promise. I love you, I love AmFed, but I have to go after what I want, and I don't want to be a back-room banker anymore. I want to prove myself. Papa, I've been valuable to you, I know that."

Agosto frowned and Clare knew that in spite of his strong feelings about women and their role, he was too fair to deny what she said.

"California's full of nonconformists," Roberto put in. "Agosto, I think it would work. I think Clare ought to go West."

Agosto frowned, but he threw his arms in the air, a gesture of giving in. "I'm outnumbered."

Clare smiled and went to her father. She hugged him tightly, thinking: I would have gone anyway, but I'd rather go to consolidate AmFed.

"If that's settled, I'd like to drink to the new year," Roberto said, lifting his glass.

Constanza frowned. "I've never liked years that end in nines. Nines are strange numbers. I didn't like 1919 because of the horrible settlement imposed by the Versailles Conference—I mean, that's what gave Mussolini his start. God knows what will happen this year, and 1939 will probably be a disaster!"

"She's taken up numerology," Roberto joked. "If Il Duce revokes her title, she's going to tell everyone she's a Gypsy and tell fortunes."

"The way you describe the economy, I might just as well have something to fall back on," Constanza retorted. "Anyway, let's not drink to the year, let's drink to Clare and wish her good fortune in California."

Thursday, February 28, 1929

SAN MARINO, CALIFORNIA

Mark Lyons reflected on his decision to live in San Marino, an upper-class sanctuary southeast of Pasadena. In a way, San Marino was like its namesake, the tiny independent republic nestled at the foot of Monte Titano, near the Adriatic Coast, completely surrounded by the sprawling confusion of Italy's discordant provinces. The California version was also nestled against mountains, and while it hadn't been founded by a group of Christians attempting to escape persecution, it *was* founded by the extraordinarily wealthy in an attempt to isolate themselves from the larger community of Los Angeles, while still having complete access to the advantages of an urban community.

The Los Angeles basin, called the Valley of the Smokes by its original Indian inhabitants, had historically been neatly divided by the old Spanish settlers into massive *ranchos* that bore the familiar names of Sepulveda, Ventura, and La Brea.

But as the fortunes of the old conquistador families disintegrated, new barons arrived to purchase the vast, rich *ranchos* and divide them into new tracts. Though names like Sepulveda still clung to the city's map, and were mixed with other Spanish names of a descriptive nature—Palos Verdes for green hills, and Arroyo Park, which in New York would simply have been called Riverside—the lilting Spanish names on the country's map were now mixed with the names of the new conquistadores: the Firestones, the Huntingtons, the Culvers, and the Whittiers.

San Marino itself was synonymous with the word "exclusive."

The entire vast area had once been the San Marino Ranch and it was purchased by Edward Huntington in 1903 from one James de Barth Shorb. The magnificent Huntington estate was a mere half-mile from Mark's own home. Majestically situated on two hundred acres molded into a combination of English formal gardens and a peaceful Japanese garden modeled on the Kyoto Gardens, the house itself contained the most cohesive, tasteful art collection west of New York City. Edward Hungtington had whiled away his fortune as a collector, and as if in apology for his family's vast accumulation of wealth, willed his entire estate to the people of California in 1922.

But in spite of the fact that the Huntington estate was now a gallery and museum open to the public, the community retained its exclusivity. Its homes were far off the main road that went into Los Angeles. They were hidden behind tall trees and boasted beautiful well-kept grounds alive with semitropical vegetation. For three months out of the year, many had small rivers that ran through the property. Virtually all had swimming pools, and most had ten or twelve bedrooms, large reception rooms, sunny patios, book-lined studies, and teletype communications systems that linked their wealthy inhabitants to business interests.

Mark Lyons' estate was as immodest as those occupied by his neighbors, though he, unlike they, was a bachelor who owned the estate more as an investment than as a home. His life was his work, though he was only too aware of his reputation as the area's most eligible unmarried man. He traveled—usually to the Riviera in the fall or early spring. He partied, sometimes in San Marino, but more often in nearby Pasadena or Hollywood. And he spent most weekdays working in the offices of Lyons Oil, located on Broadway near the squat yellow sandstone offices of the Los Angeles *Times*, the newspaper he had just finished reading.

"She's coming to Los Angeles," he said, putting the paper down and looking across the maple breakfast table at his vice-president, Morty Levinson. Morty lived in one wing of the great sprawling house. He maintained the communications room and its adjacent office. On weekday mornings they breakfasted together and then drove into L.A. for their workday, which began at ten and more often than not lasted till six or seven, when they drove home to San Marino.

"Who's coming?" Morty asked. He was as rumpled as ever, a bullish little man with thick glasses, and though he was clean shaven, he always looked as if he needed a shave. But he had a fine mind and next to Mark himself had the best grasp on the Lyons investment portfolio. He was also a splendid negotiator, a man with a natural poker face and subtle sarcastic sense of humor.

"The Countess Clare Marina Sforza-Tonelli," Mark replied, studying her picture in the paper. There was no need to explain further, because Morty had met Clare Marina years ago, and he knew all about Count Sforza.

"Why's she coming to the Coast?" Levinson asked. Then added, "Aren't there enough parties in the East these days?"

Mark smiled. No one who read magazines and papers hadn't heard of the countess's relentless social life. In the past two years her name had been linked to an endless string of wealthy and prominent men; gossip about her abounded in spite of the occasional grudging comment regarding her business successes. "She may have the reputation of a social butterfly, but I've met her twice and she's anything but a ball of fluff. Actually," he admitted, "I'm the one who suggested she come West."

"You've been keeping things from me, but since it's your suggestion, I assume you know why she's coming."

"The story says she's coming out here to shape up the banks owned by AmFed and invest in motion pictures," Mark answered. "I'd say AmFed is planning to expand in California."

"AmFed and everyone else," Morty grumbled.

"It's a big state."

"Why do I have the feeling you have more than a passing interest in her?"

"She's intriguing," he answered, setting the paper down.

"And a real knockout."

"Yes, she is," Mark agreed.

"Does this mean there is some sort of romance brewing?"

Mark flushed and shook his head. "I hardly know her, that's the problem."

"Problems get solved."

"Sometimes," Mark answered thoughtfully. "You see, I think . . . no, I *know* she worships the memory of her husband." He didn't add to his statement because he didn't have to; Morty would understand: what kind of serious relationship could he have with Clare Marina unless she knew the whole story? And, he admitted, telling her that story would be extraordinarily difficult.

"We've got those Navy guys coming in at eleven. I'd like to go over the financial briefs on the way into town," Morty announced, changing the subject. "You have studied the Navy's proposals?" he pressed.

Mark nodded abstractedly. The Navy wanted to purchase a large undeveloped field on which he held a lease. Something about the need to retain oil reserves for the future security of the military. "I've given it some thought," he answered.

Morty shrugged. "I'd give it more than some thought if I were you. I think you'll get the best price now."

Mark laughed. "Why? Is the bottom going to drop out?"

"I don't like the looks of things. It could, you know. I'm a cautious man, Mark. I believe in the Torah and what it says about investment. I believe you invest one-third in property, one-third in gold, and one-third you keep liquid. I don't like the proliferation of pyramid companies and the continuation of an ever-rising market."

Mark nodded. "What goes up must come down?"

"A cliché, my friend, but it usually works that way." He shook his head. "We've got an inactive government, and inactivity doesn't solve problems." Morty shook his head. "You know, your countess is smart."

"That was a thought leap," Mark observed.

"Yeah. If there's a crisis brewing, it's smart to get her out on the Coast to strengthen AmFed and diversify. It'll give them balance."

"She's smart," Mark acknowledged. "And I like her."

Saturday, March 16, 1929

ON THE TRAIN WEST

Clare Marina sat in her private compartment in Car 9 on Southern Pacific's *El Capitan* heading west. She studied piles of documents and files spread out on the small wooden table set up by the porter.

Emil sat placidly across from her, watching as the high desert landscape of southern Arizona sped by. He had tired of his picture books, but enjoyed looking out the window, and that, Clare decided, was because the scenery was so completely different from anything either of them had ever seen.

"The banks in California have too much land," Clare said abstractedly as she put aside her papers.

"What, Mama?"

A few months short of his fifth birthday, he was a precocious child. His eyes flickered with interest. He was a handsome boy and Clare decided he looked a great deal like his grandfather Agosto and a little like her own brother, Anthony. In a small, unstated way, she was glad he did not resemble his father, because if he had, he would have been a constant reminder of Emiliano Sforza, who still haunted a corner of her mind.

"I said the banks in California have too much land. What I mean is, too many of their loans are guaranteed by land, and too much of their solvency is based on real estate."

Emil blinked and then yawned.

"I know you don't understand," Clare said. "Sometimes Mama just talks aloud. My father used to talk aloud to me too, long before I really understood." Her mind strayed to her trip to Italy with her father in 1915 and to his endless long conversations on the train about the coming war, the economy, and the banks. But then, she had been almost twelve at the time and doubtless she remembered that trip better than Emil would remember this one.

"I miss Grandpapa," Emil murmured. "And Fabiana too."

"You'll find friends in California," Clare said brightly. "And maybe soon Grandpapa and Fabiana will come and visit."

Emil smiled. "Soon?"

Clare laughed softly. "We have to get settled first." She reached across the table and took his hand. "I'm glad I sent Sylvia ahead. This is the first time we've traveled alone for ever so long." She smiled at her son. He was growing up, his vocabulary seemed to increase daily, and he sometimes seemed to grow before her eyes. He was a wonderful child, with wavy soft brown hair, huge brown eyes, a pensive sober expression, but also, when he chose, a warm loving smile.

"I liked the Indians on the train platform in Albuquerque," Emil announced. "Are there Indians in California?"

Clare shook her head. "I don't think so, Emil. But there are oranges you can pick right off the trees, and movie stars too."

Emil grinned. "Tom Mix! Will I see Tom Mix?"

Clare nodded. "I suppose you might," she said carefully, remembering that Tom Mix was only a few years younger than her father. "But he's not as young as he looks in the movies, you know. And you must remember, Emil, movies are make-believe."

"It's really his horses I want to see, Mama. I want to be able to ride like Tom Mix and do stunts on horses!"

"That's dangerous, and you have to practice a long time," she said, squeezing his hand and glad that he had at last found a reason to look forward to their new life.

"Can I have a horse, Mama?" His eyes were huge and questioning. He loved animals, and heaven knew, all the while they had lived in Manhattan, she had felt guilty because he was deprived of owning them, though she had arranged for him to take riding lessons on a pony in Central Park on Saturday mornings.

"Perhaps, Emil. I suppose it depends on where we live."

"I want to live where I can have a horse."

Clare nodded. "It would be a nice fifth-birthday present, wouldn't it?"

"I already got an electric-train set from Grandpapa."

"And a baseball glove too."

"That was from Auntie Fabiana. You gave me those books."

They had celebrated Emil's birthday in advance the night before leaving New York. It was a combination birthday and farewell party. Clare almost cried thinking about it. Her father had wept. Clare pushed her sentimental thoughts aside and concentrated on the present. "Well, I intended to give you something more when we got settled, Emil. And if possible, I'll get you a horse. And if we can't have a horse, then I promise you a dog or a cat."

"Like Vanderbilt?"

"Vanderbilt's an old cat. No, a little kitten."

"I'd like both a horse and a kitten," Emil replied.

Clare laughed. He had sensed his good bargaining position and was now working on two presents instead of one. "You're a little devil," she said affectionately.

He slid under the table and emerged next to her on the dull blue plush seat of the railway compartment. Clare put her arm around him and he snuggled up next to her. "I love you, Mama."

Clare felt tears forming in her eyes as she hugged him tightly. "I love you too," she answered softly.

Friday, April 5, 1929

LOS ANGELES

"What do you think, Emil?" Clare led him through the rambling house. "This area is called Bel Air and this is a unique house. It was built three years ago, and the plans were designed by Frank Lloyd Wright. He's a famous architect."

The house was crafted of golden stone that blended with the natural beauty of the area. It had gently curved walls, skylights, and in spite of the sun's heat, remained cool throughout the day.

It had large airy rooms and sat among the scrub and California pines on an acre and a half of land atop the Santa Monica Mountains.

"It's like living in the country, Emil, but Sunset Boulevard is only half a mile down the road."

"Can I have a horse?" Emil asked as they stood on the tiled patio.

Clare hugged him. "Yes," she said enthusiastically. "And a cat too!" Emil, as she might have suspected, was little interested in the house itself or its decor. But he immediately fell in love with the grounds, with the idea of being able to run free and explore.

"And next year, when you go to school, the bus will pick you up right out in front."

Emil burst into a wide grin. "I won't have to go away?"

"No, my darling. You can live at home. You won't have to go to boarding school."

Emil jumped up and down and clapped his hands. Not going away to school made him even happier than the idea of owning his own horse. Clare blinked back tears. The thought of sending him away had hung over her like a pall. They had spent too much time apart, she told herself, but now, in this new environment, in this wonderful climate, in this beautiful house, they could start a new life together. She felt suddenly lighthearted, as if a great weight had been lifted from her shoulders.

"When can I meet Tom Mix?" Emil interjected.

Clare sat down on the low wall that ringed the patio and pulled Emil down next to her. "Soon . . . soon, my darling. We'll have a housewarming party as soon as we get settled, and we'll invite everyone!"

Emil stretched his legs out and leaned against her. It was virtually the only free time they had had together since they arrived. Clare had spent all of her leisure time looking for the house, and her weekdays were entirely taken up with work. She was already in the process of ridding the banks of their large land holdings and reinvesting funds into more productive ventures. Now she congratulated herself because she knew she was on the verge of closing the deal to buy Liberty Films, a studio she felt could make a large profit, given the development of talkies. California, she thought to herself, was wonderful. It was a state filled with endless possibilities, a state that was booming, a state that had enormous natural wealth and resources. One of her investments, indeed her only sentimental investment, was an offshore fishing operation. To this she had added a cannery. She named the company Domenico and she hoped to expand the cannery into other foods, though at the moment she felt content with the fact that it produced fine-quality tinned bonito, shrimp, and West Coast lobster—all delicacies that suited Eastern tastes.

Emil was standing on the wall and looking out over the rolling mountains to the Pacific. It was an exceptionally clear day. "Are those more mountains, or are those islands?" he asked, squinting into the sun.

Clare stood up. "Islands," she answered. "One of them is Santa Catalina, which is owned by the Wrigleys. They raise cattle there and have grand parties in Avalon."

"Do they have a palace?"

Clare shook her head. "No, just a very large house."

"I like it here," Emil said with conviction.

"You like it because you can play outside all the time."

"I like it because we can be together more, Mama."

Saturday, May 4, 1929

LOS ANGELES

Crowds of people mingled on the tiled patio, others walked in the garden, and some stood around in small groups talking to one another in the spacious living room. Clare tried to circulate, moving among her distinguished quests, who included William Randolph Hearst and the lovely Marion Davies, Tom Mix, invited at Emil's insistence, several producers and directors of note, and a bevy of stars and those who accompanied them.

"I certainly want you to come up to San Simeon," Hearst blustered. "Teddy Roosevelt told me stories about your father, you know. Said, 'Look at that! One little letter of recommendation and he goes into banking! 'Course that was a long time ago. Too bad about Teddy! Stupid to die at sixty-one! That's what comes of wandering around in jungles and getting all that damned exercise. It's a killer! I never do any of those things. I just stay home and publicize the crazies who make news. Going to outlive 'em all!"

Clare smiled. Hearst was quite fit-looking, and she knew him to be sixty-six. "I can't believe you're that inactive."

Hearst leaned over and glanced at Marion. "Get all my exercise prone! It's the best kind!"

Clare blushed.

"Now, now! Didn't mean to embarrass you. My wife always

said I was crude. Comes with the territory. But I meant it about San Simeon. I've got a zoo. My own personal zoo. Little Emil would love that! Built it because no one ever took me to a zoo when I was a kid. But we haven't got cages, no sir. The animals just sort of wander around. Got twenty zebras. You can ask Emil: are zebras white with black stripes, or black with white stripes?''

Clare laughed. But she was relieved when Marion Davies signaled Hearst to join her.

"Don't forget, now, you've got a gold-edged invitation!" He waved to her as he crossed the room.

"Ah, Countess, we meet again."

Clare turned and faced Mark Lyons, who had on his arm the gorgeous blond star, Carole Lombard.

"Miss Lombard was kind enough to ask me to escort her." He smiled.

Clare smiled back, though in fact she didn't entirely feel like smiling. "How fortunate for you," she replied, knowing her comment was tinged with too much sarcasm and that Carole Lombard, whom she hoped to acquire for Liberty Films, might be miffed. Reluctantly Clare admitted to herself that she had hoped the very good-looking Mark Lyons would have come alone.

"Have you two met before?" Carole flashed a dazzling smile and ran her hand through her thick wavy white-blond hair. She was a real beauty with a full, lovely bow-shaped mouth, wide-set blue eyes, flawless skin, and a perfectly proportioned figure.

"Briefly," Clare replied, aware that her face was a little flushed.

"Good, then you can talk for a few moments. I see Irving, and I really must speak with him." She motioned toward Irving Thalberg, slipped off Mark's arm, and floated across the room.

"She's a beautiful woman," Clare observed.

"This room is filled with beautiful women. Hollywood is filled with beautiful women. But Carole's only a girl. She just turned twenty, and her life-long love will be the camera, not a man."

"Is that your way of explaining to me that you two are not attached to one another?"

"Would you be interested if we were?" His eyes danced merrily.

Clare tried to sound unconcerned. "No," she replied simply.

He stared into her eyes. They were wide and sent out signals that reflected her moods: anger, happiness, bewilderment, were all reflected in turn. Her lips were abundantly full whether she smiled or pouted. Her hair was dark and silky and she had the neck of a Botticelli model. Her figure was as good as any woman's in the room. But she was different from the others. Behind the extraordinary good looks was a fine mind. Clare Marina was a challenge, a rare woman with such an obvious sense of direction that she interested him on a level no other woman had succeeded in reaching. "I think that disappoints me," he told her. "I'd rather hoped we could get to know each other."

Clare smiled cautiously. "I should think that's unavoidable. The business community isn't that large."

"I meant on another level."

Clare ran her finger around the edge of her glass. He was certainly flirting with her, and she found she liked it. "I suppose that's possible."

He leaned over toward her. "I heard Randolph invite you to San Simeon. I'll be going up in three weeks—can I suggest he invite you that weekend too?"

"For the whole weekend?"

"It's quite an experience, one you shouldn't miss."

"I've been to many expensive homes. Is San Simeon so different?"

Mark Lyons smiled and winked. "I'll say. It's indescribable. A very luxurious study in baroque art with catsup and mustard thrown in."

"Catsup and mustard?"

"I refuse to explain. You have to experience it."

Clare nodded. "All right," she agreed.

Carole Lombard drifted back, taking Mark's arm possessively. "Darling, I have some people you really must meet."

"See you later," Mark said to Clare Marina as she moved away and began talking to her guests.

He spent a boring five minutes talking to Carole's friends—no, not friends, contacts. Carole was on her way up, and she devoted herself to finding those who could help her. "Excuse me," he said, taking his drink and walking out into the cool night air. Most of the guests had drifted inside, and he sat down alone in a chair by the shimmering swimming pool, watching as the colored lights cast reflections on the water.

"Who are you?"

Mark looked up into the questioning face of a little boy who had emerged out of the shadows. His hair was slightly tousled and his eyes looked a little tired, probably because it was late.

"Mark Lyons."

The little boy's face broke into an infectious smile. "Are you a movie star?"

Mark shook his head. "A businessman."

Emil sat down next to him. "You look like an athlete. I thought maybe you were in cowboy films."

Mark patted him on the knee. "Sorry to disappoint you. But I do own a ranch down in Santa Rosa."

"I have a horse," Emil answered.

"Do you? Did you talk to Mr. Mix?"

"Yes, but he's gone inside now. He was in the Spanish American War. So was my grandfather."

"And who is your grandfather?"

"Agosto Tonelli," Emil answered proudly. "I wish he were here. I wish he were here to go riding with me."

"You don't have anyone to ride with you?"

"Only Mama, and she's so busy all the time."

Mark looked at the child. He had seen him only once before, when he was two. Emiliano Sforza . . . but the little boy didn't look like his father. Mark shook his head as if to dispel the thought "the sins of the father." It wasn't the little boy's fault.

"Well, your mother has plenty of men friends," Mark said. "Don't they ride with you?"

Emiliano shook his head. "She only has men friends in pictures—she's always in pictures with men. But she doesn't have them for real." Emil frowned. "Pictures are make-believe," he said in an adult tone. "I think Mama is really very lonely."

29

Saturday, May 25, 1929

S A N   S I M E O N

"This is a real castle!" Emil said in awe as they disembarked from one of the twelve limousines William Randolph Hearst used to transport his guests to his mountaintop retreat.

Clare stretched and inhaled the warm dry air. She had accepted the invitation out of curiosity, and thus far it was proving an adventure. At a depot on the Coast Highway they were picked up by a train of long sleek cars and driven five miles up a narrow, winding road which passed through dense scrub, rocky mountain areas, and finally manicured green pastures. They passed herds of zebras, elks, and deer. They also passed through rigid security, for as it was explained, the privacy of San Simeon was well-guarded.

The castle and its three guest houses were built on the mountaintop, which Hearst called "The Enchanted Hill."

Outside, a huge shimmering pool glimmered in the sunlight. It was framed by an Etruscan colonnade and surrounded by European statuary. "Hearst had it built after the Olympic champion swimmer Johnny Weissmuller was a guest here. He complained because there was no Olympic-size pool."

"It's really impressive," Clare acknowledged.

They crossed the patio, which was made of thousands of hand-painted inlaid tiles and surrounded with exotic potted plants.

"Welcome to San Simeon!" William Randolph Hearst strode toward his twenty-five guests, his arms gesticulating in the air. "Come, come. You'll be shown to your rooms so you can freshen up. Then we'll have drinks on the patio."

No need to worry about Treasury agents here, Clare thought. They'd need a regiment to get past the private army that guarded the gates.

"Did you see the zebra, son?"

"Lots of them!" Emil answered.

"Well, are they black with white stripes or white with black stripes?"

Emil frowned and put his finger to his mouth, his usual thinking position. "I think it must depend on the color of their tails," he answered thoughtfully.

"Aha! Smart boy! That's the best answer I've had!"

"What is the answer?" Clare asked.

Hearst shrugged. "Damned if I know! Well, come along in. I've put you in the North Gothic Bedroom. You'll like it, it's all Renaissance and Gothic decor."

"I'm sure it's lovely," Clare replied politely. In point of fact, Mr. Hearst had a passion for buying the good with the bad and mixing them outrageously. His taste was something of a legend. In her more sarcastic days Constanza would have said that was what happened when a peasant got money.

Clare and Emil went with Mr. Hearst and the other guests staying in the main house. They passed through the giant library on their way to their rooms, and Clare noted the rows and rows of books. "What a lot of books!"

Hearst broke into gales of deep laughter. "Never read a damned one of them! Ordered them all by the yard from a bookstore up in San Francisco. That's why they all match! Called 'em up and ordered fifty yards of green books, fifty yards of yellow books, fifty yards of blue books, and a hundred yards of orange books! Wanted a good selection! But I like orange best. Actually, all my rare books are in a warehouse."

Clare bit her lip to keep from laughing.

"Randolph is a strange man," Mark had told her on the ride up the mountain. "San Simeon is the most lavish, expensive, ornately decorated mansion in North America, but Hearst insists that everyone be casual, and his idea of a casual atmosphere includes catsup and mustard bottles among the priceless antiques. You know, when he was a child, his father used to bring him up here for the summers. They camped in fully furnished silk tents, had hundreds of servants, and called it 'the ranch.' That became Randolph's idea of camping."

Clare smiled. Mark Lyons had a wealth of entertaining stories and seemed to know a lot not only about William Randolph Hearst but also about California lore and history.

"Ah, Countess, here's your room! Plenty of space for you and the boy. Remember, cocktails down on the patio!" Hearst told her.

Clare closed the heavy door and then began laughing.

"Why are you laughing, Mama?"

"Oh, I can't help it." She replied. "Oh, dear heaven, Emil, look at this room!"

Every wall had a painting by some obscure painter, though there was one by Caravaggio. The two beds were canopied horrors with tapestry coverings. The bathroom had a gold toilet, gold faucets, and marble fixtures. There was even a marble reproduction of the *David* next to the bed. The only lighting was provided by a huge silver sanctuary lamp that hung from the intricately carved Spanish ceiling.

"I do hope Lucrezia Borgia doesn't fall out of the closet," Clare said, feeling herself on the verge of laughing again. The entire place was elegantly ludicrous.

Clare opened the weekend bag she'd brought and changed quickly into a casual silk dress.

"I like it here," Emil said, bouncing on Lucrezia Borgia's bed.

"And it's in the same good taste as Grauman's Chinese," Clare said.

They went out onto the patio, where around the huge pool tables of food and liquor awaited. Emil ran off to explore Hearst's personal zoo, and Clare found herself talking to Marion Davies.

"A real countess," Marion gushed.

"I married a count. I'm really from Brooklyn."

"Fancy that! So am I. My real name's Marion Cecilia Douras, you know. But in Hollywood they say Latins aren't in any demand, so I changed my name to Davies. It looks better on the marquee and its got that old Anglo-Saxon ring to it."

"I'd never change my name," Clare replied. "My father always says a name can't bring respect, that a man must act in such a way as to make his name respected."

Marion shrugged. "Your father isn't a movie star. I do what the studio tells me." She drifted away, a sad look in her eyes, her pink drink sloshing over the sides of her glass.

"Here I am." Mark Lyons strode up to Clare. "Your hair has red streaks in the sun."

"Quite common," Clare replied.

"Oh, I doubt there's anything common about you."

His look was admiring, and Clare thought he looked dashing in white. His shirt was open at the neck, and his casual attire made him seem younger and relaxed.

"Tell you what," he suggested. "Hearst has a fantastic stable. Why don't we all go for a ride?"

"Emil would love it, but I'm not dressed for riding."

He looked at her clinging dress. "Then we'll go at sunrise tomorrow. How's that?"

She nodded her agreement and allowed him to take her arm. They began walking through the formal gardens that surrounded the patio.

"Tell me about yourself," Clare said, looking into his eyes.

"My mother was Italian," he began. "A very beautiful, very gifted woman . . ."

In the predawn hours Clare, Emil, and Mark set out on horseback to explore the ranch. They watched as the sun came up over the mountains and cast blinding reflections on the ocean in the distance. Then they rode down the hill to the beach and dismounted to sit on the sand and watch the waves crashing to shore. Emil darted off to explore clumps of seaweed deposited by the high tide.

"This is the first time in a long while that I've been completely out of touch with business," Clare admitted.

"Me too." He smiled and seemed to be studying her.

"You've never married?" Clare asked. He was most attractive, warm and friendly, and appeared unattached.

Mark shook his head. "Morty says I'm married to Lyons Oil." He winked. "Until now I never met a woman who could understand that."

Clare flushed and looked at the sand. "I've never met a man who understood my interest in banking."

"We're off to a good start, Clare Marina." He reached out to take her hand.

Clare pulled it away and looked at him steadily. "I can't be impulsive," she said slowly. "I've had bad experiences."

Mark nodded silently but decided not to say anything about Emiliano Sforza at this moment. "I'd like to see you again, soon. Come out to San Marino for dinner. Can you come next Saturday?"

Clare thought for a minute. "I'm sorry, I have an appointment. It's business, and I can't break it."

"And I'm tied up on Sunday and that week I'll be in San Francisco. How about the eighth?"

Clare inwardly determined she would make time even if she had an appointment. "The eighth is fine."

Mark bent and kissed her cheek lightly.

Clare felt a chill run through her. She found she had a fleeting wish that it had been a more passionate kiss, but then she reminded herself of her own weaknesses. I'll never be that anxious again, she vowed. One Alessandro is enough.

Saturday, June 8, 1929

SAN MARINO, CALIFORNIA

"It's very beautiful here," Clare said, looking out on the rolling lawn of Mark Lyons' San Marino estate. They'd eaten dinner alone in the dining room, talked casually, and then gone outside to enjoy the sunset. He seemed distracted, Clare thought. Not as easygoing as he'd been at San Simeon, and decidedly more distant.

Mark looked down, studying the patterns of the stones on the terrace. "I find myself very attracted to you," he began.

Clare watched him. He wasn't looking at her, and he seemed nervous, a far cry from the outgoing flirtatious picture he'd presented on previous occasions.

"You say that as if it were a regrettable illness," she commented.

Mark looked up. She was a little bemused, as if she thought he was being shy. "You don't understand. I find I want to be with you more and more, and I'm aware that things are getting out of hand."

"Out of hand!" Clare smiled, and her lovely dark eyes twinkled.

Mark shook his head slowly and put his fingers to his lips, as if to beg for her silence and attention. "I'm going to botch this," he confessed. "Clare, I don't want to do that, and you have to believe me when I tell you I don't want to hurt you."

She tilted her head. "I don't understand."

He reached across the distance between them and took her hands in his, drawing her closer to him. "I want to kiss you, I want to hold you and not let go."

"I won't stop you," she replied, searching his face, which held a hint of sadness.

Again he shook his head. "I want to, but I can't. I want to love you, but I can't love you because I think you still love Emiliano Sforza. Clare, I can't let any part of you belong to him."

Clare stood rigidly in front of him. "We were married only a few weeks, Mark, but I loved him deeply. He's Emil's father. He was a fine man, and I could never erase him entirely from my memory. I don't understand how, or even why, you'd expect me to. What possible difference could my memory of Emiliano make to us?''

"It makes a difference because he wasn't the man you remember. You had a false image of him, and I can't get further involved with you unless you know and accept the truth.''

Clare pressed her lips together and shook her head. "I don't understand you.''

"Come,'' was his only answer. He led her across the patio and into the study. He went directly to a painting that sat in the corner, covered with a white sheet. "I've told you a little about my sister, Louisa.'' Clare nodded and he could see the look of puzzlement on her face. "My sister was Emiliano Sforza's mistress. He saw her during the entire time he was engaged to you. When she discovered he wasn't going to marry her, she threatened to expose him and he had her killed by a thug named Dumini.''

Clare's mouth opened in shock and she shook her head in disbelief.

"Dumini was one of the men who killed Matteotti. I was there, I was at the window.''

"Emiliano was dead before that. He'd never have been involved with such people. I can't believe a word you're telling me.''

"I can show you letters from Matteotti. Your husband had three union organizers killed by the *ceka*, and what I'm telling you about Louisa is true. My sister was a talented artist. This was the last picture she painted. It was with her other canvases.'' He pulled the sheet away.

The painting depicted a nude Louisa—a self-portrait of a woman in pain, her facial expression distorted, her arms reaching toward a man. And the man, quite clearly, was a nude Emiliano Sforza, his facial expression coldblooded and hard.

Clare stared at the painting. Artistically, it was brilliant; but as life it was pure agony. "Oh, God,'' Clare murmured. But she leaned forward and saw that Louisa had scrawled her name on the painting, and beneath it the date September 1923.

Clare let out her breath and collapsed in the leather chair. She shook her head. "I don't believe he would have anyone killed . . . I don't.''

"You don't want to!''

Clare looked up at Mark. His face was tense, almost angry.

"Was he so good a lover?'' Mark said, a hint of cruelty in his voice.

Clare looked up at him with tear-filled eyes and nodded. "He was a wonderful lover, and the father of my son.'' She shook her head. "I now have to believe he had a mistress, and that's hurtful enough, but . . . no, I can't believe he'd have anyone killed. I'm sorry—sorry because I like you." She looked away. "Could you have Mr. Levinson take me home now?"

Sunday, July 7, 1929

BROOKLYN

Agosto Tonelli sat at the head of the table, presiding over the traditional Sunday dinner. It was, for the first time in many months, a real family gathering.

Fabiana took charge of the kitchen, directing Seraphina in the preparation of a true feast. Maria, Anthony, Jenny, Roberto Marcucci, and Constanza were all present.

"It's been a long while since the table has been so full," Agosto said as he helped himself to the cannelloni and then to an ample helping of green salad.

"Is Clare coming home in November?" Jenny asked, brushing her silky blond hair off her brow.

"Of course. She wouldn't miss the board meeting."

"I'll bet Emil has grown like a weed in the California sun," Anthony put in.

"When are you planning to have a baby?" Maria asked, looking at Jenny. "You've been married long enough—you should be having children."

Jenny stared at the tablecloth and didn't answer.

"We're young," Anthony said immediately. "There's no need to start a family just yet. There's time."

Maria did not reply, nor did she smile. Instead, she turned to her brother. "Have some more bread, Agosto. You need to eat more, and you need rest. You look tired."

"I am tired," he admitted. "I've been buying up as much AmFed stock as I can."

"Why? The market is booming!" Jenny said enthusiastically.

Agosto shook his head. "The truth is not so easily seen." Agosto deemed it fit not to mention the amount he had spent. It was nearly thirty million, and Clare was buying as well, using some of her own personal fortune.

"What do you sense, Agosto?" Maria leaned across the table. "Is there going to be difficulty?"

Agosto shrugged. "Maybe, but I know that the more AmFed

stock we have in our hands, the less vulnerable we'll be to speculation."

"But things are going so wonderfully," Jenny said. "My father has just bought a new yacht and he says the economy will just get better and better, especially if the government will just leave the banks alone."

"Your father and I do not always agree," Agosto said, trying not to sound irritated.

Jenny giggled and continued eating.

"I have funds, if you need them to buy more stock," Constanza suggested.

"I could use some of my funds," Anthony added.

"Oh, but then we can't buy the house in Newport," Jenny said, pouting slightly. "My father says real estate is a wonderful investment. And it's such a lovely house, Anthony."

Anthony fell into silence, caught between his father's good sense and his wife's material desires. She wanted to live in the grand manner like her mother, and cared little for business or indeed for his family.

"Maybe it is, maybe it isn't," Agosto said. "My father was originally a seaman, and he used to say that sometimes you couldn't see the storm but that you could feel the subtle change in the wind. A good sailor secures the sails and battens down the hatches before the squall, not after it begins. AmFed may be a public company, but there's too much speculation on the market, and the less stock there is available, the less there will be to speculate with . . . if anything happens."

"I agree," Maria said without looking up. "We should keep as much as possible in the family. Family is all you can depend on."

Agosto nodded at his sister. She was the arch traditionalist, but she was right. And Maria was more than an echo of his own thoughts financially. Over the years she had become a wealthy woman who kept her counsel. He alone realized that from the day he opened his first bank, Maria had been quietly investing. She lived on practically nothing, storing away the interest and dividends like a squirrel storing nuts. Now, as surely as he sat across from her, he knew she would use that money to buy more AmFed stock and thus bolster the company. And, he thought, looking at the silent Fabiana, she would do the same. He smiled to himself. Clare Marina had also spent a fortune helping him. They were his three women, the ones he could count on. Maria was silent and traditional and always fought with Clare, who was the born rebel. But in a way, they were alike, both bound to the family and both fiercely tenacious. And between them was Fabiana, the soft spirit who cushioned their encounters and who constantly gave love.

Agosto glanced at Anthony. He was a strong young man with a fine education. The mantle of the Tonelli empire would fall to him; AmFed would one day be his domain. Because you are my only son, Agosto thought. Yes, he decided, Anthony would be the inheritor, but he was doubly fortunate because he had Clare Marina, Maria, and Fabiana to count on. Moreover, Roberto would be invaluable. He and Constanza were more than a part of the AmFed family, they were a part of *his* family.

"Your commitment makes me proud," Agosto said. "I have a strong family that's survived personal tragedy and continued to build. Your grandparents would be proud." He smiled, blinking back sentimental tears. "Tonelli is a real American name now."

Thursday, August 1, 1929

LOS ANGELES

Clare sat propped up in bed, the Los Angeles *Times* spread out in front of her. There, staring her in the face, was a large picture of Mark Lyons and Carole Lombard. "FREQUENT COMPANIONS," read the caption. Clare folded the paper and leaned back against the pillows, feeling empty and alone.

In the days and weeks following Mark's accusation, he'd sent flowers, written notes, and phoned repeatedly. But Clare sent the flowers back, tore up the notes, and refused his calls. It won't work, it will never work, she told herself again and again. He clearly believed Emiliano had been a murderer, and Clare couldn't accept it, though she often admitted to herself that their marriage might have been unhappy had he lived. He'd never have let me help run Sforza Industries, she told herself. Then too, there was no denying Louisa's existence and Emiliano's duplicity. But a murderer? No, Clare decided, that was impossible.

And even if that were not impediment enough, there was Emil. "How would you cope with the son of the man you believe murdered your sister?" Clare asked aloud. She shook her head and closed her eyes. Lucky in business, unlucky in personal relationships.

I must stop this, Clare told herself. I must stop thinking about it and forget it. We hardly knew each other . . . it was nothing, it was good that it ended before it started. "Go away," she said aloud to the mental picture of Mark Lyons that crowded in on her thoughts. "Go away," she told her thoughts when she began wondering if there was any truth in his accusations.

"Mama!" Emil burst into her bedroom with characteristic enthusiasm. He was dressed to go riding, but his smile faded when he saw she was still in bed. "You promised," he said, pouting.

Clare smiled. "Go on, I'll get right up. It'll only take me a minute."

"Mama, have you been crying?"

Clare blinked. She'd been unconscious of her tears. "No, no," she assured Emil. "I just had something in my eye."

Saturday, October 19, 1929

LOS ANGELES

It was seven o'clock when Clare left the West Coast headquarters of AmFed at La Brea and Wilshire. The New York Stock Exchange was open till two on Saturdays, which meant that the ticker usually droned on until five in California. But at seven when she left, it was still reporting, and clearly it was running at least two hours behind.

She hurried into the house. She'd tried three times to call New York, but the lines were jammed. Clare dropped her jacket on the sofa and went directly to the phone. It was now nearly eight, so it would be eleven in New York.

"I have to get through to New York!" she demanded impatiently.

"I'm sorry, the lines are still jammed," the operator's voice announced in a weary monotone. "If you leave your name and number I'll notify you when there's a free line."

Clare did so and hung up, slamming the receiver down in frustration.

"What's wrong, Mama?" Emil came in and plopped down on the sofa.

Clare inhaled. "Trouble on the stock market," she said. How could she possibly explain to a five-year-old how totally distracted she was at this moment? She and her father had both expected an end to the boom, and certainly there had been signs of instability for months. But today's rate of selling looked bad, and because the tickers were running behind, it was hard to make a reasonable assessment.

"What kind of trouble?" Emil asked, kicking off his shoes.

"Bad trouble," Clare said. "Everyone seems to be selling."

"What does that mean?" Emil asked.

"It means many people are going to lose a lot of money," Clare answered.

"Are we? I won't lose my horse, will I?"

In spite of her grim mood, Clare laughed. "No," she promised, hugging him. "Emil, I think I'll have to go to New York."

He frowned. "Can I come?"

Clare shook her head. "I'm going to be very busy. It would be better if you stayed here. You don't want to miss school, do you? Besides, you'd miss riding Racer."

"Will you be gone long?"

"I don't think so," Clare said thoughtfully. She bit her lip. It was seven days by train and seven days back—no, it would take too long. "I'm going to try to charter a plane," she announced. "It'll be much faster."

"Oh, I wish I could go! A plane! I always wanted to fly!"

Clare stood up and stretched. "When I come back, we'll see if we can arrange for you to go up in a plane."

Emil smiled contentedly. "When will you be back?" he asked again.

"Two weeks, I hope," Clare replied. "I won't stay any longer than necessary, darling, I promise. And I'll still take you with me when I go for the board meeting in November."

Clare hurried into the small Burbank airport. She had arisen at six and eaten a quick breakfast with Emil. It was now seven-thirty, and on a Sunday morning she'd expected only the usual group of early-morning hobby fliers to be about.

She cursed under her breath. There were lines in front of the little charter operations—too many people and not enough planes or pilots.

"Good morning," the blandly cheerful vice-president of the Bank of America said to her. "Going to New York? Everybody's going to New York. There isn't a charter to be had."

"And I tossed half the night wondering if I should go," Clare replied, looking around at the grim-faced cream of the West Coast financial community.

The vice-president, whose name escaped her, shrugged. "I was ordered to go, but damned if I know what all the fuss is about. Sure, the market took a tumble yesterday, but it'll recover on Monday, it always has. It isn't like yesterday was the first loss day this year. Last February was just as bad.''

Clare listened to his comment, but only nodded. In truth, she didn't agree. Yesterday's drop was monumental, but besides the drop there were other distressing signs. The government was having trouble finding money. Yesterday's tumble was the second heaviest in Saturday trading. More than three million shares had changed hands, and the industrial index was down twelve points. There would be margin calls on Monday—a lot of them— and that would force many people to sell their shares, thus accelerating the downward plunge.

The vice-president went on burbling. "This trip is a real waste. I was supposed to be out on the green at nine. Now I'll have to wait here till the bank's plane comes down from San Francisco. Damned inconvenient.''

Clare's eyes roamed the waiting faces; then she saw Mark Lyons striding purposefully across the room, briefcase in hand. He opened the glass doors and headed for one of the hangars.

Clare didn't hesitate. She hurried after him, leaving the vice-president still talking about his golf game.

"Mark! Mark!''

He stopped and turned around. "Clare Marina! Are you trying to charter a plane?'' His facial expression was serious, and his voice conveyed concern.

"I can't get a charter,'' she said somewhat breathlessly. "Have you got one? Is there room for me? I'll pay for it, of course.''

"Lyons Oil has its own plane. The pilots are warming up the engine now.'' He smiled at her. "Of course there's room for you. I can't think of anyone I'd rather have along.''

"Not even Carole Lombard?'' Clare raised her eyebrow and looked at him.

He grinned boyishly. "You should know not to believe all you read.'' He took her arm and led her across the windy tarmac toward the hangar.

"Oh, it's large,'' Clare said, looking at the plane.

"It has quite a proper passenger compartment. Have you flown before?''

"Yes, in Italy . . . but not on a plane like this.''

He helped her up the rollaway steps into the plane. The passenger cabin was small; it had two long seats, one on each side, and she noted a small portable bar. A small steel door separated it from the cockpit. Mark opened the door and shouted above the noise of the propellers, "Okay! All aboard, Sam! Take her away!''

Clare sat down and shoved her small case under the seat. Mark sat opposite. "Coffee?"

"Do you have some?"

He produced a thermos and two cups. "Not terribly hot, but better than nothing."

The plane was backed out of the hangar and then began moving down the runway. Clare watched out the small window behind her seat till it lifted off the ground and skimmed out over the San Bernardino Mountains. "How long will it take?" she asked.

Mark shrugged. "We're not trying to set a record. We have scheduled fuel stops in Arizona, Oklahoma, and Ohio. It's about eighteen hours' actual flight time, and I have two pilots, so they trade off. With good weather we should be in New York by tomorrow morning."

"I assume there's a radio."

"Yup, we can keep in touch."

Clare leaned back. "I'm glad I saw you. I haven't even been able to get through to my father."

Mark poured himself some more coffee and refilled Clare's cup. "I sense the boom is over," he said, retreating to business, always a safe topic of conversation. "But judging from the crowd at the airport, I'd say I wasn't alone in that conclusion."

Clare nodded. "A lot of people sense this is it. Mind you, the loss of confidence isn't going to help matters."

"It couldn't go on forever. Too many people buying on margin. Christ, look at Radio. There's a speculator's dream. Ninety-four and a half for eighteen months, then zoom zoom up to five-oh-five in September. Hell, the whole country's full of people who heard the stock market is the place to get rich quick, and every one of them thinks it's possible overnight. I was in a little restaurant a few weeks ago and heard three guys talking about the prospects for GM and United Corporation, and what they didn't know was a lot more then what they did know. So what have we got?—a lot of innocents in over their heads, plus a lot of people buying because they know something's going to give and they intend to get in and get out before it does."

"According to our study, brokers' loans increased at the rate of four hundred million every single month of last summer. Our banks stopped lending for stock purchases—we've only been putting out loans for hard investments."

He smiled broadly. "And it's cost you customers, who've gone to the Bank of America."

"Which holds far too much collateral in land. If the prices drop radically as a result of selling, they'll be stuck with overvalued land as collateral on all those loans. Unfortunately, a bank can't turn a mountain of scrub into cash.''

"Seven billion out in loans . . . I knew this would happen. So did Marty. Let's say things get worse—where will you stand?''

"I'm not certain,'' Clare replied cautiously. "AmFed will certainly drop drastically, but we own huge blocks of its shares ourselves, so there can't be much speculation . . . or, more accurately, the price will bottom out at a tolerable figure. How about you?''

"About the same. I expect the price of oil to drop, but not the need for it. Face it, a lot of the get-rich-quick boys will be wiped out, a lot of small investors will go broke, and the big guys may lose half of their millions. But half of ten million still leaves you five. Half of five hundred dollars doesn't leave a small investor enough to buy groceries for more than a couple of months.'' He shook his head dejectedly. "Damn that stupid Mellon and Lamont! Mellon's a banker's banker, if you will pardon the expression. As Secretary of the Treasury the man's been a disaster. Did you see the papers yesterday? The market wasn't great on Friday, but one of the things that caused panic yesterday was Secretary of Commerce Lamont announcing that the government couldn't find a hundred thousand dollars to pay for the upkeep on that damn yacht J. P. Morgan gave them. No wonder people started selling, if the government can't find a lousy hundred grand.''

"The *Corsair*? I didn't see that story. I was at AmFed all day and I didn't read the paper last night—it seemed like old news, and I was too agitated to concentrate. I finally sent my father a wire, but I'll probably get there before it does.'' She laughed at the irony.

It was a musical laugh, Mark thought. And her marvelous eyes danced.

"You know, you're the first man who's ever had a serious financial discussion with me—besides my father.''

"Don't the people who work for you have serious financial discussions with you?''

"They have no choice,'' Clare replied. "I meant a voluntary discussion, a discussion between just friends.''

"Are we friends? Clare, I want to be.''

Clare's eyes were steady on him. "Let's try to be,'' she said seriously. She pressed his accusations about Emiliano out of her mind, admitting she wanted to be with him and thanking fate for making it easy.

"We'll be in Arizona for lunch,'' he said, leaning toward her. "Will you have lunch with me while the plane is being refueled?''

He touched her hand lightly, and she didn't withdraw it. "All right," she agreed.

A dry hot wind blew off the arid southern Arizona desert and the late-afternoon sun beat mercilessly down on them as they drove in the open car from the rough airfield into Tucson.

"It's not much of town," Mark joked. "I'm afraid the only restaurant is Fred Harvey's at the Southern Pacific Railway station."

"I think I could eat anything—I only had toast and coffee for breakfast and that was at six this morning."

"You must be hungry—it's about three now."

"Why do we have to fly so far south?" she asked.

"To avoid bad weather and wind drafts over the Rockies. There's already snow in Flagstaff."

Clare sighed. "That hardly seems possible. Lord, it must be nearly ninety! I'm perishing in this wool sweater and skirt."

He laughed pleasantly. "Flying is an impossible way to travel, and you certainly can't dress for it. Up there"—he pointed to the sky—"it's cold and down here it's a furnace. And never mind the difference between the sky and the ground. In a matter of hours we'll change climate completely. October isn't California's warmest month, unless of course we get a Santa Ana wind off Death Valley, but it's downright cold in the Midwest and usually on the East Coast."

"I didn't bring a coat," Clare replied. "In fact, I didn't even bring a change of clothes."

"You mean that bag in the plane is full of papers?"

"I'm afraid so."

"First woman I've ever met who didn't travel with a trunkload of clothes and cosmetics."

"Sorry, but the papers are more important."

"That's what I like, a woman with priorities."

The car ambled down the dusty road south of Tucson, past the glaring white San Xavier mission, and into town. It came to a rattling halt in front of the railway station, which, like most of the buildings, was designed in the Spanish style, white stucco with red tile roof. Mark helped Clare out of the car and led her into the nearly deserted restaurant. "I recommend the steak here," he said. "Good meat driven in from Texas is liable to be the only decent food."

"You order," she said, putting the menu aside.

"Two medium-rare steaks and two salads."

The waitress disappeared, and he winked at Clare. "After-dinner drinks on the plane."

"What time will we get to Tulsa?"

"Long after midnight. We'll have them pack some sandwiches here. There won't be a thing open in Tulsa. In fact, we probably won't get a decent meal till we reach New York."

"I'll live."

The waitress brought their food and perfunctorily set it down on the table.

"Good thing we got here before the six-P.M. train," Mark said. "This place is packed then."

Clare ate heartily. "I really was hungry," she admitted. Then, changing the subject: "Why are you so anxious to get to New York?"

"Lyons Oil is reasonably secure, but I have other interests. The time delays make decisions difficult. I'm afraid I have to be where the action is. And you?"

"My father will need me. He has my brother, of course, but Anthony's knowledge comes from his education, not from his gut. I love him—don't misunderstand—but he lacks experience and toughness." She smiled warmly. "Besides, my strength, if I can describe it that way without sounding egotistical, comes from being with my family. My father is the same. Maybe it's that way with all Italian families, especially those whose origins are in southern Italy. The family is everything. Even if there's dissension, there's unity."

"Is there dissension?"

"Sometimes. My brother married Jenny Stearns, and her family has been steadily buying into AmFed. Through Jenny their influence has grown."

"And they're not family?"

Clare shook her head. "Not really. I'm afraid that everything Father built will fall into the hands of others. Anthony doesn't care enough, Jenny doesn't care at all. But her mother, Sarah, does. I suspect she'd like to see her husband, Creighton, inherit my father's financial empire."

"That's an empire you were instrumental in building."

"I'm a mere woman," Clare said sarcastically.

Mark Lyons reached across the table and covered her hand with his. "You're not a mere woman," he told her. "You're a very special woman."

Mark put the basket of food down and turned to help Clare back into the plane. There were no steps, only a large wooden crate pushed up to the door so that Clare would not have to hoist herself up. "There you go!" Mark said, helping take the giant step from the crate into the cabin.

He bolted the door closed and they both sat down. Again the roar of engines, again the lift-off up into the sky.

"How about the after-dinner drink I offered?"

Clare nodded, realizing how tired she was. "I think it'll put me to sleep."

"At five o'clock?"

"I hardly slept at all last night."

"Visions of quotations running through your head, were there?"

"I'm afraid so."

He handed her the Scotch and water. "There's no ice, but the water's cold." He sat down beside her and casually put his arm across the back of the seat.

Clare sipped her drink contentedly.

"You're an intelligent woman," he said after a time. "The kind of woman who haunts a man."

"You don't mind that?"

He laughed. "What? Being haunted, or the fact you're intelligent?"

"The latter," she replied. "My experience with men has been that they want to conquer—plunder, if you like—but that they run from intellectual competition."

"I'd say that's a realistic view of the male of our species. I'd like to plunder you, as you put it. But I wouldn't run from intellectual competition. Somehow I've always thought that would make life more interesting." He leaned over and kissed her cheek, then her neck.

"Mark—" Clare's words were silenced by his kiss, a kiss that began softly and grew in intensity till she felt herself responding to it and giving way to the sensations he caused within her.

"I think I'm in love with you, Clare Marina. I think Morty's right: I think I've been in love with you for a long time."

Clare looked up into his warm eyes, then shook her head. "Mark, there's too much between us . . ." She paused for a moment, trying desperately to overcome her own desires. "I need some time . . . you've confused me. I . . . I think I have some feeling for you too, but it would be wrong now."

"And you still love Emiliano Sforza?"

Clare stared at the cabin floor. "I love a memory—it's been too long for anything else. But I've thought about your story, about all the things you told me. There's someone I must talk with before . . . Try to understand."

He released her and nodded. "I understand."

30

Monday, October 21, 1929

MANHATTAN

A cold fog engulfed the harbor and hung low over the tall buildings of the Manhattan skyline as the Lyons Oil plane landed at six-thirty A.M.

Mark and Clare Marina sat in a tiny coffee shop and waited for Mark's car to pick them up and take them into the city.

"How do you feel?" he asked.

"Apprehensive."

"Will you fly back with me?"

"If possible. It all depends on what happens." Clare stared into her coffee cup. "Where can I get in touch with you?"

Mark frowned. "Not sure . . . I don't know where I'll be staying. How about you?"

Clare shrugged. "Some Manhattan hotel, maybe the Plaza. You can get me at the AmFed offices, Broadway and Thirty-ninth."

"I'll call you in a few days. Clare, I want to see you and be with you."

"Mr. Lyons, your car is here," the messenger announced, tipping his hat.

Clare stood and brushed her rumpled dress. Then she took his hand. "Thank you, Mark . . . for everything." *I want to say more,* she thought as she felt him squeeze her hand.

"We better get into the city," he said, guiding her toward the door and still holding her hand tightly.

Remembering her girlhood, Clare said, "It's been a long while since I held hands with a man."

"It won't be so long the next time."

Clare went directly to the AmFed offices, where she waited for her father, who arrived at eight-thirty.

Agosto embraced her. "I got your wire, Clarissima. But you got here so quickly!"

"I flew," Clare told him.

Agosto nodded. "I'm glad you're here," he said, shuffling through the papers on his desk.

"What do you think will happen?" Clare asked.

"AmFed is down to 125 from 170. But that's nothing compared to what happened to other stocks on Friday." He shook his head. "The papers are predicting 'organized support.' Damned if I know where it's going to come from."

"I'm prepared to buy more AmFed stock," Clare told him. "I have over two million with me."

"You must trust your pilot."

Clare smiled. "Well, the owner of the plane anyway."

Agosto pressed his lips together. "We're going to have to play a cautious waiting game, Clarissima. One that will be very hard on the nerves. We have to use all our assets to buy at the right minute, just when the stock starts to fall. It's essential to maintain the price."

Clare nodded.

"I have private lines set up. I want you to stay here. If I call, then you buy immediately. But I warn you, Clarissima, I may not call today—it could be tomorrow or even next week. We have to be prepared to pour in millions to keep the price from dropping severely."

"You think this will drag on."

"I think it will be up and down, while steadily heading down."

"I'll stay here and wait."

"Use my private office. There's a ticker machine in there, so you can keep track of what's happening. But I warn you, if today is anything like Friday, the tape will be way behind the actual movement on the floor."

"Where will you be if I have to get in touch with you?"

"Roberto and I will be in meetings. I'll be at the Morgan Bank this morning."

Clare frowned. "Where's Anthony?"

Agosto grimaced. "He took Jenny to Bermuda for two weeks. I've wired him, but I haven't heard a word."

Clare hugged her father. "Don't worry," she said.

"This is serious, Clarissima, very serious."

"I know," she answered. "Believe me, Papa, I know."

By noon the ticker was running an hour late, and it was not until an hour and forty minutes after the exchange closed that it recorded the last transaction of the day. The final sales totaled 6,091,870 shares, the third-largest volume in the history of the market. But in spite of the monumental volume, it was extraordinarily hard to tell what was happening. A person, Clare thought, could be ruined without even knowing it. Trading aside, however, the market actually closed well above its low for the day, and it seemed that the net loss on the New York *Times*'s industrial averages was only six points.

At five Agosto called. "A shaky rally," he muttered into the phone. "Don't do anything yet."

"Are you coming back here?" Clare questioned.

"No, I have more meetings. Clarissima, go out and eat, find yourself a hotel room. I'll call you in the morning."

Clare called the Plaza for reservations, then left the AmFed offices and took a cab to Lord and Taylor. There she hurriedly bought a few outfits and a coat. Farther down Fifth Avenue she bought a few necessary cosmetics at Elizabeth Arden.

Once ensconced in her hotel room, Clare called Fabiana. They chatted for over an hour. Then she ate dinner and went to bed before nine, falling immediately into a sleep born of total exhaustion.

On Tuesday the weak rally continued. Professor Fisher, one of the happier seers of the financial world, blandly announced that "only the insane fringe of the investment community has been shaken loose from the market."

Feeling rested, if not relaxed, Clare returned to her hotel room. She sat for a long while, then called Constanza and asked her to come over alone.

"Constanza!" Clare hugged her and beckoned her into the hotel suite.

"I can't tell you how flattered I am that apart from your father, I'm the first one you asked to see. My God, this is dreary—I haven't seen Roberto for two days. Are we going to be poor, Clare? I really don't want to be poor."

Clare smiled. "Sit down, Constanza. Let me fix you a drink."

"Aren't we going to dinner?"

"After we talk," Clare said seriously.

"You look grim."

"Not grim, just tired and confused. It's always bad if something happens in your personal life at the same time there's a business crisis."

Constanza leaned toward Clare. "Is something wrong with Emil?"

Clare shook her head. "Oh, no. Constanza, I don't know where to begin. I have to talk to you about Emiliano."

"Emiliano?"

Clare handed Constanza her drink and sat down. "I know when Emiliano and I were married, you objected to me."

"I don't object to you now. I'm very fond of you."

"Then you must tell me about Emiliano. Constanza, I hardly knew him. . . . Do you know about a woman named Louisa?"

Constanza's face paled and she bit her lip. "Oh, Clare, why after all these years must you open that door?"

"I have to. It's terribly important to me. Constanza, you must tell me the truth."

"She was his mistress."

"And he stayed with her right up until he married me?"

Constanza nodded.

"What happened to her?"

"She was killed in an accident."

"An accident?"

Constanza's eyes filled with tears. "Maybe not an accident. She threatened Emiliano."

Clare drew in her breath. "And the labor organizers . . . that man Dumini . . . ?"

"I didn't want you to know all this—how did you find out?"

"It's not important, Constanza. It's only important I know the truth." Tears were already filling her eyes.

Constanza ran her hand along the edge of the sofa nervously. "My brother was a ruthless man. Yes, he employed Dumini. He told me that, and he told me about Louisa. Clare, I disliked Emiliano a great deal. It's true I didn't want him to marry you—I felt it would make my position worse. But Emiliano ruled the family with an iron hand, and he always got his way."

"Oh, Constanza, if only I'd known."

"I couldn't tell you. In the beginning there was too much animosity between us, and you wouldn't have believed me. Then I saw how you saved Sforza Industries because he'd built it. I couldn't tell you then—you'd been married only a few weeks, and I wanted you to have good memories. Then Emil was born . . ." Constanza began crying.

Clare collapsed back in her chair, shaking her head in disbelief while tears ran down her face. "Why did you help me save Sforza Industries, Constanza? There's more, isn't there?"

"Yes, there's more. You wanted to save Sforza Industries because Emiliano had built it. I wanted to save it because he built it at great cost to my happiness. It all would have been a waste, you see—Eduardo . . . everything."

"Tell me everything," Clare prodded. She wiped the tears off her face and leaned toward her sister-in-law.

"When I was very young, I fell in love with Eduardo Gallio. He came from a good family, but one that had little money." Constanza shook her head. "I loved him, Clare. I really loved him."

"But you didn't marry?"

"Emiliano wouldn't let me." Constanza's eyes took a faraway look. "Emiliano insisted I marry Ernesto Sforza, a distant but very wealthy relative who was fifty years older than I."

"Oh, Constanza!"

"I objected . . ." She shook her head. "But then Eduardo was killed." She paused and bit her lip. "I was told it was a hunting accident."

Clare reached across the distance between them and took Constanza's arm. "You believe that Emiliano . . . ?"

"He was ruthless, Clare. I married Ernesto, and he died two years later. Emiliano inherited his money and used it to build Sforza Industries."

"I didn't really know him at all," Clare said. "I was so young, so much in love."

"I hope you don't hate me," Constanza sobbed. "You've been responsible for all the happiness I've ever had. And Emil is a wonderful child, not at all like his father. He's like Agosto, you know—he's a Tonelli."

"I know." Clare brushed the tears off her own cheek. "I don't hate you," she said wearily. "I just wish I hadn't spent so long loving a memory."

"I don't think I feel like going out to dinner." Constanza wiped her face with a handkerchief.

"Let's just have something sent up." Clare ordered supper from room service and sat on the edge of the bed. She felt emotionally drained and she realized that in addition, the past few days had been a strain of another sort.

"Are you all right?" Constanza asked in a concerned tone.

"I will be," Clare promised.

Wednesday saw the fading of all optimism as the market suffered further heavy losses. The last hour of trading was a nightmare: 2,600,000 shares changed hands and prices declined as if they were going downhill on George Tilyou's roller coaster. Agosto called midafternoon and told Clare to put a million into AmFed stock. "We must try to hold the price around one hundred," he said in a tone of grim resignation.

At seven Clare returned to the Plaza, where she curled up on the giant bed and listened to the radio. The New York *Times*'s industrial average had tumbled from 415 to 384. AmFed now stood at 94, down from 125 on Monday—down a full 76 points from the previous Friday's opening price. The market had now lost all its gains since June of the previous year, and again the ticker tape had been woefully behind. Clare thanked heaven she'd come directly to New York when she heard the news that a terrible ice storm in the Midwest had totally disrupted all communications west of the Mississippi.

The knock on the door of her suite startled her, and Clare, wrapped in her newly purchased negligee, went to the door. "Who is it?"

"Mark," came the familiar voice.

She hurriedly opened the door and for a moment they stood looking at each other. "You didn't call the AmFed office," she said after a moment.

"I tried, but the lines were busy. I took a chance and called the Plaza—they told me you were registered."

Clare smiled. "I'm glad to see you."

He stepped across the threshold and into the room. "I know you said you needed time . . . I know you're as distracted as I am by what's happening . . . but, Clare, I had to see you."

He blurted out his speech and looked into her eyes. His suit was wrinkled, tiny lines around his eyes showed he'd hardly slept, and his face was stubbly from not having shaved. His square jaw was set and tense, and his handsome face was serious, his eyes pleading. "I know this isn't the best moment to say this—there ought to be candlelight and roses—but dammit, I love you."

Clare smiled and held out her arms. Mark didn't have the slow seductive powers of Emiliano Sforza or the practiced charm of Alessandro Palma. Instead, he was open and honest. And, she thought, we're equals and he accepts me as I am.

Mark took her extended hands and pulled her roughly into his arms. "I love you," was all he said before he kissed her deeply and nuzzled her neck. "I don't care about your memories, don't care about anything but making sure I don't lose you."

Clare wrapped her arms around him, the feel of his lip lingering on her neck. He pressed himself to her, and she felt a strange exhilaration, a desire to bury herself in him.

He held her away and looked at her quizzically. "You seem to have had a change of heart."

"I had a long talk with my sister-in-law. Oh, Mark, everything you told me was true."

"God, I love you," he declared. "But I'm also the second

tiredest man in New York." He took her hand and led her directly to the bed. "I've got to lie down."

"You do look terrible."

He smiled wearily. "Just what I wanted to hear. Have you got anything to drink?"

"Brandy."

"I like you—you're always prepared." His tired eyes devoured her. "I see you got some clothes."

"Only what I absolutely had to have."

"And you absolutely had to have a sheer black seductive negligee?"

Clare smiled and flushed. "Well, I thought I might see you."

He grinned. "Good direct woman. Well, I can most certainly see you, and it's the best sight I've seen in two days, I'll tell you."

Clare got him some brandy and returned to sit on the edge of the bed. "Who's the first-tiredest man in New York?" she ventured.

"I think your father. He's been in nonstop meetings with the nation's bankers. I hear he's odd man out."

"Not unusual. It's because he's Italian and the rest are Anglo-Saxon." She smiled. "Have you talked with him?"

"No, I just saw him. Looks really exhausted." Mark gulped down the brandy, then rolled over on his back and stretched out. "Mind if I spend the night?"

"Is this your idea of a seduction?" She lay down next to him and put her arm across his broad chest.

Mark chuckled. "I owe you some honesty. I feel lusty as hell when I look at you, but I'm dead on my feet."

"I'm not too chipper myself. God, last night I dreamed of ticker tape all night."

"Lyons Oil is okay, but I think I lost a bundle this morning. Motor-accessory stocks were sold heavily midmorning. All down. They're still talking about organized support."

"I know," Clare replied. "That's what all those meetings are about."

He closed his eyes, and Clare leaned over and kissed him deeply on the mouth. "Don't you dare go to sleep yet," she whispered.

Mark opened his eyes and grinned up at her as she unbuttoned his shirt and kissed his bare chest. "I like that," he muttered.

"Don't think about anything but me," Clare murmured as she slipped off her negligee and allowed the strap of her black satin nightdress to fall over her shoulder. His eyes devoured her and he lifted his hand and caressed her bare breast, watching as her dark nipple hardened.

Clare stared into his eyes. "You came in here expecting me to fall into your arms, didn't you?"

"Let's say I was hoping. You came close on the plane, but not close enough." He kissed her breast and pushed away her nightdress. She moaned as he ran his warm hands over her, and in turn she lovingly caressed him and felt him grow more passsionate.

"I love the way you touch me," she breathed into his ear.

"I love the way you touch *me*," he answered, losing himself in her. He caressed her thighs, her legs, he kissed every part of her, and Clare felt as though time were standing still, as if there were no world outside her feelings for him, outside what she felt for him. And she found herself returning all his intimacies, making love as she had never done before.

"We should have done this sooner," he whispered in her ear. "I didn't know I could feel this way. You're spoiling me. I'll never be able to make love to a passive woman again."

"You won't have to. Besides, I wouldn't allow it." She gently bit his ear, and in return, he rolled her over on her back and began alternately kissing and tickling her.

Clare giggled and struggled with him, then clung to him as his caresses became more intimate.

"I love you too," she declared.

He gently ran his hands from her hips to her knees and back, and she moved seductively to his touch. "Now," she breathed, "now," but he waited a bit, kissing her and relishing her inflamed response to his caresses. Then, unable to hold back, he entered her, and felt her lift herself to him. She made lovely animal noises and wrapped her long legs around him. He felt her throbbing against him in the same instant he himself knew satisfaction.

After a time, he withdrew from her and simply held her tightly in his arms. "When this is over, we'll get married," he mumbled as he fell asleep.

Clare laughed softly into the pillow. His proposal was as offhand as his seduction. "I accept," she said loudly enough to make him open his eyes and smile at her. She touched his hair gently with her hand. "You can go back to sleep now," she said with satisfaction.

At three the phone rang and Clare jolted up in bed, shaking her head and fumbling for the telephone. "Papa?" she responded as she heard her father's voice.

"Can you meet me at the Federal Reserve Bank at seven A.M.?"

Mark stirred and started to say something, but Clare pressed her fingers over his lips. "Of course, Papa. I'll be there." She replaced the phone. "Morning's going to come too soon," she said, snuggling back down against Mark.

Mark left early and Clare met her father, who briefed her on the meetings and predicted a grim day. His prediction, Clare knew by evening, had been an understatement if anything. By five o'clock she knew that this was the day history would record as the true day of panic.

"Thursday, October 24." The announcer's cool voice droned out over the crackling airways. The floor of the exchange had been characterized by disorder, confusion, and fear as 12,894,650 shares changed hands. Fortunes were lost; prices shattered a thousand dreams. "The mystery of the stock market," her father had once told her, "is that there is always a buyer for those who want to sell." But today, Clare thought sadly, in spite of the huge number of stocks traded, there were many that had no buyers at all. AmFed dropped to eighty-eight, and Clare and Agosto poured in another two million to maintain the price.

The bad news flooded over her. The tape had run woefully behind all day. The uncertainty of not knowing what was happening had led more and more people to dump their stocks. Brokers' lines were jammed with margin calls, and by eleven-thirty A.M. panic, pure and simple, had grasped the populace. The police had to subdue a crowd that gathered on Broad Street outside the exchange. At twelve-thirty the gallery of the exchange was closed. But at noon the banks did make a move. It was the long-awaited "organized support."

At ten P.M. the phone rang and Clare hurried to answer it. It was her father, and he sounded as if he had aged ten years in the past four days. "Put in another two million," he told her. "And don't call the broker, go there!"

"Yes, of course, Papa. What's happening, what about the meeting?"

"We went to 23 Broad and met with Lamont. National City Bank, Chase, Guaranty Trust, Bankers Trust—they finally agreed to pool resources and go out on the floor to try to support prices. As you know, Whitney, the floor broker for Morgan's, ordered ten thousand shares at way above market price. Of course, given the damn ticker, no one was sure what the market price was."

"I heard that . . . and I saw the final ticker. It seemed to have

worked—the market was booming toward late afternoon—but
then it went soft again.''

"You don't sound any more convinced than I am," her father
observed.

"It's just the flood of bad news. I think the support is too little
too late, and what difference does it make to all those people
who were already forced to sell?"

"Exactly. I believe in trying to maintain confidence, but it's
too late for that now. Clarissima, this is a disaster.''

"Will I see you tonight?"

"No, Clarissima. Nor tomorrow either. It's mad down here.
It's ten o'clock and every light in every building is still on.
Everything is behind, everything. And I have more meetings,
and more meetings after that.''

"I know. The whole board of AmFed, except me, is sleeping
on cots in the boardroom.''

"Well, you can't sleep with all those men!''

"Believe me, I'm perfectly happy at the Plaza. Papa, you
need to get some rest.''

"I'll catch a few winks, don't worry.''

"Well, I do worry.''

"Have a good weekend," he finally said.

Sunday, October 27, 1929

MANHATTAN

"Do I look better now?" Mark leaned over and kissed her on the
cheek.

"Oh, much. It's surprising what eighteen hours' sleep and a
shave do for you.''

"The last six days have been miserable. God, six million
shares on Friday and two million during the short session on
Saturday.''

"I love the *Times*!" Clare cast the paper aside, allowing it to
fall on the floor next to the bed. "All that blubbering about the
banks rushing in and how they stand ready to prevent a recur-
rence of the panic! It's a joke, Mark, a very bad joke. It's not
just the market! There's going to be a ripple effect that turns into
a tidal wave. All the depositors will be taking their money out of
their accounts to live on because they lost so much during the
selling panic . . . and God knows how many loans will be

called. The value of everything is going to drop to rock bottom. Those banks that have land as collateral aren't going to be able to sell it. There aren't going to be any buyers.''

"You sound very gloomy for a woman who has just been made love to.''

She took his hand and kissed it. "I'm afraid no matter how much I love you, as soon as we're finished I start thinking again.''

"As long as it isn't me.''

"It isn't, I promise you that. You're a wonderful lover.''

"Are you going to tell your father about us?''

Clare rubbed her fingers over his hand. "Not right away, if you don't mind. Mark, we have to get to know each other under more normal circumstances. Besides, my father's very traditional. I'm afraid he wouldn't approve of our present intimacy.''

"Italian fathers are that way. As for getting to know each other under normal circumstances, I can hardly wait.''

Clare laughed in spite of the undercurrent of apprehension that seemed to be perpetually sweeping over her.

"I saw that AmFed went up yesterday.''

"Only a half point, I put my two million into stock yesterday.''

"I feel absurdly unreal. I'm lying in bed in the most expensive hotel in New York with the world's most stunning woman, a woman who yesterday poured two million into her business. I myself have lost at least that much and been forced to spend another four bolstering Lyons Oil. Other people are jumping off buildings, the entire economy is collapsing, and I'm lying here enjoying myself. Makes me feel like Nero. What do you want to do today? God, am I glad the market's closed. I wish they'd close it for a week.''

"The zoo?''

Mark burst out laughing. "Sorry, no. Too much like where I've been all week.''

Clare giggled and kissed him. "It's unseemly to spend the whole day in bed.''

"I know. Let's ride the Staten Island ferry.''

"All day?''

"All day till it's time to go to dinner at Delmonico's.''

"Can we afford that?''

Mark shrugged and hugged her. "I think we should each pay for our own dinner.''

"Agreed. By the way, why aren't you attending all the weekend meetings?''

"Brought Morty in from the Coast on Friday. Fresh blood. You make mistakes when you get too tired.''

"I wish my father would get some rest."

"Is your brother back?"

"Yes, but Papa wouldn't send him to meetings alone. He's working with Roberto."

"I thought you'd sleep late this morning," Sarah Ainsley Stearns said as she looked up from her breakfast.

"I've got a meeting at eleven." Creighton pulled the chair across the floor, making a grating sound; then he sat down and poured himself coffee.

"You've been away all week." Sarah ran her hand through her short hair. "But I suppose it's necessary."

"Necessary? Do you have any idea what's happening?"

"Of course I do."

"Well, then, you should understand why I haven't been here. In any case, tomorrow I'm making a move that should make you extremely happy."

"Oh?" She arched her eyebrow and leaned over.

"I'm buying heavily into AmFed. I'm buying enough to get a seat on the board."

"And then what? Is a takeover possible?" Her features became suddenly animated.

Creighton scowled at her. "Not immediately. Let's just say it puts me in a good position. I'm buying in primarily because I think it's safe."

"Buying in will help maintain the price," Sarah observed.

"Yes, and you did always want to be part of the Tonelli empire, didn't you? Or perhaps it might be more accurate to say you just wanted the Tonelli empire."

Sarah pressed her lips together, but she didn't answer.

"You're quite transparent, my dear. I told you when Jenny and Tony married that I'd get what you wanted, but not for you. I've always known how you felt about Agosto, Sarah. Indeed, I've always known how you felt about me. I don't like being second best. I intend to be first. You married Jenny off to Tony so she'd have what you wanted. Well, Sarah, I'm going to break Agosto Tonelli eventually. Tony won't have anything to inherit, but my son will."

Sarah's mouth opened and she stared at her husband. "I hate you," she said, blinking.

"Ainsley's a dead name, Mrs. Stearns. I'm going to see to it that Tonelli is too."

Tuesday, October 29, 1929

MANHATTAN

"There's no end to it," Clare said dejectedly as she put down the latest figures. It was nearly eleven P.M. and the numbers kept changing. She rubbed her eyes; she'd been at the AmFed building since seven in the morning.

Today 16,410,030 shares had been traded. The entire mechanism of the exchange was in total disarray. Everyone was selling and there were no buyers. The industrial averages were down forty-six points. And losses on individual issues were far greater. She sighed. In the past two weeks it had been a slaughter of the small speculator; today began the slaughter of the professionals and the well-to-do. The only consolation was that AmFed was holding.

When her father called, she pleaded with him, "Papa, you must get some rest."

"I can't rest. Those bastard bankers who were supposed to hold up prices are out there selling, Clarissima. They should close the exchange and clean up this mess. Nobody knows what the hell is going on, because everything is so far behind."

"AmFed is holding. Though by my calculations it ought to have gone down at least a fourth of a point."

"Stearns bought in—a lot."

"Oh," Clare replied, feeling more than a little ill-at-ease. "Is that good?" she asked, prodding for his reaction.

"I'd say so, if it helps hold the price up."

"Please, Papa, slow down."

"I will," he promised, and then the phone clicked.

On Wednesday the market rallied slightly, and feeling optimistic, Richard Whitney announced that the exchange would not open till noon on Thursday and that it would be closed all day Friday and Saturday to allow everyone to catch up. Clare, like those on the floor of the exchange, greeted the news with relief.

"Darling," Mark said when he called her, "I think things are leveling out, or perhaps I should say leveling down. In any case, I have to get back to the Coast. Want a lift?"

"Oh, Mark, I can't. I'm still needed here. This thing is far from over."

"I know. It could go on for months. But I've done all I can here. Morty's staying in town, of course. It's just that one of us has to go back."

"I wish it didn't have to be you."

"I love you and I'll be waiting for you on the Coast."

"I love you too. Mark, go see Emil. I miss him terribly."

"I will, I promise. When will you be back?"

"I'll stay now till the board meeting on November thirteenth. I'm sure Papa will want me to go back to California after that."

"I'll be waiting."

Tuesday, November 19, 1929

LOS ANGELES

Clare pushed through the crowd on the train platform. The redcap followed in her wake carrying her suitcase and muttering darkly about a sudden drop in income. "People sure don't tip like they did last month," he said. "Bad times coming. Yeah, I feel it—real bad times coming."

"Clare!" Mark called her and she looked in the direction of his voice to see him standing with an armload of flowers while Emil streaked toward her at breakneck speed.

"Mama! Mama! Mr. Lyons brought me to meet you! Mr. Lyons took me riding this morning in Griffith Park!" He threw himself into her arms.

"Oh, I missed you!" Clare kissed him and ran her hand through his hair.

"And I missed you," Mark said when he reached her. He kissed her on the cheek and she smiled up at him, grateful that while Emil was with them he restrained the passion she could see in his eyes.

"That's a radiant smile," he told her, gently squeezing her arm.

"It's been a while since I smiled," she answered.

"I've got the car. Let me take you home." He turned and handed the complaining porter some change, then lifted the suitcase. "You came back with more than you left with," he said, laughing. "Oh, here—these are for you."

Clare took the flowers. "Considering your seduction scene

and proposal, I didn't think you were such a romantic," she whispered.

"You'll find out how romantic I am soon enough," he whispered back.

Clare took Emil's hand, and they crossed the station platform. "It's beautiful," Clare said, breathing deeply. "Heavens, the last four days I was in New York it was threatening to snow. But it *is* hot. I wish Los Angeles had a proper station."

They climbed into Mark's Pontiac, Clare and Mark in the front, Emil in the back.

"Mr. Lyons has a ranch, Mama. Mr. Lyons wants us to go to the ranch with him in a few weeks. Can we?"

"I suppose so," Clare answered. "But for the next few days, Mama will have a lot of work to do."

"Sylvia says a lot of people are losing their money. My teacher said the stock market has crashed. Mama, what's happening?"

Clare turned around and smiled at Emil. "You're becoming a question box. I'll try to explain it all to you later. It's very complicated."

Mark turned the car and they traveled along Hollywood Boulevard and then along Sunset, which skirted the Santa Monica Mountains.

"I can't wait for a hot bath." Clare sighed. "I thought the train trip would never end."

"I thought you would never arrive," Mark answered. "Three hours late! Emil and I had to drink three sodas at the Pig and Whistle.

"We were delayed, we sat on a railway track outside San Bernardino for what seemed like forever while they put another engine on the back of the train for the trip over the mountains."

"Were you able to keep in touch?"

"Reasonably well. My father sent wires, which they brought me at practically every station. There's certainly no good news."

"Down, down, down—the bottom has certainly fallen out. And as you said, the ripple effect hasn't even started yet. Wait till the foreign loans are called."

Clare leaned back and closed her eyes. "It's going to be terrible," she said, half under her breath.

The car turned into the circular drive and they climbed out and went into the house.

"I'm going out to play," Emil announced as he disappeared through the open patio doors.

"Do you want something to drink?" Clare asked Mark.

"Yes, but I want a kiss first." He took her in his arms and kissed her deeply and she leaned against him, returning his kiss.

"Thank you for not doing that in front of Emil," she said when he released her.

He smiled. "It'll take time for him to get to know me."

Clare went to the bar and prepared two drinks. "I've wanted this all the way from New York," she said, sipping it.

"What, couldn't you get a Mickey from the porter?"

Clare shook her head and laughed. "No, damn, the compartment across the hall had three Treasury agents! The porter said, 'I don't sell no hooch!' "

Mark roared, "Just your luck, you get the only train from New York to California with Treasury agents. How's your father?"

"Tired. I'm really very worried about him."

"He's been through a lot."

"We've all been through a lot. The trouble is, it's not over."

He nodded knowingly. "Projecting six months ahead, I'd say AmFed and Lyons have both bottomed out, though. Personally, you and I don't look to be in such bad shape."

"I'm not certain about AmFed," Clare said cautiously. "The stock appears stable enough, but I have some worries about why."

"I'm afraid I don't quite understand."

"I'm not certain I do," she said with hesitation. "Call it woman's intuition for the moment. I know that Creighton Stearns put a lot into AmFed. I suppose I'm afraid that the Stearns family will try to exert more control over the company."

Mark nodded silently. "And that's bad?"

"Not now. My father still has firm control. I suppose it's the future I'm worried about. Anthony is . . . He's a wonderful person, I love him, but . . ." Her voice trailed off.

"Yes, I remember you talked about your brother before."

"It's my old fear: I'm still afraid that someday the control of AmFed will slip into the hands of the Stearns family. I don't think I could stand that, Mark. It's the business my father founded."

"Surely your father realizes you're more competent than your brother. Christ, look what you've put into AmFed already."

Clare sank into the chair and looked at him. He was totally unlike any man she'd ever known, and he looked truly shocked by the implication of her words. "My father is Italian," Clare said simply. "Sons inherit."

31

Friday, June 27, 1930

LOS ANGELES

The Long Beach oil fields stretched for endless acres between
the sea and low dry hills. Great jets of fire spurted into the air as
the natural gas burned off, and it was impossible to close out the
noise of the constantly cranking rigs that brought the black ooze
from beneath the ground.

"They look like giant black grasshoppers," Clare commented
as she took in the scene. There were hundreds of the huge dark
metal pumps, each going up and down in discordant motion.

"And it smells, too! I didn't promise you a tour of California's
prettiest landscape, did I? I told you it was awful—a real but
quite necessary blight on the scenery."

"I can't disagree with that." The sky was all but obliterated
by the smoke, and the fumes and noise combined into a totally
unpleasant whole.

"Black gold," Mark said appreciatively. "More and more
factories are switching over, and there's a demand from overseas
too. In spite of faltering prices, there's an increased market. This
is going to be the fuel that makes America run, Clare. I'd wager
that in a few years more and more factories will switch from coal
to oil. It's a cleaner fuel, easier to get at. It's an amazing source
of energy, and right now, right here, we're producing more oil
than any other state in the union."

She slipped her arm through his. "It's exciting," she said
enthusiastically. "But I must confess the fumes are giving me a
headache."

"Then let me take you away from here. I have a rather nice
refuge in mind. Not too far down the Coast Highway."

They climbed into Mark's Jordan Playboy, one of his four
cars, and drove down the two-lane highway, past Terminal
Island and then onto a long undeveloped stretch of road that

wound through the hills, dipping now and again to follow the ocean's shore.

"I love the look on your face when you talk about oil," she told him.

"I see the future, I see the growth and development it can bring. I've felt that way since I sank my first well, since I saw it gush up. God, it's a feeling like no other. It's filthy, messy, hard work. Then it comes, a spraying black fountain. God, it's beautiful!"

"It's your passion," Clare said.

"You're my passion too. And I've seen that same look in your eyes, my woman. The world of investments fascinates you the way oil fascinates me. Risk excites you, Clare."

"You're right." She squeezed his arm. "We're two of a kind."

"That's why we're so good together. Hey, don't sit so close. I'll become so distracted I can't drive."

"Where are we going?" Clare asked after a time.

"Laguna Beach . . . nice hotel, the waves crash up on the rocks practically under the windows of the dining room. Then we can walk on the beach.

"It's a little windy."

"But not cold. I love the sea, probably because I grew up in the Midwest, where you have to make do with placid and often muddy lakes."

After a time they came to the small community of Laguna Beach. It was nestled between the mountains and shore, and the hotel with its glassed-in dining room was, as promised, built out over the great jagged rocks against which the waves hurtled, sending masses of white foam back into the blue-green water.

When they finished lunch, Mark took her out onto the beach. "See, the wind's died down," he said, sitting down on the warm dry sand.

Clare sat down next to him. "It's truly beautiful here." She sighed, breathing in the fresh salt air.

"I did bring you here for a reason." He took her hand and held it.

Clare smiled and looked into his face. "May I ask the reason?"

"Because your name is Clare Marina, because you told me you were named for the ocean waters your grandfather loved so much."

"Oh, you are a romantic."

"Clare . . . clear, brilliant—that's what it means in Latin. Your grandfather chose an appropriate name."

"Now you're flattering me."

"The first time I made love to you, I was dead tired. The first time I proposed, I was nodding off to sleep. This time I wanted to have the right setting."

He leaned over and kissed her, and she put her arms around him and returned the kiss.

"Does that mean yes?" he asked as he kissed her neck.

"I think we must do *something*—everyone is talking about us."

"Ah, yes. Desirable, wealthy bachelor seen frequently with desirable, wealthy countess."

Clare leaned against him. "Would you settle for an engagement? I know it's already been eight months. I love you—you know that—but we've both been so busy."

"I can't disagree with that. I've hardly seen the light of day since last November."

"And there's Emil, Mark. He adores you, but I still think he needs more time to get used to the idea of having a father."

"There's your family too," Mark said, grinning. "Presumably it'll take them a while to adopt me."

"All those reasons. I think we should announce our engagement and get married . . . oh, perhaps in the spring next year."

"I don't know if I can wait that long." He nuzzled her neck.

Clare laughed and ran her hand across his cheek. "Wait? You haven't waited at all!"

He pushed her gently back on the sand and kissed her neck. "I still promise you an interesting wedding night."

"Oh, do stop. We can't make love here," she teased.

"How about in a hotel room overlooking the sea?"

"In the middle of the afternoon?"

"Why not? We have little enough time together."

Clare took his hand and pressed it to her lips. "Not many men would understand my involvement with AmFed. I'm a lucky woman to have found you."

"Not many women would tolerate my schedule," he replied. Then, kissing her ear, he whispered, "Let's go fight about who's the busiest."

Friday, July 4, 1930

STATEN ISLAND

Roberto Marcucci stuffed a hot dog into his mouth and tilted his head upward to watch the fireworks display. "I love the Fourth of July!"

Constanza looked around at the milling crowd. There were hundreds of children oohing and aahing at the display. The adults sat on the grass, eating and watching the night sky. "It's an odd holiday, the Fourth of July. To look at people you'd never guess they were celebrating a revolution."

"But you're enjoying it, aren't you?"

"I must say I am."

Roberto swallowed the rest of his hot dog. "Hey, there's Agosto!"

Agosto strode toward them. He kissed Constanza on the cheek and slapped Roberto on the back. "My favorite holiday!" he said cheerfully.

"Happy birthday! Your fifty-fourth, unless you've given up counting!"

Agosto grinned.

"Lots of people," Roberto said, shaking his head. It's been a tough year, so it's good to see them enjoying themselves."

"It's good to see so many people who're employed. The bread lines depress me. God, not even I thought things would go this far." Agosto shook his head.

"Don't talk about it. Forget it for today."

"I'm trying," Agosto responded.

"Hey, Agosto!" Joe Castellano from the Jersey City branch bank hugged Agosto warmly. "The wife and I want to thank you for the layette you sent when the kid was born. There's so much to buy when it's the first one."

Agosto nodded and flushed with embarrassment.

"Don't be so modest!" Castellano shouted. "You know how bad times are! You know the stuff will get passed on." Castellano shook his head. "I doubt there's one guy here who isn't supporting four, maybe five unemployed relatives."

"Damned administration!" Roberto mumbled. "God knows what it will take to get this country going again."

"It'll get worse before it gets better," Castellano said.

Agosto agreed. "As long as we can hold the line."

"Agosto! Agosto Tonelli!"

"Over here!"

"Got a telegram for you," Bruno Andretti, the secretary of AmFed's board, announced. "It's from Clare Marina, but I was under strict instructions not to deliver it to you till the fireworks display was under way."

Agosto took the telegram and ripped it open.

PAPA! HAPPY BIRTHDAY. I'M ENGAGED TO A WONDERFUL MAN. MARK LYONS OF LYONS OIL. HIS MOTHER WAS ITALIAN. YOU'LL LOVE HIM. PAPA, I'LL BRING HIM HOME IN NOVEMBER FOR THE BOARD MEETING. SEND A ROCKET UP FOR ME! LOVE, CLARE.

Agosto grinned from ear to ear.

"Must be good news," Roberto guessed. "I haven't seen you smile like that since . . . ah, since last Fourth of July!"

"Clare's getting married!" Agosto announced with joy. "I don't know him personally, but I know he's one hell of a good businessman!"

Saturday, August 2, 1930

NEWPORT

"Newport is really quite dull these days," Jenny lamented, a tone of exasperation in her voice. "But I'm glad we came anyway. You needed a rest, you know. You practically live at the office."

Anthony slid up in the bed and puffed the pillow behind his head. "My father needs me. Lately he's been under a terrible strain."

"Everyone's tired! And I'm tired of being around tired, boring people." She pouted and thrust her lower lip out. But she didn't reach down and pull her nightdress strap up. It fell over her shoulder and left the curve of her lovely white breast exposed. "You know, we just never have any fun anymore."

"The economic situation is very serious," Anthony returned. "People have lost a great deal and they're still losing." He shook his head dejectedly. "God knows where it's going to stop or how it's going to end."

"Well, we still have plenty of money and I don't see why we

have to live like hermits just because a few people are out of work. Daddy says what the nation needs is new blood and new ideas. He says the people who lost the most deserved to lose because they were all trying to get rich quick.''

"That's true of some, but not of all,'' Anthony replied.

"Well, I don't know what it has to do with us.''

"I told you, my father needs me. I shouldn't even have come up here this week, I should have stayed in New York.''

"Spoilsport,'' she said, tossing her blond curls. "I think you should talk to your father . . . I think he ought to be considering turning over the reins.'' She moved closer to him and ran her hand seductively across his chest. "You're more on top of things than he is, you know. You're younger and stronger.'' She combined her last comment with a sweep of her hand that sent a chill of anticipation through him.

"Don't do that unless you want to play,'' he said, lunging toward her. His hand reached for her breast, and he caressed the exposed curve, then pushed her dress away still further till she was full revealed and he could kiss her nipple.

"Oh, Anthony . . .'' She giggled and pressed her self against him. He ran his hands over her and she moved against him till he could wait no longer.

"You're beautiful,'' he whispered as he entered her. She moved about and sighed, and he came quickly—too quickly. But she seemed to respond and indeed she seemed quite satisfied as she nestled in his arms afterward.

"Daddy thinks you should insist on being put in a position of greater responsibility, and after all, Daddy's on the board. It's the perfect time, you know. Clare's not only in California, but now she's engaged. And your father really does need a rest. You said so yourself.''

"Sometimes I wish she were here,'' Anthony said.

"You don't need her, you know. You're perfectly competent yourself. Let her stay in California. Out of sight, out of mind.''

Anthony frowned. "What does that mean?''

Jenny sighed deeply. "Nothing really. I just meant that you're a man, you can't spend your whole life being told what to do by your sister and father.''

"I don't,'' Anthony protested.

"You do! All I hear is Clare this and Clare that! What if your father signed his controlling shares over to Clare instead of you?''

"That won't happen.''

"Well, what if something happens to him? What if something

happens before you take over—then where will you be? Clare will come back to New York and she'll tell you what to do and how to do it. AmFed will be hers, not yours, because she'll find a way to make you let her run things, even if she does get married. Besides, now that Daddy's on the board of AmFed, he'd be there to help you. Mummy and Daddy both say you're a very bright young man and that you ought to be taking over soon.''

"I don't really know if I'm ready."

"Well, if you don't do something, you're going to lose AmFed to your sister. After all, now she owns shares in Lyons Oil, and when she marries, there's a real possibility of some sort of merger that would give her and her husband real power."

"Clare's not like that. She cares about AmFed. She really cares about it."

"Maybe. But you'd be the laughingstock of Wall Street, I can tell you. Everyone would say that you were in charge but that Clare pulls your strings. I'm telling you for your own good: you should talk to your father now. Look at my grandfather—he died unexpectedly in that ghastly explosion. You never know, Anthony. People don't live forever, and it's better to have things in hand before anything happens."

Anthony scowled. "Clare doesn't pull my strings," he insisted, ignoring the rest of what Jenny had said.

"Then prove it by talking to your father," she challenged. "Take over AmFed's daily operations now. There's no real reason to wait. Then your father could take a long-needed and well-deserved vacation."

"He could take one now. He could leave Roberto in charge."

"Roberto may be competent, and he may be vice-president, but he's not your father's son. Your father wants you to take over eventually—you know that. What you need is the experience, darling."

Anthony rolled over on his back and stared at the ceiling. The morning light was coming through the slit in the curtains, and outside he could hear the gardener as he began to mow the lawn that surrounded the Newport mansion. It was certainly true that his father needed a rest. And Anthony had been working at his father's side for the last ten months. He also felt he had a good grasp on AmFed's day-to-day operations—except for those on the Coast, which Clare controlled. Perhaps, he reflected, Jenny was right.

Sunday, September 7, 1930

BROOKLYN

"So you want me to turn over the chairmanship of AmFed to you." Agosto Tonelli leaned back in his chair. It was his favorite after-dinner repose, his feet up on the footstool, a stogie in his mouth. Billows of pungent cigar smoke curled around his head.

"You need a rest," Anthony reiterated. He was standing by the window looking out, trying to imagine Emmons Avenue as it had been when he was a child.

"I'd be the first to admit that I'm tired, but I'm not ready to retire."

This was a difficult conversation, Anthony thought. Roberto was sitting on the sofa across from his father. The look on his face was nothing short of bemusement. Fabiana, Maria, Constanza, and Jenny were in the kitchen. Jenny didn't like being with the other women; she'd be straining to hear the outcome of the discussion between the men. Unconsciously Anthony bit his lip. "I'm twenty-six," Papa. "I've been with AmFed for four years and on the board of directors for fourteen months. I've got a good education."

"I know. I paid for it," Agosto returned.

"Clare Marina's only thirteen months older than me, and she's running the entire California operation."

Agosto shrugged. "Till she gets married. When she gets married, she'll probably step down. Besides, it's different. She bought heavily into AmFed with her own money, she's on the board because she's a major stockholder, and she's running the California operation because she's—"

"Smarter than I am," Anthony said, finishing his father's sentence. "You always treat her differently. Clare gets everything! It's not right, Papa. I'm your son!" His voice was low and firm and he wondered if his father could hear how hard it was for him to control himself.

"She's insightful and she's had more real experience. You have business out of books, but Clare has experience actually dealing with it."

"So why am I on the AmFed board? I thought I was there to

514

get experience! I'm the youngest member, the boss's son, and everybody thinks of me as a glorified office boy."

"Is that how you feel?"

"Sometimes. I don't make decisions, I rubber-stamp them. Clare makes decisions."

Agosto sighed audibly and Anthony turned around.

"How can I learn if I never have any real responsibility?"

Agosto smiled. "It's good to hear you talk this way. I was never sure what you wanted to do. I was never sure you really cared."

"I do!" Anthony said emphatically.

"I'm glad, but you're still too young to take over the business. A twenty-six-year-old! We'd lose the trust of our investors. Wall Street bankers would laugh. Granted, it would be the first laugh most of them have had since October!" He grinned; then immediately his face grew more serious and he shook his head. "We have an obligation to our shareholders to provide experienced leadership, especially now. The situation is getting worse, not better."

"Maybe we need new ideas and fresh blood!" Anthony countered, aware that his impatience was showing.

"You telling me I'm getting old?" Agosto asked tersely.

"Not old, just bogged down. Maybe instead of trying to hold the line we should be expanding, buying up—"

"With what?" Agosto thundered. "I've spent nearly fifty million bolstering AmFed stock so it wouldn't be vulnerable to speculation! That's what started this whole business. This whole mess was caused by people expanding when they didn't have the money. It started with banks lending too much, with worthless stocks as collateral. It started because instead of working hard as they should have, a million or so people thought they could get rich quick with scraps of paper. Work! They didn't want to work, they wanted to live off the interest of those scraps of paper. Now most of that paper isn't worth shit! No, AmFed and our banks will continue to invest, but those investments will be cautious and we'll go back to the philosophy I started this company with: we'll invest in those who are willing to work! We'll invest in little businesses where a man's strong back, his imagination, and his ambition are his real collateral."

"AmFed certainly has interests in other areas," Anthony returned sarcastically. "Clare bought a movie studio, and she's bought into oil too. She's got holdings in Seattle Power and Electric that aren't worth spit!"

"But they will be, because this country's going to run on

electricity and oil and she had the insight to buy cheap and the financial ability to hold on. But that's her money, not AmFed's. As for the studio, which *is* AmFed's, I'd say that was a pretty good investment. As this nightmare wears on, people are going to need entertainment, and believe it or not, they'll find ways to pay for movies. There's going to be a lot of nickels and dimes spent on Saturdays, I can tell you. They add up.''

"There, you see—you're sitting there telling me what fine investments Clare has made, but I don't have the opportunity to make my own. I don't even have the opportunity to fail!'' Anthony said in frustration.

Agosto's face knit into a frown. Clare's place on the board was secure because she had invested much of her inheritance from Emiliano Sforza in AmFed, and in addition, had made other personal investments, most of which had amazingly survived the downward spiral of the market. Anthony, he conceded silently, had a point. He had no personal fortune, only the shares he had been given in AmFed.

"You're my son,'' Agosto said in a calmer, more compassionate tone. "You know that you will inherit all my shares, and you know those shares will give you control.''

"I only want some leeway now, a chance to gain some experience.''

"Well, you don't start out as chairman of the board. But I'll tell you what we'll do. We'll go to the lawyers tomorrow and I'll sign my controlling shares over to you in trust. And I'll put you in charge of our Eastern interests, so you can get your damned experience without leaving New York. What do you think, Roberto?''

"We could move Casale out to Chicago to deal with the Midwest.'' He smiled and winked at Anthony. "It's good to know you need experience, Tony.''

Anthony looked at his father and smiled. "Do you really trust me?''

Agosto nodded, his lips pressed together. "Trust is earned, but you're my son, and I have faith in you. There's one proviso.''

"Yes?'' Anthony queried.

"If anything did happen to me, Clare is to be left in charge of the West Coast division, at least until she marries.''

"Of course,'' Anthony replied. "I wouldn't try to change that.''

Monday, September 15, 1930

LOS ANGELES

Dear Clare,

I know that I don't write you often, but I simply had to write today, darling. I'm sure your father will write to you soon and tell you the big news. But I couldn't wait! Anthony is just so excited and proud, and I know you will want to share in his happiness.

Your father has signed all of his AmFed shares over to Anthony in trust and put Anthony in charge of all the Eastern operations. Of course, your father will remain chairman of the board, and now, with my father on the board too, it's just a fine tight family corporation. Isn't that wonderful, Clare? Of course, it's been decided that you will remain in charge of the West Coast operations—at least as long as you want. I know that will make you happy! Although I must confess I never knew why you wanted to be so involved and I've never understood why you weren't content just having fun and spending all that money. But that's not the end of the news. This is the really big news, Clare: I'm pregnant! Anthony is simply overcome with joy and Agosto is so happy! They all want a boy, of course, but personally I would like a girl. A mother can have so much more fun shopping with a daughter!

I think that's all my news for now. I do hope we will see you soon. Love to Emil.

Yours,
Jenny

Clare Marina held the letter tightly. It was laden with innuendo and fairly dripped with Jenny's ingenuous enthusiasm. "Simpering bitch!" Clare said under her breath as she tore the letter up in little pieces.

"I gather that's not good news," Mark said, cocking an eyebrow.

"No, it isn't."

"Want to talk about it?"

517

"My father's signed his shares over to Anthony to be held in trust."

"You expected that."

"It's Jenny's tone. It's the beginning, Mark."

"Your father's still in charge."

"I know. I'm just uneasy about the gathering forces."

He walked over to her and kissed her hair. "Fight your battle when the time comes. Never wear out your troops ahead of time."

"I won't let it happen," Clare said firmly. "As God is my witness, I won't let it happen. Mark, I will never let them have the company my father built!"

Sunday, November 16, 1930

B R O O K L Y N

Agosto stood proudly at the head of the table. Around him sat Jenny, Anthony, Clare, Mark, Emil, Fabiana, Maria, Roberto, and Constanza. "Proud!" Agosto said. "I'm proud to give my blessing to this engagement!" He lifted his wineglass and toasted Clare and Mark, and everyone joined in.

Mark's face reddened. "Thank you, sir," he said, smiling boyishly.

Clare reached under the table and took his hand. He was every inch a man, but she had to admit that at thirty-seven he still had a certain mischievous youthful smile and attitude that made him irresistible. Fabiana fell in love with him at first sight, Constanza couldn't take her eyes off him, Jenny tried her charms and failed, and even Maria seemed taken with him. As for Agosto, they were alike in some ways. They talked and talked about business, and clearly her father liked him.

"Will you come home to get married?" Fabiana asked.

Clare shook her head. "We'd like just a quiet ceremony on the Coast—just family. You'd love California, Fabiana."

"Mr. Lyons has a big, big house," Emil announced knowingly, "and a ranch, and horses, and everything!"

Clare caught the look of envy on Jenny's face and vaguely wondered why. She was such an acquisitive girl. Like her mother, Clare thought. But Jenny didn't want for anything. Still, Clare's happiness seemed to bother her.

"Clare's still plenty young enough to have babies," Maria put in. "You should do that, Clare, you should have more children."

Clare only smiled. For once the suggestion didn't seem barbed, and the feel of Mark's hand on her knee made it seem a rather nice suggestion.

"I'm happy for you two," Anthony said sincerely.

"Nobody asked, but I certainly approve," Constanza announced.

"I feel settled," Agosto announced. "Like all the loose ends are tied. The future of AmFed is secure, my daughter's going to be married. Things are as they should be."

Clare glanced at her father, wishing he hadn't made his last statement. She and Mark had arrived in New York on Wednesday and the board of shareholders' meetings had taken all of Thursday, Friday, and Saturday. She had yet to see her father alone, to confront him with her feelings about the Stearns family and his signing over shares to Anthony. "I doubt it will do any good," Mark had told her. But she insisted, "I still have to talk with him."

"Let's open another bottle of wine!" Agosto suggested. "Clare doesn't look happy enough yet!"

"I am happy," she persisted. Mark glanced at her. He was certainly attuned to her moods, she thought. He had surely felt her tense when her father talked about the future of AmFed.

After dinner, the men gathered in the parlor, as was the custom. Fabiana, Constanza, and Maria went into the kitchen for coffee and Clare went up to her former room to look for an album of photographs she wanted to show Mark.

"So this is your room," Jenny said, standing in the doorway. She looked about, and Clare, who had emptied an old chest looking for her photos, could see the disdain on Jenny's face.

"Yes, this is the room. Should it be grander, Jenny?"

Jenny half-smiled. "Mine certainly was. Goodness, the mirror's so small."

Clare shook her head. Jenny was not easily put off. "I never spent that much time looking at myself."

Jenny giggled. "Well, I certainly imagine you'll have plenty of mirrors now! Mark is very rich! You're quite lucky, you know. Imagine finding two rich men. Of course, you'll give up the West Coast operations when you get married. You haven't set a date, have you?"

Clare looked up. "No. What makes you think I'll give up the West Coast operations?"

Jenny smiled. "Don't you know? It's in the papers your father signed. They say you can remain in charge till you marry."

Clare felt her hand tremble as she gripped the photo album. She was sure the color had drained from her face, but she fought for control. Jenny's expression was close to triumphant and Clare refused to react and give her pleasure. "If I were you, Jenny, I wouldn't spend so much time worrying about *my* future."

"Worry? Oh, I'm not worried. We all know how very happy you're going to be."

Clare forced a smile. "Yes, we do, don't we?" she said bitterly as she pulled herself up and left the room. "Not tonight," she whispered under her breath. "I mustn't lose my temper tonight." But she vowed: I'll talk to my father in the morning.

32

Monday, November 17, 1930

N E W Y O R K

Clare climbed out of the cab at Thirty-ninth and Broadway, crossed the street, and entered the AmFed Building. As she rode the elevator to the executive offices, she momentarily regretted not telling her father she was coming. She'd thought a great deal about what she was going to say—it would be so anticlimactic if he were out. Words reeled through her mind. Over and over she had rehearsed this conversation. Over and over she had arranged and rearranged her arguments.

"Clarissima!" Agosto shouted as she was ushered into the executive suite. "What are you doing here?" He rushed out from behind the desk and hugged her. "I thought you and Mark would be busy today. Why didn't you tell me yesterday you were coming this morning?"

"Papa . . ." Her voice trailed off and she fought to maintain her resolve.

"Is something wrong? What could be wrong?—you're going to get married!"

"Papa, believe me when I tell you I love Mark. But marriage isn't everything, and I have to talk to you—alone."

"Clarissima, here, sit down. Now, tell me what's wrong."

"Papa, it's about Anthony. I want to talk to you about your having signed the controlling shares over to him in trust. I know you said I could remain in charge of the West Coast as long as I wished. But, Papa, that's not what the documents actually say— they say until I marry, Papa. I am getting married."

Agosto frowned and looked troubled. "It's only wording, Clarissima. I naturally assumed that when you married, your husband would make you happy, you'd give up running the West Coast operations of AmFed to be a wife and have babies."

521

"I will never get married if I have to give up AmFed," Clare said, struggling for control. "I helped build AmFed!"

He held out his hands to her. "Clarissima, what are you talking about? You won't have to be in business when you get married. And as for signing the controlling shares over to Anthony, it's only paperwork, something I've done because I'm nearly fifty-five. You always knew your brother would inherit. Clarissima, women should not be in business. But if it makes you happy, you can stay in charge of the West Coast as long as you want. I've come to accept the fact that the business climate on the West Coast is different." He shook his head. "I even saw a picture of a woman from California wearing long pants." He shook his head. "I don't know what the world's coming to."

"Its senses," Clare replied. "Papa, it's fine that you say I can stay in charge. But what if something happens to you? Papa, the way those documents read, I could be replaced. Papa, since I was a little girl I wanted to be a banker—I *am* a banker. I've done a good job, a better job than Anthony!"

"You'd still be on the board, you have your own shares. And of course you've done a good job. But it's not a job for a wife and mother, Clarissima. Do you know what a banker is? A banker is a gray man, a conservative man, a man who tries never to offend anyone, a man who leads a very private life. But above all, a banker is a man. Banking and finance, Clarissima, are a man's world. In all of this country you are the only woman in banking, you are almost the only one in big business. Clarissima, I've understood that it made you happy after Emiliano died to be involved. But you won't need that when you marry Mark."

"I will need it! And what about the future?"

Agosto's face flushed in deep red. "I told you! You can stay on! I'm not dead yet!" he shouted back at her angrily. "I'm not dead, but I am living to see my children fight over the spoils from a lifetime of my work! I won't go back on my word, Clarissima, I won't take the West Coast away from you. But I believe—and I believe it with all my heart—that a woman must be with her husband!"

"I'm not fighting with Anthony over what you've built! I'm worried about Creighton Stearns. I don't want to see control of AmFed fall into the hands of the Stearns family."

"Clarissima, Creighton Stearns is an asset to the corporation. I'm ashamed because you think your brother would let that happen. Clarissima, he *is* your brother, your blood. We're a family. You do him a dishonor, and I'm ashamed of you. I trust Anthony, and my judgment is that Creighton Stearns is an honorable businessman and that his sole reason for investing in

AmFed was to make a good investment." He dropped his head and stared at the carpet. But his face was still beet red and Clare could see he was shaking.

"You are wrong!" Clare stormed back. "Anthony has no backbone! All of AmFed will fall into their hands! Papa, you're making a terrible mistake! And don't talk to me about your judgment! You don't know! When I told you I loved Emiliano, you told me what a fine man *he* was. Well, he wasn't a fine man! He had a mistress whom he had murdered! He had labor organizers murdered! But it was your judgment that Emiliano was a 'fine man.' Papa, you were wrong about him, you're wrong about Creighton, and you're wrong to believe that if he's left alone Anthony could run things."

Agosto lifted his head and looked at her stonily. "In all my life, Clarissima, I never hit you." He spoke evenly, though his tone was low and menacing and his fists were tightly clenched. "I would like to slap you now for what you've said about Anthony. As for Emiliano Sforza, I don't have the faintest idea what you're talking about, but I caution you to remember you're speaking of the dead, and of the father of your child."

"Go ask Constanza about Emiliano. Find out just how good your judgment is," Clare said, pressing her lips together.

Agosto scowled at her. "I'll ignore what you say about me. Clarissima, go back to California and the West Coast office if it means so much to you. And tell Mark that you're too stubborn to give it up for the mere pleasure of having love and a family. Sooner or later you'll realize that no matter how hard you fight and struggle, no matter what gifts of intelligence you have been blessed with, you are still a woman and a mother and that alone is your place and role. What would your mother say if she could hear you accusing your brother of having no backbone? What would she say if she saw you neglecting your son to run a business? What would she say if she knew you'd give up a good man if marrying him meant losing AmFed?"

"She would probably say, 'Good luck!' " Clare screamed. "Did you think you made her happy having her for a decoration? Did you think she liked being nothing? Did you think she was truly happy?" Tears of anger and frustration ran down Clare's face, hot tears over red flushed cheeks.

"Your mother was the perfect wife! And she was far from nothing!"

"And she hated it!" Clare shrieked. Then, seeing the look of pain on her father's face, she lowered her voice. "She loved you, but she hated being the perfect wife."

"Clarissima!" His hand was lifted and Clare backed away.

"She told me to be different. She told me that in a letter before she died. 'Clare, dare to be different! Don't be like me!' Does that sound like the voice of fulfillment, Papa?"

"Go away! I loved and honored your mother and I knew her better than you. I will not have you destroying her memory with your jealous temper! Go away, Clare."

Clare let out her breath and turned, hurriedly wiping the tears off her cheeks. "The Stearns family will get it all," Clare declared. "Papa, Anthony doesn't care that much, he never has!"

Agosto looked away from her, then shouted, "Go back to California, Clare. And stay there!"

Tuesday, November 18, 1930

The plane's engines filled the passenger cabin with a low droning sound. Clare huddled in her seat, while Mark sprawled out across from her, Emil sleeping soundly at his side.

"You look miserable," Mark observed.

"My father and I had a terrible fight. I said terrible things to him." She ran her hand across her forehead.

"And he told you that you should be a proper wife and mother?"

Clare nodded.

"If you two didn't love each other so much, you couldn't hurt each other so deeply. He says what he says because he believes it, and you fight back in anger and say things you don't mean."

"Always," Clare said dejectedly.

"I used to do that with Louisa. I had all the right weapons in my arsenal."

"I told my father about Emiliano . . . I told him he had no judgment. Oh, God, Mark, I even told him my mother was unfulfilled because of him."

"Was she?"

Clare shook her head. "It wasn't as simple as that. She gave me everything, she encouraged me to study, she read to me. She was a beautiful, brilliant woman who had no self-confidence. It was like an illness, her fear of going beyond her traditional role. I used to watch her. Not only did she always tell me to be different, but I used to watch her and think. I have to be different, this can't be all there is, it's not fair that men run everything."

"It's not," Mark agreed. "But you'll never make your father see that. Clare, you're fighting tradition. You told me that your brother would inherit. Now that I've met your father, I know he will. I like your father, but he's of the old generation, He's not going to change, and you can't change him."

"It's the wording in the documents. As long as Papa's alive, he'll let me run the West Coast office. He's given in to that much, but those documents read 'until I marry.' Oh, Mark, my father's not well. I know Creighton will do something—Anthony's so weak. If Creighton were in control, he'd move quickly to get me out of management."

"You're a threat."

"He can manipulate Tony, but not me."

"Clare, does this mean you won't marry me in the spring?"

"I'm so confused, Mark. I love you—you have to believe that."

"I do. But I also want you to marry me. I want us to live together and have children. I want us to be a family. Clare, don't change your mind about marrying me."

"I won't," she promised. "Maybe Papa will change his mind, maybe he'll talk to Constanza . . ."

"Maybe the sun won't come up," Mark said, reaching across the distance between them to take her hand. "You two are just alike, stubborn to the core. Clare, marry me and fight your fight when the time comes."

"I don't know what I'd do without you."

Wednesday, December 10, 1930

N E W   Y O R K

Agosto shook his head in disgust. Businesses were failing all over the country—122,000 since October of twenty-nine. The industrial averages were below 275, down from 500 before the crash. And now the Bank of the United States, one of the nation's largest, had collapsed.

He closed his eyes and thought back to March. Some 35,000 unemployed had demonstrated in the streets of New York. The police had intervened, but scores and scores of people were injured. Now there were even more people unemployed, demonstrations continued, soup kitchens attempted to feed the hungry; there were bread lines everywhere. It was going to be a terrible Christmas, but then, he contemplated, it had been a terrible year.

"Are you working late?"

Agosto looked up to see Anthony standing in the doorway. "Not really, just examining the evidence of another disastrous day."

"It's not good, is it?" Anthony commented. "Hell, the Bank of the United States was huge. A lot of people were wiped out, lost every cent of their savings."

"It's going to be a bad winter."

"You ought to go to Florida. A lot of people go down for a few weeks."

Agosto's eyes snapped. "Not a lot of people, just a few of the people you know. Most people can't afford carfare. In any case, I was talking about the economy, not the weather."

Anthony didn't reply. Lately his father had been extraordinarily bad-tempered and seemed to harp on the way he lived, urging him to live more modestly and curb Jenny's spending.

"Why don't you come home with me?" Anthony asked. "It's late. You don't want to go all the way back to Brooklyn, and we have plenty of room."

"Most houses on Park Avenue do have plenty of room."

Anthony ignored this mild sarcasm. "Please come. We'll have a simple dinner."

"I don't want to put you out," Agosto replied. Then, almost as an afterthought: "How's Jenny?"

"So-so. The doctor says she's fine. But she still gets sick in the morning. Anyway, you're not putting us out—we do have servants. You know what we could do? We could walk over and look at the Empire State Building. It's really coming along! Then we could take a cab over to the apartment."

Agosto nodded. "I suppose a little exercise wouldn't hurt me."

"It's good for you," Anthony enthused. He checked himself just before reminding his father that he went to the health club three nights a week and often played tennis on the indoor courts.

They left the AmFed Building and walked in the brisk December air to the Empire State Building, which was scheduled to be finished next year.

"You know," said Agosto, feeling somewhat more cheerful, "I remember the first skyscraper built by old Stearns— Creighton's second cousin, I believe. Everyone thought the sides would fall down if there was a storm. But the damn thing stood up!''

Anthony thrust his hands in his pockets. ''Heard from Clare?'' he asked, trying desperately to sound casual.

''I don't want to discuss Clare,'' Agosto said firmly.

''Well, you gotta admit she has flair. The streets are full of apple sellers, hundreds of banks have gone under, and she's made four million on miniature golf, of all things!''

Agosto only grumbled. ''I don't care if she makes two hundred million. Anyway, I don't approve of investing in fads.''

''So far, it's been a hundred-and-twenty-five-million-dollar business this year. You didn't mind when she invested in the studio—you were the one who said people needed entertainment.''

''That's different,'' Agosto grumbled.

Anthony stopped dead and looked up at the towering structure. ''It's not right, Papa. It's not right that the family should be at odds like this, especially you and Clare.''

''I was defending you and your wife, not to mention your mother.''

''Clare's my sister, Papa. Frankly, she practically got me through school when we were kids. She was always the smart one. No, not just smart, Papa. Clare's a genius.''

''She's a woman and she's getting married. She ought to give up working.''

''She's just like you. That's the trouble, Papa, she's just like you.''

Agosto grunted. ''You're a good brother. I wish she were as good a sister.''

''She *is* a good sister, Papa. Write to her, tell her you're sorry.''

''Why? So we can have another big fight over what happens if I die?''

''No, so our family will be a family again,'' Anthony said simply. ''Papa, this isn't right.''

''Your sister thinks your wife is simpering and ambitious.''

Anthony shrugged. ''I know they don't like each other, but I love both of them in different ways.''

''So you came and kidnapped me from my office on the pretext of looking at the monumental facade just so you could talk to me into writing to Clare?''

Anthony smiled. ''Something like that. Papa, in two weeks it'll be Christmas.''

Agosto didn't answer, but he half-nodded his head.

Tuesday, December 23, 1930

LOS ANGELES

Clare sat curled on the sofa, her father's letter in her hand and tears in her eyes.

Dear Clare,

Anthony came to my office yesterday and we had a long talk. Naturally, Anthony isn't the only one who talks to me about you. Fabiana urges me to write too. So I've decided to write and wish you a Merry Christmas. But I warn you now, Clare Marina, this letter does not mean that I'll discuss the arrangements I've made, nor will I change them. I don't want any more of your temper and I want none of your talk about what will happen if I die. I have faith in your brother. And he is a good brother, perhaps more loyal than you deserve.

I did talk with Constanza. I am shocked that you never shared with me the pain you must have had about Emiliano. In that instance, I admit my judgment was bad, but that doesn't mean it's bad all the time. I haven't changed my mind about Creighton. He's a rich man, he's Anthony's father-in-law, and I see no reason why he would have designs on AmFed, as you irrationally believe. These matters I will not discuss now or in the future.

I suppose I should say that I love you and miss you. That is the truth, of course.

Love,
Papa

Emil studied the expression of sadness on his mother's face, then asked, "What's the matter, Mama?"

"It's just a letter from your grandfather," Clare said abstractedly. It wasn't the letter she had wanted, and it certainly skirted any kind of apology. He still didn't understand, he never would, she decided. Mark was right, there was no changing her father's mind. But of course Anthony was right too: a family is a family, and theirs was being destroyed by mutual rancor.

"Will we see grandpapa soon?" Emil pressed.

"I hope he'll come in June for Mama's wedding."

Emil smiled brightly. "He'll come if you write."

Clare reached out and hugged her son. "Yes," she murmured. "I'll write, I'll tell him how much we both miss him."

Thursday, March 5, 1931

NEW YORK

"You should stay home," Fabiana cautioned. "You never take care of yourself, Agosto, never. All these months of strain and working till all hours of the night. You should go to a physician and have a good checkup, and then you should have a long long vacation."

"Why does everyone want to send me on vacation?" Agosto replied in irritation. Then, ignoring his throbbing head, he traveled into Manhattan and went directly to the Federal Reserve Bank at Wall and Broad for a meeting.

"You don't look well," Lamont observed.

"Just a headache."

"Have you the limo?"

Agosto shook his head. "Now that we're finished here, I think I'll walk a bit, then grab a cab uptown."

"Are you sure? I could have you driven."

"Absolutely. The fresh air will do me good."

Agosto walked out of the building and up Broad Street to the corner of Wall. He inhaled deeply, aware of the brisk March wind. The Treasury Building loomed in front of him, its flags flying in the breeze. He shook his head slightly, but it was no use. It pounded relentlessly, exactly the way it had when he was recovering from malaria so many years ago. He thrust his hands into his pockets and started walking toward the soot-darkened Trinity church that looked down on Wall Street as if endowing its inhabitants with some kind of blessing. Wall Street, the financial heart of America, began in the cemetery of old Trinity and ended in the river. He half-smiled at the ironic symbolism.

"Jobs! Jobs! Jobs!" a group of men chanted.

Agosto looked up to see a ragamuffin band of rowdies approaching. They carried placards with the hammer and sickle emblazoned across a red background, and they waved their signs ominously and chanted, "Jobs, jobs, jobs!" over and over.

Vaguely Agosto wondered how, when they were out of work, they could afford such elaborate signs.

"Hey, there, you!" One of the larger men lurched forward and grabbed him roughly by the lapels of his gray suit. "You're one of them! You're one of them bankers who's stole our savings! Look at you, you have money in your pocket for lunch! You have enough to buy lunch for all of us!"

"There ain't no bankers in bread lines!" another yelled. "Even if they close their doors, they got money!"

"Our money!"

"Jobs! We need jobs!"

Agosto grimaced. Hungry men had a right to protest. And God knew that bankers were fair prey: they hadn't stopped things when they could. Still, these men were clearly communists, and just as clearly, there was absolutely no point in standing here like a babbling idiot trying to explain where the blame in economic collapse should be placed. "Get your hands off me," Agosto said, scowling. "The police will be here any second, and I warn you—"

"You warn us!"

The tall burly man gave Agosto a mean shake and Agosto pulled himself up and raised his own fist threateningly, aware of the sudden numbing ache of his arm and the fierce pounding in his left temple. The man's face became a sudden blur, became Paolo's face, contorted with anger and frustration. Paolo's face weaved before him, and when he looked around, all the faces were Paolo's. He shook convulsively and gasped as his legs buckled beneath him and he fell to the hard pavement, aware only of the fact that he felt absolutely nothing.

"What's wrong, old man?" He heard the shout but couldn't move.

His eyes seemed to take things in, but he couldn't speak or move even his finger. Faces stared down at him, and then the faces were dispersed by police brandishing clubs. He heard screams, and still he lay there, a prisoner in his own body, his eyes seeing, his ears hearing.

"Is he dead?"

"Not yet."

Then the screaming wail of the ambulance, and Agosto closed his eyes, moving his lips only once to whisper, "Paolo . . . I didn't mean it."

The doctor lifted the sheet and examined Agosto's feet. Using the pointed end of a safety pin, he ran it along Agosto's sole. He talked to himself, then straightened up and turned to face Anthony and Jenny, who stood at the far end of the room. "That's the fourth time I've given him that examination, and there's no reaction. Your father's had a massive stroke. He's completely paralyzed."

"How long will he be that way?" Anthony could hardly speak.

"I suggest we step outside," the doctor said, motioning them toward the door and into the hall.

The doctor fidgeted with his white jacket, then looked at Anthony's over the top of his horn-rimmed glasses. "The prognosis isn't good. He'll probably suffer a second seizure, then he'll be gone. In any case, he won't recover either speech or movement. We feel there's a blood clot near the brain."

Anthony trembled, then crossed himself. "Oh, God," he groaned.

"You can stay with him. I don't think he can hear, but you can hold his hand. He might be like this for some time, you know. I'm afraid there's not much that can be done. . . ."

Anthony nodded and blinked back tears. He pushed his way past the doctor and went directly to his father, sitting down on the side of the bed and taking Agosto's limp hand.

"Papa . . . oh, Papa . . ." The tears flowed down his face.

Jenny hovered behind him. "You'll have to call a board meeting right away," she said in a small voice.

"How can you think of something like that now?" Anthony whipped around to face her.

"It's what your father would want, Anthony. AmFed can't go leaderless, especially not now. You must call a board meeting and put Daddy in charge, at least for a while. I'm sure that's what your father would want." She nodded toward Agosto, whose vacant brown eyes only stared into space.

"I really don't want to talk about this now."

"He can't hear you. And it's important to get these things settled. Think what it will do to the stock if there isn't immediate action."

"Why are you babbling on about your father?"

"Because you're too young—that's what your father said."

Anthony looked at Agosto pleadingly. "Oh, God," he sobbed, "I don't want all this responsibility! I just want him to get well. Papa, get well, I don't want to run this corporation, I never wanted to run it!"

"For heaven's sake stop that!" Jenny said coldly. "You heard what the doctor said. Anthony, go and call Daddy immediately."

Anthony shook his head. "Clare!" he suddenly said. "I have to call Clare."

"It's more important for you to call Daddy first."

Anthony squeezed his father's hand. "You call him," he said. "But call Clare first! I'm not moving, I'm staying right here."

Anthony bent over his father and pressed his father's hand to his own face. "Don't die, Papa . . . please don't die. I love you, I care about you, and I can't get along without you. Papa, I don't want to run AmFed . . . please, don't die. . . ." Anthony closed his eyes, and Agosto blinked ever so slightly.

LOS ANGELES

"Who?" Clare shouted into the phone. The line was terrible, crackling and clicking. "Talk louder. I can't hear you! . . . Jenny? What is it? What's the matter?" Clare Marina drew in her breath. "When? How?" she stammered into the damnable phone.

"He's had a stroke, a massive stroke, and he can't move, speak, or hear. Anthony says you must come immediately, but I don't know if you should hurry or not. The doctor says he may live only a few hours. Now, Clare, you mustn't worry, everything will be fine. My father will see to that. You just come and be with Agosto—if you can get here soon enough, that is."

"Jenny!" Clare screamed into the telephone, but the line went utterly dead. She stood for a long moment with the phone in her hand like a deadweight. She leaned against the table for support as tears began to tumble down her face. After a moment she shook herself and in spite of her shock dialed Mark's number.

"He's still up in Santa Barbara with the exploration crew," Morty Levinson told her. "I thought you knew he wouldn't be back till the weekend."

"Can you reach him?"

"He's absolutely out of contact, somewhere up in the hills."

"I have to get to New York," Clare said, almost sobbing into the phone. "My father's had a stroke. I have to get to New York."

"Our plane's not doing anything—want me to fly you out?"

"Can you fly it?"

Morty laughed. "Are you serious? I'm a New Yorker. I can't even drive a car. The most mechanical thing I do is use the can opener. I meant I'd get you a pilot."

"Oh, could you? I don't care how much it costs. I have to get to New York."

"Well, stand by, I'll have a car pick you up in . . . say, an hour."

"Yes," Clare answered gratefully as she put the receiver back on its cradle. "Emil!" She ran upstairs and into her son's room. "Emil, we're going to New York now, in an hour."

"In a plane?"

"Yes, in Mr. Lyons' plane. Now, hurry, get out your suitcase and put your underwear and some shirts and your suit in it. Mama has to pack her things. Can you do that, can you hurry?"

"Will Mr. Lyons be coming too?"

"No, he's still in Santa Barbara." I wish to heaven he were coming, Clare thought, her mind straying to Mark. "Do it quickly, Emil," she told him.

"Mama, you're crying. What's the matter?"

"It's Grandpapa. He's sick."

Emil bit his lip. "Very sick?"

Clare nodded. "Please, Emil, just hurry." She turned and fled the room.

Friday, March 6, 1931

MANHATTAN

"You really must do something, Anthony. Mummy says you must, and Daddy says it's absolutely essential."

"Roberto's there, he knows what to do. Jenny, this is no time to discuss this."

"Well, the doctor said he probably can't hear. For goodness' sake, Anthony, you know it's all over the papers. My father says the investors will panic. You know how important confidence is. Roberto's a fine vice-president, but a vice-president is a vice-president. Your father's never going to get well. Daddy says you have control of the company because the documents have something about incompetence in them—no, incapacitation, that's it."

"Jenny, in the name of God—"

"Darling, I know you're tired, I know you haven't slept for twenty-four hours, but you don't realize how important this is. Daddy just wants you to sign some papers. . . ."

"All right, tell him to bring them!"

* * *

Agosto tried desperately to move his lips, to blink, to speak. He did them all in his mind, but he couldn't even command his eyes to open. "Don't do it, Anthony!" he cried out inside himself. "Wait for Clare!" But nothing worked. He felt even his ability to hear slipping away. But he could still hear Anthony sobbing, "I don't want this responsibility. Papa, please help me!"

Creighton Stearns was trim, distinguished-looking, and fifty-two years old. His steel-gray eyes, generous head of dignified white hair, and broad shoulders gave him a youthful appearance. Everyone said he was a banker's banker, a man who never swore, seldom drank, and was a model of proper manners and decorum.

Creighton Stearns looked at Anthony kindly, and his strong hand gripped Anthony's shoulder. "You haven't had a wink of sleep for twenty-four hours, son."

"I can't leave him," Anthony answered hoarsely.

"Son, I know this is hard for you. I'm sorry to have taken you away from his side."

Anthony looked around. They were in the hospital boardroom. It was quiet and fresh-smelling, lacking the medicinal odors of Agosto's room. The decor was colorful, and Anthony blinked, realizing that for the entire past twenty-four hours he'd been in glaring white surroundings.

"I can't stay," Anthony said, his eyes focusing on the door.

"I wouldn't ask you to unless it was important, Anthony. Give me your attention for just a few minutes. I know your father is seriously ill—"

"He's going to die!" Anthony blurted out, and again he began to shake and feel ill. He'd done nothing but drink black coffee and smoke cigarettes while the doctors were with his father; the rest of the time, he'd been by the side of the bed praying and sobbing.

"Perhaps, but we all hope not. After all, we're all very fond of your father. We're family, you and I. And you must listen to me. It's already in the papers, and the entire financial community is aware that Agosto owns the controlling shares outright. Agosto's shares are in your name in trust. They are yours now because he's incapacitated. Son, the value of the stock will drop if we don't do something. There could be a shareholders' panic. What's more, people might lose confidence in the banks and make massive withdrawals."

Anthony rested his forehead in his hand. His father-in-law's words hardly penetrated his thoughts. "What do you want me to do?" he said wearily.

"Just sign these papers. They'll give me control, and that will show the financial community that there's a steady hand on the tiller, so to speak." Creighton smiled, rather proud of his use of sailing terminology. "Of course, it's only temporary, until you're a little older and a little more experienced. It's still all in the family, son."

Anthony nodded and took the pen his father-in-law offered. He scribbled his name on four different sets of documents.

"I want to go back to my father," he said, getting up.

"Of course," Creighton replied, patting him gently on the back. "I promise to look after everything. Don't worry about anything."

"Thanks," Anthony said, hurrying from the room. He rubbed his eyes and made a silent wish for Clare to come. He felt like a child and he wanted to lean on her and have her hold him.

33

Saturday, March 7, 1931

MANHATTAN

Clare hurried down the hospital corridor. It seemed as if she had been running for two days. The plane trip had been a nightmare; there were storms over the Rockies that caused delays, she'd been unable to eat or sleep, and her mind had never slowed down. Emil followed in her wake, asking endless questions she couldn't answer.

"It might be best if you left the child outside," the nurse at the door suggested.

"I want to see Grandpapa!" Emil announced in a loud voice.

"Sh." Clare lifted her finger to her lips pleadingly. "Please, Emil, Mama has to see him first. Please be good, sit over there, and I'll call you in just a few minutes. I promise." She looked at her son, then bent over and kissed him. "You've been terribly good, Emil. Please be patient just a little longer, to help Mama."

Emil nodded and obediently went to the chair against the wall and sat down.

Clare opened the door and entered quietly. Poor Anthony, he was sitting by the bed holding Agosto's hand. He was fast asleep.

"Tony," Clare whispered.

He blinked open his eyes and for a second stared at her as if she were an apparition. Then he stood up and all but collapsed against her. "Oh, Clare, I feel like I've been waiting for you forever!"

Clare ran her hand through his thick curly hair. In so many ways he was a little boy. His eyes were red and swollen from crying and lack of sleep. He shivered slightly in her arms. "I'm here, Tony. Please tell me what's happening . . . tell me how this happened."

Anthony nodded. "He's asleep now. Clare, he was attacked

536

. . . well, set upon by a mob of protesters. He had a stroke . . . that's all I know. You know how doctors are.''

"Tell me exactly what the doctor said," Clare pressed.

"That he won't regain movement or speech, that he'll have another . . . That he probably can't even hear." Anthony broke down again and Clare blinked back her own tears.

"I didn't know what to do, Clare. Creighton said I should sign the stock over to him, that the stock would drop if I didn't, because Papa's incapacitated.''

Clare went cold at his confession, but she couldn't say anything to Anthony. He was beside himself already; he was worn out and obviously close to a total breakdown. "Where's the rest of the family?''

Anthony sniffed and wiped his swollen eyes. "They're downstairs in the chapel with a priest.''

Clare bit her lip. "Has Papa received extreme unction?''

Anthony nodded.

Clare patted him on the back gently. "Tony, leave me alone with him for a few minutes. Please, go have some coffee or join the others in the chapel.''

Anthony nodded and Clare turned to her father, who lay in the bed, his eyes open and staring at the ceiling.

"He can't close them," Anthony said, shivering. "He just lies there staring at the ceiling hour after hour. He sleeps with them open. I can tell when he's awake—there's more of a flicker in his eyes, like he's trying so hard to speak to me, but can't.''

Clare knelt down and took her father's hand in hers. "Oh, Papa," she whispered. "I love you, I really do. I know we've hurt each other, but I love you." Clare closed her eyes. She could hear Anthony leaving the room, and the steady sound of her father's breathing.

"Oh, Papa, if you could only talk to me." Clare's eyes searched his face. "Papa, I don't know what you want me to do." She smiled gently at him and passed her hand over his forehead. In his brown eyes she thought she saw the flicker that Anthony had spoken of. "It's me, Papa. It's Clare Marina. I'm here, Papa, and I won't leave you, I promise.''

She laid her head on his chest. "I've made so many mistakes, Papa. I didn't want to fight with you, I didn't want to hurt the family. I wanted to protect what you built, Papa. I wish I could make you understand, but none of that matters now." She lifted her tearstained face, and to her surprise,' Agosto made a low, guttural sound in his throat. He strained to lift his head off the pillow. "No, Papa, just lie still," she whispered.

But Agosto continued to strain, and then, as if by some

miracle, he managed to move his lips, even though there was no sound. He seemed to be mouthing the word "wrong," then "I was wrong." Clare saw him mouth a long sentence and she knew it was in Italian. "Keep your own counsel," Agosto was saying. "Protect the family."

"Oh, Papa . . . ." Clare held his hands, but Agosto began to shake violently in a spasm that rocked his paralyzed body. Clare screamed and nurses came running, followed by two doctors. She fought for an instant to stay at her father's side, but then gave way when she saw him collapse back against the pillows, his face ashen, his eyes fishlike.

Clare leaned against the wall, her whole body shaking. Anthony was first back with Emil, then Fabiana and Maria, who were summoned from the hospital chapel on the floor below.

Fabiana knelt by the side of the bed sobbing. "Oh, Agosto, I love you, please don't die, please." Great tears rolled down her round face, and she dabbed at them with her sleeve.

Maria stood stoically by the other side of the bed, crossing herself and saying a prayer aloud for her brother. "God forgive me for being a hard woman, God forgive me for not telling you how much I loved you! Agosto, I never thanked you enough. There were so many things I never told you. . . ."

Anthony let out an audible groan. Then Agosto's lost voice called out in a long garbled wail, "Clarissima . . ." and his head fell sideways, his fingers slack in Fabiana's hand.

The doctor held Agosto's hand for what seemed like an eternity, then put it down and closed Agosto's eyes. "He's passed on."

Clare covered her face with her hands and began to sob violently, aware only of one of the nurses leading her away, and finally of being held in her brother's arms as they cried together.

Wednesday, March 11, 1931

Clare, Anthony, Jenny, Constanza, Fabiana, and Maria sat in the first row of the little church in Sheepshead Bay. Behind them the pews were filled to capacity and the crowd overflowed out onto the street. Wall Street luminaries sat next to the baker, the shoemaker, and the greengrocer. Men and women alike sobbed when Roberto Marcucci delivered the eulogy. Poor Roberto, tears streamed down his face and he fought to keep his voice from cracking.

The priest delivered the final blessing, and slowly the assembled mourners filed out of the church.

Clare Marina stood flanked by her aunts and her brother.

"Agosto Tonelli was the finest man I ever knew," Joe Castellano from the Jersey City branch bank said, weeping. He wiped his cheek with a big black handkerchief. "He was like family," he added as he hugged Clare Marina.

Bruno Andretti fairly shook with emotion. "It's the end of an era," he mumbled.

Clare felt as if she were in a dream. The managers of American Federal Banks had come from all over the United States, had come at their own expense in a time of great hardship to pay their last respects to Agosto Tonelli. It was a procession of more than three hundred and fifty men. Each of them, Clare thought, had been handpicked by her father.

"It never mattered how busy he was—he always had a personal relationship with us," Joe Castellano told her. "It's what saved us—it's the strength of AmFed."

"Your Papa, he worked too hard," ninety-year-old Salvatore Giuliano muttered as his son Sal pushed his wheelchair up to the Tonelli clan. "But I come out to his funeral . . . I don't come out nowhere anymore, but I come to Agosto Tonelli's funeral. I come because Agosto Tonelli, he make the word 'dago' a compliment! He showed them . . . he showed them what an Italian boy could do!"

Clare let her tears flow freely beneath her heavy black veil. She looked at AmFed's managers, at all the people from the neighborhood, she listened to the words of her grandfather's friend. She glanced briefly at Crieghton Stearns. He looked so out of place, so stiff, so emotionless.

I won't let you win, she vowed. I can't. I can't let you win.

Thursday, March 12, 1931

N E W   Y O R K

"Oh, Clare! I got here as soon as I could." Mark held her tightly in his arms as they stood in the hallway of the Tonelli home. "I had to take a commercial flight."

She pressed against him. The feel of his tweed jacket was

rough on her skin. She smelled his pipe tobacco, a sweet lingering odor; whenever she smelled it, she thought of him, and when he left her, the smell was there for hours to remind her he'd been there. "I'm terribly glad you're here," she finally managed.

Mark held her back and studied her face. It was filled with anguish.

"I've finally stopped crying," she murmured.

He took her hand and led her into the living room. "Where is everyone?"

Clare shrugged. "Fabiana's at Maria's house. Anthony's gone back to the city with Jenny." She sighed. "I'm glad we're alone."

Mark sat down on the sofa and pulled her down beside him. He kissed her, then held her. "I wanted to be with you. Talk to me, Clare. Tell me everything."

"It was a massive stroke . . . he was in a coma." She bit her lip. "Mark, he spoke to me before he died. He told me I was right."

"I'm glad," Mark answered, not quite understanding.

"Creighton persuaded Anthony to sign over his father's controlling shares. He tricked him. Anthony was so tired and under so much stress, and Creighton told him the stock would drop in value if there wasn't a steady hand at the helm."

"Bastard. That happened before you got here?"

Clare nodded. "I phoned Creighton this morning. I actually had to make an appointment to see him! Oh, Mark, it's all happening. . . ." She looked up at him with her long dark eyes. "Mark, if I marry you, he'll enforce the will. I'll be right out of management."

"He'll take you out of management anyway as soon as the will is probated in a year's time. He'll then have the controlling stock firmly in hand."

"I know that. Mark, I have to stay in management for that year. I have to fight this."

"Clare, we could still be married."

"We can't. It's the wording in the documents. If I marry, I can be replaced."

"You'd still be on the board."

"Mark, that's not good enough. I have to have access to the inside. Roberto says Creighton's a dangerous fool. Oh, Mark, this is what I feared most—it's all fallen into their hands."

He lifted his eyes and looked at her. She was wearing a frilly gold dress and her hair was loose. She looked small and vulnerable and he wanted to take her in his arms and make love to her.

But instead he sat rooted on the sofa, knowing that however small and vulnerable she looked, she had a will of steel.

"Clare, I love you. You know I'd planned a spring trip to South America. It was going to be our honeymoon."

"It's not fair of me to ask you to wait for an eternity."

"I'm not sure I can stand over a year of stealing weekends, trying to be together as often as possible. That's not marriage. I want children, I want to be with you on more than a hit-and-miss basis."

"I understand," she said in a voice that was hardly a whisper. "I have to save AmFed, I have to get it back."

He shook his head. "You haven't many weapons in your arsenal, Clare. Your father was the major stockholder. What can you do against the combined shares of the Stearns family and those shares Anthony signed over? I know I told you to wait to fight the battle, but I didn't foresee Anthony signing over his shares. Clare, it's hopeless. I don't see what you can do."

"Fight," Clare answered. "I can start buying more shares. I have to get proxies."

"Clare, you can't buy that many shares."

"I have to try."

Mark shook his head. "Clare, marry me as we planned. I'll help you, I have money. More than you right now."

Clare shook her head. "No, I can't take your money. I have to do this myself."

"Clare, I've waited a long while for you. Now you won't marry me because you're afraid of being replaced. This is a battle you can't win, and it could go on for years. I've seen enough proxy fights to know that. Clare, I know how important this is to you, I know your passion for the business world, so I'll make you my partner in Lyons."

"No, I can't. Oh, God, I'm losing you too!" Tears filled her eyes. "Mark, give me some time."

He stared at the floor. "You're choosing to marry AmFed, Clare."

"I have to get it back! My father built it! The family built it! I won't let them have it!"

"Clare, I have to think about this." He shook his head, overwhelmed by her determination.

Clare turned away from him. "I *have* to do this," she repeated.

"I know how much it means to you, but you won't take me, you won't take my help, and logic tells me you can't win this fight alone. Clare, love is a partnership too."

She turned away, sitting stock-still. "Go now, then. Don't make this harder for me."

Friday, March 20, 1931

BROOKLYN

Emil sat on the edge of the bed and watched his mother stuffing clothes into their suitcases.

"You're angry," Mama.

Clare didn't look up. "Yes, Mama is angry. That man is truly a bastard! He's no better than a common thief!"

"What man?"

"Creighton Stearns. He's stolen control of this company. He's practically ordered me back to California instantly. God knows what he'll do next!" Clare fumed and fought to hold back tears. She'd had her meeting with Creighton this morning. Polite, cold, despotic—a thousand adjectives ran through her head. He'd sent Anthony on vacation to "get over the shock of his father's death." He'd already begun making minor changes.

"Are we taking the train?" Emil's voice broke into her thoughts. Clare nodded.

"Is Mark coming with us? Will we be back in time for your wedding?"

"Oh . . . ." Clare looked at Emil in horror.

"What's the matter, Mama?"

Clare bit her lip and tossed her last remaining dress on the top of the suitcase. She walked over to Emil and sat down next to him, looking into his soft brown eyes. She shook her head. "Mama's not going to have a wedding."

Emil looked at her and frowned. "I like Mark," he said defensively.

Oh, how to explain this to a child? "I like him too. But, Emil, something awful has happened. This man . . . he's trying to take away your grandpapa's company. Mama can't let him do that. AmFed belongs to the Tonellis."

"Won't Mark help you?" Emil's eyes seemed so huge.

"It's something I have to do alone."

"I'll help you, Mama." He threw his arms around her neck and nuzzled her.

"Oh, Emil," Clare said, "oh, I hope Mark comes back to us." She held her son tightly. She had worked so hard to make sure Emil accepted Mark, then sent Mark away without even thinking of Emil. "I'm not a very good mother."

542

"I love you," Emil mumbled.

Clare tried to smile at her son. He was growing up so fast. He looked so like her father.

Friday, November 20, 1931

NEW YORK

It had been eight months since Clare's last tense meeting with Creighton Stearns. I'm stronger now, she thought to herself. I'm stronger and I have real complaints. I know what he's been doing, I've experienced the results.

"Do sit down, Clare Marina." Creighton smiled solicitously without revealing his teeth, then glanced at his watch in that damnable nonverbal way that as much as said: I don't have much time for you.

Clare sat down in the blue chair on the other side of the massive oak desk. Her father had never liked a private office, but Creighton had wasted no time building himself one. And, she noted, Creighton's desk was on a slight platform, so that no matter where you sat, he was always at a slightly higher elevation.

"You wanted to talk to me before the meeting," he said, lighting a long cigarette, which was extended by a gold holder.

"You've moved Tony from head of the Eastern division," she said plainly. "Why?"

"Oh, my dear. In order to put the boy in a position of greater visibility."

"With less responsibility," Clare observed evenly.

Creighton's facial expression didn't change. "He's a young man, a boy really, and, need I remind you, the new father of a lovely daughter. He and Jenny need time together, time to have fun."

"He's a twenty-six-year-old man," she said coolly.

Creighton gave a half-shrug.

"When are you going to move me?" She stared at him, her eyes hard.

"I can't move you. Your father's will is still in probate. And as I'm sure you know, the documents were quite clear. You were to remain in charge of the West Coast division till you remarried."

"I'm certain that doesn't please you."

"Naturally not. You have your own investments, I have no way of knowing if there's a conflict of interest."

"You're the only one with a conflict of interest. You and your Anglo-Saxon dynasty! Tell me, Creighton, have you tried to get Tony to change his name yet?"

"Oh, it's true that I'm not crazy about ethnics, my dear, but I wouldn't do that. In any case, I have a son at Harvard, remember? My dynasty, as you call it, will carry on. There'll always be a Stearns in charge."

Clare glared at him, though his declaration hardly surprised her. Sarah might have initiated the idea, but Creighton had taken charge of the plotting. "In the last five months you've moved seven Italians out of managerial positions, men who were lifelong friends of my father's. You've given up the bonus program, and you didn't even have the annual picnic this year."

"Frills. These are hard times, Clare, or hadn't you noticed?"

Clare pressed her lips together and stood up. "You've lost a lot, Creighton. You've ruined the morale of the employees, and you've lost a great deal of money."

"I don't want to listen to the hysterical rantings of a female!" Creighton said, looking angry for the first time.

Clare walked over to him and stood beside his desk. She could feel her own face flushed with anger. "You're not replacing Roberto Marcucci!"

"I am," he said, looking up at her. "I have the votes, my dear, because I have the controlling shares, and I'm going to do just that."

"You're a bastard!" Clare hissed, stomping her foot and bringing her hand down on the table.

"I don't believe young ladies should swear."

"I don't believe anyone has the right to steal and I'm not surprised you don't want to listen to me! Well, Creighton, I'm not your 'dear,' I've already begun fighting you, and I intend to continue. I'll fight you till my last breath, Creighton. I'm going to get AmFed back!"

"You're being tiresome, Clare."

Clare felt her hands double with tension. She suddenly picked up the inkwell and threw it on the desk, causing ink to spatter across Creighton's papers and all over his shirt. "I'll win!" she said, whirling around. "Damn you, I *will* win!"

LOS ANGELES

Clare Marina sat in the pleasant sunny dining room and sipped her coffee. Outside, Emil was riding Racer. Good thing, she thought. He'd ask hundreds of questions if he saw this morning's Los Angeles *Times*. Its business section carried a large photograph of her, beside which the headline read, "BILLION-DOLLAR FAMILY FEUD!"

Clare reread the article:

The Tonelli family feud features the heirs to a billion-dollar banking fortune in a corporate battle that could threaten thousands of jobs in California and across the nation.

On one side of the bitter dispute is Anthony Tonelli and his father-in-law, financier Creighton Stearns, a major AmFed shareholder. On the other side is the globe-trotting beauty of the financial world, the Countess Clare Marina Sforza-Tonelli, Anthony Tonelli's elder sister.

In the middle is AmFed, a sprawling holding company which is the major stockholder in American Federal Banks, AmFed Securities, AA&C Real Estate, Liberty Films, Anaheim Animation Films, Salinas Salad Growers, Jerusalem Steel, Annan Rubber, Universal Motors, and Domenico Canneries, among others.

Since her father's death, the Countess Sforza-Tonelli has waged a $250,000 campaign, charging her brother and Creighton Stearns with incompetence.

"The management team brought in by Stearns is not acting in the best interests of the shareholders. My father didn't build AmFed to pay for the high living of those on the board of directors," the countess is quoted as saying in a full-page ad she took out in papers across the nation in a bid to rally shareholders.

The countess goes on to question the consultant salary taken by Stearns, the dismissal of management selected personally by her father, and several recent losses.

The countess and her brother both own 3.5% of AmFed stock, but Anthony Tonelli inherited an additional 10.5%, which has been signed over to Creighton Stearns in trust. This effectively gives Anthony Tonelli and Creighton Stearns control unless the countess can rally shareholders to sign over a whopping 11% of proxies.

Can the countess win? Some think she can. She's won the support of two big institutional shareholders who support her accusations concerning Stearns's mismanagement. Both the Columbus Day Heritage Fund and the Sons of Garibaldi say they will give her their proxies, though neither would state publicly the number held.

Clare put the paper down and sighed. "Poor Tony," she said, shaking her head. "It's not really you I'm warring with." He loves me and I love him, she thought. But there's a foreign element between us, and it's seeking to tear us apart and break our family apart.

Clare checked her watch. Roberto Marcucci was due within the hour. He's been such a help, she thought. He and Constanza had temporarily come West to assist her. Creighton, true to his word, had fired Roberto. And, faithful to his threat, he would place a motion before the shareholders to have her taken out of management. Her father's will had been probated, and full ownership of the controlling shares was now in the hands of Creighton, who had simply made a figurehead out of Tony.

34

Saturday, September 10, 1932

LOS ANGELES

A warm September sun beat down on the colored stones of the inlaid patio. Clare stretched out on a lawn chair and stared off into the garden. The battle lines are drawn, she thought. In almost exactly two months she and Creighton would face off before the shareholders of AmFed. She'd placed a motion before the shareholders to have him replaced; he'd placed a motion before them to have her taken out of management. He could have done that at a board meeting, of course, but Creighton was smarter than that. To have her dismissed behind closed doors would be dangerous. No, he wanted the shareholders' backing, he wanted to do it publicly, he wanted the issue settled once and for all.

"A gentleman to see you," the maid announced from the doorway of the house. "I told him you were busy."

Clare looked up. She hated visitors on her morning off. There was so little time for relaxation. "Is it my broker?" she asked, thinking that was the only man who might come unexpectedly.

"No, ma'am. It's a Mr. Lyons, Mr. Mark Lyons. I asked him for his card, but—"

Clare stood up. "It's all right, tell him to come in, and please, no phone calls." She ran her hand through her hair and brushed out her skirt.

"Clare . . ." He paused on the edge of the patio. He was wearing white trousers and an open-necked shirt. He was tanned, and he smiled warmly and held out his arms.

"Mark!" Clare ran to him and leaned against him, listening to the beat of his heart, letting herself feel warm and secure for just a moment. She looked up into his face. His eyes caressed her, and she could feel his love flowing over her. It had been so long, she'd almost given up hope that he'd return.

547

"I have this problem," he said seriously.

Clare stood close to him. "Tell me."

"Well, you see, I'm desperately, hopelessly in love with this beautiful genius. For an entire year I've been running away in South America, but Morty says I'm restless, annoying, and a real son of a bitch. He told me if I didn't come back to you, he'd kill me. I can't make it without you, Clare. I surrender. Be my mistress for as long as it takes."

Clare put her arms around his neck and he kissed her passionately, moving his lips against hers. "Oh, Mark, do you mean it? I love you. I've missed you so. Emil's missed you too. I was wrong to send you away, and I prayed you'd come back."

He held her close and gave her another intimate kiss. "I mean it. I've been away too long."

"I can tell," she said as he pressed her close.

"Will the snoopy maid mind if we go upstairs?"

"You're terrible. It's nine o'clock in the morning."

"At least tell me you can't wait either."

"I can't wait either," she said, taking his hand and leading him into the house.

"Have there been many men in my absence?" He flipped the lock on her bedroom door and carried her to the bed. "Good, it's unmade. I always liked the way you looked on rumpled bedsheets."

"None. I love you, you know that."

"You'll have no trouble telling I've been celibate." He took off his shirt and trousers, then his shorts.

Clare giggled, feeling suddenly alive and lighthearted for the first time in months. "You always make me laugh. I've seen you look like that ten minutes after we've finished making love."

He smiled. "Well, then, you'll have to take my word for it. You were always there, on my mind. I slept with you a hundred times in my dreams, but there were no realities." He unbuttoned her blouse and kissed her neck, then took off her bra and kissed her breasts again and again.

Clare put her arms around him and wiggled so he could take off her skirt and panties.

"I like it when you do that," he said into her ear as he kissed it and licked it with his tongue.

He moved his hands over her softly, then with more pressure as his own desire grew. She touched him lightly, running her hands over his back, then his hairy chest. Then she touched him intimately and he smiled at her. "It's going to be awfully quick if you do that," he joked, playfully touching her.

"That goes for me too."

He returned to her breasts, then slid down her body and kissed her thighs, her legs, and even her feet. He slid back up, kissing her again, then entered her, kissing her ears. "I can't wait . . . it has been too long," he breathed. "Clare, I'll never leave you again."

Friday, November 4, 1932

LOS ANGELES

Clare's desk was strewn with documents and pads of paper covered with figures.

"How goes it?" Mark asked, not really needing to hear the answer. Her facial expression was sufficient. It was intense, but her eyes, always her most expressive feature, held a hint of despair.

"I don't have enough proxies yet," she confessed "I only need a little more—one-percent. It sounds like so little, but it represents so much."

He put his hand on her shoulder. "You don't know how all the shareholders will vote—you only know what you have for certain." "Clare, what do you intend to do?"

She reached up to her shoulder and touched his hand. "This is the only shot I'm going to have. I forced this shareholders' meeting, Mark, and by forcing it, I made it necessary for Creighton to try to dismiss me publicly. He has to have a vote of confidence now . . . he has to prove that the shares he has are in fact enough to swing the vote. Some of the shareholders I haven't got proxies from may back me, others may back Creighton. But if I can't win, at least I'll speak my piece." She shook her head. "I'm so worried about Tony."

Mark glanced at the letter from Fabiana that lay among Clare's notes. "He's drinking heavily, isn't he?"

"Did you read the letter?"

"No, Morty heard about it in New York last week. I didn't want to mention it to you—you've got enough on your mind."

"*Heard* about it? My God, does everyone on Wall Street know?"

Mark nodded. "Come on, Clare. Your family was respected but never really liked by the establishment . Tony's young, he's got a temper, and there are a lot of mean jokes on the Street—

men's jokes—about how you're trying to emasculate him in this shareholders' war.''

"Oh, dear heaven. Tony just can't take that. I didn't know.''

"He's not helping to stop the gossips any, falling down drunk every night at the club.''

"But jokes—how can people be so cruel?''

He bent down and kissed the top of her head. "They make the same jokes about me, you know. There's a rumor that if you fail in your takeover bid, you'll come after Lyons Oil next. I think they call me your 'slippery tomcat.' And according to rumor, I'm every bit as emasculated as Tony.''

"Oh, Mark!''

"Clare, I'm secure. Don't worry about me. But you know you're operating in a man's world. You're threatening a whole system. You might as well know how men talk when they're together.''

She nodded. "You're strong, but Tony isn't. Fabiana says his relationship with Jenny is terrible. She's taken the baby and gone home.''

"That doesn't change Creighton's position.''

"This is destroying my family. Fabiana's given me her proxies. Tony hasn't seen her in weeks . . .''

"Come on, leave your desk for a while, come and sit with me on the sofa.'' He pulled her down close to him and put his arm around her. "I took Emil to the zoo today. It's not the world's best. When we're in New York, I'll take him to the Bronx Zoo.''

"You mean a lot to him,'' Clare said earnestly. "He's never had a man to take him places, except for Tony when we lived in New York. Oh, God, this makes me terribly sad. Tony is being torn apart.''

"Clare, you can't make him strong.''

"I didn't want this fight to break up his marriage. I'm not fond of Jenny, but I know Tony loves her.'' Clare shook her head. "Fabiana said that's why Jenny left. She left and said she'd only come back if Tony votes with Creighton. She's literally blackmailing him.''

"Maybe that's why he's drinking. He's finding out what she's like.''

"She's his wife, and there's a child.''

"If you'd known about Emiliano Sforza, would you have stayed with him?''

Clare shook her head. "I don't think so.''

"I know divorce isn't permitted.''

"Tony wasn't married in a Catholic ceremony, so a Church

annulment might be possible. But that's not what I want to see. I know he loves her.''

"He's pulled in too many directions. Maybe once it's over . . .''

"I hope you're right.

"See, you've done it again. I wanted to talk about you and me and Emil, and you worked the conversation back to Tony and next week's shareholders' meeting.''

"I'm sorry,'' she replied, forcing a smile.

"I know you have a one-track mind right now. But, Clare, you haven't answered my first question. What will you do if you lose?''

"I'm going to give up. I'm going to marry you. I can't go with this any longer. As I said, this is my one shot.''

Mark smiled. "Is that a solid decision—you won't change your mind?''

Clare shook her head. "Win, lose, or draw, I'll marry you.''

"And that brings me back to Emil. Clare, when we're married, I want to adopt him. I want him to be my son legally.''

"Oh, Mark . . . I hadn't thought about that.''

"Clare, after the shareholders' meeting we're going to be starting over. I'd like it to be a really new beginning.'' He kissed her and ran his fingers around her lips. "I want us to be a family.''

B R O O K L Y N

Fabiana paused in front of the old Tonelli house—Domenico's house—where she'd lived with Paolo when they were a large family that consisted of old Domenico, Gina, Maria, Donato, and little Tina. Agosto, Cecilia, Clare, and Tony were part of the family too, but they hadn't lived in the same house.

Fabiana remembered Sunday dinner when Agosto and Cecilia were there, Sundays when Tina, Clare Marina, and Anthony cluttered the living room with their toys and clambered over their grandfather to listen to stories. Those were happy times, Fabiana thought. Times when the family was together and strong, when they all worked to make Agosto's bank a success.

Now it was all changed, and the house had changed too. It needed paint, and the garden was unruly and uncared for. And out on the avenue, Domenico's vegetable store was run by people who had been hired to do the work that was once lovingly done by members of the family.

Fabiana pushed open the gate and walked into the unkempt yard. The old Tonelli house was inhabited only by Maria: Maria, who had sometimes resented her; Maria, who kept her silence and who lived with bitterness and disappointment, wearing them like a medal that proclaimed her survival. Maria lit votive candles for a husband she had not loved, mourned a daughter she had rejected, and cried for Agosto, whom she worshiped even though she had nagged him incessantly for thirty years. Maria, Fabiana well knew, held the key that would solve Clare's dilemma.

"You've come calling on a Friday?" Maria said, ushering Fabiana into the house, which had the odor of some other time and place. A faded house with faded furniture, a mantel full of mementoes: a bouquet of faded silk flowers that Agosto had brought her from Cuba; a tintype of Agosto in his uniform; an Italian doll she had bought in Italy when she went to Clare's wedding; a picture of Tina at the age of ten, holding hands with Clare Marina; and a picture of Tina in her Communion dress.

"Must I wait until Saturday?" Fabiana asked.

"No, it's just that you usually don't come on Fridays."

Fabiana laughed. "You're addicted to routine."

"Things should happen when they are supposed to happen."

"And the way they should happen," Fabiana said pointedly as she sat down. "Maria, I have come to talk business with you."

Maria frowned. "I have no business," she said curtly.

"You have no business living this way," Fabiana said, looking about. "I know you. You own stock, a lot of stock. You were buying stock in AmFed all the time, and you had family stock in the bank before that, and it was converted into AmFed stock. And, Maria, you have always collected money—not spent it, but collected it like the gray squirrels on the lawn who collect nuts before the winter."

"What I own is my business," Maria said coldly. "I have what I want and need. I do not live frivolously—there's no need."

"Traveling or spending your winters in the sun would deprive you of your misery," Fabiana said, "and you enjoy your misery, Maria."

"Have you come to call on a Friday to insult me?"

"No, I have come to talk to you about Clare. Maria, Clare needs your stock in AmFed. If she doesn't get it, AmFed will be taken over by Anthony's wife's family."

"Clare only wants it to prevent Anthony from having what is

rightfully his," Maria said acidly. "He is the son; he is Agosto's son, and it is he who should inherit. Sons run businesses, and women have babies. Clare is unnatural."

"Clare is brilliant and the Stearns family will not allow Anthony to run AmFed. Clare wants to keep AmFed in the family. Clare doesn't want what Agosto built to go to others, Maria. And, Maria, Clare is right."

Maria shook her head emphatically. "Clare is unnatural. She doesn't behave as a woman should."

"Have you enjoyed behaving in such a way? Have you enjoyed always being told what to do and how to do it? Have you enjoyed having every decision made for you?"

"It is right. To try to change it is wrong. We have great advantages: men to look after us, to provide for us and to—"

"As Donato did for you?" Fabiana asked. "Or as Paolo did for me?"

"They were weak. But Agosto took care of us, he saw to everything."

Fabiana nodded. "I don't deny that, Maria. Nor do I deny that you and I are from another generation; we are a society of women, Maria. Women who go to church together, women who help one another birth babies, women who market together and gossip together." Fabiana sighed. "Women who grow old together and who only have each other because we've been excluded from the society of men, Maria. We are of the old tradition, but we are in a new country and Clare is both like us and different from us. She has one foot in her traditions and another in a quite different world, a world I do not have the mind to understand, but a world I have the eyes to see. Maria, use your eyes, if not your heart."

Maria didn't reply. She ran her fingers over the worn material of the sofa and then touched her black dress of perpetual mourning.

"Have you truly forgiven Clare for Tina's death?"

Maria looked Fabiana in the eye. "Yes, I accept that it was not her fault."

"Good. Maria, I want you to think on these things. I want you to think about family and what it means. I want you to do one thing right in your whole life."

Maria looked away. "I will consider what you've said," she agreed.

Saturday, November 19, 1932

MANHATTAN

"Nervous? You must be—you haven't touched one bite of your breakfast."

Clare nodded. "I just don't know, Mark . . . I don't know what's going to happen. I'm close to having enough proxies, but there are still undecided votes. What I say and how I say it could be the deciding factor, at least for those who haven't already mailed in their proxies."

"Shareholders' meetings aren't easy. Have you got any indication of the numbers attending?"

"I called the AmFed office at eight. The final tally is around nine hundred and fifty."

"Your battle has brought them out of the woodwork."

"I'm terrified."

Mark glanced at his watch. "The shareholders' meeting is at two o'clock, right?"

"Board members have to be there at one-thirty."

He smiled. "What a place to have the meeting. I can think of better things to do in the grand ballroom of the Waldorf."

She smiled faintly. "So can I."

"It's essential that you try to relax. You've got to be composed."

"I'm only too conscious of that! Otherwise Creighton will be muttering about the instability of the female of the species." Clare folded her hands and looked at them, then said thoughtfully, "Mark, can you get a car to take us to Brooklyn?"

"If you want to see Fabiana, she's coming into New York for the meeting."

Clare shook her head. "No, I want to go someplace . . . just walk around a little."

"You're very mysterious."

"Humor me."

They drove across the Brooklyn Bridge and past the familiar landmarks. "Where to?" Mark asked. "Brooklyn's a rather large place."

"Ocean Avenue," Clare answered. "I'll tell you where to stop."

Mark glanced at Clare. Her facial expression was comtemplative and her eyes seemed to drink in the streets as she directed him. She was like a piece of metal being drawn to a magnet, or a homing pigeon circling the familiar.

"Look, there's old Mr. Romano's bakery." Clare pointed to a building. "Here," she said. "Stop the car here."

"At this American Federal Bank branch?"

Clare's eyes flooded with tears. "It's not a branch, it's the very first bank. We lived upstairs."

Mark stopped the car, and Clare Marina climbed out. He followed her as she walked up to the old building and touched it almost reverently.

"My father and Roberto repaired the masonry themselves. Donato painted it. Mama . . . Mama worked here sometimes."

"You were just a baby then."

Clare smiled through her tears. "I know all the stories." She touched the brass plaque; it was green with age. "See," Clare said, trembling. " 'THE ITALIAN BANK, *FOUNDED MARCH 7, 1904.*' "

"Clare, you're getting upset. You're crying, and the share-holders' meeting is just a few hours off."

Clare ran her hand over the sign and shook her head. "No, I'm finding the strength I need, Mark. It's here, it's in this place."

He put his arm around her and they stood for a long while in front of the bank on the corner of Emmons and Ocean avenues. Then finally Clare turned to him and looped her arm through his. "I'm ready now."

The long black limousine purred to a stop in front of the Waldorf. Mark, Constanza, Roberto, Fabiana, and Clare climbed out.

"We'll all be sitting in the second row," Mark told her. "I'm glad you relented and signed over a few proxies so I could come."

Roberto grabbed Clare and hugged her. "Clarissima, I'll be there. You look for Roberto if you're nervous."

Fabiana kissed her. "Good luck, Clarissima. Trust in God."

Constanza smiled and hugged her. "Pretend you're back in Italy. You've done this before, and you can do it again." She smiled, then whispered, "That dreadful man can't win!"

Clare tried to smile, but she could only think of Anthony. "I have to go," she whispered. "Thank you all. I'll look for you. I'd rather be with you than at that long table with Creighton Stearns, in front of all those people."

Clare took a deep breath and turned away, hurrying through the glass doors, clutching her briefcase. Mark and the others were going to wait in the lobby, but they would be there when the meeting started.

"Clare! Clare Marina!"

Clare stopped just short of the doors to the grand ballroom. "Zia Maria!" she said in surprise. "What are you doing here?"

"Waiting for you," Maria said in clear annoyance. "And you are almost late. I've been here half an hour."

Clare glanced at her watch. "I only have a few minutes."

"Clare, what would you do with Anthony if you won?"

"Zia Maria, I don't have time to discuss this now."

"Tell me, what would you do with Anthony if you . . . if *you* controlled AmFed?"

"I'd put him back in charge of the Eastern division so he could go on learning, but I don't know what's going to happen. I don't think I have enough proxies."

Maria opened her shopping bag and took out a long brown envelope. "Here," she said. "They're signed and notarized."

"Zia Maria . . . how many are there?"

Maria looked down. "The lawyer says I own one and a half percent of the shares of AmFed. You, Clare Marina, may think I'm an old fool, but I'm not so stupid that I don't invest. All these years . . . all these years I bought what Agosto bought, and I used the interest to buy AmFed stock. I'm giving them to you to save this company for the family. Fabiana says I have to."

"Zia Maria!" Clare's eyes filled with tears. "I knew you had shares, but I didn't know you had so many. I thought you didn't want me to have control."

Maria didn't smile. "The world is changing, Clare Marina. I don't have the mind to understand, but I have the eyes to see. Now, go and get Agosto's company back, Clare Marina."

Clare hugged her aunt and kissed her. "I shall never forget this," she whispered.

"We must stick together, Clarissima."

"Zia Maria, go sit with Mark and the others . . . go sit with the family."

Clare watched for a moment as her aunt went in search of the others; then she went into the ballroom. It was transformed. On a high dais was a long table. On its white tablecloth glasses were set out, decanters of water in front of each place. Below the dais, rows and rows of chairs—chairs that would soon be filled with AmFed's stockholders.

Creighton Stearns sat imperiously in the center of the long table. Clare sat to his right; Anthony, looking pale and ill, was to his left. All the other board members were on either side of them.

Creighton Stearns called the meeting to order and the secretary first read out the provision relating to voting: "AmFed is represented by 278,854,296 common shares and 40,494,737 preferred shares. Each share of the capital stock, whether common or preferred, entitles the registered holder thereof to one vote on each ballot taken at this general meeting of the shareholders of the company. Such votes may be given in person or by proxy. The shareholders have, by such means, the right to elect all directors of the company, to appoint auditors, and to vote for, vote against, or abstain from any other matter of business that may properly be brought before this meeting. Only shareholders of record on the company's books as of January 1, 1932, will be entitled to attend or to register a vote at this annual and special general meeting, to be held this day." He paused and drank some water, then continued in his monotone. He recited the rules for those holding proxies, quoted the bylaws, and paused again. Then he turned back to face the large audience. "I will now call on the chairman of the board, Mr. Creighton Stearns, to present the annual report and financial statements."

Creighton stood up, smiled, and opened his folder. He droned on for nearly an hour, making constant references to the annual report. Clare glanced down at her family. Maria was stony-faced, Fabiana smiled, Mark winked.

At last Creighton finished and the secretary stood up again. "The next order of business is the first motion placed before this meeting. I will read the motion as submitted on your printed ballots."

Clare stared at her papers as the secretary read out her motion to have Creighton Stearns removed as chairman of the board.

"Would you care to speak to your motion, madam?" He turned to her.

Clare struggled to her feet, aware of growing tension. "Yes," she replied, trembling. Talk directly to me, Mark had said. Try to look around, make eye contact, but talk to me. Clare took a deep breath. "I have made this motion because I believe Creighton Stearns to be incompetent. He has removed well-trained, informed management and replaced them with a management team that will do his bidding. He is draining this company of capital by paying himself high consultant fees. My father did not found this company for the sole benefit of the executives who run it. He founded it to benefit small investors, people who worked with their hands and who had no collateral but their calluses.

"I further charge that Creighton Stearns has made extraordinarily bad decisions, that since he has taken over, AmFed, a company that withstood the stock-market crash and increasing assaults on the market, has begun to lose money. He is arbitrary in his choice of personnel, and among our employees morale is at an all-time low. It is for these reasons I recommend his immediate removal.''

Clare sat down and looked at Mark. He grinned and made a "perfect" sign with his fingers.

"Will you speak against the motion?" the secretary asked Creighton Stearns formally.

Creighton, not even red-faced, stood up and blandly replied, "I have brought in a crack management team to replace family friends who were hired by the Tonellis. I have made no bad decisions—it's only that times are bad and AmFed is beginning to feel the effects of the deep depression that envelopes this nation. I refute Madam Countess's charges utterly and absolutely. I suggest she makes these charges only to take the company away from her brother, who has chosen to put me in charge." He nodded toward Anthony, who stared vacantly at the floor. With that, Creighton Stearns sat down, the smiling vision of confidence.

"You will now cast your ballots," the secretary intoned. "Those supporting the motion to replace Creighton Stearns as chairman of the board will vote 'Yes.' Those against the motion will mark their ballots 'No.' Those wishing to abstain will so mark their ballots.''

People lined up, and their proxies were added to those that had already been mailed in and counted.

The seven accountants and four observers pored over the ballots. It seemed to Clare as if it would take forever. The shareholders' meeting was adjourned for coffee. An hour passed before the shareholders were called back into the ballroom.

The secretary, flanked by the head accountant, stood up. He cleared his throat. "The results of the motion made by the Countess Clare Marina Sforza-Tonelli to have Creighton Stearns removed as chairman of the board of American Federal Corporation are: 24,110 abstentions. In favor of the motion: 169,242,210. Against the motion: 150,082,713. I declare the motion carried.''

Clare sat stock-still for an instant, even though the room broke into pandemonium. I won by a little over nine million five hundred thousand votes. That's three percent of the stock, she mentally calculated. But Maria had given her only one and a half percent. Clare looked past a red-faced Creighton Stearns, who was banging down the gavel.

"I adjourn this meeting for one hour!" he shouted angrily. "Then Madam Chairman can take over!"

"Anthony . . . oh, Anthony!" It was the answer, the only possibility.

Anthony's eyes seemed glazed; he looked at her and nodded silently.

"You voted your shares with me," Clare said as she pushed away from the table and hurried to take his hand. "Oh, Tony."

"It's our bank," he managed. Then, shaking his head: "Papa built it."

Clare led her brother through the crowd of reporters who flooded the room. "Mark!"

In a second they reached each other, and the press gathered around, cameras clicking.

"Countess, how does it feel? You won!" one of them shouted.

"Come on, Countess, a nice pose alone! Come on! You've beaten your brother, you're chairman of the board!"

Clare stiffened. "Gentlemen! Gentlemen, please." She tossed her head back, took off her hat, and shook her hair loose.

The crowd of reporters shoved and pushed into position, but after a moment they were silent.

"One at a time," Clare said.

Cameras clicked again, and Clare leaned against Mark's shoulder.

"Well, you won! How does it feel to win?"

Clare hesitated for a moment, then drew Anthony closer.

Maria, who actually smiled, Fabiana, Roberto, and Constanza stood in a protective circle around her and Tony and Mark. They were family, and they were together. "Take this picture," Clare said, turning to the photographer for the *Times*. She smiled through her tears. "Don't say *I* won. This battle was fought for my father, Agosto Tonelli, for my aunts, for my brother. Say it was a victory for the Tonelli *family*."